the
KING'S
DERYNI

Deryni books available from Ace

DERYNI RISING

DERYNI CHECKMATE

HIGH DERYNI

KING KELSON'S BRIDE

IN THE KING'S SERVICE

CHILDE MORGAN

THE KING'S DERYNI

THE KING'S DERYNI

KATHERINE KURTZ

ACE BOOKS, NEW YORK

THE BERKLEY PUBLISHING GROUP
Published by the Penguin Group
Penguin Group (USA) LLC
375 Hudson Street, New York, New York 10014

USA • Canada • UK • Ireland • Australia • New Zealand • India • South Africa • China

penguin.com

A Penguin Random House Company

This book is an original publication of The Berkley Publishing Group.

Ace Books are published by The Berkley Publishing Group.
ACE and the "A" design are trademarks of Penguin Group (USA) LLC.

Library of Congress Cataloging-in-Publication Data

Kurtz, Katherine.
The king's deryni / by Katherine Kurtz. — Ace hardcover edition.
pages cm
ISBN 978-0-425-27668-6 (hardcover)
1. Deryni (Fictitious characters)—Fiction. I. Title.
PS3561.U69K495 2014
813'.54—dc23
2014016850

FIRST EDITION: December 2014

PRINTED IN THE UNITED STATES OF AMERICA

10 9 8 7 6 5 4 3 2 1

Cover illustration composite by SFerdon/Shutterstock, Christopher Brewer / Shutterstock,
Christos Georghiou / Shutterstock, Fun Way Illustration / Shutterstock,
Sign N Symbol Production / Shutterstock.

Eleven Kingdoms map copyright © 2003 by Grey Ghost Press, Inc. www.derynirealms.com.
Graphic design by Daniel M. Davis, Ann Dupuis, James A. Davis, Martine Lynch.

For the many followers of the Deryni,
and especially the fans who faithfully gather
in Chat on Sunday evenings
at 7:00 p.m. (eastern standard time)
at rhemuthcastle.com, especially
Bynw, Shiral, Evie, The Bee, Jemler, Desert Rose, cynicalmedic,
Alkari, AnnieUK, Laurna, kirienne, Elkhound,
DomMelchior, Aerlys, Jerusha,
and the many others whose names have momentarily slipped my mind.
(It's been a long day.)
You know who you are!

The Eleven Kingdoms

Atlantic Ocean

Northern Sea

Gulf of Northarch

Gulf of Kheldour

Bay of Klaggen

Lough Cloome

Lough Bay

Cassan

Klaggen

Kilshane

Kierney

Uradnba

Meara

Rathaïkin

Cloome Mts.

Cloome

Culleine

Colan

Druime Macha

Connait

Cashien

Jenas

Concaradine

Danoc

Desse

Rhemuth

Arx Fidei

Eirian R.

Mollins R.

Gwynedd

Valoret

Haldane

Iendour

Iendoug Mts.

Rhengarth R.

Rhengarth Plain

Carcashale

Iomaire Plain

Ianmoull Plain

Rhendall

Eastmarch

Rheljarains

Ilynbourn Meadows

Iomaire Plain

Iilynbourn Plain

Connel Mountains

Tolan

Kheldish Mis

Kheldour Rhomb

Marley

(Old Kheldour)

Claibourne

Stavenham

Kutnin

Sasovna

The Fertile Crescent

Rheolour R.

Ratan

Ianmoull Isle

Tigre

Torenth

Beldouria

Csorra

Sostra

Western R.

Sostra

Corwyn

Coroth

Coroth River

Arjenol

Kheïrene

Beldour R.

Beldour

Abandour Pass

Brustarkia

Arjenol

Czalsky

Jandrich

Truvorsk

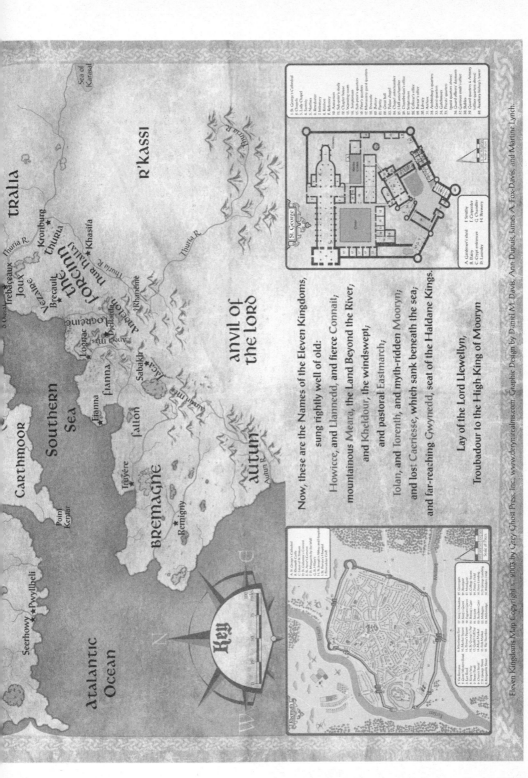

PROLOGUE

"That the generation to come might know them,
even the children which should be born. . . ."

—PSALMS 78:6

I N the four years immediately following the accession of Brion Haldane King of Gwynedd, the new sovereign perforce focused his energies on perfecting the statecraft learned at his father's knee, and also honing the martial skills he would need as a warrior and leader of men. He had come to the Crown at fourteen, of age in law; but for a warrior-king, the true rite of passage into adulthood came only with the accolade of knighthood.

He would receive that accolade on his eighteenth birthday, conferred by both his royal uncles. Richard Haldane Duke of Carthmoor, younger half-brother of the late King Donal, was reckoned one of the most accomplished knights of his generation, and had ultimate responsibility for the training of all the young boys and adolescents who came to court to hone their warrior skills in royal service. In his hands, Brion Haldane had been but another squire as he completed his apprenticeship, wearing no crown when he bowed himself to the discipline his uncle imposed; and he had learned his lessons well.

Slated to assist Duke Richard was King Brion's other uncle: his mother's brother, Illann King of Howicce and Llannedd, come with his son and heir, Prince Ronan (himself only recently knighted), to likewise lay his royal hand on the sword that conferred this public recognition of his nephew's true coming of age.

Many were the noble witnesses to this royal rite of passage. In addition to his family—his mother, his surviving brother, and two younger sisters—some were young men like the king himself: Ewan Duke of Claibourne, but three-and-thirty; Sir Phares Donovan and Sir Jaska Collins, among the last knights to be made by Brion's late father; Sir Joris Talbot, eldest son of Meara's royal governor; and Sir Jamyl Arilan, a favored companion of the king, knighted by Duke Richard but two years before, whose late uncle Seisyll had served both Brion and his father before him.

Others had been his father's friends and confidantes: Tiarnán MacRae and Jiri Redfearn, both with sons now preparing for royal service, and several of the great earls: Jared McLain Earl of Kierney, Caulay MacArdry Earl of Transha, and Sir Kenneth Morgan, now Earl of Lendour, who had come to his title through his young son, Alaric Morgan, who was sired on a Deryni heiress and destined to become the king's magical protector and companion—if he could be kept alive that long. For though young Alaric was heir to a great duchy, one of only four in the land, he also was not yet eight years old, with powerful enemies who would risk much to see him dead.

Meanwhile, Brion King of Gwynedd had enemies of his own, both east and west. Happily for his young reign, none of these had yet dared any overt measures to undermine his crown—none, at least, that had required direct intervention. Separatist factions in Meara, to the west, continued to skirt the edges of rebellion, but nothing had flared that was beyond the ability of the provincial royal governor to quell it. That would change, as it always did in Meara—King Donal had been obliged to mount expeditions into Meara on a regular basis—but for now, all was quiet in the province.

So it was, as well, in Torenth, to the east—at least so far as anyone knew. Not long before Brion's accession, the Kingdom of Torenth had suffered serious upheavals in the highest echelons of power: the still-unexplained death of King Nimur's eldest son, Crown Prince Nimur, and the subsequent setting aside of the second son, Prince Torval, in favor of Prince Károly, the meek and bookish third son. Torenth had offered no official statement beyond the bare announcement of Prince Nimur's passing, but the House of Furstán was Deryni, and used its magic openly—which could explain much. Persistent rumor had it that the true cause of

Prince Nimur's death had been a magical experiment gone horribly wrong, and that his brother Torval had been present, and was driven mad by what he had seen and experienced.

Whatever the cause, this unforeseen shift in the Torenthi succession had left Torenth ill equipped to take advantage of the youth and inexperience of Gwynedd's new king. Both Prince Nimur and his brother had been grown men, well capable of backing up an aging sire in declining health; and neither would have hesitated to take up the Torenthi cause, which was the eventual re-conquest of Gwynedd.

That assumption appeared not to hold true for Prince Károly, the new Torenthi heir, who was a decade older than Brion, but had received only a rudimentary portion of the education for kingship that was lavished on his two elder brothers—and his own heir was young yet, and certainly lacking in the training of a future king. Of a certainty, Károly would have set about remedying that deficiency while Brion scrambled to complete his own training for kingship, but thus far, Torenth had made no move beyond the usual border incursions that tested periodically at Gwynedd's eastern defenses.

Old King Nimur had even sent an envoy bearing his congratulations on King Brion's knighting—Count János Sokrat, aged but little since his visit for Brion's fourteenth birthday observances—but no Torenthi royalty accompanied him this time around. The king's advisors duly noted the Torenthi presence, and the absence of any over-large escort, and concluded that the visit was unlikely to spawn any great threat. Brion, so advised, put the matter out of his head and set about readying himself for the ceremony.

Chapter 1

"Blessed art thou, O land, when thy king is the son of nobles . . ."
—ECCLESIASTES 10:17

STANDING in his own great hall at Rhemuth, surrounded by men sworn to uphold him, Brion King of Gwynedd knew that the faintly queasy sensation in his gut came of no rational fear for his safety. Nonetheless, the sight of a foreign king standing between him and his throne, armed and crowned, could not but give one pause, especially when that king was accompanied by another prince regarded as one of the most puissant warriors in all the Eleven Kingdoms.

That the two men were his royal uncles only partially reassured, for blood greed had been the downfall of many a young king come prematurely to his crown, with still much to learn of his craft as monarch and warrior—and Brion had been but fourteen at his coronation, hardly four years before.

Nonetheless, all experience before and since that day declared that Brion King of Gwynedd need harbor no such misgivings about these two men. For as long as he could remember, Prince Richard Haldane, younger half-brother of his late father, had been his teacher, his mentor, his most merciless critic when Brion failed to do his very best.

As for the goodwill of his other uncle—the one who wore a crown of his own—that, likewise, was beyond question. Illann King of Howicce and Llannedd was the beloved elder brother of Brion's mother, the Dowager Queen Richeldis, come especially to honor this milestone in his nephew's young reign. He stood now at Richard's left, peacock-bright in the colors of Howicce and Llannedd amid all that Haldane crimson. Both he and Richard were the sons of kings, of blood equally royal to Brion's own, yet they had come to their feet at their nephew's approach, inclining their heads in respect.

The man who had presented the royal candidate, and had fixed the golden spurs to his heels, was also of blood both ancient and royal. Ewan Duke of Claibourne was a direct descendant of the last prince of Kheldour, to the north, and one of only four dukes in Gwynedd. Assisting him had been the scion of another great ducal family: Jared Earl of Kierney, deputizing for his ailing father, the Duke of Cassan. Like the royal uncles, both of these men also wore noble coronets upon their brows, and all of them bore steel at their hips.

By contrast, Brion King of Gwynedd wore no crown or other emblem of his royal estate, no rich raiment or even any weapon. With his sable hair caught back severely in a warrior's knot, he had donned the robes traditional to any candidate for knighthood: the unadorned inner robe of white, signifying the purity of his honor, partially covered by the stark black over-tunic symbolic of the grave to which all eventually must come.

Over both lay the bloodred mantle: fittingly, in Brion's case, of Haldane crimson. To such blood had he been born—blood which, even more than any mere knight, he must be willing to shed in defense of his realm, even unto death. At his coronation, the new king had pledged his life to his kingdom: reckoned a man, in law, for the governing of his realm, and well enough prepared in mind, but all too aware that he wore still the body of a half-grown youth, with much yet to learn of the warrior he must become, if he hoped to keep his crown.

That he had kept it thus far was due, in part, to his royal uncles, to the princely dukes flanking him, and to the loyalty and courage of the sandy-haired man standing close beside the throne: Sir Kenneth Morgan Earl of Lendour, who bore the great state crown of leaves and crosses intertwined as if it were no more burden than its mere weight of gold and precious stones, though he had saved it and Brion's life on more than one occasion.

And the towheaded boy at Kenneth's side, who had proudly carried the golden spurs now affixed to the king's heels, and assisted in their fastening, was cut from the same cloth as his sire: quick and earnest, utterly devoted to Brion, and so much more than he appeared to be, for all that he was only seven years of age. Because his mother had been heiress to a great duchy, Alaric Morgan would be Duke of Corwyn when he came of age, one of the most powerful men in the land. But Alyce de Corwyn had also been Deryni, possessor of powers both feared and resented by ordinary folk—which meant that many feared who and what young Alaric was, and what he might become.

The Church, in particular, had made its position abundantly clear regarding Deryni, for those trained in that heritage were believed to wield extraordinary powers that could compromise another's free will and even enslave the soul of the unwitting. Several of Gwynedd's bishops, some of whom were present today, had been particularly vocal in their condemnation, and one of them had nearly been the death of Alaric's mother before he was even born.

Yet King Brion's father, only days before his death, had commended the boy Alaric to Brion's especial attention and care, promising a legacy of benign magical powers to be employed in Brion's service, and further powers to be imparted for Brion's own use.

Was it true? Brion was not sure he remembered all that had been told him, but he believed and hoped that further knowledge would be revealed to him in due course—hopefully, well before he really needed it! And it was all somehow linked to the blond boy holding a crimson pillow beside the throne of Gwynedd.

But that was for the future—with any luck, some years in the future, when Alaric Morgan was grown. For now, Brion returned his full focus to his uncles, from whom he was about to receive the knightly accolade, which only another knight might bestow.

"Your Royal Highness," a herald intoned, addressing Richard, "having been invested with the spurs, the noble squire Brion Haldane now presents himself before the throne of Gwynedd to request the accolade from your hand, that he may henceforth be recognized as a knight."

Richard inclined his head, a faint smile curving within the sable mustache and close-clipped beard as his eyes met Brion's, Haldane grey to Haldane grey. In that moment, wearing Haldane crimson and a royal diadem, with one hand resting on the hilt of the sword at his hip, he very much resembled his late brother.

"Kneel now, Brion Haldane," he commanded.

With a nod of his head that was more jerky than intended, Brion moved forward to kneel on the scarlet cushion that young Alaric Morgan now set atop the first step of the dais; before, it had borne the golden spurs. As he settled himself and looked up, Richard turned to the crimson-clad duty-squire standing behind him: Brion's younger brother and heir presumptive, the twelve-year-old Prince Nigel, who extended the hilt of the sheathed Haldane sword, borne by many generations of Haldane kings. He retained the jeweled scabbard as his uncle drew forth the blade in a hiss of fine steel, clasping it to his breast in wide-eyed awe as Richard raised the blade and briefly brought the sword's cross-hilt to his lips in salute.

Richard paused then as King Illann reached across to rest his bejeweled hand atop Richard's, in pointed reminder that *this* knighthood came by way of *two* lines of royal kings and noble knights. The significance was not lost on Brion or, indeed, on any of those present.

Very briefly, as the flat of the blade descended toward his right shoulder, Brion closed his eyes and prayed that he might be worthy of this new charge, then lifted his gaze to Richard's once more, as the flat of the blade touched his right shoulder and Richard spoke.

"In the name of the Father, and of the Son"—the blade lifted to touch the left shoulder—"and of the Holy Spirit"—the blade arched upward to briefly rest atop Brion's head—"be thou a good and faithful knight. Amen."

As the blade lifted again, to briefly rest over Richard's right shoulder, he glanced aside at Illann with a speaking glance. Smiling, Illann offered the new knight his right hand and said, "Arise, Sir Brion Haldane, and be invested with the further symbols of your new estate."

Murmurs of approval rippled among the assembled witnesses as Brion clasped his uncle's hand and got to his feet, grinning as he accepted the bear hug that the older man offered. Richard, after passing the Haldane blade to Prince Nigel, likewise offered the new knight a quick embrace. As he did so, a beaming Dowager Queen Richeldis joined them from the sidelines, flanked by Brion's two younger sisters. Xenia, the adoring thirteen-year-old, proudly bore the white belt across both hands like some holy relic: the most visible outward symbol of the honor her brother had just received. Silke, who was nine, had been entrusted with a single red rose.

Composing himself to a properly kingly mien, Brion bent to kiss his mother's hand, then straightened and lifted his arms to either side so that she and his sisters could pass the belt around his waist and under his mantle, stark white against the sable of his over-robe.

"Congratulations, my son," his mother murmured, as she fastened its jeweled clasp. "May this belt be always a reminder to keep your honor spotless."

When she had kissed him on both cheeks and hugged him close, Silke shyly presented him with her rose, which he tucked into his belt. He then accepted a kiss from each of his sisters, in turn.

After that, as the women drew back, Brion turned back to his uncle and again sank to his knees on the scarlet cushion. At the same time, the aged Archbishop of Rhemuth came forward, coped and mitered in cloth of gold, to stand as witness. Richard had retrieved the Haldane sword from Prince Nigel, and now laid it across both palms, extending it to Brion. In response, the king laid his hands atop Richard's in oath, looking him in the eyes.

"Here before God and these witnesses, and with my hands upon the sword of my fathers, I, Brion Donal Cinhil Urien, knight, do make this reaffirmation of my coronation vows," he said steadily. "I solemnly promise and swear that I will do my utmost to keep the peace in Gwynedd and govern its peoples according to our ancient laws and customs; that I will, to the best of my ability, cause law and justice, in mercy, to be executed in all my judgments, so that evil and wrongdoing shall be suppressed, and the laws of God maintained. All this I vow, on my honor as a king and as a true knight, so help me God."

With that, he bent to kiss the blade between his hands, crossed himself in response to the blessing uttered by the archbishop, *In Nomine Patris, et Filii, et Spiritus Sancti,* then waited while his uncle slipped the sword into its jeweled scabbard and laid it back across his hands. As he stood, shifting the sheathed sword into the crook of his left arm, Kenneth

Morgan brought forward the state crown of leaves and crosses inter-twined, inclining his head as he lifted it slightly between them.

"Sire, I return the crown of Gwynedd into your good keeping," he said.

Smiling, the king bent slightly so that Kenneth could set the crown upon his brow, then turned to face the waiting court. At the same time, Ewan Duke of Claibourne declared: "My lords, I present to you Sir Brion Haldane, King of Gwynedd, Prince of Meara, Lord of the Purple March, and now, by God's grace, a knight!"

A roar of approbation erupted from the assembled court, along with an energetic stamping of feet, only abating when the smiling Brion lifted a hand for silence. As he did so, Duke Richard moved from in front of the throne to make way for his nephew, and Kenneth took his place beside the throne with half a dozen others on whose counsel the king relied. King Illann retired to a noble chair set among those of his sister the queen, her two daughters, and also his own son. Young Alaric Morgan, his official duties now complete, retreated into the charge of Sir Llion Farquahar, the young Corwyn knight who looked after him when his father was otherwise engaged.

"That was nicely done, Master Alaric," Sir Llion murmured, as he shepherded the boy toward a side door. "Now we'd best get you changed into proper tourney clothes. And you have a pony waiting to be groomed."

"But the king is going to make more knights," the boy replied, cran-ing his neck back over his shoulder to glimpse the senior squires gath-ering at the back of the hall with their escorts of family and supporters. "And then there will be birthday gifts."

Chuckling, Llion smiled faintly as he ushered the boy out into the garden colonnade adjoining the great hall.

"Have you not had enough pomp and ceremony for one day?" he teased. "I thought you were keen to beat Airey Redfearn and Aean Mor-risey in the ring-tilting—and your cousin Duncan will be eager to have you cheer him on."

"That's later this afternoon," Alaric said reasonably. "We have plenty of time."

"And why would you want to go back into that hot and crowded great hall?" Llion countered lightly, as he scanned the handful of others who had sought the cooler climes of the garden. Fortunately, no one was close by.

"Well, I—just like to watch people," the boy said uncertainly.

"Hmmm, yes. And I have no doubt that some of them would derive great satisfaction from watching *you*—though I very much doubt that 'like' has anything to do with it." Llion glanced around again, and kept his voice low. "Did you not notice Bishop de Nore glaring at you the whole time you were standing there beside your father, because you were close to the king? And it is quite possible that there are Torenthi emissaries among the observers, who almost certainly would be Deryni. They don't hate you in the way that de Nore hates you, but it certainly would be to the advantage of *their* king if the King of Gwynedd did not have a future Deryni duke being brought up in the safety of his court."

The boy glanced down at his feet, clearly unhappy with the direction the conversation was taking.

"Alaric," Llion murmured, drawing the boy closer into the shelter of one of the columns, "you know what could happen. Your father or I cannot always be there to protect you—but even if we could, it makes no sense to deliberately expose yourself to danger."

"I know, but—"

"No 'buts' about it, lad," Llion returned. "There is no point courting an incident. Time enough for that when you're grown, if you feel you must. For now, however, we need to prepare for the tournament. I know that I don't intend to dirty *my* court garb. Let's go upstairs and get changed."

The boy rolled his eyes and sighed with the indulgent acceptance of any well-mannered seven-year-old, but he was already bestirring himself to head toward the entrance to a back stair, Llion trailing after him as the murmur of distant voices from the great hall faded behind them.

Meanwhile, those voices betokened the ongoing business of the king's court, which must be concluded before the assembled nobles might retire to the tournament field. Though the conferring of knighthood customarily took place at Twelfth Night court, usually the one following a candidate's eighteenth birthday, Brion had still been but seventeen at the Twelfth Night just past. Exceptions were often made for good cause, especially in the case of a king or prince, but Brion had declined to exercise that prerogative, even though his uncle, Duke Richard, had declared him easily ready in level of strength and skill.

"I am happy enough to wait," the king had said, in the lead-up to Christmas court. "My brother Nigel is to receive his squire's spurs this year. He should not have to share that day with the knighting of an older brother. I shall hold a birthday court and tournament instead, and receive my knighthood at that time."

Accordingly, Prince Nigel Haldane had duly received his promotion to squire at the previous Twelfth Night, ahead of all others moving from page to squire. It had given the two brothers opportunity to serve as squires together for six months, albeit as senior and junior squire. It had also underlined their love, which shone proudly in Prince Nigel's gaze as he attended the throne today—and had provided the younger prince with a prize vantage point from which to observe this, his elder brother's official coming-of-age as a warrior as well as a king.

The king now took center stage in the further ceremonies of the day, by which additional young men would receive the knightly initiation. In a display of largesse unseen in recent memory, the newly dubbed Sir Brion Haldane conferred the accolade on six worthy candidates from lesser noble families throughout the realm: promising younger sons whose modest circumstances would have precluded taking up this honor without royal patronage, and whose gratitude would reinforce their loyalty in the years to come. All six had served the royal household as senior squires at least since the previous Twelfth Night, refining the skills acquired at various provincial courts and learning the ways of royal service, as they submitted themselves to the discipline of Duke Richard's impeccable tutelage. For each candidate, the same care was applied as had been given the king, with the six new knights then taken into personal service to the king, as household knights. The measure met with great popular approval.

Following these formalities came a less formal birthday court, with presentations of felicitations both personal and diplomatic, and often more tangible tokens of esteem. Similar to what had occurred on his fourteenth birthday, the young king received gifts appropriate to his now-adult status: new items of armor and weaponry; swords and daggers; a finely illuminated compendium of religious houses in the southwest from his uncle the King of Howicce and Llannedd; a brace of brindle coursing hounds from the Emir of Nur Hallaj; a fine R'Kassan stallion from the Prince of Andelon; a hawk from the governor of Meara, delivered by his eldest son; a little recurve bow inlaid with ivory and a quiver of fine hunting arrows from the King of Torenth, delivered by his envoy, Count János Sokrat; half a dozen lengths of gold-shot crimson silk from the Hort of Orsal; and divers gifts of gold and precious jewels from other representatives of the ambassadorial corps, with delegates from as far away as distant Bremagne.

"I thank all of you for your kind gifts," Brion said to the assembled court, when all the presentations had been made. "You have been most generous, and I shall treasure these tokens of your esteem. But having concluded the formal part of our proceedings, I now invite all of you to join us for a light collation before we adjourn to the tourney field, for I have a hankering to test my new knights." He nodded to the other newly knighted men, not bothering to control his smile. "I look forward to an interesting afternoon, gentlemen!"

Chapter 2

"My son, hear the instruction of thy father, and forsake
not the law of thy mother."
—PROVERBS 1:8

S EVERAL hours later, all the company had adjourned to the
tourney field in the lower ward of the castle. Sir Kenneth Morgan
was among those who came down with the others to share in the
king's celebrations, riding the occasional run at the quintain, but also to
watch his own son in the competitions.

The boy was good—far better than any lad of only seven summers
had any right to be, even one with so illustrious a lineage. As young
Alaric Morgan wheeled his pony and started his seventh run at the rings,
child-sized lance leveled squarely at the dangling target—and snared his
seventh ring!—rider and mount seemed to move as a single entity.

Watching from behind a fence rail at the sidelines, the boy's father gave
an approving nod and glanced up at the blond, mop-headed young knight
perched on the fence beside him: Sir Llion Farquahar, who had become
almost like a second son to him, and who looked after his true-born son.

Earlier, immediately after the ceremony that made a knight of Brion
King of Gwynedd and six others, the king and his new knights had
enjoyed a mock melee battle against a like number of older knights,
fought with blunted weapons and courtesies never accorded in true
combat. At Kenneth's urging, Llion had volunteered to be one of the
seven riding against the king—and helped to trounce the royal side.

Now, while the squires in training rode at the quintain across the
field, or galloped down a flag-marked lane with wooden swords in hand,

and tried to whack head-sized sacks of wool from stout posts set at the
height of a man, the duly humbled Sir Brion Haldane was taking challenges from individual knights—and making challenges, and winning far
more often than he lost. For the pages, who were only early in their training for eventual knighthood, Duke Richard had arranged a competition
of ring-tilting. Alaric, though not yet old enough to have entered formal
page's training, was outperforming boys nearly twice his age.

"He's riding very well today," Kenneth observed, well aware that Llion
could claim a good deal of the credit. Since taking service with Kenneth
nearly five years before, following his own knighting in Corwyn, the
young knight had been the boy's riding master and constant companion
when Kenneth was otherwise occupied—an arrangement that seemed to
please all concerned.

Llion nodded agreement, but he did not take his eyes from his young
charge as the boy circled around to return to the start of the run. "Aye, he is,
my lord—though I've learned not to be surprised at his knack with animals.
The true test will be whether his accuracy holds for ten runs. These are
smaller rings than we've been using up at Culdi. I'll need to remedy that."

Kenneth said nothing, only hiking himself up onto the fence rail with
Llion to watch as a squire set a new ring and the next boy began his run.
Airey Redfearn and his twin, Prys, were several years older than Alaric,
already official pages at court, and had six rings each, though the former
had also missed two rings. One more miss would put Master Airey out of
the competition.

"Llion, Llion!" came a young and urgent voice from Llion's other
side, as a boy in the sky-blue and silver of the Duchy of Cassan pelted up
behind them and scrambled onto the rail between the two adults. "What
did I miss? How many has Alaric got? Do you think he'll take all ten
rings? Oh, hello, Uncle Kenneth."

"Hello, Duncan."

The tousle-headed boy who snuggled into the curve of Kenneth's arm
was only a few months younger than Alaric: Duncan McLain, the younger
grandson of Andrew Duke of Cassan, whose sister had been Kenneth's
mother. He was also Alaric's favorite cousin.

"In answer to your most pressing question," Llion said, chuckling, "he has seven, and—oh, dear!" he murmured, as Airey Redfearn not only missed his third ring but tumbled from the saddle as his pony jinked and bucked at the end of the run. "Well, that's young Airey done for the day."

"Ow, bad luck!" Duncan said. "That pony is nasty! Airey is much better than that!"

"Aye, he usually is," Llion agreed. "Let's see how Alaric does on *his* next run. He's next after Ciarán MacRae."

"Is Ciarán any good?" Kenneth asked, just as an older page with a shock of bright red hair shot from the start and neatly took his next ring. "Well, answering my own question, obviously he is."

"I don't think he has any misses yet," Llion replied.

"He's nice, too," Duncan chimed in. "Look! Alaric is lining up for another go."

All of them fell silent as a new ring was set and a senior squire signaled ready. With a nod, Alaric collected the shaggy mountain pony and started his next run—and snared the ring smartly. As the lance lifted, they could see the new ring glinting in the sun as it slithered down the shaft to stack atop the first seven. Young Duncan let out a delighted whoop and waved energetically as his cousin pulled up at the end of the run and glanced back in their direction, flashing a gap-toothed grin. Atop a rail on the opposite side of the ring run, a dark-haired older boy in Haldane page's livery looked decidedly less pleased.

"Hah, Cornelius Seaton is soooo jealous!" Duncan muttered under his breath.

Kenneth refrained from comment, but he could sense Llion considering a fitting response. Both were well aware that the said Seaton scion, regarded as one of the more promising of Duke Richard's latest crop of pages, had been unceremoniously dumped from his pony on his very first run at the rings.

"Is it charitable, do you think, to take delight in another's misfortune?" Llion asked after a beat.

"He hates Alaric," Duncan said stubbornly, lower lip outthrust. "He does everything he can to make Alaric look bad."

Llion merely slipped an arm around the younger boy in sympathy, but Kenneth allowed himself a tiny grimace, well aware of the long-standing antipathy between the two youngsters—and its cause. Though Cornelius's father, Sir Errol Seaton, was regarded as a decent enough man, and recently had been appointed to the crown council, his mother was a sister of the powerful Bishop of Nyford, Oliver de Nore, who had made a career of persecuting Deryni. Their youngest brother had been the disgraced priest Septimus de Nore, executed on the testimony of Kenneth's late wife, for his part in the rape and murder of a child. Kenneth had assisted in the investigation of the crime, and had no doubt that the testimony had been honest, but he could understand the family's resentment. Still, Alaric could not help being his Deryni mother's son. . . .

"I hope he falls off the fence!" Duncan muttered darkly, folding his arms across his chest and glaring at the offender.

"Who, Cornelius?" Llion said mildly, as Kenneth glanced down at the sulking Duncan. "I should think it would be sufficient to hope that he eventually reaps what he sows—as shall we all." He reached up to gently tousle Duncan's sun-kissed brown hair. "But in answer to your previous question, I think Alaric shall, indeed, take many more rings, if he continues to ride as he has thus far. Do you intend to ride again?"

Duncan ducked his head sheepishly. "I can't win," he said glumly. "I missed the ring on my fifth run."

"Ah, but winning is not the only point of this exercise," Llion countered. "If you don't practice, you cannot improve. Your cousin was not always as skilled as he appears today; nor will he always ride the perfect set. And it isn't even always up to the skill of the rider. Ponies can stumble, or act up—as yon Cornelius has cause to know very well. He's actually quite a good rider."

Duncan wrinkled his nose in distaste, but also nodded grudging agreement. "I suppose," he said, then glanced up winningly at both adults. "I wonder if the list master would let me continue. After all, I didn't fall off—I only missed a ring. You're allowed to miss three before you're out."

"Which means that you could still score nine, if you don't miss any more," Llion agreed.

"And if I don't fall off!" Duncan retorted, rolling his eyes, though he was climbing down from the fence rail as he said it.

"You won't fall off!" Llion called after the boy as he took off toward the ring lists.

Kenneth set a comradely hand on Llion's shoulder as they watched Duncan disappear amid the milling pages and ponies at the far end of the lists, smiling as the younger man turned to glance at him.

"He *won't* fall off, my lord," Llion said somewhat defensively. "His seat is as good as Alaric's, and the pony is rock steady."

"I know that," Kenneth replied, giving the other's shoulder a reassuring squeeze. "I was simply appreciating your skill with children. You need to be a father, Llion."

The young knight looked momentarily startled, then a trifle bashful. "One day, perhaps I shall, my lord. I do enjoy children. But I'm young yet, and my first duty is to you, and to your son. There will be time enough for a wife and children of my own when Alaric is farther along in his training."

"Loyally spoken," Kenneth agreed. "But do keep in mind that the two are not mutually exclusive."

"No, my lord, but right now, I think it more important to help ensure that your son survives to adulthood—and that the king survives."

Kenneth nodded, glancing over to where the king was readying for his next joust, conferring with his two uncles. "Yes, that *is* the challenge, isn't it?" he murmured under his breath.

The two returned their attention to the milling youngsters nearer the start of the ring run, where Duncan had just taken a ring, to the delight of Alaric, who punched his lance into the air in approval. Then they watched as squires set up a new ring while Alaric lined up for his run. Thus far, he was the only one in the youngest age group to ride a perfect set—and as Kenneth and Llion watched, Alaric took his eighth ring.

"Good lad," Llion murmured.

Back at the senior lists beyond, the king was preparing to ride a *pas à barrière* against Sir Jamyl Arilan, under the keen scrutiny of Duke Richard and Prince Ronan, his cousin. Earlier in the afternoon, Brion had unhorsed Ronan, but Jamyl was far more experienced at the *pas*. On this sultry June afternoon, with the major competitions finished and their prizes given, the crowd was thinning, but many had stayed to watch the new royal knight's performance—save for Kenneth and Llion, whose attention was divided between him and Kenneth's son. The boy's runs were closer together now, as other contenders were eliminated.

"Steady, lad . . . ," Llion breathed, all but holding his breath—and then exhaled as Alaric took another ring.

"Good!" Kenneth said, lifting a hand to wave as his son turned to watch the squires position a new ring and saw him. Grinning, the boy saluted with his ring-laden lance, then quickly returned his attention to lining up for the next run. "What was that, eight, nine?"

"This will be the tenth, my lord," Llion replied, not taking his eyes from his young charge as Alaric gigged his mount, starting forward, and the tip of his lance dropped toward the target. "No misses, thus far—and *that* is ten! Well done!" he called in a louder voice, lifting a clenched fist in salute as a patter of applause also acknowledged the performance—mostly from young girls and even the king's sisters, Kenneth noted. But then, Alaric was a very attractive boy, with his silver-gilt hair and pale eyes.

"Well done, indeed," Kenneth agreed. "That's an excellent showing. Have any of the others done as well?"

"Not in this youngest age group, or even the next older," Llion replied. He jutted his chin in the direction of the glowering Cornelius, who had jumped down from his fence-rail perch and was stomping off to join the other pages. "Some of the others are none too happy, of course—especially that one. I've seen a few of the oldest pages ride very well and take lots of rings, as one might expect—some of those about ready to move up to squire—but I wasn't able to keep track of exact numbers. Still and all, this has been quite an extraordinary achievement for a lad who technically isn't even a page yet."

"Well, Duke Andrew means to make him one at Michaelmas, when he turns eight," Kenneth said. "We've already discussed it, and Alaric is ready. The king is eager to have him at court, of course, but even he agrees that Alaric is probably better off learning the basics away from court."

"Aye, away from the likes of yon Cornelius and his ilk," Llion muttered fiercely.

Kenneth sighed, but in resignation. "Unfortunately, that's true," he agreed. "Once he has to fight his own battles, with boys his own age and even older, it won't be easy, being who and what he is. Pray God, we can shelter him until he's ready to do that." He shrugged lightly. "But look, the king and Jamyl are finally ready to go."

Over in the adult lists, the king was, indeed, preparing to engage, saluting his opponent at the far end of the *barrière* and then releasing his mount to the charge in an explosion of thundering hooves. Jamyl was a few years older than the king, and had received part of his training at King Illann's court, where jousting was more common, but Brion easily held his own; neither scored more than a grazing hit of lance to shield.

"They're testing one another," Kenneth murmured under his breath, watching both men keenly.

"Aye, this next run will be more in earnest," Llion agreed.

"Jamyl is good, though," Kenneth said. "I've ridden against him."

"So have I," Llion replied, "and tasted dust more than once. But then, so did he," he added with a grin.

As the pair wheeled for another run, Alaric came trotting up happily on his pony, his stack of ten rings borne proudly on his junior-sized lance.

"Papa, did you see me?" the boy crowed. "Did you see?"

"I did, indeed, and you did very well," Kenneth replied somewhat distractedly, reaching down to take the pony's reins. "You mustn't gloat, though. Come up and sit with Llion and me. The king is going to have another go at Sir Jamyl."

Again baring his gap-toothed grin, Alaric let Llion take his lance to lean it against the fence, then clambered up to sit in the curve of his father's arm, between him and Llion. Kenneth could feel him tense as the pair began their second run, always concerned for the king. This time, Jamyl's lance shattered against the king's shield with a force that sent the royal rider reeling precariously in the saddle, but Brion managed to keep both his seat and his weapon. As he drew up at the end of the *barrière* and turned, gentling his excited mount, he saluted with his lance, grinning.

"Again, Jamyl!" he shouted. "You're going to have to do better than *that*. And I still think I can take you!"

"You can try, Sire!" Jamyl replied, good-natured laughter in his voice as he trotted over to the sideline and discarded what was left of his lance, then selected another from a rack.

"I shall do more than try!" Brion returned.

Again they took their places at either end of the *barrière* and prepared to engage, suddenly loosing to the charge, lances lowering as their horses gathered speed. This time, both lances shattered against shields, but it was Jamyl who reeled in his saddle, though he, too, quickly recovered his seat and pulled to a halt, tossing aside his shattered lance as he turned his mount.

"Well struck, Sire!—but perhaps we should call this a draw," he called, raising the visor of his tournament helm. "You very nearly had me that time! Give an old man a break!"

Brion guffawed and handed off the stub of his lance to his brother Nigel, who was squiring for him, then trotted his horse back to meet Jamyl midway, halting knee to knee with him to clasp forearms across the *barrière*.

"Old man, indeed!" the king declared. "But you'd better not be saying that just to salve my pride."

"I think not, Nephew," Duke Richard said, chuckling as he walked out to join the pair. "It was well ridden—both of you. But your lady mother asks that this please be the last challenge of the day. You know how she dislikes the heat and dust. She would like to award the rest of the prizes, so that our guests can retire for a few hours to refresh themselves before the evening's festivities."

Brion glanced toward the reviewing stand, where his mother and sisters were conferring with King Illann, then laughed and leaned toward Jamyl conspiratorially. "What she means is, she doesn't want her hall polluted by a bunch of sweaty, smelly men who've been in armor all afternoon."

"Can you blame her?" Jamyl replied, grinning.

"No, but I really wanted to trounce you, Jamyl," Brion responded, turning beseeching eyes on his uncle. "Can we not ride one more pass, Uncle? Please?"

"Only if you wish to incur the resentment of an exasperated queen," Richard replied. "Be content with a draw, as Sir Jamyl suggests. Either of you could do far worse. Part as equals, knight to knight."

For a moment, Brion looked like he might continue to protest, but then he quirked a reluctant smile and pulled off his helm, handing it down to Richard.

"Oh, very well. I accept the draw." He pulled off his gauntlets and tossed them into the helm Richard offered up. "And I suppose there's an element of grace encompassed in the knightly vows I made today. Something about courtesy to ladies, as I recall. I daresay that queens fall in that category, and especially one's mother."

He turned in the saddle to glance back at the reviewing stand and, as his mother rose, raised a hand in salute and then brought it to his breast and bowed over it. Duke Richard was smiling as he and Nigel led the king's horse over to the sidelines for Brion to dismount.

"Well, that's settled happily enough," Kenneth said, handing the pony's reins to Llion. "Or maybe not."

Across the yard behind them, his attention had been caught by a cloaked, dark-clad figure sitting motionless astride a coal-black R'Kassan steed with bardings as black as his master's garb. The lower part of his face was obscured by the veil of a black headdress worn in the desert manner, but the eyes were a piercing blue above the swath of black.

"Llion, why don't you take Alaric over to the watering trough to clean up a bit? They'll be calling the pages for the prize giving soon." Not taking his eyes from the newcomer, he plucked Alaric from the fence rail and set him on his feet. "Better collect your rings, son, and then go with Llion. I'll join you directly."

He did not wait to see whether the pair obeyed him; only grabbed the reins of his waiting mount and swung up, the horse already moving as he settled into the saddle. He could sense curious eyes shifting in his direction as he set off briskly across the mostly empty field, obviously headed toward the mysterious black-clad rider, who did not move from his place. As he drew abreast of the man, halting stirrup to stirrup, the black-swathed head inclined in greeting.

"Kenneth."

Chapter 3

"Because thou hast been my help, therefore in the shadow
of thy wings will I rejoice."
—PSALMS 63:7

"WHAT are you doing here?" Kenneth whispered, his gaze flicking warily around them. "Can they see you?"

The black-clad man lifted one hand to pull down the veil from the lower part of his face. As he did so, Kenneth caught the flash of a dark tattoo at the inner wrist, of a small, equal-armed cross.

"They can now," the man said softly, a faint smile moving in the close-clipped dark beard. "I shouldn't want your companions to think you addled, talking to thin air. I've come to pay my respects to Gwynedd's new premier knight—and perhaps cross lances with him, though I fear I may have arrived too late for that. Please ask if he will meet me in the center of the field, so I may offer the congratulations of my Order. Beyond that, the others need not know who I am."

"You seem very certain he'll agree," Kenneth muttered, though he found himself already backing his mount to turn and head in the direction of the king. Instructions from Sir Sé Trelawney were not easy to ignore— and in all fairness, the Deryni knight had always been an unfailing friend to Gwynedd and its royal line, and to the kin of Kenneth's late wife. Most recently, at least so far as Kenneth was aware, Sé had made an appearance at Brion's coronation, apparently seen by only a very few, and then had held brief but intense private converse with the new king later that evening.

Now Sé had returned, this time in view of the whole court, with yet another mysterious mission regarding Gwynedd's king. For a Knight of the

Anvil to make an appearance in the West was regarded as a singular honor, given the near-legendary prestige of the Order, at least in more eastern climes. During the reign of King Bearand Haldane, Anviler knights and members of the Order of St. Michael had held back Moorish incursions and policed the sea lanes against marauding pirates; and later, they were said to have given refuge to fugitive Michaelines after the suppression of that order, some of whom had been Deryni. No one knew how many of the present Anviler order might be Deryni, but the presence of any foreign Deryni in Gwynedd would always be cause for concern, if it became known.

Which made Kenneth's next task all the more delicate. The king knew that Sé was Deryni, but his father had not known; and the Sé Trelawney of today was not the Sé Trelawney knighted by Donal Haldane some sixteen years before. Complicating matters was the presence of Duke Richard and the king's younger brother, Nigel, standing nearby—and Jamyl Arilan, sitting his horse just behind the king. Though Kenneth had learned that Jamyl was Deryni (though he was forbidden to speak of it), he doubted anyone else at court knew, even Brion. And he did not know whether Jamyl was aware of Sé Trelawney.

"Kenneth, you're too late," Brion said good-naturedly, still a-horse as he tugged at the buckle of a vambrace. "Uncle Richard tells me I must bow to the wishes of the ladies. A pity, because I'd hoped you and I might cross lances today."

"You may wish to reconsider, Sire," Kenneth murmured, with a nod of acknowledgment to Duke Richard. "Yon black knight wishes to convey his respects, and hopes that the newly knighted Sir Brion Haldane might consent to meet him on the field of honor."

He jutted his chin in the direction of Sé, who had tucked the veil of his headdress back into place as Kenneth crossed the field, once again obscuring his lower face, and now was donning the helmet previously hung at his saddlebow. Both the king and Richard gave the newcomer careful scrutiny, the latter with something more akin to suspicion, for the rider's attire suggested origins far to the east, perhaps from the lands of Gwynedd's enemies. Jamyl, too, looked keenly interested.

"Who is he?" Richard demanded, bristling slightly. "He looks Torenthi."

Shaking his head, Kenneth smiled and leaned his elbows easily on his high pommel, beginning to enjoy the exchange. "He is not Torenthi," he replied, turning his gaze to Brion. "He is a friend, I assure you. Your father gave him the accolade, though he is no longer in service to Gwynedd."

"To whom is he in service, then?" Jamyl interjected, unable to contain himself any longer.

"Not to any enemy of ours," Kenneth assured him. "His service is to God, if you will. He is a Knight of the Order of the Anvil. But he prefers that his more particular identity not be made public. The king knows him."

Brion had begun nodding as Kenneth spoke, obviously making the connection, and turned his grey gaze on his uncle.

"Yes, I do know him, Uncle," he said quietly. "Pray, go to my lady mother and beg her indulgence for one last bout. For I think I owe much to this man."

"But—"

"Just do as I say!" Brion retorted, the steel of command in his voice. "And Jamyl, make certain that no one interferes. *No one!* Nigel, I'll have my helm and gauntlets back." He retrieved the gauntlets from the helm that Nigel timidly offered up, then handed the helm across to Kenneth. "Ride with me."

He pulled on the gauntlets as they slowly made their way toward the center of the field, never taking his eyes from the now-helmeted rider in black, who had tossed his cloak back on his shoulders and was selecting a white-painted tournament lance from a rack tended by a nervous-looking squire. A white belt gleamed against the black of boiled leather tournament armor, and a blank shield now adorned his left arm, borrowed for the occasion.

All around them, spectators were congregating along the sides of the field. The queen had risen and moved to the front of the royal pavilion, to stand anxiously with one hand on Duke Richard's arm. King Illann and Prince Ronan stood uncertainly to her other side, quietly conferring. Across the field, nearer the junior lists, Jared had pulled Llion to one side by the bicep and clearly was interrogating him. Llion, in turn, had both hands set firmly on young Alaric's shoulders, and was shaking his head.

All this Kenneth noted, the while watching Brion sidelong as the two of them rode out to meet the rider in black. All around them, a hush of anticipation was settling over the field. It was not uncommon for newly fledged knights to accept challenges in honor of their coming of age as warriors—Brion had been doing it all afternoon—but clearly, this challenger was new come to the field, and unknown to virtually everyone save Kenneth and, apparently, the king. When the rider had come within a few horse lengths of the king, he halted and slowly dipped his lance in salute, letting its tip rest lightly on the ground.

"Hail, Brion of Gwynedd," he said quietly, blue eyes ablaze within the shadows of his helm. "I offer you the reverence accorded a king, but my business today is with Sir Brion Haldane. Will he honor me with a *pas à barrière?*"

"You . . ." the king whispered wonderingly. "You were at my coronation."

"And told you then that I should be there for you, when you have need. Today your need is to demonstrate that you are not afraid to face a seasoned warrior in battle. Your men are watching. . . ."

He jutted his chin toward the outer boundaries of the tourney field, where the elite of Gwynedd's fighting men were gathering along the rails: battle-hardened veterans and those newly belted, and also the squires and pages, Gwynedd's future knights.

"Shall we?" Sé said softly.

With a glance at Kenneth, the king nodded gravely. Nodding in return, his opponent lifted his lance and wheeled to head for the far end of the *barrière* along which the two would ride. Kenneth accompanied the king to the opposite end and dismounted, giving his mount to Nigel and holding the head of the king's horse while Brion selected a lance.

"I know he's a Knight of the Anvil," Brion said quietly, staring down the *barrière* as Kenneth helped him seat the lance. "Anything I should know about their jousting strategy?"

Kenneth only shook his head and chuckled as he reached out to adjust a stirrup buckle. "Nothing *I* could tell you, my prince. They spend hours every day, honing their fighting skills. He will probably trounce you right royally—which is as it should be, on this, your first day as a newly dubbed knight. But he won't humiliate you. What he does, he will do for your own good, to remind you how much you still have to learn."

"I already know *that*," Brion muttered under his breath.

He bent helm to lance far enough to tap the visor into place, then let Kenneth lead his mount into position, to the right of his end of the *barrière*. At the far end, his opponent sat statue still, white-painted lance at rest in one gloved hand, stark against his black raiment.

Heart pounding as if it were he, about to face Sé Trelawney, Kenneth moved back a few paces, easing toward the sidelines with Nigel. He had no doubt that Brion would be taught an important lesson today, but the means had yet to be shown. What he did know was that Deryni did not come much more puissant than Sir Sé Trelawney, especially when honed by the rigorous training of the *Equites Incudis*. Could the less experienced king take a pass from the Anviler knight? That remained to be seen.

The two eyed one another for several long seconds, holding their increasingly fractious mounts at either end of the *barrière*, until suddenly, as if by unspoken command, both loosed their steeds in the same instant and came thundering down their respective lanes, lances dropping between horses' necks and shields. The weapons were especially designed for tournament use, to break away on impact—and did, both of them shattering halfway along their lengths as blunted tips struck squarely against shields with a tremendous crash of wood against metal.

Gasps reverberated amongst the onlookers, and several men started onto the field, but it immediately became clear that both riders were still seated. Duke Richard had moved with the others, but pulled himself up and signaled the others to pull back, for the king was grinning as he pulled up his mount at the far end of the *barrière* and saluted his opponent with what was left of his lance.

"Again!" he shouted, casting the shattered weapon aside and calling for a fresh one, which a squire was already running to provide. When his opponent saw what the king intended, he, too, took up a fresh lance and rode to his end of the *barrière*.

The outcome of the second run was not so evenly decided. Though both men started well, horses running strong and true, the blunted tip of Brion's lance wavered just at the last instant, striking off center and skittering off the blank shield and over Sé's shoulder. Sé's lance hit more squarely, shattering against Brion's shield with such force that the king reeled in the saddle, losing a stirrup, and only managed to stay a-horse by throwing his lance aside.

Sé, seeing this, immediately circled tight and urged his mount into a breathtaking leap up and over the *barrière*, to crowd hard against Brion's mount while he menaced the weaponless king with the jagged remnant of his own lance.

"Have a care, Sir Brion!" he said sharply. "In real battle, this could have been a more deadly weapon, in the hands of a real enemy, and you might well be dead! A tournament is practice for real combat! Never throw away your weapon while an opponent remains armed!"

With that, he cast the lance stub aside and backed off.

"Now, shall we give it one more try?" he said lightly, before turning to trot back toward his end of the *barrière*.

Shocked almost mute by his opponent's horsemanship, and how quickly Sé had pressed his advantage, Brion managed to gasp out a shaken, "Very well," and turned his mount to return to Kenneth.

"How did he *do* that?" he muttered under his breath, as Kenneth put another lance into his hand. "Do you think he used magic?"

"You know he did not, my prince," Kenneth said sharply. "What he *has* done is to share some of his experience with you. Gentlemen may play at war games, and even go to war, but in true battle, it is hard men who stay alive. You use whatever weapon is at hand. Remember that."

"Believe me, I am not apt to forget it," Brion said, adjusting his grip on the lance as he moved into position for the final run.

This time, as both men thundered straight and true along either side of the *barrière*, Sé's lance again shattered against the king's shield with jarring force. Brion's lance also struck squarely, but instead of breaking away as intended, it bowed in the instant of impact and then skittered over the top of the shield to graze the left side of Sé's helm, its hand guard walloping the faceplate with enough force to jar the black knight from his mount and wrench the lance from Brion's hand as Sé fell. Only narrowly did Brion avoid tripping up his own mount as they scrambled clear of the tumbling lance.

Amazingly, Sé managed to land on his feet, shield still on his arm and still clutching what remained of his lance. He brandished it like a sword as the king came around tight, working to control his mount. In that same, heart-pounding moment, as a collective gasp rippled among the spectators, Sé summoned his own mount with a shrill whistle and, as it galloped toward him, discarded his broken weapon and vaulted back into the saddle. Without pause, he then doubled back sharply, still at the gallop as he bent low to retrieve the lance-stub from the dust.

By then, Brion was pulling up in confusion, uncertain as Sé set his mount back on its haunches in a flurry of dust and gave the king ironic salute with a flourish of the broken weapon before casting it aside. As his horse settled, abruptly as still as a statue, he let fall his borrowed shield, then dropped his reins to pull off his helm, allowing his mount to move a few steps closer to the king as he hooked the helm's chin strap to his pommel.

"Well ridden, my lord," he said, as he gathered up his reins. "And in all, I think we both have learned useful lessons today." He glanced around at the debris of shattered lances, then returned his gaze to the king.

"I will share with you this caution, however. It would be prudent to have a word with those who craft your tournament and practice weapons. Your lance ought to have broken away as mine did. I should hate to see some worthy squire or page in your service take serious injury or death from such a fault."

Speechless, Brion could only nod, sweeping off his helmet with both hands. Kenneth had come running to his side by then, Nigel trotting wide-eyed behind him, and Brion handed off the helmet to Kenneth, who passed it on to Nigel.

"But I salute you, Sir Brion of Gwynedd," Sé said then, laying his right hand flat over his heart and bowing over it, "and I wish you many years of victory in battle. Until next time, may God hold you in the hollow of His hand."

With that, he wheeled and galloped from the field, cutting between groups of men who only gazed after him with mouths agape, too stunned even to think of trying to impede him.

"What just happened?" Brion said low to Kenneth, a slightly dazed look on his face as Kenneth laid a hand on the king's bridle.

"I believe—not to put too fine a point on it—that you were just put in your place, my prince," Kenneth said with a strained smile. "But I suggest that, if you wish to avoid awkward questions, you make little of this when we return to the dais. You comported yourself well against a very seasoned knight. Make no acknowledgment of anything more, lest you compromise his usefulness." He glanced back at the junior lists, and then at the royal pavilion.

"But I—ah—believe we still have prizes to award," he said, setting a hand on young Nigel's shoulder and indicating that he should go on ahead. "A goodly number of young men and boys are eagerly waiting to have the king recognize their accomplishments today. Shall we go back?"

Chapter 4

"A wise son maketh a glad father . . ."
—PROVERBS 15:20

As Kenneth took the head of the king's horse and began leading it slowly back to the royal pavilion, Brion pushed back his arming cap and started pulling off his gauntlets, his mood subdued and thoughtful. Duke Richard came out to meet the pair as they approached the royal pavilion, but the king brushed off his demands for an explanation and merely assured him they would talk later.

"I've taken no harm," he assured his uncle in a low voice, as he swung down from his mount and handed his gauntlets to Kenneth. "And I do apologize for the delay. Please gather the squires and pages for their prize giving."

"But, who was he?" Richard insisted.

"A friend of Gwynedd, Uncle. A Knight of the Anvil. Beyond that, you will have to ask *him*. Now, please see to the squires and pages."

More members of his family and immediate entourage tried to press him for details as he and Kenneth moved into the royal pavilion, but again he brushed them off, merely reiterating that he was unharmed, and wished to proceed with the conclusion of the afternoon's activities. Kenneth cleared a path as the two of them worked their way to the rear of the pavilion, where a body squire was waiting with towels and a basin of clean water.

Pulling off his arming cap, Brion plunged his head into the water and scrubbed vigorously at face and neck and hands, then toweled off and slicked back his hair before donning a gold circlet. Richard, meanwhile, had begun gathering the squires and pages as requested.

Kenneth stayed by the king's side as they returned to the front of the pavilion, where Brion took his place in the center chair between his mother and King Illann. Politely but firmly, he declined to comment on what had just transpired on the field. Brion's younger sisters, Princesses Xenia and Silke, settled onto stools at their mother's feet, raven hair glistening in the sunlight like blackbirds' wings, with several ladies-in-waiting ranged to either side. Moving to his customary place behind the chairs, Kenneth politely fended off all questions.

"It is not for me to say," was all the comment he would make, good-natured but firm, when pressed for information about the king's mysterious opponent.

At Duke Richard's summons, all the squires and pages in the competition began gathering in front of the dais, many of them with fathers or other male relatives trailing along to gather at the edges. Among them Kenneth noted the glowering presence of Sir Errol Seaton, whose son Cornelius had turned in a less than stellar performance.

Briskly Richard began moving among the boys, rapidly sorting them into some semblance of order, by age. Most of them had varying numbers of rings looped over an arm: booty from the competition. Conversation immediately ceased as a herald thumped on the floor of the dais with his staff of office and called for attention.

"Pray, attend the words of the king."

Brion smiled and sat forward, glancing to Duke Richard, who was standing among the pages. Most of them wore Haldane page's livery and looked much older than Alaric and Duncan, who stood together with Llion in their house livery of Corwyn and Kierney. A few were senior pages, nearly ready for squiring. The dozen or so squires were grouped to one side, including Duncan's brother Kevin, but some of the squires clearly were no longer children.

"I see that we're starting with the pages," the king said easily, looking over the sea of Haldane crimson. "Uncle, I understand that these young gentlemen competed at the rings."

"They did, my Liege," Richard said formally, still annoyed at his nephew's refusal to identify his opponent. "The rings were a handspan wide, fixed so that they would not rotate during a run," he added, for the benefit of King Illann and Prince Ronan. "Contestants were given ten runs in which to take as many rings as they could, but a fall disqualified from further participation, as did three consecutive passes without taking a ring."

"A worthy practice for future knights," Brion said with a droll nod, glancing at his royal guests. "As you know, the exercise teaches hand and eye coordination, as well as horsemanship. Mind you, the rings will be smaller when you compete as squires, lads," he reminded the assembled boys, "and as some of you found out the hard way, it's more difficult than it looks. How many of you were unhorsed during the competition? All those who fell off, please move over by Duke Richard."

Fully a third of the boys moved sheepishly to the duke's side, Cornelius Seaton among them, though many of them bore at least a few rings. Cornelius had none, and looked none too happy about it. Brion merely raised an eyebrow, shaking his head lightly as he pursed his lips and scanned them.

"Well, I see that some of you at least managed to snag a ring or two before tasting dust. That's commendable, but I know that all of you can do better in the future. It isn't that you will never fall off your horses—my uncle will tell you how often I used to land on my backside when I was first beginning my training—and even the best rider gets dumped occasionally. Today I learned that some riders, like my last noble opponent, even manage to land on their feet, and then vault back into the saddle. Uncle, you must learn how that is done—and then begin to teach it!"

Duke Richard only bowed slightly in agreement, lips tight-pressed.

"In any case, with practice, *all* of us will improve," the king went on. "And remember that it is also important to learn *how* to fall off your horse and not injure yourself." His grey eyes held a twinkle as they swept his listeners. "Happily, all of you seem to have survived *that* lesson, at least for today."

He smiled, then turned his attention to the rest of the pages. "Now, any of you who managed to stay on your horse but missed taking any rings, please step forward."

Two of the younger boys shuffled clear of the others, looking hangdog.

"Well." Brion looked askance at the pair. "I suppose that boys who can ride but can't hit a target might serve as couriers, or perhaps carry banners." He drew a breath and let it out with a dramatic sigh. "But since you aspire to be knights one day, lads, your use of weapons *will* improve." He made a shooing motion in the direction of the first group. "Join the ones who can't ride. All of you still have much to learn."

With that, he turned his attention to the remaining pages, of which there were nearly a dozen.

"Very good. I see that the rest of you all managed to stay mounted and take at least a few rings. Move closer now, right up to the dais."

Alaric shuffled forward with the rest, clutching his rings close to his body. Duncan stayed close beside him. Though both had known Brion Haldane since birth, viewing him almost as an elder brother or uncle, it was different standing before the king.

"Now, all of you raise your left arms and show me your rings." The royal gaze swept the quickly upraised arms. "I see. Now, if you have five or less, lower your arm and take three steps back."

Two boys stepped back.

"Six or less."

Airey Redfearn and another boy retreated.

Brion surveyed the rest of those standing with upraised arms, then pointed to a boy standing near Alaric, who stood a head taller than he. "Ciarán MacRae, how many rings do you have?"

"Eight, my lord," the boy said brightly.

"Eight. That's very good, but I see boys with more than that." He glanced at the others. "Anyone with eight or less, step back."

Ciarán and two more stepped back, including Duncan, and several of them cast interested glances at the stack of rings on Alaric's arm. But piled together, it was hard to judge how many there really were.

"Paget Sullivan, how many have you got?" Brion asked the oldest of the remaining boys, a tall twelve-year-old.

"Ten, Sire," the lad replied.

"Ten? Excellent work! And you, Aean Morrisey?"

"Only nine, Your Grace," the boy admitted.

"Ah, but nine is still very, very good. Well done, Aean. And young Alaric Morgan? It looks like you have quite a stack there. How many?"

"Ten, Sire," Alaric said confidently.

"Ten?" The king glanced over his shoulder at Kenneth and raised an eyebrow. "He really took ten? How old *is* he, Kenneth? He isn't even officially a page yet, is he?"

"No, my prince—but he will be eight at Michaelmas. Earl Jared and I are training him—and Sir Llion." He smiled as he jutted his chin toward Llion, standing with Duncan and trying to be invisible.

Brion shook his head, half in disbelief, then glanced at his mother, who had come to her feet and was holding a laurel wreath, looking faintly disapproving. Princess Xenia held a small silver cup.

"Interesting. Very well, I'm giving the prize to Paget Sullivan, because he was the best of the pages competing, with ten rings. Alaric, you aren't yet an official page, so I'm disqualifying you from the official competition. Paget, come and get your prize."

Alaric looked astonished and a little affronted, but after a glance at his father, he simply lowered his arm to cradle his rings and stepped back so that Paget could approach the queen.

"Congratulations, Master Paget," Richeldis murmured, setting the wreath atop his curls and then handing him the cup. He, in turn, bowed and kissed her hand.

"Thank you, Your Majesty."

"Thank *you*, Master Paget. I look forward to following your career."

Paget adjusted the wreath as he rejoined the other pages, grinning as he turned the cup in his hands. Alaric started to head back to Llion as the rest of the pages began to disperse, but at the sound of the king clearing his throat, all of them stopped and turned.

"Did I give anyone permission to retire?" Brion asked sternly.

A dozen pairs of eyes darted back to the king, and several boys murmured, "No, Sire."

"I didn't think I had. Alaric Morgan, come back up here, please. And young Duncan McLain, as well. And Earl Jared, where are you? And Earl Kenneth."

Wide-eyed, Alaric went forward, bowed, and looked around bewilderedly as his father, Duncan, and Jared joined him. Brion was conferring with one of his aides as they did so, and turned back to them with something in his hand.

"Alaric, I said that you were disqualified from the *official* pages' competition," Brion said, "but your performance certainly merits recognition." He crouched down to beckon both boys closer. "Let me see those ten rings."

Dutifully, Alaric held out his arm and watched while Brion counted.

"Good Lord, there really are ten. And Duncan, how many have you got? You're even younger than Alaric, aren't you?"

"Yes, Sire," Duncan whispered, showing the king seven rings.

"How old are you?"

"Seven, Sire. And a half."

"And you took seven rings? I think there were only four or five others who did that well, and everyone except Alaric is *much* older than you are. Both of you did very well." He put a silver coin in Duncan's hand and a gold one in Alaric's. "Thank you, gentlemen. I look forward to the day when you wear my livery. Jared, Kenneth," he got to his feet and nodded to both men, "well done."

Kenneth gestured toward Llion, standing farther back in the assembly. "Sir Llion Farquahar deserves most of the credit, Sire. He is responsible for much of the day-to-day drill for these lads."

Brion nodded toward Llion. "I do beg your pardon, Sir Llion. My thanks to you as well. Well done."

Llion bowed to acknowledge the compliment, and the king signaled that the fathers and sons might withdraw.

"We'll have the squires up here next," Duke Richard said, as the pages retreated and the squires began to assemble, Kevin among them. "Rather than rings, they jousted at the quintain, and a few of them managed stay mounted *and* hit the shield—which is no mean feat when trying to avoid the swing of the sandbag. A few even splintered lances." He winked at his nephew, his good humor apparently restored. "Some of them did very well, my prince. In a few years, I have no doubt that some of them will have earned the accolade."

"I certainly should hope so," Brion said with a snort.

Chapter 5

"That thou mayst walk in the way of good men,
and keep the paths of the righteous."
—PROVERBS 2:20

THE feast that night in the great hall was less in the nature of a further celebration than it was a hearty meal to replenish weary warriors after the exertions of the day, which had been hot and tiring.
A contented if somewhat bruised King Brion presided informally from
the high table, surrounded by members of his family and his dukes and
earls, including Kenneth and Jared. He had also invited King Illann and
Prince Ronan to sit at the king's table.

Also seated with the two earls were Jared's son Kevin, who had done
well in the squires' competitions, and half a dozen knights of their combined households, including Sir Llion and his counterpart for Earl Jared's
household, Sir Tesselin of Harkness, who looked after Kevin and Duncan.

Women were few in the hall, for the knights attending from outside
the city mostly had not brought along their wives or daughters, but one
end of the high table was graced by the presence of the Dowager Queen
Richeldis and her two daughters. In addition, Richeldis's brother Illann,
for some years a widower, had finally decided to remarry, and had brought
along his future queen to meet his sister and her family, though she
had declined to attend the knighting ceremony or the afternoon's tournament. The Countess Amielle sat demurely with the other royal ladies,
rather than her intended, but she was a sultry, voluptuous beauty much
younger than Illann, with dark eyes and masses of titian hair caught up in

a netting of slender gold cords. While her manner in no way invited inappropriate attention, she had managed to turn the heads of not a few young and not so young men of the court. Kenneth had met the lady the day before, when the visitors arrived, but had found himself comparing her to his late wife.

"I think I am quite content to remain a dour old widower," he said to Jared, as he took his place at table with him and their other knights. "However, there is no doubt that she will considerably adorn Illann's court."

"Not my type," Jared said flatly. "What about you, Llion?"

Llion shook his head, slightly amused. "I think she may be trouble for Illann, once she is entrenched at Pwyllheli, my lord."

"You think so?" Jared cast a glance over his shoulder at the royal ladies, then back at his companions. "You may be right. We shall hope not."

They settled into their places as servers brought out the first course. Alaric and Duncan served their fathers at the beginning of the meal, bringing basins and ewers and towels for hand washing; but then, by virtue of their impressive performances in the afternoon's ring jousting, they were allowed to take places at table and share in the meal. Wide-eyed and famished, they stuffed themselves on roasted beef, capon, stewed onions, and fresh-baked bread, along with well-watered ale, but after less than an hour both boys were visibly drooping. Duncan nearly nodded off into his trencher, saved only by a sharp kick from his elder brother, and Alaric was finding it ever more difficult to keep his eyes open. Their plight soon came to the notice of the adults.

"Tesselin, why don't you and Llion take the boys up to bed?" Jared said after a speaking glance at Kenneth, gesturing with his cup of ale. "Yes, Kevin, you may stay awhile longer," he added, at his elder son's obvious objection.

"I'll take them," Llion said, rising. "I confess I'm tired myself, and Tesselin looks like he's enjoying himself. Let's go, lads."

Neither of the younger boys put up any serious resistance, despite the unprecedented novelty of being allowed to eat with the grown-ups. By the time they had paid their respects to the king, Duncan was all but asleep on his feet, and Alaric's yawns were becoming more and more difficult to suppress.

With Llion bringing up the rear, the two boys trudged up the turnpike stair and down several torch-lit corridors, going first to the quarters being shared by Earl Jared and his two sons. There Llion helped the younger of those sons strip off his belt and tunic and crawl into the big canopied bed—asleep as soon as his head settled into the pillow. Llion smiled as he paused to pull off the boy's boots and tuck a McLain plaid around him. Then he and Alaric made their way to the modest suite always reserved for Earl Kenneth and his immediate party when they were in residence at the capital.

Alaric paused just long enough to wash his face and hands, letting Llion pull off his boots and outer garments while he blearily checked in his belt pouch for the gold coin he had won at the tournament that afternoon. Then he crawled happily into the bed his father would later share with him. As he drifted off to sleep, he was briefly aware of Llion gathering up his discarded clothes and unrolling the pallet where he customarily slept at the foot of the bed.

SOME little while later—he could not have said how much later—Alaric became abruptly aware that something vital in the room had changed. His eyes popped open to faint moonlight and awareness of an unmoving, black-clad form sitting right on the edge of the bed beside him—not Llion or his father or, indeed, anyone in his father's household! His stunned first impression of a high-collared black robe suggested a priest, of which very few bore much goodwill toward a half-Deryni child.

Jolted fully awake between one heartbeat and the next, Alaric flung himself toward the far edge of the bed, scrambling for safety, and groped for the dagger that should have been beneath his pillow but wasn't. Frantic, he twisted to escape the hand that clamped onto the neck of his shirt and dragged him back, both his small hands locking around the powerful wrist. But even as he drew breath to scream for help—*Where was Llion?*—golden luminance flared around the man's head, far brighter than any moonlight, and he found himself ensorcelled in the gaze of a pair of jewel-bright blue eyes.

"*Do not cry out,*" the man said softly, though the gentle tone belied the compulsion in that simple command. "Relax."

Despite his best efforts to the contrary, Alaric could feel his indrawn breath softly leaving his lungs, his body going limp, resistance draining away like water through a sieve.

"Good lad!" came the whispered response, as a faint smile parted the close-clipped beard and mustache and the man's free hand reached out to briefly brush his brow, the Deryni aura dying away. "You're quite safe. We have actually met before, but you were only a baby then. At your baptism, your parents laid you in my arms before God and bade me serve as one of your godparents. 'Tis a vow I take most seriously."

Alaric stared at the man, mouth agape, trying to take it all in, but he knew, without knowing how he knew, that the man's revelation had put to rest any remaining alarm, along with the last of his resistance. As he drew a deep, deliberate breath to marshal his wits, letting it out slowly as his mother had taught him, he opened his hands around the man's wrist and drew them apart in an exaggerated gesture of yielding. The man, in turn, released his handful of shirt, nodding as he briefly smoothed the crumpled linen.

"I apologize for the somewhat unconventional introduction," his visitor murmured, sitting back and reaching behind him briefly. "I would have approached through your father, but this seemed more expeditious. And earlier this afternoon, I was somewhat occupied. This is yours, I think," he added, and produced the dagger Alaric had been looking for, offering it hilt first across his forearm.

"Who *are* you?" Alaric whispered, as he accepted the dagger and laid it aside. "It was you who fought the king this afternoon, wasn't it? And where is my knight?" he added, suddenly remembering Llion. "Does Sir Llion know you're here?"

The man smiled faintly and nodded. "Excellent. A duke should always have concern for his men. Your Sir Llion is keeping watch in the other room. He has been instructed not to speak of me, so do not ask, for he may not answer. And yes, it was I who fought the king this afternoon."

Alaric's eyes widened at the implication, for the man clearly was Deryni—he could sense the man's shields, now that he was fully awake—but curiosity was fast replacing whatever fear was left. Something about his Deryni visitor seemed oddly reassuring, almost . . . familiar. . . .

"You said you're my godfather," he said softly. "But, who *are* you?"

"You are to be the king's protector; I am *your* protector," the man said, lifting both hands to show the inner wrists, and the ink-black crosses tattooed there, each hardly bigger than a man's thumbprint. "My name is Sir Sé Trelawney. Perhaps your mother told you what these mean."

All at once Alaric remembered a sunny afternoon in that long-ago last autumn before his mother died, watching her bent over the illuminated capital she was just finishing: the opening page of a book she had penned for his father, of poetry written by his sister Delphine—what had been their last Christmas gift for him. Alyce de Corwyn had looked up and smiled as her firstborn came into the room, laying aside her brush and beckoning for him to come and sit beside her on the padded bench, for she was heavily pregnant with his sister Bronwyn.

Embracing him briefly, she had smoothed his hair and kissed him on the forehead, then bade him watch while she took up pen and a scrap of parchment and inked a tiny, equal-armed cross, exactly like the ones on the insides of both Sir Sé's wrists.

Men who bear these marks are vowed Knights of the Anvil, she had told him, *sworn before God to serve the Light. There is one such man—his name is Sir Sé Trelawney—whom you may trust with your life and your very soul, if he offers you assistance.*

"You're a—a Knight of the Anvil," Alaric whispered. "Mama said that I can trust you."

"Indeed, you can," Sé replied, smiling faintly as he lowered his hands and briefly glanced away: an angle that enabled Alaric to glimpse the dark, silver-threaded hair sleeked back in a braided warrior's knot. "She was a remarkable woman, your mother—like a sister to me. We grew up together—she and your Aunt Marie and your Uncle Ahern, who both sadly died before you were born—and your Uncle Jovett Chandos and I. After Marie died, I—went away. But I promised your mother that I should always be there when she had need. When she died untimely, I made your father the same promise—and I make it to you, now: that so long as I have breath within me, I shall always be there for you, when you have need."

"Is that why you've come?" Alaric managed to whisper, unable to look away.

"In part." Sé gave him an inclination of his head. "I came to see the king knighted—but I also watched you ride," he added, smiling at the boy's hopeful look. "You did very well."

"I didn't see you," Alaric retorted, almost challenging.

Sé chuckled. "That is because I did not wish to be seen," he said lightly. "And in time, it may be that you shall acquire the same skill.

"But other skills must come first. I have come to see whether some of those other skills perhaps can be awakened, to help you protect yourself while you take the time needed to grow up. This asks a great deal of you, I know. You do not yet have the years to learn all that you *should* know— and I do not know how much your mother was able to teach you before she passed. But you will be coming to the king's court in another year or two, away from your father's protection. There will be those who will try to kill you before you can grow into the role intended for you."

Alaric shivered a little, for he knew full well who some of those were, who would prefer to see him dead, but no one had ever phrased it quite that way before—that people would try to kill him.

"What must I do?" he whispered.

"For now, simply allow me access to your mind," Sé said softly. At the same time, Alaric felt a gentle probing at his shields, quickly withdrawn.

"Good, you do have shields," Sé went on. "Quite good ones, actually. Fortunately, most of your enemies do not, for they are human—and Deryni enemies should be few, at least for now. But the strength of your shields means it is likely that you also have an awakening of at least the beginnings of other skills. To know for certain—and to begin teaching you how to use them—I must slip past those shields and probe deeper. And to do that without hurting you, I must have your help, and your complete trust."

Wide-eyed, Alaric took a deep breath, then reached out to take Sé's right hand, keeping his gaze fixed on Sé's as he brought the Anviler's hand up to touch his forehead—for that was how his mother had always begun their teaching sessions.

"Do what you need to do," he whispered, closing his eyes.

MEANWHILE, in the castle hall, the ladies and the king's uncles had retired for the night and many of the king's guests were beginning to take their leave, for the hour grew late. Nonetheless, at the king's invitation, most of the new knights created that day had joined him and Jamyl and Prince Ronan at the high table to drink increasingly exuberant toasts. Kenneth and Jared were part of the company, and had been finishing last cups of wine and thinking about leaving the younger men to more serious drinking when Kenneth saw the travel-worn man in Cassani livery paused in the doorway of the hall, scanning faces as he removed his cap. One look at the messenger's expression told Kenneth that the news was not good.

"Jared," he murmured, setting a hand on his cousin's arm and glancing pointedly in the direction of the doorway, "one of your father's men has just arrived—and on urgent business, by the look of him."

Even as Jared and the king swiveled to look, Jared coming to his feet, the man spotted them and started in their direction, breaking into a trot to traverse the length of the hall.

"Is it my father?" Jared demanded, as the man reached them and bowed over the cap he clutched to his breast, first to the king and then to Jared.

"Aye, my lord—but he was yet alive when I left him three days ago," the man added hopefully, though his lips tightened as he glanced at his dusty boots and twisted at the dusty cap. "But he took a turn the day before that. He cannot speak or move on his right side. Your lady wife bids you return as soon as you may, for the surgeon does not think he will long endure in this state. I fear it is the end, my lord. I'm very sorry. He is a good man."

Jared's face had gone very still as the man spoke, but he clasped the man's shoulder distractedly as he turned to the king.

"I must return to Cassan at once, Sire," he murmured.

"Of course you must."

"Prince Ronan, please make my apologies to your father and all his party."

"I shall," Ronan agreed, "and I daresay he will understand."

"Kenneth, will you ride with me?" Jared went on, already edging back toward his men, who also had risen with their lord. "Sybaud, choose four men to ride with us. Kevin must come as well—and perhaps Llion and the rest of the household knights could accompany Tesselin with the younger boys," he added to Kenneth. "Will you bring Xander and Trevor?"

"Of course." Kenneth's nod to the pair set them on their feet. "I must speak to Llion as well. We'll assemble in the stable yard in half an hour."

A few minutes later, having given orders to the men Jared had chosen to accompany them, Kenneth was slipping into the modest suite allotted to himself and Alaric. To his surprise, he found Llion sitting in a chair before the dark hearth, his gaze vague and unfocused. The young knight looked a little bewildered as he glanced up.

"Llion?" Kenneth murmured. "I expected you would be long asleep by now."

"The fault is mine," said a low voice as Sé emerged from the shadows nearer the door that led into the sleeping chamber. "I had business with my godson. I hope you do not mind."

Kenneth started back slightly, surprised to find Sé here, then glanced at Llion, who seemed still unaware of Sé's presence, and had started to get up.

"I am always glad to see you," Kenneth said tentatively, as Sé came to set a hand on Llion's shoulder and the young knight subsided. "What is this all about?"

"I came to see the king knighted, as you know—and I may not stay long—but I also wished to see how the boy is progressing," Sé replied. "Some of his powers are stirring already. He yet lacks the focus to *compel* the truth, but that will come as his powers mature. In the meantime, I believe he will know, increasingly, when he is being lied to."

"Already?" Kenneth murmured, but it was not so much a question as a statement of confirmation. "I hope you've stressed the need for discretion. That particular talent brought his mother little but trouble."

"Aye, but she used it in the king's service, in the cause of justice," Sé pointed out. "I have no doubt that she counted the risk well worth while."

Kenneth fought down a lump in his throat and looked away, more than a little troubled. "I know that—and I loved that she was willing to make that sacrifice. But Alaric is still so young. . . ."

"He is young, but he has a strong instinct for self-preservation," Sé pointed out, "and I have reinforced that. He will not *invite* trouble. But reading the truth will be an increasingly valuable skill for him."

"I don't doubt that," Kenneth replied, glancing back at Llion, oblivious near the door. "What have you done to my knight?"

Sé smiled faintly. "He will remember nothing of this visit, unless you wish him to do so, of course. Or if you prefer, I can leave him with knowledge of who I am, so that we need not go through this deception every time I come. In that case, I would also set compulsions that will keep him from speaking of any of this—the way Alyce did with you, when the king came to Alaric's Naming."

Kenneth remembered the night well—and the prohibition against speaking of it to outsiders had been gentle, as Alyce had been gentle. He had no doubt that the precaution had probably protected all of them who had been involved. She had looked so beautiful in the candlelight, surrounded by the glow of her magic. . . .

"Yes, do that," he murmured, turning half away. "And thank you for what you are doing for her son, Sé."

"Your son as well," Sé said, smiling faintly as he lifted his right hand to his heart and bowed slightly over it. Then he went to Llion and touched his forehead, briefly closing his eyes. When he turned back to Kenneth, he held out his hand.

"God keep you safe, Kenneth," he said softly, as their hands clasped. "I think it best that he does not remember this visit, but he will be ready for the next."

Grateful beyond speech, Kenneth let himself be drawn into the open doorway as Sé departed, watching as the Anviler knight merged with the shadows and disappeared. After gazing after him for a moment, Kenneth turned back into the room, where Llion had stirred and was moving about the outer chamber, tidying various pieces of equipment.

"Llion, could I see you outside for a moment?" he said quietly, motioning with his chin.

With a look of question, Llion put aside a folded shirt and followed Kenneth into the corridor.

"I must ride for Cassan tonight, with Jared," Kenneth said in a low voice, after he had drawn the door closed. "Duke Andrew has been taken ill, and Jared is likely to be duke far sooner than we had hoped."

The young knight's face fell. "I *am* sorry to hear that, my lord," he murmured. "Duke Andrew is a good man. Shall I get the boy ready to travel?"

"Not tonight," Kenneth replied. "Jared and I will leave shortly, with a small escort that can move fast. I'll take Xander and Trevor with me— and we'll take Kevin with us; but Jared is leaving Duncan and Tesselin with you. He has asked that the two of you bring the boys with the rest of our party. Set the best pace you can, but remember that they're only seven. With any luck, at least Jared and Kevin and I will arrive before Andrew passes."

"You think he's going to die?" Llion asked softly.

"He has had a long, full life," Kenneth replied, "and you know his health has not been good, these past few years. I think this may well be his time. But it will be the end of an era."

Llion crossed himself in silent agreement. "God grant him a peaceful passing," he murmured.

"May He grant it, indeed." Kenneth allowed himself a weary sigh. "I'll change into something more suitable for hard riding, then say good-bye to Alaric. I'd take him along, but seven is young for the kind of speed we'll be trying to make. You might check with Tesselin and Jared's men, see if you can give them a hand. You should make the best time you can, but you *are* allowed to stop for food and sleep along the way."

"Aye, my lord."

Returning to the inner chamber, Kenneth moved as quietly as he could, changing his court attire for more serviceable riding leathers, sturdy boots, a light mail shirt. He was doing up his leather vambraces when he became aware that he was being watched. As he turned toward the bed, Alaric eased up on his elbows.

"What're you doing, Papa?" he whispered.

Forcing a faint smile, Kenneth sat down on the edge of the bed beside his son. "I must go back to Culdi with your Uncle Jared, lad."

"Now? In the middle of the night?"

"I'm afraid so. Uncle Andrew is very sick."

The boy plumped back onto his pillow, looking away briefly. "He's going to die, isn't he?"

"I suspect he is," Kenneth admitted.

"I don't want him to die."

"Well, neither do I. But we all have to die someday. And he's had a long, full life. He's seen his son grow into a fine man, and watched his grandsons grow nearly to manhood. . . ."

"He still shouldn't have to die."

"No, he shouldn't, and maybe he won't for a while yet. But if it *is* his time, Uncle Jared would like to see him one more time, to say good-bye. So I'm going to go with him and Kevin, to help them get there fast."

"When will you be back?" Alaric wanted to know.

Kenneth shrugged. "Difficult to say. But it really doesn't matter, because Llion and Tesselin are going to bring you and Duncan—just not quite as fast. You'll leave tomorrow, and probably get there several days after we do."

Alaric perked up immediately. "We get to go with Llion?"

"Yes."

"Will it be an adventure?"

"Hopefully, not *too* much of an adventure," Kenneth said with a faint smile. "You shall have a proper escort of household knights. If I thought there might be trouble, I wouldn't let them bring you."

"I shall need to ride a horse, Papa. My pony would be much too slow!"

"I believe Llion is organizing that as we speak. He'll find you and Duncan some steady, reliable mounts. Your ponies can stay here, for now. I'll send someone for them later in the summer, maybe even in the autumn."

"You mean after Uncle Andrew is dead," the boy said sadly, then sat up abruptly. "May I go tell Duncan?"

"No, you may not. Duncan and his da are having much the same conversation that you and I are having, except that it's his grandfather they're discussing, not my brother-in-law, and it's Uncle Jared's father. Jared and I plan to be on our way very shortly, so you need to get your sleep. Today was a busy day, and tomorrow will be even busier."

"Can I at least watch you leave?"

Kenneth started to say no, but then relented and reached down to scoop up the boy in his arms and set him on the floor.

"Just until we leave," he agreed, "and you're to do as Llion asks, once I've left, as though his instructions came from me."

"Yes, Papa."

"Now, bring me my sword, so we can get down to the stable yard," he instructed, with an affectionate swat to his son's backside.

Chapter 6

"Now a thing was secretly brought to me . . ."
—JOB 4:12

A little while later, when Earl Jared McLain and his elder son rode out of Rhemuth Castle, accompanied by Lord Kenneth Morgan and a small escort of their combined household knights, two kings and two princes were among those who gathered in the castle yard to bid them Godspeed, for Prince Ronan had gone to wake his father at the news. Atop the battlements above the gate, the young sons of Jared and Kenneth leaned out to wave farewell, watched over by Sir Llion Farquahar and his Kierney counterpart, Sir Tesselin of Harkness. Despite the late hour, news of Duke Andrew's failing health had spread quickly, for the imminent passing of a duke had implications for all the Eleven Kingdoms. Accordingly, even the queen and her daughters and ladies had betaken themselves to the chapel royal to offer prayers for the stricken duke, and for the safety of those traveling to bid him farewell.

GIVEN the unexpected ending to the evening, it was well after midnight by the time the king and his guests retired and Sir Jamyl Arilan could safely set about his other duties—duties not to the king but to a secret organization to which he was sworn by oaths far more binding than those he owed his sovereign. Ascending a spiral stair to an upper floor, he made his way quietly past the royal library and paused outside the door of a neighboring guest chamber to listen, setting his hand flat against the wood while his mind probed for a presence beyond.

When he had confirmed that the lone occupant was deeply asleep, he slid his hand down to the door latch and exerted power, breathing a faint sigh as the latch lifted with a soft *snick*. A moment he paused to listen again, lest the sound had been heard; then he slowly pushed the door open far enough to slip inside, closing it behind him and setting the latch back in place. Beyond, from the direction of the canopied bed, he could hear breathy snores.

He allowed himself a wordless prayer of thanks that his entry had not been detected, even as he tiptoed close enough to gently touch the sleeper on the brow, deepening the sleep and setting controls in case the sleeper should stir when he returned. He had performed this office often in the past, so that his late uncle and the even later Michon de Courcy might have safe access to the room and what it hid—the guest chamber was often in use when providing accommodation to visitors—but this was the first time Jamyl had facilitated his own use of the room. The estimable Lord Michon had passed two years before, his absence still felt keenly among those Jamyl was on his way to meet; and Jamyl's Uncle Seisyll had slipped away shortly after Twelfth Night, following several months of declining health. The pair had been senior among those who comprised the Camberian Council. The eldest now was Prince Khoren Vastouni, seriously contemplating retirement, and after him Oisín Adair. Jamyl, at twenty, was the youngest.

Sobered by this thought, Jamyl moved softly into the center of the room, nearer to the window, and took his stance in the center of the Kheldish carpet that lay there, reaching with his mind for the now long-familiar coordinates of the Portal matrix beneath. Then, after a last glance at the unmoving lump in the bed, he briefly closed his eyes and tweaked the energies—and controlled the slight surge of vertigo as he was suddenly . . . elsewhere.

"Enjoyed the feast, did you?" said a pleasant baritone from the shadows to his left, before Jamyl could even draw breath.

Instinctively, Jamyl glanced in that direction, grinning as silvery light flared in the hand of the speaker. Though Stefan Coram owned only a few more years than Jamyl, and was senior in the Camberian Council by only a matter of months, he was perhaps the most powerful Deryni Jamyl had ever met: a fitting replacement for the redoubtable Michon de Courcy, whom Jamyl had known since childhood and from whom Jamyl had received much of his training.

"I wish it *were* the feast that kept me," Jamyl retorted, stepping from the Portal to exchange a handclasp with the other man. "A messenger arrived from Culdi several hours ago. The Duke of Cassan is dying—may already be dead, for all we know. Earl Jared and Kenneth Morgan rode out shortly after they received the news. After that, it took a while for everyone to settle in. Caused quite a stir, as you can imagine—but then, Duke Andrew's absence from the king's knighting had already caused a lot of speculation."

"Cassan, eh?" Coram raised one white-blond eyebrow. "Well, he's had a long and distinguished life, and Jared McLain has served his apprenticeship, that's for certain. He'll wear the coronet well." He gestured with his handfire toward a pair of burnished metal doors, half again as high as a man. "We'd best go in. They're discussing Meara—which is hardly anything new, but they're also waiting for Khoren, hoping he'll have further news from Torenth."

Jamyl looked at him sharply. "Do we have another Festillic claimant?"

"Perhaps not *this* time round," Stefan replied.

"No? I thought we had confirmation that Prince Hogan's new wife is carrying another son."

"Oh, she is," Stefan confirmed. "Whether she can deliver this one alive remains to be seen. Khoren's contact in the Festillic household reports that she went into labor nearly three days ago."

Jamyl grimaced, for while he could hardly wish ill on any innocent babe still in its mother's womb, or even on its mother, a male heir for the Festillic pretender to the throne of Gwynedd could only cause problems for his own prince. But he said nothing as the doors parted for him and Stefan.

Inside, four heads turned to note their arrival, momentary anticipation subsiding as Jamyl's presence registered.

"Ah, it's Jamyl," the lone woman observed.

She and the three others were gathered around the great, eight-sided table of ivory that dominated the octagonal chamber, and appeared to have been poring over a map spread in the table's center. Above the table, suspended from the center boss of the faceted dome that lit the room by day, a crystal sphere cast a stark light that quite overpowered the more golden glow from candle sconces set at the angles of the room.

By this light, the Lady Vivienne looked distracted and a little haggard, aged beyond her years in a robe of faded russet and a close-fitting wimple. Barrett de Laney wore his customary scholar's robes, the scarlet of the great university at Rhanamé, but the harsh lighting emphasized the angles of his lean, ascetic features, his sightless eyes like pools of darkness under the shadow of his brow.

Rhydon, somewhat older than Jamyl or Stefan, managed to look both serious and a trifle rakish, wearing his long facial scar like the badge of honor it was. He had sustained it in protecting the king, little though the king realized it—just as the king must never learn the full extent of Jamyl's assistance on that fateful day. Oisín Adair, the oldest of those present, was probably the one Jamyl knew least well, but he clearly had been leading the discussion, one hand poised on the map before them.

"No word yet from Khoren," Oisín said, in answer to the unspoken question in Stefan's lifted eyebrow, as he waved the pair to vacant chairs. "Jamyl, while we wait, I was sharing some intelligence regarding recent developments in Meara. You may recall that I have been nurturing a friendship with the royal governor, who indicates that the king probably will need to begin thinking about a campaign next spring—or at least a royal visitation."

"Well, at least we got him safely knighted," Jamyl murmured, as he took his seat to Oisín's right and Stefan continued on past Barrett to sit. "He made a good showing at the tournament as well. But I had hoped he would have a few more years before Meara reared its ugly head."

Vivienne quirked a faint smile as she glanced at their most recent inductee. Though Jamyl was junior to all of them, he had served an exceptionally useful apprenticeship beside his late uncle, Sir Seisyll Arilan, thereby gaining valuable access to the inner workings of Gwynedd's court—and close friendship with the king.

"Oh, hardly ugly, dear boy," she said lightly. "Sometimes bleak, I will grant you, though parts of the coast can be quite agreeable, at least in high summer. But then, you probably have never been to Meara."

Several of them chuckled at that, and Jamyl rolled his eyes, smiling as he did so, but shook his head in agreement that, indeed, he had not visited that benighted province.

"Take heart, lad," Oisín said at his left. "If you continue to serve Brion of Gwynedd, 'tis likely you will be obliged to become familiar with Meara all too soon."

"A pesthole!" Rhydon muttered under his breath, leaning back to fold his arms across his waist.

"Indeed," Barrett agreed, and returned his attention to the map beneath his hand, sweeping southward along the mountains that marked Meara's border with the Connait, though the sightless eyes gazed at nothing. "Unfortunately, I fear that the pestilence festering in Meara will continue to plague the kings of Gwynedd for as long as there are descendants of the old Mearan royal line."

"Surely, there can't be many left," Jamyl said. "I was under the impression that King Donal's last foray into Meara pretty much wiped out the last of them. And didn't Prince Judhael disappear after that? Is he even still alive?"

Barrett shrugged. "Alive, yes, though in exile since that time. And I would venture to say that his threat is greatly diminished."

"Be plain about it, Barrett," Rhydon muttered. "They say that his mind has gone."

"Can that be any great surprise?" Vivienne replied. "After all, that venture cost him a daughter and a granddaughter."

Rhydon snorted. "A proper prince would have taken that as a call for vengeance."

"For those Mearans faithful to the cause, Judhael *is* a proper prince, *and* their rightful lord—not Brion of Gwynedd," Barrett pointed out dryly. "Which is why we must not discount Judhael. And however sound of mind he may or may not be, he has a grandson of the same name nearing his majority. Furthermore, the Princess Caitrin might yet marry and produce an heir."

"There may be some truth to that last," Oisín said thoughtfully.

"Had it not been for Donal Haldane's last Mearan campaign, she would have married Sir Francis Delaney, the younger brother of the Earl of Somerdale. Fortunately for Donal, Delaney met his end in the same engagement that saw Judhael's daughter and granddaughter hounded to death. We have Morian to thank for that," he added for the benefit of Jamyl, who had been but a boy at the time. "Yes, Morian du Joux, or ap Lewys, as he was born, whose father was Lewys ap Norfal. Lewys was quite a thorn in our sides, in his time, but fortunately the son serves us well. He has mostly made his career at the governor's court in Meara, serving Haldane interests."

Jamyl only nodded. He was well acquainted with the stories of how Lewys ap Norfal had been expelled from the Camberian Council many decades before, and had later perished in a magical endeavor gone horribly wrong. And he had heard of Morian, who apparently had mostly lived down his father's reputation.

"In any case," Oisín went on, "recent rumor has it that the Princess Caitrin now wishes to marry Derek Delaney Earl of Somerdale, the elder brother of her previous betrothed. This match—nay, any match—does not meet with the approval of her mother, who has been serving as regent-in-exile since her husband's descent into . . . let us say ineffectiveness rather than madness. Aude of Meara believes that enough Quinnell blood has been spilled in the now-lost Mearan cause. If Caitrin should fail to produce an heir, the last of the Mearan succession would rest in that last surviving grandson, the younger Prince Judhael—and they say that Aude has been grooming him for the Church, to the point that he intends to take holy orders."

Vivienne sniffed. "At twelve, I think it far more likely that young Prince Judhael may awaken to more worldly ambitions, but at least that is probably for the future."

"We shall see," Oisín replied noncommittally. "I worry more about Caitrin. Her mother's health is said to be failing. Once Aude is gone, Caitrin may well marry—and any children she might bear would—"

He broke off as the double doors suddenly parted and the last of their number silently entered the chamber, not meeting anyone's gaze. In contrast to his usual, sometimes flamboyant attire, Prince Khoren Vastouni tonight was clad all in black, his greying hair ruffled in a silvery halo around his flat-topped black hat. As he slid into his seat to Vivienne's left, she touched a hesitant hand to his shoulder, at which he shook his head.

"What has happened?" Barrett asked quietly, cocking his head in the other's direction.

"'Tis over," Khoren said in a low voice, clearly steeling himself for the news he must deliver. "Both the Lady Roshane and her child are dead."

Vivienne gasped and sat back in her chair, her face draining of color, and Stefan bit at his lip.

"It *was* a very long labor . . . ," Barrett said tentatively.

"Aye, but that alone was not the cause of her death," Khoren replied, gazing up sightlessly at the glowing crystal far above their heads, his tone flat and detached. "Hogan had summoned his aunt to attend the birth: the very ruthless Princess Camille Furstána—or Mother Serafina, as she now styles herself." He briefly closed his eyes, as if to blot out the memory, then leaned his head against the high back of his chair.

"The Festils are nothing if not tenacious, whether by birth or by marriage," he went on. "When it became clear to the Lady Roshane that her strength was failing, and that she could not deliver, she seized her husband's hand and bade them cut the child from her womb." Vivienne gasped, and Jamyl felt his gut do a queasy roll. "Hogan held her head and blocked the pain, weeping, and Camille did the deed—all for naught, as it happened. The child, a prince, never drew breath—and could not have long survived, in any case. The head was nearly twice the size it should have been, and there were . . . other deformities. My informant was present at the birth, but would not elaborate. Perhaps it is better that way."

As he raised a hand to cover his eyes, a collective sigh whispered among his listeners.

"Well," said Rhydon, after a beat. "It could be argued that there *is* a positive side to all of this. One less male heir to strengthen Hogan's claim on Gwynedd."

"That is a monstrous thing to say!" Vivienne snapped.

"Nonetheless, it is true," Rhydon said coldly. "The Festils have long memories, and they will not lightly give up what they regard as rightfully theirs."

"What they stole in the first place!" Stefan said under his breath.

"Be that as it may," Rhydon replied, "eventually, your Brion Haldane will need to contend with Prince Hogan. But at least it will not be with a son at his back. At least not this time."

"He does have issue from that von Soslán affair," Barrett pointed out. "Two boys among them, as I recall."

"They are of no import," Vivienne said flatly. "All of the children of that union are bastards."

Jamyl sat forward. "Hogan has children besides Charissa?"

Vivienne shrugged. "There were several by the von Soslán woman. The two were even married briefly, though his mother had the marriage annulled as soon as she found out, and King Arkady also disapproved. Kethevan, she is called.

"For some years after that, Hogan refused to take another wife, though he continued to live with his inamorata, and she bore him many children. I believe that three survive. Eventually, he was reconciled with his mother, and agreed to marry a woman of appropriate rank."

"That would be Larissa de Marluk, who bore him the Princess Charissa," Barrett offered. "There was also an identical twin who died shortly after birth. Then after Larissa died in childbed of a stillborn son, he married another highborn woman, Roshane of Fallon. Alas, poor lady, *her* first child was stillborn, and the second. . . ." He sighed. "But it all matters little, now."

"These surviving von Soslán bastards," Jamyl said thoughtfully. "Might they still present a threat?"

Khoren shook his head. "Festillic house law is quite specific. Charmed though Hogan may have been by the Lady Kethevan, she was not deemed of sufficient rank to contract a royal marriage. Hence, the children of that union may not inherit. None are in the Festillic succession, or have dynastic rights."

"That could change, of course, were Hogan to become more ambitious, or more desperate," Barrett observed dryly. "Blood *is* blood, after all."

Chapter 7

"Thine own friend, and thy father's friend, forsake not . . ."
—PROVERBS 27:10

IR Llion and Sir Tesselin left with the second Culdi party at mid-morning of the following day, with both their young charges now well mounted on reliable rounceys. The journey would take nearly a week, since Tesselin kept the pace moderate in the beginning, but it would give ample opportunity for the boys to become accustomed to full-sized horses.

"They shall never be satisfied with ponies again," Llion remarked to Tesselin, after they had been on the road for most of the first day. The boys were riding farther ahead with Sir Froilán Lascelles, the other young knight in Jared's household.

Tesselin snorted. "Oh, ponies have their uses, even for grown men. There's nothing better in rugged mountains. Of course, I come from that kind of country."

"Well, so do they—Duncan, at least," Llion replied. "Still, I suppose it was time—and you saw how Alaric performed at the tournament. Nor was Duncan far behind, and neither of them yet eight."

"Aye, they're fearless at this age," Tesselin said with a chuckle. "But ponies are small and quick and maneuverable—and closer to the ground. There's more scope for error on a full-sized mount."

"True enough." Llion scanned ahead, where the boys had been joined by one of the squires. "But somehow, I don't think there will be much difference, once they're riding full-sized horses regularly." He glanced aside at Tesselin with a sly grin. "Remember, I've been training Alaric since he was four; I know what he can do."

Tesselin shrugged amiably. "You may be right. Still, it's a transition all of us have had to make."

FOR Alaric and Duncan, the initial headiness of embarking upon their first almost-adult adventure had settled into tedium by the second day, underlined by increasing physical discomfort. While they had been thrilled to be given full-sized mounts for the journey, and had sat their horses proudly as they headed north along the river, it soon became abundantly clear that there was a vast difference between a few hours of riding for pleasure, or even for training, and spending hour after hour in the saddle, mile after mile and day after day. Llion and Tesselin halted the party every few hours to rest the horses and allow their riders to get down and stretch cramped limbs, but by the second day, the boys were finding it increasingly difficult to summon up serious enthusiasm when it was time to remount and press on.

"I suppose it just takes practice," Alaric murmured aside to Duncan, on one such occasion midway through the second day, as they watched two of their escort knights cinch up the horses' girths again, getting ready to resume travel. "It doesn't seem to bother the men."

Duncan nodded, rubbing surreptitiously at his backside. "I think those saddles are too big for us," he replied. "We were used to our old saddles."

"Yes, but our saddles are pony saddles," Alaric pointed out reasonably. "They're too small for these horses."

"That's true," Duncan agreed. "My da says it's always better to have a sore backside than for your horse to have a sore back."

"Aye, my da says that, too."

As they walked back over to the horses in question, Llion came to join them.

"All right, lads. Ready for a leg up?"

Both boys put on stoic faces and accepted the offered assistance, settling gingerly into saddles as they resigned themselves to several more hours before they would stop for the night.

T HEY stopped that night at the manor house of a minor baron called Murchison, whose lady provided them with simple but plentiful fare before they bedded down in the stable loft. The boys slept reasonably well in the sweet-smelling hay, but every muscle of legs and backs protested as they clambered down the next morning to break their fast.

But they knew better than to complain. Both boys hoped to see Duke Andrew a final time. Fortunately, their initial stiffness slowly subsided to a dull ache as they worked sore muscles and settled into their usual pace, though conversation was sparse, each rider alone with his thoughts.

The long hours in the saddle allowed Alaric ample time for his own contemplation, often on matters far different than any of his adult companions or even his cousin might imagine. Often he found himself thinking about his visit from Sir Sé, and the glimpses of memory he had retained of that most unusual night. Though he could dredge up nothing in the way of earlier memories of Sé himself—after all, he had been but a babe when the Anviler knight held him at his christening—he had no doubt that his mother had been referring to Sé when she drew the little cross on the scrap of parchment. Somewhere in his collection of childhood treasures, in a small chest in his room at Culdi, he was certain he still had that scrap of parchment, because of its association with his mother. He vowed to retrieve it when they arrived back at the Kierney capital.

He was less certain just what Sé had done to him, though he had vague impressions of gentle . . . *prickling* inside his head. What had remained, however, was a gradually growing awareness that he now could begin to distinguish when a person was telling a lie.

There were degrees of lying, he soon deduced, and he had to concentrate to distinguish the more subtle nuances. Sometimes, listening to the escort knights during meals, or as they bantered back and forth behind and ahead of him, he simply *knew* that some of the stories they told one another were utter fabrications—though it often was clear, even without using his emerging powers, that the men frequently were telling varia-tions on the truth that would make them appear more clever, or better fighters, or more accomplished with women than had actually been the case. He gathered that such boasting lies, if not carried to extremes, were deemed more or less acceptable. On consideration, he decided that it hardly seemed worth the effort to distinguish shades of truthfulness in such tales.

There were also the social lies, told to avoid giving offense or hurting someone's feelings. These, too, were deemed acceptable, though one must be careful not to overdo. Less benign—and less obvious—were the misdirections that, while not precisely lies, could almost escape detec-tion, even by a Deryni—and Sé had warned him how a clever person might avoid the direct lie by simply telling only part of the truth.

Alaric was witness to one such deception when their party stopped to water the horses and have a loose shoe reset at a livery yard near the Mearan border. The ostler seemed civil enough, if sparing of speech, and readily provided the requested services, willing enough to accept the coin Llion offered in payment; but when asked which of two roads out of town led to Culdi, Alaric had the distinct impression that the man had been less than forthcoming. He said nothing as their party moved out on the designated road, but as the others picked up the pace ahead, he eased his mount alongside Llion's.

"Llion," he said quietly, motioning the young knight to lean closer, "you should ask someone else for directions. I think that man sent us the wrong way—or at least not the shorter way."

Llion looked at him oddly, but drew the two of them aside to let the others pass, indicating to Tesselin that they would catch up.

"And why would you be thinking that he sent us the wrong way?" Llion asked, when the others had moved on out of earshot.

"I just . . . think he wasn't telling all the truth," Alaric said uneasily, fiddling with the ends of his reins. "He didn't much like us; I don't know why."

"We *are* near the Mearan border," Llion pointed out, "and we've ob-viously come from the direction of Rhemuth. Did it occur to you that the man might have Mearan sympathies?"

"I hadn't thought of that," Alaric conceded. "But he still sent us the wrong way. I just—knew."

"I see. I don't suppose this might have something to do with . . . what you are?"

Alaric glanced at Llion sidelong, then reluctantly nodded.

"It's all right," Llion said, peering ahead where the rest of the party were passing between a pair of cottages that faced one another across the road, to disappear around a bend beyond. "I'm not afraid of you; you know that. Your mother told me that your gifts would begin to emerge, as you got older. Did you read his mind?"

The boy shook his head emphatically, but did not look up.

"It doesn't work like that."

"Then, what *does* it work like?"

"It's hard to explain," Alaric murmured. "I'm . . . learning how to tell when a person is lying. I've—been practicing since we left Rhemuth. I don't necessarily know what the truth *is*; I just know a lie when I hear it."

"And you think that this is *not* the way to Culdi?" Llion asked quietly.

"I'm just saying that you should ask someone else for directions, to make sure."

Llion simply sat his horse for several seconds, obviously considering, then glanced in the direction of the cottages, where the last of their party were riding out of sight.

"All right, we'll ask directions up ahead," he said, touching heels to his mount. As the animal moved out, Alaric followed suit, wondering whether he had over-reacted. Maybe the ostler *had* been telling the truth.

They quickly reached the cottages, where a thin, sour-faced country-woman with her hair tied back in a kerchief was draping a braided rug over the low, dry-stone wall beside the cottage on the right. She looked up as the two riders drew rein, and let out an exasperated sigh.

"Och, I thought ye'd all passed by, with yer great clouds o' dust!" she grumbled, taking up a rush-woven rug beater.

"Dear me, I *am* sorry," Llion murmured contritely, backing his mount a few strides and motioning Alaric to do the same as the woman raised her beater and gave the rug an energetic whack, which made the horses toss their heads. "If I told you we weren't with them, you'd know that isn't true, but please believe that I do apologize for the extra work we've caused you." As she gave the rug another whack, glaring at him, he added, "Shall I do that for you, Mother, since our men are responsible? It's no bother. I used to help my own mother with the rugs, back in Corwyn."

As he swung a leg over the pommel and jumped down, then handed his reins up to Alaric, the woman lowered her arm and stepped back, astonished and suddenly wide-eyed as he approached.

"Nay, nay, sor, ye mustn't do that," she protested, backing away as she eyed his white belt and sword. "It weren't fittin', fer a gentleman like yersel' . . ."

"Nonsense!" Llion said, smiling as he gently took the beater from her hand and urged her back from the rug-draped wall. "It is entirely fitting for a gentleman to come to the aid of a lady needing assistance, especially if his own men were responsible for her distress." He limbered the rug beater tentatively, then whacked it hard against the rug with a resulting cloud of dust, grinning as he glanced back at her in approval. "An excellent implement, dear lady! I'll have this clean for you in no time at all."

To Alaric's surprise, Llion proceeded to do just that, beating the rug rhythmically and energetically for several minutes, until no more dust flew. When he was finished, he presented the beater to its owner with a bow, then gathered up the rug itself and carried it inside, the woman following in bewilderment. Alaric stared after them uncomprehendingly, even standing in his stirrups to lean forward and peer after them.

They were gone but a moment. When Llion emerged, the flustered goodwife simpering behind him, he was drinking something from a fist-sized wooden cup, which he handed up to Alaric, mouthing for him to drink it when the boy raised an eyebrow in inquiry.

"Madam, that is some of the finest buttermilk it has ever been my privilege to sample," Llion said as he turned back to the adoring goodwife—though Alaric guessed that only Llion's impeccable good manners had allowed him to offer the compliment; they were neither of them over-fond of buttermilk.

Alaric's emerging skill in detecting lies confirmed his observation, but he also realized, as he dutifully drained the cup, that this was one of those social situations when an untruth was not only acceptable but considered gracious. He bowed over the cup as he handed it back to Llion, who bowed similarly as he placed it back in the goodwife's work-worn hands.

"Our thanks for your hospitality, Mother," Llion murmured, "and I wonder if you could tell us if this is the most direct road to Culdi, for I confess that we do not know this area well."

The woman curtsied in turn, and clasped the cup to her breast like a sacred relic as she pointed down the road in the direction that the others had gone.

"Aye, sor, this *will* take ye to Culdi," she said, to Llion's nods of encouragement, "but there be a faster way, just beyond the next village—or ye can go back to the last fork. Tha road ahead joins up wi' the turning ye passed at the last fork. Turn right a' th' church, and ye'll save near half a day's ride. They say 'tis a mite harder going, mind ye, but yer horses look fit an' well fed. Och, and there micht be bandits."

"I see," Llion said, looking incredibly fascinated with what she had just told him, but also taking his reins from Alaric and swinging up into the saddle. "Well, I don't think bandits will bother so many armed men, but thank you for the warning. And again, I apologize for the dust."

"'Tis nae bother, sor," the goodwife replied, grinning ear to ear as she dipped in a curtsy. "God bless ye, sor."

"And you, Mother," Llion replied, lifting a hand in smiling salute.

As they headed off after the others, holding back to a walk for the first little while to avoid more dust, Alaric glanced searchingly at the young knight riding at his side.

"Llion, I don't understand," he said quietly.

"What do you not understand, my lord?"

"She was only a common woman, but you treated her like a lady of the court."

Llion drew rein abruptly, reaching across to grab the boy's reins and stop him, too, though he did not look at the boy. His clenched jaw told of . . . anger? When he did not speak immediately, only taking a long, slow breath in and out as he stared down at his horse's mane, Alaric whispered, "Llion?"

At once the young knight released Alaric's reins, his gloved hand clenching and unclenching, but he still would not meet Alaric's gaze as he finally spoke. "You never had the chance to meet my mother, did you?" he said, as he shook his head and leaned heavily against the pommel of his saddle, gazing into the middle distance with a sigh. "No, of course you didn't. She died when I was still very young, so my father had to teach me the early lessons of courtesy that would have fallen to her. I am told that, when first they met, she was a 'common woman' very like the one back yonder—or leastways, of common stock; she was younger.

"But my father fell deeply in love with her, and she with him, and they married despite the objections of his family. He made her a knight's lady, and treated her as such until the day she died, bearing my youngest brother. After that, he honored her memory, and taught his sons to do the same."

He turned his gaze on Alaric. "In honor of his love for her, he taught us to honor all women for her sake, with the respect we owe to our mother, our sisters, our queen, and the mother of our Lord. Courtesy costs nothing to give, but it is coin of inestimable worth to the recipient. It is a lesson I have tried never to forget."

Alaric had listened slack-jawed at this glimpse into the personal life of the young knight he trusted with his life, and thought he understood a bit more, why his parents had chosen Llion to be his governor.

"I—I didn't know," he managed to murmur. "Llion, I'm so sorry. I meant no disrespect."

"I know none was intended," Llion replied, forcing a smile as he reached across to briefly clasp the boy's shoulder in reassurance. "But many were . . . unkind to my mother during her lifetime, because of her common birth. Yet she was one of the noblest women I have ever met, then or since. She—"

The approach of several of their knights, returning from farther up the road, interrupted whatever else he might have told Alaric about his mother. Alaric, for his part, was happy for the interruption, for he was well aware that the conversation might have caused his friend embarrassment.

"Ach, now we've tarried too long, and the others are anxious," Llion said breezily, as he glanced down at the boy with a sheepish expression and signed that they should head for the others. "And that's their job, after all."

Froilán was in the lead, and drew rein as the pair approached.

"We were beginning to be concerned," the Kierney knight called. "What kept you?"

"We stopped to ask directions again, just to be certain," Llion said. "And a good thing, too. We wanted the other road, after all. This one does go to Culdi—eventually—but the other is quicker by half a day. We can cut across at the next village."

Froilán shrugged. "Good that you asked, then. But the others are waiting. We'd best ride."

T HE discussion did not come up again during the remainder of the journey, though Alaric thought about what Llion had told him. There was no privacy to tell Duncan about any part of it, either, though Alaric would like to have been able to talk about the Truth-Reading, at least. They spent nearly a week traveling to Culdi, sometimes camping just off the road, but more often requesting hospitality at noble houses along the way—which was always given generously, when it was learned that the two boys were kin to the old Duke of Cassan, who was dying. That news inevitably brought dismay, for Andrew McLain was admired and respected throughout the north.

Much to the relief of everyone in the party, the McLain patriarch was yet among the living as they made the final approach to Culdi, toward the end of June. On the last night before they expected to arrive, Llion sent word ahead to ask for an update on the duke's condition. The reply came late the next morning, when they were only a few hours out. The bearer of the news was Kenneth's son-in-law, Sir Walter Lithgow, who was the husband of Geill Morgan, Kenneth's second daughter by his first wife.

"Sir Walter, what news?" Llion called, as the other drew rein in a cloud of dust.

Walter gave a weary shrug and shook his head. "He still lives, but for how long, who can say? He eats but little, he speaks not at all." He sighed. "It is but a matter of time, I fear."

The two boys caught only the tail end of the exchange, for they had been riding toward the rear of the party with Tesselin, but it was enough to dampen their spirits for the rest of the ride to Culdi.

"He's going to die, isn't he?" Duncan said tremulously, for he was particularly fond of his grandfather, and Alaric likewise held the old duke in close affection.

They arrived late in the afternoon, on the heels of a brief spattering of rain that was just enough to leave the air close and sticky, even in the hills above the town. The guards at the castle gate gave impeccable salute as the dusty band clattered across the ramp that bridged the dry moat, with Walter in the lead, but the demeanor of the grooms who came to take their horses was somber, befitting the deathwatch for a duke.

"Any change?" Walter asked one of the men, as he swung down from his mount.

"None for the good, my lord," the man replied. "The duchess and his sister attend him, along with Lady Kierney."

"And Lord Jared? Lord Kenneth?"

"Lord Jared is receiving petitioners in the hall." He shrugged apologetically at Llion's look of surprise. "The lives of the common folk do go on, my lord, even if the life of their liege lord and chief is winding to its close. Lord Kenneth is with him, along with Master Kevin."

"Of course," Llion replied, also dismounting, and signaling Alaric and Duncan to do the same. After a brief visit to their fathers in the hall, and a happy reunion with Kevin, Tesselin stayed with Jared and Kevin, while Llion took the younger boys to see Lady Vera, who came out of Duke Andrew's sickroom to greet the pair with warm hugs.

"I have missed you so much!" she whispered, as she knelt down to enfold each in the curve of an arm. "Was your journey exciting?"

As both boys nodded earnestly, Duncan whispered, "Sometimes we slept in *barns*, Mama! And Llion let us ride big horses!"

"*Did* he?" Vera replied.

"An' at the king's birthday tournament, he gave us prizes!" Alaric chimed in, digging into his belt pouch. "Duncan got a silver coin, 'cause he only got seven rings, but I got a gold one! Look!"

As he pulled it out to display on his open palm, Vera gravely inspected it, then cocked her head at him.

"That *is* a very fine prize. How many rings did you take?"

"Ten!" Alaric said proudly. "Paget Sullivan took ten, too, but he's twelve."

"Ah, twelve," Vera said, nodding as she glanced up at Llion. "Well, it appears that both of you did very well, and against boys much older than you. I think we can look forward to having two more very successful warriors in the family. Llion, I'm sure we have you at least partially to thank for this fine showing."

"I had excellent material to work with, my lady. And they were very grown-up on the ride here."

"Mama, how is Grandrew?" Duncan broke in, using the grandchildren's pet name for their grandsire. "Can we see him?"

"Not just now, my love," Vera said softly, shaking her head sadly. "He's sleeping. Perhaps later."

"Is he *very* sick?" Alaric whispered.

"I'm afraid he is, darling. But you'd best go with Llion now. All of you smell of horse—you, too, Llion—so it's baths for the lot of you!"

Duncan rolled his eyes, but Vera got no argument from any of them, for the boys did like baths, especially on a hot day. And later, for just a few minutes, their Grandmother Jesma called them in to see Grandrew, who recognized his grandsons and Alaric and pulled them close in a loving hug before slipping back into sleep. After that, the entire enclave settled into the long-drawn process of waiting.

Chapter 8

". . . Well done, thou good and faithful servant . . ."
—MATTHEW 25:21

ANDREW McLain Duke of Cassan lingered for another month, in and out of sleep, never speaking, taking but little nourishment, wasting to a frail shadow of the fierce warrior he once had been. His womenfolk made him as comfortable as they could—his wife of more than half a century, his only remaining sister, and his devoted daughter-in-law—but it became increasingly clear that this was the duke's final battle, in which victory would not be his. In the final days, his sleep became more fitful, his breathing shallower. Toward the very end, a few at a time, his grandchildren and nieces and nephews were brought to his bedside by Jared to say their last good-byes.

He passed peacefully on the afternoon of the first day of August, surrounded by his extended family, lucid enough in his final hour to give a last blessing to his son and heir; he had long since received the last rites of his faith, the viaticum to sustain him in his final journey.

When he had breathed his last, a solitary piper outside his chamber window began the slow, mournful strains of a *corranach* to mark his passing, and grim-faced runners set out to carry the news into the surrounding countryside. In the preceding days and weeks, as word spread of the likely outcome of the old duke's illness, many of Andrew McLain's retainers from all over Kierney and Cassan had already gathered outside Culdi town, camping in the fields. More would come in the hours ahead, but less because he had been their duke than because he had been their chief.

Just at dusk, as the lament of the *corranach* faded into silence outside the old chief's window, three McLain chieftains came marching up to the manor house from the town below, bearing torches and accompanied by three pipers, to fetch the old chief's heir. Hearing the skirl of the pipers' approach, Jared slung a McLain tartan over one shoulder and took up his father's sheathed sword to greet them, his eldest son and his wife falling in behind him as he followed the newcomers down the hill, a torchman leading the way and the other two flanking him, the pipers behind. Other members of his family followed, Kenneth and the two younger boys among them, down to the gathering place before the town, where more torches awaited them, ranged in a wide horseshoe shape.

The pipes abruptly ceased as the chiefly party came into the mouth of the horseshoe and halted. There a household herald in the livery of Cassan proclaimed the titles that came to Jared McLain from the king: Duke of Cassan, Earl of Kierney, and half a dozen subsidiary honors. In time, and at the king's pleasure, these honors would be confirmed in the king's presence, and in a manner befitting his exalted rank, but for the moment Jared merely promised to exercise his rank and privileges according to the laws of Gwynedd and the will of the king.

More important in this place, however, were the highland honors, to be confirmed according to different custom. Formal investiture would take place later, after the late chief's interment in the ancient McLain burial grounds at Ballymar; but for now, as many of his clansmen looked on, a clan bard declaimed the new chief's illustrious lineage, direct descendant from a long line of noble chiefs stretching back nearly three hundred years: from Andrew, son of Arnall, son of Roger, son of Andrew, son of Duncan, son of Arthur, son of Charles, son of Angus, son of Iain. . . .

For Alaric and his cousin Duncan, standing with Alaric's father, it was a time of both puzzlement and excitement mingled with the sadness, beginning at the very moment of the old duke's passing. Grandrew, as the children had called him, would be greatly missed, to be sure; but he had been old and sick, and even such young children sensed that his passing had been a blessed release from the prison of his failing body. They stood dutifully if dry-eyed amid the myriad members of Jared's extended family while the formalities of his accession were proclaimed, not really paying close attention, because they had heard the lineages recited since infancy, and could rattle off noble pedigrees as well as any herald, for that was part of the training of a noble youth, especially boys.

In due course, the clansfolk came, one by one, to bow heads before the new chief and clasp his hand in homage, giving similar salute to Kevin, who was now the heir. Eventually, the pipers and many of the torchmen escorted Jared and his family back to the manor house, where a modest repast had been laid out to offer hospitality to those who had come so far and waited so patiently.

The occasion could hardly be aught but subdued, with the old chief lying dead in another chamber. While the women withdrew to prepare his body to lie in state overnight in the castle chapel, Jared and the old duke's other nearest male relatives began organizing the guard of honor that would keep watch while the people came to pay their respects. With Llion and Tesselin pressed into service to assist in the chapel, Alaric and Duncan took advantage of the evening's informality to raid the long tables for chunks of bread and cheese and a few apples—items that could be secreted inside tunics and carried off for more private consumption—for the looks the pair had been exchanging since leaving Andrew's death chamber had made it clear that each had things to tell the other that were best said in private.

Slipping away from the others, the pair made their way out to the castle garden and into the white-gleaming mortuary chapel which was the final resting place of Alaric's mother and also an infant McLain daughter who had not long survived her birth. The little chapel did not often attract the attention of the adults in residence at Culdi, for there was a proper church not far across another courtyard, but its miniscule size had long made it a favorite place of refuge for the noble children of the ducal household, especially Alaric and Duncan. Tonight, it at once became the safe haven where the pair could compare notes on the day's events—for it quickly emerged that both boys had sensed the presence of unexpected visitors attendant upon the passing of Andrew McLain's spirit into the next realm.

"You mean, you saw something, too?" Duncan whispered, as the two of them hunkered down behind Alyce's tomb, backs against the side of the massive sarcophagus and knees drawn up under chins. The flicker of votive candles and the steadier flame of the chapel's vigil lamp lent the illusion of animation to the carved alabaster effigy atop the sarcophagus, almost as if Alyce de Corwyn only lay sleeping above them. "Well, *did* you?" Duncan persisted, when his cousin did not immediately answer.

Alaric nodded gravely and glanced at Duncan sidelong. "I saw *something*. What did *you* see?"

"I dunno," Duncan admitted. "I didn't exactly . . . *see* them. Not with my eyes. But I'm sure they were there." He glanced at the chapel door nervously. "We aren't supposed to talk about such things."

"It's safe enough in here," Alaric replied. "There's no one to overhear."

"Yes there is," Duncan countered, jerking his chin at the Presence lamp, then quirking a sheepish expression. "I guess He knows all about it, though."

"Well, if they *were* angels, like we think, of course He does," Alaric agreed. He fell silent for several seconds, then added, "Let's ask your mama. Maybe she saw them, too."

"Maybe," Duncan said uncertainly, though he scrambled to his feet and followed as Alaric rose and started toward the chapel door.

They had no opportunity to ask her that night. When they returned to the room where Duncan's grandfather had died, they could see Lady Vera inside with the widowed Gramma Jesma and Grandrew's sister Nesta, the three of them tenderly preparing the body for its waking through the night and on the morrow, but Sir Walter turned them away—and, in fact, personally escorted them back to Alaric's chamber, where he put them in Llion's charge.

"Lady Vera has duties to perform this evening, lads, as do I," he told them. "Besides that, it's been a long day for everyone. 'Tis time both of you were in bed. I'm sure Sir Llion will agree."

"I do, indeed," Llion said. "Duncan, if you'd like, you may stay here tonight with Alaric. There will be a lot going on tomorrow, and you'll both need a good night's sleep. Wash up now, and go to bed."

Bed was the last thing that either boy had in mind at that point, but experience and common sense had taught the pair that it was best to at least appear to go along with the instructions of their elders—and this certainly was not the time to test the limits of Llion's patience. Besides, Llion was usually right. Accordingly, both boys did as they were bidden, and soon had slipped safely into sleep.

Morning found their resolve undiminished by the interruption of sleep. Bright and early, when the pair had washed and dressed in clean shirts and breeches and wolfed down some bread and hard-boiled eggs in the castle hall, they crept up to the solar room where Duncan's mother habitually spent the early part of her days. That morning, gowned in the plain black of mourning, the new Duchess Vera was bent over a writing desk set to catch the light from a window that looked down on the castle garden, her honey-brown hair caught back under a black caul. She looked up as they eased the door open and peered inside, smiling and laying aside her quill as she opened her arms to her son.

"Ah, there you are, my love. Come in, come in, both of you." She caught Duncan in a quick embrace, kissing the top of his head, then gave Alaric a hug and a kiss as well. "I see that Llion brought you the clean shirts I had him lay out for you. Duncan, you'll want to put on your plaid before the funeral, to honor your grandfather. Did both of you sleep well?"

"Mama, we saw angels last night," Duncan said baldly, as he drew back to look at her.

Vera tensed almost imperceptibly, then nodded to Alaric. "Please go and make sure that you latched the door, love. I assume that you saw them, too?"

Alaric nodded solemnly, then scooted off to obey when Vera jutted her chin toward the door. As he returned, she drew the two of them into the window embrasure to settle onto a bench to either side of her, each in the curve of an arm.

"Now, quietly, tell me all about it," she murmured, giving each a re-assuring hug. "We should have a few moments before anyone comes. Just what do you think you saw?"

They told her, haltingly at first, but then in whispered, fervent phrases that could leave little doubt.

"There were two down by the end of the bed, with their hands held up like when Father Paschal says Mass, an' there was light all around them!" Duncan murmured, wide-eyed, as Alaric nodded emphatic agreement and chimed in.

"An' there were two more, one up by Grandrew's head. One was really big, an' he had swoopy wings that nearly scraped the ceiling. They were dark green like that old rooster's tail, out in the vegetable garden. An' there was light all around 'em, too, but nobody else seemed to notice!"

Through several elaborations on this theme, Vera listened without interruption, nodding in encouragement until the pair finally wound down and merely stared at her hopefully.

"Four of them, you say?" She raised an eyebrow at their nods of agreement. "Who do you think they might have been?"

The boys exchanged uncertain glances.

"I'll give you a clue. Do you remember that night when Auntie Alyce and I took you down to the garden chapel in the middle of the night?"

Both boys went wide-eyed.

"Archangels?" Duncan breathed. "Really?"

"Why did they come?" Alaric wanted to know.

"Because I invited them," Vera replied softly, "and because they chose to come."

Duncan's eyes went even wider. "Why would they do that?"

She smiled and hugged both of them closer. "Because angels adore holiness," she told them, "and the time of a soul's passing into the next life is *very* holy. I wasn't sure you would see them, but I knew *I* would. And I would like to think that Grandrew may have seen them, too."

"Did Papa see them?" Alaric whispered uncertainly. "Or Uncle Jared?"

Vera smiled a little sadly and shook her head, giving Alaric another hug. "I don't think so, dear. Most times, it's only Deryni who can see them, and then only if they're focused and really *want* to see them—and if the angels are willing to be seen. But sometimes even humans feel the brush of the angels' wings when someone is passing. It helps them remember that God's love is with them, even in death."

"Do you think Papa maybe felt the wings, then?" Duncan asked, cocking his head.

"I'm sure he knows that God was with Grandrew, love—and that Grandrew is now with God."

"Then, death is not such a *bad* thing," Alaric said thoughtfully. "Not if you go to be with God."

Vera nodded thoughtfully. "It can be a *sad* thing, for those left behind," she clarified. "And sometimes it comes far sooner than seems right. And sometimes the dying itself can be very, very hard. But Grandrew's passing was as peaceful as any I have seen. He was a good man, and lived a long, full life. Now he is resting for a time in God's love."

"What happens when he's rested enough?" Duncan wanted to know.

Vera suppressed a chuckle at the question: seven-year-olds wrestling with the great conundrums pondered by wise men throughout the ages.

"We don't know that, my love. But God knows His plan for each of us. And the plan for the two of you, right now, is to get yourselves ready to attend Grandrew's funeral. Would you do that for me, while I finish dressing? Duncan, I've laid out that sleeping lion brooch with your plaid—and yes, I *know* that the wool is itchy and hot in summer. Alaric, tell Llion that I said you should put on one of your heraldic surcoats, in honor of your great-uncle. And both of you should wash your faces and comb your hair."

The boys did as they were bidden, Alaric pulling on his Corwyn surcoat over his shirt and breeches and then rejoining his cousin when it was time to go downstairs. To his surprise, he found his father and Llion in urgent consultation with Jared and a knight he recognized from his father's manor at Morganhall: Sir Calix Howard, who had married his former nurse, Melissa, and stayed on at Morganhall to protect the household there. Alaric's two Morgan aunts lived at Morganhall—Aunt Delphine and Aunt Claara—and also Claara's granddaughter Clarice Fraser, who was six.

More important, his sister Bronwyn lived at Morganhall, and she was only four. He adored Bronwyn, and hoped nothing had happened to her, but the serious expressions on the faces of the grown-ups sent him pelting across the hall to join them.

"Papa, what is it?" he blurted. "Has something happened to Bronwyn?"

"Nay, nay, she is well," his father replied, circling his son's shoulders with a reassuring arm and giving him a quick hug. "It's your Aunt Claara. She's taken a bad fall and broken her hip. Now, hush while Sir Calix finishes telling me about it."

Calix, a short, sturdy man in his fifties, with grey-streaked side-braids mingled with his hair, glanced uncertainly at his lord's son and heir, then at Kenneth.

"Shall I really continue, my lord?" he asked in a low voice.

Kenneth inclined his head. "Alaric is the future Duke of Corwyn, Calix. He needs to be exposed to life in all its misfortune as well as its triumphs."

"Very well, my lord." Calix ducked his head in agreement. "But whatever the outcome, I fear you will need to make some changes at Morganhall. Lady Delphine declares that she is perfectly able to continue running the estate, as she has long done, but she will need help in the daily management of the household. That has always been Lady Claara's function."

"I understand," Kenneth said.

"And you will need to engage several more maids to help with the care of the children," Calix went on. "My Melissa will help, of course, along with our own daughter, but more hands will be required. And if Lady Claara should not survive this, I think it likely that Sir Paxon will soon come to take little Clarice back to his own people."

"Aye, that would not surprise me," Kenneth agreed. "And given what has happened, perhaps 'tis time to reconsider Bronwyn's care, though I had thought to delay a bit longer."

At Calix's look of question, Kenneth went on.

"It has been in my mind for several months, Calix. The timing is ill, but it has always been my intention eventually to move my daughter to Lady Vera's care, as was the wish of my dear wife." He cast a sidelong glance at Jared. "But right now, Vera will have her hands full, settling into her new station. I cannot ask that of her yet."

"That need not be a concern just now," Jared said low, speaking for the first time. "She must accompany me to Ballymar, of course, to bury my father, and we'll progress through Cassan on the way back here. But I fully intend that Twelfth Night shall see us back in Rhemuth. By then, you should know what changes are required at Morganhall—and I assume that you still intend to visit Lendour and Corwyn this year, as you usually do?"

Kenneth sighed and nodded. "Now, more than ever—especially if I must shift personnel to Morganhall." He glanced at Llion, who was waiting expectantly. "We'll leave immediately after the funeral, Llion. If you'd be so good as to begin making the arrangements. . . ."

"You needn't stay for that," Jared interjected. "Family must come first. Andrew would understand."

Kenneth shook his head. "No, Andrew is my family as well: my mother's only brother. I can spare a few more hours to pay my final respects. Have I time before Mass to write a quick letter to the king? He should know of my change of plans."

"Use my writing room," Jared replied, with a gesture toward the withdrawing room off the great hall. "Someone will call you when they're ready in the church."

Chapter 9

"Even a child is known by his doings, whether his work be pure,
and whether it be right."

—PROVERBS 20:11

A S it happened, there was more than enough time for letter writing, for the start of Duke Andrew's Requiem was somewhat delayed owing to the sheer number of local folk come to pay their respects to their late duke. Accordingly, it was mid-afternoon before Kenneth could lead his party out the gates of Culdi, riding hard along the route they had traveled only weeks before. As on the journey north, Alaric rode a small horse rather than a pony, but this time with no other child along to keep him company. Fortunately, he was accustomed to interacting with adults, and rode in turn with several of his father's knights besides Llion.

Other than boredom and the hardship of the road, then, their southward journey was uneventful. They reached the ancient Morgan seat nearly a week later, to find that Claara seemed to have survived her injury, but was unlikely ever to walk again. After spending a few minutes at her bedside, and greeting his daughter, Kenneth conferred briefly with Father Swithun and the household steward, Master Leopold, then asked Delphine to join him in his quarters.

"I'm sure you've thought about this in the past several weeks," he said, pouring her a cup of ale. "Calix tells me that you're going to need additional help, if you're all to remain at Morganhall."

"Of course we shall remain at Morganhall," Delphine said indignantly. "Morganhall is our home."

"And that is why I'm making arrangements to bring in some assistance."

Delphine nodded, her momentary indignation appeased. "Good. I'm perfectly willing and able to continue managing the estate, but help would be welcome, especially now. Leopold and Calix are treasures, but they are still only two men—and it would ease my mind considerably if we had more of a male presence here. I had been meaning to mention it the last time you were here, but none of us like to admit that we're getting older. Now, with Claara virtually an invalid—well, we *could* use the additional help."

Kenneth nodded. "I already have some men in mind."

"I am very glad to hear it," Delphine replied. "I should hate to see the estate fall into decline. It would be good if there were something left by the time all of us are gone—perhaps a dowry for Bronwyn. God knows, Alaric shan't need the income, what with his duchy and with Lendour after you. But we must think about these things."

"Indeed, we must," Kenneth agreed. "I shall have this resolved before the winter snows. Can you manage until then?"

"With God's help. Your daughter Zoë sends us supplies from time to time, and men to help with the harvest. Will you go to Lendour when you leave here? I know she would love to see you and Alaric."

He smiled. "And I am pining to see my grandchildren. I must make my annual visit to Lendour, in any case—and to Coroth, as well."

Delphine nodded. "And what of Bronwyn? This is the only home she's ever known."

"I know that," Kenneth replied. "And you and Claara are the only mothers she's known. Alyce wanted Vera to have the care of both the children, in time. But now is not the time, with Vera and Jared busy burying Duke Andrew."

"I'm aware of that," Delphine said. "And don't mistake me. Bronwyn is a delight, and I don't regret a minute of having her here. But you need to make permanent arrangements sooner rather than later. She's very attached to Claara's granddaughter. Clarice, she's called. Her father will probably arrive any day now. I sent him word soon after Claara's accident, when it became clear that Claara would not be able to care for her any longer."

In fact, little Clarice's father arrived the following afternoon: Sir Paxon Fraser, a handsome knight in the service of the Earl of Rhendall. After he had greeted his young daughter and paid his respects to his mother-in-law, he joined Kenneth in the solar room that overlooked the castle garden.

"Have a seat and take some ale, Sir Paxon," Kenneth said, pouring from a glazed pottery pitcher into a pair of treen cups. "It's cold from a spring in the cellar. Just the thing for a sultry afternoon."

Sir Paxon smiled nervously and sat, taking the cup Kenneth offered and lifting it in salute.

"Thank you, my lord. Good health to you." He took a long quaff and, at Kenneth's gesture of invitation, held out his cup for a refill.

"You appear to have ridden hard," Kenneth remarked. "Am I to gather that the Earl of Rhendall keeps you quite busy?"

Sir Paxon gave a genial shrug. "He keeps all his household knights busy. But I have no complaints. He is a good overlord, and has given my son a place as page in his household."

"Mine is soon to enter Duke Jared's service," Kenneth said, jutting his chin in the direction of the garden below as he sipped at his ale. "And I gather that our daughters have become fast friends. I am hoping I can persuade you to let her stay here awhile longer, while I sort out more permanent arrangements."

Paxon glanced into the garden below, where the two girls were playing with a clutch of gangly stable kittens. Nearby, in the shade of a pear tree near the garden wall, the mother cat had found a comfortable perch on Alaric's chest as he sprawled in the cool grass.

"The girls *are* close in age, aren't they?" Paxon replied. "And they seem to get on well. How old is Bronwyn? A little younger than my daughter, I think?"

"She will be five in December," Kenneth replied, trying not to dwell on the reminder that, in December, it also would be five years since Alyce's untimely death. "How old is Clarice?"

"Six, nearly seven. And she can be a handful. With Claara laid up, Delphine certainly won't be able to keep up with the pair of them."

"Delphine assures me that she can manage for the present, if she has help," Kenneth replied. "I intend to leave for Lendour within the week to secure that help. I have retainers there that I can spare. It would only be for a few months—a year at most," he added hopefully. "I had already planned to move Bronwyn to the care of Vera McLain, as was her mother's dying wish. But frankly, this is not a good time, with Jared just come into his ducal rank. I assume you heard that Duke Andrew passed a few weeks ago." Paxon nodded that he had.

"Jared and Vera won't even be back in this part of the kingdom until late autumn," Kenneth went on. "You would be doing me a great service if you'd allow Clarice to stay here until I can make my arrangements. But I do understand, if you'd prefer to have her with you."

Paxon sighed and sat back in his chair, toying with his cup. "It isn't that, my lord. My own duties keep me often in the field, and she and her grandmother adore one another, so I'd prefer not to deprive them of one another's company—especially not now." The younger knight looked up with another sigh. "But there are additional factors to consider. Clarice has a brother she hardly knows; I should like to remedy that. Granted, Kian has his duties as page, but they would be in the same household; and the earl has a daughter only a few years older than Clarice: Meraude, she's called. Exposure in an earl's household is far more likely to fetch my girl a good marriage."

"All true," Kenneth agreed. "Morganhall can't compete with the household of the Earl of Rhendall." He sighed. "But we're only talking about a year, maybe less. Claara has survived this current crisis, but one cannot predict the future. And Delphine is not getting any younger, either. Children in the household will help to keep both of them young, but it's only a matter of time before my sisters pass on. For that matter, I'm not getting any younger myself, Paxon, and I have two young children to think of. At least the three grown daughters are settled."

Paxon nodded slowly. "I do sympathize, my lord. Suppose that, for now, we simply leave matters as they are. For now, I shall leave Clarice here with her grandmother, and we'll discuss this again in the new year."

"Thank you," Kenneth said, extending his hand. "I do appreciate it."

• • •

ALARIC, for his part, found his days at Morganhall little different from the routine at Culdi or Rhemuth, aside from the opportunity to become better acquainted with his sister. He had seen Bronwyn but little in the first few years of her life, as she changed from infant to toddler, but his father usually did bring him to Morganhall to visit her several times a year.

Lately, however, she was becoming increasingly precious to her elder brother, much more a companion and playmate and less a nuisance. He welcomed the opportunity to help teach her her letters, and to tell her about what he remembered of their mother—of whom Bronwyn had no memory whatsoever. He told her, too, about participating at the king's birthday court, and riding at the tourney, and the sad journey to Culdi. But she had not known Duke Andrew, so his passing meant little to her on a personal level. Nor had she yet met the king.

A love of riding the two of them shared, however, even though Alaric was far more advanced. Llion found her a natural rider, and commended the instruction she had received from Sir Calix and Master Leopold. Bronwyn was managing quite a feisty pony, and clambered right back into the saddle whenever she fell off, which was seldom.

Alaric, by contrast, was deemed to have progressed beyond ponies, by dint of his experience on the rides from Rhemuth and Culdi. Though he would continue to ride ponies when training with other young riders, Llion decided to continue some of his instruction on horses. To that end, Alaric was given the occasional use of a steady and reliable Llanner mare called Dilys, belonging to Sir Calix, and began learning to jump the mare over obstacles in the field.

He soon found that taking a full-sized horse over hedges and ditches was somewhat different from popping one of his ponies over pre-set fences in a riding ring—with the result that he, like Bronwyn, sometimes "dismounted" well before he had intended, and from a greater height than that to which he was accustomed.

"That looked painful," Llion said, catching Dilys's reins as Alaric picked himself up from a particularly abrupt dismount.

"My balance was off," Alaric muttered.

"So it was," Llion replied, and gave him a leg up. "Try that one again."

But he far preferred riding in the field to going round and round in an arena. He and Llion rode out most mornings, usually with one or another of the other household knights, and Llion gave him sword drill every day, in-between other activities.

Nor was more academic training neglected, though it was not Llion who provided it. For a change of pace, and to keep his mind engaged as well as his growing body, Aunt Delphine had him read family histories to her, and practice his scrivening, and even taught him the Torenthi alphabet.

"You will wish to learn at least a little Torenthi," she told him, "since Corwyn's nearest neighbor outside Gwynedd is Torenth. It's a challenging language, but there is much to learn from Torenth."

"But, they're our enemies," Alaric objected.

"No, some of their leaders merely have other objectives than we do in Gwynedd," she replied tartly. "You will find that true of many people you think are enemies. Besides, many of them are Deryni, as your mother was. And it is also a very good idea to know your enemy," she conceded with a wink.

Flashing her a cheeky grin, he returned to copying out a list of simple words in Torenthi.

She also gave him exercises in accountancy, which he would need in the management of the estates he would eventually inherit.

"I know this is not your favorite pastime," she told him, as he labored over yet another column of figures she had set him to add up, "but one day, the numbers will mean something to you, when they pertain to the production of crops and animals and timber and such, coming from your lands. A knowledge of accountancy is part of the job of every noble lord, be he simple knight or a duke holding vast estates, as you will be."

The perverse pen he was using chose that moment to deposit an ugly blot on his figures, and he flung it down in exasperation.

"Here, now, none of that, young man," Delphine said, putting the quill back in his hand and, at the same time, applying a blotter to the mess. "As a future duke, I know you think that you will always have others to do your accounting—and you *will* have clarks aplenty to carry out most of these tasks. But you must be able to go over an account and see for yourself whether the figures are accurate, or whether your reeves and stewards are cheating you.

"It does happen," she added, as the boy looked up in indignation. "Subordinates sometimes assume that a duke cannot be bothered to concern himself with such details. But many a fine estate has been run into the ground by dishonest stewards, especially when the master or the heir is young—or set apart for some other cause. You know what I'm talking about, young man."

She gave him a gimlet glance, only nodding as his lips parted in a silent gasp of sudden suspicion.

"Aunt Delphine," he whispered, carefully laying aside his quill, "are you saying that people might try to take advantage of me because I'm . . . because my mother was . . ."

Delphine gave a wry grimace and nodded jerkily. "I loved her dearly, child—you know that. But other than the time she spent at Arc-en-Ciel—and there were problems even there, at least at first—I don't know whether she ever felt truly safe."

"There were problems at Arc-en-Ciel?" Alaric said in a small voice. "I thought that religious houses were sanctuary."

Delphine snorted in a most unladylike fashion. "From the outside world, they are. But no one had reckoned on that beastly Septimus de Nore. He was one of the chaplains there."

"De Nore?" Alaric interjected, eyes narrowing. "He's that priest who was executed for his part in the killing of a boy at court."

Delphine allowed herself a curt nod.

"He was. How much do you know about that, love?"

"Well, not a great deal," the boy admitted hesitantly. "It happened before I was born. But sometimes the pages at court talk about him—to scare the younger boys, I think. The boy's name was Krispin, wasn't it? He was drowned in a well in the stable yard. My mother helped find out who did it, and the guilty men were hanged—and *gelded*," he added, with a look of awed disbelief.

"Do any of those boys mention *how* she helped find out?" Delphine asked.

"She—used her Deryni powers," Alaric whispered, thinking of the power he himself now was beginning to sense, to tell when a person was lying. "The old king commanded her."

Delphine nodded slowly. "And de Nore's brother is Bishop Oliver de Nore, who hated your mother for the rest of her days, and will seize any opportunity to vent his spleen on you as well, because you are your mother's son. Be careful, love, because he will see you destroyed, if he can."

"I—have a bishop who wants me *dead*?" Alaric said in a small voice.

"He would be happy if *all* Deryni were dead," Delphine replied. "I hope that one day your father will tell you of the full extent of what your dear mother suffered because of her race. You *cannot* be too careful. The old king protected your mother, and the young king will try to protect you—but you must always be on your guard."

Alaric swallowed at a lump that suddenly had materialized in his throat. He knew that Delphine and his mother had been close, especially in those final weeks, but he had begun to learn much more of their relationship in the past few days, and was suddenly aware just how much more precarious was his situation than he had thought. He also had no doubt that Delphine had loved his mother very much, and loved him as well.

Turning back to the writing desk before him, he ran his gaze over the numbers that had defeated him earlier, then picked up his quill without another word and bent again to his task. This time, when he finished and laid aside the quill to push the results across the desk to Delphine, the old woman smiled.

"Exactly right, my love," she said, reaching across to clasp his shoulder in affection. "Your mother would be very proud, and your father will be proud as well." She smiled and cocked her head in sudden inspiration. "Can you keep a secret?"

"What kind of a secret?" Alaric wanted to know.

Delphine's mouth curled upward in conspiratorial glee. "It's a gift for your father, something I've been working on for several months. Would you like to see it?"

At his silent nod, she rose and went to a tall cabinet behind her, root-

ing behind a cupboard door until she emerged with something wrapped
loosely in a piece of raw silk.

"It's very nearly done," she said, unfolding the bundle as she sat. "I
had to wait until you came back to Morganhall before I could finish it.
Tell me what you think."

From the folds of silk she withdrew an egg-sized silver locket with a
filigree face. This she opened before handing it to Alaric. Inside, painted
on a flat oval of ivory, was the miniature portrait of a fair, beautiful
woman with golden hair caught in ringlets at the nape of her neck, and a
golden circlet across her brow. The blue eyes were familiar and beloved to
Alaric, and he caught his breath in wonder.

"Maman!"

"Ah, then it's a good likeness," Delphine said, beaming at his delight.
"Now see if the inside also meets with your approval. It opens from the
left, so that it can fold out as a triptych. The locket belonged to my
mother, your grandmother, Madonna McLain. I doubt you remember
her. I've simply changed the portraits."

Grinning, Alaric touched a reverent finger to the likeness of his
mother, then carefully opened the next level of the locket. The left side
displayed a portrait of his sister Bronwyn, merry-eyed and full of life, but
the right side was vacant.

"Your likeness will go there," Delphine said, reaching behind her to
produce a third ivory oval, handling it by the edges. "I only finished it
last night. I knew you would have grown since last I saw you, so I wanted
to wait until you returned to do the final touches. But your mother's vis-
age is forever in my heart, as she was at the height of her beauty, and
Bronwyn is always with me. Meanwhile, you, my love, have been busy
turning into quite the handsome young man."

As she laid it on the table before him, he bent close to inspect his portrait, pleased with what he saw, then looked up with a shy smile.

"Thank you, Aunt Delphine. My father will treasure it, I know. When
will you give it to him?"

"It only wants having that last piece mounted," she said, taking the
locket back from him and laying it open beside his portrait. "I'll do that

tonight. I don't know when your father plans to leave, but he'll be able to take it with him."

Alaric was grinning widely at the shared conspiracy as she folded part of the silk over her treasure and rose.

"But, enough of that for now. You've done your sums and I've shared a secret with you. Would you like to come with me now, while I feed the chickens and gather some vegetables from the kitchen garden? You should know where your food comes from, and what's involved in helping things grow."

Smiling and eager, Alaric got to his feet and went with Aunt Delphine, happily slipping his hand into hers.

Chapter 10

"Discretion shall preserve thee, understanding shall keep thee."
—PROVERBS 2:11

OTHER things Alaric learned as well during those sultry days at Morganhall, also relating to who and what he was. He had always been good with horses, but he found that patience often resulted in unexpected rapport with birds and other small creatures—though he quickly decided that it was unfair to use his powers of persuasion in pursuit of chickens or rabbits destined for the pot, unless a person was really, really hungry.

"You can't help it, that God made you taste good," he told the hens one morning, low under his breath, while he was scattering feed in their pen. "People need to eat. Besides, most of you get to lay eggs. I like eggs."

His success with cats was somewhat less reliable, but he attributed that to the innate independence of the creatures; dogs seemed to make more ready allies. Not that his own dog was altogether an ally. The brindle hound given him by the king for his fourth birthday had mostly become Bronwyn's dog in the intervening years, since Kenneth had declined to drag the hound back and forth to Rhemuth.

"Besides, Bayard is needed here, to guard your sister and your aunts," Kenneth had said, quite reasonably. "You'll still see him when we visit Morganhall. He'll remember you."

And remember him the hound did, shadowing him whenever he was in residence at Morganhall but stopping at the gate whenever Alaric would venture out with Llion or one of the other knights to exercise the horses.

"He's doing his job," Llion reminded him, when Bayard settled yet again just inside the gate as they rode forth. "There will be other hounds in your life, over the years. This one was your first, and now he is your sister's first—and good and well that he is, to protect her when you are not here."

Alaric sighed, but he knew Llion was right. There had been a time, not so very long ago, when he would have resented his hound's shift in loyalties. But maturity was teaching him to detach from things that mattered little in the greater scheme of things. His sister's safety was more important than hurt feelings.

Something happened a bit later that afternoon that suddenly shifted more of his perspectives. He and Llion had been watching the farmers cutting hay in one of the fields, and had stopped at a stream to water the horses. He was riding the now-retired Cockleburr for old times' sake, and Llion had taken out a big, raw-boned bay from Morganhall's stables. They had gotten down to stretch their legs while the horses drank, and were preparing to mount up again when Llion's steed unaccountably snaked its long neck around and chomped hard on the young knight's shoulder.

"Stop that!" Llion exclaimed, jerking sharply at the reins beneath the bit even as he hauled off and punched the animal in the neck. Alaric had drawn back sharply at the exclamation, but at once moved closer in concern as Llion clutched at his shoulder and began rubbing it, wincing with the pain. The horse had dropped its head and begun pulling at tufts of grass by the water's edge, as if nothing had happened.

"Perverse beast!" Llion muttered.

As he slipped a hand inside the neck of his tunic to assess the damage, Alaric asked, wide-eyed, "Are you all right? Did he draw blood?"

"Apparently not," Llion allowed, with a glance at his hand. "But I'm going to have one hell of a bruise," he added, as he flexed his shoulder and resumed rubbing at the injury. "Your father said I could have any horse in the stable, but you can bet that it won't be this one!"

"I have an idea," Alaric said cautiously, "if you'll let me try something."

Llion looked at him sharply, at once wary and apprehensive. "Oh?"

"Just . . . come and sit down," the boy said uncertainly. "I may be able to take away the pain. I've done it on animals," he added, as Llion's eyebrow lifted.

The young knight gave an uneasy glance around them—there was no one nearby, save the horses—then leaned closer to his charge.

"Are you talking about using your powers?" he asked in a low voice.

"Well, sort of," the boy admitted sheepishly. "It wouldn't interfere with your free will," he assured his mentor. "And you'd still have the bite—and a bruise. But I think I can block the pain."

"You think you can block the pain," Llion repeated softly, and somewhat disbelievingly. "What does that mean, exactly?"

"I can make the pain go away, or at least ease. Will you let me try?"

Llion let out a pent-up breath and rolled his eyes heavenward for an instant, still rubbing his shoulder, then returned his gaze to the boy's.

"All right. I suppose I always knew this day would come. What do you want me to do?"

"We need to tie up the horses first," he said, gesturing toward a nearby log with protruding branches, "and then sit down. This shouldn't take long."

As Llion complied, looking ill at ease, Alaric stripped off his riding gloves and shoved them under his belt, waiting until the young knight had taken a seat on the log. Then he tentatively slipped one hand into the neck of Llion's tunic to cup his palm over the injury. At the same time, he lifted his other hand toward the young knight's forehead. Llion flinched back at first, for common wisdom held that physical contact usually went with the exercise of Deryni powers, but Alaric only quirked him a self-conscious smile and shook his head.

"Llion, I'm already touching you with my other hand. If I wanted to invade your mind, that would be enough—if I knew how to do that, which I don't. I promise I'm not going to hurt you."

Steeling himself, Llion let out a deep breath, only flinching a little as the boy's fingertips touched his forehead and then lay flat.

"Just close your eyes and try to relax," Alaric whispered. "Take a deep breath and let it out. Again."

Llion did his best to comply, stiff at first, but then relaxing under the boy's touch and drawing a third slow breath, then a fourth.

"That's good. Be aware of the pain now, and concentrate through it, feel it begin to recede. Try not to pay any attention to it. With each breath that you take, the pain becomes less and less, until it's only a faint, dull ache, to remind you not to overdo with that shoulder until it heals. Now, take one last breath and open your eyes."

Alaric withdrew his hands as Llion exhaled in a prolonged sigh and slowly opened his eyes. The young knight cautiously flexed his injured shoulder as he turned a disbelieving gaze on his charge.

"How did you do that?" he breathed, as he continued to flex the shoulder and rubbed at it distractedly.

"I have no idea," the boy replied. "It's just something that I can do."

"Do you know how long it will last?"

"I couldn't tell you."

Nodding, still rubbing absently at his shoulder, Llion got up from his log and reached for the horses' reins, knotted to one of the protruding branches.

"We won't tell anyone about this, all right?"

"They'd just be afraid, wouldn't they?" Alaric replied.

"They would, indeed."

The boy sighed. "Some gift, when you can't even use it," he muttered.

"I didn't say you mustn't use it," Llion said quietly, abandoning his wounded shoulder to boost Alaric into Cockleburr's saddle. "But you must be very careful when you do use it, and don't let yourself be *seen* using it. It's going to be hard enough to get you safely grown, without having to fend off people trying to get you burned at the stake."

I N the end, they lingered at Morganhall for nearly three weeks, for Kenneth was loath to leave his sisters, with Claara's health still so frail, but Trevor rightly pointed out that the end of summer was fast approaching, the first of the harvests being brought in, and Kenneth had still to make his yearly visits to Lendour and Corwyn.

The morning of their departure, after they had heard Mass and broken their fast, Kenneth bade farewell to his sister Claara and her granddaughter, hoisted Bronwyn onto his shoulders, and headed down to the yard with Delphine. Alaric was waiting with Llion and the rest of their party, who were already mounted. Xander and Trevor would be going with them, but Froilán was to remain at Morganhall for the nonce, along with two nursing sisters sent up from Arc-en-Ciel by his daughter Alazais, who was considering a vocation. In addition, four of Kenneth's men-at-arms, left behind at Rhemuth in June, had ridden up to be their escort on the road to Lendour and Coroth.

"Good, are we ready, then?" Kenneth asked, surveying the party.

"Not quite," Delphine said, pausing on the steps of the hall to take his arm. "I have a parting gift for you, brother. Alaric, would you join us?"

As Alaric did so, Delphine handed Kenneth a red velvet pouch with drawstrings, closing his hand around it.

"What's this?" he said, glancing at the others.

"Something I've been working on for several months," she replied. "Perhaps Bronwyn would like to open it for you."

Grinning broadly, Bronwyn leaned down from her father's shoulders with hand outstretched and took the bag, immediately attacking the drawstrings that closed it. What emerged, dangling from a long, braided cord of silk, was the silver locket Delphine had showed to Alaric. As Bronwyn dangled it before her father's eyes, he reached up and cupped it in his hand, looking uncertain.

"Wasn't this our mother's locket?" he asked, looking puzzled.

"It was," said Delphine. "Open it."

As Bronwyn leaned over his shoulder, both arms around his neck, and Alaric watched eagerly, Kenneth pried at the filigree cover with a thumbnail—and gaped in wonder at the tiny portrait gazing back at him.

"*Alyce!*" he breathed. "Delphine, it's beautiful!"

"There's more," she said, smiling. "Open the locket."

He did, and his expression softened. Struck wordless, he pulled his sister into his embrace and held her tight for a long moment, until Bronwyn squirmed and protested.

"Papa, you're squashing my feet."

This practical complaint somewhat broke the spell, so that Kenneth laughed and swung her down to the ground, kissing the top of her head and then pulling Alaric into an embrace as well.

"You're getting big for hugs," he whispered fiercely, "but I know you had a hand in this, or at least the keeping of the secret."

"Yes, Papa."

"I'm so glad you like it," Delphine said, obviously pleased. "I thought you would appreciate having at least some of your family with you when you are off and about in the king's service. It probably would be a good idea to keep it in its pouch when you're not wearing it."

"Delphine, this is amazing. My wife, my children, our mother's locket, and your incredible artistry, all in one package. Thank you. I shall treasure it always," Kenneth said. He closed up the locket and slipped it back into its pouch, then tucked that into the front of his tunic.

"Right, then, we'd best be off. Be sure that I shall show it to Zoë, and convey your greetings—and Claara's. Take care of our little sister, Delphine."

"I shall, dear brother."

He hugged her tight again, gave Bronwyn another hug and a kiss, then turned away to give Alaric a leg up and then mount up himself.

T HEY spent the last week in August traveling to Lendour. Riding out of Morganhall, they headed south and east across the fertile plain of Candor Rhea until they reached the Molling Valley, then turned east. With harvest in full swing, there was much for Alaric to see as they rode, and he relished the company of the adults.

The road east along the river was a good one, and they made excellent time, though they bypassed Mollingford itself and made a wide detour around the village of Hallowdale. On a previous venture along this road, returning from Zoë's wedding in Cynfyn, Kenneth, Alaric, and the three knights riding with them, along with Alyce, had witnessed the aftermath of a Deryni burning in Hallowdale's village square: a horrific sight that none of them would ever forget.

It was the sight of smoke that caused their detour this time, trailing upward from the distant village; but this time, at least, when Kenneth sent Xander on ahead to learn its cause, it proved to be only the smoke of burning stubble, though Kenneth still fancied he could detect a whiff of burning flesh on the summer air. (If he could have had his way four years before, the village would have been razed and the soil sown with salt to purify it.) They made camp under the stars that night, where Kenneth slept only fitfully. Alaric sought comfort curled close against his father.

But another day's travel took them back along the river road and onto the plain that lay before Lendour and the mountain fastness of Castle Cynfyn, where outriders from the Lendour capital met them the following afternoon, for Kenneth had sent word ahead that they were coming.

A proper welcoming party was waiting for them the next morning as they approached the castle itself: the castle's seneschal, Sir Deinol Hartmann, and Kenneth's son-in-law, Sir Jovett Chandos, with his father, Sir Pedur. Perched on the saddlebow before Sir Pedur was the grandson adored by both men: Kailan Peter Chandos, Zoë's eldest child, who was nearly four.

"Welcome, Kenneth, Master Alaric," Sir Pedur called with a grin, as Kenneth and his party approached. "Shall I give you a grandson to ride with you?"

For answer, Kenneth spurred on ahead to take Kailan from his other grandfather's arms and hug him close, to the boy's delight. Alaric, too, was grinning as he joined his father and fell in beside him as they continued on into the town and through the castle gates. He liked Kailan, who was only a few months younger than his sister Bronwyn.

But it was Zoë herself whom Kenneth most longed to see: darling Zoë, eldest daughter of his first marriage and heart-sister to Alyce, the love of his second marriage, who was waiting for him on the steps to the castle hall with her own daughter in her arms: Alyce Maria, born but a few months before. Beside her, Jovett's beaming mother held both hands of a sturdy toddler with a shock of coppery curls like Kailan's: Charlan Pedur, Kenneth's second grandchild. Kenneth was grinning as he handed Kailan off to a waiting squire and sprang off his horse to mount the steps and enfold grandson, daughter, and granddaughter in his embrace.

"Darling Zoë, she's beautiful!" he exclaimed, after he had saluted each of them with a kiss and stroked the downy hair on the baby's head. "And she is, indeed, worthy of her name." He turned to pump Jovett's hand as the infant's father came up the steps behind him with Alaric and Llion. "Jovett, you make beautiful daughters as well as handsome sons!"

"'Tis most pleasant work, I assure you, my lord," Jovett replied happily. "Come inside and refresh yourselves—all of you," he added, with a sweep of his arm toward Xander and Trevor and the rest of Kenneth's party, who were dismounting in the yard behind them. "The cooks have been busy for several days, preparing for your welcome. For a while, we feared we should not see you this season."

"Aye, we feared it, too," Kenneth replied, as he moved into the hall amid happy members of his family. "But Duke Andrew's passing is now resolved, and Claara's condition appears to have stabilized. As I said in my letter, however, Delphine will need assistance at Morganhall. Have you sent anyone yet?"

"Not yet," Jovett replied, "but several men are considering whether they would like to make the move, along with their wives. Once we knew you were coming, it seemed best to hold off on making any permanent decisions."

"That's fine, then. We're well in hand," Kenneth replied.

They stayed at Cynfyn for a fortnight, while he shared the events of the past several months with his daughter and her family and set about deciding who could be spared to go to Morganhall. In the end, he recruited several semi-retired Lendour knights to join the Morganhall household, one of whom had administrative skills as well as arms acumen; and their wives would be welcome companionship for his sisters, as well as additional help with the domestic arrangements of the household. Once that was resolved, he settled into the more tedious process of inspecting the accounts at Cynfyn and attending to other necessary business of the earldom.

Alaric, meanwhile, enjoyed renewing his relationship with Zoë and becoming better acquainted with her two boys, who were technically his nephews, since Zoë was his half-sister. As for the new baby, he had no idea how to deal with her, for his interaction with Bronwyn during her infancy had been quite limited.

"Auntie Zoë, would it be all right if I called them my cousins?" he asked her one evening, after the two of them had seen the younger boys off to bed. "I don't think I'm old enough to be an uncle."

"Of course you can, darling," she said with a laugh and a hug. "Your mother and I always regarded ourselves as sisters, but the true relationship is a little complicated. And I'm sure that Kailan and Charlan will be much happier having you for a cousin—and little Alyce, when she's old enough to know what that means."

Alaric glanced at his feet, suddenly gone shy. "You named her for my mother, didn't you?" The question was more like a statement, and Zoë nodded.

"I did, love. I loved her very much. Do you mind sharing her name with my daughter?"

The boy looked up in surprise. "Of course not."

"I'm so glad," Zoë whispered, and hugged him close again.

Despite their short stay at Cynfyn, Alaric was kept busy. Aside from interacting with his "cousins," and sharing some of their lessons, he continued his weapons training with Llion, sometimes under the eagle eye of Jovett and Sir Deinol. More important, he was at his father's side when, the day before they were to depart for Coroth, Kenneth convened a formal earl's court to continue his son's exposure to the people who, one day, would become his vassals.

"He's turning into a fine young man," Sir Deinol remarked later that night, when the children had gone to bed and Kenneth had opened several bottles of R'Kassan red to share with the men charged with the daily running of the Lendour estates. Llion, to give them privacy, had gone to see to final arrangements for their departure in the morning.

"I see shades of his uncle, Lord Ahern, in some of his determination and focus," Deinol went on. "He's quite the horseman for a boy his age."

Jovett snorted. "He is quite the horseman for a lad *twice* his age. Ahern would have been proud." He sighed. "I still miss him."

"So do we all," Kenneth said quietly, trying to put from mind the young earl's untimely death, after overcoming injuries that would have defeated a lesser man. "But what he accomplished was possible, at least in part, due to the encouragement and devotion that all of you gave him. If my son is truly cast in Ahern's mold, it's that same encouragement and devotion that will help enable him to reach his own potential."

Jovett gave a shrug, as if to dismiss the compliment, and Deinol looked slightly self-conscious, but Kenneth continued.

"Do not minimize your parts in this, gentlemen. I am well aware what a trial it has been, for Lendour and for Corwyn to have a succession of minor heirs. If we can keep him alive long enough to enter into his manhood, I have no doubt that Alaric will become an earl and a duke worthy of your devotion."

"My lord, we are content for now that *you* are our earl," Deinol returned.

Kenneth smiled faintly. "Thank you, Deinol. But we all know that I am but a caretaker, until my son comes of age."

"If you are a caretaker, my lord, it is for a son who will be a worthy successor to his very worthy father one day," Pedur retorted. As Deinol and Jovett nodded their agreement, Pedur lifted his cup. "To the young Lord Alaric, and to his estimable sire!"

"Hear, hear!" Deinol said, likewise lifting his cup in salute, as the others did the same.

THEY were in Coroth, the Corwyn capital, in time for Alaric's birthday at the end of September. Jovett had traveled with them, and also two more of Cynfyn's young knights: Jardine Howard, one of Duchess Vera's uncles, and Phares Donovan, whom Kenneth had knighted several years before. Again, Kenneth had sent word ahead that they were coming, so an escort met them as they approached the city along the river route, led by the ducal chancellor, Sir James of Tendal, and one of the ducal counselors, Sir Crescence de Naverie.

"Well met, my lord!" Sir James called, as his party drew rein and turned to merge with theirs. "And Master Alaric, welcome back to your duchy."

Alaric beamed at the greeting, and fell in beside Sir Crescence as they continued on toward the northern city gate, Llion riding to his other side.

"I must say that your timing could not be better, my lord," Sir James remarked to Kenneth, as they passed into the city. "Usually, you and Master Alaric come earlier in the summer. We have never had the honor of his presence on his feast day. 'Tis a very special celebration in Coroth."

"Indeed," Kenneth replied, as Alaric also looked at him in question. "And aside from it being his natal day, what makes it so special?"

"Ah, well, then, 'tis Michaelmas," James replied, "when the knights in charge of training the squires and pages lead all the boys in a special procession to Saint Michael's shrine at the cathedral. Sir Llion will remember," he added, with a glance over his shoulder in Llion's direction. "There they dedicate their weapons to knightly service and receive a special blessing from the bishop. It's perhaps a quaint custom," he admitted, "but the boys do seem to enjoy it, to have their future warrior status so ratified. Perhaps young Alaric would like to take part, since he is our future duke."

As he glanced hopefully at Alaric, the boy cast a fleeting look in Llion's direction, then inclined his head in a dutiful nod of agreement.

"It would be my honor, Sir James. Perhaps Sir Llion will consent to instruct me regarding the ceremony."

"I am certain that Sir Llion is well capable of that," Sir Crescence replied. "Quite clearly, he has taken the inspiration of Saint Michael very much to heart." He gave Llion a nod. "It is always a pleasure to acknowledge the success of one of our Corwyn knights who has made good, Sir Llion. And we have heard of your charge's proficiency a-horse. Perhaps afterward, in honor of his feast day, he would consent to compete with some of our pages here at Coroth."

"Perhaps some friendly ring-tilting," Llion replied, with a tiny smile in Alaric's direction.

"Excellent!" Sir James replied. "I shall ask Lord Hamilton to arrange it."

THEY supped in the great hall that night, with Alaric seated beside his father in the place of honor. His regents made much of him, and he tried to do justice to the meal set before him, but he soon found himself stifling yawns of increasing tenacity. One of the slightly older pages, a hazel-eyed lad with curly auburn hair and a smattering of freckles, noticed him struggling to stay awake, and leaned closer as he presented a savory pie.

"You look like you'd rather have a bed," the boy whispered.

Alaric shrugged a little self-consciously.

"I'd hoped it wasn't too obvious," he whispered back. "We had an early start. How are you called?"

"Jernian," the boy replied with a faint grin. "I think I'm named for one of your ancestors. My father is, too."

Alaric cocked his head at the boy. "Oh? Who is your father?"

"Airlie Kushannan," the boy replied, jutting his chin in the direction of a fit-looking man sitting farther along the table, with the same auburn hair. "He's Earl of Airnis, now that my grandfather is gone."

"Your grandfather?" Alaric repeated, taken aback. "Not Lord Síoda . . . ?"

Jernian looked surprised. "You didn't know?"

"No one told me. When did it happen?"

Glancing around uneasily, for he was on duty, Jernian put his platter on the table beside Alaric's place and said quietly, "Come outside, where we can talk."

Outside, the two of them settled awkwardly on one of the lower steps into the great hall. Alaric was no longer sleepy.

"What happened to Lord Síoda?" he said, when Jernian did not immediately speak.

Jernian sighed. "I'm sorry. I thought you would have been told. He took ill shortly before he was to leave for the king's knighting. That's why he didn't attend. He wasn't sick for very long," he added, at Alaric's expression of dismay. "And he *was* nearly seventy." He briefly glanced aside. "I do miss him, though."

Alaric glanced down at the steps beneath his feet. "I shall miss him, too. Did you know that he served Duke Stíofan, my mother's great-grandfather?"

"Yes."

"Whenever I came to Coroth, he would tell me stories about my heritage, and when my mother was a little girl. I always looked forward to it."

Jernian nodded, smiling faintly. "He was a man of great honor, and he lived a good, long li—"

He broke off as he noticed that Llion had appeared in the doorway from the hall, and scrambled to his feet.

"Coming, Sir Llion," he said quickly. "I know I'm shirking my duties. But he didn't know that my grandfather had died."

"No need to make apologies, lad," Llion replied, coming down the steps to join them. "I saw Alaric had left, and I wanted to make certain all was well."

Alaric nodded. "I'm perfectly fine. I'm tired, is all. May I be excused?"

"Of course." Llion offered his hand to assist the boy to his feet. "And thank you, Jernian. I'll be certain you aren't reprimanded for leaving your post."

"Thank you, sir."

"I'll see you in the morning," Alaric called after Jernian as the older boy headed back into the hall. "Perhaps you can guide me through this Saint Michael procession tomorrow."

Jernian only cast a grin over his shoulder as he disappeared into the hall.

"Llion, did you know that Lord Síoda had died?" Alaric asked, as the two of them headed up the stairway that led to the residential apartments.

"Not until this evening," Llion replied. "You were fond of him, weren't you?"

"Yes, I was."

What he did not mention, as Llion helped him undress and ready for bed, was that Síoda Kushannan had told him, on their last visit, that his mother had been Deryni. "That means that both of us are half-Deryni, lad," Earl Síoda had said, "though my mother was from a far less illustrious line than yours. Perhaps, if God gives us time, we can both explore what that might mean for Corwyn. We can talk more on your next visit."

But for Síoda Kushannan, there would be no "next visit." Only as Alaric was settling into his bed did it occur to him to wonder whether any spark of that long-diluted Deryni blood might run in the veins of young Jernian, who carried the name of a Deryni duke.

Chapter 11

"For I was a witty child, and had a good spirit."
—WISDOM OF SOLOMON 8:19

ALARIC was up early the next morning, to dress in the formal attire that Llion had laid out for him.

"Your father and I discussed the best way to convey your status, and we agreed that the livery of a Lendour page is probably most appropriate," Llion told him, as Alaric did up the laces on his linen shirt. "Eventually, you *will* be Duke of Corwyn, of course, but he did not think this the time to make an issue of it."

"I understand," Alaric said, as he let Llion slip the red and white Lendour tabard over his head. "Some of the other boys have been pages or squires for years, and have earned their status. You've taught me well, Llion, but I still have much to learn."

"You shall be an official page to a duke by Twelfth Night," Llion replied with a smile. "And meanwhile, it is no small thing to be an unofficial page to your father."

"And it is no small thing to be your student!" Alaric said loyally, as the door opened and his father entered. "Let them watch me at ring-tilting this afternoon."

"Just don't show them up too badly," Kenneth said, smiling as he closed the door behind him. "The boys and even the squires you contest today will become the men you will one day rule, and childhood grudges can last a long time."

Alaric cocked his head. "Are you saying that I should not do my best?"

"No, just be mindful of *how* you do your best," Kenneth replied. "Every man wants his lord to be the best, but these are still boys, who have trained together for years, some of them. You are still something of an outsider to them, so you must prove your worth. Here, I've brought you something to wear for the ceremony."

So saying, he produced an oblong object swathed in wrappings of checkered wool. "Lord Hamilton gave this to me last night, and bade me give it you," he said, folding back the wrappings. Inside was an ivory-hilted dagger with silver mountings, its blade sheathed in a plain leather scabbard. "Apparently it belonged to your great-great grandfather Stíofan. It would have gone to your Uncle Ahern, if he had lived. In any case, Hamilton and his predecessors have held it in trust for the next duke—which will be you."

He offered it across his left forearm, hilt first, and Alaric grinned ear to ear as he took it. The quillons of the weapon were deeply engraved with a design that included gryphon wings.

"This belonged to Duke Stíofan?"

"So they told me. Be sure to do him proud. But we'd best be going now. They'll be waiting downstairs."

"Yes, of course."

Alaric thought about what his father had said as he slipped the dagger's fittings onto his plain leather belt and followed him down the turnpike stair, Llion bringing up the rear. Ring-tilting was planned for the afternoon, and he knew that he was good. Not to do his best went against everything he had been taught.

But then it came to him how he might still level the field a bit, and give an honest striving that would not compromise his honor. Grinning, he drew Llion aside at the bottom of the stairs and whispered his plan in his mentor's ear. Llion laughed aloud and nodded his approval. "I'll tell him," he said.

But before the strivings of the afternoon must come the morning's procession to the cathedral to pay their respects to St. Michael. Horses and ponies stood saddled in the castle yard, where several dozen squires and pages had already congregated. Most were in the black and green livery of Corwyn, but a few wore the colors of their fathers' houses.

Young Jernian, in the green and white of Airnis, spotted Alaric almost as soon as he and Llion emerged from the great hall, and waved a cheery greeting.

"It appears that we're meant to ride down to the cathedral square," Llion said aside to Alaric. "If you'd like, why don't you ride with Jernian, if that's permitted, and I'll join your father. I see Giles with a pony for you. That's what all the other pages seem to be riding."

Craning his neck, Alaric said, "I see him."

By the time he had worked his way over to the groom, Lord Hamilton was shouting for everyone to mount up. Alaric was surprised at how quickly the seeming chaos of the castle yard turned to order. When Giles had given him a leg up, Alaric eased his mount over to Jernian with a tentative grin.

"Good morning," Jernian said brightly.

"Good morning," Alaric returned. "Since you've done this before, I'll assume that you know where we're meant to go. May I ride with you, or is there some special order?"

"Only that we ride by twos, first the pages and then the squires," Jernian said amiably. "You do me honor."

Alaric shrugged a little self-consciously. "No reason that you should feel honored. I'm only a page, like you. And not even an official one, yet."

"The honor still is mine," Jernian said, smiling slightly as he bowed in the saddle. "After all, you are my future duke."

"And a friend, I hope," Alaric countered.

Jernian inclined his head. "That, too."

They set out very soon along the winding avenue that led down to the cathedral square with Lord Hamilton leading the pages and squires, followed by a bevy of knights and grooms and the fathers of some of the boys. Some of the women of the town had turned out to line the route, to wave gaily colored kerchiefs and cast late-blooming flowers in their path, honoring the warriors they would become.

Dismounting before the great west portico, the young riders gave their mounts into the care of the grooms and allowed Lord Hamilton to shepherd them into a proper procession between the choir and assorted clergy. To preside over the ceremony was Coroth's bishop: the silver-haired Esmé Harris, wearing a golden cope embroidered across its back with an image of St. Michael, the wings sweeping onto his shoulders. His golden miter was embroidered with a six-winged seraph at front and back.

A thurifer led the way in cassock and surplice, swinging a great brass censer that trailed billows of sweet-smelling incense, perfuming the cathedral as he came. Next came a crucifer with a jeweled processional cross, flanked by a pair of lantern bearers. Following came a knight carrying a silk-embroidered banner of the archangel.

A choir of young boys followed, gowned in Corwyn green beneath their white surplices, singing a hymn to the angels: *"Benedicite Dominum, omnes angeli ejus . . ."* Bless the Lord all ye His angels. You that are mighty in strength, and execute His will, hearkening to the voice of His orders, alleluia, alleluia. . . .

The squires and pages followed this band, with the bishop bringing up the rear. Processing down the center aisle, they made their several reverences before the high altar, then continued into the south transept to halt before the side chapel that housed the armored image of the saint, fierce and more than life-sized, with sword uplifted to slay the cringing dragon pinned beneath one booted foot. There the boys formed two lines before the statue and knelt, the pages in front and the squires behind, while the bishop came to stand before them, flanked by the two lantern bearers. The boys of the choir gathered to one side.

"In Nomine Patris, et Filii, et Spiritus Sancti, Amen," the bishop intoned, signing himself with the cross as everyone did the same. *"Dominus vobiscum. . . ."*

"Et cum spiritu tuo," the choir answered.

What followed mostly ran together in Alaric's mind—readings from sacred writ and prayers invoking the blessing and protection of the great archangel whose feast this was—but kneeling by Jernian's side, he comported himself as a dutiful page, doing what the others did, careful not to put himself forward in any way that would make him stand out from the others. His bright hair already did that. And of course, everyone attending knew who he was.

To his relief, no one made direct reference to his identity; not even when the pages and squires were invited to come forward in single file to place their daggers on a low table at the feet of the statue, returning then to kneel again with clasped hands before the archangel's statue. Next, while the bishop knelt at a prayer desk off to the right, the choir began a low, melodic chant invoking the presence and protection of the archangel.

"*Alleluia, alleluia, Sancte Michael Archangele, defende nos in proelio. . . .*" Holy Archangel Michael, be our shield in battle, alleluia, alleluia. . . .

For an eight-year-old, the ceremony soon bordered on the tedious, even though Alaric knew it was his duty. Head bowed over his clasped hands, he let himself drift with the harmony and even daydream a bit. He remained vaguely aware of the others kneeling beside and behind him, of the bishop at his prayer desk, the fathers and other knights standing behind them.

Something changed, however, when the bishop rose and took up the great brass thurible, charging it with fresh incense as the choir began another invocation that elaborated on an ancient text.

"*Per intercessionem beati Michaelis Archangeli, stantis a dextris altaris incensi. . . .*" At the intercession of blessed Michael the archangel, who stands at the right hand of the altar of incense. . . .

As the bishop brought the censer over to the statue, swinging it from side to side, Alaric certainly was not expecting anything unusual to happen. But as the bishop saluted the statue of the archangel with incense and then turned his attention to the daggers at its feet, all at once Alaric became aware of . . . *something* suddenly looming behind and all around the statue of St. Michael, overshadowing and engulfing it, larger than a man.

Startled, it was all he could do not to jerk his head upward in surprise, though he sensed that nothing physical had changed. Nor was anyone else reacting to anything out of the ordinary. Certainly not the bishop, looking almost bored as he trailed incense smoke over the daggers, the censer's chains clinking brass against the brass.

Forcing down a faint queasiness in the pit of his stomach, Alaric cautiously dared a glance upward, careful not to move anything but his eyes—and quickly averted them as he caught the distinct impression of fire shimmering around the statue like a vast, fiery cloak . . . or folded wings.

Suddenly light-headed, he made himself draw a slow breath to steady his nerves. Then he cautiously looked upward again, for in the afterimage of his mind's eye, he had also formed the vague impression of gauntleted fists folded over the quillons of a massive golden sword within the column of fire. Sidelong vision seemed to be more distinct than head-on, but he lowered his gaze again when, quite deliberately, part of the fire abruptly swept down like an arm, to pass above the daggers laid out on the table at the saint's feet.

Alaric stifled a gasp at that, thankfully masked by the choir, though he remembered to keep his face impassive. The bishop still seemed unaware, calmly turning away to hand off the censer to a waiting server. But when Alaric glanced back at the statue, the overlay of fire was gone.

Exhaling cautiously, he lowered his eyes and tried to collect himself, only now recalling the apparitions he and Duncan had seen at Duke Andrew's deathbed. He wondered whether this had been a similar vision, whether anyone else had seen it.

He followed the others dutifully as the ceremony came to a close, the bishop giving all of them a final blessing and then gesturing that each boy should retrieve his dagger before filing out in silence. Jernian was rubbing at his eyes, looking a bit bemused as he and Alaric headed down the stairs before the great west portal. Had he, too, perhaps seen something?

"That was interesting," Alaric said quietly, looking for and then spotting his father and Llion, who were waiting with their horses and Alaric's pony. "Is it always done that way?"

"What do you mean?" Jernian replied. He was still rubbing at his eyes.

"Oh, with the bishop presiding, and all those prayers to Saint Michael," Alaric said vaguely. "Do you have something in your eye?"

"It's nothing," Jernian said with a shake of his head. "Maybe some ash from the incense. Why do you ask about the ceremony? Don't they keep Saint Michael's feast in Rhemuth?"

Alaric shrugged, but he could not shake the feeling that Jernian was dissembling. "I'm sure they must do. Most knights have a devotion to Saint Michael. I'm just glad his feast doesn't happen in the summer, with all that incense. I expect it might get plenty warm."

"Oh, it would, and it does." Jernian grinned self-consciously and turned his attention to Kenneth and Llion as they approached the two adults. "Look, here's your father."

Alaric thought about what he had experienced while they rode back up to the castle, but realized that any serious discussion probably would have to wait until he returned to Culdi. Though he and Duncan had told Aunt Vera about the angels at Duke Andrew's deathbed, he had not mentioned it to his father or Llion, who were not Deryni.

As for Jernian, he still was not certain, though the older boy might well have a bit of Deryni blood through his great-grandmother—if, indeed, Earl Síoda's mother had been Deryni. But until he knew Jernian better, it was probably a good idea not to talk too much about Deryni. In general, Corwyners seemed predisposed to accept Deryni, and had revered Duke Stíofan, but it was not something on which Alaric wished to gamble his life just now. Meanwhile, he had ring-tilting competitions to think about.

In the end, he had very little time to think about anything *except* ring-tilting for the rest of the afternoon. Most of the squires and pages at Coroth were more than competent, he soon discovered; especially the squires. But at least initially, he beat the other pages handily, even on a horse instead of a pony like most of the other boys rode. Riding a horse was the leveler he had chosen for himself, to give himself a slight handicap, for horses were less nimble when it came to snagging rings.

But even so mounted, it soon became clear that he was a better rider than most of the other pages, even the ones soon to become squires. Only the two oldest squires, due to be knighted by his father on this visit, were consistently better. Poor Jernian was not a good rider at all.

"Are you all right?" Alaric whispered to the older boy as he bent to give him a hand up after a particularly awkward-looking unplanned dismount. "That looked painful. Did the pony stumble?"

"No, I just fell off," Jernian said cheerfully. "I haven't got very good balance. And it doesn't help that I don't see the rings that clearly. Lord Hamilton says I have the makings of a good strategist, though. I'm very good at theory. And it doesn't hurt that I'll be Earl of Airnis one day."

"I suppose you're right," Alaric said thoughtfully.

Something he had not done before was to ride at multiple rings in a single run, as the squires did after the first few passes at single rings. The best of them could take all three rings most of the time. One squire called Edgar of Mathelwaite, a baron's son and heir, rode well enough, but seemed to take perverse pleasure in gloating when one of the other squires took a spill or missed a ring, especially the younger ones. Alaric insisted on trying it, and managed to keep up reasonably well—until they switched to smaller rings.

"Llion, why have I not been practicing at multiple rings?" he asked under his breath, when he had ridden another pass and taken only one ring.

Llion only raised an eyebrow and pretended to adjust a spur strap. "For one thing, it takes far more personnel to attend to three rings—or else much more time between runs. And while it does help with hand-eye coordination—and it looks very dashing!—it doesn't much reflect real battle experience. Sword-work will be much more important."

Alaric allowed himself a heavy sigh.

"Having said that, you'll get some experience at multiple rings when you train at Rhemuth," Llion went on. "I know that Duke Richard favors it. For now, the smaller rings are more important than trying to take several of them in a row."

Alaric gave a grudging nod. "You did say back in Rhemuth that I needed to start riding at smaller rings."

"True enough," Llion agreed. "And you do. But you've still given quite a respectable showing against lads considerably older than you are, and riding an exercise that you'd never done before."

"Point taken," Alaric said. "But I do like to win."

"And so you shall, in the future," Llion replied. "But part of the purpose of today's exercise was not necessarily to win, but to show yourself more than competent at your present level of training—and to accept the limitations of your training."

Alaric rolled his eyes.

"I know that exasperates you," Llion went on, "but grace in training is important. Meanwhile, you have shown skill and heart before your future knights. And remember that there will always be *someone* who is better than you, whether with sword or lance or even as rider. Right now, the occasional defeat will only hurt your ego. When you're grown, even one defeat could mean your life."

"I know, but—"

"There is no *but*," Llion said flatly. "Never forget that the ultimate purpose of all training is to keep you alive. Incidentally, those hours and days in the saddle on the way here have paid off. You rode *very* well. An excellent performance, lad, whatever you may think."

As he clasped Alaric's shoulder in approval, the boy managed a wan smile.

"Thank you, Llion." He arched one eyebrow. "But you *will* get me smaller rings, for when we resume training back at Rhemuth, won't you?"

"I will," the young knight agreed with a smile.

T HAT night, at supper in the hall, they dined on succulent Michaelmas goose in honor of the day, after which Kenneth and the regents convened a ducal court to confer knighthood on the two most senior squires. Reamonn de Naverie, the son of Sir Crescence, was a tall, soft-spoken young man with dark hair already receding at the temples. What hair he had, he wore braided and clubbed in a warrior's knot. With Kenneth's permission, Reamonn's father conferred the accolade, inviting Jernian and a slightly older page called Viliam to buckle on the spurs. By the response in the hall, young Reamonn clearly was well respected at court, and more than ready for the honor.

The other knight to be made was Gilles Chopard, son of Sir Miles, the council's secretary. A little older than Reamonn, Gilles carried himself like a warrior born, and wore braided sidelocks in the Torenthi fashion. Though Sir Miles was offered the opportunity to give his son the accolade, he deferred to Kenneth, saying that he would rather his son be knighted by the father of his future duke. Gilles agreed.

Hence the second knighting was carried out, again with Jernian and Viliam tending to the spurs. Both new knights were then belted by the beautiful redheaded wife of Earl Airlie, who reduced both young men to speechless blushes as she murmured compliments while she buckled the white belts around their waists.

After that, the assembled nobility of Corwyn drank the health of the two new knights, and then the health of their future duke and his father. A little later, the formalities of court having finished, both new knights came to commend Alaric for his very fine showing in the tilting yard. A few of the men, aware that it was his birthday, gave him tokens by which to remember the day: a pair of dark green riding gloves, ostensibly from the pages. A supple black belt worked with interlace and adorned at its tongue with a brass fitting depicting a Corwyn gryphon—that, from the squires. And from the council of regents, a cardounet board inlaid with contrasting woods, light and dark, along with a set of pieces carved from walrus tusk and jet.

"Jet isn't exactly a stone," Jernian's father told him, as Alaric fingered one of the black archers and wondered at its lightness. "It washes up on the beaches, polished by the sea. Some folk believe that it once was wood from forests that were drowned by the tides. Sometimes you can see the wood grain in rough pieces. But it carves nicely. I hope you will enjoy this set."

"Thank you, my lord, I know I shall," Alaric said, smiling as he replaced the piece with its fellows in its wool-lined box. "Incidentally, I was sorry to hear about your father's passing. I so enjoyed his company on previous visits. I hope it was gentle."

"Thank you, lad, I believe it was," Lord Airnis said, clearly touched as he stepped aside for the next well-wisher to approach.

A little later, Sir James of Tendal, the duchy's chancellor, came over with several of his fellows to give him a far more intriguing present than any mere game set.

"This will give you access to the ducal library," Sir James said, laying a large key in his hand, adorned with a green silk tassel. "It is housed in the so-called 'Green Tower,' on the top floor but one, where many of the books and scrolls belonging to your great-grandfather Stíofan are stored. He was quite a collector."

"They are among the duchy's great treasures," Sir Crescence added, as the wide-eyed Alaric inspected the key, "so none of the volumes may be removed from Coroth until you come of age. But you are welcome to use the library whenever you are in residence."

"Of course, you will need to learn several other languages, if you are to avail yourself of all the library's treasures," Father Tividan said with a faint smile. "I am told that Duke Stíofan was a prodigious scholar."

"All the more reason to keep applying myself to my studies," Alaric replied with a smile. "Thank you, all of you, for this very special gift."

The gift giving done, the adults soon retreated to the tables to take up some serious celebratory drinking in honor of the two new knights, and the pages and squires were dismissed from their table duties. Alaric had just tucked the library key into his belt pouch for safekeeping, and was contemplating an inspection tour of the Green Tower when Jernian and Viliam came over to inspect his new cardounet set.

"Viliam's father is a baron," Jernian said, by way of introduction. "Both of us are passionate for cardounet. Could we have a closer look?"

Inspection led to setting out the pieces on the board, which soon evolved into a hotly contested match between the two, with Alaric looking on in growing amazement. Very quickly it emerged that Viliam, like Jernian, had aspirations as a strategist—and both of them were very good, indeed. Several times, one or another of the other pages and even a squire or two drifted over to watch, but they would soon lose interest and move on. The tension was almost palpable as the two played, briskly, passionately, obviously often matched.

Finally, Viliam let out a dramatic groan of defeat and tipped over his priest-king, conceding the game. Jernian merely sat back and folded his arms across his chest, looking very pleased with himself.

"But . . . you still have moves," Alaric said to Viliam.

"Yes, but he has me in six more moves," Viliam explained with a sigh, indicating the pieces that, when played out, would lead to an inevitable conclusion.

"But he did play very well," Jernian chimed in. "We've been doing this for several years, and we're fairly evenly matched, if the truth be known. He nearly had me, ten moves back, but then he had to get sneaky with his war-duke."

As he gave the other boy a good-natured dunt in the bicep, Viliam snorted, though he was also smiling.

"War-dukes are sneaky; no offense, Alaric. And you can bet that I'll not make *that* mistake again!" he said to Jernian. "Another match? Or you, perhaps?" he added to Alaric.

Before Alaric could answer, Jernian said, "I'd love to, but Alaric probably would like to take his set back to his quarters. It's getting late."

"No, you can play again, if you like," Alaric said. "But only if one of you agrees to play me tomorrow night. And you must teach me more about strategy while I'm here. I always thought I was a reasonably good player, but you two are amazing. It isn't just a game for you, is it? How did you learn to play so well?"

Viliam gave a grin like a cat with a mouse as he began resetting the pieces to begin again. "We've had a Torenthi tutor for the past year. It was originally a Torenthi game, you know."

"You have a Torenthi tutor," Alaric repeated.

"He's actually my father's steward," Jernian replied. "He's quite old now, but he was a master player when he was younger. When he brings the accounts to Father every quarter, he stays for about a week, and I pester him to tutor Viliam and me. Torenthis take the game very seriously."

"It's all about tactics and strategy, after all," Viliam agreed. "My father says that's one of the most important parts of being a good general."

"Do you want to be a general?" Alaric asked.

Viliam shrugged. "Dunno. Maybe." He flashed a winning smile. "But I want to be a squire first. You have to be a squire before you can be a knight. And you have to be a knight before you can even think about being a general."

"I don't want to be a general," Jernian said. "I can't see well enough. But I can be a strategist or tactician on a general's battle staff. Maybe even for the king." He cocked his head at Alaric. "Have you met him? The king, I mean."

Alaric suppressed a smile, for he sensed it would not do to tell his new friends that it would be his job, one day, to guard the king's life, and to be his Deryni protector, that already the king held him in special favor.

"I've met him," he said simply. "My father has known him almost all his life. We attended his knighting celebration in June. I'm not an official page yet, but I got to ride in the pages' competition," he offered.

"You rode at Rhemuth?" Viliam asked, wide-eyed.

"Well, I rode against other pages," Alaric admitted.

"How'd you do?" Jernian wanted to know.

Alaric shrugged. "They only rode at single rings. Not nearly as challenging as what we rode today." He gave a sheepish grin. "I did better than I did today, too. I guess I need to keep practicing. Sir Llion has promised to get me some smaller rings. And I want to start riding at multiple rings, too."

Both his companions nodded sagely. "That's hard," Viliam said. "But Lord Hamilton says that's what it takes, if we want to be knights. And sword practice. And knife-work, and hand-to-hand combat—wrestling and such. Lots of sword practice. That's much more important than lance work. And the book learning."

"I do just fine on the book learning," Jernian chimed in.

Across the hall, Alaric saw Llion watching him, and nodded as Llion caught his eye.

"I'd best say good night now," he said to his two new friends. "I'm not sure what they have planned for me tomorrow, but Sir Llion seems to be looking for me. Play as long as you like," he added, with a glance at the cardounet board. "Just don't lose any of the pieces."

Jernian snorted. "My father would kill us both," he said under his breath, though with a grin.

Both older boys bobbed briefly to their feet as Alaric rose, but they were deeply immersed in a new game before Alaric even cleared the hall.

Chapter 12

"My son, gather instruction from thy youth up; so shalt thou find wisdom till thine old age."
—ECCLESIASTICUS 6:18

It was, indeed, late as Alaric joined Llion and his father; far later than he had thought.

"I wanted to make a quick visit to the library," he told them, as they trudged up the spiraling turnpike stair to their quarters.

"Tomorrow," Kenneth replied. "It's been a busy day, and you need your rest."

"But I'm not tired," Alaric said. "Honestly, I am not."

"Well, I am," Kenneth said. "And I'd like you to be able to sit in tomorrow when the regency council meets. You need to begin learning how a ducal estate operates."

"Oh," Alaric said, surprised and pleased that he was to be included. "In that case . . ."

The reality, the next morning, was far less exciting than he had anticipated or hoped. Sir Trevor came to escort them to the council chamber, Llion also accompanying them. Though the men of the council greeted their future duke warmly when he and his father came into the room, inviting him to sit in the high-backed chair carved on the back with the ducal arms, they soon settled into the business of the ducal court, where Alaric soon got the impression that he was all but invisible.

The proceedings quickly became mostly incomprehensible to even a precocious eight-year-old. Alaric listened dutifully, and tried not to fidget while his officers reported from their various departments. His father, of course, advised and made decisions based on the reports. But by the time they adjourned at midday for a light meal, he was nearly ready for a nap, for all that he had slept very well the night before.

"Well, what did you think?" Kenneth asked, as they headed down the stairs with the others.

"I think that I need to learn a great deal more patience, Papa," Alaric admitted. "Must I go back this afternoon?"

"No, you did well, but it was asking a great deal of an eight-year-old. I merely wanted you to get an idea how it will be, as you grow into your role as duke. Llion, after the two of you get something to eat, why don't you take him up to see the library, and then make arrangements for him to join the pages' training."

"Aye, my lord."

Llion ate, but Alaric was too excited to do more than wolf down a slab of bread smeared with butter and honey as he willed Llion to eat faster. When Llion finally got up from the table, Alaric grabbed an apple and stuffed it into the front of his tunic as he allowed the young knight to lead the way from the hall, following him across the castle yard.

On this final day of September, the weakening autumn sun still managed to glint color off the narrow, green-glassed windows of the top floor that gave the tower its name. Looking up, Alaric could not be certain how many floors there were, but he guessed four or five. Sir James had told him the library was on the top floor but one.

The entrance to the tower's stairwell seemed black as pitch, after the sunlit yard. The narrow stair spiraling upward to the left was built into the thickness of the tower wall, with a thick rope strung through iron rings set into the outer wall, rough under his left hand. The central newel was carved with a spiral that turned the opposite direction from the stair. Though narrow loopholes pierced the outer wall of the stairwell at each turning, casting the occasional bar of daylight across the stone treads, he was glad of Llion's torch following behind, and took up a torch of his own at the first landing, lighting it from Llion's. The flare of extra light revealed several closed doors at each new landing as they ascended, doors that seemed to beckon him.

"Llion, have you any idea what lies behind these doors?" he asked, his voice instinctively hushed in the narrow stairwell.

"Not specifically," Llion replied. "Of course I mostly grew up here at the castle, from the time I was about eight. When I was a page, we used to sneak around in the corridors when we weren't required for lessons or drill or table duty. Some of us would play loyal guards, and a few got to be treacherous enemy infiltrators, and the guards would try to capture the enemy agents. We thought it was terribly grown-up and important—and it *was* good practice, I suppose. The lower levels here are mostly guest quarters, I think. Maybe a few offices. And storage at ground level."

"Were you ever in the library?" Alaric asked.

"No, but I'm given to understand that it's quite extensive. Your grandfather Keryell used to spend several months in Coroth every summer, as your father has tried to do, administering his late wife's estate. That would be your grandmother Stevana. Usually, he would bring the three children with him—your mother, your Aunt Marie, and your Uncle Ahern—and they would play in the corridors and in the castle gardens. I was only just starting out then, as a very junior page, but I do remember serving him at table."

They had been climbing steadily as Llion spoke, pausing at each landing to inspect the doors, but came at last to one that was slightly different from the others, with a painted sign affixed to it that read *Bibliotheca*, and below that, the painted image of an open book.

"This must be it," Alaric breathed, holding his torch aloft to take in the sight.

"So it would seem," Llion agreed.

Even as he spoke, Alaric was digging into the pouch at his waist to produce the key, which he fitted to the brass-rimmed keyhole. The key turned easily in the lock, and the door swung inward on well-oiled hinges.

The room beyond was dark, save for a few slivers of sunlight showing around the shutters that closed off the windows. Lifting his torch to cast better light, Llion made his way over to the nearest one and lifted the bar on the shutters, then folded them back. More light streamed in; and with that, plus the torches, Alaric was able to make out a few details.

"Shall I open more shutters?" Llion asked, turning in the bright window.

"No, this is fine."

Moving on into the room, holding his torch high, Alaric could see that the walls were lined between the windows with tall bookshelves secured against the walls. Nearly all of them bulged with assorted volumes. Clustered in the center of the room, a succession of waist-height scroll cabinets also provided table space, though he could see a writing desk tucked under the window to the left of where Llion waited. He longed to explore, but it was clear that even beginning to acquaint himself with the ducal library would take far more time and knowledge than he currently had available.

"So much to learn," Llion heard him murmur, as he circled along the shelves and trailed his fingertips across the backs of bound volumes at eye level. Some of the texts undoubtedly would be esoteric works that were well beyond his present capability, if he could even read them. Most seemed to be in the common tongue or Latin, but some were in Torenthi or even R'Kassan.

Here was a battered copy of the *Annales* of Sulien, and one of the *Lays of the Lord Llewellyn*. And here, a beautifully bound double volume labeled *Praedictionum Nestae* and *Fatum Caeriessae*.

Another shelf held military works: *The Road to Killingford*, by Sir Rhupert Calder of Sheele, and Sir Thomas Riordan's *Essential Cavalry Tactics*. The latter was one of Duke Richard's favorite sources for teaching battle strategies, usually for squires rather than pages, and Alaric had absorbed the information like a sponge, whenever he was able to sit in on one of the royal duke's lectures.

Crouching down to peer at a scroll lying on a bottom shelf, he puzzled at the Torenthi lettering along its side and realized that it was a copy of something by or about the great Torenthi battle genius Jurij Orkény. He couldn't be sure, of course, because it was written in Torenthi, but it *could* be Orkény's classic *Failed Battle Tactics*, written shortly after the Battle of Killingford. He had heard it mentioned back in Rhemuth, but he had never actually seen a copy. Not that he could read this one.

Reluctantly leaving the Orkény in its place, he moved on to the next bookcase, which held more general titles pertaining to estate management and husbandry, livestock breeding—and stacks of account rolls going back decades. The duchy's history stretched back nearly two hundred years, and before that had been part of the ancient kingdom and principality of Mooryn.

There were more account scrolls in the cases in the center of the room, dozens of them, and he found family histories there as well. Here was a *Vita* of Duke Jernian, and another of Dominic, Corwyn's first duke, so old that the ink was fading. So much to learn! He was eager to begin exploring, but he knew that these, too, would have to wait, for he could not remove any of the works from Coroth, at least until he came of age. But maybe he could borrow some of them, while he was here.

"That's fine, Llion," he finally murmured, lifting his torch high as he turned back toward the silhouette against the opened window. "We can go now. I've seen what I came to see."

Moving back into the open doorway, he waited while Llion closed and re-barred the shutters, then let him pass onto the landing, locked the door behind them, led the way back down the winding stairs. Right now, acquainting himself with all the volumes in the library seemed a lifetime's occupation. But at least it was there, and it was his. He had all the time in the world.

Down in the practice yard, they found Lord Hamilton and Sir Robert of Tendal, the chancellor's son, overseeing sword practice with the pages, who were whacking at heavy oak pells with blunted iron practice swords. Alaric watched with Llion for several minutes, then took up one of the practice swords and began whacking at one of the pells not in use, striking in rhythm with the others. After a while, Sir Robert came over to observe his form, standing silently beside Llion, then called him aside and handed him a wooden practice sword and a padded practice helmet.

"Your form is good," he said, putting on his own helm. "Let's try something a bit different. Do your best to hit me," he instructed, raising his own practice sword *en garde*.

Alaric did his best, parrying most of Sir Robert's offensives and nearly landing several attacks of his own. Robert seemed pleased with his skill, and signaled him to resume drill while he drew Llion aside to confer. Later that evening, over a simple supper, his father passed on compliments from both Robert and Llion, and expressed his paternal pride.

"He was very favorably impressed," Kenneth allowed. "And Llion, he was very complimentary about the instruction you've given. When we return to Rhemuth in a few weeks' time, son, you should have no difficulty joining Richard's lads."

In the days that followed, though he sometimes sat in on council meetings with his father, Alaric fell easily into the routine observed by the other pages, especially the tilting at multiple rings. Drawing a pony from the reserves at the stables, he worked with the animal for an hour in the ring, then returned to the tilting yard to ride against the other pages. And excelled.

After a week, under Llion's tutelage and still riding at the larger rings, he was taking at least two rings out of three. Occasionally, Llion would slip in a smaller ring with the others, and often as not, he would take it. The other pages acknowledged his abilities with good grace, and with growing respect for their future duke.

Through it all, his friendship with Jernian and Viliam continued to flourish. Both were older than he—Jernian was ten, and Viliam twelve—but the difference in age soon ceased to be a factor, for all three boys were precocious. Though Jernian continued to be hopeless at ring-tilting, and regularly took tumbles from his pony, his sunny disposition made it difficult to hold the failing against him, especially when balanced against his academic acumen—and it helped that he was a future earl. Viliam, by contrast, could expect to wear a baron's coronet in due course, was an excellent rider, nearly as good as Alaric, and excelled at the more usual pursuits expected of a future knight. But both of them had an astonishing grasp of tactics and strategy for their age, and repeatedly gave Alaric good trouncings at the cardounet board.

"That's partly because I can see the board properly," Jernian allowed, apparently conjuring an abbot out of nowhere to take one of Alaric's archers.

"So can I," Alaric replied, "but—where did *that* come from?"

"He's been sitting there for six moves," Viliam said good-naturedly.

Alaric sighed and tipped over his priest-king in defeat.

"I am beginning to think farther ahead," he said, indicating the board, "but obviously not far enough—or soon enough. How did you learn that? Was it your Torenthi tutor?"

"In part," Viliam admitted. "And I've read several of the classic works. Let me see what I can come up with, to give you an edge. Meanwhile, I do believe that young Jernian needs humbling. Are you up for a match, my friend?"

The younger boy was already rearranging the pieces to their starting positions, and grinned wickedly. "We'll see who needs humbling."

Indeed, the two were still playing when Alaric finally excused himself and headed up to bed.

The next time they were to play, two nights hence, Viliam handed Alaric a dog-eared sheaf of vellum pages stitched together along one long edge.

"That's Ulger de Brinsi's *Elements of Basic Strategy*," Viliam said, as Alaric riffled through the pages, peering more closely at the diagrams. "Apparently, his principles apply for armies as well as cardounet."

"Who was he?" Alaric asked.

"He was a Thurian master player," Viliam replied, "trained at the court of Prince Kirill Furstán, who became his patron. Anyway, Ulger wrote this treatise for Kirill's sons, who were mad keen on the game and later became master strategists for one of King Kiprian's generals in the Great War. Fortunately, they were both killed early on, or all of us might be speaking Torenthi."

"And I don't think Kiprian had read Ulger," Jernian chimed in.

Viliam chuckled at that, then resumed. "Anyway, it's a good place to start with formal strategy. If you could read Torenthi, I'd loan you Count Koltan's masterwork. He was amazing."

"You read Torenthi?" Alaric asked.

Viliam shrugged. "Enough to read Koltan. A lot of the terminology translates directly, once you master the alphabet."

"He reads Torenthi," Jernian muttered, "and Bremagni, and—"

"Just play," Viliam retorted, with a good-natured dunt to Jernian's arm. "You'll scare him away."

Alaric grinned, now thankful for the lessons in rudimentary Torenthi that his Aunt Delphine had given him. "It will take more than that," he said. He glanced again at the vellum manuscript. "Let's see how I do with Ulger. And thank you, Viliam."

"Always pleased to recruit another serious player," Viliam replied, "and you do show promise, Duke of Corwyn. Now, Jernian, make your first move."

Cardounet became their regular pastime after supper. Now and again, one or another of them would be assigned to table duty, delaying the start of play, but the work was not onerous, and none of them resented taking their fair turn. Alaric read and re-read the Ulger treatise, and his game slowly improved. So did his tilting at multiple rings, though he could not credit Ulger with that.

"You're developing a more discerning eye," Llion told him. "Excellent. I've noticed that the squires do it with a sword as well as a lance. I think we shall try that tomorrow."

WHILE Alaric continued his training, also sharpening his acumen at cardounet—and, thereby, his grasp of strategy—Kenneth was attending to the business of the duchy. Sometimes he rode the nearer boundaries of the duchy with a few of the regents, conducting regents' courts and assizes. On the first such foray north, Jovett rode with him, along with Phares Donovan and Jardine Howard, for all three men had spent several weeks acquainting themselves with the operations of the duchy, so that their practices back in Lendour would be in harmony.

More often than riding the boundaries, however, Kenneth sat on local courts and heard the domestic disputes of petitioners. In addition, he would receive periodic reports from his regents back in Lendour, and letters from Zoë. Correspondence came as well from Morganhall and Culdi, and also an occasional letter from the king.

He received one such letter midway through October, on a blustery afternoon made more pleasant by the pitcher of mulled wine he was sharing with several of his fellow regents in a sheltered corner of the courtyard adjoining the castle gardens. All of them looked up as Llion joined them brandishing a letter sealed with Haldane crimson. Alaric had gone riding on the beach with the other pages, in what promised to be one of the last such jaunts of the season, for the weather was starting to turn.

"When did this arrive?" Kenneth asked, as Llion handed over the letter and, at Kenneth's gesture of invitation, sat between Crescence de

Naverie and Airlie Kushannan. Both Udauts were also present, father and son, and the elder Udaut poured a cup of wine for Llion as Kenneth cracked the seal on the letter.

"Within the hour, my lord," Llion said. "It came by ship—which probably docked earlier this morning, but someone at the harbor only just got around to sending it up."

"We'll hope that it isn't urgent, then," Kenneth said, skimming over the usual salutations.

I am advised that no immediate escalation of hostilities is likely in Meara, Brion had written—or, a clark had taken his dictation, for the missive was not in Brion's hand—*but we continue to monitor the health of the Lady Aude. For when she dies, it is likely that Caitrin will marry, and perhaps produce another Mearan pretender.*

At this point, the hand changed, and also the tone.

On another matter, I trust you will have heard by now of the death of Prince Hogan's wife, and the loss of the prince she was carrying. We now hear that Hogan has remarried the woman he had taken to wife in his youth: the Lady Kethevan von Soslán. His wedding gift to his new bride was to create her Countess of Soslán and to legitimate their children, though Festillic house law will not allow them to succeed to his titles and pretensions. Perhaps you might make discreet inquiries into Torenth, for it would be useful to learn how the Torenthis regard this news.

In the margin, Brion had written, in his own hand: *Duke Ewan wrote that part, as he is far more astute in such matters than I am.*

Kenneth smiled as he skimmed over the rest of the letter, which inquired regarding the health of Kenneth and his son, then ended by reiterating the request that Kenneth should see what more he could find out about the Festillic pretender's domestic arrangements.

"It appears that we need to make some discreet inquiries into Torenth," he said, as he passed the letter to Crescence. "Apparently Hogan Gwernach has remarried his first wife and legitimated her children by him. Had you heard anything about that, Laurenz?"

The elder Udaut shook his head. "No, but that does not mean that it is not true. I can certainly put out some feelers. There may be some gossip down by the harbor. And I can send some men across the border to see what they might turn up. Have we any idea when or where this might have taken place?"

"Nothing was mentioned," Kenneth replied, "but my guess would be late summer, and probably somewhere up in the north of Torenth, since his superior title is Duke of Truvorsk."

"And Pretender of Gwynedd," said Airlie Kushannan, with a wry lift of one tawny eyebrow.

"Aye, that, too," Kenneth conceded.

"I'll see about it," Laurenz said, rising. "These things take time, but juicy gossip like an irregular royal marriage will tend to travel fast."

h ARDLY a week later, one of the men sent out to investigate the rumors returned with news both surprising and shocking.

"This was unusual enough that it was making the rounds all along the waterfront across at Furstánan," said Sir Seamus O'Flynn, dropping his saddlebags beside the table as he pulled up a stool across from Kenneth and Laurenz, who was his brother-in-law. "Hogan Gwernach has, indeed, married the Lady Kethevan and legitimated their surviving children. In addition, he gave titles to the two sons. The eldest, Zimarek, became Count of Tarkhan. The other son, Mikhael, is now Count of Sankt-Irakli."

Laurenz cocked his head at the newcomer as Airlie Kushannan and Crescence de Naverie joined them. "This is hardly unusual, under the circumstances. You have more?"

"Oh, aye. Much more." Seamus, who was heir to the Earl of Derry, poured himself a cup of ale and tossed it back before continuing. "To further celebrate the nuptials, which lasted a week, Hogan staged a grand tournament in which both his sons competed. For the younger, Mikhael, it was mostly for show. He is but seventeen, and only received the accolade a few months before the wedding. He prefers books to the sword, and only rode a pageant course or two before retiring from the field, content to watch from the stands with his parents.

"For Zimarek, it is a somewhat different story," Seamus went on, allowing Kenneth to refill his cup. "Zimarek fancied himself quite the warrior. At two-and-twenty, he had half a dozen very successful tourney seasons under his belt. He rode well against all challengers—until a black knight rode onto the field."

"Seamus, you are enjoying this far too much," Crescence said sourly. "Who was this black knight?"

"That's the odd thing. No one seems to know. But he was able to put the point of his lance right through the visor of Zimarek's tourney helm."

The statement left all his listeners momentarily speechless, including Kenneth.

Then: "A black knight killed Prince Hogan's son?" Airlie Kushannan breathed, then added, "I assume he *was* killed."

Seamus gave a curt nod and drained off half his ale.

"And they don't know who he was?" Laurenz asked.

"Witnesses said it's very likely he was Deryni," Seamus said. "Apparently he melted into the crowd before anyone could apprehend him. But whoever he was, he did Brion of Gwynedd a favor. That's one less Festillic pretender to deal with."

"Hardly a serious threat," Crescence said. "Zimarek couldn't inherit his father's pretensions."

"Stranger things have happened," Laurenz replied. "In any case, the point is moot. The man is dead."

"And they have no idea who the black knight was," Kenneth said thoughtfully, wondering, though he did not voice it, whether it possibly could have been the same black knight who had challenged Brion in June. Fortunately, none of those present had witnessed the bout; but Llion had, and Xander and Trevor. Llion would not and could not mention it, but Xander might, or Trevor. But only Llion and possibly Alaric knew the identity of the king's black knight.

Seamus took another deep draught and shook his head. "If anyone knows, that information has not reached the portside taverns. Hogan is still well regarded in Torenth, even if few believe he can actually regain the Crown of Gwynedd." He shrugged. "Of course, it's unlikely that Zimarek actually could have been accepted as Hogan's heir. But now, we shall never know."

"There *is* still that other son," Airlie Kushannan reminded them.

"Aye, but he hasn't the fire in his belly to take the Crown, even if the legal obstacles could be overcome," Crescence said. "No, if Hogan is to make a try at winning back the Crown, it will have to be with his daughter at his side. And that should be a while, because she is only five."

"That's one blessing, then." Kenneth breathed out in a long sigh. "Very well. I doubt this changes anything in the short term, but the king should know what we've found out. And let's keep our scouts out awhile longer. Any additional information could be useful."

"That can be done," Airlie agreed.

"Meanwhile, I probably should think seriously about heading back to Rhemuth," Kenneth continued. "I had never planned to be away this long."

Laurenz Udaut inclined his head. "You will be missed, my lord, but we do understand. Had it occurred to you that you might return by sea? It's getting late in the season, but you could skirt the coast and then sail north to Desse."

"That's true," Kenneth replied. "It would save horses—and our backsides. We've already done a good deal of riding this season."

"I'll see about a ship," Airlie said. "I believe we have a smaller one due within the week, bringing over wine from Fianna. The cargo was intended for the market in Corwyn, but it could be profitably diverted to Desse."

"That would be ideal," Kenneth replied. "Thank you."

He shared the news with Llion shortly after the meeting broke up, sharing nothing of his speculation regarding the black knight, and the young knight offered no speculation of his own. By suppertime, Xander and Trevor had also heard the news, with Xander remarking on the coincidence of Brion's challenge by a black knight, but neither offered any theory of who either man might have been.

"Good riddance, I'd say," Trevor muttered darkly, echoing Seamus's remarks. "That's one less Festillic pretender."

Thereafter, conversation turned to the preparations that must be made for their return to Rhemuth by ship.

Chapter 13

"He that saith he is in the light, and hateth his brother,
is in darkness even until now."
—I JOHN 2:9

THE expected ship made port two days later, and its crew began making immediate arrangements to divert to Desse, offloading some of its cargo and taking on new consignments to accommodate the changed schedule. Some of the crew aboard the ship had heard about the death of Prince Hogan's son, but no one had any information that Kenneth and his council did not already know.

Meanwhile, in preparation for his imminent departure, Kenneth held several final courts and, on their last night in Coroth, promoted several pages to squire. After supper that evening, while Kenneth and Llion drank with the men who would resume running the duchy, Alaric watched moodily as Jernian and Viliam set up the cardounet board for a final set of matches. He would miss their camaraderie. He had few friends near his own age besides Duncan and Kevin, and they were cousins, so it hardly counted. Back at Rhemuth, he had none, really—and more than one who hated him.

"Alaric, you look like your best friend just died," Jernian observed.

Forcing a wan smile, Alaric propped his head against one hand and sighed. "It's almost that bad," he replied. "I shall miss the two of you."

"Well, then," Viliam said. "We aren't dead *yet*. But we shall miss you, too. We haven't been able to find *anyone* else to play as passionately as you do."

"I'm no match for either of you," Alaric said, straightening one of the archers on the board. "I can't be much challenge."

"On the contrary," Jernian said. "You're getting quite good—at least compared to most players."

"They must not be very good."

"No, they aren't," Viliam said flatly. "We live in eternal hope, but you . . ." He glanced at Jernian. "Shall we give it to him now?"

"I think so. Otherwise, he's apt to get all mawkish on us."

Alaric glanced between the two of them in question. "What *are* you talking about?"

"We have a parting gift for you." Viliam reached into the front of his tunic to produce a much-folded sheet of parchment. "Jernian copied out most of it, and I did most of the translation. But neither of us knew some of the Torenthi words, so you're on your own for that." He handed the parchment to Alaric.

"I did include some diagrams," he went on. "Those should help. It's the opening section of Count Koltan's *Elements of Strategy*—or as much as would fit on that piece of parchment. He had to write really, really tiny, so it's going to be tedious to read. As if Koltan isn't already tedious."

A pleased grin slowly spread across Alaric's face as he realized what a very special gift the two had prepared for him: a gift nearly as precious as the friendship the three of them had shared in the previous weeks.

"You copied out part of Koltan for me?" he said, unfolding the packet.

"You'll have to start learning Torenthi," Jernian warned. "It won't be easy."

"The best things are rarely easy," Alaric replied, casting an eye over the tight-crabbed script and then peering more closely. "I do know the Torenthi alphabet, though, and a few simple words. My Aunt Delphine taught me."

Viliam sat forward eagerly. "Does she play cardounet?"

Still grinning as he shook his head, Alaric refolded the parchment and slipped it into the front of his tunic. "I shall ask her, the next time I see her. She's very clever. But this is a wonderful gift, Viliam. Thank you, both of you. I shall study it on the voyage to Rhemuth, and I shall think of the two of you. We sail in the morning, you know."

The faces of both older boys fell. "We know," Jernian said.

"And that's why we must play tonight," Viliam said, pushing the board slightly closer, to invite Alaric to play the whites. "Your move, Duke of Corwyn!"

In the game that followed, Alaric came very close to beating Viliam, and was almost certain that the older boy had not held back to give him a better chance.

Viliam and Jernian then played a fast, brilliant match at which Alaric could only shake his head in wonder. And when Alaric did finally play Jernian, he actually won.

"Viliam, did you see that coming?" Jernian demanded, as Alaric sat back to savor his victory.

The older boy only shook his head and gave a tiny smile. "Only toward the end, my friend. But it wasn't *my* place to tell you. Nicely done," he said to Alaric, extending his hand for a congratulatory handshake. "You're actually a very quick student. I shall look forward to our next game."

On that happy note, Alaric retired for his last night at Castle Coroth, dreaming of strategies when he finally fell asleep.

NEXT morning they rode down to the docks several hours before the tide was to turn, accompanied by most of the regents. Alaric rode ahead of the adults with Jernian and Viliam, who had been given special permission to come along, ostensibly to attend Jernian's father.

The ship waiting at the quay was a sleek cargo cog called the *Gryphon*, middling in size, with faded green sail furled along her wide yardarm and Corwyn's long sea pennant of green-black-green floating lazily from the top of the mast. Aboard the ship, members of the crew clearly were stowing equipment and cargo and readying for departure, but a considerable commotion was brewing quayside, where several men in green knitted caps apparently were trying to load a horse that, quite clearly, did not want to be loaded. They could hear its squeals and the frenetic clatter of hooves on stone well before they got close enough to see the cause.

"Whatever are they doing to that horse?" Viliam said, trying to stand in his stirrups for a better view.

"Frightening it half to death, it would appear," Alaric retorted, then gigged his pony as close as he could get without trampling bystanders.

"You there, stop that!" he shouted, as he threw himself from the saddle and began pushing his way between the nearest of the sailors. "Can't you see she's afraid?"

Struggling his way closer, he could see that the distressed animal was a magnificent grey mare of obvious R'Kassan breeding, apparently disinclined to put even one dainty hoof on the boarding ramp leading into the dark hole of the hold. Two men on the ramp had a long rope looped around the mare's hindquarters, trying to make her move forward, and another was tugging at a rope attached to the mare's headstall, but a new explosion of frenzied resistance sent one of the men into the water with a dull splash.

"Easy, lad!" another man cried, putting out an arm to block his way. "D'ye want to get killed? She's a demon, she is!"

"She isn't a demon, she's just frightened," Alaric replied, focusing on reaching out to the mare with his mind as well as his hand. "Papa, I can gentle her. I know I can."

"Yes, I believe you can," said Kenneth, who had worked his way closer to the drama at quayside, with Llion and Lord Hamilton close behind. "Gentlemen, why don't you back off and let my son give it a try? He really is very good with horses. What have you to lose?"

The men looked dubious, but they backed off dutifully at a nod from Lord Hamilton, one of them tossing an end of the come-along rope to his mate in the water and another edging his way around the mare to hand Alaric the end of the lead. A second lead trailed from the headstall and was tangled under the mare's feet, but she had ceased her plunging as the men backed off, and now was merely snorting and blowing, rolling the whites of her eyes as she turned her attention to this new threat in the shape of a boy, gathering up the slack of the lead rope in his hands.

"So, what's this all about?" he crooned. "No one is going to hurt you. There's a good girl. Aren't you the fine, fierce battle steed? I'm sorry if you were frightened, but you needn't be worried. I know, it's a big, dark, scary hole, but I promise that there's nothing aboard the ship that wants to eat horses. You're very, very beautiful, and I'm sure you're very, very fast. . . ."

As he talked to her, mostly nonsense just to catch and hold her attention, he gradually eased closer. She whuffed a few times, and whuffed again to get the scent of him as he held out his hand to her velvety nose. But when he had stroked her neck a few times, at the same time gathering up the rope tangled under her feet, she seemed to sigh and lean into his caress, even half closing her eyes.

"That's better," he murmured. "Now let's go inside. It's just a big barn, really, and they've got lots of oats and hay for you." He took a few steps toward the loading ramp, and she followed obediently, before he could even tug on the lead. "Good girl! Just keep walking. And once we've got you bedded down, they'll give you a nice rubdown and a good feed."

With that coercion, the mare walked calmly into the hold of the ship and let herself be tethered in a waiting stall next to a dun gelding, who whickered greeting across the divider. A stableman immediately brought her a wooden pan of oats, stroking the mare's neck as she tucked into it. He then showed Alaric how to pass the canvas support sling under the mare's belly and secure it.

"How far is she going?" Alaric asked, as they fastened the last buckle.

"Nyford, I think," the man replied, then added, "You do have a way with horses, lad. I heard her carrying on outside."

"She was just frightened," Alaric replied, smiling as he gave the mare a final pat. "She should be fine now, especially with another horse for company. But I'll be aboard until Desse, so call me if there's any problem whatsoever."

The man nodded. "I will, young sir. And who should I ask for?"

"Just ask for Alaric Morgan," the boy replied, with a cheery smile as he turned on his heel and went back out the loading ramp to the quay.

His father and the regents were waiting as he emerged into the sunlight, and several gave him pleased huzzahs. The crew had mostly returned to the rest of their duties, but the man he had spoken to out on the quay touched two fingers to the edge of his cap and nodded in approval. Kenneth and most of the rest of their party had dismounted—only Llion and Xander would be accompanying them, along with four men-at-arms—and the regents were in the process of taking their leave.

Some of the partings were poignant. Trevor Udaut had served Kenneth since his knighting, some four years before, and had spent much of his time going back and forth between Rhemuth and Coroth as Kenneth's liaison with the regents, for his father, Lord Laurenz, was part of the council. Now Trevor was leaving Kenneth's service to remain in Coroth, for he had married the year before and now had a wife and twin daughters. In due time, he would succeed his father as Baron Varagh, but more immediately, he was to become the council's most junior member.

"You will be missed in Rhemuth," Kenneth told him, as Trevor clasped hands with him at the gangplank with his young wife and his parents. "But you have family responsibilities of your own now. You don't need to be traipsing all over the kingdom with me."

"Xander is still a bachelor, my lord," Trevor replied, with a smile and a nod at Xander. "He'll take good care of you. And Alaric will need Llion less and less, as he shifts into official training as a page."

"That is very true," Kenneth agreed. "And meanwhile, I shall rely on you as another pair of safe hands here in Coroth, to keep my son's duchy safe."

"You have my word on it, my lord," Trevor said with a smile. "Godspeed."

"And keep you safe as well," Kenneth replied, turning to another of the regents.

A further farewell was of particular poignancy for Alaric, for he must say good-bye to Jernian and Viliam, who stood now near Jernian's father as Alaric prepared to board.

"You must write if you find someone to play cardounet with you," Jernian said.

"Of course I will," Alaric replied. "And when I come back next summer, I intend to trounce both of you!"

"Oh, yes?" Viliam retorted.

"Oh, yes!" Alaric answered, tapping the breast of his tunic, over the bulge of the Koltan transcript. "I have the magic formula, and I intend to master it!"

"I hope you do," Viliam said honestly. "Godspeed, Duke of Corwyn."

"And God bless both of you," Alaric replied, just before Llion hustled him aboard. Kenneth had already gone up to the afterdeck with Xander, and seemed to be deep in conversation with several of the crew.

Llion stayed with Alaric at the ship's rail as the crew began to cast off the mooring lines, first the bow and then the stern, the pair of them watching as the tide caught the bow and slowly began swinging the ship out from the quay. Once they were clear, men belowdecks ran out the oars to row a few dozen strokes that moved the ship into a patch of wind as sailors aloft began to unfurl the great, green sail.

High atop the mast, the narrow green-black-green pennon of Corwyn's maritime service lifted and writhed on the growing breeze, and the heavy canvas of the sail bellied and snapped until the crew could secure the sheets. But once they trimmed the sail and ran the oars back in, the ship's speed increased and they began moving briskly on into the harbor, headed out between the great sea jetties of tumbled granite.

"Listen, and you can hear the bells on the sea buoys that mark the harbor entrance," Llion said, gazing toward the end of the nearer jetty. "The one on this side has a deeper voice than the other, so you can tell them apart in the dark or in rough seas. Do you hear it?" At Alaric's rapt nod, Llion swept a hand toward the lighthouse towers bracketing the harbor mouth, horizontally striped green and white.

"And those towers have fire platforms at the top, where beacons can be lit at night to mark the harbor mouth and warn ships off the rocks. The harbor at the Isle d'Orsal has similar ones."

Something suddenly shuddered underneath the bow, scraping along the keel toward them, and Alaric leaned out in some alarm to look down.

"That's only the harbor chain," Llion told him, pointing as they passed over the submerged shadow-line of massive chain—"There!"— and watched it recede into the gloom behind them. "When it's raised, big ships can't pass. It's part of Coroth's sea defenses."

Alaric's delighted grin said far more than words as the two of them watched the lighthouse and jetty recede and they passed into open water, now skirting westward along the rolling pasturelands of Tendal. After a while, with admonitions to keep a good grip until Alaric was sure he had his sea legs, Llion abandoned him and went up on the afterdeck where Kenneth and Xander stood chatting with several of the crew. Their four men-at-arms were gathered nearer the bow, one of them already looking a trifle queasy as the light chop of the enclosed harbor gave way to more rolling swells.

But Alaric found the experience exhilarating. The wind was fresh, the sun pleasant, and a decided nip of autumn was in the air. He had been aboard ships before, tied up in the harbor at Coroth, but he had never been at sea, and he squinted happily against the wind and the sea spray, glad of the wool cloak and cap Llion had insisted he wear.

After a while, when he was beginning to tire of watching the slow crawl of the distant shore, Llion came back down to fetch him onto the afterdeck. There he found his father and Xander talking with a man Alaric could only assume must be the ship's master: a wind-burnt, bandy-legged individual with a thatch of wiry grey hair escaping from underneath his salt-stained leather cap. The battered cockade affixed to the brim might once have been the green of Corwyn's sea service. The worn leather jerkin and breeches under the man's cloak of faded black obviously had weathered many a storm.

"Alaric, meet Rafe Winslow, master of the *Gryphon*," Kenneth said, indicating the captain.

"Honored, milord," the captain replied, touching two fingers to his cap. "And that shaggy fellow at the helm is Henry Kirby, my first mate," he added, jutting his chin at the tall, lanky man steering the ship. As Kirby also gave Alaric a nod, white teeth flashed in his full beard and mustache, which were bleached rusty-brown by the sun and rain.

"Welcome aboard, my lord," the man said. "Would you like to take a turn at the tiller?"

Alaric's eyes got round, but he came immediately to place both hands on the weathered oak, moving at Kirby's direction to stand between the man's two burly arms.

"Can you feel the pressure of the current?" Kirby asked. "She's got a heavy touch in this weather, but she's a good ship, very responsive."

Alaric concentrated, letting his hands move with Kirby's in fine response to the waves, and thought he felt what the helmsman was talking about. He grinned as he glanced up at the man, then murmured his thanks and ducked out to let Kirby resume full control.

"Thank you, Master Kirby, but it might be best if you did the steering."

The adults chuckled at that, the captain clapping him on the shoulder in good-natured approval. Soon a cabin boy began bringing out cups and a jug of ale, and then folding canvas stools, so the men could take their leisure, but Alaric politely declined their invitation to join them, excusing himself to explore the ship instead. The crew were mostly friendly, some of them aware of what he had done to assist with loading the grey mare below. He headed down to see her, spending a few minutes stroking both horses, but it was stuffy belowdecks, so he soon went back topside to scan the distant shoreline once more.

He soon learned that, once the cargo was safely stowed and the sail was set, there was very little for the crew to do when they were not on duty, so many of them were relaxing on deck, a few fishing off the sides. He could see a lookout up in a little cage atop the mast, and two more at the bow, but the frantic activity attendant on getting the ship under way had ceased. The men-at-arms had settled to sit with backs against the forward deck platform, except for one who was retching over the side.

"Some men just don't take to the sea," one of the sailors told him. "It isn't their fault. He'll feel better, once we anchor for the night. Lucky for him, this is a calm sea today."

Alaric found himself wondering what it would be like if it were *not* a calm sea, but he decided to say nothing, lest he damage his credibility as a sailor. After a while, he found an out-of-the-way spot to sit at the base of the afterdeck platform, with a view of the shoreline crawling by. There he settled down and pulled out the Koltan extract that Viliam and Jernian had given him, and spent the rest of the afternoon puzzling out the first few lines. They dropped anchor that night in a tiny bay tucked into the coastline at Trevas, dined on a hearty fish stew and crusty bread washed down with ale, and sailed again shortly after dawn.

This became part of his routine for the next few days: morning sword drill on the main deck with Llion and Xander and the men-at-arms, and sometimes his father, then several hours immersing himself in Koltan. Occasionally, one of the sailors would give him a fishing line to hold, but he never caught anything, and concluded that fishing actually was rather boring. One afternoon he spent several hours with one of the sailors learning about simple splices and knots.

He also visited the cargo hold at least once each day to check on the grey mare, usually wheedling an apple from the ship's cook to split between the mare and the dun gelding. On the third day out, after a stop at the Carthmoori port of Kilchon, he looked up from his reading to see Henry Kirby, the steersman, towering above him.

"Do you read for pleasure, young sir, or has your knight set lessons for you?" Kirby asked casually.

Alaric gave the man a wry smile. "For pleasure, though some of this is hardly pleasant. I don't suppose you read Torenthi."

"As a matter of fact, I do." Crouching down, Kirby reached across to angle the manuscript toward him. "We trade with Torenth, so I had to learn the lingo. And if you want to be a master one day, and captain your own ship, you learn to read it as well as speak it. Is this Koltan you're reading? Don't tell me you play cardounet?"

"Yes, and yes," Alaric said in surprise. "Friends in Coroth copied out part of the beginning of his *Basic Strategies*—and tried to translate it for me. But I don't think their Torenthi is as good as they'd like it to be. We played a lot, though, while I was there. And I'm much better now than I used to be."

"May I see that?" Kirby asked. "Do you mind if I sit?"

Shaking his head, Alaric handed over the piece of vellum, which Kirby studied for several minutes. Then:

"This is useful, as far as it goes. A pity they didn't have room to copy more for you." Kirby looked up. "Would you like a match? I have a board and pieces in my cabin. It's a game that seafarers play a lot."

"Thank you, but I doubt I'd be much challenge for you," Alaric said, though he was pleased to be asked.

"Nonsense. If you don't play, you can't learn. Let me get my board. We've time for a match before I must go back on watch."

Without waiting for an answer, Kirby unfolded himself and went below. Across the deck, Llion had been watching, and smiled and nodded as he caught Alaric's eye. But the boy was given no opportunity to contemplate that for very long, because Kirby emerged very quickly with a small cardounet board under one arm and a leather pouch in that hand.

"Here we go," he said, folding back to a cross-legged seat beside Alaric and plopping the board between them. "You probably aren't used to pieces like mine, but you can help me sort them and set up."

He pulled apart the drawstrings and upended the bag over the board, spilling out an assortment of black, white, and brown tiles, which he quickly began sorting. As he did so, Alaric soon saw that the brown tiles were actually suede leather backings for black or white tiles, which all had symbols painted on them to represent the traditional pieces.

"I suppose you're used to fancy game pieces carved like the figures they represent," Kirby said, as he began sliding the white tiles into position on his side of the board. "These are easier to play with at sea; they don't slide off the board as easily in weather. And frankly, it keeps your concentration sharper, because you must pay more attention to the pieces."

The explanation made sense, and Alaric immediately pitched in to help, first turning all the rest of the brown tiles, then sliding the black ones onto his side of the board, for Kirby clearly had already chosen the white side.

"I've taken the white, so that you don't have to waste time deciding what first move *you* would make," the helmsman said, looking up at him when the board was set. "And no reading my mind," he added casually. "Fair is fair."

With that comment, he sent his war-duke over the front of the white line to challenge Alaric's archers.

This opening move, plus the allusion to his Deryni powers, put Alaric on the defensive at once, though there had been no hostility in Kirby's statement; only an acknowledgment of fact, that seemed not to bother the helmsman in the least. It did, indeed, take more concentration to keep the pieces straight without the shapes to remind him which was which—and Kirby did not coddle him or give him extra advantages. As he had said, fair was fair.

Kirby trounced him handily in their first match, and in the second, and the third. But each time, Alaric learned something new. Sometimes he was able to answer one of Kirby's moves with a move of his own that came straight from Koltan, which always brought a smile to Kirby's lips and a nod of approval. The helmsman was a good player and a good teacher, and pointed out the boy's mistakes in constructive and sometimes even humorous ways.

"Now, *that* was fairly pathetic," Kirby said sympathetically, taking Alaric's war-duke after Alaric had moved the piece directly into the potential path of one of Kirby's knights and then not covered it in his next move. "When you're a real duke, you'll need to look ahead better than that."

"What?" Alaric yelped. Then: "Oh," he said, breathing out with an exasperated sigh.

"But you won't forget *that* again, will you?" Kirby said.

They played again the next day, and the next, sometimes on deck and sometimes down in the cabin, by lamplight. The pair became a regular sight on deck, when Kirby was not on duty: the shaggy-haired helmsman and the towheaded lad young enough to be his son, with heads bent over the cardounet board.

Kenneth was glad to see him so occupied, and he and Llion would watch the pair for hours from up on the afterdeck, as the ship continued westward along the rocky coast, calling at the ports of Kentar and Dunluce and finally rounding the Point of Kentar to enter the Eirian Estuary. High above, on the point, the Abbey of St. Ultan's looked down on the sea, and they put in briefly at the abbey's tiny harbor to take aboard two monks of the *Ordo Verbi Dei*, bound for Nyford.

And to Nyford they came, at midday the next day, tying up at the quay along the northern bank of the Lendour River where it met the Eirian. The groom in charge of looking after the horses aboard had asked Alaric to stand by when they offloaded the grey mare, for it was uncertain how she would react after nearly a week at sea.

It was well that they had taken the precaution, because the mare all but exploded as the groom tried to lead her from the hold, nearly going over backward and into the water as her hooves hit the ramp and she skidded, screaming.

Fortunately, Alaric was waiting nearby, and immediately slipped in beside her to grab the headstall and haul her down, crooning endearments all the while. He became airborne a few times, but he hung on doggedly as she gradually danced to the end of the ramp and onto the stone paving of the quay. At the same time, Kenneth and Llion came down the passenger gangplank and rushed to assist him, Xander right at their heels. No one noticed, until the mare had stopped dancing, that a party of mounted men had ridden up quayside, their leader robed in episcopal purple and wearing the flat, broad-brimmed hat of a bishop.

"You there! Back off, all of you! Take your hands off my horse!" the bishop cried, his voice rising on an angry note as he gestured for two of his men to take charge of the animal. "Why, don't tell me it's the Earl of Lendour? What an unpleasant surprise."

Kenneth whirled to confront the speaker, his heart sinking as he recognized Oliver de Nore, the Bishop of Nyford, who of all the men in the world probably hated Kenneth Morgan and his son more than any other.

"Yes, I'm Lendour," Kenneth said defiantly. "And you probably have my son to thank for the fact that your horse is not now in the bay, or hobbling on a broken leg."

Startled, de Nore turned his attention to Alaric, who was doing his best to become invisible while being separated from the mare, who still was rolling her eyes and dancing on the slick cobbles.

"So," de Nore breathed, furious, "the Deryni spawn of the Deryni witch. Did you lay hands on my horse, *boy*?"

"She was frightened. She might have hurt herself. I only meant to help," Alaric replied, taken aback, though he kept his head high.

"Help?" de Nore repeated. *"Help?"* He paused to draw a deep breath, then: "You have ruined her," he said in a low, dangerous voice. "She is contaminated by the mere contact with your Deryni cursedness!"

"Then, I'll take her off your hands!" Kenneth snapped, as Llion reached Alaric and seized him by the upper arms, pulling him back from the growing altercation. "I'll buy her. I'll give you twice what you paid for her, whatever that might be!"

De Nore's eyes narrowed as he glared back at Kenneth, and his men stirred uneasily all around him.

"You'd like that, wouldn't you?" he muttered, low and dangerous. "But, no. There's a better use for a horse ruined by the likes of your devil-spawn son. I shall give her to feed the poor." Alaric gasped. "There are plenty of worthy poor in Nyford. Gareth, fetch me a compliant butcher from the town market!"

"No!" Alaric shouted, squirming unsuccessfully to escape from Llion as one of the mounted men immediately wheeled to trot off in the direction of the town. "No! You can't! Papa, stop him! He *can't*!"

"Can I not?" De Nore backed his horse a few steps as his men interposed themselves between him and the boy—and the boy's father, who had gone white. "The horse is my property, Kenneth Morgan Earl of Lendour!" he said coldly. "You are an officer of the king's law, and the law says that I can do whatever I please with my property—and today it is my pleasure to provide some free meat for the poor of this town."

"My lord, be reasonable," Kenneth said desperately. "Choose another horse. There's another in the hold. Take that one, and give me the mare."

De Nore had begun to laugh now, obviously enjoying the moment. "But this isn't about just *any* horse, dear Morgan," he said. "It's about *this* horse, which your son cares about, and which has been sullied by his filthy Deryni powers. I can't touch *him*, but I can do whatever I please with my own property.

"So it pleases me to watch him suffer, the way his mother made my brother suffer—or at least a little of the way my brother suffered. Can you even imagine what that must have been like for him, trussed up naked like an animal and thrown headfirst into that well to drown?"

"It was the king's judgment, Bishop!" Kenneth retorted. "Not my son's, and not even my wife's."

"But it was your wife's filthy Deryni testimony that condemned him!"

"No, it was the *law* that condemned him. It was his *guilt* that condemned him," Kenneth snapped.

"He is no less dead," de Nore said, with a dismissive shake of his head. "My brother cannot have been guilty of the crimes with which he was charged. Ah, here's my man with that butcher. Come here, Butcher, I have work for you."

The soldier sent to fetch the man had carried him on the crupper behind him, and let him down onto the ground before de Nore. The man looked around curiously before turning his attention to the bishop, then pulled off his cap to bow over it.

"My lord?"

"Yes, Butcher, I wish to make a gift of meat to the poor of Nyford," de Nore said, pointing at the grey mare, which now was standing quietly with two of de Nore's men at her head. "Put that horse down, here and now, and then you can take away the meat."

The butcher glanced at the mare, then did a double-take. "I don't understand, Excellency. Is the horse injured, or unsound? She looks a fine specimen to me."

"I wish to have it butchered. Just do it."

"But, my lord—"

"Just do it!" de Nore snapped. "Or do you wish to forfeit your right to ply your trade here in Nyford?"

The butcher sighed and shook his head. "As you say, my lord." Then he began walking toward the mare, drawing his butcher's blade from a heavy leather scabbard at his waist, but holding it close against his leg.

Alaric tried not to look, still struggling in Llion's arms and now held by several more of his father's men, but Llion leaned down to whisper in his ear.

"You cannot stop this, my lord, and neither can your father," he said. "But do *not* let de Nore see you cry. Don't *ever* let him see you cry! Can you do that?"

His words were like a jolt of icy water, instantly sobering the boy. Red-faced and breathing hard, he quit struggling and straightened, his eyes narrowing in sheer hatred for the man who was ordering this thing. If he had had the killing use of his powers, de Nore would have toppled from his horse at once, blasted by the very magic he so feared.

But Alaric had no such use of his powers yet. He was Deryni, heir to incredible magic, but he was still only a boy, barely eight years old.

Mercifully, the butcher knew his business, and his knife was sharp. The mare only tossed her head once as the blade slit her throat, more startled than frightened—and then confused, as blood spurted from the silky grey neck, gushing onto the cobbles and spreading beneath the mare's dainty hooves until she slowly sank to her knees, to her side, and then was still. So quickly was it over.

The momentary silence was almost palpable as, for a long moment, Alaric returned his gaze to the bishop, willing him nothing but ill. Then he shrugged off Llion's restraints and turned on his heel to go back aboard the ship, Llion following close behind him. Kenneth, also glaring at the bishop, walked slowly across the several yards that separated them and stopped a few paces away. Xander accompanied him, a hand on the hilt of his sword.

"Be assured," Kenneth said to de Nore, "that the king will hear of this."

"My dear Earl of Lendour, I have done nothing wrong," de Nore replied, leaning casually against the high pommel of his saddle and smiling faintly as he gazed down at the other man.

"And on this day, you have done nothing *right*," Kenneth retorted. "That was pure spite, against a child who was not even born when your brother met his fate. And it was senseless cruelty against one of God's innocent creatures."

"The boy is Deryni," de Nore said coldly. "His very touch is corruption. And he laid his hands on my property, polluting it beyond redemption." He glanced at the crumpled grey mass nearer the water, sprawled in a pool of congealing blood. "At least it will feed the poor."

"You sanctimonious bastard!" Kenneth's voice was low, dangerous. "You had best have a long talk with your confessor, because you will surely answer for today's work when you stand before the Judgment Seat!"

De Nore sat upright in his saddle, a look of cold disdain contorting his features. "How dare you?"

"Ask *yourself* that question," Kenneth retorted. "And do not expect God's mercy, when you had none for that poor, dumb beast!"

"How *dare* you?!" de Nore repeated, as Kenneth turned on his heel and stalked back toward the ship, Xander at his heels. *"How dare you?!"*

Kenneth was shaking with fury as he and Xander went back aboard. They found Alaric with Llion in their cabin, with the boy weeping in the young knight's arms.

"How could he *do* that, Papa?" the boy sobbed. "He just—*murdered* her, for no reason!"

"Unfortunately, he had a reason," Kenneth murmured, sitting down beside the pair and pulling his son into his embrace. "He did it to hurt you, for being what you are. And he did it because of what your mother did, to bring his brother to justice. I know, it makes no sense to you and me," he added, as Alaric looked up indignantly. "But I told you before that Bishop Oliver de Nore is an enemy. I just didn't think we'd confront him here."

"There's no way that any of us could have known that the horse was de Nore's, my lord," Llion said quietly.

Alaric snuffled and wiped at his eyes with his sleeve. "That shouldn't have made any difference," he said. "All I did was ease her fear, keep her from injuring herself. And what he did was *wrong*! The *horse* didn't have anything to do with his stupid brother."

"Nor did you, and it *was* wrong," Kenneth agreed. "Unfortunately, it was not illegal. The horse was his, to do with as he pleased."

"Not to just butcher it," the boy muttered.

Kenneth sighed, for morally, he could not disagree with his son. But like it or not, de Nore had been within the letter of the law.

"It was wanton destruction of one of God's beautiful creatures," Kenneth agreed, "and be assured that I shall tell the king about this, when we reach Rhemuth. But don't expect that he can do anything about it, either. I wish it were otherwise, but . . ."

Shaking his head, he gave the boy a final hug and gave him back into Llion's embrace, then turned and went out of the cabin with Xander, back up to the deck, where the *Gryphon*'s crew were preparing to depart. A few minutes later, as the men cast off their lines and rowed out to catch the wind, Alaric and Llion also came back up on deck, and the boy watched silently from the rail as the port of Nyford receded, along with the sight of the butcher and his men cutting up the bloody grey carcass on the quay.

Alaric did not play cardounet that night. He took to his berth early, though he slept only fitfully. Next morning, he was at his sword drills with Llion, but his practice had a new intensity. Even Xander remarked on it, as he and Kenneth watched from the afterdeck.

"He's still angry, my lord."

"Aye, he's feeling guilt from yesterday, which he shouldn't," Kenneth said quietly. "But perhaps it has underlined for him the constant danger that will surround him increasingly, especially now, when he's too young to use his powers to protect himself."

"It's a delicate balancing act, isn't it, my lord?" Xander murmured. "But I know he'll be equal to the challenge."

"I hope so, Xander. I do hope so," Kenneth replied.

Chapter 14

"Obey them that have the rule over you, and submit yourselves:
for they watch for your souls . . ."
—HEBREWS 13:17

THE waters of the Eirian grew calmer, once they passed its confluence with the River Lendour, but the prevailing wind sweeping down the estuary meant that they often were obliged to augment sail with oars as they skirted the western coast of Carthane. Accordingly, the crew were more often engaged, swapping off on rowing duties, and the steersman Henry Kirby was less often available to play cardounet. When he and Alaric did finally play again, the last afternoon before the ship was to dock at Desse, Alaric played distractedly, and Kirby called him on it.

"Are you still moping about that horse, lad?" he said sharply.

Startled, Alaric looked up at the older man, then dropped his gaze to the board again.

"Laddie, laddie, you may be Deryni," Kirby went on more gently, when the boy did not speak, "but you're still only a boy. Even a Deryni can't change what happened. But maybe you *can* change what happens the next time. It's your move, by the way."

Recalled to the game, Alaric reached toward one of his archers, hesitated, then deliberately moved his abbot instead.

"It's more than just the horse," he finally said, almost whispering. "I made a serious mistake, Henry. This time, it only cost a horse, but it could have been a person." He swallowed audibly. "It could have been *me*."

Kirby nodded, moving his priest-king. "That is true. And what was your mistake? In life, as in cardounet, we must learn from our mistakes. What was yours?"

Alaric exhaled slowly, considering, and moved one of his archers. "I underestimated how much de Nore hates Deryni. And I underestimated how much he hates me, in particular, because of my mother. If I hadn't been with my father, it could have been a fatal mistake."

Kirby moved his war-duke, not looking up. "That is also true. Fortunately, you *were* with your father. But tell me, given all the other things that you did or did not do, and knowing what you did at the time—or did not—could you have done anything differently?"

As he looked up, frank challenge in his eyes, Alaric made himself go back over his actions for at least the dozenth time.

"It would have been wrong not to have gentled the horse when we were loading her at Coroth," he said slowly. "I probably saved her from serious injury. She might even have died."

Kirby nodded. "That is so."

"But in Coroth," Alaric continued, "I was among my own folk, who know what I am and accepted that. And I was safe enough on a Corwyn ship." He managed a mirthless smile. "It doesn't seem to bother *you*, that I am Deryni."

"No, it does not. But what about Nyford? What did you know about Nyford, before we even docked there? And what did the folk in Nyford know about you?"

Alaric hung his head. "I knew that they don't like Deryni in Nyford, that there have been persecutions there," he whispered. "And I knew that Oliver de Nore was the bishop there, and that he hates me."

"And?"

"Well, who would have guessed that the mare was intended for de Nore?" the boy said, almost belligerent. "If I'd known, I never would have shown my face."

"And it's quite a distinctive face, with that shock of blond hair, and traveling on a ship out of Corwyn with your father, who is also well-known," Kirby said mildly. "Don't beat yourself up about it, lad, but you must learn to think ahead, to anticipate these kinds of coincidences. This time, it only cost a horse's life. Next time . . ."

Alaric looked away. Kirby was absolutely right. It was an error born out of kindness and a natural inclination to be helpful, but he had not thought through all the possible consequences, especially there in Nyford, where they did not like Deryni.

"I understand," he whispered. "I didn't think far enough ahead. Thank you, Henry."

"Right, then," the helmsman said briskly. "Now, are you going to move that war-duke, or do I have to take it with my archer? Not *this* move, lad. Three moves ahead."

Alaric's gaze immediately darted back to the board, and he soon saw the threat. "Oh!"

"Don't just say 'Oh.' Move the blasted war-duke out of harm's way! Sometimes the best defense is a quick evasion."

I T was just past noon the following day when they put in at Desse, which was the northernmost port on the Eirian that was navigable by seafaring ships. Here the *Gryphon* would be offloading cargo and taking on new before its turnaround to sail back to the Southern Sea. It would also be bidding farewell to its prominent passengers.

Kenneth had sent Xander and one of the men-at-arms—the man who was not a good sailor—on ahead at the last overnight stop to secure horses, so the pair were waiting at dockside with the requisite mounts as Kenneth, Alaric, and Llion came down the gangplank with their remaining men, all carrying their saddlebags. Alaric's spirits had improved somewhat after a good sleep, his last aboard the ship, but he knew he would miss Henry Kirby. Nonetheless, he was once again in good humor as they mounted up and headed north along the river road, eager to resume his young life.

The weather had definitely turned while they made their way northward along the coast from Coroth and then up the estuary. The nip of autumn was in the wind sweeping down the valley of the Eirian, and the horses were full of themselves, so Kenneth let them have a good gallop out of Desse to help the horses settle before reining back to the usual pattern of walking awhile and trotting awhile. It was good to be back in the saddle, good to be back on dry land.

It was also good to keep moving, though this was a time of year that Alaric loved. All along the river road, the trees were ablaze with scarlets and ochres and tawny golds, many of their branches already going bare. At times, the horses crunched through carpets of fallen leaves. On the slopes across the wide river, crops had been harvested and farmers were burning off the stubble. The fields to the east likewise were short shorn and dotted with golden haystacks. All too soon, winter would be upon them.

They reached Rhemuth just as the sun was sinking behind the leafy avenue of scarlet and gold leading from the river to the city gate. It had been market day, but the cathedral square was emptying, most of the vendors packing up their wares to head home, the shops lowering their shutters. As they rode into the yard at Rhemuth Castle, servants came at once to take charge of their mounts. Leaving Xander and Llion to get their party resettled into the quarters they used when resident in Rhemuth, and sending Alaric with them, Kenneth went immediately to the king.

"And that was all we could do," he concluded, when he had told Brion of their run-in with Nyford's bishop. "It was nothing a young lad should have had to witness, much less be the cause of, but de Nore was within the letter of the law."

Brion sighed. Ordinarily, he would have had at least one advisor with him, but matters concerning Deryni were best handled out of the public eye, at least until he knew better what was involved. And since the king himself had—or would have—Deryni powers someday, much if not all depended on the son of the man sitting before him.

"It was an unfortunate incident," Brion finally said. "And it must have been very distressing for Alaric. But you're right: de Nore was within his rights, much as it pains me to say that. We know that he reserves a special resentment—nay, a hatred—for your son—and why. But there's nothing you could have done differently, to change the outcome."

Kenneth only sighed and bowed his head. "No, there wasn't. I knew that must be your answer, but I had to tell you." He studied his lap for several seconds, then looked up. "But, tell me of your news, my prince," he said, putting on a more pleasant face. "You'll have had my reports regarding the situation with Prince Hogan. Has there been additional on that? And what further news of Meara?"

"A long and complicated story," Brion replied, standing. "You'd best come and talk to others of the crown council. And I suspect that a good meal would not go amiss, after your days at sea. We'll catch you up over supper."

YOUNG Alaric would be privy to little that went on at the king's table that night, for Llion made arrangements for meals to be brought up to their quarters. The next morning, however, while Alaric broke his fast with his father in the great hall below, Llion set about scouting the lay of the land regarding pages at court.

"As you may recall, he was to become a page to Duke Andrew at year's end," Llion told Sir Ninian de Piran, heir to the Earl of Jenas, who was Duke Richard's deputy for the training of royal pages. "Now he will be Duke Jared's page. The duke is expected back at court for Twelfth Night. In the meantime, Alaric is progressing well—I had him training with the pages at Coroth—but I don't want him to lose his edge while he waits for Duke Jared to take him on."

Sir Ninian gave the younger knight a knowing nod. "I saw him ride at the king's birthday tournament," he said. "An impressive showing. I understand that you are responsible for much of his training?"

"His sire works with him when he can," Llion allowed, "but—"

"But *you* are the one who works him every day," Ninian said, smiling faintly. "I also saw *you* ride at the tournament, Sir Llion. Credit where credit is due. If the time should ever come when Lord Kenneth tires of your services, you would be most welcome on Duke Richard's staff."

Llion shrugged somewhat sheepishly, pleased at the compliment. "I shall keep that in mind, sir, but I expect that Master Alaric will need me for yet a few years."

"But less and less, as he takes up his formal training as page and squire," Ninian countered. "Still . . ." He paused to consider for several seconds, then: "Bring him along to the practice yard this afternoon. I want to see what he can do when there is no competition. It may not be an easy few months for him, because he's obviously more advanced than the other boys his age—and some of them may still be smarting from the trouncing he gave them at the tournament."

Llion made no comment, only murmuring his agreement as Ninian continued on his way, but he was thinking of one page, in particular, who had not been happy with Alaric's performance, or with his own very poor one. And when Cornelius Seaton learned of his uncle's run-in with Alaric, Llion suspected that sparks would fly again.

B OTH Llion and Kenneth were present later that afternoon, as Sir Ninian prepared to put Alaric through his paces on the practice field. Unfortunately, so were half a dozen of the other pages, Cornelius Seaton among them, lined up on a fence to observe. Not being in competition this time, the other boys had no direct or immediate reason to resent the newcomer, but that did not prevent whispered commentary among them, and glowering looks from several of them.

But Alaric rose to the challenge. His own pony was still here at Rhemuth, though it had been ridden little during his absence. Nonetheless, half an hour in the arena soon had boy and pony back in harmony. He was riding patterns in the arena when Ninian showed up carrying several wooden swords and a pair of practice helmets, which he dumped at Kenneth's feet. Llion was in the center of the ring, calling instructions to his charge.

"Lord Kenneth," Ninian said with a nod.

Kenneth nodded in return. "Sir Ninian."

After a few minutes of watching with the boy's sire, Ninian took up one of the practice swords and moved into the ring. Llion saw him and immediately signaled Alaric, who turned his pony and came to halt smartly in front of the pair.

"Alaric," Ninian said, with a nod. "I already know that you ride well and you're good at snagging rings with a lance. I saw your performance at the king's birthday tourney." He glanced in the direction of the other watching pages and raised his free hand in summons. "Paget, Airey, could you please set up a couple of rings for me?" He returned his attention to Alaric, reversing the wooden sword to offer it to him hilt first.

"I'm going to ask you to do a different exercise for me now. I understand that you saw squires riding at rings with swords while you were in Coroth."

Alaric gave a nod as he took up the sword. "Yes, sir."

"And did you get to try it?"

"Yes, sir."

"How'd you do?"

Alaric dared a faint smile. "It was a good challenge, sir. And I did fairly well."

"All right, let's see how you do here."

"Yes, sir," Alaric murmured, and lifted the wooden sword in salute before turning his pony to take position at the far end of the arena, opposite where Paget and Airey were setting up the rings.

Ninian and Llion withdrew to stand beside Kenneth. The boy glanced in their direction when the older pages had finished and withdrawn to sit on the fence again, and, at the older knight's signal, he kneed his pony into a gallop, sword extended. He took the first ring neatly, and then the second, pulling up then to turn and glance at Ninian, who nodded his approval.

"Again."

Dutifully Alaric saluted with the sword again, then trotted over to where Airey and Paget were climbing down from the fence.

"Nice riding," Airey said, as Alaric tipped the sword down to let the rings slide off.

"And a good eye," Paget added.

"Thank you," Alaric replied, then trotted back to the opposite end of the arena to wait while the two older boys reset the rings.

This time, when he rode at the rings, he only knocked the first one from its peg, but he continued on to snag the second. His brow was furrowed as he pulled up and turned, but he trotted obediently out to meet Ninian, who was striding toward him, and smiling slightly. Llion followed behind him with the two practice helmets and more wooden swords.

"You may have noticed that I had Paget substitute smaller rings on that run," Ninian said. "But you didn't let it break your concentration. Get down now, and let's see how you perform on the ground."

Alaric complied immediately, first handing his sword to Llion, then jumping down to put on the helmet that Llion offered, also pulling on a padded glove for his sword hand. The sword Llion handed him was similar to the one he had used to snare the rings, but with a light basket hilt to protect the hand. Turning, he saw that Ninian now was similarly helmeted and armed. As Llion led the pony back to where Kenneth was watching, Alaric wondered what Ninian had in mind.

"All right, this is to assess your level of training, not to get you hurt," Ninian said, making a few practice swings to limber up. "I have twice the reach that you do, and I can hit much harder, but I want you to spar with me as if I were a pell that can move to block your blows. That means that I want you to land solid blows. And don't worry, you aren't going to hurt me."

"Yes, sir," Alaric said somewhat uncertainly.

As Ninian lifted his sword to the vertical and gave a nod, Alaric gave it a tentative whack, then another from the other side. But after the first few contacts, Ninian's sword started moving more actively—in no way aggressive, but inviting the boy's attacks from a variety of directions.

Alaric responded with increasing confidence, and shifted several of his exchanges into more serious attacks. He never quite managed to land a blow on the knight, who countered most of his ripostes with ease, but he was left with the feeling that he had done far better than Ninian had expected.

"That's quite good," Ninian finally said, backing off a few paces and giving casual salute with his sword, which Alaric returned. "I think we'll put you with the older pages for arms drill." He tucked his sword under his arm and pulled off his helmet, then summoned Airey Redfearn with a raised arm.

"Mind you, you're good enough to spar with some of the squires," he went on, "but they're mostly much taller than you are, so that would put you at a distinct disadvantage. In the real world, of course, you'll have to face whoever decides to lay into you, but training at this stage is not so much about winning or getting beaten; it's about learning, and hopefully not getting hurt too much in the process."

As Airey Redfearn approached at the trot, Ninian handed him his sword and helmet, and Alaric also turned over his equipment.

"All right, you can go fetch your pony now, and put him away for the night," Ninian said. "And I'll expect you in the classroom in the morning with the other boys."

He nodded to Kenneth and Llion as the boy trotted toward them, then turned to go with Airey.

Chapter 15

"My son, if thou wilt, thou shalt be taught: and if thou wilt
apply thy mind, thou shalt be prudent."
—ECCLESIASTICUS 6:32

I N the days that followed, while Kenneth conferred with the king and his crown council and caught up on developments in Meara, Llion kept close watch on the progress of his young charge. Alaric had accepted that he would be joining the pages' training at Rhemuth, and did his best to fit in, but it was difficult.

As Llion had warned him, he soon discovered that his knowledge and skills were well above those of most of the other boys near his age. Furthermore, because of his father's rank, and because he was already slated to enter page's service with Duke Jared right after Twelfth Night, he was not obliged to share accommodation in the dormitory rooms allocated for other pages. Clearly, some of the others resented that. But that alone was not what soon set him apart from them.

"No one likes me, Llion," he muttered to his mentor after the first week, when he was getting ready for bed.

"Well, you *are* the new boy," Llion said lightly, though he suspected he knew the true source of his charge's difficulties. "The others have been together for many months now, some of them for several years. And even though you're much younger than most of them, you did make a rather impressive showing at the king's birthday tourney—and when Sir Ninian evaluated your training. There's bound to be some resentment."

"I don't think it's that," Alaric replied.

Llion sighed. Aside from the run-in with Bishop de Nore, the boy had been mostly sheltered until now, secure in the company and protection of loving parents and loyal retainers in the immediate household; Llion would certainly give his life for his charge, if required. But what young Alaric Morgan was beginning to experience went far beyond resentment of his titled privileges, his emerging skills in the field, even his physical attractiveness—and the boy *was* handsome, God knew, with his pale hair and eyes, his regular features, his mannerly demeanor. Young girls were already beginning to notice, and not a few not-so-young ones.

"Well, envy almost certainly is a factor," Llion allowed. "And a bit of that is natural, though maturity hopefully teaches all of us to put aside petty jealousies. You also wear your own clothes instead of Haldane livery. That makes you stand out."

"That isn't all that makes me stand out," the boy muttered.

"No, it isn't," Llion agreed.

"But, that isn't fair," Alaric said after a beat. "You're talking about me being half-Deryni. I can't help that! And I don't *do* anything. I *can't* do anything yet."

Llion quirked an eyebrow at him. "No?"

Alaric glanced at his feet. "Well, there's the Truth-Reading," he admitted reluctantly. "And the pain blocking," he added. "But that doesn't hurt anyone. Besides, no one but you knows I can even do that yet. Some of them just hate me; I can sense it. Especially Cornelius. He definitely hates me. And a lot of the others are afraid of me."

"That *is* true."

"Well, what do I *do* about it?" Tears were glittering in the boy's grey eyes as he looked up. "They don't even *know* me."

"It's difficult, I know," Llion said gently. "Unfortunately, there are some who will always dislike you—because of simple jealousy, in many cases, but also because they don't know you and they're afraid to know you, because of what you are. All the telling in the world won't change some people's minds."

"That doesn't answer my question, Llion," the boy murmured, knuckling away his tears. "What can I *do*?"

With a heavy sigh, Llion came to sit on the bed beside the boy, slipping a comforting arm around the rigid shoulders. "Well, one thing you *cannot* do is force the other boys to be friends with you." He rolled his eyes in grudging amendment. "Actually, it's possible that you *could* force at least the outward semblance of friendship, once you've come into your powers. But if you were ever found out, that would only prove to those who hate your kind that Deryni are not to be trusted."

"Then, what *can* I do?"

"Simply be the very best person you can be, as your dear mother would have wished. Say little and observe much. Be courteous and thoughtful, a man of honor. Try to be good-natured and helpful to the other boys, but never do less than your best, even if some are envious. It's something you must learn," he added, at Alaric's dubious grimace, "because you're the one who must live with these lads—and with the men they will become. When all of you are grown, they'll remember how you treated them now. It would be good if you could trust at least a few of them at your back. Do you understand?"

"I suppose so," Alaric murmured, sighing. "But growing up is harder than I thought it would be."

IN the coming weeks, as they began counting down to the feasts of Christmas and Twelfth Night, Alaric thought about what Llion had told him. Though he tried hard to implement what Llion had suggested, he could see little real change, but at least he better understood what might be causing the other boys' antipathy, and consoled himself with the expectation that he would soon be returning to the relative safety of his Uncle Jared's household.

Thus fortified, he decided not to mention the conversation to his father, and indeed, would have found it difficult to do so, for Kenneth was much closeted with the king and the crown council, or out on the king's business, and often returned late to his bed, if at all. A visitation to Valoret with the king kept him from court for more than a week. Kenneth also made a quick visit to Morganhall to check on his sisters, with only Xander and a pair of armsmen to accompany him.

"I would take you and the boy, but I don't want to interrupt his training," he told Llion, before setting out. "I know this is a difficult time for him, and I'd prefer to avoid the impression that he's getting any more special treatment than he already is."

"Yes, my lord."

But a week later, the afternoon following Kenneth's return, he asked Alaric to accompany him to the practice arena. To Alaric's surprise, Llion was already there, cinching up the saddle on a compact bay Llanneddi mare he had never seen before.

"I wanted your opinion on this mare," his father said. "Llion pointed her out to me, when I got back from Morganhall. She's old enough to be sensible, but she still has many good years in her. What do you think?"

As his father came to hold the mare's head and stroke the velvety nose, offering her an apple, Alaric eyed the mare appraisingly, running a hand along the bright bay hindquarters and down one white-stockinged leg. Some of his earliest and happiest memories were of walking through horse fairs with his father and Llion and occasionally other knights of the household, watching and listening while his father haggled with horse dealers over the merits and faults of various steeds. Though Alaric was still learning the finer points of equine assessment, the mare looked like a good example of her breed: not perfect, by any means, and perhaps on the small side for a grown man, but then, Llanners ran small. This one was bigger than most.

"Whose horse would this be, Papa?" he asked, for he knew that it was important to match horse and rider.

Kenneth inclined his head. "Yours, perhaps?"

Alaric felt an anxious flutter in the pit of his stomach, for he could not suppress the sudden image of the doomed grey mare at Nyford, blood blossoming against her satiny coat as she sank into death, but he ducked his head and made himself put it from mind, concentrating instead on his inspection of the animal. At least this animal was bay, not grey.

"Well, she looks a little narrow through the withers, but at least for me, that might be an asset while I'm still growing." He swallowed and managed a brittle smile as he glanced up. "My legs still remember those big-barreled livery horses from the summer. Good chest, though," he went on more confidently, "and good legs."

"Let's put you up on her and see how she goes," Kenneth said, giving the mare's bridle to Llion and moving to the animal's side. "Here, I'll give you a leg up."

Smiling tentatively, Alaric moved to the animal's near side and allowed his sire to boost him into the saddle. Across the arena, he was aware of several of the older pages and younger squires taking places on the fence rail, but he tried to put them from mind as he gathered the mare's reins and moved out.

For the next little while he put the mare through her paces. He was heartened to find that his hours in the saddle going to and from Culdi and Morganhall and Coroth had left him confident and easily capable of handling the larger animal. The mare was responsive and even-tempered, her gaits far smoother than the livery mounts' that had served them on their peregrinations. Alaric could picture himself riding her for some years. But he also knew there would be a price to pay.

"Well, what do you think?" his father asked, as the boy brought the mare to a halt beside the fence where his father sat with Llion. "Shall I tell Master Oisín we'll keep her?"

Alaric glanced across the arena, where he could see the horse dealer likewise sitting on the fence with Paget Sullivan, Airey Redfearn, and several of the younger squires, including Prince Nigel, obviously watching them. Unfortunately, Cornelius Seaton was also among their number.

"I like her very well, Papa," he said quietly, with a covert glance at Llion. "But I . . . don't think it would be a good idea if I had such a fine horse just now, while I'm at Rhemuth."

"Oh? And may I ask why not?"

Alaric ducked his head, reluctant to mention his reasons, but aware that his father probably should be apprised of them—and perhaps even knew already, anyway.

"Well, some of the other boys already don't like me very much," he said hesitantly. "Llion says some of it may be because they're envious. None of the other pages at court have such fine horses."

"Son, you are a future duke," his father said patiently. "You are heir to a great fortune and a noble name, and there will always be those who will resent you for it."

"That's—probably part of it, sir," Alaric almost whispered, blinking hard to keep back tears.

Kenneth nodded slowly, casting a sidelong glance at Llion. "I see. And the other part of it would be that some of them don't like you because you're very accomplished and very clever, and because you are your mother's son as well as mine."

Alaric glanced up quickly, shocked.

Kenneth sighed and shook his head. "I'm very sorry, son," he said quietly. "I knew this time would come, though I had hoped it would be later. But don't you ever let them see you cry!" he said fiercely, though his voice did not rise.

"He's bearing up well, sir," Llion assured him. "He'll be all right."

"He'll be better than all right," Kenneth said under his breath. "He'll be superb! And he deserves a superb horse."

"Yes, sir, he does," Llion agreed. "But perhaps not just now. He'll only be at court for a few months. Perhaps best if we wait."

Considering, Kenneth shifted his gaze from Llion to Alaric and back. "Aye, that's probably true. Very well. Llion, you also deserve a superb mount, so the mare is officially yours for now, if anyone asks. And once you and Alaric move up to Culdi to train with Jared, he can have access to it, with no one the wiser here at court. You *are* his riding master, after all. And meanwhile, I'll have Master Oisín on the lookout for another horse for you."

Llion allowed himself a pleased grin, and Alaric, too, found himself greatly cheered.

"That is uncommonly generous, my lord," Llion said. "Thank you."

"It isn't generous; it's expedient," Kenneth replied. "I've been remiss in not finding you a suitable mount of your own—which I did promise, when you first entered my service."

"I am content, my lord," Llion objected. "You have been most generous."

"Nay, 'tis only your due," Kenneth said. "Old Cockleburr has been retired for several years now, and you're still soldiering on with borrowed horses. Besides, it reflects badly on *me*, if my son's knight is not well mounted." He jutted his chin in Llion's direction. "Give the mare a try, so that our deception will hold, and I'll go and speak with Master Oisín."

"Very good, my lord," Llion agreed. "Lad, you'd best get down now, so I can put this lady through her paces."

Alaric was grinning as he complied, and held on to the stirrup for Llion as the young knight swung up. As Llion settled into the saddle and then moved out, Kenneth watched him for a few minutes, nodding approval as Llion eased the mare into a canter. Then, with a nod and a smile at his son, he headed off across the arena toward Master Oisín.

THE ruse held in the remaining weeks leading up to Twelfth Night. Alaric did ride the mare once or twice, for lessons in the arena, but Llion made a point of taking the little bay out for daily rides, and for his own weapons practice, and always rode the mare when he needed to accompany Kenneth on missions for the king. So far as he could tell, others at court accepted the supposition that Earl Kenneth was a generous lord, and that Llion simply indulged his young charge from time to time.

Since Llion continued some of Alaric's private training, especially in areas in which Alaric was well ahead of his age-mates, this averted some of the too-close contact that the lad had dreaded. On his own, Alaric even began venturing guarded interactions with a few of the other boys. Some, like Cornelius Seaton, would always remain implacably against him, but a few encounters seemed to hold the potential for more positive relationships, perhaps even a kind of friendship.

"You handle that pony well," said a voice from the fence, as Alaric pulled up after yet another successful run at the rings with a wooden sword. "Is he the same one you rode at the king's birthday tournament?"

Alaric turned his attention to the speaker: Paget Sullivan, a tall, gangly lad with auburn hair and bright blue eyes, slated for squiring at the upcoming Twelfth Night festivities. There was reserve in his gaze, but no apparent hostility.

"Aye, he is," Alaric acknowledged, reining the pony closer and halting. "Would you like to try him?"

The other boy looked surprised, but then a faint smile curved at the corners of his mouth. "May I, truly?" he asked.

For answer, Alaric swung one leg over the pommel of his saddle and jumped down, offering the reins with an answering smile.

"Of course."

"Thank you." The older boy reinforced his reply with an amiable nod and climbed down from the fence.

"You're Paget Sullivan, aren't you?" Alaric said, as the other set his foot in the stirrup.

Young Paget flinched, then put his raised foot back on the ground and partially turned toward Alaric.

"I am."

Alaric gave the older boy a nod of approval. "You took ten rings at the king's birthday tourney. That was impressive."

Paget turned to face Alaric squarely, his expression softening a little. "Thank you. As I recall, you also took ten rings." He glanced around to see who might be listening, then added, in a lower voice, "Cornelius Seaton was practically livid. He hates you, you know."

Alaric shrugged. "I've given him no cause, other than to exist."

Paget snorted. "That's more than enough for Cornelius. He doesn't much like me, either—probably because he considers me a rival, which I am. Come to think of it, there aren't many of the other pages he does like, much less respects."

"I gathered that," Alaric said. "But I've heard that he's actually pretty good at ring-tilting—when he isn't getting dumped from his pony."

"Don't let *him* hear you say that," Paget murmured, casting a nervous glance under the pony's neck to where the said Cornelius had just come in from riding a set of runs at the rings, and negligently threw his lance aside to nearly hit one of the younger pages. "He does have a fearsome temper."

"You'd better ride, then, before he sees us talking," Alaric said, wisely keeping the pony between him and Cornelius.

Tight-lipped, Paget again set foot to stirrup and, this time, sprang up into the saddle. Gathering up the reins, he then cast a conspiratorial grin down at the younger boy. "He'll remember that this is your pony, you know. As soon as he sees me ride out, he's going to know I was talking to you. But if you don't mind, I don't!"

"Enjoy your ride," was all Alaric said, though he smiled as he said it.

"Thank you—and not just for the ride," Paget returned with a nod.

With that, he kneed the pony into motion and took off across the arena, heading toward the stand where the practice lances were racked up. He nodded amiably to Cornelius as he passed, seizing a lance on the trot as he continued on toward the ring lists. Fortunately, just as Cornelius recognized the pony and cast a poisonous glance in Alaric's direction, Llion came up beside his charge.

"May I ask what that was all about?" Llion asked, leaning nonchalantly against the fence.

"I told Paget Sullivan he could ride my pony," Alaric replied. "He's nice. But apparently Cornelius Seaton doesn't like the fact that I talked to Paget." He grinned up at Llion. "I don't think I care."

Smiling, Llion gently dunted Alaric on the bicep. "Good lad! It appears you may have made a friend. Just watch out that an old enemy has not become Paget's enemy as well."

"I think they already didn't like each other much," Alaric replied. "But I'll watch Paget's back—and mine."

"See that you do," Llion replied. "It could be worth both your lives."

"Our lives?"

"Just remember whose nephew Cornelius is," Llion said darkly.

Chapter 16

"A man that hath friends must show himself friendly . . ."
—PROVERBS 18:24

O the relief of all, Alaric's act of generosity seemed to provoke no serious repercussions. Cornelius Seaton performed extremely well that day, even outriding Paget Sullivan, and seemed more caught up in his own success than in paying much attention to who was mounted on what pony.

The incident also seemed to mark a subtle change in the attitude of Paget Sullivan. Paget's outward attitude around the other boys altered little, and he was careful not to appear too friendly; but neither did he exhibit any sign of dislike or fear or even resentment. And one dreary afternoon midway through November, when Alaric chanced to be reading in an archway of the colonnade skirting the royal gardens, he looked up to see Paget approaching from the direction of the great hall, apparently lost in thought and unaware of his presence.

"Hullo, Paget," he said softly, as the other drew abreast of him.

The other boy looked up with a start, expressions of surprise, uncertainty, and uneasiness briefly flitting across his face.

"Hello," Paget replied, glancing around to see whether anyone else was in sight or earshot. When he saw no one, he cautiously ventured a little closer. "What's that you're reading?" He jutted his chin at the manuscript in the other boy's hands.

Alaric shrugged. "Just an old treatise on battle tactics from the Great War. It was written by one of the Torenthi generals who survived Killingford. I have permission to borrow manuscripts from the royal library," he added, at Paget's raised eyebrow.

"Is it in Torenthi?" Paget moved closer still, to glance down at the scroll open on Alaric's lap. "Good Lord, it is. You can read that?"

"Only a little, but I'm learning. My Aunt Delphine taught me the script; she's my father's sister," Alaric added, lest Paget construe this somewhat unusual accomplishment as something learned from his Deryni mother. "And Sir Llion helps me sometimes. He grew up near the Torenthi border, so he speaks a little of their tongue. A lot of their military terminology is very close to ours, once you puzzle out the different alphabet."

Paget raised both eyebrows this time, then flicked a glance at the stone bench beside Alaric, clearly intrigued that an eight-year-old, even a Deryni, should spend his own time in such esoteric pursuits. "Could you show me?"

Flashing a tentative hint of smile, Alaric gave a nod and scooted a little aside to make room, shifting the manuscript so that Paget could have a better view of it, and searched for a passage that he had already puzzled out.

"The general's name was Jurij Orkény—see, there's his name." He pointed to it and sounded out the pronunciation. "Say it."

"*Yu-ri Or-kay-nee*," Paget repeated dutifully.

"That's very good. You now know two words in Torenthi."

Paget chuckled dubiously. "Two whole words."

"Don't scoff," Alaric said lightly. "It's probably more than Cornelius knows."

Stifling a snicker of agreement, Paget settled closer to look at the name again. "Orkény. Actually, I think I've heard of him. I'd just never seen it written—and certainly not in Torenthi."

Alaric nodded. "He was on the general staff of Prince Nikola, who didn't survive the battle—which is a good thing, because besides being the brother of Prince Arkady, who soon became King of Torenth, Nikola was supposed to marry Roisían of Meara."

Paget snorted. "Meara! Trouble, even then. You do know that there's apt to be another Mearan campaign in the spring, don't you?"

"I'd heard that," Alaric said carefully. "If they go, my father will be riding with the king. They're hoping it will just be a visitation, though—perhaps a royal progress. Rumor has it that old Aude of Meara is dying, and that Princess Caitrin will marry as soon as the body is cold. That would not be a good thing."

Paget looked at the younger boy in surprise. "Who told you that? And how does an eight-year-old know about such things?"

Alaric turned a guileless gaze on the older boy. "I'm going to be a duke someday, Paget. I'll need to know about such things. Besides, I overheard my father and Sir Llion discussing it one night, when they thought I was already asleep." He sighed and shook his head. "I hope there isn't another war."

"So do I," Paget allowed. "My father is getting too old for battle, but I have uncles who—" He broke off at the sound of footsteps, accompanied by the dark silhouettes of three cloaked figures approaching from the direction of the kitchens. Two of them were the king's sisters, the Princesses Xenia and Silke, but the third was Cornelius Seaton, who was carrying a handled basket from which all three were partaking: tarts, by the look and aroma.

"Your Highnesses!" Paget blurted, springing to his feet as Alaric, too, rose, cradling the manuscript against his chest as both of them bowed.

Xenia, the older of the two girls, looked flustered but returned them a prim curtsy. Silke, who was only ten, broke into a wide grin and ran to bestow an exuberant hug on Paget.

"Paget! What are you doing here? Oh, hullo, Alaric. Cornelius, bring some of the tarts for Paget and Alaric." Turning back to the pair, she added, "Cook doesn't know we took them. But it was so boring, with all the rain, and the tarts smelled *so* nice. Here, have one. Go ahead."

His face blank and neutral, Cornelius dutifully brought the basket, which Silke snatched from him and thrust at both boys. Though Paget delved into its depths, indulging the younger princess, Alaric mutely shook his head and stepped back, noting the poisonous glance Cornelius gave him.

"What's the matter, *Deryni?*" Cornelius muttered, when Silke had seized Paget's hand and begun dragging him and the basket back in the direction of her elder sister. "Afraid you'll be caught with stolen tarts, and get into trouble?"

Alaric shook his head again. "Sticky fingers and old manuscripts don't go well together."

"Old manuscripts? Let's see that," Cornelius demanded, reaching for the vellum scroll in Alaric's arms. "What have you got there?"

"Leave it!" Alaric ordered, pulling back farther. "It's the king's manuscript, and I have permission!'

Cornelius froze just before his hand could touch the vellum, then drew himself up haughtily. "So, that's the way it is," he whispered. "Invoking the king's name." He sniffed disdainfully. "Well, I won't fight you in front of the princesses, but I won't forget this, either, *Deryni*!"

With that, he turned on his heel and followed Paget and Silke, putting on a pleasant expression as he rejoined them. At Silke's insistence, Paget went with the three, but not before casting an apologetic glance in Alaric's direction. Alaric, after a few deep breaths, settled back with his manuscript until Llion came to find him for dinner. By then, it had become too dark to read anyway. He told Llion about the incident while they were cleaning up.

"I didn't know what else to do," he said, on finishing his account. "It's one thing if he tries to beat me up. It's quite another, if he tries to drag Paget into it. They're both due to be advanced to squire at Twelfth Night, but if Duke Richard catches them fighting, he'll be very cross. He could even hold them back."

"A run-in with Duke Richard might be just what Cornelius needs," Llion replied, "though it wouldn't improve the dispositions of his parents or his uncle the bishop. And it would hardly be fair to Paget, who seems to be a fine young man. I've been watching him, since the two of you struck up a friendship, and I'm impressed with what I've seen."

"Well, what can I do?" Alaric asked. "Now that we're indoors most of the time, because of the weather, there are all kinds of opportunities for Cornelius to lie in wait somewhere, and jump us. And he's much bigger than I am."

"Let me have a word with your father about this," Llion said thoughtfully.

"Llion . . ."

"I'll be subtle," Llion promised.

Much later that night, when even Kenneth had retired to his quarters, Llion took the opportunity to speak to him about his son's dilemma. Alaric pretended to be deep asleep in the adjoining chamber, but Llion suspected that his charge was far more aware than he appeared. He decided to proceed, nonetheless. Best if the boy knew just how dangerous the situation could become, if Cornelius Seaton was not set straight very soon.

"My lord, there is something you should be aware of," he said to Kenneth, as he pulled the connecting door mostly closed and the older man began to disrobe for the night.

"Oh?" Kenneth's glance at Llion was met with a telling glance in the direction of Alaric's bed, at which Kenneth gave a knowing nod.

"Aye, my lord. Ordinarily, I would take this to Duke Richard, but I don't want the situation to escalate. Are you aware of the hostility of young Cornelius Seaton toward your son?"

Kenneth gave a heavy sigh and sank down on a stool so that Llion could pull off his boots. "What has he done? And what has *Alaric* done?"

"Neither has actually done anything—yet," Llion replied, pulling off the first boot. "But you may or may not be aware that our lad has been spending a bit more time with Paget Sullivan, Sir Evan Sullivan's boy. I might even venture to call it a friendship—which is difficult for Alaric, for reasons you know."

"And?"

"And Cornelius has taken exception to this association, and apparently threatened at least Alaric—to the extent that both boys have been avoiding dark corridors, and keeping a wary eye out for Cornelius."

Kenneth allowed himself another heavy sigh as Llion pulled off the second boot. "Dammit, Llion, can't you keep this situation under wraps until I can get Alaric safely shipped off to Culdi with Jared? I'm trying to help the king plan a Mearan expedition that we all hope will not turn into a full-blown campaign."

"I'm aware of that, sir. It isn't so much Alaric I'm worried about, as it is Paget. But if Cornelius goes after either of them, and gets called on the carpet by Richard . . . well, his father—or his mother—will have words with her brother the bishop, and you can bet that everything will be blamed on the 'Deryni brat.'"

Kenneth allowed himself a third great sigh. "Very well. The weather is worsening, but Jared should arrive shortly. I'll see about getting Alaric sworn as his page as soon as the formalities of his own new office are taken care of. Meanwhile, see that you keep a close rein on my son. The last thing we need is an incident. And keep an eye on young Paget as well."

"Very good, my lord."

FORTUNATELY, the worsening weather curtailed much outdoor activity as winter settled in, greatly diminishing the likelihood of mishap in the practice arena—and encounters with Cornelius—though horses and ponies still must be fed and groomed, and stalls mucked out. After morning stable duties, while the squires retired to the king's council chamber for lectures, the pages would take over the great hall for arms drill. Most of the exercises involved work at the pell, or vaulting onto the back of a wooden horse, sometimes with sword in hand, but the training was beginning to include instruction in hand-to-hand combat and even wrestling. Alaric paid close attention to those sessions, and even sparred with the younger pages, but always under Llion's watchful eyes. One boy, called Quillan Pargeter, seemed particularly well matched in size, strength, and physical ability, and did not appear to be intimidated by Alaric's lineage, either noble or esoteric. After a while, the two had formed a tentative camaraderie that gave Llion hope that an actual friendship might develop.

Afternoons offered challenges of a more intellectual nature, and sometimes new perspectives. Most afternoons, Duke Richard drafted various of Gwynedd's seasoned warriors to give instruction in military history, heraldry, and noble deportment. In addition, the chamberlain rehearsed the boys regularly in proper table service, and one of the king's chaplains gave them occasional religious instruction. Alaric had hoped he might be excused from the latter, for many priests preferred not to deal with Deryni, but Father Henry was evenhanded and neutral. It was another indication that perhaps, eventually, he might hope to be accepted.

But court was still a very complex and unpredictable place, as he kept

being reminded. One midday early in December, still mulling the previous afternoon's lesson on cavalry tactics by a Marley veteran, Alaric
fetched his Orkény manuscript and betook himself to one of the deep
window embrasures in the great hall, looking out onto the snow-
powdered gardens. His father had taken Llion on an errand for the king,
so Duke Richard had excused him from the morning's hand-to-hand
practice. Some of the squires had come early to afternoon weapons drill
and were sparring farther up the hall. He was immersed in his document,
snugged up warmly in a fur-lined mantle, when the king came strolling
through the hall with Sir Jamyl Arilan, and chanced to notice the boy
sitting there.

Alaric sensed rather than saw the royal gaze at first, and looked up to
see the king smile and nod as he caught Alaric's eye and started toward
him. The boy immediately sprang to his feet, giving a graceful bow over
the manuscript clutched to his breast.

"Good afternoon," the king said, coming up into the embrasure as
Sir Jamyl took up a posture of casual vigilance in the opening at floor
level. "What have you there? The light isn't very good on a day like this."

"Begging your pardon, Sire, but my Torenthi isn't very good, either,"
the boy replied, smiling. "But I keep at it. Winter is a good time for such
pursuits. There isn't much else to do in one's free time."

"Hmmm, perhaps Duke Richard is giving you too much free time,
then," the king observed, though he was smiling as he said it. "What's
that you're reading, anyway?" he asked, reaching across to tilt the manuscript toward him. "That's Orkény's *Memoirs of the Great War.* 'Failed
Battle Tactics,' my uncle calls it. Good Lord, you don't mean to tell me
you're trying to read it in Torenthi?" The king looked up incredulously.
"You do know that we have a translation."

The boy looked startled and a bit appalled.

"No, Sire, I didn't know," he said in a small voice.

"Well, we do. Practicing your Torenthi is one thing, but—tell me,
have you gotten much out of the original?"

Alaric swallowed and ventured an uncertain nod. "I think so, Sire.
I've tried setting up some of the battle scenarios on a cardounet board,
but the scale is a bit small to be certain what he was doing."

"Well, I've only read Orkény in translation, but I do understand his strategy," the king said, glancing back thoughtfully at his companion. "Jamyl, please ask my uncle to join us in the withdrawing room. Young Morgan, come with me."

Wide-eyed, still clutching the manuscript to his chest, Alaric gave an obedient nod and followed as the king struck out across the great hall floor and Sir Jamyl Arilan headed in another direction. He could feel the stares of the squires as he went, though no one dared to break from training exercises.

Up to the left of the dais they went, passing then into the withdrawing room behind, where the king customarily held more private audiences. Alaric had been there once before, at that Twelfth Night when his father was created Earl of Lendour.

Today, in addition to serving as the king's winter writing room, the chamber was arranged with maps spread across several trestle tables, with troop markers and tallies such as Alaric had never seen up close. As they entered the room, the king gestured toward a senior squire sorting documents at the writing table nearer the fire.

"Godwin, bring out the maps that would cover the action of the Battle of Killingford, if you will. Young Master Alaric has discovered Orkény, in the original Torenthi, and would like to see the battle laid out properly—and I should like to see now much he understands."

A flurry of activity ensued, as Godwin and another squire hastily cleared away the markers from the map table and unrolled another map atop the first, weighting its corners with river-polished stones. When the king had briefly explained the correspondences for the various markers and tokens, he gestured for the boy to set up the arrays for the start of the battle.

Alaric began slowly at first, as he familiarized himself with this particular map, then with growing confidence. He was unaware that the king's uncle had arrived until he looked up and saw the royal duke standing at the king's side, with Jamyl looking between them from behind. All three of them were wearing expressions of varying disbelief, as were the two squires, both due to be knighted at Twelfth Night.

"I—believe this is correct, Sire," Alaric murmured, casting hesitant looks at all five men. "I had to guess at a few of the terms that didn't seem to be quite the same in Torenthi, but this scenario seems consistent with what I'd learned elsewhere."

"Interesting," Richard said, stroking his close-clipped beard as he studied the board. "You need to shift this and these," he went on, adjusting several markers, "but I can see how you were misled, given that you don't actually read Torenthi. Or do you?" he asked, looking up with narrowed gaze.

"Not really, sir," Alaric whispered. "Well, a few words. My Aunt Delphine, my father's sister, taught me Torenthi lettering, and then I just—sounded out some of the terms. And Sir Llion speaks and reads a little. Oh, and I learned a bit from reading about cardounet strategy," he added as an afterthought. "But no one seems to play much here. At least the other boys don't."

Richard turned to glance at Jamyl. "You play, don't you, Sir Jamyl?"

Jamyl inclined his head. "I do, sir."

"Perhaps you could find someone to play with Master Alaric."

"I am certain that can be arranged, sir."

"Fair enough," Richard agreed. "Now, run the battle, lad. I know you haven't yet been taught the standard way of doing that—or at least I assume that you haven't—but show us how you think it went on the day."

Tentatively at first, Alaric explained the course of the battle, moving pieces, shifting markers, and finally ending with the Torenthi army routed, though at what cost to both sides, he had only just begun to comprehend, as the battle unfolded on a proper map. When he had finished, he looked up apprehensively, certain he must have got most of it wrong. To his surprise, both Richard and the king were nodding in approval, exchanging pleased smiles. Jamyl had clasped his arms across his breast, but was not quite covering his own smile behind one upraised hand. The two squires looked disbelieving, but the respect in their eyes was genuine.

"Innis, go and fetch me the translation of Orkény's battle memoirs," Richard said to the taller of the two squires. "Godwin, leave us. Jamyl, you can go as well." And as the pair beat a hasty exit, followed by the young knight, he said to the king, "Well, it's clear that we have something of a tactical prodigy on our hands, Nephew. *Must* we let Jared have him for the next few years?"

Brion nodded, smiling faintly. "I fear we must. Kenneth has been quite adamant about that. He needs time to grow. I told you about young Seaton. And there are others who resent him as well." He glanced at Alaric, who was trying hard to make himself invisible while two Haldane princes discussed his shortcomings. "Alaric, what do *you* think?"

The boy cleared his throat nervously and ducked his head in agreement. "I—think it would be good if I served Duke Jared for a time, Sire. People in the borders are more tolerant of my kind. Here, you would be spending a great deal of energy trying to keep me safe. And begging your pardon, Sire, but neither you nor Duke Richard can be everywhere at once. I've heard about what happened to Krispin MacAthan—and that was at a Twelfth Night court, surrounded by people who should have been able to prevent it but couldn't."

Brion gave a snort and glanced at his uncle. "Eight years old, Richard. My father has left me a formidable weapon, *if* we can get him safely grown."

"Truly," Richard agreed. "Then, until he does go with Jared, may I take over his training, at least for the theoretical aspects? I should like to continue with analyzing Orkény. Sir Llion can continue with his physical training. He's doing an admirable job."

"What say you, lad?" The king turned his attention on Alaric. "Would you like to have some private tutoring from Duke Richard?"

Alaric allowed himself a slow, pleased grin. "I should like that very much, Sire."

"Excellent," Richard said, as the door opened and the squire Innis returned with a scroll under his arm. Just beyond him, Godwin waited in the open doorway, looking uncertain. "Is that the translation?"

"Aye, sir, it is."

"Good. I'm giving it on loan to young Master Alaric, who will begin reading this instead of attending lessons with the other boys." He intercepted the scroll and handed it off to Alaric, also gesturing for Godwin to enter. "I shall expect you every afternoon for an hour before supper, lad, beginning tomorrow. Godwin, Innis, you can put back the room. We'll be wanting it in the morning for a staff meeting."

LATER that evening, when the castle slept at last, Sir Jamyl Arilan repaired to the room he had made his own in the months since the king's knighting: the room next to the royal library, where lay the Transfer Portal by which he could gain access to the chamber where the Camberian Council met. As rationale for claiming the room, he had made it known that he desired to conduct research in the royal archives next door—and indeed, he did avail himself of the assembled records on a regular enough basis that no one questioned his interest.

On this occasion, however, he gave the library door not a second glance, instead letting himself into his own room and setting the latch behind him. He lit several wall sconces before reclining on the canopied bed that occupied most of the room.

For several minutes he simply closed his eyes and concentrated on the flicker of the torchlight behind lowered lids, letting the wavering patterns of light and shadow propel him deep into trance, at the same time sending out a very focused and specific call. Then he roused from trance and sat more upright, propped against the pillows with arms crossed on his chest, waiting.

Beyond the closed door, he could faintly hear the normal night sounds of the castle at rest, and the occasional shuffle of footsteps passing. Then, all at once, the very air in the room seemed to grow quiet, expectant, just before a shadow shifted at the foot of the bed and a cloaked figure winked into existence.

"This had better be important," a soft whisper breathed, as golden light briefly flared around the head of Stefan Coram, confirming his identity.

At once Jamyl slid to his feet and came to clasp hands with the other man, wrist to wrist.

I couldn't risk leaving the castle, Jamyl sent, mind to mind, *and it isn't something the entire Council necessarily needs to know, at this point. But I knew you would appreciate the intelligence.*

Stefan cocked his head in question.

Imagine the king's surprise, Jamyl went on, *when he discovered that young Alaric Morgan, his half-breed Deryni duke, has been reading Orkény in the original Torenthi.*

He reads Torenthi? Stefan interjected.

Enough to get the gist of Orkény's battle tactics—and that's difficult enough to do in translation. I don't know whether to attribute it to being half-Deryni or just being bright, but it certainly bears watching.

Stefan made a silent whistle under his breath.

Anyway, Brion gave him the translation, and we'll see what happens next. Probably not a great deal right away, because Kenneth is adamant that the boy should begin his official page's training with Duke Jared—and I can't say I disagree. Having a Deryni openly at court is going to be difficult on many levels; best to let the boy get some years under his belt before he has to contend with the hostility that will only increase as he gets older. The Seaton boy is already making life difficult for him from time to time, following in his uncle's footsteps.

Stefan only shook his head, resignation in his pale eyes.

I don't envy the boy the next few years—but you're right: we don't need to involve the full Council at this point. Keep an eye out for him, if you can. Until he matures, he is still very much an unknown quantity, and may or may not prove an asset to our operations.

One other development that might prove useful, Jamyl replied. *A relationship, one might even venture to call it a friendship, seems to be developing between Alaric and the son of Sir Evan Sullivan, Oisín's friend.*

Then I'll mention it to Oisín, so that he can make the necessary adjustments if the friendship continues. Stefan smiled as he gave Jamyl's wrist an affirming squeeze. *Well done, friend. It will be interesting to see how this all plays out.*

Chapter 17

"Withhold not good from them to whom it is due,
when it is in the power of thy hand to do it."

—PROVERBS 3:27

THE remaining weeks until the feast of Christmas and the festivities of Twelfth Night court passed quickly for young Alaric Morgan. With his training now conducted exclusively by Llion and Duke Richard, he had little need to interact with the other boys, which he mostly counted as a distinct blessing, but it also meant that he had scant opportunity to pursue his friendships with Paget Sullivan and Quillan Pargeter. And even when the older page summoned up the courage to ask whether Alaric might consent to be part of Paget's squiring party, Alaric felt obliged to decline.

"I wish I dared," he told Paget, one cold December afternoon shortly before Christmas, "but it does no good to rub Cornelius's nose in the fact that I'm getting special treatment—and from Duke Richard, at that. And I don't want to get you into more trouble with Cornelius, when I'll only be at court for a few more weeks. You'll still have to train with him, once I'm gone."

"That's true," Paget said, ducking his head. "I wish you were staying at court, though. I want to read that battle treatise when you're finished with it," he added, almost defensively.

Alaric smiled faintly and gave a gentle buffet to Paget's bicep. "Careful, you're about to become a Haldane squire. It wouldn't do to be looking up to a mere page—and a Deryni one, at that."

"That doesn't bother me," Paget said, a little flustered. "Not the fact that you're only just becoming a page *or* that you're Deryni. I've decided you aren't that scary, Alaric Morgan. Not now that I've gotten to know you a bit. I don't understand why most people are afraid of your kind."

"Maybe it's one of life's great mysteries," Alaric said lightly. "But I do promise that I'll try never to do anything that will make you afraid of me. And if you like," he added with a smile, "I'll ask the king whether you may have custody of the Orkény treatise when I go to Culdi."

A look of uncertainty flashed across Paget's handsome face. "You would do that for me?"

"Of course. That's what friends do for friends."

Paget's uncertainty slowly shifted into relieved acceptance as he shyly offered his right hand.

"Thank you," he whispered. "And you *are* my friend, Alaric Morgan."

A testing of Alaric's resolve not to frighten came far sooner than he might have hoped—not involving Paget directly, but impossible to hide or even temper with much restraint. It was the week before Christmas: a rare, sunny day, but snow was thick on the ground. Earlier, Alaric had enjoyed a vigorous ride-out with his father and Llion outside the city walls, with a stop on the way back at a silversmith's establishment near the cathedral, to see about a commission for the king.

Early afternoon found him and Llion ensconced in a window embrasure in the great hall, where Llion was setting up for a game of cardounet with a set loaned by Duke Richard. Llion was not a keen player, but he was more than competent, and always gave his young charge a good game. He had also read both de Brinsi and Koltan. A firepot was set on the floor of the embrasure, which kept the worst of the chill at bay.

Down in the great hall itself, Jiri Redfearn and a pair of younger knights were putting half a dozen junior squires through sword drill with practice equipment moved inside for the occasion. Some of the young-sters were taking turns vaulting onto a wooden horse with wooden swords in hand, then leaning down to whack at a helmet set atop a wooden crosspiece. Others, wearing practice helmets, hacked at thick wooden pells with live steel, occasionally sending splinters flying—a step up from the drills with wooden swords. The adult supervision was essential, for the youngsters' control was sometimes less than exacting.

That should have been sufficient to avert disaster. Nonetheless, the rhythmic thud of blades against leather and wood was suddenly punctuated by a less solid thump and a sharp cry of pain.

Llion came to his feet and was on his way onto the floor even as activity ceased. Alaric likewise had risen to peer down into the hall. Jaska Collins was pushing his way through the gaggle of stunned and frightened squires to where Jiri and Phares Donovan had gone to the aid of the injured squire. The lad had one gloved hand clapped to his left arm, where bright blood had blossomed against his white shirt.

"Easy, lad, let me have a look," Jiri murmured, easing the boy's hand far enough aside to assess the damage as Jaska pulled off the boy's helmet.

"*Jesu*, I'm bleeding like a stuck pig!" the boy gasped, eyes screwed shut as he grimaced with the pain. His face was as white as his shirt. "How bad is it?"

"I think it will want some stitching," Jiri allowed, "but it doesn't look too bad."

"Nolen, fetch Duke Richard's battle surgeon!" Phares ordered one of the older squires, himself bolting toward the stairwell that led to the duke's quarters. "I'll get the duke."

Llion, meanwhile, had taken Phares's place, and was helping to support the boy while Jiri jammed a wadded cloth to the wound to apply pressure. The injured squire was a studious fifteen-year-old called Maxen of Coldoire, whose father was a vassal of the Earl of Marley. He also was one of the few older boys who had occasionally had a kind word for Alaric.

"Maxen, let's shift you over here to sit down," Jiri said, as he and Llion began walking the injured boy to one of the window embrasures, to sit on the step up. "How did this happen?"

"I think—my sword must've hit a knot," Maxen managed to murmur. "The hilt twisted right out of my hand—I couldn't stop it! And then the blade—"

He grimaced and sucked in breath between clenched teeth as Jiri checked the wound again, then reapplied pressure. As running feet heralded the arrival first of Master Donnard, Duke Richard's battle-surgeon, and then the duke himself, Alaric stepped down from his window embrasure and tried to edge closer to the action. He sensed Maxen's pain and fear—and was well aware that he could ease it, if only they would let him—but Jaska started moving the other boys back from Maxen to make room.

Llion also stepped back as Donnard took his place, he and the duke both listening as Jiri murmured what had happened and Donnard took a quick look at the wound, then opened his surgical kit and began selecting instruments. Very shortly, a kitchen boy appeared with a bowl of steaming water and some clean cloths over his arm. Maxen's face was tight with the pain as Duke Richard cut away the sleeve, and Alaric started to edge his way closer, trying to position himself where he had a clear view.

"Maxen, look at me! I know you can do this!" he said, his voice calm yet powerful with conviction.

Master Donnard faltered in his preparations, glancing quickly at the duke, but Richard only shot Alaric a stern look and shook his head minutely.

"Careful," he murmured.

"Yes, sir," Alaric whispered, as his stomach did a slow, queasy roll.

But Duke Richard mercifully said nothing further; merely turned deliberately back to Master Donnard, who had commenced to wash out the wound.

"You'll need more light," the duke said, and motioned for several of the other squires to come closer. "Some of you, bring some torches, and a few of you can help hold him steady. It's time you learned about another facet of being a warrior. One day, hopefully not too soon or too often, you may have to do this for one of your men. Charles, Harry, give Master Donnard a hand."

The torches came, and the two squires Richard had named positioned themselves to one side and behind their wounded fellow, one supporting Maxen's back and the other bracing the unwounded arm. Alaric desperately wanted to join them and help, but he knew he dared not; and he was greatly aware that Llion had returned to stand behind him, hands tightening on his shoulders, holding him back.

"Right, then," Donnard said, taking up his needle. "I'll try to make this as quick as possible, lad."

Fortunately, Donnard was quick, indeed, and soon had closed Maxen's wound with half a dozen tidy sutures. A scar the boy would have, to remind him of his carelessness—or ill fortune—but Donnard assured him, as he waved off his assistants and finished tying off the bandage, that if he followed instructions to keep the wound clean, he should heal quickly.

"Very well," Richard said, giving Maxen a hand up and motioning for the rest of the boys to disperse. "The rest of you lot, return to your drill—and try not to repeat Maxen's mistake." He pulled off his own mantle and put it around Maxen's shoulders. "Maxen, you can sit here and watch for the rest of the session. Jiri and Phares, Jaska, try to keep a closer watch this time. Sir Llion, please bring that firepot from the next window for Maxen, then bring your young charge and come with me."

Alaric's heart was in his throat as Richard led him and Llion beyond the dais and into the king's withdrawing room, which was unoccupied at that hour. As soon as the door closed behind them, Richard turned to fix the boy in his stern gaze.

"Now, suppose you tell me just what you thought you were doing out there," he said quietly, though there was steel in his voice.

Alaric swallowed. "I—thought I might block his pain, sir."

"Llion, could he have done that?" the duke demanded.

"I don't know, Your Highness," Llion said, which was true but ambiguous.

Richard gave a heavy sigh and turned to briefly lean against the writing desk, gazing at the surface between his two hands as he considered his reply. Then:

"Alaric, apparently I need to remind you of a few unpleasant truths. There are those at court who do not like Deryni. Some have what they consider to be legitimate reasons; some are simply ignorant gits. My brother intended that you should be an asset to his son, my nephew; but if you flaunt what you are, even for what you regard as good reason—and I will not deny that it would have been a kindness to young Maxen, to lessen his pain while Master Donnard patched him up—if you flaunt your powers, those who hate your kind may take it in their minds to eliminate you."

Alaric could not bear to look at the duke, whom he greatly respected, and found himself hovering on the verge of tears. But Duke Richard did not relent.

"I trust I need not remind you what happened to young Krispin MacAthan," the duke went on. "He was precisely your age when narrow-minded men consumed by hatred of your kind contrived to take his life, and in circumstances whose details I hope you do not learn for many years. I do not know whether you are the only Deryni at court—my nephew has not confided in me in that regard, if even he knows—but I do know that whatever other Deryni might be here, they are discreet, they do not call attention to their powers—and that is what enables them to survive. Do you understand what I am saying to you?"

Alaric nodded slowly, still not looking up. He had nearly made a serious mistake, in his instinctive impulse to try to help Maxen. He could see that now. The line he must walk was even more delicate than he had imagined: to learn to use his powers, as they emerged, but to exercise the uttermost discretion in how and when he used them. At least until he was old enough and skilled enough to protect himself.

"Good, then," Richard said softly, when it became apparent that the boy was not going to speak. "I trust we shan't need to have this conversation again for many years, if then. I don't know who is training you, or even whether *anyone* is training you; I have no idea what provisions my brother made for seeing you to manhood. But be careful, lad. You have powerful enemies, and neither the king nor I will always be able to protect you."

"Yes, sir," Alaric whispered. "It won't happen again."

"I am very glad to hear that," Richard replied. "Llion, you keep a tighter rein as well."

"Aye, my lord," Llion murmured, similarly cowed by the duke's justified anger.

"That's all, then. If I were you, I would lie low for a few days—both of you."

With only a nod for answer, Llion set his hand firmly on his young charge's shoulder and marched both of them out of the room, heading up the nearest stair to return to their quarters, rather than going through the great hall. When they were safely behind the door, Alaric moved blindly to the window and stood there for the better part of an hour, gazing out at the rooftops of the castle complex, not speaking. Llion sat down to wait. When the boy finally turned, he gave Llion a long, searching look, as if somehow surprised to see his mentor still there, then returned his gaze to the view out the window.

"I only wanted to help," he said. "Was that so very wrong?"

Llion allowed himself a sigh. "Not so *very* wrong, no," he replied, after a beat. "But not so very wise, either. Do you understand that?"

Sighing, Alaric nodded and turned to sink down on his haunches against the wall beneath the window, hugging his arms around his knees, not meeting Llion's gaze as he slid to a sitting position.

"Alaric," Llion said softly, "what you tried to offer to Maxen was an act of kindness, to ease his pain—except that you are who and what you are. Aside from the danger to *you*, there might have been a danger to Maxen. There are those who would view such a 'kindness' as a corruption, the imposition of an evil power—a taint that might haunt young Maxen for the rest of his life."

Alaric had looked up in horror as Llion spoke, his eyes wide.

"But, that isn't true—"

"Of course it isn't true," Llion replied. "But many believe that it is. Remember the grey mare, lad. They would say, 'Oh, Maxen of Coldoire. He let a filthy Deryni lay hands on him, to spare him pain. Do not trust him, because a godless Deryni sorcerer has corrupted him. The devil has besmirched his soul.' That is what some would say."

Llion had not raised his voice, but his tone cut like a lash, underlining ugly words that both of them had heard all too often. Alaric flinched as if struck by physical blows, and buried his face in his folded arms atop his knees. After a moment, Llion realized that the taut shoulders were shaking in silent sobs. Sighing, he moved quietly to sit beside the boy, enfolding the taut shoulders and holding him close until the sobbing finally ebbed.

"Alaric, you did nothing wrong," Llion said at last. "You must learn better discretion, but your heart is true. With time, they will forget—those who even understood what you offered. And in another fortnight, we shall be away from here, at least for a time."

They did not go downstairs for supper that night; and later, when Kenneth and the king returned, Llion told the boy's father about the incident, and all of them resolved to be more careful in the future.

T HE final days of Advent approached at last, and with them all the preparations for the great feasts of Christmas and Epiphany. Late Advent also brought a reunion of Alaric with his beloved cousin Duncan, who arrived a week before Christmas with his parents, his elder brother, and an escort of bordermen from the highlands of Cassan, colorful and exotic in their tartans of green and black and white.

The first night of their arrival, ducking out early from the feast to welcome the new Duke of Cassan and his family, the two boys betook themselves to Alaric's room, in the apartments he shared with his father and Llion, where they could be assured of privacy to catch up on all that had transpired during their separation. First, of course, was the very disturbing interview with Duke Richard, warning him not to use his powers openly, which went double for Duncan.

"You can block pain?" Duncan whispered, wide-eyed.

Alaric nodded slowly. "I think I started on animals, and then I did it for Llion, when his horse bit him."

"A horse *bit* Llion?" Duncan repeated, wide-eyed.

"Well, it was one of the stable horses, not any of our regular mounts—and I did distract him."

"Can you show me?" Duncan wanted to know.

"Not here, not now," Alaric replied. "After Twelfth Night, when I go back to Culdi with you. It isn't safe here."

Duncan accepted the decision with good grace. "That's probably a good idea. Maybe Mama can help, too."

"I'm hoping she can."

Alaric's report of beginning to Truth-Read was also relegated to another day and time, before they shifted to the less dangerous topic of pages' training at court, and identifying friend and foe among the other pages and squires, and Alaric's apparent aptitude for military tactics.

"You really tried to read Orkény in the original?" Duncan asked disbelievingly, when Alaric had told him how he came to receive special tutorials with Duke Richard.

"Well, how was I to know it had been translated?" Alaric countered. "I found the Torenthi version when I was rummaging around in the royal library, and the king had already said that I could borrow anything I liked. Aunt Delphine's tutoring proved useful, though. I was able to puzzle out the most important points well enough to impress Duke Richard."

"Which is no easy feat, from all that I've heard," Duncan replied. "You must tell me all about it."

In the coming days, Alaric would do precisely that, but mostly, since regular pages' and squires' training had been suspended for the Christmas interval—other than Duke Richard's continued tutelage of his new protégé—the two played like the boys they were, haunting the stables and the castle kitchens, exploring the vast corridors of Rhemuth Castle, and secretly observing life at court.

On the day after Christmas, having heard Christmas Mass in the chapel royal on the feast day itself, they accompanied their fathers in the traditional procession that marked St. Stephen's Day, when the king and his family rode down to the cathedral in their finery and crowns. There, after a Mass in honor of the first Christian martyr, St. Stephen, it was the custom of the king to hear informal petitions on the cathedral steps while the queen and her ladies distributed largesse to the city's poor. On this occasion, while the new Duchess Vera attended on the dowager queen and the king's two sisters, assisting in the distribution of alms, the boys served among the pages helping to carry the parcels of food and clothing.

Kenneth and Jared attended as part of the king's entourage, though it was Brion himself, assisted by his uncle, who actually received the petitioners. As Kenneth and Jared observed from the sidelines, Kenneth found himself reminiscing about another St. Stephen's Day, now nearly a decade past, when, with the late king's permission, he had asked for the hand of Alaric's mother.

"I'll never know where I found the courage to actually ask her," he told Jared quietly, as they watched a young widow present a petition to the king and bask in his undivided attention. "Granted, I knew that Donal desired the match. I was a safe pair of hands, and I was aware that he had already informed Alyce of his wishes, so I knew she wouldn't turn me down. But I'd never dared to hope that our marriage would go so far beyond what one usually expects of an arranged marriage. She made me feel like a young man again, Jared."

"I know you miss her," Jared said quietly.

"Every day." Kenneth allowed himself a heavy sigh, then braced himself with a smile. "And lately, with her gone, I've been feeling like an *old* man—not that there's anything I can do about that. At least she left me with a son." He jutted his chin at Alaric, who was handing a bundle to a boy about his age, in tattered clothes and with rags wrapped around his feet. "He'll be a fine man, won't he?"

"Of course. And you have a beautiful daughter, too—and beautiful grown daughters."

"I do," Kenneth said softly. "I only hope I live to see all of them grown. I *am* getting old, Jared."

"Nonsense."

"No, I'm fifty-three years old, and I haven't stopped since I came of age. I've served three Haldanes, and hope to serve at least one more. But I don't like the feel of this latest Mearan venture."

Jared looked out over the cathedral steps again, at their sons attending on the queen. "From what I've heard, it isn't apt to become a full-blown military campaign," he said softly. "I was picking up rumors as we rode down from Cassan. Princess Aude could hang on for months, maybe years. And so long as she does, she won't let Caitrin marry, and the Mearan succession stops with her father."

"Aude has a grandson, Princess Onora's boy."

"Young Judhael is destined for the Church, quite possibly a bishopric. He's been in a seminary for several years."

"Princes have left seminaries before. Cinhil did."

"True enough. But Caitrin is the one with fire in her belly. However, if she doesn't marry—and she *is* getting on in years—there will be no fiery candidate for her to promote."

Kenneth stretched in the weak December sun, allowing himself a heavy sigh. "Somehow you manage to reassure me." He saw the king rising, and shifted his attention to the squires starting to bring up the horses. "It looks like we're done here. I don't know about you, but I'm looking forward to a hot meal when we get back. You cannot fault the Haldanes for their charity, but I have often wondered why they chose Saint Stephen's Day to exercise it. It's always one of the coldest days of the year."

Chapter 18

". . . Lo, I am come to great estate . . ."
—ECCLESIASTES 1:16

KENNETH spent the next week briefing Jared on the plans for a Mearan visitation and listening while the new duke shared his observations with the king. In addition, the king was busy working with Richard and the chancellor on plans for Twelfth Night court, the most important administrative date in the court calendar.

Unlike many a Twelfth Night in the past, that of 1100 dawned clear and not too cold, enabling many visitors from outlying regions of the kingdom to make the trip to the capital. It was the first of a new century and the first since the king's own knighting. The mood was festive in the great hall of Rhemuth as the court assembled and noon approached, but one of the attendees spelled potential trouble for the Morgans, father and son.

It had occurred to Kenneth that Bishop de Nore might make an appearance, since his nephew was being promoted to squire. Sure enough, de Nore was there among the attendees with his sister and her family, hard to miss in his purple cassock and purple skullcap and great purple cloak. Not on the dais, where the archbishops would sit, but prominent enough by his mere presence, attended by a chaplain and two dour, black-clad household knights.

Llion spotted them just before court was to begin, and came to warn Kenneth and Alaric, who were waiting at the rear of the hall with Jared and his family, since the king had decided that the ceremony of Jared's reception as Duke of Cassan should take precedence over the rest of the court's

business. Kenneth was attired in the crimson and white of Lendour, with
Lendour's coronet on his brow, and bore the ducal coronets of Cassan on
a cushion of azure silk, ready to come forward at the king's command.
Alaric stood at his side with the lesser coronet of Kierney on a similar
cushion, and wore a surcoat of the Corwyn duchy to which he was heir.

"I suppose he does have a legitimate reason to be here," Kenneth said
sourly, not looking in the direction of the supposed man of God who
seemed to serve quite a different God from that revered by Kenneth and
his son.

Llion snorted. "Yes, to taunt you and the boy," he muttered. "Do you
think the king is aware that he's here?"

"I'm sure someone will have told him," Kenneth replied. "Jiri or
Tiarnán will have seen him, or even Duke Richard. But there's little that
de Nore can do in the full sight of the court, with the king present."

"So we hope," Llion muttered.

Kenneth gave a grimace, and Alaric controlled the urge to crane his
neck for a look at his nemesis, but Kenneth shook his head minutely.

"Do not let him intimidate you," he said quietly. "Stay focused. And
Llion, I want you to circulate into their general vicinity. Make certain
that de Nore sees you. Hopefully, that will discourage anyone from getting carried away by an excess of zeal."

At that moment, the chamberlain thumped the foot of his staff on the
oak floor to call the assembly to order. As Llion headed off in the direction of the de Nores, the crimson-clad dowager queen and her daughters
entered the hall from behind the dais, attended by several ladies-in-waiting
and a few pages. A second thump as the waiting courtiers settled themselves, and then the herald's cry:

"Pray attend His Majesty, Brion Donal Cinhil Urien Haldane, King
of Gwynedd, Prince of Meara, and Lord of the Purple March."

At this declaration, the king himself entered the hall from the side,
preceded by Duke Richard bearing the sword of state and accompanied
by the twelve-year-old Prince Nigel, who was currently Brion's heir presumptive. As was customary at important formal courts, Brion wore Haldane crimson and gold, with the Haldane lion *rampant guardant* bold
upon the chest of his robe and the snow-white leather of a knight's belt

circling his waist. A crimson mantle lined with silver fox was fixed to his shoulders, and the state crown of intertwined leaves and crosses confined the sable hair, which fell loose to his shoulders. Three of the king's gentlemen attended him, taking places behind and around the throne: Jiri Redfearn and Tiarnán MacRae, who were legacies from the old king's reign, and Jamyl Arilan, one of the king's younger boon companions.

Gwynedd's two archbishops followed behind the king and his brother—Desmond of Rhemuth and Paul of Valoret—coped and mitered in festive white and gold, pausing before their chairs of state set to the right of the dais, where the latter gave the assembled company his blessing before all took their seats. First on the agenda, before the expected knightings, and the taking of new squires and pages, came the official recognition of the new Duke of Cassan.

Bare-headed and arrayed in the blue and silver of Cassan, with the sleeping lion and roses upon his chest, Jared stood in the midst of his tartan-clad bordermen, flanked by his wife and his elder son. Duncan, his younger son, bore the sheathed ducal sword across his palms, waiting with Kenneth and Alaric.

The herald glanced at the king and, at his nod, turned his attention to the party waiting at the back of the hall—and at Jared's nod, drew himself up to rap with his staff on the great hall floor.

"Your Majesty, the late Duke of Cassan having passed into the company of his ancestors, his eldest son and heir, the high and mighty Jared Douglas McLain Earl of Kierney, now become chief of all the McLains, makes bold to present himself and his house before the throne of Gwynedd, that he may be recognized in his estate and enter into your homage for the lands and honors of Cassan."

"Let him approach," the king replied with an eager smile.

The ducal party moved slowly forward, led by Sir Tesselin of Harkness carrying the banner of Cassan. The Cassani bordermen followed directly behind him, sweeping apart to line a wide aisle through the center of the hall, down which Jared, his lady, and his two sons slowly moved, Duncan leading with his father's sword, to halt half a dozen paces from the stair, where all of them made their reverences.

"Your Majesty," Jared said, taking another step forward with another, lesser bow, "I regret to inform you of the passing of my father, the high and mighty prince Andrew Tairchell McLain Duke of Cassan, and request that you recognize me as his successor and permit me to enter into your homage for the lands now accruing to me. In token thereto, I surrender up my sword."

Rising, the king lifted his hand in summons for Jared to approach. Bowing again, Jared took his sword from Duncan's hands and ascended the dais steps to kneel at the king's feet and offer up the sword across his palms. As Brion received the sword, passing it into Prince Nigel's keeping, Jared lifted his joined hands in the ancient gesture of homage and fealty, waiting until the king's hands had encircled his own before speaking.

"I, Jared Douglas McLain, do enter your homage and become your liege man for Cassan and Kierney. Faith and truth will I bear unto you and your lawful successors in all things, so help me God."

"And I receive your homage most gladly, Jared Douglas McLain," Brion replied, "recognizing you as Duke of Cassan and Earl of Kierney, and I pledge you my loyalty and protection for so long as you keep faith with me and my house."

With that, the king released Jared's joined hands and held his open palm out to Prince Nigel, who set a heavy gold signet in his hand. This Brion slid onto Jared's left forefinger.

"Receive this ring as a seal of fidelity to the oath you have sworn, and as a symbol of your authority."

Gesturing for Kenneth to bring forward the ducal coronets, he took the one intended for Jared and placed it on his brow.

"Receive this princely coronet as a mark of my esteem and trust, and as a symbol of your rank," he said, turning then to take back Jared's sword from his brother Nigel and lay it across Jared's hands.

"And finally, as a sign of my charge to defend the lands I have entrusted to you, I return your sword."

"All these charges I shall respect and keep in honor, my Liege," Jared said, then kissed the cross-hilt before slipping the sword into its hangers at his waist.

He kissed the royal hand, then rose to turn and beckon Vera forward. Taking up the smaller ducal coronet, he set it on his wife's tawny hair, kissed her on both cheeks, then beckoned for Kevin to join them. Alaric followed with Kevin's coronet, wide-eyed and proud to be part of this historic occasion.

"Sire," Jared said, lifting a hand toward his elder son, "I present my son and heir, Kevin Douglas McLain, and ask that you grant him the courtesy title of Earl of Kierney, to hold that style and title until he comes of age, and then to hold it in truth, eventually to succeed me."

"I am pleased to grant your request," the king said. "Young Kevin, kneel and swear fealty to your father."

Straight-backed and solemn, Kevin came to kneel before his father and offered up his joined hands, which Jared enclosed in his. The eleven-year-old's voice was steady as he made his oath.

"I, Kevin Douglas McLain, do become your liege man of life and limb and earthly worship. Faith and truth will I bear unto you, to live and to die, against all manner of folk, so help me God."

"And I, for my part, will be a faithful liege to you, Kevin Douglas McLain, giving justice and protection so long as you keep faith with me, so help me God."

Jared reached across, then, to take the coronet that Alaric offered, placing it on his son's head and then raising him up to kiss him on both cheeks.

"Congratulations, son. Now the *real* work begins!"

"I will not fail you, my lord," Kevin replied, eyes shining.

There followed the more usual activities of a Haldane Twelfth Night court, for which Alaric, Duncan, and Kevin retired from the dais to rejoin Tesselin and the Cassani men. Duchess Vera was invited to sit with the queen and her ladies.

First came the new pages to be enrolled for pages' training: five wide-eyed seven- and eight-year-olds in clean white tunics and black britches and boots, each to kneel before the king, state his name, and make his promise of loyalty before receiving the scarlet page's tabard that would mark him for the next half-dozen years as a Haldane page. Kenneth had joined the king on the dais, so Alaric watched with Duncan and Kevin, dreaming of the day when he, too, might wear the king's livery—though now he knew, from hard experience, that a page's life was about far more than a smart surcoat.

Next up were the pages being promoted to squire. Alaric found himself standing on his tiptoes to see past Llion, grinning ear to ear as Paget Sullivan came forward with his father to make his pledge of fidelity to the king, then allowed his father to buckle on the blued-steel spurs of a squire. Alaric could imagine his friend's pride as he received his squire's dagger from the king's own hands and kissed the blade in salute.

When Cornelius Seaton likewise had been invested, along with a new boy from Howicce, the queen came forward to bid all three boys exchange their pages' tabards for the more elegant scarlet tunics of a Haldane squire, with the king's cipher embroidered on the left breast. Paget was beaming as he adjusted its folds and cinched it with the plain red leather belt that squires were allowed. The tunics were for more formal occasions and court functions; at other times, a hip-length crimson vest sufficed, over the same white tunic that the pages wore, but even the crimson vests bore the king's cipher: a privilege coveted by all the boys in training. The fathers of the boys looked on in pride as the king gave a final admonition to the newly liveried squires.

Sir Evan Sullivan looked appropriately proud, as did all the fathers. Sir Errol Seaton appeared to be gloating, and Bishop de Nore was not far away, accompanying father and son as they melted back into the crowd. He cast a contemptuous glance at Alaric as he followed his brother-in-law and the new Seaton squire back to his sister.

"That should be the worst of it," Llion murmured close beside Alaric's ear.

Alaric said nothing, only ducking his head in agreement.

The knightings came last, with only three young men slated to receive the accolade on this day, for a number of candidates had elected to be knighted with the king, the previous summer, even if a bit early. First to be called forward was Claud de Saeva, son of the king's castellan, Sir Robert. Claud had grown up in the castle, training from early childhood with the royal household, so he was well qualified for the honor. Godwin Godreddson was the second son of Captain Godredd Colbertson, an officer of the Marley heavy cavalry, and esteemed for his tactical sense, as Alaric had discovered when called to the king's withdrawing chamber to explain Orkény's battle tactics.

The third and final young man slated for the accolade was Innis de Pirek—or Innis Pirek-Haldane, as was more technically correct, for his family was descended from a distant Haldane cousin, though young Innis had elected to put aside that part of his name, lest he be accused of curry-ing special privileges in the Haldane court. His elder brother, knighted several years before, still used the name—Sir Michael Pirek-Haldane—and their father, Sir Quentin Pirek-Haldane, was the Earl of Carthane. Earl Quentin had made the long ride to Rhemuth for his younger son's knighting, but he did not look well. He leaned heavily on his elder son's arm as they followed Innis and the Carthane banner forward. A squire in the colors of Carthane carried the sword intended for the candidate, with the straps of the golden spurs looped over the quillons.

"Who presents this candidate?" Brion asked, as the party drew up before the dais.

"I do, my Liege," Earl Quentin said steadily, though he was weaving a little on his feet. "This is my beloved son, Innis de Pirek, as he prefers to be called, and I ask that you grant him the accolade of knighthood."

"I am happy to grant your request, my lord," Brion said easily. The Haldane sword was cradled in his left arm, with the tip extending over his left shoulder, and he nodded to the earl's elder son.

"Sir Michael, if you would be so good as to invest your brother with his spurs. And perhaps one of our new squires might bring the earl a stool?"

Instantly Paget Sullivan scrambled to fetch a stool for the Earl of Car-thane, setting his hands under the older man's elbow to help him ease onto the seat and then staying close when Earl Quentin seemed a little light-headed. Both of them watched avidly as Sir Michael knelt to buckle the spurs on his brother's heels.

"I wish Earl Quentin to know how much I esteem his son's abilities," Brion said easily, scanning his audience while Michael worked on the spurs. "Young Innis has demonstrated an admirable tactical instinct in the past few months, and I am minded to take him with me on an exercise in the spring. I doubt he shall see any heavy action, but the experience will be good for him. Thank you, Sir Michael," he said, as Michael finished with the spurs and rose. "Innis?"

As he gestured toward his feet, young Innis de Pirek mounted the dais steps to kneel before him and Brion shifted the sword into his right hand, raising the blade above the candidate's head.

"Innis de Pirek-Haldane, son of Quentin, in the name of the Father"— the sword descended to touch the candidate's right shoulder—"and of the Son"—the blade arched to the left shoulder—"and of the Holy Spirit"— the blade lifted to touch briefly on the crown of Innis's head—"be thou a good and faithful knight."

With a deft flick of his wrist, Brion raised the sword to kiss the holy relic in the pommel, then reversed it smartly and passed it to Duke Richard, hilt first, before extending his hand to Innis.

"Arise, Sir Innis de Pirek, and be invested with the other symbols of your new rank."

Sir Innis rose, beaming as he was directed to one side to allow the queen and the two princesses to gird him with the white belt. While they did so, Alaric noticed that the new knight's father was weaving on his stool.

"Llion?" he whispered, jutting his chin at the earl as Llion glanced down.

Llion went to the earl immediately, crouching at his side to ask whether he was all right. Young Paget looked worried; Michael, the earl's son, had gone forward to present his brother with the sword. Innis was kneeling now before the king, setting his hands between those of his sovereign.

"I, Innis de Pirek, do become your liege man of life and limb," Innis was saying.

"My lord," Llion whispered to Earl Quentin, trying not to make a scene, "you are not well! Let me take you to a place where you can lie down."

"No!" the earl whispered fiercely. "I will hear my king make his oath to my son!"

"But, sir—"

"*No!*"

"And I, for my part, will be a faithful liege to you, Innis de Pirek, giving justice and protection"—

The earl had been clinging hard to Llion's shoulder as he strained to hear the king's return oath, but Llion felt the hard grip loosen as the king spoke the final words, "so help me God." He sensed the exact instant in which the old man became a dead weight in his arms, as the spent body relaxed against his, and he deftly caught the coronet before it could fall to the floor, looking up in sorrow as Michael and then Innis turned and saw them.

"No! God, no!" Innis cried, dashing back to his father to fling his arms around him and hug him close, Michael following to hover close above them, looking stunned. The king, too, came down off the dais, concern in his eyes, followed by the diminutive Archbishop Paul, who removed his miter as he came and handed it off to a courtier before sinking to his knees to pray for the dead man's soul.

"I felt him pass, Sire," Llion said softly, drawing back to let the earl's two sons, descendants of Haldane kings, tenderly cradle their father in their arms. "I would guess that it was his heart. But he was determined to see you knighted, Sir Innis."

"He had been ill for some months," Michael said dully, "but he insisted on making the journey from Carthane. I am his heir, and I know he loved me, but Innis was always the favorite." He set a heavy hand on his brother's shoulder, shaking his head. "But at least he got his final wish, Innis: to see you knighted."

"Yes, and he would wish to see you confirmed at once," Innis said softly, tears in his eyes as he then looked up at the king. "Sire, my brother is now become Earl of Carthane. Is it possible to—acknowledge him right away, in our father's presence?"

The king glanced uncertainly at his uncle, but the older man only nodded slowly. "It can be done," he murmured. Coming down from the dais, he took off his fur-lined mantle and shook it out before spreading it on the floor beside the dead earl. "Let us have a few more mantles, please," he added to the watching court, even as the king himself was removing his and adding it to Richard's.

Several more mantles followed the royal ones, many hands helping to shift the old man's limp body onto this makeshift couch, and even young Alaric took off his small mantle of Corwyn green and rolled it into a pillow for Sir Innis's dead father. The king gave him a wan smile as he accepted the offering and tucked it under Sir Quentin's neck. Archbishop Paul took advantage of the lull in activity to come closer to the deceased, kneeling to anoint him with oil as was proper, then signing the body and himself with the sign of their faith before withdrawing.

Meanwhile, Sir Innis took off the sword he had just received and laid it in his father's hands like a cross, and Michael retrieved the signet ring from the earl's dead hand, passing it to his brother. Seeing the coronet still in Llion's hands, the king signed for him to bring it as he returned to the dais and took his place before the throne, then beckoned for the new Earl of Carthane to approach. Sir Michael handed off his own sword to his brother, then came to kneel before the king, his brother standing behind him with the sword across his hands. The shocked queen and the two princesses had moved closer to witness the event about to unfold.

"We shall follow the same general form that we used for Duke Jared," the king said to Sir Michael in a low voice. "You may begin when you are ready, by informing me of the earl's passing."

Michael managed a curt nod, bowing his head briefly, then boldly lifted his eyes to those of the king.

"Sire, I regret to inform you of the passing of my father, Quentin Pirek-Haldane Earl of Carthane, in the hour just past, and request that you recognize me as his successor and permit me to enter into your homage for the lands now accruing to me. In token thereto, I surrender up my sword."

Turning to retrieve his sword from his brother, Sir Michael offered it to the king across his two palms, and Brion duly received it and passed it into Duke Richard's keeping. As Michael then offered up his joined hands, Brion clasped them between his own before nodding for the new earl to continue.

"I, Michael Pirek-Haldane Earl of Carthane, do enter your homage and become your liege man for Carthane. Faith and truth will I bear unto you and your lawful successors in all things, so help me God."

"And I receive your homage most gladly, Michael Pirek-Haldane," Brion replied gravely, "though I receive your news with a heavy heart. I acknowledge you as Earl of Carthane, and pledge you my loyalty and protection for so long as you keep faith with me and my house."

With that, the king released the earl's joined hands and, with only a flick of a glance toward Sir Innis, opened one hand to receive the signet ring that lately had adorned the hand of the old earl.

"Michael Earl of Carthane, receive this ring as a seal of fidelity to the oath you have sworn, and as a symbol of your authority," he said, slipping it onto Michael's left forefinger. "Receive, also, this coronet of your new rank, as a mark of my esteem and trust," he went on, taking the coronet from Llion and setting it on Michael's brow.

"And finally, as a sign of my charge to defend the lands I have entrusted to you, I return your sword to you." He received the sword from Duke Richard and laid it across Michael's hands. Michael kissed the crossing of hilt and blade and then thrust it into the hangers on his belt.

"All these charges I shall respect and keep in honor, my Liege," Michael said steadily. "And now, with your permission, I beg leave to attend to my dead father, and pray that you will not long allow this sadness of mine to intrude upon the festivities of this house. There is a time for everything under heaven, and my father's time is now with the angels."

"Rise and go with God, Earl of Carthane," the king said quietly, extending his right hand to the earl and raising him up to bestow a fierce embrace.

In answer, the earl bent to seize the royal hand and kiss it, then turned with tears in his eyes to join his brother and the men of Carthane who were gently shifting the old earl's body onto a litter to take it from the hall. Silence followed the sad cortege as they made their way out, only slowly giving way to the murmur of comment when the doors had closed behind them.

In light of these developments, Jared decided to delay taking Duncan and Alaric as pages that day. The feast that followed court likewise was subdued.

Chapter 19

*"If they obey and serve him, they shall spend their
days in prosperity . . ."*
—JOB 36:11

T HE mild weather ushering in the new millennium did not last. A
series of winter storms that swept in from the north and west left
the mountain passes blocked and even the river roads all but im-
passable, well into February.

Accordingly, little further news of Meara arrived in Rhemuth for
more than a month. Jamyl Arilan might have provided the king with
more recent information, gleaned from his access to the Camberian
Council, but he dared not even hint of such knowledge, lest he compromise his true identity. However, he did contrive to keep the Council
apprised of the king's reaction as further Mearan news at last began to
trickle in to Rhemuth; the Council, in turn, gave Jamyl guidance on how
to advise the king if he did, indeed, decide on the Mearan venture.

"We've finally had word that the Mearan marriage *did* take place,"
Oisín informed Jamyl late one February night, as the latter slipped into his
place at the great ivory table in the Council's meeting chamber. It was just
the two of them tonight, and Oisín looked tired in the wan light of the
great crystal above their heads. "The weather has been atrocious, even
over on the coast, but Morian managed to pick up some information."

Jamyl sat back with a sigh, shaking his head. "So she went and married Delaney. Brion will be livid when he hears."

"Just make certain he doesn't hear it from you," Oisín retorted. At
Jamyl's withering glance, he shrugged and allowed himself an ironic

smile. "I'm not questioning your competence, Jamyl, God knows. But you can't deny that it will be difficult not to let on, while you wait for more usual confirmation." He glanced briefly aside, then gave Jamyl a nod. "I think that's all I can tell you for now. Has anything changed regarding the king's plans?"

Jamyl shook his head. "No, there *will* be a progress into Meara, regardless of what Caitrin does right now. However, I expect that Brion will become a bit more focused, once he learns of the marriage."

"That's likely so," Oisín agreed. Gathering his resolve he rose. "Well enough, then. You'd best get back before you're missed. Let us know when word of the marriage reaches Rhemuth—and we'll hope that Caitrin does nothing too rash."

"And Brion," Jamyl replied with a grimace.

T HE news, when it finally reached Rhemuth early in March, arrived in the hands of Sir Caspar Talbot, with an official missive from his father, the Mearan royal governor. The young knight found the king and Jamyl sparring in the castle hall with blunted swords, along with nearly a dozen other knights intent on keeping their skills honed through the winter. Kenneth had partnered up with Jared, who was providing him with a serious workout. Duke Richard had assembled his squires to observe the adults at practice, giving them a running commentary. Alaric and Duncan watched avidly from a vantage point in one of the window embrasures.

"Uh-oh, here comes trouble," Alaric murmured aside to Duncan, as he spotted Sir Caspar, making his way along the sidelines of the hall. "I don't recognize the man, but that's the Mearan governor's badge on his sleeve—and he does *not* look happy."

Richard, too, had seen the new arrival, and immediately broke off his commentary to head toward Sir Caspar, at the same time shouting "Hold!" and raising both arms in visual signal to underline his shout.

All fighting immediately ceased, and the king pushed his leather practice helm back on his head to look at Richard in question, then noticed the newcomer approaching.

"Ill news from Meara, Sire," Sir Caspar announced, holding up a sealed missive. "Aude is dead, and Caitrin of Meara has declared her intention to marry the Earl of Somerdale."

Scowling, Brion handed off his practice sword and helmet to a squire and held out a hand for the letter, cracking its seal with a grimace. His jaw tightened as he skimmed the text. Then:

"Crown council, in my withdrawing room, now!"

Those thus summoned immediately set aside practice equipment and streamed after the king as he stalked off in the direction of the withdrawing room. At Richard's gesture, Prince Nigel also scurried after with the king's real sword, put aside before beginning practice. Kenneth and Jared exchanged glances as they, too, followed the king, close behind Duke Richard. As they entered the room and slid into their customary seats, Brion had already taken his place at the head of the table, and was drumming his fingertips on one chair arm.

"Well, gentlemen, it appears that our spring progress into Meara will, indeed, be more in the nature of a visitation and fact-finding mission," the king said, eyeing all of them as they settled around him. "If we are very fortunate, Caitrin will be content merely to marry, and will prove barren."

"May we have particulars, Sire?" Jiri Redfearn asked.

Brion took the sheathed sword that his younger brother handed him and thumped it onto the table in front of him. "You may have such particulars as I have," he said, passing the letter to Jared, who shared it with Kenneth as the king went on. "Apparently Aude of Meara passed away at Laas, just at the turning of the year; Lucien Talbot isn't sure precisely when. She must have had some inkling that she was dying, because Judhael came up from the Connait to be with her. By Twelfth Night, they had buried her with their Quinnell ancestors, and Judhael had convened a shadow court at Laas, whereupon Caitrin announced her intention to marry the Earl of Somerdale, Derek Delaney."

"Delaney," Tiarnán murmured. "Wasn't she betrothed to another Delaney, some years back?"

"Aye, Francis Delaney," Kenneth said. "There was never any official betrothal, but it matters little. He was captured and executed during the 1089 rebellion."

"He left a son, as I recall—just a lad," Jared said.

Jiri Redfearn nodded. "Aye, another Francis. They say that Derek adopted the boy, and treats him like a son. And Caitrin apparently dotes on him as well, like the son she has not had."

"Well, he is *not* her son," Richard said irritably, "and it behooves us to ensure that she does not have one of her own—or daughters, either. In Meara, the women are almost more dangerous than the men!"

The comment elicited a medley of snorts and ironic laughter, but it was no more than the truth. Mearan princesses had been the death of far too many in the past century.

"So, what is it that you propose to do, Sire?" Tiarnán finally asked. "She has announced her intention to marry, which almost certainly means that she intends to breed more Mearan pretenders, and eventually to take up her father's cause and make her own bid for an independent Meara."

"That is what I hope to discourage," Brion replied. "I am disinclined to hound anyone to death, as my father was forced to do, but I won't have her undermining the political stability in Meara, such as it is."

Jared snorted. "Meara hasn't been stable for years!"

"No, and it will never *be* stable, so long as soi-disant Mearan pretenders keep periodically reviving the old claims," Richard said irritably. "I confess that I was never able to figure out why Donal didn't just sweep through and clean out the last of them, once and for all."

"Perhaps because they are also our blood, Uncle," Brion said mildly. He leaned back in his chair, considering. "I think, perhaps, that it's time to pay a visit to my very troublesome cousin Caitrin."

*A*ND once you locate her, what then?" Queen Richeldis said to her son, when she summoned him to her quarters later that evening. "Did it occur to you that she might simply wish to experience the domestic pleasures permitted other women? To marry and bear children of her own?"

"Children who might well threaten my throne one day," Brion replied. "Did you not see enough of that when Father was alive, with his ceaseless forays into Meara to put down one rebellion or another?"

Richeldis looked away, her face bleak, shuttered. "He and his father did terrible things in Meara, terrible things!"

"Was it terrible to hunt down rebellious subjects who threatened the throne?" Brion countered. "I don't understand these royal Mearan women. They simply will not give up. My grandmother Roisían was the senior heir to Meara, as declared by her own father, who was the last independent Prince of Meara—and I am *her* senior heir. Why will they not accept that?"

"Do you think that barging back into Meara to thwart your cousin's marriage plans will make them accept it?"

"Mother! I am Prince of Meara. If I enter my own lands, I do not *barge*."

Richeldis gave a self-righteous sniff. "Many Mearans would beg to differ."

Rolling his eyes, Brion got to his feet. "It's clear we shall not agree on this. However, I do intend to make a progress into *my* principality, and to seek out my cousin. We shall be leaving within a few weeks, as soon as the weather allows."

I N fact, various contingents of the king's intended party departed at varying times throughout the next fortnight, for there were logistic arrangements yet to be worked out for the expedition. Jared and his sons would be among the first to depart, for he had been charged with assembling a suitable escort of Cassani borderers to ride with the king from Culdi. Kenneth, his son, and a pair of aides would travel part of the way with Jared, for Bronwyn must be fetched from Morganhall, to also take up residence at Culdi.

But for the newly acknowledged Duke Jared, one task yet remained to be performed before they left Rhemuth, in a slight change from his original intention. The day before they were to ride out, Jared asked the king for the use of his withdrawing room, and invited both the king and Duke Richard to join him and Kenneth in witness to an important occasion in the lives of two young family members.

"As you know," Kenneth said to the two Haldanes, "it has long been my intention that Alaric should begin his formal page's training in Jared's household with his cousin, away from the pressure of court." He glanced aside where Jared and Sir Tesselin were shaking out the folds of two child-sized tabards in the blue and white of Cassan. "We would have waited to do this at Culdi, later in the spring, but I knew that Duke Richard would wish to be present."

"What I would have *preferred*," Richard said with a droll drawl, "is that your Alaric would have passed directly into my supervision. He has astonishing potential, but I do understand the—ah—unique circumstances that make it preferable to keep him sheltered a bit longer," he added, with a good-natured nod to Kenneth. "Boys can be nasty brutes at his age. And the border training will do him good for a few years."

"It will," Brion agreed. "And I'm sure the lads would like to show off their pages' tabards here, before they leave," he added, grinning. "I well remember when I first received mine. I had been begging for it for months."

Richard snorted. "He gave his father and me no peace. But he was a very good page and squire," he said fondly, "and he's turned out to be quite a passable knight, and a first-rate king."

Brion chuckled and shook his head. "We'll see if you feel the same way after I've been to Meara and back." He turned his attention to Jared and clapped his hands. "Jared, are you going to take these lads as pages or not? If you don't do it quickly, my uncle is likely to snatch them right from under your nose."

Jared turned and shot the king a grin, then began gathering his immediate household with a summoning motion, at the same time donning his coronet. Duchess Vera and Kevin had joined him, Vera with the two Cassan tabards over her arm, and Kevin was straightening out two narrow lengths of McLain tartan. Llion and Tesselin had charge of the two incipient pages, who were dressed in clean white tunics with black breeches and boots. In addition, a handful of Jared's bordermen were assembling in the doorway to the chamber, jostling for vantage points from which to witness the ceremony about to take place. As the king and Richard joined the party, along with Kenneth and several of his men, Jared cleared his throat and waited for the room to settle.

"Thank you for coming," he said. "Today marks an important first step in the making of future knights, as I take two new pages into my service. Duncan, please come forward."

Grinning ear to ear, Duncan came to kneel at his father's feet, eyes aglow with excitement as Jared drew his sword and set the point on the floor between them, right hand resting on the pommel.

"Duncan Howard McLain, place your hands on my sword and hear the responsibilities of a page of my house."

Duncan did as he was bidden, setting his two hands on the quillons of the sword as he gazed up at his father with wide-eyed awe.

"Will you promise loyalty and service to me and my house," Jared said, "accepting the discipline and instruction of those set in authority to train you, to learn the ways of a gentleman and future knight?"

Duncan nodded earnestly. "I will, Your Grace, so help me God."

"Then receive the tabard of a page of Cassan," Jared replied, nodding to Vera, who came closer to slip the blue and white tabard over their son's head. Duncan was beaming as his head emerged from the neck opening and his mother helped him straighten it, front and back.

"This will be your livery for when you're on duty," Jared added. "Try to keep it reasonably clean. And when you are not on official duty"—he also took a narrow length of McLain tartan from Kevin's hands—"wear this around your waist, to remind you and all who see you that you serve under the protection of the Chief of the McLains."

This, too, Duncan donned, knotting the length of tartan around his waist under the tabard. When he had finished, he took the right hand his father offered him and rose to be enfolded in a one-armed hug; Jared still held his sword in the other, under the quillons.

"Congratulations, son," Jared murmured, drawing Duncan to his side, to take a place beside his brother Kevin. "Now, let's have young Alaric up here."

At his command, and at Kenneth's added prompting with gentle pressure to his shoulder, Alaric made his way to Jared, sinking to his knees to place his hands on the quillons of Jared's sword.

"Alaric Anthony Morgan," Jared said solemnly, "is it your desire to enter into service as a page of my house?"

"It is, Your Grace," Alaric said steadily, never taking his eyes from Jared's.

"Then, hear the responsibilities with which I charge you," Jared said, "for to be a page is to be at another's beck and call, to come and to go at another's will, that you may learn the ways of a gentleman and future knight. Therefore, will you promise loyalty and service to me and my house, accepting the discipline and instruction of those set in authority to train you?"

Alaric nodded gravely. "I will, Your Grace, so help me God. And as heir to Corwyn and Lendour, I also desire to swear you fealty, saving what duty I owe to my father and to the king."

So saying, he lifted his hands from the quillons of the sword and joined them palm to palm, intent and entreaty in his eyes. Jared was somewhat taken aback by the request, for the boy had not discussed this with him beforehand. With a glance at Kenneth and the king, who moved slightly closer, he crouched down to the boy's level, one hand still poised on the hilt of his sword.

"You are not of an age where that is expected or required, son," he said quietly. "Why do you wish to do it?"

Alaric's gaze never wavered from his. "You know what I am, sir," he said steadily, "and that there are those who wish me ill. My father and the king are about to go into Meara for some months, and I will remain in your household."

"But I, too, am going to Meara," Jared pointed out.

"Yes, sir, but if it is known that I am also under your personal protection, even though you are away, those of your household may be more diligent in guarding my safety."

Considering, Jared cast another glance at Kenneth and the king, then got to his feet, passing his sword to Kevin by the pommel.

"The boy is astute beyond his years, Sire," he said to the king. "If you have no objection, I am minded to grant his request."

Brion nodded over his crossed arms. "I have no objection, and will bear witness to this exchange."

"Thank you, Sire. Tesselin"—he nodded to the young knight, standing with Llion near the doorway from the room—"please ask such others of our household who are present to join us."

At once Tesselin ducked his head outside briefly with a low-voiced order, then moved farther inside to make room for nearly a dozen other knights and men-at-arms who had been congregated there to witness Duncan's reception of his page's tabard.

"Come in, gentlemen, come in," Jared said as they jostled for position. "I wish you to bear witness to another oath today, since some of you will be called upon to uphold it while I am absent in Meara with the king. In addition to my son Duncan, I have just taken young Alaric here as a page to the House of Cassan. He has asked, and the king has agreed, that he might also enter into personal liege fealty to me, since he will be residing in my household while his father and I are with the king."

He held them with his gaze for several seconds, that the import might sink in, then returned his gaze to Alaric, taking the boy's joined hands between his own.

"I am prepared to receive your oath," he said with a nod.

Alaric swallowed visibly, his eyes never leaving Jared's. "I, Alaric Anthony Morgan, heir of Corwyn and Lendour, do become your liege man of life and limb and earthly worship, to serve you in good faith and without deception, saving my allegiance to my father and to our lord the king, so help me God."

"And I receive your oath and fidelity, Alaric Anthony Morgan, heir of Corwyn and Lendour, and I pledge to you the same protection and fidelity that is the right of my own sons. So say I, Jared McLain Duke of Cassan, so help me God."

With that, he raised Alaric up and enveloped him in a bear hug, then pressed him to arm's length and nodded to Lady Vera.

"Right, then. I believe this young man needs a tabard, my lady. And the sash of Clan McLain."

Chuckling in gentle amusement, Vera brought forward the tabard and pulled it over Alaric's head, helping him straighten it, then knelt to tie the sash of McLain tartan around his waist.

"That was a very brave thing you did," she whispered so that only he could hear, "and a very smart thing. I am very proud of you."

So saying, she gave Alaric a hug, then drew Duncan likewise into her embrace and hugged him, too.

"My lord," she said to Jared as she rose, "I thank you for adding two

such courtly pages to our household. I shall make certain that they perform their duties diligently in your absence."

"Their duties *and* their studies," Jared amended with an arch nod.
"And thank you, Sire, for witnessing this ceremony."

Brion inclined his head, smiling. "It was my pleasure."

"And now, all you lot, get on with your preparations," Jared added to
his men, with a shooing motion. "We leave in the morning."

T HAT night, though supper in the king's hall was in nowise out of
the ordinary—simple but hearty fare for those still resident at the
royal court in the winter aftermath of Twelfth Night—both new pages
proudly wore their tabards to serve their fathers at table, and even assisted
with service to the king. In truth, such service mostly required standing in
readiness to perform tasks that were few and simple, but the pair nonetheless basked in the heady awareness that today they had, indeed, passed from
the lowly realm of feckless boys to that of very junior pages to a duke.

This change in circumstances did not go unnoticed by the other
pages, most of them in service to the royal household, but it was sufficiently different from their own status that even the most resentful of the
older boys were too taken aback to decide immediately how this difference might be turned to advantage within their own ranking. By the next
morning, when both boys left Rhemuth with their fathers, it was too late
to devise suitable boyhood torments.

Only Paget Sullivan made the effort to rise early and bid farewell to
his new friend—and was rewarded for his loyalty with custody of the coveted Orkény translation.

"You're *sure*?" Paget breathed, as Alaric gave it into his keeping.

"I told you I would," Alaric replied. "And I told Duke Richard; he
said it was all right. Besides, you'll make much better use of it than I will,
for the next few months."

"Thank you," Paget replied, grinning. "And Godspeed."

Chapter 20

*"Many will entreat the favour of the prince: and every man
is a friend to him that giveth gifts."*
—PROVERBS 19:6

IN the excitement of setting out for new adventures as official members of a ducal household, it is likely that neither of the new Cassani pages realized the timeliness of their departure. Indeed, since both boys rode in the same party as their respective fathers, little would change for either of them, at least for the next few years. Eventually, Alaric knew he would return to court to continue his training—and would have to deal with the bullies and bigotry he was temporarily leaving behind—but Duncan was slated probably to spend his life either in the service of his father and brother or, because he was academically inclined, to take up a life in the Church, as was often the choice of second sons. For the present, however, both looked forward to new experiences.

Because Lady Vera and a maid were among their number, they traveled at a more moderate pace than might have been the case otherwise. Further, the weather worsened only a day out of Rhemuth, so that they were obliged to halt earlier and often. When they reached the turnoff for Morganhall, Kenneth took Xander and two of his men-at-arms and struck off eastward, so that he might retrieve his young daughter and bring her along to join her brother in the ducal household at Culdi.

"But, may I not go along?" Alaric objected, when it became clear that his father intended to leave him behind.

"That is no longer solely up to me," his father replied. "You are page to a duke now, son. I'm sure he wishes to be certain that Llion and Sir

Tesselin have a suitable summer training schedule in place for you and his sons, before he and I head off with the king. I'll only be gone a week or so. You'll see your sister soon."

Quite clearly, the decision brooked no further discussion, so Alaric accepted with good grace, riding on cheerfully in the easy company of Llion and his two McLain cousins. Other than for the intermittent rain, the rest of the ride to Culdi was uneventful, much to the secret disappointment of the boys, though they heard Jared profess himself relieved that no untoward incident had marred their journey.

By the time the Morganhall party rejoined them, a week later, all three boys had settled into daily tutelage with Vera on their reading and ciphering and history, ably assisted by Kenneth's middle daughter, Lady Geill Lithgow—regarded as an aunt, like Zoë, because of her age, though she, too, was a half-sister to Alaric. Geill's husband, Sir Walter, had been in Jared's service for some time, and was delegated to work with Llion, Tesselin, and Jared's seneschal, Lord Deveril, in supervising the martial training of all three boys in their fathers' absence.

The three of them were practicing at the archery butts set up in the castle yard when Kenneth and his party arrived, with Bronwyn perched ahead of her father on his saddlebow. Alaric gave a whoop of delight when he spotted father and sister, and cast down his bow to race to his father's steed. By the time he got there, Kenneth had already handed Bronwyn into the waiting arms of a smiling Sir Walter. Alaric caught his sister in a delighted bear hug as Walter, in turn, eased her to the ground.

"You're here, you're here!" he cried, as Duncan and Kevin also came running to share in the reunion.

T HIS indulgence in domestic harmony would last only a short time. The king arrived a fortnight later, accompanied by a modest personal guard of Haldane lancers and close companions of his immediate household: Jiri Redfearn and Jamyl Arilan. He had left his uncle as regent in Rhemuth, along with Prince Nigel and the Dowager Queen Richeldis.

With Kenneth and Jared now added to the king's party, they took a further week to finalize their plans for the expedition and wait for the weather to break, ending their stay at Culdi with a more formal meal in the castle hall on the night before they were to leave. Kevin proudly served the king at table, ably assisted by Duncan and Alaric. The air was festive, charged with anticipation, with the young king quickly putting all three boys at their ease.

"They could almost be my brothers," he remarked to Kenneth, as they watched Alaric take away a basin and towel after serving both men. "I'm not so very much older than they are."

Kenneth only smiled, well remembering how very nearly Brion and Alaric might have been brothers in fact—though he was not about to tell that to the king.

"I pray that he will always love you like a brother," he replied. "It will make life a bit easier for him."

One final formality remained at Culdi, before sending the king and his party on their way. Early on the morning they were to leave, Vera had arranged for her chaplain, Father Geordan, to celebrate a Mass; and because both Duncan and Alaric had recently turned eight, Geordan and Father Nevan, Jared's battle-surgeon, had been preparing both boys for their First Communion: an important rite of passage for eight-year-olds, and one fondly anticipated by both the boys' fathers. It enabled both Alaric and Duncan to receive this adult sacrament at their fathers' sides, and then to kneel beside them for a final blessing before the adults mounted up to depart.

"They looked quite grown-up in their pages' livery, didn't they?" Jared remarked to Kenneth, as the royal column took shape in the castle yard.

Kenneth smiled as he handed Bronwyn down to Llion. "They did, indeed," he replied. "You take good care, now, poppet," he said to his daughter, "and mind Llion and your Aunt Vera."

"I will, Papa," she called, grinning and waving as Llion carried her back from the pack of milling riders.

It was a dull, soft morning late in April as the royal party rode westward out of Culdi town. Young Caspar Talbot, the Mearan governor's son, had agreed to serve as guide. Sir Jamyl Arilan carried the Haldane banner before them, Jiri Redfearn at his side, and the others followed

after. Duke Jared had provided an escort of twenty fierce Kierney borderers, their green and black tartan muted in the morning mist, and brought,
as his aide, Sir Rhupert MacInnis, a brother of his late first wife, who had
become a frequent companion in recent years. Father Nevan also accompanied them, to serve as battle-surgeon as well as their chaplain. Kenneth
brought Xander of Torrylin as his aide, and also his two Lendouri
armsmen.

In all, they were nearly fifty strong. The children and Duchess Vera
watched them ride out, waving from the battlements above the gatehouse, for the weather looked increasingly uncertain.

T HEY were spared actual rain for the first few days, and made good
time, though they never saw the sun. They spent the first several
nights under canvas, camped in fields along the way, but a deluge on the
third day caused them to seek better shelter. That night and the next,
they huddled in a farmer's barn—mostly empty after the long, hard winter, but at least it was dry, and the king and his immediate companions
were able to find comfortable sleeping space in the hayloft. The days still
were chill and sometimes drizzly, but they made reasonable progress.

The Cùille was running high as they skirted closer along the river,
making the ford at Tandorello difficult and dangerous, but they crossed
without mishap. By dusk they were approaching the modest keep of Trurill, which lay not far short of the Mearan border. Trurill's baron, Sir
Brothen de Paor, received them courteously enough, if a trifle dour as he
eyed the Haldane banner and the several score of well-armed men in his
sovereign's train, but nonetheless, he invited the king and his immediate
companions to sup with him and his family.

"Unfortunately, we canna accommodate *all* your party, Sire," the
baron told them, looking vaguely ill at ease as he ushered the king into
his hall. "Had we known ye were coming . . ."

"It was a decision of the moment," Brion said easily, "but I have no
wish to place an undue burden on your hospitality. With your permission,
my men will make camp in the field outside your walls."

"No, no, Sire, they must at least use the stable yard and barn; there are not so *very* many of them," the baron replied, clearly relieved. "Perhaps some may wish to sleep in the hayloft. But we can provide for you and your officers." The sweep of his hand included Kenneth and Jared and several more of the king's companions. "The fare will be simple, for winter is not long past, and 'twas harsh here in the borders, but we do well enough in Trurill. Pray, allow me to present my sons," he added, as he gestured forward a pair of strapping, dark-eyed young men who had eased within earshot. One wore the white belt of knighthood, but the second did not, though he looked to be of age for the accolade.

"My heir, Sir Baylor, and Brice, my second son," the baron went on, as the pair made respectful bows. "It had been my hope to see Brice knighted this Twelfth Night past, but the harvest was nae sae good. I ha'e three daughters as well, but they and their mother will present themselves later."

The women did, indeed, join the party later, when the company sat down to supper at the modest trestle tables hastily erected in the baron's hall. The king, seated in the place of honor between the baron and his lady, was served by two of the baron's daughters, dark-eyed and buxom and eager to please. The meal was modest but ample, the wine surprisingly good—and taken in moderation by all present.

"The ladies fancy you, Sire," Sir Caspar whispered, in a teasing aside to the king, as the two of them made their way back from a visit to the privies.

Brion gave him a startled look, but Caspar shrugged and allowed himself a tiny smile.

"This is not the royal court, Sire, and notions of propriety are . . . somewhat more flexible here in the borders."

"But surely, no well-bred girl—"

"Sire, remember who you are. Few well-bred border lasses would pass up the opportunity for close congress with a king, and perhaps a chance for the Crown matrimonial—or even a royal by-blow, for that matter. Believe me, Sire, you could have either of those girls in your bed tonight, and likely with her father's blessing. Maybe both of them. The baroness, too, for that matter."

Brion snorted and shook his head, uncertain how much to believe.

"Caspar, you are a bad influence!" he muttered, though he was trying to keep from grinning as he said it. "We'd best return to our hosts, lest you tempt me to unseemly thoughts. Besides, we have a wayward princess to find. I trust you've noticed how the subject has never come up."

They rejoined the low murmur of casual conversation as they resumed their places at table. The baron had seen Brion's cup refilled. As if on cue, the baron's youngest daughter brought out a lute and accompanied her elder sisters in several duets. While the singing was pleasant enough, and the girls were attractive by country reckoning, the king gave them only polite attention, and barely sipped at his wine, for he was impatient to resume conversation.

Shortly thereafter, when the ladies at last retired, Kenneth deftly nudged conversation toward Meara and its politics, for the baron and his kin had been skirting the issue all through dinner.

"Aye, we did hear that the old princess died," Brothen allowed, in answer to Brion's pointed look of question. "I reckon she must have passed around Christmastide—but the news didna reach us here in Trurill until well after the turning of the year. The winter was harsh here, an' the roads nigh impossible, an' we had worries of our own; lost a lot of livestock. But we heard she'd been poorly for the past year, so 'twas no surprise."

"We had heard that her health was failing," Jiri said neutrally. "I believe she had been living with her daughter?"

"Aye, in Cloome, this past se'nyear and more."

"And her husband?" Jamyl asked.

Brothen gave an uneasy snort. "Him? They say old Judhael is no' right in the heid, that he sees almost no one." He arched a shaggy brow. "He doesna call himself prince any longer, ye ken. For a time, he kept his grandson close beside him, but young Judhael is twelve now, an' bookish, an' they say he means to take holy orders."

"That is probably wise," Brion said noncommittally. "Tell me, did the elder Judhael attend his wife's funeral?"

"Och, aye. Both Judhaels did," Brothen said. "An' Caitrin as well. They were at Aude's side when she passed, an' she gave the young lad her blessing—her grandson, he is. After, they buried her at Laas, wi' the rest o' that line. All the old nobility o' Meara came to pay their respects. Gave her a right proper send-off."

"Surely all souls deserve a proper send-off," Father Nevan said quietly.

"Aye, they do," said Baylor, the elder son, tension in his jaw. "And Aude knew her duty, in the end. But Caitrin—they say that no sooner were her ma in the ground than she announced her intention to wed, though she knew Aude had forbidden it, an' that her pa did not approve."

"Indeed," Brion said dryly, with a glance at Kenneth and Jared. "I don't suppose you've heard where she might be now?"

"Married by now, I'll warrant," Brice said under his breath.

"That *is* what she threatened," Jared said, with a lift to one eyebrow. "And who might the lucky bridegroom be?"

Brice looked suddenly sheepish to have spoken out of turn, and in the king's presence, and ducked his head in embarrassment.

"They say 'tis the Earl of Somerdale, Your Grace," he murmured, almost inaudibly.

"And you do not approve?" Brion asked gently.

Brice was tight-lipped as he glanced up at the king. "I have nothing against Derek Somerdale, Sire, but we knew his brother Francis, and I was to have been his page—and *he* was to have married the Lady Caitrin. He was a fine man. . . ."

The king inclined his head, conceding the assessment. "By Mearan lights, I am certain he was. I recall hearing the name, when my father returned from his last campaign into Meara. I was only young then, younger than you—too young to go to war, but—" He glanced at Kenneth. "You rode with my father on that occasion, did you not?"

Kenneth nodded. "Aye, my prince, but I was with him and your uncle, not the men who overtook Sir Francis and his party. As I recall—and remember, this was more than a decade ago—young Delaney stayed back with a handful of his men to create a diversion while his brother took the women to safety.

"In that, of course, they were only partially successful," Kenneth conceded with a shrug. "The Lady Onora was heavily with child—God only knows why she was in the field in that condition. They said she died soon after delivering a daughter, who only outlived her by hours. Onora's husband and Lord Somerdale did manage to get the Lady Caitrin to safety; both are still alive, I believe. Somerdale's brother, of course, and the others who bought them time to escape were executed in the field."

"For which the Lady Caitrin has never forgiven us," Brion said somewhat impatiently, though his tone softened as he added, "And I gather that our hosts also may not approve, especially young Brice." As Brice averted his eyes, Brion sighed heavily and cast an apologetic glance over the three Trurill men.

"Forgive me, gentlemen. It is our generation that will have to resolve this, if Caitrin's marriage is prelude to another bid for my throne. This was all meant to be settled three-quarters of a century ago, when my grandparents married. But I suppose you know that, living here in the borders, so close to the constant possibility of another war."

"Is it war you're planning, Sire?" the baron asked quietly.

Brion shook his head. "Not if I can avoid it—and that may well be up to Caitrin. I had hoped, and I know my father had hoped, that the Mearans eventually would run out of would-be heirs. It is welcome news that young Judhael intends to take holy orders; but if Caitrin has married, and if there are children . . ."

As his voice trailed off and he lifted his cup for a thoughtful sip of wine, Jamyl Arilan glanced appraisingly at young Brice.

"This Derek Delaney, the Earl of Somerdale—have you some personal quarrel with him?"

Brice looked up sharply. "Why do you ask *that*?"

Jamyl shrugged. "No particular reason. It simply seemed that the notion of his marriage to the Lady Caitrin was not to your liking."

"Her mother had forbade *any* marriage," Brothen said sharply, before Brice could answer. "Aude understood."

But their further discussion resolved nothing save to underline the necessity to press on to Ratharkin and discover for themselves what Caitrin intended.

"She cannot *truly* think that the Mearan throne might yet be restored," Jamyl said aside to young Brice, as the wine jug passed again around the table.

"Best pray that she proves barren," Brice replied softly, gazing into his cup. "For if she bears issue, the matter will not die with her." He shrugged. "But that's easy enough for me to say, I suppose. Who listens to an unknighted younger son?"

The comment passed unremarked in the continued conversation of the evening, but later, before they headed off to their beds, Jamyl managed a discreet word in the king's ear.

"It would be an unexpected mark of your favor, in return for their hospitality," Jamyl murmured. "And it might reinforce the loyalty of these Trurill men."

"Aye, it might," Brion agreed, obviously considering—and did, indeed, broach the subject as their hosts were preparing to disperse for the night.

"A word, if you will, my lord baron," he said, detaining Brothen with a light touch to the elbow. "And your sons as well. Brice of Trurill, I like your mettle," he said. "If you're minded to keep vigil tonight, in the company of my chaplain and your father and brother, it would be my pleasure to confer the accolade in the morning, before we ride out."

Brothen's jaw dropped, and both his sons looked stunned.

"You would do that for me, Sire?" Brice breathed.

"I would not offer if I did not mean it. One cannot put a price on loyal retainers along one's borders."

Thus was the deed set in motion: first, an impromptu vigil organized in the small, private chapel adjoining the baron's personal quarters; and then, following early Mass the next morning, a simple ceremony of knighthood, conferred by the king and witnessed by a duke, an earl, and half a dozen other knights from the king's household, as well as the candidate's family. It was a singular honor for a country baron's younger son, and gained the king much favor among the local folk. Baron Brothen gave his own golden spurs for the investiture, and Brice's brother lent his white belt. The proud baroness buckled the belt around her younger son's waist before the new Sir Brice of Trurill knelt to pledge the king his fealty.

"I, Sir Brice de Paor, do become your liege man of life and limb and earthly worship, and faith and truth will I bear unto you, to live and to die . . ."

After, following congratulations all around and the profuse thanks of the baron and his family, king and companions quickly broke their fast before riding out of Trurill.

"I enjoyed that," the king said brightly, full of the exuberance of youth. "I mean to do it more often, when I can. It might have been several years before Baron Brothen could afford to send a second son to court to be knighted."

Kenneth smiled, remembering his own family's sacrifices to send him to court for the accolade. "It was an act of kindness, my prince. And the baron and his kin will remember it, when the keeping of your peace in the borders might sometimes seem too much of a burden."

"Young Brice seemed a decent enough chap," Jamyl agreed. "He clearly counted it a personal tragedy of his young life, to lose Sir Francis Delaney in the last war. For the second son of a border baron, it would have been quite a step up, to enter the service of an earl's brother. Such are the lesser disappointments of war. Pray God, this act of Haldane kindness will help to counter that loss."

CHAPTER 21

"Neglect not the gift that is in thee . . ."
—I TIMOTHY 4:14

IF the king's summer was already turning tedious, Alaric's summer, or at least its beginning, was to become one of the happiest of his young life. Most mornings he and Duncan spent in formal lessons with Lady Vera, absorbed in reading, writing, and numbers, geography and history, a smattering of languages, along with the more practical accomplishments of dancing and court etiquette. Occasionally Kevin joined them for lessons, but more often he spent the mornings with Lord Deveril, the seneschal, and Sir Walter, beginning to learn about the running of Jared's estates.

Sometimes, though always behind closed doors, and never with Kevin present, Vera began to expose them to more esoteric subjects, as his and Duncan's Deryni powers continued to emerge.

They began learning to conjure handfire that summer, though Vera was quick to caution both boys that this must never be done where an outsider might see.

"You especially, Duncan, because it would be an immediate betrayal of your blood."

"Yes, Mama," Duncan breathed, wide-eyed and somber as he balanced a trembling sphere of silvery light on one outstretched palm.

"That's very good. Alaric, can you make your sphere lift into the air?"

Alaric concentrated, focused on his own sphere of greenish fire, and had the satisfaction of watching it slowly float toward the ceiling, though it got dimmer as it rose, then abruptly fizzled out.

"Suppose you try that again," Vera whispered, coming to set a hand on his shoulder. "Hold your focus. Believe it or not, this will become second nature to you, once you've got the hang of it."

The next sphere faded away before reaching the ceiling, but the third one formed, lifted, and hovered for several seconds before Vera squeezed his shoulder in a signal to relax. As the sphere dissipated this time instead of fizzling out, Alaric allowed himself a satisfied grin.

"That's very good. Duncan, why don't you try that?"

Within a week or so, their ability to conjure handfire became more and more reliable, and required less and less effort. Building on that accomplishment, Vera also began teaching them about shields—which both of them had, to varying degrees—and was pleased and somewhat surprised to find that Alaric's were already strong and well developed.

But he did not tell her of Sir Sé's tutelage, sensing that this must be kept private even from his mother's sister—and he was fairly sure that Sé had set certain protections into place behind those shields. Duncan's shields seemed somewhat more rudimentary in the beginning, but developed quickly as Vera began to work with them.

Nor were more active pursuits ignored. Between Llion and Tesselin, all three boys were kept busy with their physical training: drill with sword and lance, archery practice, wrestling and hand-to-hand tactics, riding—all the skills expected of future knights. And because their fathers were away with the king, the boys were mostly relieved of the necessity to serve at table or wait on the knights of Jared's household—for, indeed, there were few in residence, and several other pages and squires to share the work.

But Alaric Morgan was still a boy in his off hours, free to run and play like other privileged boys. (He knew that not all boys were fortunate enough to have fine ponies, and people to care for them, and adults whose sole occupation was to make his life run smoothly.)

He was also pleased to discover that he genuinely liked his younger sister, with whom, until now, he had spent only short stretches of days at a time, during their father's all too infrequent visits to Morganhall and his motherless daughter. Only recently had Bronwyn become mature enough for true interaction with her elder brother.

But they were of kindred blood, even if raised apart during Bronwyn's earliest years, and both delighted in their reunion. At nearly five, Bronwyn was quick and articulate, wise beyond her years, and adored both her brother and her two McLain cousins.

She was smart, too, Alaric quickly discovered. At Morganhall, early studies with her two aunts, alongside her slightly older cousin Clarice, had already given her basic skills in reading and ciphering, and a passionate thirst for knowledge; and Sir Calix Howard, married to her mother's former maid, had made it his personal mission to ensure that both girls rode like limpets, fearless and graceful astride their shaggy mountain ponies. They had even worn boys' clothes at Morganhall, at least for riding, though Vera quickly put an end to that notion once Bronwyn was installed at Culdi.

"That may be fine at Morganhall," she informed her new charge, as they inspected Bronwyn's small wardrobe on the day after she arrived, "but it won't do here, and it certainly wouldn't do at court."

"But, Aunt Vera—" Bronwyn started to protest.

"There is no *but*!" Vera said with an emphatic shake of her head. "Noble ladies wear skirts, even little ladies. You may ride astride, and you may even wear breeches and boots like the boys, but you must wear skirts over them. Child, you are the sister of a future duke!" she added, exasperated at Bronwyn's moue of incipient rebellion. "Don't make that face at me, madam. You must learn to comport yourself like a lady. Your mother learned it, and I learned it, and so shall you!"

It was hardly an auspicious beginning to their relationship, but Bronwyn quickly got over her pout, and was smiling about it by the time she finished telling Alaric and Duncan later that day.

"I know there are rules," she finally conceded, "but I still don't think it's fair! It's *silly* to wear skirts on a pony. I didn't have to wear skirts at Morganhall."

Alaric shrugged. "Well, she's right, this isn't Morganhall, and you *are* a duke's sister—or you will be, once I'm a duke. And she *did* say you could still wear breeches and boots under your skirts, didn't she? Count your blessings."

"I suppose," Bronwyn said petulantly. "I still think it's a silly rule."

"You think *we* don't have to follow silly rules?" Duncan said, grinning. "Come on, let's go to the stable and see the new kittens. If you ask nicely and bat your eyelashes, the head groom will probably let you have one. Kevin says that men can't resist when a lady bats her eyelashes."

"That sounds silly, too," Bronwyn muttered to herself, but she followed cheerfully as the boys took off for the stable, and did, indeed, elicit the promise of a kitten, when they were old enough, so long as Lady Vera approved.

"Do you really think she'll let me have one?" she whispered to Alaric, holding on to his hand as they headed on toward the pony paddock.

He smiled and nodded. "Probably. I've seen mice up in the living quarters, so cats are probably a good idea. You'll need to take care of it, though—and clean up after it, until it learns proper cat manners."

"Oh, I will! I promise!" she said earnestly.

In such wise did the summer progress, as Bronwyn found her stride and became more at ease in the ducal household. The boys adored her—not only Alaric, but Duncan and Kevin as well—and gladly included their feisty new playmate in their adventures, especially as the summer wore on and news came less often from their respective fathers.

S AID fathers, meanwhile, were only then nearing the Mearan border, again caught up in spring thunderstorms that forced them often to seek shelter. After several nights spent again in barns, some of them so decrepit that they pitched their tents inside, several of their party had developed serious coughs and running noses. But this last barn did not bear even considering another night.

"We thank you for your hospitality, good sir," the king said to the farmer, as they prepared to ride on—and bade Father Nevan hand over a small leather pouch of coin. "Here's for your trouble, and for the roof of your barn, and may God grant you a rich harvest in the autumn."

They left at midmorning nonetheless, hoping the weather would improve, but gave it up after only a few hours on the road, when they spied the pink granite spire and graceful walls of an apparent religious establishment tucked in a bend of the river, just before the border with Meara.

"That looks promising," Brion said, turning to beckon Jared's household chaplain closer. "Father Nevan, do you know that house?"

"I believe it is Brigidine, Sire," Nevan replied. "The Order of Saint Brigid. They are a hospital order. Grey ladies. If I am remembering correctly, this may be their mother house."

"Hospitallers, eh? Well, they can take us in, then," Brion said irritably, for rain was running down the neck of his oiled leather cloak and plastering his hair to his forehead, despite his leather cap and hood. "If ever there were travelers in need of shelter and succor, we qualify."

"We do, Sire," Nevan agreed. "Shall I ride on ahead and ask?"

"Aye, do that. Kenneth, go with him—and stress that we're perishing with the cold and wet. Cough for them, if that will help."

With an answering mock cough and a good-natured wave of agreement, for he had, indeed, been coughing in earnest, earlier, Kenneth kneed his horse after Nevan, glad of the diversion. Heads down and hoods pulled low against the driving rain, he and the young priest made their way carefully across the muddy field before the abbey walls, accompanied by the squelching sounds of the horses' hooves. When they finally drew rein before the abbey gate, Nevan leaned down to tug at the bell-pull, repeating the signal several times before a hand-sized flap drew back in the upper part of the postern door.

"Grace and peace to you, servant of God," Nevan said courteously, leaning down to the level of the opening. Kenneth could see an earnest young face peering up at them from within the hood of a dark cloak. A white coif showed close around her face.

"And God's grace to you, good sirs," she said, taking in their bedraggled state with an open glance. "Is it shelter from the storm that you seek?"

"It is, Reverend Lady," Kenneth replied, "but not for ourselves alone. I fear there are some two score of us. But be assured that the men will be content to make do in a stable or barn, so long as it is dry." He paused to press the edge of a sodden glove to his nose and mouth as he stifled a cough. "And a few of us, who have taken a chill from the rain, would greatly appreciate a hot meal and a day or two of rest in your infirmary."

"Ah, then, you know us for a hospitaller order," the sister replied cheerfully. "Please enter and be welcome."

"Thank you," Kenneth replied with a smile, even as the sound of scraping metal told of the door being unbarred. "And know that you give hospitality not only to Father Nevan and myself, but also the King of Gwynedd."

So saying, he gestured behind them, where the rest of their party were emerging from the rain, the Haldane banner limp and dripping in the hand of Jamyl Arilan. A wicket gate was open by then, and the cloaked sister now framed in the doorway turned urgently to another pair of dark-cloaked women who had joined her. Kenneth, guessing the cause of her concern, swung down from his mount and pushed back his hood as he led the horse through the open doorway and under the shelter of the gatehouse arch, where he at least was out of the rain.

"Peace be with you, Reverend Sisters," he said easily, moving aside for Father Nevan to join him. "No doubt, the thought of feeding and housing so many men and beasts is somewhat daunting. But we do carry grain for the horses."

"And be assured," Nevan chimed in, "that the king is prepared to make a generous donation to this house, in gratitude for your hospitality. The men will be grateful for shelter even in one of your barns, until this weather abates. Our Lord *was* born in a stable."

The taller of the two sisters craned a little to one side to peer past the two of them, then returned her attention to the newcomers, though she addressed herself to the priest.

"The king, you say?"

"Aye, Brion of Gwynedd," Father Nevan replied, making a small bow. "And the Duke of Cassan as well. I am Father Nevan d'Estrelldas, chaplain and battle-surgeon to His Grace. This is the Earl of Lendour. I assure you, we come in peace."

There followed a flurry of whispered consultation and scurrying to and fro, after which the sister who kept the gate came to make Kenneth and Nevan a small, nervous bow.

"Pray, bid your party enter, Father, and my lord," she murmured, with a gesture of invitation. "I shall open the gate wider, so that your men may enter, and Sister Ermengard will direct them to the stables. And our lady abbess invites the king and his officers to dine with her this evening."

"Thank you, Sister."

More cloaked and hooded sisters emerged from doorways leading into a cloister garth and the pink granite church as Kenneth and Father Nevan led their mounts on into the abbey yard to allow the full gate to open. Several younger sisters, presumably novices and lay sisters, came to take their horses as the king and Jamyl likewise entered and dismounted, followed by Jared and Xander and a slow procession of additional riders. As Kenneth and Nevan waited uncertainly, glancing back toward the king, their conductress from the gate presented them to the house's abbess: a handsome and briskly competent woman who had a familiar look to her, though Kenneth could not think where they might have met.

"I am Mother Aurelia," the woman said, and added uncertainly, "Do I know you, sir knight?"

Kenneth shook his head doubtfully, searching his memory as he gestured for Brion to join them.

"I feel certain I would remember, Reverend Lady," he murmured, as he glanced at the king. "Sire, allow me to present Mother Aurelia, the abbess of this house. Madam, the King of Gwynedd."

Brion caught the abbess's hand as she bent in a graceful curtsy, and himself bowed to kiss her ring in salute. "I am honored to meet you, Reverend Mother, and I thank you for giving us shelter from the storm. Can it be that you know my Earl of Lendour?" he added, noting the appraising looks of both parties.

"It would have been some years ago," the abbess allowed, trying not to stare at Kenneth, "and I think he was not then an earl. Have you been to Saint Brigid's Abbey near Cùilteine, my lord?" she asked Kenneth.

"Near Cùilteine? I believe I have," Kenneth said, astonished.

"Then, my memory has not failed me," the abbess said. "For I think you were in a party that stopped there with a young knight who had taken ill on the road, when I was an infirmarian there. And the king your father was in the party as well, young Sire," she added, to Brion, then sighed. "The sick lad, though—such a handsome young man he was, and so very ill," she added, glancing off into the distance of memory. "Most sadly, he did not survive."

Kenneth had gone very still as she spoke, and glanced at his boots with clenched jaws, for the distant memory, so long pushed aside, reemerged now with much of the force of his long-ago grief.

"Alas, he did not," he said quietly, then looked up briskly. "But, that was long ago, and I am sure your ministrations eased his pain. Might we please be shown to our accommodations now, Reverend Mother? I cannot speak for His Majesty, but I am greatly in need of dry clothes and a good fire."

"Of course," the abbess replied, indicating another sister waiting to convey them to their quarters. "You will be housed in our guest accommodations, and your men in the travelers' hostel. They will have to double up, but it is out of the rain. And a simple meal is being laid out in our refectory. Please join us when you have changed into dry clothing."

Brion said nothing as Kenneth sorted accommodations with the sisters in charge of guest facilities, but stayed the older man with a hand on his sleeve when Kenneth would have left him in the guest chamber assigned for his personal use.

"Do you mind telling me what that was all about?" he said, not relenting when Kenneth glanced aside with a troubled expression. "Who was it who did not survive?"

Kenneth sighed and looked around him for somewhere to sit in the tiny chamber, then sank down on the edge of the rigid cot when Brion sat and patted the straw mattress beside him.

"He was Ahern of Corwyn, elder brother of my late wife," Kenneth said quietly. "He would have been duke by now. He also, very briefly, was married to my daughter Zoë."

"Ahern? The Earl of Lendour before you?" Brion looked amazed. "I remember him. All the pages and squires idolized him. You were there when he died?"

Kenneth nodded, interlacing his fingers atop his knees. "It was a complaint of the belly—and what a loss for Gwynedd. He had survived two campaigns in Meara, overcoming a crippling injury in the first one—and then, to be taken by illness. . . ." He sighed and shook his head.

"When he fell ill on the road back, we brought him to that other Saint Brigid's to be tended by the sisters, and your father sent me back to Rhemuth to fetch Ahern's sister and my daughter. Ahern had asked for Zoë's hand during the campaign, and I had given my consent. I knew, when I left, that there was little chance of him surviving, but I did as your father bade. Of course, that was long before I knew that dear Alyce was to become my bride."

The king was listening avidly, enthralled by this glimpse of Kenneth's past. "But—did you return before he died?"

"Aye, but it did him little good, other than to ease his mind. Dear Alyce used her powers to ease his pain—and I know that Zoë's presence was a great comfort." Kenneth sighed again, his head bowing as he blinked back tears.

"He did last through the night. But the next day, when it became clear, even to him, that he was dying, he and Zoë exchanged wedding vows before he allowed the priest to administer the last rites. They had perhaps an hour as husband and wife."

Brion, too, was swallowing back emotion, and looked away. "I remember when they brought his body back to Rhemuth," he said softly. "I was about eight, and I was weeping along with all the other pages as they bore him into the chapel royal to lie in state for a day. I believe he was later buried in Lendour." He smiled. "Some of us had squabbled for the privilege of assisting at his knighting the previous Twelfth Night. I was one of those chosen, of course," he added with a wicked chuckle, glancing back at Kenneth. "But all of us were so in awe of him, and the way he overcame his injury." He shook his head. "Such a waste."

"Aye, it was," Kenneth said softly. When he did not speak further, Brion gave a weary sigh.

"Well, we'd best get into dry clothing for supper, or that abbess will thrash us both," he said, with a wry touch of humor in his voice. "I'm not certain why, but female religious always intimidate me, even now that I'm king."

Kenneth, too, had regained his usual good humor as he rose. "They don't, me. But perhaps it's because both Zoë and Alyce spent several years at a convent school. My daughter Alazais is there now. I begin to wonder whether she means to take the veil." He smiled. "But with four daughters, I suppose it was inevitable that at least one of them might do so."

A faint smile also quirked at the king's lips. "That was Arc-en-Ciel, wasn't it?" he said. "It's where you and the Lady Alyce were married."

"Aye, it was."

"But my first visit was before that," the king went on wistfully. "I couldn't have been more than five or six. My brother Blaine was with me."

"You remember that?" Kenneth asked, somewhat surprised.

"Oh, aye. Our parents took us for some ceremony or other: the daughter of a lady of the court was making vows, I think. I remember that afterward, we found a dead bird in the cloister yard. Of course we had to give it a proper burial. Krispin MacAthan was there, too. I think it was one of his sisters who'd made vows." He sighed and shook his head. "A long time ago. And now, both Blaine and Krispin are gone. Somehow, it doesn't seem fair."

Snorting at the maudlin direction their conversation had taken, he clapped Kenneth on the shoulder and also stood.

"Now, we really *had* better get into dry clothes. You don't suppose the sisters will mind if we don't break out the court garb, do you?"

"I'm certain it will be sufficient that we don't track mud through their refectory," Kenneth replied as he, too, rose. "I'll join you shortly."

T HE meal with the abbess was unremarkable, and had as its price the duty to attend Mass in the abbey church the next morning—which at least was dry and relatively warm. The guest quarters were less so, owing to a leaky roof in the king's chamber, prompting him to move into quarters in the infirmary, even though he was well, and to present the abbess with a fine purse the next morning, along with instructions to spend it on making necessary repairs to the facility as soon as weather allowed. Further inquiry revealed that the stable accommodations, at least, were a vast improvement, thus ensuring that the men and their mounts kept relatively warm and dry.

But the respite from the storm was welcome, nonetheless, and gave opportunity for those ailing from the weather to at least achieve improving health. When, after two nights at St. Brigid's, the king declared his intention to continue on their journey, he reiterated his instructions regarding the roof repairs, and declared his intention to stop there again on his way back from Meara.

"Do you think they'll make the repairs?" he said aside to Kenneth, as they set out on the road westward toward Ratharkin.

Kenneth nodded thoughtfully. "I would guess that they will," he replied. "The sisters are good-hearted, and their care of the sick and injured will be vastly enhanced by it."

"You recommend their care, then?" Brion asked, for Kenneth and another man still were coughing a little.

"I do, Sire—and you need not worry," he added, at the king's dubious grimace. "Truly. Another few days of fair weather, and we both shall be good as new."

T HEY entered Meara later that day, and the weather improved almost immediately. Brion had been to Meara once before, the summer he came of age; but that venture had been in the company of his royal uncle, the informal visit of a fourteen-year-old: resented by some, but mostly ignored by hard-line separatists still nurturing hope of an again-independent Meara.

This time, the Haldane who rode into Meara was a grown man, a king coming into his prime. Haldane kings had ridden into Meara before, with disastrous results for would-be Mearan pretenders. Now another Haldane rode into Meara to assert his mastery of his realm.

By the time they came within sight of Ratharkin's walls, spring was truly upon them, the grey of winter suddenly giving way to the glorious green that was nature in all its verdant abandon. That morning, Sir

Caspar Talbot had ridden ahead to alert the city of their imminent arrival, and returned with one of his brothers as they approached the city gates around midday.

"Sire, this is my youngest brother, Sir Arthen," Caspar told the king, as he and his companion drew rein under the Haldane banner and the two of them gave salute. "Apparently our father is in the field farther west. The sheriff, Sir Wilce Melandry, has been left in charge. He would have come to greet you in person, but he sits in court today in the city."

"No, he did right not to interrupt the processes of justice," Brion replied, glancing on ahead. "We shall join him there."

A few minutes later, as they made their way through the city gates, the king asked, "Just where is your father in the field, Sir Arthen?"

"I'm afraid I couldn't say, exactly, Sire," Arthen Talbot replied. "He and a troop of lancers headed out to Laas nearly a month ago, as soon as the roads were passable. They had hopes of intercepting the Lady Caitrin, but we've received no word of any great success."

"I see," the king said, nodding with the motion of his mount as they walked their horses into the stable yard before Ratharkin's great citadel. "And what do *you* think she's doing?"

Arthen's lip curled in a wry grimace, and he glanced at his brother. "I think she's gone and married the Earl of Somerdale, my lord. That's what I think. And then they'll go and breed up more Mearan pretenders, so that we have to ride out and kill them all, in the end."

The king snorted, but Kenneth said nothing as they dismounted, for he was remembering his last visit to Meara a decade before. He had hoped then that there would be no need for more killing off of Mearan pretenders, but the present circumstances were suggesting otherwise.

Inside the great hall of the inner citadel, the sheriff was, indeed, engaged in civil court, presiding from the grand dais at the head of the hall, where the royal governor usually sat to dispense justice. Sir Wilce Melandry, nephew of the previous royal governor, suspended proceedings and rose as the king and his immediate entourage entered, making a deep bow as the king approached. The younger man who scrambled to his feet and also bowed was Wilce's cousin, Sir Alun Melandry, who had been still a boy when his father, the previous royal governor, had been strung up from one of the great hammer beams by Mearan rebels.

In that, at least, both Melandrys eventually had seen justice served, for Donal Haldane had executed the perpetrators and later obliged those remaining to renew their oaths of loyalty upon the body of the slain governor. And when, but a few years past, Alun Melandry eventually had achieved the age for knighthood, Brion had been present when his father and Alun's cousin Wilce both had laid hands on Iolo Melandry's sword and made Iolo's son a knight.

"The cousins Melandry, well met!" Brion called, extending his hand as he strode down the hall. "I am right glad to see both of you again, and you both do me honor by your service!"

The two men showed every sign of extreme relief as the king came to clasp them both by the hands, and Sir Wilce quickly adjourned the court and drew Brion and his principal officers into the meeting chamber adjacent to the hall.

"You may remember the Earl of Lendour from his last visit, with my father," Brion said, beginning introductions all around. "Or, Sir Kenneth Morgan, as he was then. And this is Jared McLain Duke of Cassan, and Sir Jiri Redfearn, and my good friend Sir Jamyl Arilan, and Father Nevan d'Estrelldas, who serves us as battle-surgeon as well as chaplain for this venture. Now, tell me how fares my royal governor? I understand that he is in the field."

T HE king avoided voicing any specific accusations or suspicions during the briefing that ensued during the next hour, but it was clear that he was probing for information about Caitrin and her rumored marriage— or so it seemed to Kenneth. Having witnessed the exercise of royal justice a decade before, he could entertain no misgivings regarding those King Donal had left in charge in the troubled province. Sir Lucien Talbot, the present governor, certainly was sound, as were his sons. And the Melandrys, likewise, could have no scruple regarding their ongoing loyalty to the royal line which had avenged the murder of their kinsman Iolo.

Caitrin, of course, was less predictable, and certainly had no reason to love the Haldanes, whom she blamed for the deaths of her sister and niece and the man she had intended to marry, along with many more of her kin and countrymen. While she had not been in active rebellion since the last Mearan campaign, Kenneth guessed it had been more from lack of opportunity than lack of desire.

Now, with her mother no longer a tempering factor and a husband at last by her side, Kenneth thought it quite likely that, especially if Caitrin produced an heir of her body, the soi-disant Princess of Meara would waste little time in asserting her perceived rights—especially since her father seemed disinclined to do so again.

"Then, it would seem that, by now, she surely will have married Derek Somerdale," Jared said thoughtfully to one of the sheriff's scouts. "In Laas, you say."

"Aye, several months past now, Your Grace," the man replied.

"And where were Lucien and his men, when last reported?" Brion said.

"Headed down toward Cloome, Sire," the scout replied. "Caitrin's father allegedly has a stronghold in the mountains south of there, down in Pardiac."

Nodding, Brion glanced at his commanders. Their numbers were small, but he doubted that Caitrin would have made much effort to gather large numbers for herself, since she would not have expected the king to send troops into Meara. Especially, she would not be expecting the king himself.

"Then I think that we should head over toward Cloome ourselves, shall we, gentlemen? And perhaps the lord sheriff would oblige us with the loan of another score of his best men. I do not expect any serious opposition," he added, at Wilce Melandry's dubious expression, "but it would do no harm to make a show of force—if we even manage to find Caitrin and her father. All things being equal, we shall head out in the morning."

Chapter 22

". . . and mine arm be broken from the bone."

—JOB 31:22

THE letters that began to arrive in Culdi over the next several months kept Vera McLain and the ducal household reasonably apprised of progress—or lack thereof—in Meara. Most were from Jared, with instructions to share appropriate passages with the children, but sometimes Kenneth sent letters for Alaric and Bronwyn as well.

Reading the letters provided diversion and punctuation for the lazy summer days at Culdi, but the absence of more fascinating court gossip, even if worrisome sometimes, lent its own brand of ennui. The rain of earlier in the spring gave way to bright sun that was tonic to the crops maturing in the fields, but was less pleasant for humans. As the days drifted toward August, the summer heat became increasingly oppressive, and somewhat curtailed even the children's usual routines. Sometimes, after lessons and drills were finished, they would ride down to swim their ponies in the millpond below the town, or head into the cooler hills above.

On one such day, just past Lammas, the four of them ventured rather farther than was their usual wont. Llion had ridden to Morganhall for a fortnight with Kenneth's daughter Geill and her husband, both to see the first fruits of harvest brought in and to check on Kenneth's two sisters, who were not faring well in the summer heat. Llion's absence left the boys' training in the capable hands of Lord Deveril and Sir Tesselin, who had judged the day too warm for heavy exercise and released the children to their leisure.

On that particular day, the hilly heights had beckoned more seductively than the millpond. Men making hay in the golden fields beyond the town lifted their caps in salute as the youngsters passed, some of them waving good-naturedly, for the duke's heirs were well-known in the area, as were their Corwyn cousins.

Not far past the fields, where the track narrowed and began to meander upward, the four fell into single file behind Kevin, with Duncan and then Bronwyn and Alaric following. Soon they were imagining that they rode on a daring military expedition like their sires, for both Kevin and Alaric would be dukes someday, and practice was always a good thing. Just at the top of the rise, the twelve-year-old Kevin reined in his shaggy mountain pony and stood in his stirrups to survey a rather sorry looking flock of sheep grazing in the meadow beyond. Behind him, Alaric likewise drew rein between his younger sister and his cousin Duncan.

"Well, then," Kevin said to his companions, plumping back into his saddle with a calculating grin as the others kneed their ponies closer. "Time for some practice, I think! You lot probably thought those were just sheep grazing out there. They aren't, though. They're Torenthi spies. They need to be taught a lesson!"

"We aren't supposed to chase sheep," Bronwyn said, primly sitting her pony behind the boys.

"She's right; we aren't," Duncan chimed in. "Besides, they outnumber us."

"Yes, but we have the advantage of surprise," Alaric pointed out, quite reasonably.

"That's true," came Duncan's reply.

"Then, what are we waiting for?" Kevin retorted—and set heels to his pony's sides with a *whoop*, initiating a mad gallop down the hillside as he circled one arm over his head in imitation of a brandished sword. Likewise whooping, the other three fanned out behind him in hot pursuit.

Startled sheep scattered in every direction, bleating in ovine alarm. One lamb tripped over its own feet and tumbled down the hill, its mother jinking to avoid a charging pony. Alaric leaned down to lightly tap another ewe on the top of its head as he raced past, to hoots of approval from the other boys. Bronwyn, youngest of the group, was more concerned with keeping up with the boys than chasing sheep, though she rode well enough—until a heap of rags and wild grey hair suddenly reared up in front of her pony and brandished a shepherd's staff at the astonished animal and child.

The pony came to an abrupt and stiff-legged halt, wild-eyed and snorting, and Bronwyn continued over its head in a tumble of flying golden hair and tumbled skirts, to land with a thump before the pile of rags. The pony wheeled and took off in a fit of affronted bucking and squealing as a gnarled hand reached down to grab Bronwyn by the upper arm and haul her to her feet.

"Got you now, missy!" the heap of rags crowed, giving the girl a none-too-gentle shake as the other three riders whirled to ride to her defense. "What's the matter with you, galloping through here like you owned the free air and frightening an honest woman's sheep? Well, speak up, girl. What do you have to say for yourself?"

"You leave my sister alone!" Alaric ordered as he yanked his pony to a halt and glared at the old woman.

"You'd better not hurt her!" Duncan chimed in, also drawing rein. "She didn't mean any harm."

"Tell that to my poor sheep!" the old woman retorted. "Better yet, tell it to the duke, or whoever is in charge of you ruffians!"

Kevin, suddenly realizing that *he* was in charge of what the woman quite rightly regarded as ruffians at that moment, felt himself going red in the face, and ducked his head in shame as he dismounted and presented himself before the woman.

"I'm very sorry, Mother," he murmured, gentling his pony as he made himself meet her eyes. "We only meant to practice battle tactics—but we shouldn't have chased your sheep. I don't think any harm was done. Please allow us to make amends."

"Well, you can start by rounding up my sheep," she replied with a snort, grudgingly releasing Bronwyn. "They weren't bothering anyone, and they didn't deserve to be chased."

"We *are* sorry," Alaric chimed in.

"That's as may be," came the sour reply. "It still was wrong. Get down off that pony—you, too," she added to Duncan. "You'll be less frightening on foot. And catch that loose pony before you do anything else. Girl, you take charge of the beasts while the boys do the herding. I expect it was their idea anyway. Go on now, all of you!"

It took the better part of an hour to reassemble the old woman's scattered flock. While the boys doggedly began collecting sheep that wanted nothing to do with them, Bronwyn secured the ponies in the shade of a sprawling oak tree across the pasture. After a while, she began laying out an afternoon repast of bread and cheese and apples packed for them by Cook before they rode out. By the time the boys returned, sweaty and dirt-stained from their exertions, the sheep were once again grazing placidly across the pasture, nearer to where the old woman had resumed her vigil.

"Maybe we should just go," Duncan said under his breath as Kevin and Alaric flopped down on the grass and tucked into the food. "She was really angry, and rightly so."

"Aye, and we've made amends," Kevin replied. "She doesn't own the field—and I'm hungry."

As he tore off a chunk of bread and stuffed it into his mouth, Alaric leaned across to snag a bit of cheese.

"It *was* a bit funny," he allowed, as he applied the cheese to a portion of bread. "And we *were* wrong to chase the sheep."

Kevin snorted. "Aye, we were—but it *was* fun. . . ."

All three boys snickered at that, and Bronwyn rolled her eyes, but she set aside some cheese and a generous chunk of the fine manchet bread in a napkin while the others ate, and scampered off to deliver it to the old woman when everyone had mostly finished.

Kevin sprawled for a nap after that, and Duncan settled with his back against the tree to whittle at a bit of wood. Bronwyn, when she returned, began weaving a daisy crown for Kevin, whom she adored. Alaric, ever the most adventurous of their band, shinnied up the tree with an apple and perched in a fork where he could oversee the entire area. He had nearly finished the apple when he noticed the squirrel eyeing him from a nearby branch.

Slowly Alaric took the last bite of the apple, then extended the apple core on his outstretched fingers, suppressing any flicker of further movement that might alarm the squirrel.

He had been watching the creature since even before he climbed the tree, while he and his sister and cousins sprawled in the shade below and ate. Bronwyn was tidying the remnants even now, and Kevin and Duncan had gone to resaddle the ponies grazing a little farther away. In the meadow beyond, the miscreant sheep also grazed, keeping wary watch on ponies and children.

Those sheep had been trouble enough earlier, Alaric reflected sourly. Actually, the trouble had been Kevin's sudden assertion that the sheep were Torenthi spies. Though all of the children in the ducal household knew full well that chasing sheep was forbidden, that had not stopped Kevin from seizing the inspiration to practice some of the battlefield tactics he was learning as a newly fledged squire. And when Duncan joined right in, Alaric and his sister naturally had been obliged to follow suit.

Which might have gone unnoticed by everyone saving the sheep, except that their keeper suddenly had risen up like a heap of animated rags and startled Bronywn's pony, which had dumped her without ceremony—right at the old woman's feet! It would have been almost funny, if the old woman hadn't grabbed Bronwyn by the arm and hauled her upright—and then began taking them all to task for their transgression.

Grimacing at the memory, Alaric shifted minutely on his perch, startling the squirrel, and glanced down at his sister, considering whether he ought to try bouncing the apple core off her head. The old woman had been *very* cross, and had made them round up the scattered sheep—though Bronwyn's peace offering of their leftover bread and cheese seemed to have mollified her.

On the other hand, the squirrel now frozen with tail a-tremble had been exceedingly patient, and surely did not deserve to go hungry because of a flock of silly sheep.

In a burst of eight-year-old contrition, Alaric returned his attention to the squirrel and extended the barest tendril of thought as he had earlier, brushing the animal's mind with a feather touch of enticement and reassurance. At the same time, he stretched his hand a trifle closer, waggling the apple core on his fingers—and abruptly lost his balance!

Time seemed suddenly encased in thick treacle as he tried simultaneously to push the apple core within the squirrel's reach and also to catch his balance and grab for a handhold. The squirrel seized *his* victory, along with the apple core, scampering up into higher, safer branches; but Alaric's hands were slick with apple juice. His mad scramble for a better handhold—any handhold!—yielded only a double handful of leaves and twigs and a cracking sound as the branch gave way beneath him.

Bronwyn looked up and shrieked as he fell, scrambling to get out of the way, and Alaric uttered an inarticulate cry of dismay, caroming against several other branches and grabbing ineffectually for new handholds en route. But none of it was enough to break his fall—only his arm, as he hit the ground hard enough to knock the wind out of him and leave him dazed and gasping at the base of the tree.

His sister scrambled immediately to his side, pulling at his shoulders and calling his name over and over, but he could only roll onto one side and gasp for breath, eyes screwed shut and both arms clasped tightly to his chest, head ringing from the force of his fall. Only gradually did he become aware that his right arm felt odd, and was vaguely starting to ache. He opened his eyes as Kevin and then Duncan thumped to their knees to either side of him, and Bronwyn was pushed out of the way as Kevin tried to help him to sit up.

"Sweet *Jesu*, Alaric! Are you all right?" the older boy demanded, as Alaric dazedly shook his head and concentrated on trying to breathe. Duncan, meanwhile, was gently urging his cousin to roll onto his back, running his hands over arms and legs to check for injuries. He stopped as Alaric's sharp intake of breath signaled serious damage to his right forearm.

"I think it's broken," Duncan whispered, turning wide, frightened eyes on his older brother. "Kevin, what're we going to do? We weren't even supposed to *be* out here."

"We'll worry about that later," Kevin muttered, drawing his silver-mounted squire's dagger. "Help me open up his sleeve so we can see. Bronwyn—"

But the youngest member of their party had taken to her heels as soon as her brother's plight became clear, and was pelting across the meadow toward the cave haven of the guardian of the sheep, skirts hiked up and golden hair flying.

"*Now* we're in for it," Kevin said under his breath, as he cut the cuff tie of their patient's sleeve, then cast the dagger aside and started ripping with both hands.

"Ow, take it easy!" Alaric managed to gasp out, instinctively shrinking back from the hands that would have helped him.

"I've got to see how bad it is," Kevin replied. "Duncan, give me a hand!"

"I dunno," Duncan said doubtfully. "Shouldn't one of us go back and bring an adult? He certainly shouldn't try to ride like this."

Alaric groaned and went white as Kevin's fumbling ministrations jarred his injury. He was starting to catch his breath, but he had to concentrate hard to bite back tears. With a great act of will, he summoned enough focus to reach across with his good hand to touch his injury, but he winced at the new pain it caused.

"I've gone and done it this time, haven't I?" he whispered. "We're really in trouble now."

"I'd better ride for help," Kevin said uncertainly. "It's your sword arm, after all. If it's badly set, you could end up a cripple."

Alaric screwed his eyes shut and drew in a long, steadying breath, choking back a faint whimper. He knew the older boy was right, though he hadn't had to *say* it. But he opened his eyes again as he sensed Duncan scrambling to his feet beside him, and Kevin drawing back a little, on guard, fumbling for his discarded squire's dagger. Beyond them, Bronwyn had the hand of the old shepherd woman whose sheep they had chased earlier, and was leading her urgently toward them.

That the old woman was coming, in answer to Bronwyn's urgent pleas, underlined Alaric's impression that their earlier contrition, demonstrated by rounding up the scattered sheep, had been accepted, if somewhat grudgingly. And no doubt, Bronwyn's subsequent peace offering of bread and cheese had further sweetened the woman's disposition. In fact, now that no cloud of affront lay between her and her unwitting interlopers, he supposed that the woman probably was not as ancient as he had first accounted her—though it was difficult to be certain. However many years she owned, those years had not been kind to her. Still, he sensed a basic decency beneath her rags and matted hair, a trace of gentleness behind the gap-toothed grimace she offered as Bronwyn drew her nearer.

"Oh, please hurry, grand dame!" Bronwyn repeated, tugging still. "You must help him! He's my brother."

"Is he, indeed?" the old woman muttered, dropping a satchel at Alaric's right side and then easing to her knees beside it. "Well, let's have a look."

She ignored Kevin's watchfulness, and the dagger now in his hand but held close along his thigh, and began a brisk examination of Alaric's injury, probing above and below the angle of the break.

"Can you feel this?" she asked.

Alaric winced and nodded, but he did not cry out, though he did go dead white several times in the course of the examination.

"It seems to be a clean break," she confirmed, as she looked up at him, "but both bones are snapped clean through. It won't be easy to set, or pleasant." She turned her gimlet gaze on Kevin. "I can tend it, but you'd best get back to your father's and bring men with a litter. Once it's set, it mustn't be jostled before it's had time to knit a little."

Kevin's blue eyes flashed in slight rebellion. "It's his sword arm, grand dame," he said pointedly. "Are you sure you can set it properly? Shouldn't I fetch one of my father's battle-surgeons?"

She gave him a contemptuous toss of her matted head. "Not if you want it to heal straight. Most battle-surgeons would just as soon cut it off. It's a bad break. A careless manipulation, and bone could pierce the skin—and then he *would* have to lose the arm. I know what I'm doing. Now, go!"

With a somewhat cowed nod, Kevin touched Alaric's shoulder in re-assurance, then sheathed his dagger and got to his feet.

"I'll be back as quickly as I can," he murmured—and headed off briskly to where the ponies were waiting, Bronwyn staring after him. As he mounted up and kicked the pony into a gallop toward home, the old woman turned her attention to Bronwyn and Duncan.

"I shall need some wood for splints," she informed them. "See what you can find—the straighter and flatter, the better, but we'll make do with what's available. Go. I'll stay with him."

They scrambled off to do her bidding, and the woman settled cross-legged beside her patient and continued to poke and prod at the arm for a few seconds, eliciting several just-contained hisses from her patient. She then turned her attention to the satchel beside her, muttering under her breath as she rummaged into its contents. Glad for the relative respite, and well aware of the pain that was to come, Alaric kept his good hand lightly clasped to the injury and closed his eyes, concentrating on trying to put the pain from his mind.

He wasn't very good at it yet. It was something that trained Deryni could do, for themselves and for others—and he *had* managed to block Llion's pain. But the pain of a horse bite and that of a broken arm were of two entirely different magnitudes. And it was also entirely different when the pain to be blocked was one's own.

Furthermore, if he did succeed in blocking his own pain, would that reveal his true nature to his strange benefactor? He had intimated to the king that the hill folk of the borders were more accepting of fey powers such as the Deryni possessed, but was that really true? He had gained that impression over the years, but this old woman might be as bigoted as the Bishop of Nyford. It was one thing to make a sweeping statement affirming the benign nature of hypothetical strangers, and quite another to gamble one's life on such a belief.

And then there was the matter of a future reckoning, when he got back to Culdi. With his father and Duke Jared still away with the king in Meara, and even Llion temporarily at Morganhall, he would be obliged to confess to Lady Vera, how he had come to fall out of a tree in a field where he was not meant to be.

He grimaced at that thought, for while his mother's sister was a kind and gentle woman, who loved Alaric and his sister as she loved her own son and her stepson, she, too, had very strict rules about how young Deryni should comport themselves in a world that was hostile to their kind. The penalty for their disobedience was not likely to be physical, but her disappointment was apt to sting far worse than any birch switch or belt leather.

Anticipation made Alaric grimace again, and he looked up to see the old woman stirring something with a twig in one of the cups the children had tossed aside after their noon repast.

"What is that?" he asked, as she reached down with her free hand to raise his head from behind his neck.

"Something for the pain," she replied, though her gaze shifted from his as she said it. "Drink. You will feel nothing, after this."

Predisposed to accept the instructions of adults, the boy laid his good hand on hers, where it held the cup, and started to set his lips to the rim. But then some inkling of her true intent crossed the link of their physical contact and he froze, his eyes darting to hers in sudden, shocked comprehension.

"It's poison!" he gasped, pushing the cup aside. "You want to kill me!"

As he drew back in alarm, his head slipping from her grasp to hit the grass with a thump, he sent out a tendril of thought as he had done for the squirrel, and felt her hostility. He tried to roll away from her, cradling his injured arm as he attempted to sit up, but her touch on his shoulder seemed to drain strength from him. As he subsided, helpless, he could feel her fingers twining in his hair, lifting his head upturned, her other hand again bringing the cup toward him: the cup that he now knew held his death, if he drank it.

"But, why?" he managed to whisper, tears runneling tracks down the dirt on his face. "I never harmed you. I never wished you ill. It can't be for the *sheep*!"

She only shook her head, tight-lipped, shifting her hand to pinch at the hinges of his jaw and force his mouth to open.

"Please, no," he whimpered, as the cup came nearer.

But in that instant, reason or reality or divine providence suddenly prevailed. Sunlight filtering through the tree's leafy canopy flashed bright gold on the plain band his assailant wore on her right hand, and the maniacal gleam in her rheumy eyes abruptly went out. With a muted little cry, she flung the cup aside and released him, burying her face in her hands as her shoulders shook with sobs.

"I'm sorry, Darrell," she whispered, pressing the ring against her lips. "I am *so* sorry! Oh, forgive me, my love, my life. . . ."

Astonished, Alaric shifted onto his back and watched her cry herself out, sensing that the moment of immediate danger had passed, grimacing against the pain as he tried to cushion his broken arm with his good hand. When she finally dried her eyes on an edge of her tattered skirt, he caught her gaze with his. Once upon a time, he realized, she had been a fine-looking woman.

"You know what I am, don't you?" he asked softly.

She gave a curt nod, but shifted her gaze from his.

"This . . . Darrell—was he killed by a Deryni?"

She shook her head, stifling another sob. "No," she whispered. "*He* was Deryni, and died to save another of his kind."

Alaric gave a wary nod. "I think I understand." He drew a deep breath. "Listen, you don't have to help me if you don't want to. Kevin will bring the battle-surgeon, even though you said not to. I'll be all right."

"Without a sword arm, young Deryni?" She drew herself up with returning dignity. "Nay, I cannot let you chance that. My Darrell would never approve. How can you carry on his work without a proper sword arm?"

As he raised one fair brow in question, she tucked a small leather pouch back into her satchel and began pulling out rolls of surprisingly clean bandages.

"I shan't offer you another painkiller," she said with a sour smile. "I will not ask you to trust me in that, after what has already passed between us. I *will* set the arm, though. And I give you my word that it will heal straight and true, if you follow my instructions."

"Your word . . . yes," he replied. "And I sense that your word is a precious bond, as was *his*." He turned his head as Duncan and Bronwyn returned with an assortment of more or less straight pieces of wood.

"Ah, good. Let me see what you've found," she said briskly, as the two children laid the wood to her other side. "Yes, this one will do, and this, and this. You, boy—do you have a knife, like your brother?" she asked Duncan, holding out her hand as he produced a short eating-dagger. "It has an edge, does it?" she went on, testing its blade with approval. "Take those four bits of wood and whittle them smooth along one side. Carve off all the knots and twiggy bits, and make them the length of your friend's arm from elbow to fingertips."

Alaric found himself drifting a little while the splints were prepared, but he roused when the old woman bade Bronwyn cradle his head in her lap.

"Girl, you try to ease him now," she said gruffly, probing above the break and sliding one hand down to his wrist. "A pretty girl can take a man's mind from the pain. My Darrell taught me that."

He had stiffened at her first words, anticipating the pain to come, but he only turned his face to his sister's and closed his eyes, making himself draw a deep breath, bidding his tension drain away as he let it out. After another breath, he thought he felt a tentative touch from an alien mind, just at the edge of awareness, but he managed not to shrink from it, sensing no threat in the touch.

Then she gave his wrist a slight squeeze of warning and began pulling the arm straight, at the same time rotating it slightly and guiding with her other hand as she eased the ends of bone into place. He could not suppress the hiss of indrawn breath between clenched teeth, and his back arched off the ground with the pain; but he did not cry out, and the injured arm did not tense or move except as she manipulated it.

He lasted until Duncan had helped hold the splints in place while she bound his arm to them, immobilizing the arm from bicep to fingertips, but he finally passed out as she tied off the last bandages and eased the bound arm gently to his side.

The next thing he knew, he became aware of voices talking about him, as if he were not there, and gentle fingers probing lightly at the dull ache beneath his bandages.

"Nay, boys will be boys, sir," he heard the old woman saying. "The young lord fell out of the tree. I but lent my poor skills to right his hurt. He will mend well enough."

Alaric opened his eyes to see Macon, Duke Jared's retired battle-surgeon, glancing up at the split tree limb above their heads—and beyond him, Jared's seneschal, Lord Deveril. A contrite and silent Kevin watched from beyond Deveril's elbow, looking like he wished he were anywhere but here.

"An expert job, m'lord," Macon said approvingly, with a glance up at Deveril. "If nothing shifts, he should heal as good as new." He glanced at the boy's benefactor. "You didn't give him any of your hill remedies, did you, Mother?"

The old woman shook her shaggy head. "No, sir. He is a brave lad, and would have nothing for his pain. A fine soldier in the making, that one. He will fight many a battle in his manhood."

Lord Deveril looked at her strangely as Macon motioned for men to bring a litter nearer, stepping aside so that they could set it down along Alaric's left side.

"Aye, he likely will, at that," Deveril replied, almost to himself.

Macon, meanwhile, had produced a tiny, stoppered glass flask from his belt pouch, and gestured for Bronwyn to raise her brother's head as he drew out the stopper.

"Here, lad, drink this down—the whole thing. No need to feel the pain while we jostle you home—though it would be no more than you deserve, after such a damn-fool stunt."

Alaric needed no further encouragement to do as the battle-surgeon ordered, upending the flask with his good hand and draining it. Very quickly he could feel the potion going to work, allowing him to drift into a not-unpleasant fog of blessed easement from the pain as the men shifted him onto the litter, Macon steadying his injured arm. He felt some jostling as they secured the litter to the pair of horses brought to convey it, but he was fading fast—though still focused enough to beckon the old woman closer as his rescuers prepared to move out. She took his good hand and bent down at his gesture, straining to catch his words.

"Thank you, grand dame—for *all* that you did," he whispered. "I will—try to carry on *his* work." With that, he pressed his lips to her ring in salute . . . and drifted into semi-consciousness as the litter began to move and his hand relaxed.

Chapter 23

*"He shall set his children under her shelter, and shall lodge
under her branches."*
—ECCLESIASTICUS 14:26

O N the journey home, his mind dulled by Macon's painkiller, the eight-year-old Alaric was in no condition to ponder the likely further consequences of the afternoon's misadventure. Kevin, however, had been made well aware of Lord Deveril's displeasure, and his apprehension quickly conveyed itself to his brother and cousins. With his father and Earl Kenneth away with the king, he knew it would fall to Duchess Vera to decide on a suitable punishment for their disobedience in riding out so far from home.

To the surprise of all, no summons came that evening. Kevin, as the oldest, was ordered to his room with scant supper and not a word from his stepmother. Duncan and Bronwyn likewise were sent to bed without further comment. Vera did look in on Alaric, but by then Macon had given him another potion to ensure that he slept through the night.

It was the next morning, after a meager breakfast of bread, sliced ham, and watery ale, that Alaric at last found himself summoned to Duchess Vera's solar. Macon accompanied him, after helping him wash and carefully change into a fresh tunic: someone else's, far larger than himself, to allow for the bulk of the bandaged arm. His arm ached, even supported by a sling, but Macon offered him nothing further for the discomfort, and he was not bold enough to ask for anything.

His sister and his two cousins were already in the solar when he and

Macon arrived. The three were standing awkwardly in the center of the room, their faces solemn and contrite. Duchess Vera sat straight backed on a wide, low bench before the window, Lord Deveril attending her. She looked drawn and tired, and very, very sad.

No one was invited to sit. No one spoke at first. Bronwyn was sniffling, obviously fighting back tears. Kevin and Duncan would not look at him, and seemed inordinately interested in the toes of their boots.

"Dear, dear children," Vera finally said after a moment, in a very low voice. "I am so very disappointed in all of you. What on earth were you thinking?"

Alaric joined his cousins in contemplation of footwear, for he had no excuse.

"Did Lord Deveril not make it clear that you were not to go so far from home?" she said after a moment, when none of them offered an explanation. "Kevin, was this the responsible behavior of an elder brother? You are twelve years old, beginning your squire's training. You are nearly a man. If I cannot trust you to look after your brother and your cousins, how can I possibly trust you to look after your father, when you serve him as squire? One day, you will be Duke of Cassan, my love. Is your word so little worth, that you will disobey those put in charge of you while you are growing? And chasing sheep. Really."

Kevin swallowed audibly, head bowed in shame, then lurched forward to sink to his knees at his stepmother's feet.

"Forgive me, Maman," he whispered, bending his forehead to her knee. "We just—" He raised his head and shook it, drawing a steadying breath. "I have no excuse, Maman. I am oldest and should have known better. I will accept whatever punishment you see fit."

Vera nodded slowly, gently setting a hand on his shoulder as she glanced at Duncan, her own son.

"And Duncan, my love—what have *you* to say for yourself?"

Duncan hung his head and also came to kneel at his mother's feet.

"I'm sorry, Maman."

"And it won't happen again?"

"No, Maman."

"And Bronwyn? You're the youngest, but you usually have better sense."

"She did, Maman," Kevin interjected. "She told us we shouldn't chase the sheep, but we didn't listen."

Vera cast him a withering look, shaking her head, then gave an exasperated sigh.

"What *am* I to do with you? All of you should have known better. And boys, you have a responsibility as gentlemen to protect your cousin, and to keep her safe. Bronwyn, I don't know what to say."

"I'm very sorry, Auntie Vera," Bronwyn whispered, as the two brothers nodded their agreement, eyes still downcast.

"Very well. The three of you may go. Alaric, please stay. Kevin, I feel certain that your father will have a few things to say about this misadventure when he returns. I shall do what I can to intercede in your behalf, but all of you were disobedient, and you knew better. That cannot go on. I'm certain that Lord Deveril can find some extra chores for you today, to remind you of your folly. All of you could have been killed. Go now. I have nothing further to say to you."

The three of them scrambled to their feet with alacrity and headed for the door, Deveril following casually after. At Vera's nod, Macon also left, closing the door behind him. Alaric, who had yet to speak, gazed at his aunt in apprehension as the others departed, but she beckoned for him to come and sit beside her on the bench. Alaric did as he was bidden, well aware that his own disobedience had led to far more serious consequences—and fearful that his punishment was likely to be commensurate with that seriousness.

"So, what went on out there?" Vera asked softly, when the boy had settled gingerly beside her. "Tell me about the old woman who set your arm."

Alaric swallowed hard, but he was not eager to go into overmuch detail.

"She was only an old shepherdess, a widow woman," he said carefully—which was true, as far as it went. "We did chase her sheep, when we first got there," he admitted, "but it was just for fun. We weren't thinking. But we rounded them back up immediately, when we realized what we'd done. Bronwyn even took her a peace offering: some of the food we had left, after we ate. She liked that. And even Macon was impressed with how well she set my arm," he added brightly, hoping that might mitigate the circumstances.

"You do realize how easily this could have gone otherwise," Vera said dryly.

Alaric hung his head. "Yes."

"It still could go badly, if you don't take care and do what Macon tells you. The king would not be happy if his Duke of Corwyn ruined his sword arm from a foolish, childish prank."

Alaric swallowed hard and nodded, then dared to cast a quick glance in her direction. To his relief, she was smiling faintly.

"Your arm isn't the only reason I'm concerned, my love," she said after a moment. "When you ride so far afield, without anyone knowing where you're going, things can happen—as you discovered, to everyone's regret. People are not always what they seem, and you know that many people do not like Deryni. If that woman had discovered what you are, or had taken a true dislike to you, she might have done you serious harm."

Alaric swallowed painfully and again averted his gaze, well aware that she could very well have made him seriously dead. He had been totally at her mercy. The incident had taught him a powerful lesson, but he wasn't about to betray the old woman, who had spared him—or worry Lady Vera even more.

"I'm sorry that we disobeyed by riding out so far, Auntie Vera—and that we chased the old woman's sheep," he whispered. "And I'm sorry that we put Lord Deveril and Macon to extra trouble. It won't happen again."

"Have you apologized to Deveril and Macon?" she replied.

"Not yet," he admitted sheepishly, with a quick shake of his head, "but I will."

"See that you do," came her reply, and then, after a beat, "Does your arm hurt?"

He looked up sharply, for it *did* hurt—though he had somehow managed to put the pain from his mind under her interrogation. "A bit," he admitted.

"Then, I think it's time you learned how to control your pain," she said, drawing him around to rest his head in her lap. "Lie back and make yourself as comfortable as you can." She waited while he settled, sprawled on the bench and with his arm well supported. "Once you learn to control your own pain, it is only a short step to easing the pain of others. A useful skill, don't you think?"

"Yes," he whispered, though he decided not to mention Llion and the horse bite. As he settled into the comfort of her embrace, she laid one hand gently across his brow and bade him relax. At the nudge of her powers against his shields, he felt his eyes fluttering closed and willed himself to open to her instruction.

The next thing he knew, she was urging him to sit up. Surprisingly, his arm no longer hurt. At the same time, he realized someone was knocking on the solar door—Macon, come to take him back to his room for a light meal and a nap. He ate and napped several times in the course of the rest of the day, before falling into bed in the deepest sleep of all, and did not rouse until the morning.

NEXT morning, little though he wished to do it, he was obliged to deal with the obligatory letter to his father, informing him of the accident. What made it worse was that he could not write it himself, with his arm all splinted and in bandages, but had to dictate it for Father Geordan to write down. Thus framed, and filtered through Father Geordan's perspective, it somehow took on the aspect of a confession—which perhaps was inevitable, since the young priest had helped prepare him and Duncan for their First Communion, before their fathers' departure. He later learned that Kevin and Duncan likewise had been obliged to write letters to their father, and decided that the exercise probably was part of their punishment for disobedience. To his great relief, Lady Vera never again mentioned the circumstances of his accident; only did her best to ensure that its physical effects were minimal.

THUS began what would be several months of recuperation. And when Llion returned, a few days after the accident, Alaric was obliged to confess his failings all over again.

"I see," Llion said, scowling, for he had already spoken with Lord Deveril and Macon. "I assume that I needn't reiterate how foolish it was, to go so far afield."

Alaric only shook his head, for he could not bear to meet Llion's gaze, to read the disappointment on his mentor's face.

"That's far worse than the fact that you had the accident," Llion went on. "You could have broken your arm anywhere. God knows, there are enough trees to fall out of, closer to home."

"We just didn't think," Alaric said bleakly. "It wasn't *that* much farther from where we usually ride. Things just . . . got out of hand."

Llion gazed at him for a long moment, saying nothing, then came and put an arm around the boy's shoulders to hug him close.

"I won't tell you to be more careful, because I know you didn't intend to fall out of the tree. But do try to exercise better judgment in the future. If you'd broken your neck instead of your arm, I don't know what I would have done. I do know that I should miss you very much."

This affirmation of Llion's genuine affection and concern loosed the floodgate of tears that neither Lady Vera nor the disapproval of Lord Deveril and Macon had been able to dislodge. For several minutes, the future Duke of Corwyn sobbed like the boy he still was, burying his face against Llion's shoulder and shaking with finally unpent emotion. Llion said nothing; only held him close until the tears ceased, then offered him a square of linen to dry his eyes and blow his nose.

"Feel better?" he asked quietly, as Alaric awkwardly wadded up the linen square and let Llion take it from him.

The boy only nodded self-consciously.

"Don't dwell on it," Llion said. "We'll not speak of it again. Far more important is to get you healed and healthy again. Why don't we go downstairs and get something to eat? And then you can have a nap."

"I'm not a baby, Llion," Alaric said, faintly affronted. "Despite the tears."

"No, but you have a broken bone. Give your body time to heal."

"I suppose."

T O Alaric's surprise, it seemed to require a great deal of energy to knit a broken bone. He had expected to take his injury mostly in his stride, like the lesser injuries he had sustained in his young life, but he mostly ate and slept for the first week or two, disinclined even to attempt anything else. Vaguely he wondered whether Lady Vera was responsible for that, and finally summoned up the will to ask her, one sunny morning early in September, when she informed him that he might begin to resume very light activities, so long as he did not use his injured arm.

"Aunt Vera, is it because of you that I've slept so much lately?" he asked, as she handed him a copy of a treatise on stable management.

A faint smile curved at Vera's lips as she glanced out the window.

"The original of that text is in R'Kassan," she remarked, "but we're fortunate enough to have a translation. I think the content will be far more useful to you than struggling with another language, at least for now."

"Then, you *did* make me sleep," Alaric said.

"Plenty of food and rest are the best ingredients for healing a broken bone," Vera replied with an inclination of her head, looking him up and down. "They're also useful for growing, in general—and I do believe you're having another growth spurt. Isn't that the tunic I gave you just last month?"

He looked down at his tunic. The seam of the right sleeve had been opened to accommodate his splinted arm, but the left sleeve hit well above his wrist.

"Maybe it shrank?" he said doubtfully.

"No, you've grown," she replied, plucking at a fold of the fabric at the shoulder. "It's binding at the chest, too."

He grinned and shrugged. "I guess I *have* grown."

"Well, at least some good has come of your summer's adventures," she said with a smile. "Bring me the tunic in the morning, and I'll see what can be done with it. Perhaps one of Kevin's old tunics would fit, without ripping out the sleeve seam."

At his pleased nod, she added, "Good, then. Off with you, now. And I believe you'd best see Llion about resuming light exercise with Duncan and Kevin. Just be careful of that arm!"

He had already resumed the portion of his academic pursuits that did not involve writing, for reading was the only thing he had really felt like doing in the initial weeks after his accident. But when he presented himself the next morning in the stable yard, expecting to be eased slowly back into physical training, he soon discovered that Llion and Lord Deveril did not regard a broken arm as any reason to slack off. Ponies still must be groomed, even if it took at least twice as long using only one hand.

Nor did he receive much sympathy from Kevin and Duncan, who had taken on that duty during the first few weeks of his recovery—and quite rightly, Lord Deveril pointed out, since all three boys had been party to the disobedience that led to the injury in the first place. He was not yet permitted to ride, either, for a fall could undo all the healing he thus far had accomplished.

Furthermore, the injured Alaric was expected to resume sword drills with his left hand—which, as he accustomed himself to the initial awkwardness, he decided was actually no bad thing, as Kevin reminded him in an annoyed snit distinctly lacking in sympathy. And that, too, was entirely appropriate, since injury to a warrior's preferred arm in battle might well require that he shift to his off arm to save his life.

It was a sound rationale; and whether or not that was the reason for Lord Deveril's firmness, Alaric did not complain, because the discomfort of his arm grew less with every day that passed, and the steady intake of nourishing food fueled a spurt of growth that brought its own discomfort, measured in aching limbs.

By the end of September, he had gained a full three fingers in height, also adding enough in girth that Duncan made him a new belt for Michaelmas, which was also his ninth birthday. It was crimson leather, "For when you become a royal page," Duncan told him. "But you can wear it now, if you want. Papa won't mind. You *are* going to be the king's page, after all."

"Well, eventually," Alaric replied, smiling delightedly as he fingered the soft, supple leather. "I'm happy enough to be Uncle Jared's page for now, though—and my father's. Papa says I needn't go to court for another year."

"You can at least try it on now," Kevin pointed out. "Bronwyn, put it on him. A warrior should always be armed by a lady."

"That's true," she agreed, taking the belt from her brother and waiting while Alaric undid his old one of plain brown leather. "And you have to start paying attention to these things, 'cause you're going to be a duke someday. Auntie Vera says you will represent the king, so you must always look your best."

Alaric only rolled his eyes as his sister passed the new belt around his waist and drew the tail through the brass ring at one end, then looped it up behind and then down through the slipknot taking shape at the ring.

"I know that. But the king isn't here, so I don't have to represent him yet." He glanced at Duncan and grinned. "But thank you for the belt, Coz. The old one really was getting too small."

Duncan grinned back and gently dunted his arm with a clenched knuckle—then winced as he realized he had hit the arm that was injured.

"Ow, I'm sorry, Alaric! Did that hurt? I forgot it was your broken arm!"

"It's all right," Alaric murmured, flexing the fingers of that arm to demonstrate. "It's mostly healed now, see? No sling, no bandages. Llion even has me doing light sword drills again. I'm fine."

The one thing that was disappointing was that his father had not returned in time for his birthday. He had written other letters to his father besides the one telling of his broken arm, but he received few letters in return, and nothing to indicate that Kenneth even knew about the arm.

"Maybe the letters aren't finding him," he said to Lady Vera, one afternoon early in October, after receiving a letter that only commented on the various places the king's party was visiting. By now, he was recovered enough to write again, albeit carefully; but he knew his father would have been concerned about the arm.

"That may well be," Vera replied. "I've had letters from Jared as well, and all the news is very general. I have no idea where they actually are—though I gather that they have not found the Lady Caitrin yet."

Alaric sighed. "It must be hard, just relying on the reports of scouts in the area. Do you think they shall ever find her?"

Vera shrugged. "I hope that they do. 'Tis strategic business, so Jared doesn't dwell on much detail. I do know that they continue to search, and I gather that they hope soon to locate her. But Meara is wild and vast. It may be that they eventually will return empty-handed."

Chapter 24

"To deliver thee from the strange woman, even from the stranger which flattereth with her words."
—PROVERBS 2:16

I N Meara, meanwhile, the king's progress through that troubled province was yielding little but frustration. But though Kenneth Morgan and the king's party were empty-handed thus far, their fortunes were about to take an unexpected turn, though not as anyone would have hoped.

A week out of Ratharkin, they had chanced upon Meara's royal governor, Sir Lucien Talbot, and his party, who still were scouring the land for the elusive Caitrin. Among Lucien's party was an old companion of the king's father: the Deryni Sir Morian du Joux, whom Kenneth had met on his previous foray into Meara a decade before, when the province had been in open rebellion. On that occasion, it had been Morian who came closest to tracking down Caitrin, and who had captured and interrogated the brother of the man now said to be Caitrin's husband, discreetly lending his talent to the king's service.

What made this encounter particularly interesting was that Kenneth knew Morian to be Deryni, though he was not certain how many others of the present king's party were aware of that fact. Brion did seem to know, and shortly after Morian's arrival summoned Kenneth along with Jared and Jamyl to meet with Morian and Lucien Talbot in a private chamber of the manor house where they were staying.

Morian had aged appreciably since their last meeting; his once-dark hair was gone steel-grey, grown long and clubbed back in a warrior's knot. But the keen blue-violet eyes were as piercing as ever, and Kenneth had the distinct impression that they missed nothing.

"So, tell me what you've discovered, Lucien," Brion said, waving the newcomers to seats and taking one himself. "Do you know where she is?"

"We have had reports that she may be in the area around Laas," Lucien said.

"We've been to Laas," Brion replied. "I've no doubt that she came through there, but she was long gone when we arrived."

"Then, she may well have headed down toward Cloome," Morian volunteered. "I spoke with several local folk who interacted with her household, and a few reported that they thought she planned to go there. She knows you are in Meara, Sire," he added, at Brion's look of skepticism. "Cloome is close to the border with Pardiac, where we have known for some time that her father maintains his headquarters. But since he's made no move in some years, some felt it best to let sleeping dogs lie."

At his glance toward the royal governor, Lucien grimaced and folded his arms across his chest.

"Sire, I have kept the peace in Meara for those ten years and more. If I had thought Judhael still posed a threat, I would have acted."

"That's as may be," Brion agreed, "though my father would say that Mearans never give up. And even if Judhael has given up, his daughter now has married, which suggests that *she* still intends to fight. If she should produce an heir . . ."

"That is part of what brought us to Meara ten years ago, my prince," Kenneth pointed out, shifting in his chair. "Her father had risen in rebellion, and her sister had borne a succession of would-be future claimants to the throne of Meara. Thankfully, only one of them still survives: another Judhael. She died bearing yet another short-lived child. Her father may have set aside his aspirations, but Caitrin's marriage tells me that *she* has not."

"Aye, if she has her way, she'll be breeding by now," Jared said sourly. "Just what we need: another Mearan pretender."

Scowling, Brion turned back to Morian. "You say she may have headed back toward Cloome. I'll ask you to take a small party and investigate your suspicion, find out if that's where she's gone." Morian gave a nod, rising. "We shall follow a day behind you," Brion went on. "Lord Faas of Glyndour has a manor in that area, as I recall. We'll meet you there, and hope that you have good news."

"Very good, Sire."

THE king was as good as his word, and three days later met up again with Morian and his scouts at Castel Edain, just outside Cloome, where the local baron had given hospitality to the royal party.

"Still nothing concrete, I fear," Morian reported. "She is believed to be still in the area, but no one seems able to pin down her exact whereabouts."

Brion sighed, pulling the neck of his damp tunic farther open in hope of gaining some respite from the heat, for it was a still, sultry day toward the end of a hot summer, and he was ill pleased with their continued failure to find the elusive Mearan princess.

"I am getting very tired of this," he muttered under his breath, then sighed again. "We'll take a break today, I think. Anyone else fancy a ride along the beach? Perhaps we'll catch a sea breeze and cool off."

Half an hour later, he was leading a small party along the hard-packed sand west of Cloome. A little back from the king and his immediate companions, Jamyl Arilan rode at the head of half a dozen well-armed Haldane lancers, but Brion was comfortably attired in lightweight riding leathers, as were Kenneth, Jared, and Morian. Two more armed Cassani borderers also rode with them.

"It's still too hot," Brion muttered, with a devilish side glance at Kenneth and Jared. "What say we generate a bit of a breeze of our own?"

With that, he kicked his horse into a canter along the forbidding cliffs that limned the beach, laughing gleefully and increasing his speed as Kenneth and Jared fell in behind and flanking him, followed by Morian and their two guards. Jamyl and the others followed at a more leisurely pace, for they knew the moods of their liege lord, and when to give him space.

So it might have resolved as it usually did, with the king eventually pulling up to allow his entourage to catch up with him. Except that as he led the way sharply around a rugged headland, he found himself nearly upon perhaps a score of riders clustered around something large and mottled grey, that had washed up on the beach. Though a few were in riding leathers, most of the riders wore fighting harness, two of whom were afoot with swords drawn, hacking at whatever it was that lay in the gently foaming surf.

Taken aback to be so suddenly confronted by so many armed men, and by the flash of drawn swords among them, Brion pulled up sharply and yanked his mount around in a tight circle, glancing back as Kenneth and Jared quickly fell in to either side of him and Morian also joined them. The two borderers had set hands to sword hilts, but the rest of the king's party were still far back on the beach, out of sight around the jutting headland.

"Keep your distance!" one of the stranger riders ordered, hand going to the hilt of his sword as two of his companions moved to back him up. Behind them, more of their fellows were fanning out to either side to confront the newcomers.

"Peace, gentlemen, we mean you no harm," Brion said reasonably.

"And you'll receive none, so you be on about your business!" a second man retorted. "Turn back *now*!"

"Mind your tongue!" Morian snapped, moving slightly ahead of the king to shield him.

"And you mind yours!" said another man, clearly in authority, who kneed his horse between two of the armed men. "For an interloper, your words are very bold."

He appeared to be somewhat older than the others of his party, with streaks of grey in the dark hair pulled back in a clouted braid. His forked beard likewise was braided. Brion surveyed him appraisingly as he kneed his mount a step closer to assert his leadership.

"He speaks for me," he said evenly. "And who might you be, sir?"

"Do not answer," said a lighter voice from behind the line of men. "That is for him to answer first, since he is on my beach."

As a speckled grey nosed its way next to the Mearan leader, Brion was startled to realize that its diminutive rider was, in fact, a woman, wearing riding leathers and riding astride. The thick plait hanging over one shoulder reached past her waist, tarnished chestnut brown that glinted silver in the sunlight, with a blue ribbon twined in the strands. Though he had never seen Caitrin of Meara, the tight-lipped, rather plain-looking woman before him matched the descriptions he had heard. Could it be that, after so many weeks, they had finally stumbled upon the elusive princess?

"Peace, Morian," the king said quietly, signing for the older man to draw back a little. "The lady is clearly mistaken, for this is *my* beach."

"*Your* beach?"

But the woman's retort was only barely audible in the sudden flurry of movement and exclamation as her men reacted, surging forward to envelop the king and his immediate companions, even as Jamyl Arilan and the rest of the king's escort came cantering around the beachy point and at once shifted into a gallop, drawing their swords as the king's danger became apparent.

At the same time, more of the Mearans overwhelmed Morian, engulfing him and his mount, yanking the animal to its knees and Morian to the ground, even as the Deryni knight's magic belatedly began to flare around him.

Caitrin, for her part, allowed her noble companion to seize her reins and take them on a dash for safety with half a dozen of their men, for the king's additional men were now approaching at the gallop.

What followed was more mayhem than true skirmish, for no one seemed able to decide whether or not fighting was to be done in earnest, though Morian's attackers appeared to have no doubt. At the approach of Jamyl Arilan and his men, more of the Mearans crowded after Caitrin and her escort and galloped off—except for the half dozen men swarming over Morian, two of whom were the men Brion had seen afoot, hacking at the thing on the beach. Seeing the other Mearans withdraw, Kenneth and Jared, along with the king, concentrated their efforts on coming to Morian's rescue, cutting one man down and wrestling the others away from the downed Deryni.

By the time it was over, a Mearan lay dead and three more were pulled struggling from the stricken Morian and held in close custody. One of Jamyl's men had been pulled from his horse, but was picking himself up, apparently uninjured. Morian, as Kenneth and Jared dismounted and rushed to his aid, lay flat on his back and bleeding from half a dozen superficial wounds, but had both hands clasped around a bloodied shaft of spiraled ivory, thick as a man's thumb, that pinned him to the sand through his upper chest. As the king hastily dismounted to join them, he was horrified to see bloody froth bubbling from between Morian's lips as Jared lifted the injured man's head to prop against his knee.

"Dear God, what have they done to you?" the king whispered, pulling off his gloves as he bent over the wounded man.

A pained, ironic chuckle rasped from Morian's lips. "I fear they have killed me, Sire," he whispered. "And it was a quite focused hatred aimed specifically at me, not at you. An attack of opportunity, to be sure, for I am known in Meara. And it is known that I was responsible for a long-ago action done in your father's service, not yours."

"But, what—" The king looked up in question at Kenneth, who had joined him kneeling at the dying man's side. "What is he talking about?"

"Sire, I have always been faithful in the service of your house," Morian rasped, before Kenneth could answer. "A decade ago, I rode with your father against the Mearans, and hunted down highborn Mearans risen in rebellion against the Crown of Gwynedd. Some of them I was obliged to kill. Ask *them*, when I am gone," he added, jutting his chin toward the captive Mearans.

"When—No!" the king cried, gingerly touching the ivory shaft protruding from Morian's chest. "Dear God, what *is* this?"

"Magic to slay a wielder of magic," Morian whispered. "What they found on the beach—it is called a narwhal." He flicked his glance in the direction of the butchered grey carcass lying off to one side in the foaming surf. "In ancient times, their tusks were sometimes mistaken for unicorn horn: potent magic."

"Sire, you must not pull it!" Jared said sharply.

Brion's hand flew backward in alarm. "Because it is magic?" he whispered.

"No, because it is all that holds his life within his body," Kenneth answered, setting his hands over Morian's. "Morian, can aught be done?"

The Deryni weakly shook his head. "Perhaps in times gone by, when there still were Healers . . . but no more." He drew breath painfully as he returned his gaze to the king's. "Do not go to war over this, Sire. The attack was against me only."

"But, *why?*" Brion asked.

Morian briefly closed his eyes, summoning strength. "I am known and hated in Meara, Sire, both for what I am and for whom I serve. Somehow, I have always known that one day . . ." He winced and drew another bubbling breath, then turned his gaze on Kenneth.

"You dared to love a Deryni woman, Sir Kenneth," he whispered. "For love of her, let me go."

"You're sure?" Kenneth murmured.

Morian nodded. "Do it, my friend. It will be a kinder death than if you attempt to save me. Either way, I cannot survive this."

With that, he pulled his hands apart in surrender, lips moving in an unspoken prayer as he briefly turned his gaze toward the sky above.

Kenneth glanced at the king, whose head slowly bowed in resignation, then at Jamyl Arilan, who had come to kneel across from him. Jamyl's faint nod gave him courage to return his gaze to the dying man, and to shift his grasp onto the blood-slick shaft of ivory.

"May God give you mercy, as I do, Morian," he whispered, steeling his resolve as the dying man's gaze again returned to his. "Go with God, go in peace."

With that, he gave the shaft a mighty tug, at the same time twisting to free it from Morian's flesh, backing it out in the direction of the ivory spiral. Hot blood bubbled from the wound for a few seconds more, and from between Morian's lips, along with a faint, anguished groan, but Kenneth only shifted one hand to grasp one of Morian's, his eyes never leaving Morian's as the dying man drew a few more labored breaths and then was still.

Kenneth took a deep breath and bowed his head for a moment in wordless prayer for the dead man's soul before crossing himself and closing the dead man's eyes, then looked up at the king.

"He's gone."

"Yes, and those responsible will be punished," Brion said, reaching across to take the ivory shaft from Kenneth's hand.

He fingered it with distaste for a few seconds, then rose and turned toward where several of his men were holding the Mearans responsible for the attack on Morian. The tide had turned, little wavelets beginning to skim across the sand as he headed toward them. Meanwhile, Kenneth and Jared deputized several men to carry Morian's body over to the horses and secure it, then strode after the king.

Jamyl Arilan had taken charge of the prisoners, and had them forced to their knees as the king approached, Kenneth and Jared behind him. One of the borderers was also afoot, with drawn sword. The prisoners' wrists were bound behind them, but they glared up defiantly as the king came to a halt before them, with the narwhal tusk in his hand like a weapon.

"I suppose you men have what you consider to be good reasons for attacking my knight," Brion said evenly, lightly tapping the tusk against the side of his leg.

One of the men snorted. "He was Deryni. That is well-known in Meara."

"That is no justification for unprovoked murder," the king replied.

"No?" another prisoner replied. "Then, call it a delayed execution, for he has slain many a Mearan patriot in the past decade and more."

"Then, you will not object if your own executions are somewhat less delayed," Brion retorted. "Jamyl, bring them!" he ordered, turning then on his heel to return to where another borderer was holding his horse, in the deepening surf.

Chapter 25

*"Mercy and truth preserve the king: and his throne
is upholden by mercy."*
—PROVERBS 20:28

THEY returned later that afternoon to Castel Edain, where Jiri and Sir Lucien Talbot had been growing anxious.

"I had thought you only gone for a ride on the beach, Sire," Jiri said, coming onto the great hall steps with Lucien and Baron Faas as the king's party clattered into the stable yard. "What has . . .?"

His voice trailed off as he saw the bundled shape strapped across the saddle of a horse, and another as well, and the three dour strangers in battle harness who rode with bound hands, each accompanied by a grim-faced Haldane rider. The king's face was stony, Kenneth's troubled, Jared's unreadable, Jamyl's blank with suppressed anger.

As the royal party dismounted, men-at-arms beginning to unstrap the bodies on the horses, Lucien made his way to Jamyl, who was closest, keeping one eye on the king.

"What has happened?" he murmured. "Who was killed, and by whom?"

"The one who matters is Sir Morian," Jamyl replied, jerking his chin toward one of the bodies. "The other one was part of the attacking party, as are the prisoners. We found Caitrin. Unfortunately, some of her men recognized Morian and overwhelmed him before anyone could intervene. Ask the king about the narwhal tusk he is carrying—if you dare."

Jamyl knew that the royal governor had worked closely with the

Deryni Morian in the past decade, and could sense him making the connection.

"A narwhal tusk? Dear, merciful *Jesu!*" he whispered. "The Mearans killed him with a *unicorn horn?*"

Jamyl inclined his head curtly. "They pinned him to the sand with it. Morian knew the wound was mortal, once the horn was pulled. He asked Lord Kenneth to release him. Kenneth is carrying a great burden right now."

"I should say he is," Lucien replied, then appeared to pull himself together. "Right, then. Lord Faas has a chapel here. The body can lie there overnight."

"There're apt to be more bodies in the morning," Jamyl said. "I believe the king plans to execute those responsible for Morian's death."

"Those are a different matter," Lucien said coldly. "We'll bury them, but insurgents don't deserve anything fancy."

T HE king had a Mass said for Morian that evening in the chapel, celebrated by Father Nevan. Afterward, in further discussion with the royal governor, they learned that Morian had family not two days' ride from there.

"A wife and several children, mostly grown," Lucien said. "He lived a quiet life, but he put his many skills always in service of the Crown. Your father greatly esteemed him."

"As did I," Brion retorted, still angry at the waste of Morian's life. "Very well, we'll take him there in the morning," he said. "First, though, I mean to question those who killed him."

"Of doubtful usefulness, without Morian's . . . 'skills,'" Jamyl said quietly.

Brion blew out breath in an exasperated sigh. "I know that, Jamyl, but we must try. Morian asked that we not go to war over this, but I can't help wanting revenge for his death. It was an unprovoked attack."

"So it seemed to me, Sire," Jared said. "Thank God that *you* were not the victim."

"There is that." Brion sighed again, then rose.

"Let's get on with it, then. We'll talk to the prisoners."

• • •

JAMYL also was present during the questioning that followed, though he said little, other than to clarify a few points. The prisoners were frightened, but maintained that it had been an attack of the moment, when they realized that Morian was among them. Several of the men had lost loved ones in the Mearan expedition of a decade past. One of the men, the one who actually rammed the narwhal tusk into Morian's body, had lost an adored older brother directly at Morian's command, as he tried to cover the escape of Caitrin's sister and newborn child.

"It does explain a great deal," Jared said quietly, when the prisoners had been taken back to the dungeon where they were being held. "It was manslaughter, I will grant you, but hardly murder. And certainly a crime of passion. No one could have expected such a confrontation before we came upon them so suddenly."

"They still have killed a trusted vassal," Brion said doggedly.

A short silence ensued, after which Lucien said quietly, "What will you do, Sire? Do you intend to execute them?"

"I don't know," the king replied. "I'll decide by morning."

When they had dispersed to a joyless supper, Jamyl drew Kenneth aside, where they could not be overheard.

"Sir Kenneth, you must try to persuade him not to execute the men," Jamyl said quietly. "Their attack was unfortunate, but it was not premeditated. Morian had the right of it, when he said we should not go to war over his death."

Kenneth fixed the young Deryni with his gaze. He had been wondering whether Jamyl had used his powers to Truth-Read as the prisoners were questioned, but he also knew that Jamyl would never reveal himself to the king or anyone else in their party. He was also aware that he himself could not disclose any evidence that might exonerate the prisoners. Not if it meant betraying Jamyl.

"That was my sense of it," he said quietly. "And I was the one Morian chose, to release him. But you know the king, and how he refuses to let go of a notion, once his mind is set. I will try to persuade him, but realize that I hold little hope of it."

"I know you will do what you can," Jamyl replied.

Later that night, when all had retired save an honor guard of four to keep watch beside Morian's body, Jamyl went onto the roofs at Castel Edain and sought out a quiet spot where, even if someone else took it in mind to indulge sleepless wandering, they were not apt to notice him. It was risky, what Jamyl planned to do, for he had no Portal to facilitate his contact with Stefan Coram, but he and Stefan had worked together often enough that he knew he had a good chance of breaking into Stefan's sleep to communicate the events of the day.

He found a secluded niche beside a chimney and sank down on his hunkers, leaning his forehead against his clasped knees as he closed his eyes and took a few deep breaths to center and relax before sending out the call. He sustained it for several minutes before settling back to wait. Very shortly, he felt the telltale tingle of another mind touching his.

I assume that this is important, came the thought insinuating itself into Jamyl's mind.

Just a quick bit of information I thought the Council should have, Jamyl returned. *Morian is dead, speared by a Mearan partisan with a narwhal tusk—or a unicorn horn, as common superstition would call it.*

Stefan's shock and dismay came through as a burst of unfocused static that made Jamyl wince with its intensity. Then:

That is the absolutely last thing I would have expected to hear from you. Review it for me.

Jamyl complied, quickly recounting the incident in question.

I think he means to hang those responsible, he finished. *Which is hardly just, because it really was a completely unforeseen and unforeseeable occurrence. If anything, it's the circumstances that were at fault. But I can't tell Brion how I know this.*

No, you can't, Stefan agreed. *Well, do what you can. I'll inform the Council. I suppose you have no idea when you'll be able to make a proper report.*

None. If he hangs the Mearans, it could spark another full-scale rebellion. But I'm hoping it won't come to that.

Good luck, then.

An instant to disengage the communication. Then Jamyl was back in his body, drawing a deep breath to settle back into normal consciousness.

Casting out with his Deryni senses, he was relieved to find no one on the roof. He took another few seconds to fully shake off the effects of his focus, then rose to make his way to the bed assigned him.

I N the end, further unexpected events the next morning swayed the king's resolve where the reasoning of his closest confidants could not. They were assembling in the stable yard of the manor house, where Brion was eyeing several beams that protruded from the stable loft, when one of his men came running into the yard from outside.

"Rider approaching, Sire, under a white flag."

"Who—?" Brion started to say.

But Jamyl was already moving into the gateway to peer out, two of the Cassani bordermen swinging onto horses to ride out and investigate. The men returned several minutes later with a young man bearing a parley banner. The lad could not have been more than fifteen or sixteen, but he rode proud and straight as they led him before the king. Jamyl watched but said nothing.

"And who is this?" Brion asked the bordermen.

"Risto of Glenmor, Majesty," the young man said, before the men could reply. "I come in peace, on behalf of the Princess Caitrin of Meara. Will you speak with her?"

The king could not have been more surprised if the young man had suddenly sprouted horns and a tail. He glanced at his officers—at Kenneth and Jared and Jiri—then returned his attention to the Mearan envoy.

"Very well."

"You will guarantee her safety, and allow her to depart in peace?" the young man said boldly.

Kenneth could sense the king tensing next to him, and the royal jaw tightened, but Brion gave a curt nod. "I will respect the truce."

"Then, I will bring her," the young man said, and backed his horse a few paces before turning sharply to canter off over the nearby ridge.

"*Caitrin* is asking to parley?" the king said incredulously.

"Further evidence," said Jamyl, "that yesterday's attack was entirely unplanned."

"But she *is* a Mearan," Jared pointed out.

"And our intention, from the beginning, has been to find her and speak to her," Kenneth said. "It appears that we now have that chance, Sire."

"Here she comes," Lucien Talbot said, low.

As a small party came over the ridge, again preceded by the parley flag, Brion swung onto a horse and moved into the open gateway, flanked by Kenneth, Jared, and the royal governor. Jamyl and a handful of his knights gathered behind, alert for any sign of treachery. More men were up in the gatehouse with bows, should any of the Mearans take it in their minds to violate the truce.

As the approaching party drew closer, more Mearans appeared from over the ridge behind them to pull up in a line across the track. Only four riders continued forward behind the young man carrying the parley flag. One was the man they had seen before, with the forked beard, one was cloaked and hooded, the other two were armed retainers. When they drew to a halt, perhaps twenty yards out, the envoy and armed men held back while the older man and the hooded figure continued forward to within a few horse lengths of the king and drew rein.

"I am Derek Delaney Earl of Somerdale," the man said, gentling a restive mount. "May I know whom I have the honor of addressing?"

"You are in the presence of Brion King of Gwynedd and Prince of Meara," Lucien Talbot said stiffly, indicating the king.

As Delaney inclined his head in acknowledgment of the introduction, if not its content, and Brion silently did the same, the earl's companion pushed back her hood with a gloved hand and lifted her chin defiantly. It was the same plain-faced woman of the previous day, though the ribbon woven through her long plait today was black, and skirts billowed around booted legs, though she still rode astride.

"We truly regret the manner of our meeting yesterday," Delaney said, before the woman could speak. "The presence of Sir Morian du Joux among your number was a great shock to all of us, for he has been responsible for the death of many a loyal Mearan."

"He was my loyal servant," Brion said pointedly, "and your men attacked him without provocation." He glanced at the woman beside Delaney. "May I know the identity of your fair companion?"

Delaney inclined his head again. "My bride of some months, Caitrin Countess of Somerdale."

As Caitrin allowed him a curt dip of her chin, Brion made a more courtly bow of his own.

"Lady."

"Why have you asked for this parley?" Jared said stiffly.

"Why, to retrieve our men, of course," Delaney replied. "We are on our wedding progress through these lands. The last thing we expected was to come face-to-face with one who has done such infamy against the people of Meara."

"If he did infamy," Brion said, "it was done in time of war, in the service of the king my father, to safeguard the greater well-being of the people of Meara."

"We shall never agree on *that*," Caitrin said, speaking for the first time. "A decade ago, when your father invaded my land, your Morian hounded my sister to death, along with her newborn child."

"And the past cannot be changed," her husband interjected, with a note of somewhat long-suffering patience, Kenneth thought. "But we truly intended no hostility yesterday, Brion of Gwynedd. My wife and I are celebrating our marriage, as any couple might do. Can we not resolve this as reasoned men?"

"Your men attacked us without provocation," Brion replied. "How can I construe that as anything but hostile?"

"It was not deliberate, nor was it ordered," Caitrin said, though more temperately than before. "But you must understand that Morian du Joux was hated and reviled by my people."

"*Your* people?" Brion retorted. "Lady, Meara is *mine*."

"No, it is my father who is Prince of Meara," Caitrin said stubbornly. "I can never acknowledge any other while he yet lives."

"You claim no title in your own right?" Jared asked.

Caitrin managed a brittle smile. "What would be the point? My father yet lives, and I am a new bride of . . . a certain age. I pray for the blessing of children, but do you think it likely that my aging body will produce challengers to your claim against my father's throne?"

"This discussion is pointless," Brion said coldly. "Your father *has* no throne. *I* am Prince of Meara."

"I will not dispute that with you while he yet lives," Caitrin replied. "I ask only that you give back my husband's men and allow us to go in peace."

"Your husband's men killed one of mine," Brion said doggedly. "Justice must be served."

"Then, temper justice with mercy," Caitrin's husband countered. "I regret that life was lost, but it was a passion of the moment, against one who has greatly wronged many Mearans. Surely that does not require their deaths as well. One of my men also died."

"What do you suggest?" Lucien interjected, with a glance at the king.

"Flog them," Delaney said coldly. "They behaved like wayward boys, brawling in the presence of my bride, and one of them died for it. But the rest do not deserve to die."

Brion gave a heavy sigh. Kenneth sensed his frustration and uncertainty. It was a terrible burden laid upon a young man only just come into his full adulthood, but he was also a king, and must always weigh the greater good in his decision.

Brion glanced aside at Lucien, backing his mount a few paces, and motioned Kenneth and Jared closer.

"What say you?" he murmured. "They killed Morian, but we did kill one of theirs as well. I don't want to go to war over this. Not right now."

"The decision must be yours, Sire," Lucien whispered.

"I know that. I'm asking what you would do. You live among these people."

Lucien inclined his head. "I would flog those responsible and release them to their lord."

Brion shifted his attention to Kenneth and Jared. "Do you concur?"

"Aye," Jared murmured.

"Kenneth?"

"Regrettably, I must agree."

With a heavy sigh, the king motioned to Jiri Redfearn, waiting in the gateway. "Bring out the prisoners and prepare to administer punishment."

And so it transpired. The Gwynedd men grumbled when they realized what was to be done, and the Mearan men could not believe their
good fortune, but the prisoners were soundly flogged and then released,
backs bleeding and wrists still bound, into the custody of Derek Delaney,
who sternly marched them back to the safety of his own line, accompanied by his wife and the parley banner. The king watched them go,
watched the waiting men take the flogged ones up behind them on their
horses. No one moved from the gatehouse arch until all the Mearans had
disappeared over the rise.

"Very well," Brion finally said. "I didn't like that resolution, but it's
done, as Morian would have wished. We now have the sad duty to return
him to his family."

Chapter 26

"Lord, now lettest thou thy servant depart in peace . . ."
—LUKE 2:29

THEY were two days taking Morian home, with his body well wrapped in cerecloth and sheltered under a canopy atop a light cart drawn by a pair of sturdy cobs. It was not an ideal arrangement, for the summer heat was still upon them, but nothing could be done about the weather. Despite their good intentions, the body was beginning to bloat by the time they finally approached the modest manor house outside Ratharkin. Lucien said it was called Breitfahr.

At Lucien's recommendation, Brion had not sent a messenger ahead to warn Morian's family that they were coming, for he believed that such ill news should be delivered in person. But as they rumbled through the gatehouse to the yard before the manor house, several liveried servants came onto the porch before the great hall, followed by a tiny woman clothed all in black, with her grey hair unbound to tumble down her back.

"Lady Cloris!" Lucien called, immediately drawing rein to dismount and bound up the steps to her. As they met, she let herself be enfolded in his arms, wordlessly laying her head against his chest.

"I knew he was gone," she murmured, as Brion, too, mounted the stair, followed by Kenneth and Jared. "How did it happen?"

Brion shifted uneasily from one foot to the other. "I am so very sorry we must bring you such news, my lady," he said awkwardly. "The encounter was altogether unexpected, and his attackers were more successful than any of them would have dared to hope."

She pulled back a little to search all their faces, then gazed beyond them to where the cart had stopped in the yard with its sad burden.

Within the hour, after being coffined, Morian's body lay in the little church nearby, under a guard of honor by half a dozen of the king's men. Soon after, the dead man's son arrived: an intense, fit-looking young man of a like age to Jared, with wavy red hair tied back in a queue and a red beard to match. Sir Halloran du Joux seemed personable enough, as he sat at table with the family that night, though he spoke but little, but he kept watch through the night with Lucien, Jared, Kenneth, Jamyl, and the king himself.

The next morning, after a solemn Requiem Mass, they buried Morian in the nearby churchyard, next to the graves of several of his children and a sister who had predeceased him. After, the widow walked back to the manor house beside Kenneth, for she had learned of his part in her husband's passing.

"Lord Kenneth, I wish to thank you for the service you did my husband," she murmured, taking his arm.

He managed a faint, bleak smile as he set his hand over hers.

"It is not a service that any man is eager to perform," he said quietly, "but he invoked a plea that I could not refuse. He said, 'You dared to love a Deryni wife.' And then he said, 'For the love you bore her, let me go.'"

The lady's face upturned to him in surprise. "You were married to a Deryni, Lord Kenneth?"

"I was." He nodded, a faint smile curving at his lips. "I had not thought to marry again, after my first wife died. But the late king had other plans."

"Ah, then, it was an arranged marriage."

"Aye, in the beginning. She was a great heiress, whose marriage lay in the gift of the king, and I was privileged to be in the king's favor. But we came to love one another deeply. She gave me the son I thought never to have, and a fair, bonnie daughter who sadly never got to know her mother. She died of the milk fever soon after our daughter's birth," he added wistfully. "I still miss her, more than I can say."

"I can see that you do," she said with a sigh and a smile, laying her free hand over his. "She must have been an extraordinary woman."

"The finest I have ever known," he replied. "Would you like to see her likeness? I have a miniature, painted by my elder sister." As she smiled and nodded, he delved into the pouch at his belt and pulled out the locket that Delphine had given him. As the two of them stepped aside to let others pass, he removed it from its protective pouch and opened it, spreading its triptych before her admiring gaze.

"Oh, she *was* lovely," Cloris breathed, tilting his hand with the triptych. "And beautiful children. How was she called?"

"Alyce," Kenneth replied. "Alyce de Corwyn. And my son Alaric and my daughter Bronwyn. These are recent likenesses."

Nodding, she lightly tapped the portrait of Alaric. "I have heard his name mentioned," she said. "My husband spoke several times of a half-Deryni boy being brought up at the royal court." She looked up at him appraisingly. "You are very brave, Kenneth Morgan, to deliberately sire a half-Deryni child. It will not be easy for him—or for your daughter."

"No," Kenneth agreed with a taut smile.

"How old is the boy now?" Cloris asked.

"He will be nine at Michaelmas—only a few days from now," he added with some surprise, for he had somewhat lost track of time while they were in the field.

She, too, smiled as she closed his hand over the triptych. "A magical age, as they begin to edge into young adulthood. I remember my Halloran at nine." Behind them, said Halloran was approaching with Lucien and Jared, along with Jamyl and the king, and she glanced in their direction.

"Thank you for allowing me to gaze upon your family, Lord Kenneth," she said, turning as the king drew abreast of them. "Sire, I hope that all of you will stay to sup with us tonight in my husband's memory. It is late to start on the road now. You traveled many days to bring him home to us, and had little rest in that time—or last night, either, I think."

Brion glanced at Jared and Lucien, who had joined them. Though he would have been happy enough to make an immediate departure for Ratharkin, courtesy clearly demanded that they stay for a proper meal with the family, now that Morian was decently buried.

"It would be our honor, my lady," he said with a bow, right hand pressed to heart. "We *are* tired. And I think that, perhaps, a few of us would appreciate the opportunity to rest for a few hours before we dine. I did notice Lucien yawning at Mass."

The Mearan governor smiled and made his own bow. "Guilty as charged, Sire. And I confess that a bed would be most welcome, my lady."

"Then, I shall have our steward show you to rooms," she replied. "My son Halloran will arrange it."

Both Lucien and Kenneth took advantage of the offer of beds, along with the king and several others. While most of them followed Halloran to the next floor, Morian's widow led Kenneth to a dim, airy chamber on the ground floor, overlooking a well-manicured garden.

"My husband loved this room," she told him, as she opened the door to see him in. "There is a daybed there by the window. I can have wine or other refreshment brought for you, if you wish."

"Thank you, no," he said with a smile, flexing a stiff shoulder. "A bed is all I need—and a few hours' sleep."

"Then, I shall leave you to your rest," she said, smiling. "And thank you again for your kindness to my husband."

"Lady," he murmured, giving her another bow, hand to heart.

As she left, closing the door behind her, he continued on toward the bed, at the same time detaching his sword from its hangers. The bed was only knee-high, more of a pallet than a daybed, but it beckoned seductively as he laid the sword close along the side and, with a barely suppressed groan, sank down onto the thin mattress. After weeks in the field, any bed seemed a great luxury.

All but light-headed, he lay back and briefly closed his eyes, the back of one wrist across his brow, a little surprised at how bone weary he was. Speaking of his family with Lady Cloris had reminded him how very much he missed his children, and his longing to see them again almost overwhelmed him.

They needed him at home, too. Delving into the pouch at his waist, he retrieved the letter that had caught up with him only days before—the one telling how Alaric had broken his arm early in August. Previous letters had been written in the boy's own hand, but this one clearly had been dictated to someone else, probably Father Geordan. Unfolding it, he skimmed his fingertips down the page, though he had mostly memorized the words by now.

Dearest Papa, I hope you will not be angry when you read this. . . .

How he wished he had been there to comfort his son's pain. How he wished he had been there to prevent the ill-fated foray up to the meadow, with its perilous tree!

Almost overcome with longing and remorse, he laid the letter aside and took out the silver locket, with its triptych of his loved ones, and prised it open to gaze at the likeness of his son, of his daughter, of his beautiful Alyce, and dreamed of home. All too often he had been with the king instead of with his wife, his children! How many years he had served the Haldanes!

And yet, it was a noble service, even in its absences from those he loved the most. It was a life that had brought him great satisfactions, despite the privations. As he closed his eyes, surrendering to his utter weariness, he closed the locket in his hand and clasped it to his breast, likewise holding his loved ones to his heart.

I T was thus that Jared found him several hours later, when he came to wake him for dinner and could not rouse him.

"Kenneth?" Jared whispered. "Kenneth! Dear God, no!"

Jared shook him again and again, and even slapped his face several times, but to no avail. The loyal and steadfast Earl of Lendour had served three Haldane kings, but now it appeared he had passed away peacefully in his sleep, his faithful heart worn out in royal service. Fallen to one side lay the last letter Kenneth had received from his son; and clasped to his breast under one slack hand, Jared found the silver locket that Kenneth's sister had given him, with its portraits of his late second wife and their two children, who now were truly orphans.

"Why?" Jared whispered, as he sank down on the edge of the pallet where Kenneth lay. "Dear God, *why?*"

Despite the tears blurring his vision, Jared noticed Kenneth's sheathed sword lying close along the side of the bed and fumbled it into his hands to press the cross-hilt to his lips in salute, breathing a wordless prayer for the

soul of his dead friend and kinsman. Then he gently laid the sword along
Kenneth's side, slipping its hilt under the hand that did not hold the locket,
and retrieved the discarded letter lying close by, gently tucking that under
the hand that held the locket. He dashed away his tears with the back of a
hand as he rose and gazed blindly out the garden window, where the sun
was sinking low on the horizon in a blaze of flaming splendor.

NOT a man in Morian's hall but realized that something was terribly amiss as Jared joined the others in the room. Brion and his
men were already at table with Sir Halloran and his mother, partaking of
a modest meal, but everything seemed to move as slowly as treacle as
Jared crossed the hall, coming directly to the king's side to whisper in
his ear.

"Sweet *Jesu*, no!" Brion said aloud, his tone and a stunned expression
instantly drawing all attention to him. "Are you sure?"

"Sadly, I am, Sire," Jared murmured. He turned his gaze to Lucien
Talbot, and to Sir Halloran and Lady Cloris, seated across from them. "I
regret to report that the Earl of Lendour apparently has passed away in
his sleep," he said baldly. Beyond them, a stunned-looking Xander slowly
rose, looking like he might be physically ill.

There followed a great flurry of agitated speculation and consternation, which only ceased when Lady Cloris drew the king and Jared to one
side, along with her son.

"I am deeply sorry that this has happened, Sire," she said quietly.
"You are welcome, of course, to let Lord Kenneth's body lie in the chapel
tonight—and sadly, you have already supplied the cart and horses that
will be necessary to take him home."

The king said nothing, other than to nod his thanks for the offer of
holy space. Jared was still too distraught to speak of what had happened.

"Sire," Sir Halloran said softly, with a sidelong glance at his mother,
"I am reminded that Lord Kenneth was once married to a Deryni woman.
It occurs to me that my mother and I might offer a last service to Lord
Kenneth, as a mark of respect and in thanks for the kindness he showed
my father."

Brion cocked his head in query.

"It may be that your chaplain would object," Halloran went on, "but you perhaps are aware that it is possible for those of our kind to . . . take certain measures that delay the corruption of a corpse."

The king glanced quickly at Jared, whose grief was shifting to hopeful interest.

"Are you speaking of a preservation spell?" Brion asked. "I have heard of such."

Halloran inclined his head. "None of the rest of your party need know of it," he said quietly. "It can be done privately in the chapel, once he is laid out for vigil." He quirked a bitter smile. "We cannot avert death, Sire, or even hold it at bay, but at least its outward form can be softened for a time, for the sake of the living. It seems to me that this would be a great kindness to Lord Kenneth's young children, if they might look upon their father's face a final time without the graphic reminder of his mortality."

At the king's look of query, Jared gave a jerky nod.

"It would, indeed, be a great kindness, Sire," he managed to murmur. "I do not relish the task of telling his children that he is gone."

Halloran glanced at his mother, who nodded, then gave a slight bow. "Then, it shall be done," he said quietly.

Chapter 27

"For this corruptible must put on incorruption, and this
mortal must put on immortality."
—I CORINTHIANS 15:53

I T was mid-October by the time a lone rider galloped into Culdi: Kenneth's aide, Sir Xander of Torrylin, asking to be taken directly to Lady Vera. Alaric and Duncan, practicing their stalking skills on the battlements, saw him arrive, but by the time they could reach the stable yard, Xander had disappeared.

"Has he brought letters?" Duncan asked the groom who was walking out Xander's horse.

"I have no idea, my lord," the man replied.

"He must have gone up to the solar," Alaric muttered; and he and Duncan took off to Vera's airy dayroom, pelting up the turnpike stair to find Llion and Sir Walter just disappearing behind the closing door.

"Llion, Llion, wait!" Alaric called, for both men looked very serious. But Llion only turned and shook his head, holding up a hand to forbid further exchange, then disappeared inside with Walter.

"What do you think has happened?" Duncan whispered, wide-eyed, as Alaric drew back in confusion, for it was not like Llion to be so brusque.

"I dunno," Alaric replied. "Something bad."

"You don't suppose something has happened to one of our fathers?" Duncan ventured timidly. "Or to the king?"

"I guess we'll have to wait until one of them comes out," Alaric said, trying to keep up a brave face. But he was worried.

Very shortly, Father Geordan came trudging up the stairs, followed by a stunned-looking Kevin.

"What's going on?" Duncan demanded. "I want to see my mother!"

"Not now," Father Geordan murmured. "Alaric, my boy, come with me, please. And Kevin, you stay with your brother."

This unexpected order took all three boys by surprise, Alaric not least among them. In something of a daze, he allowed the priest to escort him through the door, which closed behind them. In the room beyond, Llion and Xander both turned somber faces toward him. His Aunt Vera was comforting Geill, his half-sister, along with Sir Walter, Geill's husband. Abruptly Alaric realized that whatever the news Xander had brought, it was something to do with his father, not Duke Jared.

"Llion?" he managed to whisper.

Both Llion and Xander came to him immediately, Llion setting a heavy hand on his shoulder as Xander murmured, "I am so, so sorry, Alaric."

"Tell me! What has happened?" Alaric blurted, on the verge of tears.

"Come and sit," Llion said softly, drawing the boy to a seat in the window embrasure. "Your father . . . has passed away. They believe it was his heart."

Alaric could only gape in horrified disbelief.

"Duke Jared found him," Xander continued, sitting on the boy's other side. "It appears that he died in his sleep. He had your likeness in his hand: the locket with your portrait, and that of your mother and sister. He also had the letter you sent regarding your broken arm. Clearly, his last thoughts were of you."

"But—he *can't* be dead! He *can't* be!" Alaric protested, dashing the back of a hand at the tears welling up.

"The king is bringing his body home," Xander said quietly, blinking back his own tears. "They should arrive in a few days. Meanwhile, I am ordered to ride on to Morganhall with the news. Unless his sisters wish it otherwise, he's to be laid to rest there with his Morgan ancestors."

This stark statement of what must be was the final straw. The boy dissolved into tears, collapsing into Llion's arms to weep himself into hiccupping exhaustion. He was not aware of when the others, saving Vera and Llion, left the room; only that, when he came to his senses, he was lying partially in Vera's lap, curled in her arms, and Llion had retreated to the window embrasure, where he was gazing sightlessly out the window at the falling night.

"I am so, *so* sorry, my love," Vera whispered, her arms tightening around his shoulders as he lifted his head.

He sniffled and did his best to compose himself as he sat up, wordlessly accepting the embroidered handkerchief that Vera offered, and wiped at his face, blew his nose. He felt hollow and empty inside, drained of emotion, but he knew he would have to go on, though he had no idea how.

"What—what will happen to me now?" he whispered after a moment.

Vera sadly shook her head. "I don't know, dearest. When the king and your Uncle Jared arrive, I expect they will have made some of those decisions. But I fear that it probably means that you will be going to court far sooner than any of us had hoped."

Alaric swallowed and nodded. "I expected that." He closed his eyes briefly, then glanced back at Llion, who had moved closer at his first words. "Llion, did Xander tell you anything else about—how my father died?"

"Only what you know," Llion replied quietly. "But if he had to die— and it's clear that this was his time—how fortunate to die in a bed, at peace, with his loved ones in his final thoughts. That is not a blessing given to every man."

"No." Alaric swallowed again, forcing himself to turn to practicalities. "Xander said that it's planned to bury him at Morganhall. Do you think that's what he would have wanted?"

"I do," Llion replied. "Your father's Morgan heritage was very important to him. Xander said that the king would have allowed him to be buried in the royal crypts at Rhemuth, but Jared suggested that Morganhall would be more appropriate: to sleep with the generations of other Morgans who have given their loyal service to the Haldanes. Xander has already ridden for Morganhall, to inform your father's sisters of his death and begin making the arrangements."

Alaric slowly nodded. "Yes, that's as it should be," he whispered, and suddenly looked even more serious, if that were possible. "What about Bronwyn? Does she know yet?"

Vera shook her head. "Not yet. Do you want to tell her, or shall I? You are head of your family now, my love. If you wish to do it, that is your right."

"Will you help me?" Alaric answered in a very small voice.

"I will, of course," Vera replied. "Would you like Llion to help as well?"

Alaric nodded and swallowed hard, reaching out to take Llion's offered hand as he rose. "Please. We'd best do it now. She'll want to know—though I wish I could have gone forever without knowing. Where is she?"

"Probably looking for supper," Vera replied, rising. "Let's go find her, shall we?"

PREDICTABLY, Bronwyn wept when she learned of their father's death. But for the four-year-old, who had spent only a short time actually living with her father, her initial grief soon faded to simple sadness: a theoretical bereavement that could be honored more in the form than in the substance.

By the next morning, she had mostly put her grief behind her—unlike Alaric, who reluctantly made himself return to his drill with Duncan and Kevin, but also spent many a silent hour walking the battlements with Llion and watching the western approach, occasionally reminiscing about the man they both had loved. They were there three days later, when a growing cloud of dust on the distant road suddenly caught Alaric's attention.

"Llion?" he said, stiffening.

Llion followed his gaze, watching as a smaller cloud of dust detached from the rest and moved at speed toward the castle, gradually resolving into an approaching rider in bright Haldane livery.

"They'll be here shortly," he confirmed, setting a hand on the boy's shoulder. "We'd best go change."

Very shortly they were down in the castle yard, now attired in the somber black of mourning. Vera had brought Bronwyn down, with Kevin and Duncan to accompany them, and Kenneth's daughter Geill stood with them as well, with her husband supporting her. Only weeks before, the couple had shared the welcome news of Geill's first pregnancy with Vera and the rest of the family, of a coming child who would never know his or her grandsire.

All too soon, the first of the riders entered the yard, accompanied by a great cloud of dust. As the king and Jared dismounted, Alaric drew himself to trembling attention, Llion at his back, his family all around him. Beyond the king, a canopied cart drawn by two horses bore what could only be his father's body, closely wrapped in a shroud made grimy by the dust of the road.

"Alaric, I am so sorry," the king said, quickly stripping off his riding gloves as he approached the boy.

With a jerky nod that was both an acknowledgment and a bow, Alaric turned his gaze to Jared, who had embraced his wife with one arm but was also watching the boy closely.

"Uncle," the boy said with a jerky nod. "Xander said that you were the one who found him. Is it really true that his passing was peaceful?"

"So it appeared," Jared replied. He drew the silver locket from inside his tunic and extended it to the boy. "This was in his hand. And he also had the letter you had sent regarding your broken arm." He jutted his chin at the arm in question. "I see that you are mostly recovered."

Alaric gave a vague nod as he accepted the locket, but all his focus was on his father's body as he moved between Jared and the king to approach, clasping the locket close. Drawing near, he reached a hand to almost touch the dusty shroud, but then let the hand fall heavily to his side.

"Xander said that he's to be buried at Morganhall, with his Morgan ancestors," he said softly, turning slightly toward the king.

"I did offer a place in the royal crypts at Rhemuth," Brion replied, "but Duke Jared felt that your father would have preferred Morganhall."

Alaric managed a jerky nod. "It is a kind offer, Sire, but Duke Jared is right. He belongs at Morganhall." He paused to swallow painfully. "May I—make one personal request?"

"Of course."

"My mother lies here at Culdi. If it is possible, might he lie beside her for the night? He's already with her, I know, but it would . . . give me comfort."

"That can certainly be done," Jared murmured, with a speaking glance at Vera, who had drifted closer to join them. "And a funeral Mass early tomorrow, before we leave for Morganhall, so that the household may pay their respects."

Alaric said nothing; merely gave a jerky nod, then turned on his heel to flee the yard with Llion. He tried not to think about the body of his beloved father, wrapped in its dusty shroud, and reminded himself again and again that Kenneth Morgan no longer occupied that all too mortal flesh.

H E did not make an appearance at table that evening, though he did allow Llion to have a meal brought up for him, and forced himself to pick at it. Later that night, after it was dark, he took Llion with him when he went down to the familiar garden chapel where his mother's tomb lay. The door to the chapel stood open to the night, candlelight spilling out across the threshold. Silent Lendour men with torches stood to either side of the doorway. Just as he and Llion approached, Vera came out of the chapel with Duncan and Kevin, followed by Sir Walter with his arm around a sobbing Geill.

The sight caused Alaric to hold back until they had passed, resolutely avoiding their gaze. Only when the sound of their footsteps on the gravel had faded did he again move toward the open doorway.

"Shall I wait outside?" Llion asked quietly.

"Please."

Reluctantly the boy moved into the rectangle of light, nodding nervous acknowledgment to the two Lendour men, and drew a cautious breath as he stepped through the doorway. Someone had set fat pillar candles in floor stands at either end of his mother's familiar effigy, and a black-draped catafalque had been drawn close beside it, bearing an open coffin. A banner of Lendour lay across the lower half of both, like a coverlet. The red of the banner looked almost black in the candlelight.

"Come ahead in," said a quiet voice behind and to his right, speaking from the shadows.

He started at that, but a quick glance revealed the speaker to be the king, clad all in black, who had been standing quietly with another man whom Alaric did not know. The stranger remained in the shadows as the king moved quietly to the coffin and beckoned for Alaric to join him.

"Come and look," the king said. "It isn't what you're probably expecting."

Bracing himself, and wondering what the king meant, Alaric came to stand beside him—and drew a startled breath as he dared to look into the coffin. To his surprise, his father's body had been laid out in a long robe embroidered with the Lendour arms rather than the grimy shroud in which he had traveled from Meara. Though a veil of fine gauze covered the face, Alaric could see the contours of the familiar profile through the gauze. A similar veil had covered his mother's face, the last time he had looked upon her.

"He did pass peacefully, Alaric," the king said softly beside him. "There's no evidence to suggest otherwise. Would you like to see his face?"

The boy swallowed hard and gave a nod of acceptance, and the king lifted the veil and folded it back above the head. Looking closer, Alaric was heartened to find the sight not at all as dreadful as he had imagined. In fact, by the flickering light of the watch candles and the many votives set around the perimeter of the tiny chamber, he could almost imagine that his father merely slept, here beside his beloved Alyce. The skin had a faintly pearlescent glow to it, almost like the alabaster of his mother's effigy.

"There has been a preservation spell placed upon your father's body," the king said softly. "Not by me, but . . ." He cast a thoughtful glance at the stranger in the shadows, then set a hand on Alaric's shoulder and guided him to a bench set against the chapel's south wall.

"Sit with me for a while," the king said quietly. "You're probably wondering about the spell. It has to do with what happened shortly *before* your father passed, for he was not the only man to die in my service in Meara."

As Alaric looked at him in question—and at the stranger still standing in the shadows—the king turned his gaze back to the banner-draped coffin beside the sepulcher.

"Several days before your father's death, when we had finally found Caitrin of Meara, the encounter cost us the life of Sir Morian du Joux. He was a Deryni in my service, who had also served my father. Yes, there are—or were—other Deryni in royal service," he said, glancing again at the stranger in the shadows. "Morian's son has yet to decide whether he will take up his father's mantle, but he and his mother were kind enough to set the spell on your father's body. Sir Halloran, will you come and meet Lord Kenneth's son?"

The man in the shadows pushed himself away from the wall and moved slowly into the brighter candlelight around the bier. He was taller than the king, and somewhat older, with pale eyes and a thatch of wavy red hair that glistened in the candlelight, and bearded likewise. He was also the source of a quick but powerful probe against Alaric's shields, withdrawn at once, when it became clear that the boy had shields of his own and had sensed the attempted intrusion.

"You're Deryni!" Alaric blurted, instinctively pressing closer to the king.

Halloran gave an awkward little bow and a hint of a smile. "So I am—and so are you, I see. My father spoke of you in passing: the half-Deryni lad who will one day be Duke of Corwyn."

Alaric darted a glance at his father's coffin, now able to detect a tingle of power like unto that of Halloran himself. It was not a magic yet accessible to a boy of only nine, but he had heard of such spells, and now was seeing firsthand what one could do.

"It—appears that I have you to thank for the spell placed on my father's body, Sir Halloran," he said tentatively. "Especially for my little sister's sake, and for my other sisters. It is a great kindness."

"It little compares to the kindness done by your father to mine," Halloran replied. His tone was such that Alaric immediately glanced at the king, then back at Halloran.

"What— May I ask what he did?"

Halloran glanced at his feet, shifting uneasily, then lifted his gaze to the king. "Sire, perhaps it would be better if you spoke of this, since you were present. By your leave, I shall wait outside."

"Very well."

Brion waited until Halloran had left the chapel, pulling the door closed behind him, then glanced aside at Alaric.

"I hope that you will not fault Sir Halloran for declining to explain," the king said. "His father did not merely die on the Mearan expedition. Those responsible for his death sought his life because he was Deryni, and your father . . . Tell me, have you been taught about the coup de grâce?"

"I know what it is," the boy said cautiously. "Did my father give it to Sir Halloran's father?"

"Not . . . exactly," the king answered, "though he did help speed Morian on his way, at his request. It is a solemn duty that most warriors will eventually have to face. Have *I* done it?" he added, apparently anticipating Alaric's next question. "No," he admitted. "But I know it probably lies in my future—and yours. If one is to be a leader of men, especially of fighting men, one also assumes a responsibility for their well-being. Sadly, that sometimes includes easing them on their final journey."

"I understand," Alaric whispered. And he did, in an abstract sense. He had seen wounded animals dispatched at the end of a hunt, to end their suffering, and occasionally had been present when a foundered horse had to be put down. (He tried not to think about the grey mare.) He knew the necessity to give a suffering animal the mercy stroke, but he could not imagine what it must be like, to deliberately end a man's life. Killing in the heat of battle was one thing; he thought he could do that, when the time came. But the coup . . .

"May I—know the circumstances of Sir Morian's death?" he said hesitantly.

Brion nodded. "You have a right to know." He drew a fortifying breath and crossed his arms on his chest. "You're aware that we had gone to seek out Caitrin of Meara. Morian had been doing advance scout work, and joined us shortly after Ratharkin. We had poor hunting for many weeks, but we finally stumbled upon her with a small party on the shore near Cloome. There was great surprise and confusion on both sides at first, but Caitrin's forces initially outnumbered ours, and they immediately pressed their advantage, for they recognized Morian.

"None of us saw exactly what happened, because all of us were under attack. Morian's attackers overwhelmed him, and dragged him from the saddle. And one of them . . . managed to stab him through the chest with a narwhal tusk. Do you know what a narwhal is?"

Alaric shook his head.

"Well, it's a kind of whale, though it can easily be mistaken for a seal or a walrus, especially when it's dead," the king went on. "What is particularly distinctive about narwhals is that they have a long, spiraled horn, as big around as a man's thumb, and sometimes taller than a man. Sometimes they have two. The ancients, occasionally finding narwhal tusks, came to believe that they were actually unicorn horns: powerful defense against magic."

"But—where did the Mearans get a narwhal tusk?" Alaric asked.

"Sheerest happenstance on their part, I suppose, and damned fool bad luck on ours," the king replied. He paused to draw a deep breath. "It was a very hot afternoon, so I had decided to take a ride along the beach with just a few men: your father, Duke Jared, Morian, and two guards. Jamyl was following with a more suitable escort: perhaps six or eight armed men, I suppose. I wasn't entirely stupid.

"But there were only the six of us in our immediate party. As we rounded a little headland, we ran smack into a much larger body of armed men. Some of them had found a dead narwhal washed up on the beach, and were in the process of hacking the horn off the carcass, though we didn't know that initially. And of course, we didn't know who they were, or that Caitrin and her new husband were with them. But they recognized Morian, especially after I'd spoken to him by name. I shan't make *that* mistake again."

Brion sighed and glanced away briefly. "Anyway, it all happened very quickly, and I doubt even his attackers thought they'd succeed in killing him. When Jamyl and the rest of our escort came around the headland, most of the Mearans fled, though we did kill one, and captured a few more.

"But by then, the deed was done. Morian . . . was still conscious, but he knew his wound was mortal. We all did. The narwhal tusk had pierced his lung, and it was the only thing holding his life in. So he—asked your father to release him, for the sake of the Deryni woman he had dared to love."

Alaric's mouth had fallen open as the king spoke, and he caught his breath in wonder.

"He knew about my mother?"

Brion nodded. "He did. And Kenneth agreed to do as Morian asked.

He could do no other. The end was very quick, very gentle. Morian—did not suffer further."

He sighed and shook his head, forcing himself to continue.

"For that act of mercy, Morian's family later would return the favor. His body—was not in the best of condition by the time we got it back to them. The heat had begun to take its toll, so we buried him the very next morning after arriving at his home. But then, when your father died that afternoon, Morian's widow and his son offered to place the preservation spell on his body, to spare you what they had experienced. They believed that he would have done the same for Kenneth, had he been able. I hope you don't mind."

Alaric shook his head, numb with the knowledge, and stunned that such a thing was even possible. "How long will it last?" he whispered.

"Another week or so, I am told," the king replied. "Sir Halloran has asked leave to return to his family in the morning, but he assures me that the spell will last long enough to see him safely to Morganhall, so that his sisters and his daughters can bid him a proper farewell. Incidentally, I did not see Bronwyn with the rest of your family, when they came earlier. Did they decide not to let her see him?"

"I don't know," the boy whispered. "Probably. I didn't know he would look . . . this way. I thought she would be frightened."

"Would you like me to bring her, in the morning before Mass?" the king asked gently.

"Would you?" the boy replied.

"Of course."

Alaric looked at his feet, suddenly awkward. "I'll come along, if I may."

"Are you sure?"

He nodded. "I'm the older brother. That's part of my job."

"Very well, I'll bring both of you," the king said.

Chapter 28

"The memory of the just is blessed . . ."
—PROVERBS 10:7

T HE king was as good as his word, and brought both Alaric and Bronwyn to visit their father early the next morning. Llion accompanied them. Bronwyn held back with him at first; but then, at the urging of the king, who crouched down to her level, she let him pick her up and carry her over to gaze into the coffin. She was wide-eyed and curious, a little timid, but not at all frightened, for it was, after all, her father, lying next to all she knew of her mother.

She gazed silently at his veiled face for several minutes, saying nothing, then turned away to bury her face against the king's shoulder. Alaric had stood stonily on the other side of his mother's effigy, not really looking, but when the king made to carry Bronwyn from the chapel, the boy tarried, resting his hands lightly on his mother's effigy.

"Alaric, are you coming?"

"In a few minutes, Sire," the boy murmured. "Will they close the coffin before it's taken over to the church?"

"Yes."

"Then, I'd like a few minutes in private," came the reply. "Could Llion stay?"

"Of course."

With a speaking glance at Llion, the king carried Bronwyn from the little chapel and closed the door behind them. Llion, with a nod to his young master, took up a position with his back against the door, hands clasped behind him and head bowed.

It was deathly quiet in the little chapel, as was fitting in this place of death. The vigil lights of the previous night had burned out, other than the Presence lamp above the little altar, but the soft morning light streamed through the open window above, bathing Kenneth's body and his wife's effigy in a golden haze.

Bracing himself, Alaric trailed one hand along the cool alabaster of his mother's effigy and moved around to the prie-dieu set beside his father's open coffin. Kneeling there, he awkwardly signed himself with the cross as he bowed his head in wordless prayer, because he knew he should. The king had said that Halloran's spell would last until Morgan-hall, but it might not. Delays sometimes happened. Alaric knew that this might be his last chance to say a proper good-bye to the man who had given him life and the love of a precious father.

He crossed himself again, then leaned forward to fold back the veil covering his father's face. Again, especially in the soft glow of morning, it was easy to imagine that some semblance of life lingered, that his father only slept beside the silent effigy of the mother who also had died all too untimely.

"Oh, Papa," he breathed, tears welling in his eyes. "Why did you have to leave? I needed you *here*, with *me*!"

He briefly closed his eyes at that, fighting back the tears, which he knew would change nothing. Then, vision still blurry, he slipped a hand into the neck of his tunic and pulled out his father's silver locket, now hanging from a leather thong around his neck. Fumbling it open, he took out the tiny miniatures of himself and his sister, which he earlier had pried loose from their settings, and let the locket dangle as he glanced briefly at the two likenesses.

"I've thought about it, Papa," he whispered, fingering the two minia-tures, "and I want you to have these, so that you won't forget us." He was biting at his lip as he leaned forward to slip the tiny keepsakes into the front opening of his father's robe, close to the heart. "And when we get to Morganhall, I'm going to ask Aunt Delphine to paint a new one of you, to keep in the locket with the one of Mummy." He swallowed painfully. "I guess I don't really need pictures to remind me of you, because you're always in *here*"—he touched his chest over his heart—"but I'll have them to look at when I'm really missing you."

He gently reached out to brush his father's cheek, then bent to press a final kiss to the cold forehead, remembering a similar kiss he had given his mother in farewell.

"You should go to her now, Papa," he whispered very softly. "I think she's been waiting for you. I only wish she could have waited a little longer, because I still need you so much!"

He could feel his throat tightening, and sensed the tears starting to sting again behind his eyelids, but he pulled himself together by an act of sheer will as he straightened to draw the veil back into place across his father's face. He was composed if somber by the time he rose and made his way back to Llion, and held his head high as Llion opened the door to admit the men waiting to close the coffin.

THE funeral cortege left for Morganhall directly after the Requiem Mass celebrated at Culdi in Kenneth's behalf. His now-coffined body again traveled in the canopied cart, escorted by his son and Llion, the king, the Duke of Cassan, and an honor guard of Cassani borderers. The king retained two of his Haldane cavalrymen as personal guards, but sent the rest back to Rhemuth with Jiri and Jamyl to report to Duke Richard and advise him regarding the Mearan venture.

Kenneth's daughter Geill and her husband did not accompany the party going on to Morganhall, for Walter feared that the hurried journey might endanger her pregnancy. Vera likewise remained at Culdi with Bronwyn, who was deemed too young for further exposure to death, and also Kevin and Duncan; all had already said their good-byes. The burial at Morganhall would be strictly a family affair.

Obliged to travel slowly because of the cart and its cheerless burden, they took several days to make the journey to Morganhall. Kenneth's sister Delphine was waiting to receive them, along with his daughter Alazais, just arrived from the Convent of Notre Dame de l'Arc-en-Ciel. With

her had come the abbess, Mother Iris Judiana, and several other sisters
who had known and admired Kenneth. Though all the sisters were
garbed in the distinctive sky-blue habit of their order, with a rainbow-
embroidered band along the front edge of the veil, Alazais wore deepest
black; for though she had been in residence at Arc-en-Ciel for some years,
and was establishing herself as an illuminator of note like her sister and
sister-in-law before her, she yet remained a secular member of that house.
Claara did not come down for the reception, being still confined to her
bed, but the Morganhall knights brought her downstairs in a litter later
that evening, to visit her brother's coffin and dine with the new arrivals.

That night, over a simple meal in the great hall, Jared reiterated his
account of Kenneth's passing, for the benefit of the Morgan women gathered there. Meanwhile, the coffined body lay in Morganhall's tiny chapel.
Llion kept vigil, since he had heard the story all too many times. Alaric
was allowed to sit with the adults, flanked by his Aunt Delphine and Lady
Melissa, his former nurse, but it was mostly a rehash of what folk had
been saying for the past week, and he found himself nodding off early.

Zoë and her husband arrived the next afternoon with Xander, exhausted from their helter-skelter dash from Cynfyn, where they had left
their young children with Jovett's parents. Zoë's reunion with her sister
Alazais was joyous, but tinged with the sorrow that all of them shared as
Jared retold the story and tears were shed anew.

After a little while, Alaric could bear it no longer, and excused himself
to go with Llion up to the rooftops, as had long been his place of refuge
when life became too intense.

"I couldn't stand it anymore, Llion," he muttered, as he plopped
down behind one of the parapets and Llion crouched beside him. "They
just keep repeating the same things that I've heard before. He was my
father. With him gone, nothing is ever going to be the same."

"No, it won't," Llion agreed. "But he was Zoë's father, too—and
Alazais's, and Geill's. And Bronwyn's, not to mention being grandda to
the grandchildren that will never know him. Do you think that things
will be the same for any of *them*?"

"No," the boy whispered.

"Then, what is your true concern?" Llion asked after a moment, shifting to a seated position beside him. "Are you worried about what will happen to you now?"

Alaric had clasped his arms around his drawn-up knees, and rested his chin on his knees. "I suppose. Llion, I'm going to miss him *so* much. . . ."

"Of course you are. You loved him, and you always will. But life *will* go on."

"At court now, I suppose."

"That's true. But you knew that."

"But it wasn't supposed to happen so soon!" Alaric blurted. "I was supposed to have a few years at Uncle Jared's court!"

"Yes, well, I think that would have been a good idea, too, but the king has changed his mind, under the circumstances. I'm sure you'll get a few weeks' reprieve, possibly even a few months, until your arm has completely healed, but my guess would be that you'll go to court permanently after the first of the year."

Alaric lifted his chin indignantly. "It's already been decided, then?"

"It has been discussed," Llion allowed.

"When?"

"Over the past week or so, when you were safely abed. I won't lie to you," Llion added, when the boy looked at him rebelliously. "Like you, I must answer to a higher authority—and at this point, I'm not even sure who that is, since my service was directly to your father. The difference is that one day, provided I've managed to get you safely to adulthood, there won't be a much higher authority than you."

"I hadn't even thought about *your* service," Alaric whispered. "Llion, they won't take you away from me, will they?"

Llion shrugged. "I don't know. I don't think so. Sir Ninian de Piran offered me a place on Duke Richard's training staff, if ever I should leave your father's service—though I don't think any of this was what he had in mind. For the present, however, I do answer to Duke Jared and the king, as you do. And they've determined that, with your father gone, you'll be safest, and get the best training, if you are directly in the king's service. Believe me, there are far worse fates than to be the king's personal page, and then his squire, until you become his Duke of Corwyn."

Alaric turned his face away for a long moment, then lifted his chin to gaze out at the night. "I suppose that part is all right," he agreed. "And if you join Duke Richard's staff, I'd still see you. But will you still be my knight, Llion?'

"Always, my lord," Llion replied with a smile. "And your friend, if you'll have me."

The boy managed a faint, tentative smile. "Then I suppose I do still have control over *something*," he said, and awkwardly extended his good hand. "Thank you, Llion."

LATER that night, the last before Kenneth Morgan's burial, Alaric dressed carefully in his old Lendour surcoat over a black tunic and breeches, and buckled on the small sword he was allowed to wear for formal events, along with the dagger that had belonged to his Corwyn grandfather. To that he added the tartan sash of his Cassani page's service, for he knew how proud his father had been of that. Then, around his neck, he hung the leather thong on which he had strung his father's gold Lendour signet, quietly given him by the king shortly after they returned from Meara with Kenneth's body. It was Alaric's now, for he had become Earl of Lendour at his father's death, though he was still years away from being able to actually claim the title.

Llion, for his part, kept to his all-black attire, though with Kenneth's Lendour badge prominent on one sleeve, since both of them intended to take a turn at keeping vigil beside the coffin.

Down in Morganhall's tiny chapel, Xander and three other knights from Lendour had already mounted a guard of honor at the corners of the closed coffin, facing away from it, heads bowed and hands clasped at their waists. The banner of Lendour covered the coffin, its white and crimson folds billowing down the sides.

But when Alaric started to enter the room, he realized that Jovett was also present, at the back of the chapel, in quiet conversation with another dark-clad man. Jovett turned as Alaric paused in the doorway, Llion also holding back, then quickly came to meet them. His companion remained in the shadows. The four guardian knights did not lift their heads.

"Alaric," Jovett said quietly, also nodding to Llion.

"Llion, please keep watch at the door," the other man said, emerging from the shadows to join them.

Llion immediately moved to the side of the doorway, half turning to keep an eye on the stair from which they had just emerged. By the light of the candles set at the head and foot of the coffin, Alaric felt a thrill of recognition as he saw that Jovett's companion was Sé Trelawney.

"You!" he whispered. "I prayed that you would come!"

Sé inclined his head. "Would that it were in happier circumstances. I am very sorry that this has happened."

Alaric shrugged and briefly averted his gaze. "So am I. But thank you for being here. He would appreciate that, I know. In fact, you have always been there when he needed you—and I thank you for that as well."

Suddenly making a connection that had not occurred to him before, he glanced at Jovett, then at Sé again. His consternation must have shown on his face, because Jovett smiled faintly and folded his arms across his chest.

"Yes, I am," he said quietly. "And we'll speak of this at a more appropriate time. In the meantime, I trust that you'll keep your sudden enlightenment to yourself."

"Of course," the boy murmured, wide-eyed.

"And more immediately," Sé interjected, "I gather that you've come here for the same reason we did: to pay honor to your father." He glanced approvingly at Alaric's sword and mourning attire. "Shall we rotate in, then, and allow our colleagues from Lendour to take a well-deserved break?" he asked, jutting his chin in the direction of the oblivious Lendouri knights.

Alaric only nodded solemnly, suddenly aware that Sé must have controlled the knights as he had done to others in the past. He wondered whether Llion was also controlled, but his mentor seemed well aware of what was going on, with none of the dazed look about him that characterized the guardian knights. Which meant that Llion knew about Sé—and now, Jovett as well—and that Sé trusted the young knight to keep their confidence.

"Gentlemen, Lord Alaric and these other knights will take over for a while," Sé said to the men, opening his arms to include all of them in a

vague shooing motion toward the door. "Sir Xander, please remain outside the door to give us some privacy."

Without demur, the four lifted their heads and filed out of the room,
Xander pulling the door closed behind them. Jovett started to move into
one of the guard posts around the coffin, but Alaric caught his sleeve and
glanced at Sé. Before they began their vigil, there was one other thing he
needed to do, here in the presence of his father.

"Sir Sé, Jovett, before we proceed, could I ask your indulgence?"

Both Deryni paused, exchanging glances, and Llion also looked at
him in question.

"Earlier this evening," Alaric said carefully, "Sir Llion agreed to be
my knight. We clasped hands on the bargain, but with his permission, I
should like to make the arrangement more formal, in front of witnesses.
If he's still willing, that is."

At once Llion sank to one knee before him, lifting his joined hands to
the boy in the traditional gesture of vassal to lord.

"You know that I *am* your knight, my lord," he murmured. "Will you
receive my vow?"

Alaric nodded and clasped Llion's hands between his, and the two
Deryni moved closer to witness.

"I, Llion Farquahar, do become your liege man of life and limb and
earthly worship," Llion said steadily, his eyes never leaving Alaric's. "Faith
and truth will I bear unto you, to live and to die, so help me God."

"And I, Alaric Anthony Morgan, pledge to be unto you a true and
faithful lord," Alaric replied. "So help me God."

Before Llion could rise, Jovett also knelt and offered up his joined
hands.

"Alaric, I, too, am your man, as I was your father's man," Jovett said,
nodding as the boy shifted to enclose his joined hands. "And I vow to
serve and protect your interests in Lendour, for so long as you shall need
me. So help me God."

"Thank you, Jovett," Alaric whispered. "With an elder brother guarding Lendour for me, I could not be better served." He glanced aside in
surprise, for Sé had also knelt, but not to offer his hands. Instead, he
slipped his sword from its hangers, and now offered the hilt to him.

"My fealty is already given to a higher Lord," Sé said softly, "but I promise you my service in time of need, as I promised your mother and your father before you. Will you accept what I may give?"

Nodding, Alaric laid a hand on the cross-hilt of Sé's sword. "I shall always treasure whatever service you may give," he said. "And thank you, *all* of you."

"Right, then," Jovett said, standing. "I know that Kenneth would approve what has just been done. Now we should pay our respects, as is fitting and proper."

"Amen to that," Sé replied, as he and Llion also rose.

So saying, he moved into position at the foot of the coffin, touching a reverent hand to the Lendour banner before clasping his hands at his waist and bowing his head. The others followed suit, Jovett opposite Sé, and Llion and Alaric taking places left and right. Thus they stood for the next hour, each meditating on the life of the man they had come to honor.

S IR Kenneth Kai Morgan Earl of Lendour would be buried at noon the next day, in the selfsame crypt where his beloved second wife had lain while her tomb was being prepared at Culdi. It also was not far from the grave of his celebrated kinsman, the loyal Sir Charlan Morgan, who had died at the side of King Javan Haldane, so many years before.

Sir Sé Trelawney was among the eight knights who bore the coffin from the chapel at Morganhall to the nearby church. Aside from Alaric, Llion, and Jovett, no one marked his particular presence, in part because he did not wish them to, but in part because, in his stark black robes, he looked much like any of the other knights who performed this final service for their liege lord.

Alaric walked behind the coffin with his Aunt Delphine, the king, Duke Jared, and the delegation of sisters from Arc-en-Ciel, along with two of his half-sisters: one who had studied at the convent and with Alaric's mother, the other now resident at the convent, though she had not taken vows. His Aunt Claara, still confined to her bed, was carried down to the church on a litter, to weep beside the coffin as Father Swithun cele-

brated the Requiem Mass to send Kenneth on his final journey. As a special tribute of their own, the sisters of Arc-en-Ciel sang the Mass
responses, Alazais and Zoë joining their number, and at the end offered
the hauntingly beautiful funeral antiphons that had been sung at the
funeral of Marie de Corwyn, so many years before:

*"Alleluia. . . . Chori angelorum te suscipiat. . . . In paradisum deducant
te angeli. . . ."*

Alleluia. May choirs of angels receive thee. May the angels accompany
thee to paradise. Give rest, O Lord, to Your servant, who has fallen asleep.
Remember me, O Lord, when You come into Your kingdom. . . .

When the Mass was ended, the king, a duke, and four more knights
who had been close friends of the dead man carried his coffin down into
the crypt of the church. Sé held back from this last service, lest his ano-
nymity be compromised by such confined proximity to those who might
know him, for space was tight down in the crypt; but he had already paid
his respects the night before, and had disappeared by the time the immediate family emerged from the little church.

L ATER that evening, in the aftermath of a long and emotional day,
the king summoned the members of Alaric's extended family for a
private meeting in the castle's great hall. While the arrangement for the
boy's future had been quite clear between the king and Kenneth, the rest
of the family—and Alaric himself—needed to be informed of the king's
plans.

"I know that it was your father's wish that you serve for at least a few
years in Duke Jared's household," he told the boy and said duke, as they
gathered before the fireplace. The evening had grown cool, and the
season definitely was turning. Zoë and Jovett, Alazais, and Delphine
Morgan were also present, along with Llion. Claara had made her apologies and retired to her room, for the day had taken much out of her.

"Sire," said Jared, "you're aware of the reasons he wished this to happen. The court at Rhemuth is not without its dangers for a boy of Alaric's
lineage."

"I am well aware of the increased dangers at court," the king replied, "but with his father gone, I believe that his training for the future would be best served if he were at my side."

"But you cannot guarantee his safety," Zoë said baldly. "Remember what happened to Krispin MacAthan. I was there. And it was not widely known that he was Deryni."

"With all respect, my lady, *none* of us can guarantee his safety," the king replied. "But because of that, and because I greatly value your goodwill, and that of your family, I am willing to offer something of a compromise. I am willing that Alaric should remain in Duke Jared's household until the new year. He could join the royal household at Twelfth Night court. That will give all of you time to get used to the idea and make the necessary adjustments, and for me to confer with my uncle and the rest of my household officers about the best way to go about integrating a new page into my court. Granted, there will be resentment, but there is precedent for a king attaching particular pages and squires to his personal retinue."

"Until Twelfth Night, you say?" Jared said quietly.

"Aye, and he will be well into his tenth year by then," the king replied. "If he continues to grow as he has over this past summer, he should be able to hold his own with any bullies he encounters."

"Bullies near his own age, perhaps," Jared said sourly. "But what of the sort who killed Krispin MacAthan?"

The king's jaw tightened. "That is why I shall place him under my personal protection. And he will become older and more capable with each passing day. He has a powerful destiny to fulfill, Jared, and many obstacles to overcome. We must not cripple him by protecting him overmuch."

"I am willing to go at Twelfth Night," Alaric said quietly, speaking for the first time.

All eyes turned toward the nine-year-old.

"I have always known that it would be a challenge to get me safely grown. May I ask one favor?"

Brion inclined his head. "Of course."

"I should like to retain Sir Llion as my knight—not to serve me as he has, as governor, but to be present and accessible to me at court, so that I have at least one person besides yourself, in whom I can trust utterly."

"That is entirely reasonable," the king agreed. "I assume that, with your knight resident at court, I may also utilize his services from time to time?"

His wink, directed at both the boy and Llion, defused any hint of affront on his part, but Delphine still drew back in an expression of indignation.

"Alaric! You are speaking to your king!"

"Let be, my lady," Brion immediately replied, smiling as he reached across to pat her hand in reassurance. "He is my future duke, and I shall always expect him to speak his mind. He did so courteously, and he is entirely right in his concern. I am well aware of the pressures he will face at court, far beyond those of any other page or squire in my service. Llion, have you any particular concerns that you would care to offer?"

"I do, Sire," Llion replied, with an inclination of his head. "Both Alaric and I are grateful for your understanding, but if I may, I should like to offer a practical arrangement that would benefit all three of us." At the king's nod, he continued. "Sir Ninian de Piran offered me a position on Duke Richard's training staff, if I should ever leave Earl Kenneth's service. My service is now to his son, but circumstances still would allow such a position, if Duke Richard agrees. He gave me to understand that His Highness would also support such an appointment. If you agree, of course."

The king glanced in question at Jared, who nodded.

"I should prefer that he stay with me for another few years, but this is acceptable."

"And apparently Alaric is in agreement." The king gave a curt nod. "Very well, then, I shall expect the three of you at Twelfth Night."

THE king departed for Rhemuth the next morning with his two guards. Jared remained at Morganhall with Alaric and Llion for several more days, confirming the present arrangements for Lendour, at least until the king should decide otherwise, and installing Xander at Morganhall to oversee that holding—again, until the king might determine otherwise, though Morganhall was Alaric's now, and must be held in trust for him until he came of age. When Jared and his party finally rode out of Morganhall, Jovett and Zoë headed east toward Lendour. The holy sisters and Alazais rode a little way with the ducal party before turning off toward Arc-en-Ciel. Shortly after they had disappeared from sight, Llion glanced sidelong at Alaric and eased his horse a little closer, keeping his voice down. They were riding at the tail end of the ducal procession.

"It was good to see the holy sisters again, even if in such sober circumstances," he remarked.

Alaric absently agreed that it was.

"I loved their singing at the funeral. They sounded like angels."

Alaric made a vague sound of agreement, though his mind was elsewhere.

"I was a little surprised that your sister Alazais was not wearing the habit of the order," Llion went on. "When I asked Zoë about it, she laughed and told me that Alazais has never taken vows."

"No, of course not," Alaric replied, only now beginning to pay casual attention. "She's been studying manuscript illumination, you know, as Zoë and my mother did."

"Has she?" Llion said thoughtfully.

"Aye, and Father Swithun says that she's gotten very good—perhaps as good as Zoë or my mother. She's even begun taking commissions."

"Indeed."

"I gave her a commission," Alaric said after a beat, glancing down at his reins. "I was going to ask Aunt Delphine to do it, but I'd forgotten how good Alazais is. In fact, I left Father's locket with her, and asked her to make me a portrait of him to go inside." He cast a sidelong glance at Llion. "There's room now. I put the ones that Aunt Delphine did of me and Bronwyn in Father's coffin, next to his heart." He paused a beat. "Was it wrong to do that?"

"Not at all," Llion replied, with a faint smile. "And Alazais is going to paint a new miniature of your father?"

Alaric nodded happily. "She said she'd try to have it done by Twelfth Night. And if she does, she'll bring it to Rhemuth for me. She promised to come and see me received as the king's page."

"Did she, now?"

Something in his wistful tone made Alaric look up sharply, suddenly aware that Llion's seemingly idle questioning seemed to be focused rather precisely on his youngest half-sister.

"Why do you ask about Alazais?" he said, after glancing at the riders ahead of them, to be sure they could not be overheard. "Do you fancy her?"

"No, I—" Llion looked suddenly flustered, a faint blush staining his cheeks as he feigned intense interest in his horse's mane.

"Llion, tell me!" Alaric said quietly, but quite emphatically. "And don't lie to me, because I'll know. If you do fancy her, I think it's wonderful. And if you marry her, we'd be brothers."

Llion's face went from rosy to sheet-white. "My lord, I would never presume. . . ."

Alaric abruptly reined in his horse, reaching across to snag Llion's reins as well. Ahead, the rest of the ducal party were continuing on. It was a straight, open part of the road, so he thought it unlikely that anyone would turn back immediately to check on them.

"Llion, it is not presumptuous to take a fancy to my sister. You have a right to a normal life. You're a knight, and a very well-regarded one. You'll be on Duke Richard's staff, and provisions will be made for you. *I'll* make provisions for you. The pair of you could live at court, and she could continue to paint, and serve the queen—and a new, younger queen, once the king marries. Now, answer me truly. Do you fancy her?"

Llion managed an awkward swallow and nodded. "I do, my lord."

"And does she fancy you?"

"I—I think so, my lord. It was only in the last few days that we actually talked much, but we've known one another for several years."

"Yes?"

"We first met at Zoë and Jovett's wedding celebration. I doubt you remember that. But we both were young then, and I was only recently entered into your father's service, and I never would have presumed—"

"Well, you aren't presuming now," Alaric retorted, "and I think my father would have approved." He glanced ahead, where Father Nevan had noticed them lagging behind and was turning his horse back in their direction.

"We'll speak more of this later," he said. "We'll see her at Twelfth Night, if all goes well, and I'll talk with her then. If both of you want it, then we'll make it happen."

With that, he set heels to his horse and trotted on ahead to rejoin the others, Llion close beside him. He had not noticed any particular interaction between Llion and Alazais in the days surrounding his father's funeral observances, but then, he had been a bit preoccupied. Still, the thought of having Llion as his brother made him very happy. And helping make it happen was something to look forward to, when he must move permanently to the court at Rhemuth, with all its challenges.

Chapter 29

*"If they obey and serve him, they shall spend
their days in prosperity . . ."*
—JOB 36:11

THEY arrived back in Culdi late in October, with much to accomplish before Twelfth Night. Since Alaric's arm now was mostly healed, Llion immediately eased him back into light training with Duncan and Kevin, to rebuild his strength. The familiar drills were more difficult than Alaric remembered, after several months of inactivity, but they gave him comfort, for he knew that his days in the ducal household were numbered.

Shortly after Martinmas, Llion had him begin sparring with Tesselin and Walter and other knights of Jared's household, and occasionally with Jared himself. Alaric tried not to think too much about the changes looming ever nearer, once he moved to court, and pushed himself as hard as he was able. He knew he would have much to prove among the royal pages and squires at Rhemuth, especially as the king's page.

Tutoring with Father Nevan also resumed, along with continuing lessons in history and languages. As for his Deryni training, Vera resumed cautious sharing of what she could, but her own training had been sketchier than she might have wished—and they were running out of time.

"I wish we could have worked more on Truth-Reading," she told him one grey morning early in December, when Jared and Kevin and many of their retainers had gone hunting. She and Alaric were standing in the little mortuary chapel, close by his mother's tomb, and Duncan was keeping casual watch outside, pretending to be absorbed in the patterns of icicles that festooned the edge of the roof. "That's a particularly important skill for you to master, because the king knows it's a Deryni talent that your mother had, and he'll expect you to have it as well."

"Won't that be dangerous?" Alaric asked.

"No more dangerous than simply existing, where everyone knows what you are," she said with a shrug and a faint smile. "I hope I need not remind you to be extremely discreet—and it's best if you remind the king to be discreet as well, not to draw attention to your powers. That's what got your mother into so much trouble."

Alaric laid a gloved hand gently over the still, cold hand of his mother's effigy. "He wouldn't put me into danger unless there were no other way," he said softly.

"No, I would hope that he would not." Vera gathered her cloak more closely against the cold and lifted her gaze to the stained glass above the effigy. "Fortunately, many will underestimate you while you are still young—and if, while Reading the truth, you can learn to keep your features neutral, no matter how outraged you may become, you will be that much more effective.

"It will not always be easy, I know," she went on, noticing his grimace of distaste. "But that must be your goal: to Read the truth, without anyone being the wiser, and then report your findings to the king in private. It can be a very valuable asset: to know if a vassal is telling a lie—for a duke as well as a king," she added, smiling faintly. "In the old times, it was quite common for the Haldane kings to have Truth Readers in their households. And even the Regents had captive Deryni to Truth-Read for them."

"But, they *made* them do it," Alaric said sullenly. "They made them betray others."

"Yes, unfortunately, they also forced their captives to misuse their powers," she went on, "which only reinforced the common belief that Deryni were too dangerous to be allowed to live openly. It's a very dangerous tightrope you will have to walk, my love. But I know that you can do it."

They kept Christmas at Culdi that year: the last that Alaric was likely to spend in the bosom of a family, for some time. He would remember it as a happy time, if tinged with apprehension. Jared gave him a new dirk with a tawny cairngorm set in the pommel; Kevin and Duncan had made the scabbard, embossing the black leather with a subtle interlace design. Alaric put it on the red belt Duncan had made him for his birthday. (The Corwyn dagger was too precious and conspicuous to wear every day, but he continued to wear the Lendour signet on its leather thong.)

The ladies of the household also gave him gifts. Little Bronwyn, with guidance and a little assistance from Vera, had hemmed him a handkerchief of fine linen. Vera and the ladies of the ducal household had been industrious during the long winter nights and were able to present him with a new linen shirt and several wool under-tunics to see him through the winter at court.

"But don't grow too much until the spring," Vera warned him, as she made him try on each garment. "We've made them a little large, but you'll be glad of the extra layers, when it's really cold."

And, indeed, frigid temperatures soon became a serious concern. The weather turned filthy two days later, casting serious doubts as to whether the roads would be passable in time for the journey to Rhemuth. Vera had to bow out of the trip owing to a heavy chest cold.

But Jared duly organized the expedition despite snow and ice, and led his modest contingent into Rhemuth two days before the planned spectacle of Twelfth Night, with banners flying. He took both Alaric and Duncan with him as pages, and Kevin as his squire, for a duke was expected to travel with a suitable retinue. Tesselin rode as his personal aide, as well as half a dozen Cassani bordermen. Llion accompanied them, of course, for he would be entering the king's service along with his young master.

It seemed strange to be back at court without his father, but to Alaric's surprise and delight, the apartment formerly assigned to his father was now become his and Llion's. It was more than Llion would have merited on his own, but Alaric was, after all, a future duke and earl.

"I'll keep my old bed, of course," Alaric said, as the two of them stashed their saddlebags in the apartment. "I suppose you ought to take my father's bed, rather than your old trundle."

"I couldn't," Llion said. "It wouldn't seem right."

"Nonsense," Alaric replied, quite reasonably. "Your job is still to help protect me, as my father did. Plus, you'll be on Duke Richard's staff. That's something of a promotion. And I believe you said something about marrying my sister?"

At Llion's sudden look of owl-eyed dismay, Alaric grinned. "Good. I didn't think you'd make her sleep on the trundle bed with you. Don't worry. I think we'll be fine here."

Llion could not argue that point, and dutifully moved his things into the small sleeping chamber previously occupied by Kenneth. Later, when he and Alaric joined Jared in the great hall for the evening meal, the duke drew them to places near his own chair, close to the king's.

Alaric wore his Cassani page's tabard, expecting to serve Jared one last time, but instead Jared seated him at his right hand, to underline his future rank, and bade him wear the Lendour signet outside his clothes, as further reminder to the court of who he was and would be. Kevin and Duncan served them, as squire and page. The experience was bittersweet for Alaric, because he knew how much was about to change. Further, it was appearing less and less likely that Alazais would be attending Twelfth Night court, much to the disappointment of both Alaric and Llion.

The day of Twelfth Night dawned even colder and more blustery than any the previous week, with portents of a new blizzard to come. The sky was a dull, sullen white, pregnant with snow, and it suited Alaric's mood as he washed and dressed for court, again donning his Cassani tabard and the McLain sash, though he layered them over several of the new wool under-tunics for warmth, and slung a fur-lined cape over that.

This time, the Lendour signet remained under his clothing. His new dirk rode at his right hip on the belt Duncan had made for his last birthday; he knew it would be allowed, at least for court. Llion put on a long grey court robe with his Lendour badge bright on the sleeve, though the latter was covered by his own thick cloak. They were nearly ready to head down to the hall when a knock sounded at the door, which immediately opened to admit Jared.

"Good, you're about ready," the duke said, casting a critical eye over both of them. "Beastly day out, which should cut down on attendance, but I've managed to arrange for some major concessions. I hadn't realized how much influence dukes have. The king wishes to see both of you in his withdrawing room at once."

The king was not the only one waiting when Alaric and Llion entered the room behind the dais. Brion was standing before the fireplace amid a sea of Haldane crimson worn by himself, Duke Richard, Queen Richeldis, and Prince Nigel. Duke Richard's deputy, Sir Ninian de Piran, was also present, but stayed near the door, wrapped up in a tawny cloak lined with fur.

"Ah, there they are," the king said, raising an arm in summons as Jared ushered the pair into the room. "Come here, lad. We have business to transact before court."

Mystified, Alaric allowed Jared to escort him before the king, glad of the warmth from the fireplace. Brion was already dressed in his full court attire, including the state crown of leaves and crosses intertwined, and Richard and Richeldis likewise wore the coronets of their rank. Nigel wore his crimson squire's doublet.

"Excellent," the king said, as Richard eased closer and the queen sank onto a stool. "Llion, stand there beside Jared. Some of what I'm about to do concerns you."

Alaric glanced back over his shoulder as Llion moved closer, though the young knight looked just as bewildered as Alaric felt. Jared's hand was heavy on his shoulder, and he wondered whether he had done something wrong.

"Duke Jared informs me that you are somewhat apprehensive about court this morning," the king said, bracing his thumbs in the front of his bejeweled white belt. "I am told that it might have something to do with the likely presence of a certain bishop of your unhappy acquaintance.

"Yes, I am well aware of the incident with my lord of Nyford last year," the king added, at the flicker of concern that sparked briefly in the boy's grey eyes. "I am also aware that his nephew has been an ongoing source of aggravation for you. Be assured that young Cornelius is being watched very closely. And I am happy to report that the weather appears to have prevented His Grace of Nyford from attending court this year."

Alaric mostly managed to contain a sigh of relief. De Nore and Cornelius had, indeed, been on his mind increasingly, as the time drew nearer to leave Duke Jared's protection and join the king's household. But though he knew that dealing with them and others of their ilk would become an increasing necessity of his life, the older he got, he had thought himself mostly resigned to it.

"I'm guessing that you are relieved to hear that," Brion went on, rightly gauging the boy's reaction. "Duke Richard and I have made a further decision that should ease any lingering concerns. You will not be participating in the public ceremony of reception as a Haldane page." At Alaric's expression of surprise, he went on. "We have conferred with Duke Jared, and we have agreed that, since you have already gone through a semi-public ceremony when you became Duke Jared's page, it would be appropriate simply to receive you now, privately, in order to avoid drawing particular attention to your change of status when we go into court. That will become apparent as soon as you appear in Haldane livery, of course, but at least it avoids putting you into the center of attention right away. May I assume that this meets with your approval?"

Alaric shot an inquiring look at Jared, who nodded, then gave a quick nod of assent.

"Yes, Sire."

"Very well, then. Jared Duke of Cassan, do you relieve this page of his duties to your house?"

"I do, Sire, though I am sorry to lose his service," Jared said, removing his hand from Alaric's shoulder.

At the king's nod, Llion reached around Alaric's neck to unfasten and remove the cloak covering his Cassani surcoat, which Jared then pulled off over the boy's head and handed to Llion. When he would have removed the McLain sash as well, Alaric's hands darted to it protectively, and he glanced quickly at the king.

"Sire, is it permitted to keep the sash, if Duke Jared agrees? Not to wear it; just to have it. I would take it as a sign that I remain under the protection of the Chief of Clan McLain—as well as yourself, of course."

The king exchanged a quick glance with Jared, then nodded slightly.

"If Duke Jared has no objection, then I have none," he agreed. "But you do understand that I cannot allow you to wear it with your Haldane livery."

"Yes, Sire."

The king nodded to Jared again, tight-lipped, and Jared ducked his head as he bent to untie the sash and remove it, folding it in two before passing it to Llion. The young knight gently clasped Alaric's shoulder before backing off a pace with the cloak and sash.

"Very well," the king said, briskly lifting the Haldane sword from its scabbard and resting its tip on the floor between them, both hands overlapped on the pommel. "Alaric Anthony Morgan of Corwyn, is it your desire to become a page of my house, to serve me above all others?"

"It is, Sire," the boy replied, head held high. "And please understand that I am not reluctant to enter your service. It is just that I had always hoped that my father would be here to witness my oath to you—and I am grateful to Duke Jared for having me as his page for this past year and more. But Father Swithun has reminded me that there is a time for everything, in due season. And my duty now is to you, as my king and liege."

Duke Richard inclined his head in approval, and set a hand on the king's shoulder. "That was well spoken, lad. And the king shares your sorrow at the untimely passing of your father; we all do." He nodded toward Brion. "Let us take the oath and be done with it, Nephew. This lad has a great deal on his plate right now. We need not make it any more difficult for him than it must be."

Brion nodded and returned his attention to the boy, who knelt and placed both hands on the quillons of the king's sword.

"Alaric Anthony Morgan of Corwyn," the king said, "do you promise loyalty and service to me and to my house, accepting the discipline and instruction of those set in authority to train you, to learn the ways of a future knight and duke?"

"I do, my Liege, so help me God," Alaric replied, his eyes not leaving those of the king. "And because of the special circumstances of my future service, I would now offer you my fealty, as I did for Duke Jared when I entered his service. If that is allowed."

Nodding, the king shifted his hands to rest over Alaric's on the quillons of the sword.

"I am willing to receive your oath."

"I, Alaric Anthony Morgan, heir of Corwyn and Lendour, do become your liege man of life and limb and earthly worship, to serve you in good faith and without deception before all others, so help me God."

"And I receive your oath and fidelity, Alaric Anthony Morgan, heir of Corwyn and Lendour, and I pledge to you the same protection and fidelity that is the right of all my house. So help me God."

With that, the king returned his sword to its scabbard and turned to where his mother sat with a Haldane tabard now across her lap. Immediately she rose and came to them, assisting her son as he slipped the tabard over Alaric's silver-gilt head.

"Wear it well, young master," she whispered in his ear, smiling as she tugged one side into place. "I adored your mother." Then: "Brion, I should like to have this page attend me at court today—if I may."

The king raised an eyebrow. "Are you sure?" At her sidelong look of challenge, he immediately ducked his head in agreement and gave a wry smile. "Certainly, Mother."

"Excellent!" She drew Alaric to her with an arm around his shoulders. "How soon do you wish to begin court?"

"As soon as we can get everyone assembled. Where are my sisters?"

She nodded at Alaric. "Your first assignment as a Haldane page is to fetch my daughters," she said. "You know the way to my solar?"

Alaric nodded. "Yes, Majesty."

"Then, go. They were nearly ready when I left, so there should be no delay. And Llion, give him back his cloak before he leaves. We don't need any of our pages catching their death of cold. Go, lad!"

Sketching her a quick bow, and fidgeting as Llion slung the cloak back around his shoulders and fastened it, Alaric then headed out of the withdrawing room and bolted up the back stairs. He found the princesses just leaving the queen's apartment, both gowned in Haldane crimson, accompanied by a black-clad lady-in-waiting with two silver circlets looped over an arm.

After more than a year's absence from court, he almost did not recognize the elder of the pair. Xenia, at fifteen, had become a poised and haughty young woman, with masses of shiny ebon curls tumbling down her back and abundant curves where there had been few before. Silke, by contrast, was still a merry child with her ebon hair still in a single braid, whose grey eyes lit with immediate delight.

"Alaric? It *is* you!" she squealed, though he deftly fended off the embrace she attempted. "With all the snow, I wasn't sure you'd come."

The more practical Xenia cast an appraising glance over him, some of her hauteur evaporating in the face of Silke's enthusiasm. "You're taller," she said, trying not to show that she, too, was pleased. "And why are you wearing Haldane livery? I thought you were page to Duke Jared."

Alaric shrugged and smiled faintly. "I was. And now I am page to your brother the king—and your mother, today. But we'd best go. They'll be waiting court for us."

Xenia sighed and rolled her eyes, pressing the back of one hand to her forehead. "Oh, they'll be waiting *court* for us!" she repeated in a mocking tone. "We *are* Haldane princesses, you know."

"Yes, and your brother is a Haldane king," the lady-in-waiting reminded them sharply. Alaric thought her name was Lady Megory. "He'll not thank you for keeping everyone waiting."

"Oh, very well," Xenia murmured, hooking her arm through that of her younger sister. "Come, Silke. We'll let this *page* lead the way."

With that, the pair of them chivvied him on ahead of them as they clambered down the back stair to the king's withdrawing room, the lady-in-waiting following with their coronets.

T O his relief, Alaric soon discovered that being a page to the queen enabled him to be far more anonymous than a ducal heir. He carried the queen's train as the royal party entered the hall, helping her settle in her chair of state with her daughters at her feet, but after that he mostly stood attentively behind her, hands clasped behind his back, and waited to perform any errand the queen might require. While this placed him somewhat on display, he was very much in the background compared to serving the king, with ample opportunity to observe what was going on.

First, of course, after the presentations of the few foreign envoys who had braved the blizzard, was the reception of new pages, of which there were only two, but even Alaric knew that the boys were important. The first was Prince Cormac of Howicce and Llannedd, presented by his elder brother Ronan, who had become prince regent of the dual kingdoms in June of the previous year, following the incapacitation of their father, King Illann. Prince Cormac was a sturdy lad of about Alaric's age, with a shock of wiry dark blond hair, much resembling his elder brother. Queen Richeldis became wistful and almost teary-eyed as she vested her youngest nephew with the Haldane tabard, watching proudly as he swore his oath to her son.

She then bade him stand beside Alaric while she prepared for the second new page: a dark-haired lad called Xavier Howard; Alaric thought he might be some sort of cousin of Lady Vera. Meanwhile, a servant quietly appeared with a fur-lined cloak for Prince Cormac, who had come before the king in his shirtsleeves to be invested, and was shivering until the servant draped it around his master's shoulders.

"It's warmer in Pwyllheli," the boy whispered aside to Alaric, hugging the fur around his body.

Next came the new squires; again, there were only two being promoted from page. Aean Morrisey had nearly won the pages' competition at the king's birthday tournament, now eighteen months past; Justis Berringer had also performed well, though Alaric had done better, and had done as well as Aean. There was also an older squire formerly in the service of the Duke of Claibourne, who was joining the Rhemuth court to complete his training.

"I've heard of Tresham MacKenzie," Alaric whispered aside to Prince Cormac, while two Claibourne men buckled on the blued-steel spurs of a squire. "He's some kind of cousin to Duke Ewan. Supposed to be good with a sword."

A gimlet look from the queen silenced any further whispered commentary—and in good time, for the knightings were next, though also sparse this year, because of the weather and because several candidates had been knighted early, to receive the accolade along with the king two years previous. Accordingly, there were only two: a sturdy young man called Varian Lemander, who came supported by two knights of

Danoc, and a slightly older, studious-looking young man with a slight limp, waiting with his sponsors while the first knight was made.

"He's called Claud de Saeva," Alaric whispered in response to Prince Cormac's look of query. "I'm told he took a bad fall in training and broke his leg. But he's made a good recovery," he added, then pursed his lips and feigned interest in his boots as the queen glanced in his direction, though she quickly returned her attention to the candidate now kneeling before her son.

Young Cormac managed to contain his curiosity through the remainder of Sir Varian's knighting, which kept both him and Alaric from attracting any more unwelcome attention. When Claud de Saeva was then called forward, both boys watched avidly, for Cormac was intrigued by everything he was seeing, and seemed unable to resist making whispered asides to Alaric.

To their surprise, and to Alaric's acute embarrassment, the king summoned both of them to assist with buckling on the candidate's golden spurs, making comment that because Claud had endured much on his journey to knighthood, he deserved a matched pair of pages to attend to this part of his investiture. Alaric's cheeks were flaming as he knelt opposite Cormac to do the king's bidding, and he could see the faint smile twitching at the corners of Brion's mouth: certain sign that the king had noticed his exchanges with Cormac.

Afterward, when he and Cormac had retreated behind the queen's chair and the queen herself had vested the new knight with his white belt, Alaric resolved to allow himself no further breaches in the discipline expected of a royal page, though he told himself that he had only been trying to make Cormac feel more at ease in his new circumstances. Still, it was hard to keep an entirely sober demeanor, because he and Cormac would occasionally exchange glances that threatened to send both boys into gales of snickers.

But they managed not to disgrace themselves during what remained of court, when all attention was now rightly focused on the king. Fortunately, that part of court was short. When court was finally adjourned, so that servants could set up the long trestle tables and benches for the feast

to follow, the two of them headed for the nearest fireplace to get warm,
wrapping their cloaks tight. While they were there, Alaric's friend Paget
Sullivan made a point to approach and welcome him back to court, also
making himself known to Prince Cormac.

"I'm Paget Sullivan," he said, extending his hand. "We'd heard that
you were coming. Alaric probably won't have told you yet, but he's very
interested in strategy and tactics, as I am. He's also one hell of a rider.
Time will tell, whether he becomes as good a swordsman." He grinned.
"Do you play cardounet?"

All but overwhelmed by this barrage of friendly banter, Cormac
smiled back tentatively and shook his head. "Not well. Is it played a great
deal in Rhemuth?"

"A few of us play," Paget replied, with an arch glance at Alaric. "Some
better than others. I've taught Maxen while you were away, Alaric—and
Ciarán now plays a bit, too—but we all need a better challenge. Fancy a
game later on?"

Alaric quirked him a pleased smile. "That depends on the queen. She
seems to like having a matching pair of pages, so we might be kept rather
busy."

"Ah, the perils of being popular with the ladies." Paget grinned as he
glanced across the hall, where the two princesses were talking to one of
the senior squires. "But Sir Ninian has me serving Duke Richard's end of
the high table, so it looks like we'll all need to be on our toes. I'll see you
later. Highness."

With a quick sketch of a bow, Paget was on his way. Cormac, a bit
taken aback, glanced at Alaric in question.

"I gather that he's a friend," the prince said. Then: "Maybe you ought
to tell me about the ones who are *not* friends."

Alaric looked at him sharply.

"I know who you are," Cormac said softly, with a quick glance around
them. "I also know *what* you are. My father and my brother Ronan told
me all about you, and they had it from the king. I want you to know that
it doesn't bother me."

Alaric gave a snort of skepticism and turned his gaze to the fire on the
hearth before them, relieved that he would not have to have *that* conver-

sation with Cormac, but he wondered whether the prince truly understood the risks that came with being a friend to Alaric Morgan.

"I doubt he told them *all* about me," he said quietly. "And you may change your mind when you meet some of the people who are not my friends."

"Oh?" Cormac cocked his head at Alaric. "What can they do to us? Alaric, you're a future duke, which is practically a prince—and I *am* a prince. Well, not a very important prince, since I have two older brothers, but my father is still a king."

"That may protect *you*," Alaric replied, low, "but we're neither of us adults yet. We're vulnerable; *I'm* vulnerable. A few years ago, before I was born, a page at court was murdered, right out in the stable yard. The old king commanded my mother to use her powers to uncover the killers, and one of them turned out to be the brother of a bishop. He was executed. That bishop never forgave her—and he hates *me* because I'm her son."

Cormac's face had fallen as Alaric's tale unfolded. "That must be— *horrible*!" he managed to murmur. "Having a bishop hate you. But—" He glanced across the hall, where two purple-cloaked figures were moving among the other attendees, then back at Alaric in alarm. "Is it one of *them*?"

Alaric shook his head quickly. "No, no, though I expect those two don't much like me, either. Archbishop Tollendall is probably all right; he's the one who looks more like a monk. The big burly one is Bishop Corrigan. My father told me that he's a friend of Bishop de Nore; that's the one who really hates me. Fortunately, he isn't here this year, thanks to the weather, but his smarmy little nephew is."

He glanced across the hall, where Cornelius Seaton and a squire called Nolen MacInnis were staring in their direction, then rose and quietly drew Cormac with him into the outer corridor, though he stood where he could keep an eye on his nemesis.

"You might as well know that that dark-haired squire across the way is the bishop's nephew. His name is Cornelius Seaton, and the older boy with him is called Nolan MacInnis. Don't look at them. Cornelius is not happy that I've brought you out of the hall."

"Why? What business is it of his?" Cormac said indignantly, though he tried not to stare in that direction.

Alaric allowed himself a heavy sigh. "Because he hates me, and because he's already jealous that I'm even talking to you. Be warned that he *will* toady up to you, because you're a prince, and he'll try to keep you from becoming my friend." He glanced at his boots. "If that's your decision, I'll respect that. But if he tries to bully you into avoiding me, that's quite another."

Cormac pursed his lips, clearly offended that Cornelius should presume. "I choose my own friends," he said quietly. "And I don't think that anyone called Cornelius is going to be among them."

"You should at least meet him," Alaric replied. "And he *is* a squire; you'll have to deal with him, at least in training."

"Do you?—deal with him, that is."

Alaric shrugged. "I do my best to avoid him, and to do better than he does. For now, it helps that he's a squire and I'm still a page. Duke Richard and the king are aware of the problem, but I still watch my back."

"That sounds like good advice," Cormac observed, then drew himself to attention as Prince Ronan caught his eye from across the hall. "Whoops, I'm being summoned. My brother thinks he's king already. I'll see you later."

Chapter 30

"Hast thou a wife after thy mind? Forsake her not:
but give not thyself over to a light woman."
—ECCLESIASTICUS 7:26

AS darkness began to fall—early, for these long winter nights—
Alaric and Prince Cormac were instructed to remain at the
queen's bidding, serving her and the princesses at table and taking turns in attendance for anything the royal ladies might require. It was
a fitting introduction to the gentler aspects of life as a Haldane page, but
it also enabled Alaric to avoid Cornelius. Across the hall, Duncan served
his father and his elder brother, who was allowed to sit at Jared's side.
Alaric had been present at several Twelfth Night courts, but he was noticing a change in his perspective, now that he was part of the functioning
of the event.

He was tired by the time he and the other pages and squires were
dismissed for the night, but it took him a while to fall asleep. Though
back in his familiar bed, he was acutely aware that Llion no longer slept
on the pallet at his feet but in the chamber that formerly had been Kenneth's. At least when Alaric finally did fall asleep, he did not dream.

The very next day, as local visitors eyed the aftermath of the storm
and some began to depart, training resumed at the Haldane court. Duke
Jared would remain for a few days more, with Duncan and Kevin at their
leisure, for it was too short a time for them to join the training with the
Haldane squires and pages, but he was mostly sequestered with the king
and Prince Ronan, who had a ship waiting for him at Desse. Llion joined
Duke Richard's staff, and was little seen for the first few days. Alaric, for

his part, was conducted with Prince Cormac and Xavier to join the rest of the Haldane pages for a series of discussions on the history of Gwynedd and elements of protocol, conducted by Sir Ninian and sometimes Duke Richard himself.

Alaric soon decided that the sessions were intended to assess what the three newcomers already knew, because most of the questions were directed at them. The other pages seemed affable enough, if reserved. Alaric decided that it probably was because of a prince among them, and counted himself fortunate that someone else was providing the focus of curiosity. Alaric knew a few of the boys slightly from previous stays at court, and had outridden almost all of them in the competitions surrounding the king's birthday tourney nearly two years before.

This theoretical evaluation lasted only a few days, before training shifted to less cerebral activities than history and protocol.

Duke Richard was a consummate gentleman and courtier, but he was also a stern taskmaster when it came to preparing young men for eventual knighthood. Weather would prevent much outdoor activity for most of January, but the royal duke and Sir Ninian had a multitude of drills and exercises that could be pursued in the great hall by pages and squires alike; and there were always the lectures, usually delivered before the great fireplace or sometimes in the king's council room.

Duke Richard and Sir Ninian took considerable time during the next few days evaluating the skills and deficiencies of the boys newly come to Haldane training, at least regarding their weapons ability. Both archery and sword drills were a given, well suited to indoor practice. Alaric did well enough with those, though he had not yet regained full strength in his right arm.

"It will come back, lad," Sir Ninian reassured him, after watching for several minutes. "The arm is sound."

Thus encouraged, Alaric returned to the basic exercises, and grew stronger each day. He had thought that the weather would preclude any real-time assessment of horsemanship skills; not that the prospect worried him. But there were indoor exercises even for that, he soon discovered, though he knew that the duke and Sir Ninian were well aware of his own skills astride a horse; and if there had been any doubt, Llion was now working with Ninian.

Nonetheless, he had to demonstrate his own abilities just like the other boys, working through a series of drills involving a wooden saw-horse equipped with a saddle, that tested the agility of would-be riders as they vaulted from ground to saddle—first wearing hunting leathers, then shifting to boiled leather practice armor with a wooden sword in hand. That soon progressed to whacking at targets with said wooden sword after vaulting into the saddle, or retrieving weapons from the ground without dismounting.

But he apparently performed to Sir Ninian's satisfaction, such that he was soon paired with Prince Cormac, who had not done so well on the mounts and dismounts astride a false steed.

"It's easier to do this with a real horse," Cormac grumbled, as Alaric gave him a leg back up after a particularly noisy fall.

Alaric agreed, but it did no good to commiserate when Sir Ninian was watching both of them like an eagle. Cormac still would need to perform.

Fortunately, once the Llanneddi prince adjusted to the pseudo-steed, he proved to have good saddle skills, quite comparable with Alaric's own, and his skills with wooden sword and lance were of a similar level. More-over, the pair got along well: a happenstance that apparently set the king to thinking, for he soon called both boys to a private interview in his withdrawing room.

"Have a seat, lads," he said, with a gesture inviting them to sit at the table that usually displayed maps and markers. "Duke Richard tells me that both of you are doing quite well. Alaric, I understand that your arm is healing nicely."

"It is, Sire," Alaric murmured.

"Good." With his own hand, the king poured mugs of hot cider for the three of them, then pushed two of the mugs across the table.

"He also said that the two of you seem to get along very well," the king went on. "That got me to thinking that an adjustment to your living arrangements might suit both of you—provided that you agree, of course."

As the king drank deeply of his cider, Alaric glanced sidelong at the
Llanneddi prince, wondering what the king had in mind. Cormac, for his
part, looked mystified.

"Cormac, I know that you are presently billeted with the knight left
by your brother to see to your safety," Brion said, setting down his mug.
"However, I've received word that your father needs him back in Pwyllheli, so it has occurred to me that you might like to share accommodations with Alaric and his knight, Sir Llion. It was formerly the apartment
of Alaric's father, the Earl of Lendour, so it befits your rank. If either of
you would rather not," he added, at the looks of surprise on the two
young faces, "I shall understand. But it seems to me that the arrangement
would provide good company for both of you. Because of who you are, I
cannot ask either of you to share dormitory accommodations as the other
pages do, but it would give you something of the experience of com-
munal living. And Cormac, it would place you under the personal protection of Sir Llion, when you are not directly involved in training. There
are few who can match him as a teacher, as Alaric will attest."

Alaric cast a guarded glance at Cormac, who was looking pleased.

"I may change my quarters to share with Alaric?"

"You may," the king replied. "If Alaric also agrees."

Cormac glanced at Alaric and broke into a grin, echoed by Alaric as
he saw that the prince welcomed the move.

"I should like that," Cormac said. "It will be like having a brother my
own age."

The prediction was not far off the mark. By evening, Cormac had
moved his possessions into the apartment Alaric and Llion shared, and
immediately proved a lively and companionable roommate. The two
had already trained together for several weeks, and found that their physical skills were a good match. Sharing quarters was a logical progression
to their friendship. And though the prince's academic abilities were only
adequate, he seemed to have an innate ability to interact easily with
everyone he met: useful attributes for a spare prince—and also for a future duke in training.

It did not hurt that Cormac had already developed a keen interest in
cardounet. Very quickly the prince came to be included in the small circle

of boys who accepted Alaric as one of their own, and who played whenever duties and training did not interfere.

Meanwhile, training remained very much their first priority, especially
as the weather began to improve. Archery continued to be an obvious skill
that could be practiced indoors. Likewise, it was a matter of only a few
minutes to move pells into the great hall for sword drill with steel.

When weather permitted, they began riding out again, sometimes for
muddy gallops along the river road, sometimes taking to the equally
muddy fields, where they mostly avoided jumps or too strenuous riding,
for mere practice was not worth risking injury to horse or rider. Sometimes, if the tournament field was not too muddy, they began riding in
formation, which Alaric had never done before. He did not find it difficult, but it was a different sort of challenge, though he could see the usefulness of such maneuvers.

Additional new training also was introduced, especially on days when
weather kept them indoors. Wrestling had always been a part of the training of both pages and squires, and it was a useful indoor activity for a
snowy or rainy day, but after a few weeks the instructors began combin-
ing it with hand-to-hand combat, both with bare hands and with blunted
daggers.

Pages and squires trained together in the great hall, always well supervised by adult instructors, but pages were never matched against squires,
for which Alaric was grateful. His growing skill in this discipline was
such that he likely could have given a good account of himself, even with
an older and larger opponent, but he was very glad that he would not be
matched against Cornelius or some of the other older boys who seemed
to share Cornelius's antipathy toward Deryni. That day would come, he
knew, but thankfully his instructors were well aware of the need to keep
his training closely supervised for the present.

The winter gloom continued, though it was eased briefly, early in
February, when Prince Nigel turned fourteen, thus attaining his legal
majority: an event celebrated with a family Mass in the chapel royal and
a special feast to mark the occasion, when Nigel assumed the rank of a
senior squire and also received gifts appropriate to the man he was
becoming.

Many of his fellow squires and some of the pages gave him gifts as well. Alaric and Cormac, along with Paget Sullivan and Quillan Pargeter, had commissioned a traveling cardounet set made of leather, like the one owned by Henry Kirby, and presented it privately, as Nigel was heading up to bed.

"You had this made for *me*?" Nigel asked, incredulous as he inspected the gift.

"Well, it *is* your birthday, Highness," Cormac pointed out. "It was Alaric's idea."

"I played with one like this several years ago," Alaric admitted. "I thought you would like it. It's easy to transport."

"Yes, I can see that," Nigel replied. "Thank you, gentlemen—all of you."

Gradually the grey days of winter gave way to spring. Easter that year brought the usual solemnities of the season, culminating in a grand procession down to the cathedral for Easter Mass and, afterward, a visit at last from Alaric's half-sister Alazais, who had traveled in the company of two of the sisters from Arc-en-Ciel. She had brought along the new miniature of Kenneth, already mounted in its locket, but she had shifted the one of his mother inside, so that the two faced one another.

"I hope you don't mind," she told him, as she handed him the open locket. "But it seems only right that Papa and your mother should be together inside. That leaves the outside very plain, but I thought I could replace it with a new roundel with your arms on it."

Alaric caught his breath as he gazed upon the pair of them. The two styles were slightly different, but Alazais had captured the very essence of their sire.

"No, this is *wonderful*!" he breathed. "Thank you ever so much! Now the one of Mama won't get damaged."

Alazais smiled. "I'm so glad you like it. Shall I do up the new piece with your arms on it, for the front? That will also make the locket more wearable, if you choose."

"Please do!" he said happily. "How long would it take?"

"Oh, not long. I could have it for you the next time I see you."

In fact, that time would come far sooner than Alaric had anticipated. Though Alazais and her two companions had arrived in time for the festivities of Palm Sunday and the more somber observances of the Passion Week that followed, they had stayed with the sisters down at the cathedral. Alaric had noticed, but not remarked upon the fact, that Llion made himself the personal escort for Alazais and her companions during that week. In light of his previous inquiries about Alazais, Alaric was not surprised when, later that evening, Llion asked Alaric for his sister's hand in marriage.

"You mean you haven't asked her yet?" Alaric retorted.

"Not formally, my lord. I need your blessing first."

"Good God, I thought I already gave you my blessing." He cocked his head. "You do think she'll say yes, I hope?"

Llion's boyish grin reminded Alaric of those barely remembered days of his early childhood, when the two of them had first met in Coroth: he a child of nearly three and Llion a senior squire then knighted by Alaric's father and pressed into service as Alaric's governor.

"I think she will, my lord," Llion said. "We've written often in the past few months, and spent time together the past week. I still can hardly believe it's happening." His gaze turned wistful as he glanced away in memory. "I'm a younger son. When I first took service with your father, I had no idea where life might take me, much less that I'd ever be able to afford to marry.

"But your father treated me almost as another son. And he always told me I was good with children. I'll never forget how, at the king's birthday tourney, he was watching me work with you and Duncan, and he said, 'Llion, you should be a father.' It made me think. And recently it's occurred to me that I *can* afford a wife and family now. So when Alazais and I met again at his funeral . . ."

"And she *does* want to marry you?" Alaric asked, with a teasing note in his voice.

Llion only nodded, smiling. "And now that I'm to be at court, I'm hoping that a place might be found for her in the queen's household. I should imagine that the court could use a good portrait artist. You've seen for yourself how talented she is."

Alaric gave a nod, remembering the new portrait of his father, and could not disagree.

"Then, I think we'd better go find her, first thing in the morning," he said brightly. "I don't really know her all that well, because she's lived at Arc-en-Ciel for most of my life, but I'm glad she isn't going to take the veil. You and she will need to have the children that my parents didn't get to have. If you're going to marry my sister, your children will be my nieces and nephews, and you—good Lord, Llion, you'll be my brother!"

Llion shrugged and allowed himself a sheepish smile. "I suppose I will."

THEY rode down to the cathedral the next morning and found Alazais waiting in a shady arbor in the cloister garden with Sisters Iris Rose and Iris Cerys.

"You might have told me," Alaric said teasingly to Alazais, as he came to join her hand with Llion's. "And good Sisters, it appears that Arc-en-Ciel will be losing one of its daughters."

Iris Rose smiled serenely. "She did not tell us, my lord, but we have suspected for some time."

They told the king next, and then Duke Richard, and the news had spread through the court by the time Brion called the happy couple before him at dinner that evening to give his official blessing and wish them well.

There was no question of Llion leaving royal service, of course—or, Alaric's—so little would change in the short term. While details had yet to be worked out, the wedding date was tentatively set for the autumn, around the time of Alaric's tenth birthday. Meanwhile, Alaric was given leave to accompany Llion and the party that escorted Alazais and her companions back to Arc-en-Ciel a few days later.

They went by way of Morganhall, to share the happy news with Delphine and Claara, then continued on to the convent where Alazais had spent the past six years. Mother Judiana and the other sisters at Arc-en-Ciel received the news gladly, though they would miss Alazais among their number. Still, they immediately offered to help with the preparations for another Morgan bride in the autumn.

Yet to be decided was whether Alazais would marry at Morganhall, following generations of Morgan brides, or would make her vows in the chapel at Arc-en-Ciel, as her sister Alyce had done. Leaving the women to sort out the details, Llion bade his affianced bride a reluctant farewell and rode with Alaric back to Rhemuth.

L IFE at court quickly settled back into routine, though now Llion was occasionally absent for several days at a time, to visit his affianced bride. It little mattered in the short term, because Alaric and Cormac got on well, and their training kept them busy. In any case, the nature of their relationship with Llion was sure to change somewhat, once the young knight took a wife.

But if life at the court of Rhemuth was somewhat predictably routine, at least for pages and squires, developments elsewhere in the kingdom would have lasting ramifications for Gwynedd as well as for Alaric personally. That spring, an ambitious priest named Edmond Loris was elected to the see of Stavenham, far in the north: in itself, an event of little note to the boys training at court. It was some weeks before rumors began filtering south that the new bishop, previously much seen in the company of the Bishop of Nyford, was tightening enforcement of the Laws of Ramos, to the growing dismay of Deryni under his jurisdiction.

Alaric gradually became aware of these developments because he was frequently in attendance on the king. He and Llion sometimes discussed them privately, but he tried not to dwell on them overmuch.

"I doubt that this Bishop Loris even knows I exist," he told Llion toward midsummer. "And if he does, maybe he'll just ignore me, if I keep my head down. Besides, I'm under the king's personal protection."

"Aye, but you aren't always in the king's presence," Llion reminded him. "Just don't let your guard down—ever! There are too many people who would love to see you dead."

Alaric could not argue that. Besides, he knew that Llion was only trying to keep him safe.

Meanwhile, plans were moving forward for Llion's wedding. He and

Alazais had finally decided on Morganhall for the venue, and were thinking in terms of the autumn, but early in July the king called both Llion and Alaric into a private meeting.

"I'm thinking to take Alaric on a progress down to Coroth for his birthday," he told the pair. "It's been several years since his last visit, and longer than that for me, and I shouldn't like his regents to forget that he is their future duke—or that I am their king. Llion, I should like you to come with us—which means, I fear, that you will need to change your wedding plans. But if you marry before the trip, it would enable you to bring along your bride to meet your family. We'll travel by ship."

Llion's handsome face split in a delighted grin. "I hadn't expected such an opportunity, Sire. I'm certain Alazais will agree."

After much frantic riding back and forth between Rhemuth and Morganhall—and Arc-en-Ciel—the celebration was duly moved forward to mid-August, and plans went forward for both the wedding and the royal progress.

Thus it was that, two days before the designated date, Alaric found himself riding north to his father's keep at Morganhall, accompanied by the king, the eager bridegroom, and a small party of Llion's friends who would witness his nuptials with Lady Alazais Morgan. They arrived to find many of the extended family already present. Zoë and Jovett had ridden in from Cynfyn with their two eldest children, Kailan and Charlan. Duke Jared and Vera had brought Kevin and Duncan, as well as Bronwyn. Geill and her husband, Walter, also traveled with them, though Geill's baby girl, born only a few months before, had been left at home with a nurse. Somehow Alaric's Aunt Delphine had managed to find accommodation for all the visitors, but Morganhall was bursting at the seams. Aunt Claara supervised everything from a curtained bed set in a place of honor in the hall, since she was not able to walk.

The wedding of Lady Alazais Morgan with Sir Llion Farquahar was celebrated two days later, on the Feast of the Assumption of the Blessed Virgin. In honor of the feast, and in preparation for the wedding to come, local villagers had bedecked the little church just outside the keep with a profusion of summer flowers. In addition, Mother Judiana and half a dozen of her sisters from Arc-en-Ciel had come to offer their especial gifts for the happy couple.

It was Alaric's privilege, as head of his family, to escort his sister down the aisle. As the bridal party entered the church, attended by Zoë and Geill, the sisters lifted their voices in the beautiful *Ave Vierge Dorée*, the traditional hymn sung both for celestial brides and for their mortal counterparts. In return, and in tribute to the sisters, whose house had sheltered the bride for so many years, Alazais wore a simple gown of pale blue, with her flaxen hair loose and crowned with a circlet of roses in all the colors of the rainbow, as was the custom of the convent.

Little Bronwyn served as flower girl, happily scattering multicolored rose petals before the bride. And it was Alaric who proudly gave his half-sister in marriage to the man who had served him for most of his young life. Old Father Swithun married them under the selfsame rainbow canopy that had sheltered both Alyce and Zoë at their weddings.

After, Alazais and Llion led the immediate members of her bridal party—Zoë, Geill, Bronwyn, and Alaric—to the place where their father lay buried, near to the tomb of his first wife, in the tomb where his second wife had lain, and near to the tomb of Sir Charlan Morgan. There she and Llion knelt briefly by Kenneth's tomb, hands joined and heads bowed.

"Papa, I've wed your Llion," Alazais said softly, after a few seconds, smiling as she glanced aside at her new husband. "I know you would have welcomed him as a son. And I know that we have your blessing."

For answer, Llion smiled and gently kissed her hand, then bent to lay one palm flat against the ledger stone.

"Sleep in peace, my lord," he murmured. "I shall do my best to cherish your daughter."

A moment more they knelt there; then Alazais gently laid her bridal bouquet atop the tomb in tribute before they rose to depart.

Alaric lingered briefly after the bridal party joined the procession back to the castle, alone with his own thoughts concerning his father, and was surprised to find the king waiting near the church door with Duke Jared, who nodded to him and then joined the others, leaving king and page alone.

"May I walk with you?" Brion said quietly, gesturing toward the procession winding slowly back to the castle.

Alaric blinked, taken aback by the question.

"Of course. Sire, you need not ask *my* permission. You are the king."

"Aye, and you are lord of Morganhall," the king replied with a tiny smile. "When I am guest in another man's hall, I would not presume to assert my rank."

Flustered, Alaric glanced at the toes of his boots. "Sire, I am only a boy. I am not yet ten. I—"

"Alaric, you are nearly a man, and my future duke," the king reminded him, cutting across his objection. "Today you gave your sister in marriage to another worthy man. I think the days of your childhood are numbered." He glanced ahead, where the knights carrying Lady Claara's litter were falling in at the end of the bridal procession, then set his hand briefly on Alaric's shoulder. "Let us walk together."

Alaric knew not what to think. The king's tone had been serious. Though he had long been aware that his destiny was somehow entwined with the king's, he had always thought it would be farther in his future.

"I have been doing a bit of thinking about Morganhall in the past few weeks," the king said, clasping his hands behind him as they walked. "It has been yours since your father's death, of course, but your greater inheritance will be from your mother: your ducal and county lands and titles. It occurred to me that you probably will wish to gift Morganhall to Bronwyn, perhaps as part of her dowry when she eventually marries."

Alaric glanced aside briefly. "I hadn't really thought about it, Sire, but that seems a good plan."

"I thought you might approve. It has also occurred to me that your aunts are not getting any younger. Oh, I know the Lady Delphine is a formidable woman, and no one can fault her management of the estate, but perhaps it is time to give her and Lady Claara additional help. I know Llion had planned to bring his new wife to court, but perhaps she might consent to move back to Morganhall for a time; she grew up here, after all. And I cannot think of a more loyal man than Llion to guard your interests here."

Alaric fought down a sudden chill of foreboding. Surely the king did not mean to take Llion from him.

"Are you suggesting that he should move here to Morganhall?" he blurted—then belatedly murmured, "Sire."

The king shook his head, chuckling. "No, of course not—for I would also be loath to lose him. But Morganhall is close enough to Rhemuth that he could travel back and forth with relative ease. He does have some experience making the journey, you know."

At Alaric's look of question, the king looked faintly sheepish.

"Ah. Are you not aware that he had ridden to Rhemuth and back, the night your mother died, to spirit me away from here?" When Alaric shook his head, the king went on, "Are you aware that I came to see her that night, dressed as a Haldane squire?"

Alaric cocked his head, eyes narrowing in concentration. "You were *here*?"

Brion shrugged. "I was. She and I—had important work to do that night. Work having to do with . . . my inheritance. I do not know whether she was able to complete it. But she assured me that you would remember what to do, when the time came." At Alaric's continuing look of mystification, Brion shook his head and smiled faintly. "No matter. I must believe that the knowledge will come." He drew a deep breath to recollect himself, then went on.

"In any case, Llion knows how quickly the journey can be made, especially with changes of fresh horses, and when the journey is pre-planned. Do you think Alazais would mind living here for a few years?"

"I suppose not," Alaric said vaguely.

"Excellent," the king replied. "Perhaps Llion could act as official castellan while you and Bronwyn are in your minority. It would give him appropriate status, since he now is married to a duke's sister, and you would know that you have a pair of safe hands administering your estate."

"Aye, that's true," Alaric said, very much relieved.

"Good, then, it's settled," the king replied. "But come, we'd best catch up with the others. And you can announce the change at the wedding feast, if you like. Make it in the nature of a wedding present. I've already discussed this with Jared and with Llion. Jared thought it was a splendid idea, and Llion was somewhat overwhelmed by his turn of good fortune. But he promised that he would try to act surprised."

Alaric allowed himself a snort of amusement. "He never let on."

"Of course he didn't," the king replied. "He is an excellent servant of the Crown, and I have no doubt that, one day, he will win lands of his own. But for now, you could not ask for a better steward."

Very shortly, they caught up with the rest of the bridal party, and later that evening, after toasting the bride and groom, Alaric made his announcement. He did not know how many in the hall had known of the new arrangement, but by their reaction, all of them seemed to approve.

After dinner, his Aunt Delphine led the other women of their family to conduct Alazais to the nuptial chamber prepared. It was the one formerly occupied by Kenneth and Alyce, and before that by Kenneth and his first wife, the mother of Alazais, Geill, and Zoë. The sisters of Arc-en-Ciel accompanied them, singing a traditional wedding song.

Very shortly, the men then sang the new castellan of Morganhall to the bridal chamber. Alaric was among them, reckoned as a man tonight, and, after Father Swithun had blessed the marriage bed, himself closed the door after Llion before leading the rest of the wedding guests back downstairs for revelry into the small hours.

Chapter 31

"Then I was by him, as one brought up with him . . ."
—PROVERBS 8:30

HOUGH Llion was granted a week's leave to remain at Morganhall with his new bride, ostensibly to acquaint himself with the running of the estate, Alaric and the king returned to Rhemuth the very next day.

But Alaric realized, in the course of that journey, that something was changing in the interaction between king and future duke. While he was still a page in the king's service, and never allowed himself to forget that, he found that nearing the completion of his first decade seemed to make a difference in how he was treated, even though he would not attain his legal majority for another four years. Or perhaps it was because the king actively included him in the plans for the coming royal progress, which briefly would return him to his own Corwyn lands.

In any case, the change was there. And it persisted when Llion returned to court later in August, happier than Alaric had seen him in many months, even though Alazais had elected to remain at Morganhall for another few weeks, to reacquaint herself with her two Morgan aunts. Llion clearly missed his new bride, but he made several overnight visits back to Morganhall to check on her, and brought her back with him to Rhemuth early in September, shortly before they were to depart for Coroth with the king's party.

But first, at the insistence of the Dowager Queen Richeldis, yet another, more domestic detail remained to resolve before the king's departure: a slightly early celebration of her daughters' birthdays: Silke, turning twelve, and Xenia, who would be sixteen. Xenia already was a stunning young woman, and Silke still more child than woman, but both were given gifts appropriate to Haldane princesses: lengths of R'Kassan silk to be eagerly inspected and squabbled over, as well as ribbons and dainty slippers and items of simple jewelry. Xenia received her first adult coronet: a hammered silver band adorned with golden roses, which she proudly wore at the birthday supper celebrated *en famille*. Alaric and Prince Cormac served the table that evening, enduring the high spirits of the two princesses with good humor.

They left the very next day for Desse: a relatively small party, as royal entourages went, comprised of only the king, his young page and future Duke of Corwyn, Prince Cormac, a handful of household knights, and several of his immediate companions: Jamyl Arilan, Jiri Redfearn, and Llion Farquahar, the latter accompanied by his new wife and a maid. As was customary when the king left his capital for any length of time, Duke Richard would assume regent duties.

The visit to Corwyn was to be an informal one, with little fanfare or advance notice, well completed before the storms of late autumn set in. After a brisk ride down to Desse, the northernmost deepwater port on the River Eirian, they met a fast royal galley that carried them downriver and then east toward Coroth. They did not call at Nyford, for the flags flying atop the citadel above the town indicated that Nyford's bishop was in residence. Nonetheless, Alaric stood alone at the ship's rail until the port was out of sight, staring at the bustling esplanade before the city gates, remembering the grey mare.

"You do need to let that go," Llion said quietly, suddenly at his right side. "You cannot change what de Nore did, and you mustn't let it cripple you for the future."

Alaric bowed his head, not looking at Llion.

"I know that."

"Then, you need to *act* like you know it," Llion replied, a little sharply. "It was a terrible thing that he did, and he knew it would hurt you, but in the end, it was a *horse*. Save your further indignation for things that *really* matter."

"Horses matter," the boy said stubbornly.

"Do they matter like Hallowdale?"

Alaric grimaced, recalled to the vivid memory of accounts he had heard of the atrocities committed there, remembering the stench of burnt flesh.

"Oh, he wasn't directly responsible for those people being killed," Llion conceded, as Alaric dared to look at him defiantly, "but he's been preaching hatred of Deryni for years. That's the kind of intolerance and bigotry that allowed Hallowdale to happen."

Alaric's face hardened, the grey eyes as cold as the autumn sky.

"I hate him," he whispered.

"Yes, and he hates you. Do something constructive about it."

Alaric averted his gaze, biting at his lip. "I'm only a boy."

"You're a boy who will soon be a man, and a duke. And you're Deryni. You can make a difference. Think about it."

Alaric tried *not* to think about it overmuch, telling himself that, realistically, he could do little to change the attitude of bigoted bishops while he was still a child; but the conversation had begun to bring him to a more realistic sense of his own destiny. That destiny involved the king; that, he had always known. But it had also reminded him of the great influence he one day would be capable of wielding, both as a duke and a Deryni. He found himself thinking about that increasingly as the days passed, especially when he stood at the landward rail and watched the land slide past.

He and Cormac did have duties, of course, serving the king and sometimes standing a watch with the helmsman or one of the sailors atop the mast. And Llion was reluctant to let their training slacken off entirely. The galley was too small to permit much in the way of physical exercise; swordplay was out of the question, other than to practice forms. But various of the knights would grill Alaric and Cormac daily on aspects of court protocol and heraldry, and Alaric sometimes tried out his rudimentary Torenthi on some of the sailors.

When he was not otherwise occupied, he and Cormac also spent a fair amount of time playing at cardounet, sometimes with Sir Jiri Redfearn, who had been a keen player in his youth and still enjoyed the occasional match. Jiri proved to be far more loquacious than Alaric had expected, and seemed genuinely interested in the observations of the two noble-born pages regarding court life, for he had twin sons of his own at court, only a little older than Alaric and the Llanneddi prince. Sometimes, while they played by torchlight when the galley had anchored for the night, Jiri would reminisce about his own training as a page. Alaric liked Sir Jiri, who seemed not at all intimidated by what he was, or what he might become.

"Are you looking forward to your visit?" the older man asked, as he and Alaric played on the last evening before they were to arrive at the Corwyn capital.

"I am," Alaric admitted. "But it will be very different without my father at my side."

Jiri moved his war-duke, glancing sidelong at his young opponent. "It will be different, I'll grant you that," he said. "You will find that there have been some other changes as well."

"What sort of changes?" Alaric asked, surveying the board.

Jiri gave a small shrug. "They did not tell you, because there was nothing you could have done," he replied. "Several of your regents have passed away since the beginning of the year."

Alaric let his hand sink to the table beside the board.

"Who?"

"Airich O'Flynn, the Earl of Derry, was the first. He contracted a wasting disease last autumn and died shortly after Twelfth Night. His son Seamus succeeds him. He is in his early thirties."

"I think I remember both of them," Alaric said, nodding absently. "They were very kind to me. Who else? You said 'several.'"

"The Earl of Airnis, Sir Airlie Kushannan," Jiri replied.

"No!"

"Alas, yes. Thrown from his horse early this summer. His neck was broken. I believe you are acquainted with his heir, Lord Jernian."

"It isn't possible," Alaric murmured, shaking his head. "Why was I not told?"

Jiri shrugged. "It was not my decision. But I believe there has been talk of bringing young Jernian to court for a few years, since he is now an earl. I believe he is a few years older than you, yes?"

Alaric nodded numbly, thinking of his friend, who now was bereft of both father and grandfather in a very short span.

"I am told that his martial skills . . . leave much to be desired," Jiri went on. "He is shortsighted, I believe. But the trainers at Coroth report that he shows a keen affinity for strategy. If that can be developed, he could still be a valuable asset for you when he comes into his maturity."

Alaric nodded. "If skill at cardounet is any indication, he should do well." At Jiri's gesture, he picked up his priest-king and turned it in his fingers.

"It was Jernian who introduced me to the works of Count Koltan and Ulger de Brinsi," he said softly. "Did you know? Viliam, too. I was looking forward to playing with them while I'm in Coroth."

"Well, by all means, do that," Jiri said. "You've gotten quite good." He glanced down at the game board. "It's still your move, by the way."

Alaric played with new determination for the rest of the game, and even managed to play Jiri to a draw. It was no small accomplishment, given that he was grieving for his friend, who also was now fatherless.

But the next day, standing at the king's side in Corwyn green rather than Haldane crimson as the royal galley glided between the great twin lighthouses guarding the entrance to Coroth harbor, he felt for the first time that he was not quite a boy any longer, but a young man coming home. It was an impression that was only reinforced by the cheers and waves of the men waiting to greet him: his regents and the friends he had left there.

"Welcome, Sire! Welcome, Your Grace!" they called, as the ship glided to a halt alongside the quay and the crew threw lines ashore to secure her.

To his pleased surprise, the king deferred to him, inviting him to be the first to disembark, where his chancellor, James of Tendal, was waiting to clasp his hand.

"Your Grace, it has been too long," the old man murmured, pumping his hand. "So many changes . . ."

"Yes, I know, Sir James," Alaric replied, casting his gaze across the others thronged behind and to either side of the chancellor. "I only recently learned of some of the changes. Pray, present me to the new Earl of Derry, and then refresh my memory with the others."

Duly he offered his condolences to Earl Seamus, a pleasant young man with tousled curly hair, then passed among the others, shaking hands and accepting their murmured sympathies on the passing of his own father, until finally he came to Jernian, standing with Viliam, who was now a squire.

"I am so sorry, Jernian," he whispered, as he embraced the older boy briefly.

Jernian shrugged as they pulled apart. "It's done. There's nothing we can do to change it." He quirked a wry smile. "So I guess we'll just have to be orphans together. Your father will be much missed."

"As yours will be, I feel sure," Alaric replied.

"But there's a game board waiting," Viliam interjected, with his own taut smile, "and we're both eager to see how much you've learned at court."

Alaric grinned. "I've been playing with Sir Jiri Redfearn on the voyage here," he warned, "and he's awfully good."

"Did you read all of Koltan?" Viliam challenged.

"All that you gave me," Alaric retorted. "And I've corrupted several of the other pages and squires at the Rhemuth court. One of them came with us. But remember that this is a working visit for me. With my father gone, I've not got him to lean on, so I have to learn how things run."

"Understood." Viliam inclined his head. As a future baron, he was well aware of the responsibilities gradually to devolve upon the future duke. "But you *will* have *some* time to play, won't you?"

"I'll make time," Alaric replied. "And now I want you to meet my recent training partner, Prince Cormac of Llannedd," he said, stepping aside to raise an arm to Cormac, who came at his gesture to nod agreeably. "Cormac, these are my good friends, Jernian Earl of Airnis and Lord Viliam de Souza. He'll be a baron one day."

"Highness," the two acknowledged, with proper neck bows.

"Just Cormac," the prince replied, extending his hand. "In this place, I am honored to be simply a friend of your future duke."

Viliam raised an eyebrow and gave the prince a sly grin. "It is a singular honor. But we understand that you are also a student of cardounet. Fancy a match after supper?"

"If it is allowed, of course," Cormac replied. "I will abide by the custom of this court—and knowing that the two of you have duties, just as we have back in Rhemuth. *I* still have duties, even though Alaric is off the hook for a while."

Viliam arched a smile at Alaric. "I like this fellow. I think we'll all get along splendidly."

The four of them did play cardounet during the visit to Coroth, but Alaric also spent a great deal of his time attending meetings of his regency council, sometimes with the king at his side and sometimes not, and talking to his advisors, and sitting in on ducal courts beside Sir James of Tendal and Sir Miles Chopard, who customarily saw to the judicial functioning of his duchy. Meanwhile, Llion took his new bride off to meet his family for a week.

It was an exciting time for a boy completing his first decade: a boy destined for high office who, already, was venturing to try the reins of governing. Although his regents continued to make final decisions about the welfare of the duchy, they now were soliciting his opinion, considering his input, allowing him to begin assuming a public face of leadership. The king studiously remained in the background, letting the regents set the tone. Alaric little liked some of the minutiae of administration, like reviewing accounts with Lord Hamilton and Father Tivadan, but he found that he had good instincts for justice and fairness, and was pleased when his recommendations exactly paralleled the rulings handed down in several difficult judicial decisions.

"You have the knack for it, lad," Sir James said approvingly after a particularly vexing case involving purloined cattle and grazing rights and water assignments in the mountains north of Coroth. "And I think all parties in that case came away at least moderately satisfied."

The king, who had been sitting quietly at the back of the hall, also complimented him afterward.

"That was well done. I shall give a good report to Duke Richard."

Alaric enjoyed his time in Coroth, and starting to flex his wings and exercise the skills he had been training for. He also enjoyed pursuing the friendships he was developing with his age peers: few, but solid, so far as he could tell. And even those who kept their distance did so more out of respect for his rank than fear of what he was. In all, he was well satisfied with the rapport he was building among the men who served him and would safeguard his interests while he continued his education.

All too soon, his visit drew toward its close. Llion and Alazais returned from the Farquahar holding in the north, and preparations were under way for the Michaelmas observances that also marked his tenth birthday, after which they would head back to Rhemuth. But on the day before his birthday, he returned with Llion, Sir James of Tendal, and Father Tivadan from a courtesy call to the bishop, to find the king in close conference with half a dozen of the Corwyn regents before a fire in the great hall.

"Ah, you're back," Lord Rathold said, looking up as the four entered the hall. "Come join us, lad. There's been a change in plans for tomorrow."

Mystified, Alaric trotted obediently up the steps to take a seat beside the king. Jiri Redfearn was there with the regents, and also Jamyl Arilan.

"We've just received word that the old Hort of Orsal has died," Jiri said baldly. "Several weeks ago, apparently. We were discussing whether it might be feasible to attend the investiture of his successor."

"We ought to go, since we're here," the king chimed in. "The Hort of Orsal is also Prince of Tralia, just across the strait: your nearest neighbor, and a staunch friend of Gwynedd and Corwyn."

"When is it to take place?" Alaric asked.

"Tomorrow," Jiri replied with a grimace. "If we go, it would mean missing the Michaelmas observances here. But the galley can sail with the morning tide—if you wish to attend, Sire," he added, with a glance at the king.

"I think we must," the king replied. "Tralia is an important ally, and they won't be expecting us to make an appearance. Ordinarily, we would be far away in Rhemuth, with no chance to find out in time. Besides, I like Létald, the new Hort. Perhaps we should take Cormac as well: another royal to underline Létald's legitimacy."

"Is it wise to take him out of the kingdom?" Jiri said thoughtfully. "Will his brother object?"

"It's only across the strait, Jiri, and only for the day; maybe two."

"Perhaps we should allow Cormac to decide," Jamyl murmured. "I cannot imagine that there will be any danger; if there were, we should not recommend that you take Alaric. But the prince knows his brother better than we do."

"Point taken," Brion agreed with a nod. He glanced around the table at them. "We'll plan to sail with the morning tide, then, with or without Cormac. And we'd best send an emissary this evening, to let them know we're coming. Rathold, you're our diplomatic liaison. Will you go?"

"Of course," Rathold replied, getting to his feet. "With your permission, I'll go directly to the harbor. If I miss the tide, I'll be traveling with you tomorrow, and Létald will get an even more unexpected surprise."

THE king and his party sailed with the morning tide, cloaked and soberly garbed, taking along several of Alaric's regents to stand by their young lord. Prince Cormac, on reflection, elected to remain in Coroth with Jernian and Viliam, especially when he was told that he might lead the Michaelmas procession in Alaric's place. The day was blustery with the promise of autumn, and the royal galley made good time under sail.

"It's good that you should know Prince Létald," the king told Alaric, as he and Jiri stood to either side of the boy while their ship glided past the great pharos that guarded the river mouth. He wore a tunic of dark grey under his cloak, out of respect for the recent passing of Létald's predecessor, but the collar and cuffs were embroidered with silver bullion, befitting his royal stature. His dark hair was caught back in a simple queue and confined by a plain circlet of hammered gold.

"Létald himself seems a delightful fellow," the king added, leaning to gaze down at the grey water rushing by. "He's a young man still, not much older than I am, but I'm told that one does not want to become his enemy."

"No, one does not," Jiri agreed emphatically. "In that regard, he is just like his father. But his house have long been loyal friends to Gwynedd and to Corwyn: a good neighbor to have between you and Torenth, Alaric. Remember that."

"Yes, sir," Alaric murmured, glancing up appraisingly at the castle brooding on the bluff. "Is that where we're going?"

"It is," the king replied. "Vár Adony, it's called, according to your Lord Rathold. It's the Tralian winter capital. I've never been there, but my father used to take me to the summer palace, Horthánthy. We passed it a while ago, but I doubt you saw much through the mist. It's quite spectacular, though. If Vár Adony is anything like it, you'll be in for a treat. And I think you'll like Létald."

They landed shortly, where Lord Rathold was waiting with horses and a guard of honor to take them up the winding road to the castle. Since Alaric's inclusion in the royal party was intended to introduce him as the future Duke of Corwyn, he wore an over-tunic of deep green instead of Haldane livery, with the Corwyn dagger at his hip and his father's signet as Earl of Lendour on a chain around his neck: no overt declaration of his identity, since he was not yet of age, but neither was he any mere page. As they made their way toward the esplanade before the great hall doors, where the Tralian prince was greeting new arrivals, Alaric drew the occasional curious look, following at the king's elbow with Llion and Sir Jamyl, but no hostility or particular recognition. Lord Rathold was well-known at the Tralian court, and adroitly eased them into the princely presence.

Létald himself, black-clad and still in mourning for his departed father, proved to be a round-faced, energetic young man perhaps a few years older than the king, with wiry dark hair pulled back in a club at the back of his neck and a narrow gold coronet circling his brow.

"So, this is to be my new ducal neighbor across the straits," he declared to Brion, upon having Alaric presented to him. "Welcome to Vár Adony, young Corwyn. I shall look forward to our future interactions. And Lord Rathold, you are also most welcome. Sir Jiri, gentlemen."

With that, and hearty handshakes all around, Létald was off to greet other new arrivals.

"Sir Jiri, may I ask why Prince Létald wears a coronet?" Alaric said quietly, only to Jiri. "I thought we were here to see him crowned."

"Ah . . . no. He has already been invested as Prince of Tralia, shortly after his father's passing. Today's ceremony acknowledges him as Hort of

Orsal, Overlord of the Forcinn States." Jiri glanced at the boy in faint amusement. "I know, 'tis different from the way we do things in Gwynedd. The Forcinn States have, ah, unique challenges, with Torenth so close. Come, though, we mustn't get left behind."

They continued across the esplanade and followed the king into the audience hall, joining scores of milling guests who were gathering to await the court's business. At once Alaric was struck by the differences between the Tralian hall and the king's hall at Rhemuth, or even his own hall at Coroth. This hall was long and narrow, lit by a high clerestory gallery under an elaborate tangle of wooden beams that supported the vaulted ceiling. The floor underfoot, rather than stone, was of polished timber set in a herringbone pattern that drew the eye toward the dais at the far end, where a solitary chair of state was set in readiness for the man soon to occupy it.

Most striking of all were the plastered walls, where ranks of life-sized warriors watched with painted eyes, vigilant and fierce, swords in their powerful hands and long oval shields on their arms—and each one was different, given individual identity by the artists who had painted them. Some of the figures had torches thrust into brass brackets mounted in their hands, the torchlight giving a semblance of life to the painted guardians. Further illumination came from fires burning on the stone-clad hearths of half a dozen massive fireplaces along the length of the hall.

"It isn't like Rhemuth, is it?" Brion murmured aside to him as they moved among the other visitors.

Alaric could only shake his head slightly, sticking close by the king's side. The painted warriors made him vaguely uneasy.

They wandered briefly among the guests, exchanging pleasantries with a few known to Brion or his courtiers, until a squire in Tralia's sea-green livery came to escort Brion to a seat near the dais, next to the King of Bremagne and his eldest son. Jamyl and Llion attended him. Meanwhile, Alaric and his Corwyn regents were shown to seats in one of the window bays near the dais, where a page brought them refreshments. Not long after that, liveried squires began marshaling the assembled guests and witnesses to begin gathering more purposefully before the dais at the far end of the hall.

A brazen fanfare from trumpets shaped like sea serpents caused the crowd to part for a small procession down the length of the hall, led by a cleric bearing a processional cross and a gold-coped prelate whom Lord Rathold identified as Tralia's archbishop, who was attended by two surpliced acolytes.

"I have always found him to be a godly man," Rathold murmured softly to Alaric. "He will have presided over Létald's crowning, but today's ceremony is more secular in nature—though he will witness it and give a blessing. Létald's authority as Hort of Orsal will derive from the assent of the other Forcinn princes . . . who are coming now."

Indeed, another trumpet blast heralded a further, larger procession of gentlemen clad in a variety of festive attire. Some wore court robes of a sort familiar to Alaric, but one was arrayed in desert silks, another in the Eastern garb Alaric had seen on emissaries from the Torenthi lands.

"These are the rulers of the Forcinn states?" Alaric whispered.

"The rulers or their heirs. Some are too old to travel easily on short notice. The man in desert silks is Prince Hakim of Nur Hallaj, eldest son and heir to the emir Qais: a decent fellow, by all accounts." Rathold jutted his chin in the direction of the man in Torenthi attire. "The next fellow is Count Richard, heir to Regnier Duc du Joux, and the gentleman in scarlet would be Prince Ysomard of Thuria; he only succeeded to his title earlier this year, so I know little about him save by reputation. The man in purple is Prince Isarn of Logréine, and the one with ermine tails on his cloak is Grand Duke Nivelon of Vezaire, a distant relative of the late Queen Dulchesse. And the fellow in the burnoose would be Prince Mikhail of Andelon—not, strictly speaking, one of the Forcinn princes, but Andelon sometimes serves as a gatekeeper to the south, so they work with the alliance."

"And these all owe allegiance to Létald?" Alaric asked.

"It is a loose confederation, but yes. It would be in none of their best interests to break totally free of the others—not with a neighbor as powerful as Torenth close along their northern borders. The system works for them," he added.

The Forcinn princes made their courtesies to the archbishop, then arranged themselves on the dais steps in two lines fanned outward so that

Létald could pass between them. As the trumpets sounded yet another fanfare, the prince's procession slowly passed down the hall, led by half a dozen armed men who looked to have stepped from the walls of the hall. Following them came two pages in sea-green livery flanking a blonde, white-clad girl of twelve or so, who carried Létald's princely coronet on a velvet cushion, her sea-green veil held in place by a narrow gold coronet.

"The Princess Sivorn, Létald's sister," Rathold whispered. "It is customary that the Prince of Tralia comes bare-headed before his fellow princes."

Following her came Létald himself, who had donned a sumptuous robe of embroidered sea-green velvet over his mourning attire, its wide sleeves heavily encrusted with gold-couched threads and its train carried by two liveried pages also in sea-green. When he had made his reverence to the archbishop, to the two lines of princes, he mounted the steps and turned before the chair of state, waiting to sit until the attendant pages had arranged the train at his feet.

There followed a reading of the treaty whereby the Forcinn States had agreed historically to bind themselves in a loose confederation in matters concerning their mutual defense and external trade. The document then renewed the contract by which the Prince of Tralia, now embodied in Létald Sobbon Jubal Josse von Horthy, agreed to function as arbitrator and nominal overlord for said confederation, delineating the rights and duties now to be assumed by said Létald as Hort of Orsal and Overlord of the Forcinn Buffer States. This reading being accomplished, the archbishop then presented the document for Létald's assent, signified by the affixing of his signature and seal. Another trumpet fanfare signaled the accomplishment of the deed.

But the ceremony clearly was not finished. As another trumpet blare reverberated into silence, a slow drumroll drew all eyes to the far end of the hall where, to an accompanying drumbeat, an erect, middle-aged woman dressed all in white bore a glittering, princely cap of scarlet upon a black velvet cushion.

"That is Létald's mother, the Princess Maya," Lord Rathold murmured, close beside Alaric. "He has no wife as yet."

Alaric had already surmised the woman's identity, and only nodded as the princess passed between the two rows of worthies ranged along the dais steps, acknowledging their salutes, then herself made a reverence to her son, holding the cushion aloft. She then turned to give the cap into the keeping of the six Forcinn lords, who received it and knelt before Létald, each with a hand supporting it, in sign that they would support the man about to wear it. They lifted it and bowed their heads in homage as the archbishop began an invocation imploring God's blessing on Létald and all the states now owing him allegiance.

"Is that a crown?" Alaric whispered aside to Jiri Redfearn.

Jiri shook his head. "Not a crown, a cap of maintenance. The medallions suspended along the front are symbolic of the five regions over which Létald is superior."

"I understand."

When the archbishop had concluded his blessing, the princes came forward with the cap to stand around Létald's chair of state, holding the cap briefly above his head before, together, placing it on his head.

"All hail Létald Sobbon Jubal Josse von Horthy, Sovereign Prince of Tralia," a herald proclaimed, as the deed was done and the princes bowed themselves before him, "and now, by acclamation, Hort of Orsal and Overlord of the Forcinn Buffer States. *Axios, axios, axios!*"

"He is worthy," Lord Rathold translated, leaning in from Alaric's other side.

Alaric only nodded, gravely taking it all in, for many of these men would be his neighbors when he came to his majority.

At table later that evening, he sat in an honored place at the king's right hand, where he had further opportunity to observe the great and good of the region. To Brion's other side, Meyric King of Bremagne was seated beside his eldest son, Crown Prince Ryol, just come of age. The Bremagni king, perhaps in his forties, sported a head of copper-bronze curls that tumbled onto his shoulders and a curled beard twined with golden cords.

"You must visit Bremagne, my lord," King Meyric said, leaning close to Brion, and apparently in his cups. "I have another son and three comely daughters at home, and the girls all will be looking for husbands very soon. You could do far worse than to take a Bremagni bride."

Brion smiled politely and raised his cup in salute to his fellow monarch. "I am sure I could, my lord. Perhaps in a few years. My reign is yet young, and I have much still to learn."

"Then, perhaps my sons might visit Rhemuth," Meyric returned with a wink, jostling an embarrassed Prince Ryol with an elbow. "I believe you have several comely sisters . . . ?"

Other guests offered perils of a more threatening sort. "Sire, do not react," Jiri said aside to Brion a little later, when they had risen from table and were preparing to mingle with other guests, "but it appears that the King of Torenth has sent one of his sons as an observer. Prince Wencit, I believe. Do you see him, yonder?"

Brion had stiffened at Jiri's words, and cast a quick glance in the direction Jiri indicated. Alaric also managed to look that way whilst plucking an imaginary bit of fuzz from his sleeve. He had never seen the Torenthi prince, but from descriptions, he immediately recognized the slender, haughty young man in tawny silks and velvets, a little older than the king, with reddish sidelocks emerging from beneath his richly embroidered cap and a smudge of tawny mustache beneath piercing amber eyes.

"What is *he* doing here?" Brion muttered to Jiri, tight-lipped, as Wencit caught his gaze and inclined his head coolly before turning his back.

"Perhaps observing, like the rest of us," Jiri said with a sour grimace. "Or perhaps something more. I shall try to make a few discreet inquiries."

With that, Jiri moved away from the king, taking Jamyl with him, to blend casually with the milling courtiers. Brion himself seemed a little subdued as he, too, turned his back and made polite conversation with others who approached him. A little later, as Alaric prepared to top up the king's wine, Brion shook his head distractedly, darting another glance across the room in the direction of the Torenthi prince.

"I certainly would like to know why he's here," he muttered, signing for Alaric not to pour. "No more of that; it's vile stuff. A pity that neither of us is competent to read his intentions. And you're not to try!" he added, at Alaric's eyebrows raised in silent query. "It's just that his family would dearly love to take back my throne." Flustered, he thrust his goblet into Alaric's hand. "See if you can find me something that's remotely drinkable, will you? Wherever this came from, it tastes like horse piss!

And no, I've never tasted horse piss, but this is giving me a headache. Just get rid of it."

With a nod of agreement, Alaric moved off to look for something better, wondering whether the king's sour mood might have another source than the wine. As he headed toward a sideboard holding pitchers of wine, set in a curtained archway, he found himself surreptitiously eyeing the Torenthi prince, considering whether he might be able to do anything to help the king. Though he had begun to develop a little skill at Truth-Reading, he knew his training was still sketchy. Trying to Read a powerful and no doubt well-trained Deryni probably was not a good idea.

Nonetheless, he ventured a cautious and incredibly delicate feeler in that direction—and immediately withdrew as he caught the merest prickle of odd, dangerous shields he did not care to probe further. Fortunately, neither Wencit nor any of his obviously Torenthi companions appeared to have noticed.

But someone did notice. As Alaric continued on toward the sideboard with the wine, setting the king's goblet on the polished wood, he found himself suddenly yanked behind the nearby curtain, a leather-clad arm clamped across his chest from behind and a gloved hand pressed hard to his mouth. Even as his fingers flew to the restraining arm in near panic, all of his body tensing in an instinctive attempt to twist away, a voice murmured, soft in his ear, "And what, precisely, did you intend to do, if you had actually managed to touch him?"

At the same time, a familiar mental "voice" reverberated in his mind: *Are you trying to get yourself mind-ripped?*

Chapter 32

RE you trying to get yourself mind-ripped?

Stifling what would have been a whimper, Alaric all but wilted against his captor's chest with relief, for he knew both the voice and the mental touch. He had not seen Sir Sé Trelawney during Prince Létald's investiture or even during the banquet, but neither did it come as any great surprise to find the Anviler knight in attendance. He supposed that Sé's order might well have an interest in the stability of the Forcinn, just like the King of Bremagne and the Torenthi observers.

As he relaxed, letting his hands fall away from Sé's arm, the hand fell away from his mouth and the Deryni knight continued to hustle him back along the corridor and into the shelter of a shadowed doorway, where he released him. Little to Alaric's surprise, there was no one in the vicinity.

"What *were* you thinking?" Sé said softly, disapproval in his tone as he seized Alaric's shoulders and held him with his gaze. "Do you realize the risk you took?"

Alaric managed a difficult swallow, well aware that Sé was absolutely right.

"I did it for the king," he whispered.

"The king did not ask you to do it," Sé retorted. "He expressed a wish that one of you *could* do it, well aware that neither of you could. And he should not have done even that. Your powers are still developing, and your training is sketchy at best. His are all but nonexistent, until you are old enough to assist him to his powers. In the future, if he asks something you know to be beyond your ability, you must decline. You will do him no good if you try and fail and he loses you."

Alaric ducked his head. He could not disagree, but to refuse the king was not in his nature.

"I'm sorry," he said meekly.

"As well you should be." Then: "I shall come to you over the winter, and see if we can speed things along. This is not the time or place. Look for me toward Christmas."

Alaric looked up in surprise, but Sé was already backing away and bowing in farewell, right hand pressed to heart. He was gone before Alaric could draw breath to question.

Still reeling from Sé's stinging reprimand, heart still pounding, Alaric drew a series of deep breaths and simply stood with his back pressed hard against the wall for several long seconds, willing his racing heart to slow and trying to regain at least an outward semblance of composure. Only then did he square his shoulders and make his way back to the hall, where he would try again to find a wine that would please the king. He decided not to mention the encounter with Sé.

E slept poorly that night, shaken by the unexpected appearance of Sé and by his own near encounter with Wencit of Torenth, which so easily could have gone disastrously wrong. He found himself wondering if Sé had somehow intervened so that Wencit did *not* detect Alaric's clumsy attempt to probe him. He had no doubt that the powerful Deryni knight was capable of doing so, if he wished.

To his relief, the king was not inclined to linger the next morning. Alaric, for his part, had no desire to be anywhere in Wencit's vicinity, if he could help it. They sailed with the noonday tide, when the morning fog had mostly burned off and the weather looked to hold for long enough to make safe harbor at Coroth. Only as the cliffs of Tralia and the Orsal's winter palace fell away behind them did Alaric begin to breathe easily again.

On the short dash back across to Coroth, he mostly managed to put the previous night's events behind him. He chatted with Llion for most of the way and, as they sailed between Coroth's sea jetties, found his thoughts returning to more practical considerations, and wondering how Cormac had fared the previous day, leading the Michaelmas procession to the cathedral.

But as the galley's crew tossed lines ashore and warped it to the quay, he realized that he need not have worried. The prince was among those waiting quayside to greet them as they came down the gangplank, and made a point to ride beside Alaric as they headed back up to the castle. In fact, Cormac could hardly stop grinning as he recounted all the details of his great adventure.

"It's very different from Pwyllheli," the prince enthused, "but I much liked it. I was much taken by the idea of Saint Michael being the patron of knights, with a yearly ceremony to reinforce that devotion. I wonder whether my father might agree to such a custom. Though I would have to persuade my brothers first."

His sheer delight in so simple an activity underlined the sometimes bleak role Cormac was allowed at home, as a very junior prince only distantly in the succession. It was an aspect of Cormac's life that Alaric had never thought about before, and he found himself wondering whether, when Cormac returned to his brother's court, he would find it even more difficult to carve out a meaningful role. But at least for now, he could count himself a valued page in the court of Gwynedd.

The following day, Corwyn's regents belatedly celebrated Alaric's birthday with a final ducal court. There, taking advantage of the presence both of the king and of their future duke, the regents presented several squires for knighthood, which honor the king duly conferred, with Alaric's hand upon the sword. For a duke in training, it was a singular privilege, and one that he would long treasure.

He treasured, too, the time he had been given with his age-mates in Coroth, particularly Jernian and Viliam, whom he recruited to assist in the knightings, helping to buckle on the spurs. And that night, after he had supped with the king and his regents, he and Cormac were able to play a few more cardounet matches with Jernian and Viliam.

The voyage home was uneventful, though the rough weather curtailed much activity on deck, and caused many of the ship's company to spend an inordinate part of their time standing at the leeward rail, sometimes making reluctant offerings to the sea gods. Alaric suffered no such indignity. By mid-October they were back in Rhemuth, where Alaric resumed his Haldane livery and Haldane duties, settling back into his training with new focus as he counted the days until Sé should make an appearance.

October gave way to November, and November to December, and autumn duly eased into winter, with sleety rain and hard frost. The leafless branches bore a mantle of icy rime that rarely melted even at midday, then froze again. The slush underfoot was treacherous, and hardened with the dusk to a brittle layer of ice that bloodied horses' fetlocks and left bloody hoofprints where they passed, causing the royal stable masters to suspend unnecessary ride-outs until the weather should improve. Ordinary folk moved as they must. And whether by day or by night, the wintering weather chilled to the bone, sending many a denizen of the city to huddle close to fires or scurry early to their beds for warmth.

Not long into Advent, Alaric and Prince Cormac were among those who sought their beds early, though only Cormac would sleep that night. Alaric sensed Sé's presence behind the door as the two of them entered, and schooled himself not to react as a black-clad arm reached from behind the door to clasp the back of the prince's neck from behind. Even as Cormac's knees buckled, Sé was sweeping him off his feet, his black cloak engulfing the boy like the wings of some gigantic bird as he carried him to the bed that Alaric wordlessly indicated, almost as if they had planned it that way all along.

"He has come to no harm," Sé murmured, as he deposited the sleeping prince on the bed.

"I know that." Alaric closed the door and threw the bolt, watching as Sé tucked Cormac's cloak more closely around him, then covered him with a sleeping fur. A good fire was blazing on the hearth, and firepots waited beside each of the beds, flaring to life at a gesture from the Deryni knight. As an afterthought, Sé also lit a rushlight set in a niche above the bed head.

"Tell me," Alaric said, "is it always necessary to touch a person, to put him to sleep?"

"Usually, at least the first time. After that, it depends on the depth of the link one has already forged, and how much energy one is willing to expend."

Sé briefly turned his face back toward the door and gave a nod, one hand moving minutely in a gesture of warding. "That should keep us from being disturbed. Llion and Alazais are already asleep next door."

Alaric cocked his head at the older Deryni. "You put them to sleep, too?"

"Yes."

"Can you teach me?"

Sé glanced at the sleeping Cormac, his lips tightening, then nodded. "Very well. I had intended another lesson, but perhaps we can do both. Any lad brash enough to attempt Reading a Torenthi mage from across the room is probably ready to learn—if not that particular skill. You are very fortunate I was there." His tone held exasperation, but also indulgence. "Come along, then." He beckoned Alaric to join him by Cormac's bed. "Sit here beside him. He will not wake, I assure you."

Alaric had not reckoned on Cormac being his first subject, but he eagerly did as Sé directed, scrunching closer to the sleeping prince as Sé sat behind him. He tried not to tense as Sé set hands on his shoulders and drew him back against his chest, fingertips slipping forward to rest on his carotid pulse points.

"I believe I shall try the method by which we train novices in my order," Sé said softly. "Still yourself now, and open to me. Close your eyes. You may lose awareness for a time."

Alaric started, for that last statement underlined how real this was about to become—what Sé was about to do—but he did his best to comply, closing his eyes and willing himself to relax against Sé's chest. Focusing on his heartbeat pulsing under Sé's touch, he let himself drift with it, vaguely aware of the feather brush of Sé's controls slipping into place and pressing him deeper. Then he was aware of nothing.

"Well, then, *that* was interesting." Sé's murmur immediately brought Alaric back to awareness, though he had no idea how long it had been. "I see you have already begun to Truth-Read. That is a skill that will, indeed, be useful to the king, as well as yourself. Continue working on that.

"But for now, let us look at putting a subject to sleep." Sé slid his hands back onto Alaric's shoulders. "This will be the prelude to a number of additional skills that you will also learn to exercise, in time. Reach across and rest your hand on Cormac's forehead. I shall be right with you. You won't hurt him," he added, as Alaric stiffened minutely. "Nor will I hurt you."

Nodding, Alaric reached out his hand and touched Cormac's forehead, aware of Sé's presence at the back of his mind.

But he wasn't afraid. At Sé's prompting, he drew a slow, steadying breath and "reached" his mind into Cormac's, gently seizing control, astonished at how easy it was. He was also faintly aware of Sé's approval.

"Good. You may let your hand fall away now," Sé whispered. "You have him. Cormac, your sleep will be far more restful if you remove your outer garments, just as you normally do before going to bed. You need not pay us any mind."

As Cormac roused, apparently oblivious to their presence, he sat up and yawned, folding back the sleeping fur, then swung his legs over the other side of the bed. As he did so, Sé urged Alaric to his feet and drew the two of them back into shadow to watch as Cormac unfastened the cloak clasp at his throat and let it fall away, then bent to remove his boots.

Under Sé's guidance, Alaric followed Cormac's unfocused musings as he straightened and rose, pulling his discarded cloak from the bed to hang it from a nearby peg. He then unbuckled and removed his belt and dagger, hanging them on another peg, with the dagger within reach. After that, he raked both hands through tousled hair and yawned again, then padded to the garderobe across the room and disappeared behind the curtain.

"He is quite unaware that we are here," Sé said softly, "and he will remember none of this unless you wish it."

He shifted to pure thought, swiftly insinuating further teaching: the concepts that would give his pupil access to this important skill: to take control or impart communication, most often without the knowledge or consent of the subject.

Responsibility comes with that ability, Sé sent. *And prudence is essential.* The actual words unaccountably resonated in Alaric's mind, almost painfully. *If only out of common courtesy, one does not impel behavior that contradicts an individual's free will—unless, of course, it touches on your own safety or the safety of others.*

"You must forgive me if I seem to lecture," Sé murmured aloud, laying an arm around Alaric's shoulders and briefly ducking his head. "It is one of the ways we are taught, in my order. That point, regarding free will, is extremely important."

He jutted his chin in Cormac's direction as the prince came out of the garderobe, stretching and yawning again as he fumbled out of his shirt and pulled it off over his head. "This is different: a harmless training exercise, so that you may learn how to use this ability. I do hope you appreciate the degrees of acceptable interference."

Alaric nodded minutely. "I do."

"Good. Then, have him walk around the room, do things that would not be part of his usual routine before going to bed. Test your control."

Alaric looked aside, startled, but Sé only nodded and gave him a wry smile—and gently withdrew his own controls, leaving the young Deryni on his own.

Alaric drew a sobering breath, but he had no doubt that he could do this. He had no idea how Sé had done to him what he had done, but the subtle strands of Cormac's control were his to command, and not in any frivolous way.

Abruptly he decided what to do with Cormac. If he made a mistake, he knew Sé could make it right. With a few tentative tweaks of control, he was stepping out into the room, heading nonchalantly for his own bed as Cormac, in the process of pulling on a nightshirt, suddenly noticed his presence.

"Hullo. Where did you go?"

Alaric took off his own cloak and hung it on a peg by his bed. "I wanted to ask Sir Llion about something, but he was already abed." He shrugged. "It can wait until morning, I suppose." He gave Cormac an impish grin and a raised eyebrow. "Married folk!"

"Ah, well." Cormac returned the grin, but it turned into a yawn.

"Mercy, I'm tired! I think Duke Richard must stay up nights, dreaming up new ways to test us. But then, he doesn't have a bonny and buxom wife in his—" The prince's face fell, and he clapped both hands over his mouth.

"Oh God, I don't know what made me say that! She's your sister! I am so sorry!"

Chuckling and shaking his head, Alaric came over to give a comradely dunt to Cormac's shoulder. "Cormac, I'm not offended, truly. She *is* bonny—and buxom. And Llion is a lucky man to have her."

"I really am sorry!"

"Just go to bed," Alaric said. He was beginning to feel embarrassed about putting the prince up to the comment. "Get some sleep. We'll both feel better in the morning."

Still murmuring snatches of apology and shaking his head in disbelief at his presumed gaffe, Cormac climbed into his bed and extinguished the rushlight, then burrowed under the sleeping furs and pulled them close as he curled onto his side. He was asleep almost as soon as his head touched the pillow. Alaric felt a little self-conscious as he turned to where Sé waited in the shadows, but the Deryni knight only inclined his head in approval.

"Nicely done. With a bit more experience, you will learn to be less heavy-handed—and in time, all of this will become second nature when there's need."

"I shouldn't have embarrassed him," Alaric said. "He's my friend."

"He shan't remember," Sé replied. "And now that you have once established a link with him, you will have no need to touch him in the future, when you wish to resume rapport—though it will take more effort, without the contact. You'll learn, never fear." He gestured for Alaric to join him before the hearth, where two chairs were set to either side of a small table.

"When you have become more comfortable with this process, it will be the basis for compelling the truth. But that is for a later lesson. For now, you should be able to tell whether a person is lying—which is almost as useful, and not at all invasive. Do you understand the difference?"

Alaric sat in one of the chairs at Sé's invitation. "I think so."

"Good. Because if *ever* I hear that you have tried another stunt like in Tralia—trying to Read a known Torenthi Deryni from across the room!—I will come back from wherever I am, including the grave, and—" He shook his head as he, too, sat, pulling his sword from its hangers to lay it on the floor close by his feet. "Just don't ever do that again. Am I clear?"

"Yes."

"Good." With a sparse gesture, Sé shrugged out of his cloak and let it fall over the back of the chair, then conjured handfire and set it to hovering above the table. "Now, I want to teach you what I actually came here to do."

Reaching into the front of his robe, he produced a small leather pouch, which he handed to Alaric.

"These belonged to your mother, many years ago," he said, jutting his chin toward the pouch. "Go ahead, open it."

Alaric loosed the strings that closed the pouch and peered inside. By the light of the handfire above, he could see what appeared to be a jumble of small black and white cubes about the size of dice.

"Those were your mother's first ward cubes," Sé said. "You do know what ward cubes are?"

Alaric nodded distractedly. He had tipped the cubes into his hand and was fingering them curiously as he peered at them. There were four each of the black and the white, of a warmth to suggest ivory or bone or jet, like his cardounet pieces, but their weight seemed heavier, more like stone.

"I've seen ward cubes a few times," he said softly, "but I was never allowed to handle them. I do know what they do, though. . . ."

"Then let us see if *they* know what *you* can do," Sé said with a smile, scooping the cubes from Alaric's hand to place them on the table between them. "Arrange the white cubes in a square, with the black cubes at the diagonal corners, but not quite touching."

Cautiously Alaric did as Sé bade.

"Now lay your right hand flat on the cubes, covering all of them, and close your eyes."

Alaric had no idea what to expect, but he closed his eyes and tried to still his mind. The cubes felt cool at first, but then they began to tingle under his hand, only faintly at first, but then more intensely, almost vibrating.

"Keep your hand on the cubes," Sé said softly. "I'm going to touch you now. Don't resist."

Alaric drew a deep breath and let it out, making a conscious effort to relax and open to Sé as cool fingers touched his temples to either side. He briefly felt a surge of vertigo, a vague impression of reassurance and approval; then Sé's hands fell away.

"Very good," Sé murmured. "You can open your eyes now, and take your hand away from the cubes."

"What did you just do?" Alaric breathed.

"Similar to what I did before. I've given you a bit of instruction on warding. Come stand here on my right now, spread your hand over mine, and follow what I do. Wards are basically a defensive tool, and we're going to see if these will still set."

Eagerly Alaric complied, overlapping his fingers on Sé's as the Deryni knight touched his right forefinger to the white cube in the upper left-hand corner and spoke its *nomen*:

"*Prime!*"

At once Alaric felt a measured surge of power tingle through his finger, at which the cube began to glow softly in the firelight, a translucent milky-white. It had been Sé's power, but clearly the Deryni mage was expecting him to do likewise. He was ready as Sé touched the upper-right cube.

"*Seconde!*"

Again, the outflow of power as that cube, too, began to glow, but this time Alaric had contributed. He felt Sé's wordless approval as they shifted their attention in quick succession to the lower white cubes.

"*Tierce! Quarte!*"

Cautiously Alaric let out a breath he had not realized he had been holding. At the same time, he sensed a subtle change in the very air around them, and a definite depletion of his own energy. But the air itself was also charged with energy, almost like the taut, expectant stillness that follows a close lightning strike.

Sé glanced back at him, an eyebrow raised in question as he lifted his hand toward the black cube set at the upper-left corner of the large white square, but Alaric only nodded. He could do this; he knew he could.

"*Quinte!*" As Sé touched the first black cube, power went out from both of them, intertwined. The black cube flared with light: this time, a murky green-black glow under Sé's fingertip. Before Alaric could think about it too much, Sé moved to name the other black cubes in turn, in the same order he had named the white ones:

"*Sixte! Septime! Octave!*"

By the time the last cube had been named, each black cube glowed like a dark jewel at a corner of the white square. Breathing deeply and then exhaling, Sé glanced again at his pupil and nodded.

"Nicely done. This next part is a bit trickier," he went on. "Reach across and cup your left hand over my left, while we merge the eight defensive elements into four protective ones." He waited while Alaric shifted to cover both his hands.

"Are you ready? You'll feel the energy drain, if you haven't already."

"I did, and I'm ready," Alaric whispered.

Reaching slowly, Sé picked up the upper-left black cube, *Quinte*, in his left hand, and *Prime*, the upper-left white cube, in his right. Then he brought the two together as he spoke their name: "*Primus!*"

As the two cubes touched with a faint clicking sound, almost as if an attraction pulled them together over the last little distance, light flared at the joining and the two merged into a single rectangular shape, silvery in color, no longer separate black and white cubes. At the same time, Alaric had felt a distinct outrush of energy that made him wince.

"I'm fine," he assured Sé, as the older man glanced at him in concern.

Nodding, Sé picked up *Seconde* with his right hand and *Sixte* with his left, again speaking their new name as he brought them together: "*Secundus!*"

Again, the outflow of energy, the faint click as the two joined, the slight flash and change of color, though Alaric was ready for it this time.

The other two pairs followed in rapid succession: *Tierce* to *Septime*, with the whispered name, "*Tertius!*" and *Quarte* to *Octave*, named "*Quartus!*" Alaric was all but grimacing by the time it was done, but again he shook his head when Sé glanced at him in question, though he was definitely feeling the drain of energy.

"Now what?" he whispered, as Sé cast his glance over the four silver-glowing rectoids.

"Now we set them," Sé replied. "What shall we ward? You? Cormac?" He flashed a mirthless smile. "You, I think. Sit down. You should know what it feels like to be warded this way."

Alaric's eyes widened, but he dutifully sank into the chair Sé quickly vacated, watching apprehensively as Sé set the silvery rectoids on the floor around him, like tiny towers at the four quarters.

"Sit still now," Sé commanded, then pointed at the wards in succession and named them, proceeding clockwise around Alaric. *"Primus, Secundus, Tertius, et Quartus, fiat lux!"*

Alaric could feel the protection suddenly flaring up around him, a misty cocoon of silvery luminescence that rose to a glowing dome of light about an arm span across, apparently generated by the four rectoids of the wards.

"You should be able to hear me," Sé said, though his voice sounded oddly muffled. "I assure you, however, that nothing of harmful intent can pass. I could breach the wards if I chose, because I set them, but no mortal could pass."

To illustrate, he smiled and reached through the wards to touch Alaric lightly on the shoulder, then turned on his heel and went back to the bed where Cormac still lay sleeping, bending to speak softly in his ear. Immediately Cormac opened his eyes and rose, walking slowly to where Alaric sat within the bubble glow of the wards. But when he tried to reach through the wards as Sé had done, his hand seemed to be deflected by the faintly visible limits of the wards.

Sé set his hand on Cormac's shoulder and resumed control before the prince could become alarmed, and with a silent command sent him back to bed. He then returned to sit opposite Alaric, though carefully outside the wards.

"Do you have any questions?"

Alaric surveyed the wards all around him, though he was feeling a little light-headed. He was certain he would have questions later on, but he knew that Sé had given him a great deal of information to assimilate at one time: probably more than he was yet aware of. Further, the work they had already done had taken a great deal of energy. He had all but nodded off while Sé dealt with Cormac.

"You will learn to moderate the use of your power," Sé said quietly, noting Alaric's bleary gaze. "I've no doubt that you're exhausted." He rose and lifted his hands in a gesture of command, then slowly turned the palms downward as he murmured, "*Ex tenebris te vocavi, Domine. Te vocavi, et lucem dedisti.*" As he did so, Alaric could sense the wards diminishing. He could also feel himself sliding into sleep.

"*Nunc dimittis servum tuum secundum verbum tuum in pace,*" Sé continued, bringing his hands together in an attitude of prayer and bowing slightly. "*Fiat voluntas tua. Amen.*"

"Whenever we work," Sé said, turning his gaze to Alaric and setting a hand on his shoulder, "it is meet to acknowledge that God and His angels assist us. But for now, I think it's best we get you to bed. If it's any consolation, you should sleep very well this night."

Chapter 33

"A friend and companion never meet amiss . . ."
—ECCLESIASTICUS 40:23

ALARIC did sleep well. When he finally stirred the next morning, rousted by Llion, he felt deeply rested, even though the howling of wind outside the chamber and the drumming of sleet against the window glass promised a cold and dreary day. Cormac, too, seemed totally unfazed by the previous night's work or the weather, and bounced out of bed with his customary ebullience, eager to be about the day.

"Well, back to the usual routine," he declared, pulling on his boots. "Mark my words, Duke Richard will have us bashing at pells or running up and down the stairs, in this weather."

"Well, it's certain we'll have nothing to do with horses," Alaric replied, "unless it's mucking out stalls or grooming, or maybe cleaning tack." He blew on his hands and then rubbed them briskly together. "Or maybe this would be a good day to put the blacksmith to work, seeing to dodgy shoes. They could have us hold horses. At least it would be warm by the forge."

But first there was Mass before breakfast in the chapel royal for all the pages and squires—frigid enough that the holy water in the stoups had ice across the top, and Paget swore that he could not feel his toes—then a quick breaking of their fast before embarking upon variations of the physical exercise Cormac had predicted. While the squires practiced hand-to-hand combat at one end of the great hall, with much grunting and thumping, the pages were put through their paces at the pells, with

live steel. Alaric was glad of the repetitive drill, not only for the warmth
it generated but also because the mostly mindless exercise allowed him
to think about the events of the night before. (He had also found himself thinking about them at Mass, when he knew he should have been
contemplating the Sacred Mysteries. Several times he had touched the
belt pouch at his waist to reassure himself that the ward cubes were safe,
and resolved to find a suitable hiding place for them, later in the day.)

By the time the pages had switched to wrestling practice and the
squires had moved to the pells, it occurred to Alaric that the physical contact involved in wrestling might enable him to practice a bit of what Sé
had taught him.

He tried it cautiously on Cormac first, because he had already worked
with the prince and knew he could do it, even without physical contact.
Then, during a bout with Quillan Pargeter, who was a regular sparring
partner, he did manage to touch Quillan's mind, and even exerted some
control, but he lost the bout. Subsequent bouts with other regular
sparring partners were sufficiently lackluster that Sir Ninian even
remarked on it.

"You're not paying attention, Alaric. You're better than that."

Alaric knew Sir Ninian was right. And he had already concluded that
it took too long to read and then react in time to make any positive difference in a physical struggle. Besides, reading an opponent's intentions
was hardly sporting; and because much of fighting was instinctive, mind
reading was fairly useless anyway, and certainly not worth the energy in a
practice bout. Later on in his training, if the process ever became second
nature, it might just give him a needed edge in a desperate fight; but for
now, better to concentrate on his actual physical skills.

The Feast of Christmas finally came, with attendant snow that made
the next day's traditional giving of royal alms brisk but not too onerous.
Other pages were on duty while the king, his mother, and his two sisters
distributed food and clothing on the cathedral steps, though Alaric and
Cormac were present, observing with half a dozen other pages and
squires. Afterward, the king held a short court of petitions, with Alaric
and Cormac stationed nearby to listen and learn.

The weather held and even improved during the week leading up to

Twelfth Night, which also marked Alaric's first full year of royal service. The mild weather permitted scores of nobles from outlying areas of the kingdom to attend, who had been kept away the previous year.

Most unexpected amid the usual delegations offering new year's greetings was the appearance of Cormac's brother Prince Colman, with an escort of six purple-clad armsmen in the livery of Llannedd. After presenting felicitations from the court of Howicce and Llannedd, he then announced that their father, King Illann, had been obliged to abdicate the dual throne, effective this day, owing to continued ill health. The new King Ronan, previously prince regent, now was king, and would be crowned at Pwyllheli in May.

The announcement produced a frisson of excitement throughout the hall, along with a heartfelt huzzah for the new king, but Alaric's first thought, after concern for the failing former king, was that Cormac undoubtedly would be returning to his homeland for the coronation, and very probably would not be coming back. King Brion and his mother almost certainly would attend, for Gwynedd and the dual kingdoms had always enjoyed close relations, and none closer than when the late King Donal had married Richeldis of Howicce and Llannedd. He wondered whether the princesses also would attend. Both Xenia and Silke looked excited and hopeful, and summoned Cormac for a whispered conference.

After court, while servants began setting up the tables for the feast to come, said Cormac disappeared with his brother for perhaps half an hour, closeted with his Aunt Richeldis and the king. When he emerged, he looked pensive and not at all happy.

"How is your father?" Alaric said, drawing Cormac a little aside.

Cormac shook his head. "No worse, but no better. His advisors think it unlikely that he will ever be well enough to rule again. The kingdoms deserve better. So my brother Ronan now is king."

"And you are a king's brother now. That should make you happy."

"I knew it would happen eventually," Cormac said.

"Well, you will get to go to your brother's coronation, and probably even participate. That's something."

"But I shan't be a Haldane page anymore. And I doubt they'll let me come back."

"Well, you still must train for knighthood," Alaric said reasonably. "Surely your brother will want you to be part of his staff, when you're grown."

"Maybe. But Colman is the heir, until Ronan has a son. I'm still an extra prince." He quirked a dutiful smile. "But for now, I'm still a Haldane page, so I probably ought to get to work."

Indeed, both boys set themselves to their duties, for the tables were now set up, and attendees were finding seats. Prince Colman was invited to sit with the king, representing his brother. Cormac might have joined them, but he declined, to serve with Alaric.

The announcement had lent the afternoon an additional festiveness, though other factors still kept both boys on their toes. Twelfth Night court always brought out at least the local bishops—Bishop Corrigan and the Archbishop of Rhemuth almost always attended—but the milder weather also had permitted Valoret's archbishop, Paul Tollendall, to be present, along with several other bishops. Unfortunately, those included the Bishop of Nyford.

Fortunately, Oliver de Nore kept his distance from the king's Deryni page, and was served by his nephew, Cornelius Seaton. Nor was Alaric obliged to work anywhere near either of them, so he was able to avoid any untoward incidents.

But there were periodic reminders of the bishop and his spleen even after de Nore had returned to his see at Nyford, for reports trickled in periodically of incidents involving Deryni, not only in Nyford but occasionally in other outlying areas. And there were more conventional lessons closer to home, involving the pages and squires under training, that underlined the deadly necessity behind most of what Alaric and his companions were learning.

One of the most shocking examples came early in the spring, during the Lenten season, when most of the instruction of pages and squires had shifted to the out-of-doors. It was an aspect of their preparation as future knights that Alaric had somewhat anticipated, at least in the abstract, but its stark reality was stunning when it came. Though the circumstances of the specific incident did not yet affect him and Cormac directly, Paget

Sullivan was whey-faced and clearly shaken as he joined the pair in their apartment for a game of cardounet that would not be played. Llion, fortunately, was out, as was Alazais.

"Paget, what's wrong?" Cormac asked, looking up from the game board, where he and Alaric had been setting up the game pieces.

Paget came to them in some reluctance, wiping his hands against the thighs of his leggings, eyes averted.

"We really aren't supposed to talk about it with pages," he mumbled.

"What's that?" Cormac replied, cocking his head.

"I said, we aren't supposed to talk about it with pages," Paget repeated, only marginally louder, but with an edge of anger to his voice.

Alaric exchanged a guarded glance with Cormac, minutely shaking his head, then carefully resumed setting out game pieces, though he kept an eye on Paget.

"Then, maybe you shouldn't tell us about it," he said lightly.

Paget was silent for a long moment, then whispered, "No, I—need to. But you won't tell Duke Richard, will you? Or even Sir Llion?"

Both Cormac and Alaric immediately gave him murmurs of assent, exchanging glances again as Paget settled awkwardly to a seat across from them.

After drawing a long, fortifying breath, the older boy slowly began recounting how he had been taken down to the town market, where the butchers plied their trade, and obliged to observe the slaughter of cows and pigs and sheep for the Easter market—and then to wield the knife himself, to experience what it was like, deliberately to take a life.

"I suppose I understand why we're made to do it," he said then. "And it wasn't that I'd never killed an animal before, in the field; it's part of hunting, and we eat what we kill. But this was different. I'd never deliberately killed anything that wasn't already injured."

"I can't say *I* have," Cormac said uneasily. "I've never even finished an animal on the hunt. But we have to eat, don't we?"

"This wasn't about killing to eat," Alaric whispered, trying to put from mind an all-too-vivid memory of the grey mare sinking into a widening pool of her own blood, and blood dripping from the butcher's knife. "Oh, we do eat those animals you saw," he conceded. "But this was about killing men, eventually. We—"

At that moment, a rattle of the latch on the outer door heralded the arrival of Sir Llion. He apparently had come from sword practice, for he had removed his outer tunic and slung it over one arm. His sheathed sword was in that hand, with the belt wound loosely around the scabbard. Focused on mopping at his face and sweat-soaked hair, he did not at first notice as the three boys immediately came to their feet, trying not to look awkward or guilty.

"Oh, hello," he said casually, as he laid the sword across a pair of pegs on the wall. "Paget probably knows this, but sparring with Prince Nigel is becoming more and more of a workout. He—"

He broke off before the owl-eyed stares of the three youngsters, who had fallen silent and were looking decidedly ill at ease. Alaric, daring to brush at Llion's mind with his Deryni senses, could sense suspicion stirring behind the blue eyes.

"Ah. I appear to have interrupted a private conversation," Llion said easily. "I can come back later. . . ."

"No, it's all right," Alaric said, as the other two shook their heads emphatically.

"*Is* it?" Llion eyed all three of them appraisingly, then tossed his tunic and towel on a table and hooked a fourth stool close to the other three, gesturing for them to be seated. "Maybe you should tell me about it."

"Tell you about what?" Paget said defensively.

"Whatever it is that has the three of you looking so guilty."

Alaric drew a deep breath, not looking at Llion.

"Paget, he already knows."

"What do you mean, 'He already knows'?" Paget's tone had a belligerent edge. "Did you tell him?"

"No, he didn't tell me," Llion returned, apparently unfazed. "If you're implying that he might have used his powers, I don't think that's within his ability. Not yet, at any rate." At his raised eyebrow, Alaric hastily shook his head. "But I can guess the topic of your discussion," Llion went on, "because I know that Paget was taken down to the market today. Specifically, to the butchers' quarter. I take it that you found this unsettling, Paget."

Paget looked down at his hands, clasped tightly before him. "I had to kill an animal."

Llion nodded. "I believe that was the purpose of the exercise. What kind of animal?"

Paget swallowed. "A—a lamb."

"I see. Well, that *is* one of the traditional items of Easter fare. Why do you think you were required to do this, given that this is normally the work of butchers?"

Paget only shook his head, avoiding Llion's gaze, looking miserable.

"Cormac, do you know?"

The young prince also shook his head hastily.

"Alaric, how about you?"

Alaric was studying the toes of his boots, thinking again about the grey mare slaughtered at Bishop de Nore's order. He thought he knew where Llion was guiding this conversation, because they had discussed the subject of killing before. It was a necessary part of any knight's life.

"I think—it's because we need to learn what it feels like, to kill a living thing. And I'm sure it's different from ending the suffering of an injured animal."

"That's true," Llion allowed. "And . . . ?"

Alaric looked up at him in faint challenge, then glanced at his companions.

"I think it's also because we're future knights, and eventually we'll be called upon to kill men."

"Exactly so," Llion agreed. "One should never glory in the taking of a human life," he told them, "but sometimes it must be done. And it isn't always in the heat of battle, at the point of a sword or a lance. The enemy sentry you may be obliged to slay deliberately, by stealth, to prevent him sounding an alarm, is a man like yourself, with family and friends who care for him, and a liege lord whom he serves according to his oaths. And of course, there is the coup de grâce, an altogether different kind of killing, which is also a deliberate act: to end a wounded man's suffering when there is no hope of recovery."

The boys had been listening avidly to his every word—Cormac had gone alarmingly white—and Paget summoned up his nerve to ask the next question.

"Sir Llion, have you—have you ever killed a man?"

"Not that I'm aware of," Llion said after a beat.

Cormac looked up sharply, and Paget cocked his head in question.

"I don't understand, sir," he whispered. "How could you kill a man and not know?"

Llion picked up one of the cardounet pieces and turned it absently in his fingers. Alaric thought it was a war-duke. "I suppose it's a little difficult to explain, but in the heat of battle, one can't always be certain if a blow has been fatal, or even whose blow has been the fatal one."

"Then, you've been in real battles," Paget ventured.

"Let's call them real skirmishes," Llion returned. "Gwynedd has been officially at peace since I was knighted, so true battles are somewhat rare of late, but I did ride on patrol with Alaric's father a few years ago, over in the border country with Torenth, and we did end up killing a few men. They'd been raiding cattle from Corwyn lands, and had killed and raped in one notable instance. But I don't *know* that I was personally responsible. We ended up hanging a few of the miscreants, but that was execution, which is yet another kind of killing. I was not personally involved in that.

"Nor have I ever given a man the coup," he added, anticipating Paget's next question, "though I've seen it done. It cannot be easy, especially if one knows the person, but usually it is an act of compassion, to save further suffering if the subject cannot hope to recover. Hence, the term coup de grâce, or mercy stroke."

"Then, it *is* rather like finishing a wounded stag or boar," Cormac said thoughtfully.

"Yes, except that a wounded man is not a wounded animal," Llion said. "Never forget that."

"No, sir." Cormac swallowed painfully, then: "But I—think I could do it, if the person was really, really suffering, and was going to die anyway."

"Pray God that you will never need to find out," Llion said, with a note of finality in his voice. "And when the time comes when you *must* kill—and it *will* come—be certain that you do it for a very good reason."

THE remaining days of Lent seemed more somber than usual, in the wake of what had happened, and the glory of Easter and its feast perhaps less joyous than it might have been. All three boys were very much aware of the source of the Easter lamb served at the king's table. An equal if different sobriety marked their continued interaction after Easter, for Alaric was informed that he would not be included in the royal party traveling to King Ronan's coronation. The king chose the Redfearn twins to attend him, for he was taking the boys' father as his senior advisor.

It was disappointing, but at least Alaric and Paget were allowed to accompany Cormac and the rest of the royal party as far as Desse, where they would take ship for Llannedd. Both boys had become close to Prince Cormac during his stay at court. Though all of them had known from the beginning that the prince's tenure at court was only ever intended to last a year, perhaps two, the time of parting was poignant. As the royal party began to board the coastal cog that would take them down to Pwyllheli, the Llanneddi capital, Cormac held back with Alaric and Paget.

"I shall miss both of you, you know," Cormac said a little awkwardly, as they watched Queen Richeldis follow her daughters up the gangplank. "I shall miss our games of cardounet. I shall miss sparring with the pair of you. I think I shall even miss those excruciatingly awkward discussions with Sir Llion about killing things."

Paget snorted and rolled his eyes. "At least I've done *that*." He glanced sidelong at Alaric. "You and our ducal friend still have that to look forward to."

"But I think," said Cormac, "that killing, sadly, will be an important part of his life." He reached out to clasp Alaric's hand. "Be well, my friend."

"And you," Alaric replied. "Think kindly of us."

"Yes, do," Paget chimed in. "And you must let us know when you find someone else to play cardounet. You were getting pretty good, you know. And write and tell us about the coronation. You're sure to have a prime seat, probably even a part to play."

Cormac snorted and shook Paget's hand. "A page forever, at this rate. But I'll write and tell you about it. I hope the three of us can continue to be friends, even when I'm slogging away at my training at my brother's court."

"They're wanting you aboard," Alaric said, catching the look that Jiri was giving them. "You'd better go."

"Right, I'm off."

Then he was turning to trot back to the gangplank, where the king and Jamyl Arilan were boarding, along with Jiri Redfearn and his sons.

"Godspeed, Cormac," Alaric murmured, lifting a hand in farewell as Cormac paused to glance back and give them a wan smile.

BACK in Rhemuth, Alaric's life settled back into routine, though without the accustomed company of Cormac. He and Paget still played cardounet, but their training was mostly separate, as page and squire, and he found no new companion of his own age.

But he was given new worries, not long after their return, for early in May came word from Valoret that its archbishop, kindly Paul Tollendall, had passed away in his sleep. Though the particulars meant little to Alaric, Tollendall's passing meant that a new archbishop must be elected.

Immediately Duke Richard sent a courier off to Pwyllheli, where the king and his female relatives had planned to stay well into the summer. In addition, since he was regent in the king's absence, Richard made preparations for an immediate departure for Valoret to attend the old archbishop's obsequies. Alaric was not obliged to go with him, for neither he nor Richard needed an untoward encounter with Bishop de Nore, who was certain to be there. But Alaric worried in Richard's absence, keeping Llion close, and considered the ramifications if, by some horrible chance, Oliver de Nore should be elected to the vacant see of Valoret.

Richard returned, and the synod of bishops began its deliberations to choose Archbishop Tollendall's successor. By the end of June, the king and his sisters had returned from Pwyllheli, though the queen dowager had remained to assist King Ronan for a few months. Alazais was put in charge of the two princesses until the queen should return in the autumn. In addition, Jamyl brought back a new bride, the Lady Alix, who was installed, at least temporarily, in the royal household, becoming a companion of Alazais and her charges.

Meanwhile, the king fretted over the delay in electing a new primate. By early August, the synod in Valoret seemed no closer to agreeing on a new archbishop, which gave the king hope that a more moderate candidate might prevail. When the queen returned from Pwyllheli early in September, she brought along two young men sent by her nephew to train under Duke Richard. The squire, a Howiccan lad called Alphonse, was a keen archer, who began helping with the pages' archery training. The page, called Hiram, was a shirttail relative of King Ronan, and too impressed with himself to suit Alaric, but he caused no direct problems.

It was mid-September when a missive from Valoret finally came, though it was not what any of them had hoped.

"A pox on all of them!" the king muttered, when Duke Richard had cracked the seals and read the first few lines aloud to him and the crown council. "*Any* other bishop . . ."

Alaric had been the page on duty that morning, but he was sent from the room before he had time to learn more than the new archbishop's name. Immediately he went looking for Llion.

"Llion, may I speak with you?" he blurted, as soon as he found the young knight.

Llion had been giving pointers to a squire riding at the rings, and summoned a senior squire to take over before joining Alaric.

"What is it?"

"They've gone and done it," he muttered, glancing back toward the great hall. "The bishops have elected de Nore! The king just received the official notification."

And indeed, word apparently was spreading quickly, for he had already seen Cornelius, on his way across the stable yard, crowing with his friends that his uncle was the new archbishop.

Llion set his hands on his hips and let out an audible sigh, looking at the ground, a very sober expression on his face. "That is . . . unfortunate," he finally said.

"'Unfortunate'? Is that all you can say?" Alaric flounced onto a hay bale beside the ring run and briefly buried his face in his hands. Then: "What am I going to do?" he said as he looked up. "This is going to make Cornelius even more insufferable. He's already heard, and he's gloating about it to anyone who will listen."

"If he is, I expect that the king will have a few words about that," Llion replied. "And if he doesn't, I will." He sighed and shook his head. "I had truly hoped for someone more moderate."

"Well, de Nore certainly isn't *that*," Alaric said. "I just hope I don't have to go with the king to the investiture, or whatever they call it."

"I think it's an enthronement, since he's already a bishop—more's the pity. And I don't think it would ever cross the king's mind, to take you along."

CHAPTER 34

AS it transpired, there was never any question of Alaric attending on the king, for word arrived from Morganhall that very afternoon that his Aunt Claara was failing, and that Alaric and Alazais must move quickly if they hoped to see her alive again. Alaric left immediately with her and Llion, and thus had ample excuse not to make an awkward appearance with the king at Valoret, even if the king had wished him to attend.

They arrived to find Claara in her final hours, shockingly frail but still lucid, and were with her when she slipped gently through the veil in the early morning hours of the next day, comforted and supported by her sister Delphine and Alazais, her youngest niece, who sang her sweetly into eternity with a favorite hymn she had often sung with the sisters at Arc-en-Ciel. Alaric was touched by the gesture, for he knew that his aunt had suffered greatly in the two years since her fall, and was now at peace. Delphine was stoic in the face of her sister's death.

"I have known for several weeks that her time was growing short," Delphine told them over supper that night. "It is true that I might have summoned you earlier, but it would have served no purpose. And she was ready to go. I've sent for her grandchildren, and for Zoë and Geill." She gazed off into the distance. "With Claara's passing, I am now the last of my generation. When I am gone," she said to Alaric, "it will be for you to carry forward the honor of the family. We shall bury her beside her husband. It is what she wanted."

Thus it unfolded as Delphine had declared. Members of the family converged on Morganhall over the next few days to pay their respects, for Claara had been much loved. Geill and Walter rode down from Culdi with their toddler daughter Alys and little Bronwyn, who had spent her earliest years in the combined household of Delphine and Claara. Claara's son-in-law, Sir Paxon Fraser, brought Claara's two grandchildren, Kian and Clarice, much to Bronwyn's special delight, for she and Clarice Fraser had been like sisters in their early years. Kian, for his part, was thirteen and a just-promoted junior squire in the household of the Earl of Rhendall, whom Sir Paxon also served. He was also a cousin previously unknown to Alaric, though the two found little in common. Each was polite to the other, but that was all. Mostly, Kian stayed close by his father.

Zoë and Jovett were the last to arrive, the afternoon before the funeral was to take place, though they had left their three young children in Cynfyn with Jovett's parents.

"Aunt Delphine, I am so sorry," Zoë told her father's only remaining sister, as she embraced her in the yard at Morganhall. "And Alaric—my goodness, you are very nearly grown!"

They buried Claara the next morning in the village churchyard beside her husband and two stillborn sons, not far from the crypt where generations of Morgan men also lay, including Alaric's father. Afterward, while the family gathered for a light meal in the hall at Morganhall, Delphine broached the practicalities of what would now become of the estate.

"Again we find ourselves in a quandary, my dears," she said to her assembled relatives. "I am the last of my generation, and I am not getting any younger. Sir Llion is an apt castellan, of course, but he cannot often be in residence. In short, I shall need more help, unless I am to carry on until I, too, die in harness." Sir Paxon excused himself from these proceedings, for he was only a son-in-law of the deceased Claara, and had no claim to the estate beyond a few modest pieces of jewelry to be passed to young Clarice, but Alaric was permitted to remain with the adults.

Discussion among Delphine and his three half-sisters and their husbands continued the next day, after Sir Paxon and his children departed for Rhendall. Eventually, it was deemed best that Geill and Walter should apply to Duke Jared for leave to take up residence at Morganhall, to assist Delphine and hold the property in trust for Bronwyn. In the meantime, both Geill and Alazais would remain at Morganhall to assist Delphine in the reorganization of the household.

By then, it was but another day until Michaelmas and Alaric's eleventh birthday, which the family celebrated with a ride in the countryside. After that, Sir Walter headed back to Culdi to confer with Duke Jared, taking the young Bronwyn with him, and the rest of them bade farewell to Geill and Delphine before heading south. Zoë and Jovett traveled part of the way with them before turning off to Cynfyn with their escort, and Alaric and Llion made their way back to Rhemuth, where Alaric soon settled back into the routine of a Haldane page.

That endeavor would become less of a challenge with the new year, for they soon learned that Cornelius Seaton would be leaving the king's service at Twelfth Night to join his uncle's episcopal court at Valoret, as his father had already done. Meanwhile, Alaric could look forward to the Twelfth Night visit of Jared and his family, which meant that he could spend time with his McLain cousins, and see his sister Bronwyn. When they arrived, however, Kevin was not with them.

"He's gone to Claibourne to serve as squire to the duke," Jared told him. "Good experience before he's knighted."

But Duncan immediately moved into Alaric's quarters with him, and Bronwyn was taken under the wing of Alazais and Llion.

The solemnities of Christmas came and went, followed by St. Stephen's Day, when Alaric and all the McLains attended on the king and the dowager queen for the traditional observances.

During the days that followed, leading up to Twelfth Night, Jared spent many hours conferring with the king and his officers of state, mapping out strategies for the north, and Vera spent time with the queen and with Alazais. Meanwhile, formal training was suspended for the pages and squires, so Alaric and Duncan were mostly at leisure, though they did ride out from time to time with Paget Sullivan and Quillan Pargeter, and sometimes played at cardounet.

But the pair also spent many an hour alone, visiting the stables or exploring in the library, or escaping to sheltered portions of the castle's leads, where they might expect privacy, for they had much to catch up on. Like Alaric, Duncan had been pursuing his chivalric training, since a duke's son was expected to be competent in martial and courtly pursuits, and eventually be knighted, but he also had begun to consider other possibilities. He had found passion in his academic studies, and was good at them. In conversations with his mother's chaplain at Culdi, Father Geordan, he had even explored the possibility of taking holy orders.

"It *is* a traditional occupation for second sons," Duncan pointed out, when he had exhausted all his other arguments.

"Aye, and it would be dangerous," Alaric countered. "If they caught you . . . Well, you know what the law says about Deryni trying to be ordained."

Duncan nodded, looking off over the rooftops of the castle complex.

"How could I not know? They burn them. But I'm only half-Deryni, Alaric, and you're the only one who knows about that."

"So we assume," Alaric replied. "But God knows."

"Aye, He does. But if I feel the call to become a priest, doesn't that call come from Him?"

"I suppose," Alaric allowed. "But—how do you know you've been called?"

Duncan shrugged. "I don't. Yet. But I'm listening." He glanced at Alaric and grinned. "I know, it's early on. It's just something that I've been considering. But you already know what you'll be when you're grown; you've always known. You're the eldest son, so there was never any question. It's different for a second son, no matter how much your parents and your elder brother—*and* your cousin—love you."

"You could come and join my household, when you're grown," Alaric said. "If you're not to be a duke, you could always be the right-hand man of a duke."

"Maybe I will," Duncan replied, quirking him a taut smile. "One never knows." He sighed and got to his feet. "But I don't suppose we're going to figure that out today, or even tomorrow. Besides, we're only eleven years old." He cocked his head at Alaric. "Fancy a ride?"

"Of course." Grinning, Alaric likewise rose, dusting off the seat of his breeches. "We've got a few more hours of daylight—and whatever either of us ends up doing, we'll need to know how to ride. I'll race you to the stables!"

THREE days later, with the weather still holding, Twelfth Night dawned, with all the pomp and ceremony of the most formal court of the year scheduled for the afternoon. It started out well enough. The new archbishop attended that year—his first as Primate of All Gwynedd—along with several other bishops, who were entirely too numerous to make Alaric happy; but he was not obliged to serve any of them.

At opening court, after Archbishop de Nore had given the blessing, he duly took Cornelius Seaton into his household as a senior squire—which was good riddance, so far as Alaric and many of the other squires and pages were concerned, for Alaric was not the only one who had smarted under Cornelius's bullying ways. It annoyed Alaric that the smarmy Cornelius now would proceed toward eventual knighthood without the tempering influence of Duke Richard's discipline, but he told himself that there was nothing he could do about it. Cornelius immediately donned the purple episcopal livery of his uncle's household and took up squiring duties at his father's side, haughty and proud.

For his own part, Alaric was instructed to serve the queen and her daughters, as he had done the year before. Paget served beside him as duty squire. Alaric had hoped to serve Duke Jared and Duchess Vera, but that honor went to Duncan and the Redfearn twins, who now were squires. Llion, now a valued member of Duke Richard's staff, stood attendance on the duke; and his wife, Alazais Morgan, now expecting their first child, attended the queen.

When the official business of the court had been concluded—the making of pages, the promotion of new squires, several knightings—formal court was adjourned to the dais end of the hall, so that guests might pay their individual respects to the king and servants could set up the rest of the hall for the feast to follow.

The mild weather had brought foreign visitors as well as the local nobility, some of them most welcome and others less so. The Hort of Orsal, whose investiture they had witnessed only months before, appeared now with a small delegation and the gift of a Thurian harper to entertain during the feast to follow court. No longer in mourning for his father, the Tralian prince was brilliantly arrayed in velvets and silks of peacock hues, with rings on every finger and ropes of pearls about his neck, one of which he removed and presented to his fellow sovereign.

"Perhaps for your eventual bride," Létald murmured with a wink, as he pooled the pearls into Brion's hand. The prince also made a point of speaking personally with Alaric after court.

"I was very pleased to meet you at my investiture, young duke," the Hort said, shaking his hand. "We are, both of us, starting out our careers as rulers of our respective lands, and I look forward to many years of harmonious interaction. I hope we shall be friends."

"And I, Your Highness," Alaric murmured. "I was very glad that I could attend."

Another welcome and half-expected visitor was the young heir of Bremagne, whom they had met in Tralia: Crown Prince Ryol, accompanied by an uncle, Prince Joscerand, who was half-brother to King Meyric. It fell to Joscerand to unwrap and present Bremagne's gift: miniature portraits of his three royal nieces, painted on boards and handsomely framed in gilt wood.

"This is Jehane, the eldest . . . and this is Aude . . . and Ursuline," Joscerand said to the king, as Ryol handed each portrait to Brion, in turn. "My brother hopes that you will come soon to Bremagne to meet them," he added, as Brion inspected the likenesses and made the required polite but noncommittal responses.

"Most charming," Brion murmured. "Please convey my thanks to King Meyric for his kind gifts, and say that I hope to visit his kingdom very soon."

As the gifts were duly handed off to a courtier and then passed to the queen and her daughters, Alaric caught just an impression of auburn hair and pale faces before Xenia and Silke commandeered the portraits and began whispering over them, raven heads pressed together.

Other foreign guests were also seen, many of whom also offered gifts as well as Twelfth Night greetings. Two who were perhaps less welcome than most were a pair of Torenthi nobles, richly arrayed in the silk brocades and furs favored at the Torenthi court, with sweeping mustaches and braided side-locks beneath the cylindrical flat-topped hats that Alaric always associated with Torenth. Because they were Torenthi, and nobility at that, he reckoned that they most probably were Deryni. Cautious, because he well remembered his lesson with Sé, he tried to sharpen his senses regarding the two men, and caught the faint tingle of shields around both.

"Majesty," said the elder of the pair, as he and his rakish-looking companion gave the king flamboyant court bows. "I am Constantin Furstán-Arkadia. My companion is Sigismund Count von Golzcow. Our sovereign lord, *Nimouros ho Phourstános Padishah*, commands us to convey his best wishes for the new year, and to present this token of his esteem."

At his gesture, the younger man unfurled a generous length of multi-colored Moorish silk from under his arm and allowed it to cascade down the dais steps, to indrawn breaths from the assembled nobles and from the direction of the queen and her daughters.

"I recognize that Your Majesty's tastes may run to less . . . exuberant patterns," Constantin continued with a droll smile, "but perhaps the noble ladies of your household will find this one pleasing."

Before Brion could frame a diplomatic response, his mother the dowager queen rose in her place and inclined her head to the Torenthi courtier.

"My lord, we thank you for your master's most generous gift," she said. "And from my daughters' expressions, I rather suspect that we shall have . . . animated discussions regarding who shall wear it." She paused to pull a ring from one hand and extended it to the Torenthi noble with a tight smile. "Pray, convey this to your master with my thanks."

As Count Constantin took the ring, both Torenthi nobles bowed deeply and backed away, to retreat into the crowd. A glance from the queen summoned Alaric to gather up the silk and deposit it between the two princesses, but he decided to keep an eye on the Deryni who had presented it. He thought the silk itself was safe enough; he could detect no danger. But the men . . .

The next few hours passed pleasantly enough, without apparent incident. While the rest of those who wished to do so presented their compliments and sundry gifts to the king, the Twelfth Night feast proceeded, interspersed with diversions of singing and several performances by a troupe of Logreini mummers, not to mention the harper brought by the Hort of Orsal. Later on, there was dancing. Alaric and Paget, on duty serving the queen and her daughters, had a superb vantage point from which to observe all that went on, and to appreciate the finery of the young ladies of the court.

Alaric would have counted the night's festivities a resounding success, except that, when he was sent to fetch more wine for the queen's table, and took a shortcut down to the cellars, he noticed a partially open doorway into one of the storerooms adjacent to the kitchens, and heard muffled moans of pleasure coming from within.

He ducked his head and suppressed a wry smile as he prepared to scurry past. Accustomed as he was to moving in court circles, he could hardly be unaware that large gatherings at court were often the occasion of clandestine amorous encounters among the guests—and what they looked and sounded like. Pages and squires were instructed to ignore such activities whenever possible, or at least to be discreet, but he nonetheless caught the unmistakable impression of a brocade-clad male form bent into the embrace of an apparently willing partner—and white legs writhing amid a flurry of crimson skirts.

That fleeting image brought him up short to backtrack a few steps and gaze in shock, for the woman, by her dress, almost had to be the Princess Xenia, the spirited elder of the king's two sisters.

He tried to stifle his gasp, but was not altogether successful. The sound was enough to alert the man, who spun and saw him—and stabbed a hand toward him in reinforcement of a powerful command that surged hard against Alaric's shields.

"You, boy! Come here!"

Chapter 35

"Where the word of a king is, there is power . . ."
—ECCLESIASTES 8:4

INSTINCTIVELY Alaric recoiled and hardened his shields, wrenching his gaze from that of his attacker and bolting back the way he had come. It had been one of the Torenthi courtiers, he realized, as he pounded back up the stairs; and as he jerked to a halt in the doorway back into the hall, to look around wildly for the nearest adult in authority, he spied Llion conversing with Sir Jiri Redfearn before one of the great fireplaces nearby.

At once he hurried in that direction, schooling his features to show no emotion, weaving among bystanders and dancers as quickly as he could, but also trying not to create too much of a stir, for he was about to report an appalling scandal.

"Sir Llion, could I have a word?" he murmured, catching at the knight's sleeve.

Llion looked at him oddly, but let himself be drawn out of earshot of Sir Jiri, where Alaric quickly told him what he had seen.

"You're certain it was Xenia?" Llion asked, when Alaric had wound down.

"Not absolutely certain—I didn't see her face—but who else could it have been?" He was still looking around—for Xenia, for the Torenthis, for anyone whose presence might make it not be true. "Llion, only the royals wear that much red—and the queen and Princess Silke are over there. Xenia isn't." He jutted his chin in the direction of the royal dais,

where the queen and Silke were chattering with Alazais and others of the
queen's ladies, still inspecting the gift of brocade.

"And where are the Torenthis?" he continued. "I *know* it was one of
them—and if I'd not been Deryni, God knows what he might have done.
He did try to control me."

"Go back to your post," Llion said, low voiced, as he too scanned the
hall. "Say nothing until I get back to you."

With that, Llion returned to Jiri and spoke to him briefly before the
two of them disappeared through the doorway where Alaric had emerged.
The king was in very focused conversation with Prince Joscerand and his
nephew.

The festivities of Twelfth Night continued all around, but Alaric had
lost his taste for celebration. Unsettled, he fetched a flagon of wine from
a sideboard and took it back to the queen's table. Fortunately, another of
the pages had also fetched more wine, and the queen was in animated
discussion with Alazais, a goblet in her hand, though her good humor
certainly would end when she learned of her daughter's indiscretion.

Settling into his former post near the queen and her ladies, and trying
not to look as anxious as he felt, Alaric continued to scan the hall. After
a moment, he noticed Duke Richard leaving in the company of a senior
squire. Soon after that, he spotted the senior Torenthi ambassador and
several of his entourage, but not the man who had unfurled the length of
silk on the dais steps. Could it be that the missing man was the one he
had seen in the storeroom, who had tried to control him?

Very shortly, Duke Richard's squire returned to whisper urgently in the
queen's ear. She blanched, then rose and whispered to Alazais and one of
her ladies-in-waiting before following the squire from the hall, followed by
Alazais. The remaining lady took Princess Silke's hand and led her protest-
ing from the hall, just as Paget returned from some mission of his own.

"What's going on?" Paget murmured to Alaric. "Do you know?"

"Not a clue," Alaric replied. But as he glanced again at the king, he
saw that Prince Nigel had entered the hall and was whispering something
to his royal brother, who immediately excused himself from the Bremagni
princes' presence and headed briskly in the direction of his withdrawing
room. He did not look happy.

The situation clearly was deteriorating. Very shortly, Alaric's worst fears were reinforced as Princess Xenia, weeping and resisting, was hustled past him and Paget into the king's withdrawing room by a furious Queen Richeldis and a tight-lipped Duke Richard. Following at a discreet distance, and accompanied by Llion and Jiri, came a pair of stony-faced Haldane guards escorting the missing Torenthi courtier, who apparently was under close arrest.

"What's going on?" Quillan Pargeter whispered, joining him and Paget, for he had just come to take his turn serving the now-absent queen. "Who was that?"

"One of the Torenthi nobles," Alaric murmured.

"When I passed them in the corridor, it looked like he was under arrest," Quillan replied, though in a low voice, for other guests were drifting closer to their vicinity. "You don't suppose that he and Xenia . . ."

"We mustn't suppose *anything*," Alaric said sharply, for he dared not say more.

They learned little more of the incident in what remained of the evening, though they soon saw Duke Richard emerge from the withdrawing room and make his way purposefully to the rest of the Torenthi party, drawing them aside in serious discussion. Alaric noticed that several household knights drifted closer during the conversation, and soon escorted the foreigners from the hall. Duke Richard then sought out Duke Jared, and the two dukes soon disappeared in the direction of the king's withdrawing room. Duncan retreated into the nearest window bay in apparent uncertainty, looking troubled.

After that, people gradually began to filter from the hall, for the night's festivities clearly were winding down. Others of the pages and squires approached Alaric, Paget, and Quillan as the servants began to clear the remains of the festivities, curious for some explanation, but Alaric only shook his head when questioned, as did Paget and Quillan. Discretion was greatly valued in a future knight, especially those in close service to the Crown, and the three of them were well aware of their privileged positions. Even when Alaric retired to his quarters, joined now by Duncan, he could not bring himself to speak of it.

"Duke Richard did seem concerned, when he came to get my father," Duncan said tentatively. "Do you know what's going on?"

"It isn't for me to say," Alaric replied.

But it was not long afterward, while the two of them were readying for bed, that Llion came knocking on the door.

"Alaric, a word in private, if you please," Llion said, nodding apology to Duncan.

Alaric immediately went to him, silent as they moved into Llion's apartment next door, where Llion closed and latched the door behind them, indicating a chair before the fire. Alaric saw no sign of Alazais, so assumed she must still be about the queen's business, quite possibly seeing to the wayward Xenia.

"It appears that your concerns about Princess Xenia were well-founded," Llion said as he sank into a second chair. "It was not a pleasant scene, as you can imagine. The princess was hysterical. The queen could hardly speak. And the king—" Llion shook his head. "I don't think I've ever seen him so angry. For a while, I was afraid that steel would be drawn."

"It *was* one of the Torenthis, wasn't it?" Alaric said.

"Aye, the cocky one who unfurled that silk. Count Sigismund, he's called."

Alaric suppressed a shudder. "He's lucky he isn't the *late* Count Sigismund."

"He is," Llion said flatly. "But as part of the Torenthi delegation, he has diplomatic immunity. The king dares not start a war over this. Furthermore, Sigismund has declared his undying devotion regarding the king's sister, and desires to marry her."

Alaric gave the young knight a grimace. "Llion, he's probably twice her age. Does *she* want to marry *him*?"

"She says she does. She says that she adores him, and that they wish to be wed. It does appear that he had her maidenhead. Alazais was one of the women ordered to examine her."

Alaric suppressed a shudder, shaking his head. Xenia deflowered by Count Sigismund. And she had said that she "adored" him? He very much doubted that. Not that she had said it, but that it was true. Sigismund could have made her believe it. . . .

"Llion," he said hesitantly, "Count Sigismund *is* Deryni."

"You did indicate that he is."

"Then . . . it may be that he took control of her. He *could* have," he added, at Llion's look of dismay. "Especially, if he were already seducing her, flattering her, touching her. It wouldn't have been difficult to make her believe that it was what she wanted, to give herself to him."

"He could do that?"

"A properly trained Deryni could," Alaric replied. "*I* probably could—though I never would," he added hastily, wondering whether he had said too much already. "It—wouldn't be proper."

Llion was staring at him, his expression unreadable.

"You're saying that Sigismund could have forced her, not by physical strength but by magic?"

"It's possible," Alaric allowed. "And if he did, it wasn't Xenia's fault. It would be rape. Maybe she wouldn't have to marry him."

After considering for a few seconds, Llion came to his feet.

"Come with me. I think the king needs to hear about this."

HALF an hour later, with Llion's urging, Alaric had revealed his suspicions to the king. Duke Richard was also present, and looked as appalled as Llion had, only a short time before. Brion remained unreadable, though he did not contradict anything the boy had said.

"So, what do you propose I do about the situation?" the king asked, when Alaric had wound down.

"Well, if he forced her, whether by physical strength or by controlling her mind, it's still force—and that *is* rape."

"I agree," Brion said. "And how would you propose I prove that?"

"Well, maybe I could try to Truth-Read him while you're questioning him about it."

"No," the king said flatly.

"But—"

"I said no!" Brion drew a deep breath and let it out audibly. "Alaric, I don't know whether he forced her mind or just her body—giving her the benefit of the doubt, we'll simply say that she was coerced—but the end result is the same. He has had her virtue. Of equal concern to me is that he tried to force *your* mind. Neither is acceptable, and there isn't a blasted thing I can do about either one."

"I don't think his attempt to control me was serious, Sire," Alaric whispered, wide-eyed. "There wasn't time, and he can't have caught more than a glimpse of me before I bolted. I don't think he knew who I was."

"Well, he certainly knew *what* you are," the king retorted. "Otherwise, you probably wouldn't have been able to escape. And if he's asked around at all, he probably also knows *who* you are, by now. It isn't exactly a secret that the future Duke of Corwyn, a Deryni, is training for knighthood at my court." Brion drew a deep breath and let it out, briefly closing his eyes.

"What they *don't* know is how much you can do," he went on. "*We* don't know how much you can do. But I daren't risk that they'll test that question before you're grown. I can't risk losing you."

"But I *did* escape," Alaric said stubbornly. "And I'm convinced that Xenia was forced against her will."

The king looked away uncomfortably, and Duke Richard cleared his throat. "We don't know that, son."

"But—"

"We can't prove that she didn't give herself to him willingly," Richard went on. "And willing or not, Xenia is a princess of the House of Haldane. That means that she must either marry him or take the veil; the queen has declared that there can be no other resolution. Xenia has chosen to marry. For royal women, there are rarely other choices."

"But—"

Brion gave a snort, almost amused. "Think about what you're suggesting. Can you truly imagine my sister in a convent? Xenia?"

Somewhat cowed, Alaric shook his head.

"In any case, it's settled now," Brion said gruffly, getting to his feet. "If I tried to convince my mother that a Deryni seducer had used his powers to have his way with my sister, she would be unable to deal with that. And we *don't* need a flagrant misuse of Deryni powers fanning the hostility that already exists against your kind."

"But—"

"Drop it, Alaric!" the king ordered. "I've already agreed that the marriage may go forward. And once that is accomplished, I shall expel all Torenthi from my kingdom. Henceforth, they will not be allowed to enter Gwynedd save by royal license. If this Sigismund did use his powers to take advantage of my sister, it won't be allowed to happen to anyone else. Meanwhile, they are all under house arrest."

Alaric could only stare in disbelief as the king stormed from the room.

"Let it go, son," Richard said gently, not meeting Alaric's gaze as he, too, rose. "There is nothing any of us can do. Xenia will be a countess. Honor will have been satisfied. And not to put too fine a point on it, but she did make her own bed."

It seemed a cold resolution to Alaric, who rather liked both Haldane princesses, but he knew there would be no appeal from the king's decision—and the queen's. When he returned to his apartment, he shared a little of what had happened with Duncan, in strictest confidence. All aside from the matter of Xenia's fate, and whether or not Count Sigismund had used his powers to seduce her, the expulsion of the Torenthi diplomats had troubling implications for all Deryni in the kingdom.

"I do understand why the king has taken such measures," Alaric concluded. "Not only did a Torenthi Deryni use his powers on the king's sister, but he tried to control me. If he'd gotten the chance, he might even have mind-ripped me—or at least tried. But I do feel sorry for Xenia."

Duncan nodded slowly. "Bad business all around. But it surely can't have been her choice, to marry Sigismund. I mean, if he forced her . . ."

Alaric shrugged. "At this point, it hardly matters, does it? She's a king's sister, and her honor must be upheld. And the king can't very well have foreign Deryni operating openly at his court, now, can he? Other than me, of course, once I'm grown—and I'm not foreign. But for now, de Nore and some of the other bishops are already trying to crack down on Deryni in the kingdom. We'll just have to keep our heads down."

On the following Sunday, in the chapel royal of Rhemuth Castle, marriage banns were read for the coming union of Her Royal Highness the Princess Xenia Nuala Jaroni Swynbeth Haldane of Gwynedd with

Sigismund Borislav Graf von Golzców, late of the court of the Torenthi Duke of Arkadia. Only Count Constantin and a pair of bodyguards were present to stand by the prospective groom, for the remainder of the Torenthi party had been ordered to depart earlier in the week, escorted to their ship at Desse by a company of Haldane lancers. The Torenthis were less than happy with the arrangement, but were obliged to accept the measure with reasonable grace. Alaric, for his part, was ordered to maintain a low profile until after the royal wedding—and to stay well away from the remaining Torenthi lords.

On the second day of February, the Feast of Candlemas, the Archbishop of Rhemuth presided over the marriage of Princess Xenia with Count Sigismund: a quiet affair celebrated at the chapel royal, in the presence of her Haldane kin and Count Constantin, who stood as witness for the groom. The king gave his sister in marriage, expressionless as he set her hand into that of Count Sigismund. The queen wept throughout. Afterward, following a modest wedding supper, the couple took up temporary residence in an apartment adjacent to the king's, until arrangements could be made for their departure for the groom's homeland. In the meantime, keeping Count Constantin amused became the responsibility of Duke Richard.

It was hardly an ideal situation. Under the circumstances, nothing could be deemed ideal, but honor had been satisfied. Few options seemed available for the immediate future, as winter deepened and the court turned to mostly sedentary activities. The pages and squires resumed their training, now geared to academic instruction or drill in the great hall. The king's thoughts, when they were not brooding on his sister's fate, turned to more serious contemplation of his own marital future, and more thoughtful scrutiny of the portraits given him by the Crown Prince of Bremagne and Prince Joscerand. He had known from the outset that the two younger girls were entirely too young, and he was not inclined to wait while they grew to appropriate young womanhood, but the eldest . . .

He decided that he should meet the young lady in question: Jehane Julienne Adélaïde de Besançon, Princesse de Bremagne. He and his crown council had only begun logistical planning for the journey, which would also call at several other foreign courts, when an unexpected visitor made an appearance at Rhemuth just at dusk, demanding audience with the king.

"He—ah—says that he is Count Constantin's elder brother, Sire," Jiri Redfearn reported. The king was at table in the great hall with his uncle and Constantin himself, who immediately broke into a wide grin and glanced at Brion.

"And about time, too," he muttered. "May he be admitted to the hall, my lord?"

Brion looked momentarily bewildered. "But, there hasn't been time to—"

Constantin only raised an eyebrow. "My lord, we *are* Deryni. Did you not think I would notify my family of my whereabouts?"

"Yes, of course," Brion murmured, signing for Jiri to see to it as he and Richard and, then, Constantin all rose. Alaric had been serving at table at the far end of the hall, away from Constantin, and watched as Jiri quickly passed between the two long tables of gawking men set along the sides of the hall. As the great doors parted, Jiri greeted the men waiting outside, then led them back up the hall: perhaps half a dozen, wearing fur hats and fur-lined coats of bright brocades, led by a retainer holding aloft a sheathed sword with a white kerchief tied to the hilt. The man beside him, obviously the senior among them, was more richly dressed than the others, and Constantin immediately descended the stairs to embrace him.

"Brother, you come at last!"

"I should have preferred to wait until the spring, but I do appreciate the urgency. Pray, present me to your host."

"Of course." Constantin gave a little bow and turned to face the king. "My lord, permit me to present my eldest brother, Count Sergei Furstán-Arkadia, Regent of Arkadia, who has come to escort us home."

"My lord," Count Sergei said with a stiff nod.

"Count," Brion replied coolly, returning the nod. "Have you supped?"

"We have not, my lord."

"Then, perhaps you would care to join us." Brion gestured toward the other side of the table where, at his nod, squires hastily began moving benches into place. "You must be cold and weary from your journey, from . . . ?"

"From Desse, my lord," Sergei replied, removing his fur hat and shak-

ing snowmelt from his side-braids as he mounted the steps and took a
seat opposite the king. "At this time of year, it was not precisely a pleasant
voyage along the coast, but my brother indicated that the newlyweds are
eager to return to Arkadia. May I ask where they are?"

"Count Sigismund and my niece prefer to take most of their meals in
their apartments," Duke Richard said evenly, before Brion could answer.
"I am Richard Haldane Duke of Carthmoor, the king's uncle," he added,
by way of introduction. "I trust you will agree that the situation is . . .
somewhat irregular."

Count Sergei inclined his head and smiled faintly. "So I am led to
believe." He picked up a cup that Paget had hastily filled. "But I drink to all
your health, gentlemen," he went on. "And we shall endeavor to depart
soon after first light, lest we strain your hospitality unduly." He lifted his
cup. "To a peaceful night!"

It was a sentiment to which no one could take exception.

RATHER than dawn, it would be nearly noon before the Torenthi
party actually rode out of the castle yard. The count's announcement threw the queen's household into turmoil, given the short notice,
but Alazais and the other ladies-in-waiting helped organize Xenia's
belongings for transport. No one slept that night. The queen was near
hysterical, faced not only with packing a trousseau that was not yet
complete—though the remainder would be sent on, later in the summer—
but also the imminent loss of her elder daughter. Silke, soon to be bereft
of her only sister, quite possibly forever, wept inconsolably through most
of the night. Xenia alone, of the royal ladies, remained exhilarated and
focused, finally about to embark upon her new life.

All the court assembled the next morning to see off the bride and her
Torenthi groom, lining up on the great hall steps. A troop of Haldane
lancers waited in the grey March sunshine to escort the bridal party to
Desse, crimson pennons bright against the snow. Trumpeters sounded a
final fanfare for their Haldane princess as Xenia emerged with her husband at the top of the steps, muffled against the cold in a magnificent fur
hat and fur-lined robe in the Torenthi fashion, brought as a wedding gift

by Count Sergei. The king, his mother, his brother and remaining sister, and his uncle followed, and Brion himself handed the princess onto her favorite grey palfrey, stretching upward to bestow a final kiss on his sister's cheek before giving Count Sigismund a curt nod and stepping back with the rest of his family.

Alaric watched with Llion from one of the gatehouse walks as the bridal party rode out, careful to do nothing that might draw Torenthi attention to him. As Xenia passed under the gatehouse arch, she glanced back at her mother, her brother and sister, and lifted a hand in farewell, but Alaric did not think she looked quite as happy as she had when she emerged from the great hall.

"Do you think she is regretting that she married him?" Alaric asked Llion in a low voice.

"I think that, already, things may not be turning out quite as she had imagined," Llion replied softly. "Or she could be breeding already," he added with a shrug.

Alaric looked at him in alarm. Only recently had he begun to be aware of what a marriage actually entailed.

"She might be pregnant?" he said, half in disbelief.

"If I were a Torenthi count being pressured to protect the virtue of a sister of the King of Gwynedd by marrying her," Llion said dryly, "I would make it my highest priority to put a Torenthi son in her belly as quickly as possible. Or perhaps that was his plan from the beginning."

Alaric shivered, trying not to imagine what it must be like for Xenia, who surely had been an innocent, despite her protestations of worldly sophistication. Count Sigismund, for his part, had struck Alaric as a cad from the beginning, arrogant and self-centered.

"I pray that we are wrong about him, Llion," he said, watching as the last of the Haldane escort moved out of sight to pass through Rhemuth town. "And I pray that God and our Lady will protect Xenia. I wish I understood why the king insisted that they marry."

"To preserve the honor of Gwynedd," Llion replied, looking away. "It is part of the price of a crown."

Chapter 36

"But continue thou in the things which thou hast learned and hast
been assured of, knowing of whom thou hast learned them."
—II TIMOTHY 3:14

THE weather began to improve as March progressed. The winter had not been particularly hard. As the spring thaws began, indoor study and drill began to give way to more outdoor pursuits, though capricious spring rains could still wreak havoc with planned activities. Mud became the bane of stable grooms and castle laundresses.

Alaric continued to apply himself, practicing hard during the lengthening days and spending many an evening immersed in games of cardounet with Paget and sometimes with Llion or Jiri, though Llion disappeared for a few weeks just before Easter to take Alazais to Morganhall, where she would remain until after the birth of their first child. Jamyl's wife was also with child now, and suffering greatly from morning sickness.

Meanwhile, with the last of the guests finally gone and two of his knights soon to become fathers, the king began to look more seriously to his own future, especially the choice of a royal bride. He had already been presented with portraits of the King of Bremagne's three daughters, for his consideration. Alaric was not privy to what went on behind the closed doors of the council chamber, but he was one of the first ones chosen to accompany the king on his planned mission to Bremagne. Paget, now a senior squire of nearly seventeen, was also selected. The two were pleased and eager as the king called them into his withdrawing room, where Duke Richard was also waiting.

"I know there has been a great deal of speculation about who might become my eventual queen," he told the pair, "but if I'm to make an informed decision, I need to start making the acquaintance of prospective royal brides. I certainly wouldn't agree to a marriage without meeting the woman in question." He flashed them a nervous grin. "Besides, exposure to foreign courts is good experience for my future knights."

The king had determined to keep his party small on this venture, lest he frighten prospective brides, but he did take along some of his most trusted advisors: Jiri Redfearn, Tiarnán Macrae, Jamyl Arilan, and Llion. Jamyl would have been permitted to bow out, for his wife of less than a year was enduring a difficult pregnancy; but he had determined instead to send her to the family seat at Tre-Arilan for her lying-in.

"Llion has the right idea," he told the king, as they considered options over a pitcher of ale. "There's nothing either of us could do if we stayed. On the other hand, there might be a great deal we could do, if you started to choose an unsuitable wife!"

Chuckling, the king only shook his head. "Thank you, gentlemen."

They left Rhemuth early in May, riding down to Desse with a small escort to meet the king's ship *Caeriesse*. By the end of May, with stops along the way at Concaradine and Nyford, they were sailing into Coroth's harbor. There, to Alaric's pleased surprise, the king had allowed for a two-week stay before continuing on their mission.

The visit began like most previous visits, given his increasing age. Now in his twelfth year, his regents deferred to him increasingly, at least in lesser matters, and now regarded him as a young man, and their future duke in fact. There were times, to be sure, when the king met in private with Corwyn's regents, to advise and be advised. But the regents were also careful to schedule assize courts and general audiences and even a few local progresses into the countryside, where Alaric himself had nominal command. Having watched and learned at his father's knee and then at the king's side, he had a grasp of protocol and legal precedent far beyond his years. And when Llion put him through his paces in training sessions with Corwyn's older pages and some of the squires, the boy excelled far beyond what his future staff had dared to hope.

"His trainers at Rhemuth have taught him well," said Lord Hamilton, the seneschal, as he and Sir Crescence de Naverie, another regent, watched Alaric spar with a senior squire, using blunted steel and padded armor. "Given his rank, some of us feared he might be allowed to slack off from his training."

Llion snorted, for he himself had trained as a squire under Lord Hamilton before being knighted by Alaric's father. "You think Duke Richard would allow *any* of us to slack off, my lord?"

"Well, it *is* a royal court," Sir Crescence said, with an apologetic shrug. "And Alaric is a future duke. Exalted rank sometimes causes more allowances to be made than is wise."

"None of us would be doing him any favors, if we were to allow that to happen," Llion replied. "The king has great hopes for him. *I* have great hopes for him."

Hamilton smiled. "And you have fulfilled the hopes we had for *you*, young Llion. I understand that you have wed the youngest of Alaric's half-sisters."

"I have," Llion said with a grin, "and she carries our first child. With luck, I shall return before she is delivered, but if not, she is in good hands with a sister and her aunt at Morganhall."

Hamilton nodded speculatively. "You go from here to Bremagne, do you not?"

"Aye, and to several other destinations along the way."

"Ah, yes, it all begins," Sir Crescence mused. "Do you think the king will find a bride there?"

"Perhaps," Llion said. "The King of Bremagne has several daughters. The King of Fallon has a niece. And there will be other noble ladies vying for his notice, wherever else we may call along the way. But methinks this bride-finding venture is only just beginning."

The visit to Coroth also offered opportunities for Alaric to reconnect with a few of the friends he had made there. Viliam, alas, was not in residence, for he had been called back to his father's estates for further training, but Alaric did manage a few cardounet matches with Jernian Kushannan, whose skills had only sharpened since their last meeting. Jernian played with Paget as well, and trounced him handily, though Jernian was not yet fourteen and Paget was three years older.

Alaric teased Paget about the loss, but he was happy for Jernian, who had inherited his father's title two years before, and was still in much the same state of limbo as Alaric, with his own set of regents to administer his holdings. That change in status, plus his poor vision and less than outstanding physical ability, had encouraged his regents to shift his training increasingly to more academic pursuits, since he still professed himself keenly interested in military tactics.

"It will be an excellent use of his talents," Brion declared, after watching Jernian and Alaric run a battle plan on a map of the local area. "That was nicely done, lads."

"Thank you, Sire," Jernian said with a grin, as Alaric clasped his shoulder in agreement.

In all, both the king and Alaric were pleased with the course of the visit, and felt confident that the Corwyn regents were doing an admirable job of running the duchy—as, indeed, they had done, off and on, for several generations now.

It seemed a perfect visit, and was made all the more special when, on their last evening in Coroth, the king had Llion and Jiri organize a special supper for all of Alaric's regents, held in the more intimate setting of the council chamber rather than the great hall. Paget and Jernian happily served both Alaric and the king that night and, when the meal was mostly ended, moved expectantly to either side of the king as he settled into his chair and glanced aside at Alaric, seated at his right hand.

"By your leave, gentlemen, I've a mind to conduct one item of my own business before we adjourn for the evening," he said to the assembled regents, signing for Llion to join him at the head of the table. "Alaric, I have done some thinking, and I don't believe I really need a page to accompany me to Bremagne tomorrow." He raised an eyebrow at the boy, and Alaric's heart sank. "What I do need—and I had planned for it from the start—is a second squire to assist Master Paget. Would you please come and kneel?"

Astonished and delighted, Alaric scrambled to his feet and hastily moved to obey the royal instruction.

"I know he is still a few months shy of twelve," the king went on, turning his attention to the regents, "but as I hope you will agree, he is a very accomplished not-yet-twelve, as well as your future duke. Alaric, here before your regents, may I assume that you are willing to assume the duties and privileges of a Haldane squire?"

"I am, Sire," Alaric said, grinning as he lifted his joined hands to the king.

The king smiled and briefly took Alaric's hands between his own.

"I have already received your oaths," he said, "so I think we need not repeat them here." He extended his right hand to Llion, who passed him the dagger of a Haldane squire. "Take this dagger as a symbol of those oaths, and as a reminder of your duty always to protect and serve my person and my crown."

Eyes bright with unbidden tears, Alaric took the dagger and slipped it partially from its scabbard to kiss the blade, then closed and shoved it into his belt as Paget and Jernian knelt to buckle on the squire's spurs of blued-steel.

"The spurs were mine, when I served as squire to my father and Duke Richard," Brion said, quirking a pleased smile at Alaric's look of surprise. "I had two pairs, and Nigel wears the other. Wear them as a reminder of your aspiration to knighthood."

Alaric glanced back at his heels in delight as his friends finished buckling on the spurs, but he sobered as Llion brought forward the squire's doublet of Haldane crimson, ensigned on the left breast with the Haldane badge of a crowned lion rampant.

"One last thing, and we're done here," Brion said, signing for Alaric to rise. "Receive the livery of my house. Wear it with pride and honor, that all may know you serve the Crown of Gwynedd."

Alaric scrambled to his feet and held out his arms to shrug into the doublet that Llion offered—snug over his other clothes—then pressed his right hand to the badge on the left breast: the crowned golden lion rampant. He glanced around at his regents as they broke into applause and cheers.

"Surprised, are we?" Llion murmured, close by his ear.

"You know I am," Alaric replied, so that only Llion could hear. "But very, very pleased."

T HEY sailed with the morning tide. Alaric proudly wore his new livery as a Haldane squire as he took his leave of his regents and Jernian, and rode down to the harbor beside Paget, following the king.

The ship was waiting at the quay. The day was brisk, the winds fair. Brion's royal standard lifted straight from its mast as they caught the breeze and the tide. After sailing out between the twin beacons that guarded the harbor mouth, they headed due south and westerly until they passed south of the Isle d'Orsal, whose citadel dipped its banners in salute as they came abreast of it. They continued southward off the sandy beaches of Joux all afternoon, putting in that night at the Vezairi port of Trancault to sleep and take on local provisions.

"My father's first queen was Vezairi," Brion mused, as he and his immediate companions supped at an inn close to the seafront. "I'm told she was quite beautiful—and gentle, like her name: Dulchesse. Very sadly, she proved barren—or near as makes no difference. Though she did produce several babes, they were all stillborn or died soon after birth. But her father was a grand duke of Vezaire: Nivelon, I think he was called." He shrugged and lifted his cup of Vezairi white port. "That was a very long time ago."

"To Queen Dulchesse," Jiri said, raising his cup.

When all of them had drunk to the memory of the late queen, Alaric ventured a question of his own.

"Sire, have you been to Vezaire before?" he asked, for he and Paget had been allowed to sit at table with Llion, Jiri, Jamyl, and Tiarnán.

"No, never farther south than Tralia and the Hort of Orsal, though I'm told the southern kingdoms have their beauty. I imagine we'll see a bit of that on this trip, won't we?" Brion drained the last of his wine and rose.

"We'd best see about getting some sleep. The captain made it clear that he doesn't want to miss the morning tide."

They stayed ashore that night, for the king preferred not to sleep aboard ship unless there were no other options. Next morning, awakened early by the bells of nearby churches and the cathedral farther up the hill, they walked with the king in the harbor market while they waited for the tide, breaking their fast with warm bread and boiled eggs and crusty cheese from canopied market stalls. Brion remarked that he had never tasted finer, and seemed to enjoy this experience of normalcy.

They sailed with the morning tide, and spent the day watching the sandy beaches of Vezaire give way to the marshy coastline of Logreine, with its serried vineyards marching up the hillsides beyond. That night, they anchored in the chalk-cliffed bay before Fianna, where Gezelin Count of Fianna entertained them to supper at his summer house perched on a bluff above. They dined on roast capon stuffed with bread and onions and apples, along with sea bass, and succulent pork carved off a carcass turning on a spit above the fire pit in the center of the hall. To wash it down, Count Gezelin produced some of the finest Fianna red that Alaric had ever tasted, for even the squires were seated at the table with the king and his knights.

"You must take some of our wine with you when you sail in the morning," Count Gezelin said, as he topped up the king's glass. "Your father used to keep a very fine cellar, and always ordered wine from us. It is the mark of a civilized court," he added, holding up a pale Vezairi glass to the light. "This is a particularly fine vintage."

They slept again in proper beds that night, guests of Count Gezelin, and departed the next day with several cases of fine Fianna red packed with straw between the bottles.

Fallon was to be their next stop: Fallon, where the king had a niece of marriageable age, said to be intelligent and accomplished. After skirting the rocky coast of Fianna, they rounded the great cape called Jupe de la Vierge and sailed between the steep basalt cliffs guarding the bay at Niki-dari, Fallon's capital. At the quay beneath the castle heights, outriders from King Alberic were waiting with horses to escort Brion and his party up the winding road that led to the royal palace.

Said palace proved to be a soaring assortment of whitewashed domes and cupolas, gilded spires, and rich-hued glass. As King Alberic's major-domo led the way up a wide set of pristine marble stairs, Alaric was careful to maintain a fitting demeanor for a squire attending on the King of Gwynedd, but he was also taking in as much as he could of the Fallonish court, noting the livery of royal emerald-green and white on the palace retainers, the well-polished weapons, the sumptuous carving on the columns, the gilt work on the carved doors.

Vast heraldic tapestries adorned the walls of the great hall—he recognized some of the coats of arms from his studies of the great families—

and the marble floors gleamed under the broad swaths of sunlight that pierced the high clerestory windows. Their footsteps echoed on the polished marble.

The king's private reception room, to which they were led, was a cool sanctuary of white marble, arched windows, and silken tapestries, with fine Kheldish carpets underfoot and cushions of silk and velvet brocades on the chairs and benches. King Alberic himself was waiting in the wide window bay of the room, along with members of his family: a wife and grown sons, Alaric guessed, and also a thin, somewhat gangly girl in a gown of dark blue who just might be the king's niece they had heard about, though if she was accomplished, it was not in the arts of social interaction.

"Cousin," King Alberic said, coming forward to extend his hand to Brion in greeting. "Welcome to my home. I trust you will dine with us this evening, and perhaps spend a day or two as my guest."

"Alas, we may only stay the night," Brion replied. "But we thank you for your hospitality this evening."

King Alberic and his queen proved to be amiable hosts, he as tall and thin of body as she was short and stout, both of them somewhat advanced in years. Both were effusive in their welcome and distant with their offspring. Perhaps it came of presenting a niece for their royal guest's assessment whose appearance and demeanor fell somewhat short of what was usually desired in a royal consort. The Princess Kerensa Alathea of Fallon, though richly garbed and no doubt generously dowered, was rail thin and gawky, and somewhat reminded Alaric of a stork, all beaky nose and bushy brows and angled elbows. Her eyes were handsome enough, of a rather engaging sea-foam color, but the wiry hair escaping from beneath her jeweled coronet and silken veil was mouse-brown.

A sallow complexion and crooked teeth did nothing to improve first impressions, nor did her apparent inability to string together more than half a dozen words at a time, when Brion tried to engage her in conversation while at supper. Alaric felt sorry for her, and tried to be both pleasant and attentive as he helped serve her and the queen. But Sir Tiarnán, long a widower, apparently saw past her physical shortcomings, for he soon had cajoled a smile from the princess, and even had her laughing by the

time supper was over. Later that evening, as everyone retired, Sir Tiarnán
looked thoughtful, and spoke privily with the king for some little while.

"What do you suppose that's all about?" Paget whispered to Alaric as
they readied the king's chamber for the night.

Alaric shook his head. "Your guess is as good as mine, but I do think
that the princess was somewhat taken with Sir Tiarnán."

Paget looked at him owl-eyed. "You think he might be considering a
match for himself? He would aim as high as a princess?"

"It's possible. He's been a widower for many years, his children are all
but grown, he's been lonely. And she may not have many other prospects.
It might be a kindness, for her."

"And for him?"

Alaric shrugged again. "They seemed to have things to talk about.
Both of them could do far worse."

The king had nothing to say about his conversation, of course, when
he returned to the royal quarters and readied for bed; but the next morning, before they left, Alaric saw Sir Tiarnán speaking privily with King
Alberic.

Later, when they mounted up to return to the harbor, Alberic rode
down with them, along with his niece, who fell to the rear of the procession with Tiarnán. When they parted at the dock, Tiarnán kissed her
hand tenderly.

"So," the king said to Tiarnán, when they had all boarded their vessel
and the crew began raising sail and casting off the lines. "May we be
allowed to know what the lady said?"

Tiarnán did his best to look unflustered, but he kept his eyes on the
princess as the ship pulled away from the dock.

"When there is something to tell, I will share it with you, Sire," he
said quietly. "But I have great hopes."

Brion nodded. "Fair enough."

THEY were three days sailing on along the coast of Fallon, anchoring
at night in sheltered coves and occasionally going ashore. Alaric and
Paget spent a great deal of time watching from the ship's rail, taking it all

in, for neither knew when fate might again take them this far from home. Alaric might well venture this far, for a duke's duties sometimes took him far afield; but Paget would serve at the will of his king, and might well find himself back in Meara, near where he had been raised.

The fourth day found them drawing into the mouth of the River Laval, which formed a bay flanked by the Fallonese port of Ruyère to the north and the Bremagni town of Cinq-Eglise, named for the five churches that crowned its bluff. They could hear the bells ringing as they drew near, and dropped anchor just offshore to await a skiff flying the colors of Bremagne and rowed by six sets of oars. The man standing in the bow, bracing himself on the flagstaff, wore the white and blue of Bremagne.

"Ahoy, the boat!" the captain called down to him. "We seek the court of the King of Bremagne. Is he yet in residence at Cinq-Eglise?"

The man in the bow swept off his cap and made a bow. "He is. Do you come from the King of Gwynedd?"

The captain indicated Brion, standing to his right. "I do. This is Brion King of Gwynedd."

The envoy made another, more profound bow.

"My master's respect, Sire—and welcome to Bremagne. Will you come ashore? I shall take you to His Majesty."

Chapter 37

*". . . I desired to make her my spouse, and
I was a lover of her beauty."*
—WISDOM OF SOLOMON 8:2

THEY found the king with his family in the floral gardens at Mille-fleurs, the Bremagni summer palace. Across the manicured lawns, nearer to the buildings, King Meyric was lounging under a shady tree with several of his councilors of state on stools around him, watching as his two sons indulged in archery practice a short distance away. From nearby, the sweet music of a pair of lutes drifted toward them.

The king's daughters were also in evidence. Nearby, before a set of hedges trimmed with a crenellated top, three auburn-haired girls in pastel gowns were playing ball with a pack of long-eared, short-legged hound puppies, to a great accompaniment of puppy yips and girlish shrieks of excitement. Clearly, the three were sisters.

"Please wait here, Majesty," their guide said to Brion, then headed off across the grass to confer with the Bremagni king. Meyric lifted his head, glancing in their direction, then scrambled to his feet, smiling broadly as he started toward them.

The girls, meanwhile, had summoned a pair of pages to take charge of the hound puppies and were making their way toward their sire. The tallest of the three, in the lead, cast a curious look in the direction of the approaching visitors. Like her sisters, she was slender and graceful, with masses of auburn hair tumbling wild around her shoulders. Unlike her younger sisters, who tripped along close behind, she had a woman's body, and the smoldering glance of a woman as her eyes met Brion's.

Alaric sensed the king's response and glanced at him surreptitiously, catching his quick intake of breath. If this was the princess they had come to meet, Bremagne might well be the last of their bride-finding embassies.

"Cousin of Gwynedd!" King Meyric called, as he strode briskly toward Brion, with hand outstretched. "Welcome to my home!"

"Cousin of Bremagne, I am pleased to be here," Brion replied, taking the proffered hand. "I hope our arrival does not come at an inconvenient time. We were not certain whether we should find you here or at Rémigny."

"No, no, we always leave the capital for the summer," Meyric replied. "I love my Millefleurs, though it is too cold in the winter months. But you must meet the flowers of my heart, and the sturdy vines of my house." He turned to sweep an expansive arm in the direction of his offspring, all of whom were converging on the royal pair. "You have already met my eldest, Prince Ryol, at the Hort of Orsal's investiture," Meyric said. "His younger brother is Prince Trevor. And permit me also to present my darling daughters: Ursuline, the youngest of my brood; dear Aude . . . and Jehane."

The boys had offered polite bows to the visiting king. The three girls dropped him graceful curtsies as their names were spoken. Though all three were lovely, and even the younger ones were mature for their ages, it was Jehane whose green gaze immediately locked on Brion's as she rose from her curtsy.

"My Lord of Gwynedd," she murmured, as Brion came to clasp her hand and graze its knuckles with his lips.

"Princess," he managed to whisper.

They moved inside after that, to take refreshment and speak of the plans Meyric had made to entertain his royal visitor. Alaric sensed that his own king was doing his best to be personable and polite to all the Bremagni royals, but it also was clear, at least to Alaric, that the king was totally captivated by the eldest princess, and she by him. King Meyric kept up a lively conversation at first, continuing to extol the beauty and virtues of all three of his daughters, but Brion and Jehane seemed to hear little of it.

Dinner that evening was a relaxed affair, since the visitors had only just arrived, but King Meyric clearly intended to capitalize on Brion's obvious interest in his eldest daughter. That night, at table, he seated Brion at his right hand and Jehane to Brion's right, with the two younger daughters directly across from him and the boys to either end. Brion's four knights were seated across from the family.

The arrangement only enhanced Brion's first impression of Princess Jehane, and gave ample excuse, when musicians began playing later in the evening, to take the Bremagni king's eldest daughter onto the floor numerous times for dancing. Jamyl and Llion dutifully partnered the two younger girls, as did Jiri and Tiarnán; Meyric's queen had passed away several years before. By the time Gwynedd's king retired to the apartments set aside for his use during his stay, with Alaric and Paget to attend him, he was as flustered as Alaric had ever seen him, though he said not a word regarding his dinner companion.

All of them rode out hunting the next day: a more stylized and formal affair than was the custom in Gwynedd, but it provided ample opportunity for the couple to interact. If anything, Princess Jehane looked even more enchanting than she had the previous evening, in riding clothes of emerald-green that set off her eyes and her auburn hair.

The king clearly was smitten, and even Alaric and Paget found themselves falling under her spell. Jamyl and Llion, both of them very happily married men, thought her utterly charming. Brion hung on her every word, and claimed nearly every dance with her again that evening, though more of the Bremagni court joined them this time. By the time they returned to their apartments the second night, Alaric was fairly certain that the king had made up his mind.

"So, do you think you may have found your queen, Sire?" Alaric asked, as he helped the king peel off a damp linen shirt.

Brion only smiled enigmatically and shrugged, continuing to undress. "It could be, Alaric. It could well be."

The king's pattern of activities in the following days became a series of ride-outs, hunting parties, walks in the gardens, and dining in varying degrees of formality, always chaperoned, but always with opportunity for the young couple to interact. After a few days of this, Llion informed Alaric and Paget that the two of them would be joining training sessions with the squires of King Meyric's court, lest they lose their edge while the king did his courting.

It was a relief to both young men, for idleness was outside their experience since beginning their training. Details of Bremagni drill somewhat differed, but the two quickly found that the basics of combat training were much the same in both kingdoms. Paget, being nearly of an age for knighthood, soon found good sport sparring with some of the young knights of the Bremagni court, and mostly held his own with them. Alaric felt harder pressed, for he was young for a squire; but especially in exercises involving skill or horsemanship rather than sheer strength, he excelled repeatedly—and he seemed to be growing taller.

Joining the Bremagni squires also had side benefits that neither had anticipated. Both of them soon discovered that the afternoon sessions with formation riding and archery, both mounted and afoot, attracted a growing audience of the young ladies of the court, which invariably led to further interactions after practice was done for the day. Both Alaric and Paget were handsome young men, highly accomplished in their martial skills, and exotic for being foreigners. Paget, being older, became the amorous focus for several of the young ladies of similar age, and enjoyed the attentions of more than one of them in the weeks of his residence at the Millefleurs court.

Alaric, too, received his share of feminine attention, and not a few of his admirers did more than merely admire from afar. Bremagni girls, he discovered, were much more forward than their Gwyneddan sisters, and took liberties that were not always easy to ignore. He might have been largely inexperienced in matters of the heart, but his blond good looks and athletic ability, plus impeccable manners and his obvious rank by dint of his service to the King of Gwynedd, made him all but irresistible to the ladies. Much sought after on the dance floor, for he was a graceful partner, he knew better than to seek out inappropriate attentions, but that did not prevent the bolder of his pursuers from teasing.

By early July, the king had approached Jehane's father to ask for her hand. Though King Meyric heartily approved the match, and the two kings settled down with their advisors to work out the broad terms of the marriage contract, it soon became clear that keener legal minds would be required to finalize the details. Very soon, Jamyl was sent back to Rhemuth on the king's ship, to fetch suitable negotiators—who returned several weeks later without Jamyl, for the young knight had learned that, in addition to his wife nearing her term, his father was gravely ill, and likely to die.

"I'm very sorry to hear that," the king said to Sir Raedan des Champs, who was one of the newly arrived team, along with two priests from the chancellor's office, sent to work out the details of the marriage settlement. "I don't know that I've met Jamyl's father, but I did know *his* father, Sir Seisyll Arilan. I know that my father relied on him greatly. And it saddens me that Jamyl himself may soon have to deal with his own father's passing."

The three newcomers dined with the two kings that night, meeting with King Meyric's legal team, and settled down the next day to finalize the necessary documents. A particular point of contention was the actual wedding date, along with the wedding venue.

"I am perfectly willing to come to Bremagne for the wedding," Brion said, "but Twelfth Night is not at all suitable."

"It is a traditional date for royal ceremonies," King Meyric insisted.

"As it is in Gwynedd," Sir Raedan replied. "But it is also the dead of winter: hardly suitable for us to travel to Bremagne, or for His Majesty to bring home a new queen."

"Could they not travel back to Gwynedd over land in the spring," one of Meyric's courtiers suggested, "and make a wedding tour of it?"

Tiarnán shook his head. "My king cannot be away from his kingdom for that long. And an arduous journey over land, through many different kingdoms, strikes me as a needless hardship for all concerned. In late spring or summer, Bremagne lies an easy sail across the Southern Sea from Gwynedd, as Sir Raedan and the two fathers have recently demonstrated."

"There is an additional advantage to waiting until the spring," Father Creoda said quietly. "The bride is yet young. It would do no harm to delay for a few months."

"She is of age," Meyric's chancellor pointed out hotly.

"Yes, of course, of course," Creoda replied. "But she is not yet fifteen. Since one of the principal purposes of a royal marriage is ensure the succession, it stands to reason that a young woman of—ah—somewhat more mature years will be better prepared to fulfill that royal duty."

It was a telling observation, and resonated with most of those present. In the end, a compromise was reached, whereby the wedding would take place at the Bremagni capital on the first of May, after which the King of

Gwynedd and his bride would return by ship for a second blessing of the royal couple at Rhemuth cathedral, and the formal crowning of Jehane as queen.

Meanwhile, Alaric continued to expand his experience at the Bremagni court, especially regarding the fair sex. He did not see much of the Princess Jehane in those days counting down to the betrothal, for she was much occupied in the company of Brion or else sequestered with the seamstresses and other artificers who were preparing her trousseau.

The two younger princesses were a different story. Aude and Ursuline, who were thirteen and eleven, had taken an immediate liking to the handsome young squires from Gwynedd, and especially Alaric, who was closest to them in age. They were charmed that he, in turn, was fascinated by their hound puppies, and was willing to spend time chasing and rolling on the grass with them. In addition, he and Paget often found themselves recruited to join the Bremagni squires as an escort for the younger princesses and other young ladies of the court on leisurely midmorning rides in the countryside, before it got too hot.

Afternoons offered more sedentary occupations well suited to the heat: singing and playing at musical instruments, dancing, the reading and composition of poetry, artistic pursuits, sometimes archery, all interspersed with leisurely strolls in the palace gardens. To Alaric's surprise, it seemed that ladies in Bremagne did not play cardounet or other strategy games.

Fortunately, he and Paget found that gentler occupations held their own allures. In the evenings, once the service of dinner had been accomplished, there were always divers musical activities to wile away the long summer twilight: dancing, listening to singing, and sometimes mummers' plays. King Meyric was fond of dancing, and encouraged Brion and Jehane to take to the floor often, dancing nearly every dance.

The other gentlemen of Brion's party likewise were drafted as dancing partners. The handsome young squire from Gwynedd proved intriguing to ladies both young and not so young, and was much in demand as a dance partner and simply as a companion for casual conversation while musicians performed in the background.

But there was an additional dimension to Alaric's ongoing education that he had not reckoned on, and which he had not experienced in Gwynedd. Sweetly enticed into shadowed stairwells or drawn amid the leafy garden paths, he experienced the first of numerous kisses and caresses, and even more intimate attentions from several of the young ladies of court, who made it their mission to see that the handsome, bright-haired foreigner did not go wanting for feminine companionship. And finally, on one balmy evening late in July, in a fragrant garden bower, he lost his innocence between the thighs of a pretty Fallonese maid of honor whose kisses and caresses momentarily had tantalized him beyond reasoning.

Somewhat sheepishly he mentioned it to Llion the next day, though without revealing the identity of his young enchantrix. Llion only raised an indulgent eyebrow and allowed that the ladies of Bremagne were, indeed, charming—then reminded his young charge that the Bremagni king probably would take it amiss if any of the ladies of his court were to fall pregnant by one of their Gwyneddan guests.

"You're right," Alaric said uneasily. "I hadn't thought of that."

"No, it is not a possibility that comes readily to mind when all sensation is focused in one's groin," Llion replied with a droll smile. "Just remember who you are—and I don't mean that you're Deryni, though that *is* a factor. You're a future duke, which means you are all but a prince."

"Llion, I won't even be twelve for another month," Alaric objected. "And I'm certainly not a prince."

"No, but a duke is nearly as good a catch. And many a maid, and many a maid's father, would do whatever they could to entrap such a prize as yourself in marriage. That is why the king himself has been extremely discreet regarding his own romantic dalliances. You may have noticed."

Alaric ducked his head amid a welter of churning emotions. He had deduced some time ago that affairs of the heart could be complicated—he had understood what he saw, when he came upon Princess Xenia and her now-husband *in flagrante*—but his own place in such affairs was only now becoming apparent. And it had not occurred to him that the king, too, might be wrestling with carnal complexities.

"I—think I'd best confine myself to less hazardous behavior in the future," he said contritely.

"A wise decision," Llion agreed. "You do know that there are other ways to give and receive pleasure . . . ?"

Alaric nodded curtly, for the Bremagni girls had very clever hands and lips, and had taught him a great deal in the friendly twilight of Millefleurs. "I understand."

Henceforth, he conducted himself with far more restraint.

Meanwhile, as July wound toward its conclusion, the king's business moved forward as well. Early August found the two kings' respective legal teams concluding the final details of the marriage agreement, to the satisfaction of all parties. The wedding itself was set for spring of the new year, on the first day of May, at King Meyric's winter palace at Rémigny— something of a delay, but a royal wedding of this magnitude would require many preparations.

But meanwhile, the formal betrothal could now proceed, as legally binding as an actual marriage, to be solemnized two days hence at the king's chapel at Millefleurs.

The summer day dawned bright and sunny, like so many in this part of the world. Alaric and Paget had already helped pack up the king's belongings, for they would be sailing for Gwynedd on the morrow, but it had fallen to Alaric to lay out the king's attire for the betrothal ceremony: snug black breeches, low boots, and a new linen shirt sewn by Jehane's ladies and embellished with blackwork embroidery along the collar and cuffs by Jehane herself.

"It's their custom here, to dress simply for the betrothal," Alaric said to Paget, when the latter muttered that the King of Gwynedd should have more lavish attire for this important day. "I'm told we're to save the state finery for the wedding itself, when it's cooler. He won't even wear a crown today."

"It *is* warm, I'll give you that," Paget conceded. "Still, it seems like there should be *something* to set him apart."

"I suppose it's what comes of marrying in a foreign land," Alaric replied, as the king came into the room, fresh from the bath. "Different customs. Will you dress now, my lord?"

"Well, I can't go down to the ceremony wearing only a towel, now can I?" the king replied, with a boyish grin. "I suppose that must wait until the wedding night."

The two squires chuckled along with the king, who obviously was in high spirits, and helped him don the requisite attire. Brion ran an appreciative finger along the embroidered cuff of one sleeve and smiled, then buckled on his white knight's belt and sat so that Paget could comb his hair and tie it back with a white silk ribbon. The Eye of Rom gleamed in his right earlobe, and he clasped a silver bracelet to his left wrist before handing the sheathed Haldane sword to Alaric.

"I suppose I'm ready," he said, giving himself a last look up and down. "Shall we go and meet my bride?"

Very shortly, the two squires were escorting the king down to the palace gardens, and thence to a grassy clearing before a pretty garden chapel. Princess Jehane's brothers and sisters were already present, supporting the flower-twined poles of a canopy of sky-blue silk that had been erected before the steps to the little chapel. The king's knights and a small guard of honor stood to one side, and a like number of Bremagni courtiers opposite. Beyond the canopy, in stark contrast to the other guests, four tight-lipped religious sisters in black habits and veils eyed the assembled company with prim disdain.

A murmur of excitement rippled through the assemblage as the three foreigners approached, Brion in the lead. He nodded to the sisters, to Jehane's siblings, as he took a place to the right of the canopy, standing with hands clasped behind his back, looking a trifle impatient. His two squires took up positions slightly behind him, Alaric still bearing the sheathed Haldane sword.

Paget suppressed a grimace and glanced at Alaric, raising an eyebrow in question as he slightly jutted his chin in the direction of the sisters.

Alaric averted his eyes and whispered out of the side of his mouth, answering the unasked question.

"From the princesses' convent school, I think. I wonder if they don't approve of the marriage."

"By their faces, I wonder if they much approve of *anything*," Paget countered, though he fell silent as a dozen more sisters filed into place opposite the original four, wearing long white linen cloaks over their black habits, softly singing a psalm of praise.

"Jubilate Deo, omnis terra, servite Domino in laetitia. . . ." Sing joyfully to God, all the earth, serve ye the Lord with gladness. . . .

The assembled courtiers opposite the canopy settled and parted before a tall, distinguished-looking man in a white cope over pristine clericals, accompanied by a pair of candle-bearing acolytes and two deacons, one holding the Gospel aloft and the other bearing a portable desk. His handsome silver hair was pulled back in a ribbon, in a style not unlike Brion's, but he also wore a prelate's purple skullcap, and an amethyst on his right hand: almost certainly, the Archbishop of Bremagne, Alaric guessed. Looking at him, Alaric suppressed a shiver of antipathy, for he sensed that this man would not take kindly to a Deryni being so close to the man his princess was promising to marry. Instinctively he drew back a little as the king moved forward to shake the archbishop's hand, also bowing to kiss the prelate's ring, then moved aside in readiness.

The choir finished their psalm, the archbishop gave a brief blessing, then the choir began to sing the *Magnificat*, a canticle in honor of the Blessed Virgin.

"Magnificat anima mea Dominum, et exsultavit spiritus meas in Deo salutary meo. . . ." My soul doth magnify the Lord, and my spirit hath rejoiced in God my saviour. . . .

After the first line, a set of double doors parted to reveal Princess Jehane on the arm of her father, both of them clad all in white. The king wore his crown, but Jehane's head was bare, her auburn hair falling loose to her hips befitting a maiden, the fronts caught back in tiny braids and secured low on her neck with a single creamy rose.

Both squires caught their breath as the pair passed nearby, for Jehane was breathtaking. Her green eyes blazed, wholly focused on Brion as she and her father made their way under the canopy. Brion himself looked spellbound as the archbishop took Jehane's right hand from that of her father and placed it in the right hand of her intended spouse. The king moved back. Then, when the *Magnificat* had ended, the archbishop signed himself in blessing and intoned:

"In Nomine Patris, et Filii, et Spiritus Sancti. . . ."

"Amen," came the ragged response.

"Beloved children of God," the archbishop continued, "we are come here before God and one another to witness the betrothal of this woman, Jehane Julienne Adélaïde de Besançon, Princess of Bremagne, with this man, Brion Donal Cinhil Urien Haldane, King of Gwynedd and Prince of Meara."

Receiving the jeweled Gospel book from its deacon, he held it before the princess, who laid her right hand upon it.

"Jehane Julienne Adélaïde, before God and these witnesses, do you promise and covenant to contract honorable marriage with Brion Donal Cinhil Urien, here present, on the first day of May next, according to the rites of Holy Mother Church?"

Jehane's head dipped in agreement as she glanced aside at Brion with a smile. "I do so promise and covenant, so help me God."

As she removed her hand, the archbishop shifted the Gospel book before Brion, who likewise laid his hand upon the jeweled cover.

"Brion Donal Cinhil Urien, do you promise and covenant to contract honorable marriage with Jehane Julienne Adélaïde, here present, on the first day of May next, according to the rites of Holy Mother Church?"

Brion turned a rapt gaze upon the woman at his side as he said, "I do so promise and covenant, so help me God."

Bowing to the couple, the archbishop passed the Gospel to the deacon who had carried it in, then summoned forward the one with the portable desk, who presented the actual betrothal contract for signing. When both parties had affixed their signatures, and the archbishop had witnessed the document with his own, he turned to King Meyric and held out his hand.

It apparently was not the custom in Bremagne for the groom alone to give a betrothal ring; nor had Brion been allowed to supply the ring of his choice. As Alaric watched, the archbishop held two rings aloft, one of gold and one of silver.

"May these rings be blessed and sanctified, that they may be a visible reminder of the promises here spoken. *In Nomine Patris, et Filii, et Spiritus Sancti, Amen.*"

The archbishop then touched the ring in his right hand, a gold one, to Brion's forehead, then to Jehane's, then signed him with the cross, saying, "The servant of God Brion is betrothed to the handmaiden of God Jehane, in the Name of the Father, and of the Son, and of the Holy Spirit, Amen. The Servant of God Brion . . ."

Three times the archbishop repeated this formula, each time touching first Brion and then Jehane on the forehead before making the holy sign over Brion. He then did the same for the princess, first touching her forehead and then Brion's with the silver ring, before making the sign of the cross, each time saying, "The handmaiden of God Jehane is betrothed to the servant of God Brion, in the Name of the Father, and of the Son, and of the Holy Spirit."

He then placed the rings on their right hands—the silver one on Brion's and the gold one on Jehane's—and bade them join right hands again and raise them in the air, that all might see these signs of their commitment. The action reminded Alaric of the day he had watched the religious vows of one of his mother's friends at the Convent of Arc-en-Ciel, when he was a young boy. He supposed it had a similar meaning.

"So let it be witnessed," the archbishop said. "The servant of God Brion and the handmaiden of God Jehane are sealed to one another by the bonds of betrothal, and shall confirm this commitment on the first day of May next, in the sacrament of holy matrimony. In the name of the Father, and of the Son, and of the Holy Spirit."

"Amen," came the response of all present.

"Now bow down your heads and pray for God's blessing," the archbishop said, signing for the couple to kneel. "O Lord our God, who didst espouse the Church as a pure virgin, bless this betrothal"—he made the sign of the cross over the couple—"uniting these Thy servants, keeping them in peace and oneness of mind. For unto Thee belong all glory, honor, and worship, unto the Father, and unto the Son, and unto the Holy Spirit, now and for ever: world without end."

"Amen," again came the response, as all made the sign of the cross.

Festive floral crowns were then brought forward and placed upon both heads, and the archbishop invited the couple to exchange a holy kiss. The kiss was chaste, but Alaric could sense the fire only barely contained in both of the participants—a fire that smoldered in both pairs of eyes as the two parted and the assembled witnesses broke out in applause.

Chapter 38

"He that delicately bringeth up his servant from a child
shall have him become his son at the length."
—PROVERBS 29:21

THE king's ship departed on the morning tide, sailing directly north from Cinq-Eglise to make landfall at Point Kentar. The newly betrothed couple had pledged to write often, but it was understood that correspondence between the two kingdoms would become more difficult as weather worsened with the autumn, and all but impossible once winter set in.

The voyage home was uneventful. On their return to Rhemuth, the king and his party settled into the usual routine as summer gave way to autumn and preparation for winter. Alaric and Paget, now something of celebrities because of their foreign travel, were able to regale their fellow squires with descriptions of the Bremagni court at Millefleurs, and the beauty of the Bremagni girls, and also shared combat tips they had picked up in sparring with the Bremagni squires. Alaric had, indeed, grown inches during the summer's adventures, and had to request that the castle's seamstresses let the sleeves down on his shirts and tunics, and lengthen his breeches. Some even had to be replaced.

Late in September, with the king's permission, Alaric traveled to Morganhall for a week, to celebrate his twelfth birthday with his sister Bronwyn and his Aunt Delphine, as well as the small household Llion had gathered there to safeguard the holding for its young lord. The trip also offered an opportunity to meet Llion's young daughter, born during their absence.

They returned to court early in October to the news, received by courier, that the king's sister Xenia and her Torenthi husband were expecting a child in the new year. The queen delighted in the prospect of her first grandchild, though she missed her daughter, and Silke fancied being an aunt, but Brion, in private, proved less enthusiastic about the proposition.

"I knew it was likely inevitable," he told Llion and Jamyl over a pot of mulled wine that evening. "Xenia is young and healthy, and I expect that Sigismund has been an attentive and enthusiastic husband, but this means that he will get his Haldane heir."

"You could have forbidden the match," Jamyl pointed out.

"And have my sister disgraced?" Brion retorted. "I think not." He sighed. "But it's done now. Hopefully, my own marriage will soon prove fruitful, and we can secure the Haldane succession."

Llion nodded. "You do have Prince Nigel and Duke Richard still in the succession."

"That's true. It's the principle. I don't like the idea of a Haldane heir in the clutches of Torenth."

"Arkadia is less Torenthi than some parts of the kingdom," Jamyl observed. "It could have been a prince of the more immediate Furstán line who captured your sister's fancy."

Brion let out his breath with a huff. "Let's hope it's a girl."

"Aye, but *her* son could eventually try to press a claim," Jamyl countered.

"Hopefully, that will never become a problem," Llion said. "And you do have your own marriage to look forward to."

"Yes, I do," Brion said, with a wistful smile as he lifted his glass in salute.

ADVENT came and went, and the bustle of the St. Stephen's Day court on the day after Christmas. That day, as the king received petitioners on the cathedral steps for several hours, he also received the good wishes of citizens who had heard of the royal wedding to be celebrated in May.

Paget Sullivan was knighted at that Twelfth Night court, with his father presenting him and Alaric assisting with the spurs. The archbishops of both Rhemuth and Valoret were in attendance, with Cornelius Seaton in the latter's party, now wearing the livery of his uncle the archbishop and the white belt of a knight.

"When did *he* get knighted?" Alaric muttered to Paget after the ceremony.

Paget shook his head. "I don't know, but I'll find out."

Later, when the new honorees had settled down to table with their families, he beckoned Alaric to his side and reported that Cornelius apparently had been given the accolade at his uncle's Christmas court, by the visiting Earl of Eastmarch.

"I suppose it would have been difficult for him to refuse," Paget concluded.

Alaric snorted. "I suppose. One has to wonder what he was doing in Valoret in the first place."

"More to the point," Paget muttered, "I wonder how de Nore persuaded him to knight his twit of a nephew."

Alaric bit back a smile. "He *is* a twit, isn't he? Handy enough with a sword, but I guess you can get away with being a bully, when your uncle's the archbishop." He glanced around with exaggerated innocence. "But you didn't hear me say that—because I'm still just a lowly squire. You, on the other hand—" He grinned and dunted Paget playfully on the bicep. "You can call him whatever you like, because you've also had the accolade now. And you've also had the benefit of training in Bremagne as well as with Duke Richard. You could certainly take him in a fair fight—and probably in a brawl as well!"

Paget had the grace to look self-conscious, if pleased, and clapped Alaric on the back before turning to scan the hall. "Thank you for that, but I'd best get back to my da. He and some of the neighbors are finding scats. Come and chat, later. I know you met him briefly before the ceremony, but he's eager to actually talk to you. I think he likes Deryni." He gave Alaric a wink. "Can't imagine why."

Alaric shook his head and was smiling as he made his way back to the high table, to serve the queen and Princess Silke. They kept him busy enough with squiring duties for most of the evening, so he mostly managed to avoid even looking in the direction of the two archbishops, who were seated at the far end of the high table.

As for the insufferable *Sir* Cornelius, who with his father was standing watchful attendance on his uncle the archbishop, Alaric did catch Cornelius glaring at him several times, full of his own importance and apparently incensed that the former royal page was now a royal squire serving the royal ladies—and was ignoring his glares. But that royal service also insulated Alaric from any direct contact with Cornelius, which he counted as a blessing. Time enough, when Alaric was grown, to put an end to Cornelius's bullying—if it even still mattered by then.

Happily balancing the ill will of his former nemesis was the kindness of Paget's family. After the feast was mostly over, the new knight's father, Sir Evan, made a point of thanking Alaric for the friendship shown to his son during their years at court.

"Truth be known, I've found Deryni little different from any other man, when it comes to honor," he told Alaric, as the young squire topped up his cup. "I number several of them among my best clients, in Meara." He raised his cup to Alaric. "When you come to be seeking good horseflesh, I hope you will let me know."

Alaric inclined his head in thanks. "I shall keep that in mind, Sir Evan. Paget has told me of the fine horses he grew up with."

Sadly for Alaric, Paget departed for home several days later with his father and their Sullivan retainers who had come to witness his knighting, but he also took away his own copy of a work by Ulger de Brinsi on cardounet strategy that Alaric had commissioned as a knighting gift during his last visit to Coroth. Paget, in turn, presented Alaric with a finely tooled headstall for the horse Alaric promised he would eventually buy out of Arkella. Most important of all, Alaric knew that he and Paget would maintain their friendship as men. With Paget back in Meara, he would always find an ally there. For a Deryni, that was a great comfort.

FOR the remainder of the winter and into spring, Alaric settled back into his training. He grew several more inches, and the increased height and reach at last gave him the advantage he had been looking for, in hand-to-hand combat, though for a time his coordination suffered. The spurt of growth also necessitated alterations to the new set of squire's livery ordered for the royal wedding, since he would be accompanying the king to Bremagne.

But only a fortnight before the wedding party was to depart, while the king and a few of his favorite companions, including Alaric, were out on a ride to enjoy the spring weather, a messenger arrived from the east with shattering news. The king returned in good spirits to find several of his senior advisors congregated on the great hall steps, looking very solemn, indeed.

"Sire, there has been ill news from Arkadia," Jiri Redfearn announced, catching at the king's bridle before he could even get down. "It's your sister Xenia. She has died in childbed!"

"Good God, no!" Brion had gone white, and nearly stumbled as he threw himself from the saddle, and Alaric rushed to follow. "Jiri, it can't be. What happened?"

"There was a long labor—several days, they say. She was too weak to survive. The child died, too—a daughter."

Looking stricken, Brion followed Jiri through the great hall and into the withdrawing room, where Duke Richard was comforting Queen Richeldis and the weeping Princess Silke.

"I don't understand how this could have happened," he said to Richard, as he came to embrace his mother and remaining sister. "She was young, healthy. . . ."

"It is my fault," the queen said emphatically, drawing back to wipe at her tears. "I never should have insisted that she marry that—that Torenthi seducer! And to have her lie now with his kin, among strangers. . . ."

"It is not your fault alone, *Maman*," Brion whispered. "I, too, insisted on the marriage."

"Well, I want her brought back!" Richeldis declared, drawing herself up resolutely. "I want her body returned, and that of her child—my daughter and my only grandchild!"

Richard sighed. "Richeldis, we cannot just go barging into Torenth and make demands."

"Perhaps *you* cannot," she countered, "but *I* can—and I *will*, if I must. I think it unlikely that Count Sigismund would refuse a mother who seeks to bring her child home—especially a queen."

"Mother—" Brion began.

"I will not discuss this further!" she said flatly, getting to her feet. "I should prefer an escort, but if no one will accompany me, I shall go alone!"

Later that evening, with the queen and Silke now gone to their apartments, the king and his uncle holed up in the withdrawing room with Jamyl, Llion, and a few of the king's other senior knights. Prince Nigel was with them, lamenting that he yet had a year before he could be knighted and help uphold his sister's honor. Food had been brought, with Alaric assigned to serve as their squire, but no one had much appetite. As he moved among them to fill the occasional cup, Alaric wished there were something he could do to ease the family's grief.

"The timing on this could hardly be worse," Brion muttered to his uncle. "I'm expected in Bremagne in only a few weeks, so I can't go; and I can't send you because I need you to serve as regent in my absence."

"I'll go!" Nigel offered, even though he knew it would not be allowed.

Brion shook his head. "Both of us can't be out of the kingdom at the same time. Besides, Uncle Richard will need you here."

"Well, your mother *is* determined to go," Richard said.

"I'm well aware of that. And I know better than to stand against a Haldane wife."

"Allow me the honor," Jamyl said quietly.

All three Haldanes looked at him in surprise.

"Allow me to accompany the queen to Arkadia," Jamyl went on. "She'll go anyway—you shan't stop her unless you lock her up—so if she goes, she should travel with a suitable escort."

Brion gave the young knight a tight-lipped glance. "You know I had thought to have you stand as my witness at my wedding," he said quietly. "If you go to Arkadia . . ."

"If I go to Arkadia, I cannot go with you to Bremagne," Jamyl replied. "I know that. But I *have* been to weddings before, Sire—even royal ones. Take Nigel as your witness, or Jiri."

"We've already established that Nigel should not be out of the kingdom at the same time as the king," Richard said quietly.

"Then choose someone else to serve as witness," Jamyl retorted. "Summon the Duke of Cassan; he is of suitable rank, and your friend, and would be honored to so serve you. Or take Jiri, or Tiarnán. But I think I will better serve you by accompanying the queen."

Brion averted his gaze briefly, but Alaric saw the tears the king struggled to suppress.

"Sire, if I may speak?" he said quietly. At the king's gesture of assent, he went on. "Sire, it is clear that an expedition into Arkadia will take many weeks, perhaps months—and you are needed elsewhere, whatever your heart might wish otherwise."

"Your point?" Brion said impatiently.

"Send the recovery party by way of Lendour, and then northward through the Cardosa Pass. If Sir Jamyl is to be your envoy, he can pick up additional men at Cynfyn. Many of my Lendour men know that area of the borders very well. We could enlist the assistance of my brother-in-law, Sir Jovett Chandos, and some of his knights. From Cardosa, it should be an easy enough ride on to Arkadia."

"Your Earl of Lendour makes a great deal of sense," Richard said to Brion, with an approving glance at the squire. "And Lendour knights would certainly make a suitable escort for the queen. Of course, that assumes that Count Sigismund agrees to return the bodies."

"And why would he not?" Jamyl retorted. "A Haldane bride was a prize; a Haldane child would have been a veritable treasure. Quite bluntly, I doubt he feels the same way about two Haldane corpses."

Brion had grimaced at the comment, but Jiri was nodding thoughtfully.

"It could work, Sire. And I would suggest that you send the boy as well. Not into Torenth, of course," he added, with a nod toward Llion, whose mouth was opening to object, "but he and Llion know the Lendour men better than any of us. And I suspect that the queen would take comfort in their company." He glanced at Duke Richard. "Regarding the queen, will she be able for such a journey?"

Richard shrugged. "She has said she intends to go. And she is hardly an old woman. She is not yet forty."

"But she *has* borne six children," Tiarnán MacRae pointed out, "and she spends little time a-horse. It will not be an easy journey."

"No, but she clearly is determined to do it," Richard replied. He cocked his head at the king. "What say you, Nephew? I doubt you will change your mother's mind—and the weather favors such an endeavor for the next few months. Send a priest along with her, to underline the pious nature of the request. Sending her with Lendour men will also reassure the Arkadians that this is not a state matter, but a personal one on the part of Xenia's mother."

Brion sighed. "Very well. Alaric and Llion, you really are willing to accompany my mother? I had thought to have both of you at my wedding."

Llion smiled thinly and shrugged. "We serve the royal house, Sire. And this is the sort of service that dukes render to their lord." He jutted his head toward Alaric, who was listening eagerly. "Alaric will learn much from this mission, *even if he remains in Lendour*." He cast a pointed look at the boy. "And if I may, I should like to offer the services of my wife, Lady Alazais, to serve as companion to the queen," he added.

Richard snorted. "I know that Lady Alazais is fond of the queen, but she may not welcome that you have volunteered for her."

"Ah, but she has a sister in Lendour whom she sees far too seldom," Llion countered. "She is wife to Sir Jovett. Besides, most of the queen's usual ladies-in-waiting are—of somewhat more advanced years, and ill accustomed to the rigors of such a journey."

"Delicately put," the king said with a quirk of a smile. "But—is your wife not at Morganhall, with a young daughter?"

"She is, Sire," Llion replied, "but I can fetch her in less than a day. And my daughter will be in good hands with her aunt and the rest of the Morgan household."

"Then, it seems to be decided," Richard said, pushing back his chair. "I'll go and inform the queen. Brion, you probably should prepare a letter to Count Sigismund. And Llion, you'd best get yourself to Morganhall."

T HEY were ready to ride two days hence, a week before the king was to depart for Bremagne. Alaric had been excited to watch his offer of assistance be accepted by the king, and he was even more excited to be actually going along.

"You're sure you won't mind missing the wedding?" the king asked, as Alaric mounted up with the rest of the party forming up before the great hall steps. The boy was wearing brown riding leathers and a cloak of Corwyn green instead of his customary Haldane livery, and suddenly looked far older than his twelve and a half years.

Alaric smiled and shook his head. "No, Sire. As Sir Llion has pointed out, this is the sort of work I shall do for you as your duke. Besides, I get plenty of opportunity to witness court ceremony—and I've been to Bremagne. I suggest you take Ciarán as your squire, or the Redfearn twins. And take Princess Silke with you. It will give her something to think about besides the loss of her sister."

Brion glanced over his shoulder to where the black-clad princess was bidding a tearful farewell to her mother, likewise dressed all in black and already mounted on a black palfrey.

"Actually, I had already decided to take Silke along with me," he said. "She just doesn't know it yet. She's only a little younger than Jehana; they'll make good travel companions." He turned his gaze back to Alaric. "I do appreciate what you're doing, though. Just remember: you're not to go into Torenth. I cannot risk you there."

Alaric nodded. "I understand."

They soon were on their way, riding briskly eastward along the Mollingford road toward Lendour. Jamyl Arilan led the delegation, accompanied by Jiri and Llion. A priest also had joined the royal party: Father Creoda of Carbury, a solid and reliable cleric only recently attached to the royal household, who had helped negotiate Brion's marriage contract. Two additional knights brought up the rear: grizzled veterans of many a battle.

In the midst of them, and enduring the rigors of the road as well as any, was the Dowager Queen Richeldis, with Alazais as her female attendant and Alaric as her squire. The queen said little during their first day out, but she seemed to gain heart after that, since she now was doing something to bring her daughter home. She and Alazais chatted easily to one another and to the priest, Father Creoda; and even Alaric was sometimes included in their conversations.

They spent the first two nights at roadside inns along the river, but when they approached the market town of Hallowdale, Llion directed their party in a wide detour around its outskirts.

"There is no suitable accommodation there," he said flatly, when the queen asked why they could not take lodging in the town. "We'll make camp in a field, farther along the road."

"But, I don't understand," the queen said. "How could there be no lodging in the town?"

"We shall camp where Sir Llion directs," Jamyl reiterated, his face as set as Llion's. "Bad things happened here, in the past."

That night, as Alaric sat beside the fire with Llion to eat their travel fare, he was well aware that the queen had drawn Alazais aside to ask about the town. Tight-chested, he ducked his head and tried not to remember what he had been told about Hallowdale, mouthing a prayer for the Deryni who had perished that day and would have no other memorial.

They pressed on the next morning, though the mood had turned more solemn. They traveled hard, to take advantage of the good weather and open roads. It soon became clear that the pace was taking its toll, especially on the women, who were ill accustomed to riding for days on end. But the queen never complained; nor did Alazais.

On the morning of the day they were to arrive at Cynfyn, the Lendour capital, Jamyl directed Alaric to take the lead, for these were his lands through which they rode. Llion had unfurled Alaric's Lendour banner beside him, and Jamyl carried the queen's banner: the royal arms of Gwynedd within a bordure of white roses. Alaric found himself sitting straighter as they rode, and even grinning from time to time, for this was a foretaste of the recognition that would be his when he was grown.

Just at noonday, still several hours out from Cynfyn, they stopped to let the horses blow. The queen and Alazais dismounted to walk out sore muscles for a few minutes, and Father Creoda also got down. Alaric sat his horse easily, automatically scanning the higher ground around them—and did a double-take as he spied two dark-clad riders gazing down on them, motionless against the sky.

Chapter 39

"That we henceforth be no more children, tossed to and fro . . ."
—EPHESIANS 4:14

LION and Jamyl noticed the riders in that same instant, but Alaric at once signed for them to stay where they were and gigged his horse ahead, where the pair began picking their way down the hillside to meet him. He sensed powerful shields in both men, but he knew one of them even before the man reached to pull down the black desert veil covering the lower part of his face. As the two drew rein to await his arrival, the second man uncovered as well, but Alaric did not recognize him.

"Sir Sé," he said uncertainly, also drawing rein.

"Well met, Earl of Lendour," Sé said, bowing slightly in his saddle. His formal greeting told Alaric that the Anviler knight likely was here on business, and that his companion possibly did not know the extent of their relationship. Both men were dressed in the stark black of their order, with mail at their throats, shields slung across their backs, and helms hanging at saddlebows.

"Our order has become aware of a service we might render for your queen in Torenth," Sé went on. "If that is permitted."

Alaric simply gaped at Sé for a beat, glad that he was here but uncertain how much he should say before Sé's companion. In any case, it appeared that the pair knew of their mission, and were offering to go into Torenth with them, to retrieve the bodies of Xenia and her dead child.

He glanced back at the others, wary faces upturned on the road below, the knights closely guarding the queen and Alazais, who were hastily remounting their horses. Llion would know to trust Sé, but the others?

"Thank you, Sir Sé," he said as he turned back to the pair. "Sir Jamyl Arilan has command of this expedition. The queen will wish to be consulted, but I think they would welcome the assistance of Knights of the Anvil. Will you join us, Sir . . . ?"

"I am called Savion," the stranger knight said by way of introduction, smiling slightly as he kneed his horse closer to reach across and clasp Alaric's forearm. "Sé speaks highly of you and your king. Please to make us known to Sir Jamyl and your queen."

During that brief contact, despite the muffling of gloves and sleeves and mail, Alaric felt the subtle probe of the other's mind, briefly testing at his shields. But he sensed no threat; nor did he think that Sé would have exposed him to danger.

With a nod of agreement, he backed his horse off a few steps and turned to lead the way back to the waiting party. Jamyl and Llion broke away from the others and came to meet them a little way ahead of the queen and Alazais and their very wary guards.

"Gentlemen," Sir Savion said, before any of them could speak. "Our order has become aware of your mission. We are sent to escort you into Arkadia, and to assist in negotiations."

Jamyl eyed the two with suspicion. "You have access to the Duke of Arkadia?"

Savion inclined his head. "We do. And I am confident that we can persuade His Grace that he takes no profit from retaining the bodies of the late princess and her child."

"Very well," Jamyl said flatly, drawing himself more upright in the saddle. "Come with us to Cynfyn. We plan to stage the venture from there. You can explain to us over supper just how you propose to assist us."

THE queen's unannounced arrival at Cynfyn sparked both excitement and consternation, for news of Princess Xenia's death had not yet reached the Lendouri capital. But when Llion had briefly informed Jovett and the seneschal, Sir Deinol Hartmann, of the reason for their presence, also presenting the two Anviler knights, Jovett immediately drew the men into the council chamber adjacent to the great hall to get down to business. Zoë and her mother-in-law took both the queen and Alazais into their charge and whisked them off to guest chambers for a quiet meal, hot baths, and soft beds. Alaric, acutely aware that he was forbidden to accompany the party into Torenth, took his place at the high table with Jovett's father, Sir Pedur, and supped with his Lendouri retainers, trying to be personable and mature while he fretted about how the meeting was progressing.

When Llion and the others came out, Llion summoned him to the quarters they were to share. The others were dispersing to various duties.

"Jovett is going to handpick a small party of escort knights to accompany us from here," Llion said, drawing Alaric into the window embrasure in the dim-lit room. "It was decided to give the women a day to rest, but then we'll ride northward along the river to cross the mountains at Cardosa."

"Couldn't I go with you as far as Cardosa?" Alaric asked. "That's still in Gwynedd."

Llion shook his head. "I don't think that's what the king had in mind, lad. You're better off here at Cynfyn—and then we don't have to worry about you."

Alaric considered trying to change Llion's mind, but he suspected that the order had actually come from one of the others. "What, after Cardosa?" he asked.

"There it gets trickier," Llion replied. "Once we cross into Torenth, provided we encounter no resistance, Sé says it will be several days' hard ride eastward to the Arkadian capital. With any luck, the duke will honor our request and we can be back on our way within a day or two."

"And Sé thinks this will work," Alaric said, less than convinced. "Do you really think they can persuade the Arkadians?"

Llion shrugged. "Well, they're all Deryni; you tell me. But if anyone can do it, I would place my bets on Sir Sé." He cocked his head. "Do you think there's something he isn't telling us?"

"I'm sure there are many things he isn't telling us," Alaric replied with a sour smile. "I'd like to know how he found out about this expedition. But I have to trust him because my mother trusted him. And Jovett grew up with him. I do wish I could go along, though."

"In a way, I wish it, too," Llion admitted. "But the king is right not to risk sending you into Torenth before you're grown. And I somehow don't think that Sé would go against the king's wishes in this."

"I suppose."

They turned in for the night shortly after that, but Alaric's sleep was restless. The next day, he joined in the preparations for the continued mission into Torenth, shadowing Jovett as he selected the men to go along, chose remounts to accompany the party, and organized supplies.

They supped early that evening, for Jamyl planned to set out at dawn the next morning. Accordingly, most of the principals turned in soon after.

Alaric, too, retired to his chambers, for Jamyl had given him leave to ride out partway with the queen's party. He was ready for bed, checking his equipment a final time, when Llion suddenly cocked his head in the direction of the door, then went to open it and admit Sé.

Alaric straightened as the black-clad Anviler knight entered the room and closed the door behind him. Rather than his riding leathers of earlier in the day, he wore the familiar high-necked black robe of his order, fastened at the shoulder. Only now did Alaric notice how grey Sé was becoming.

"Is anything wrong?" the boy asked quietly.

"Not at all." Sé motioned him to the bed. "It's time you were abed, though. Lie down and make yourself comfortable. Llion, please give us a moment."

As Llion went to one of the chairs before the fire and settled, head against the high back, Sé came to sit on the bed beside Alaric.

"I hadn't thought to teach you this for a while yet, but I think it may be warranted, under the circumstances." He reached into the neck of his robe to pull at a length of silver chain. "I'll need this back when I return, but you can use it in the meantime." A silvery medal emerged on the chain, which he pulled off over his head. Then he looped the chain over Alaric's head and set his fingertips to Alaric's temples. "Now, clear your mind and concentrate on my voice. . . ."

• • •

IN that same hour, elsewhere in the castle, another Deryni made similar use of a spell very like the one Alaric was learning. Jamyl Arilan had used the technique many times, and now focused outward to the man in the Camberian Council who was his customary contact when he could not himself be present for meetings.

There has been an interesting development, Jamyl told his contact. *Two Anviler knights have shown up in Cynfyn and offered to accompany us to Arkadia. The one is Sé Trelawney, but I don't recognize the other one. He calls himself Savion.*

The name is not familiar, came the reply, *but I shall make inquiries. I take it that they don't simply propose to accompany the queen's party. And one must wonder how they came to know of the expedition.*

Sé seems to keep track of young Morgan's comings and goings, Jamyl said. *And in this case, he seems to be looking out for Haldane honor.*

Young Morgan isn't going on the expedition, is he? came the somewhat anxious query.

No, the king has forbidden him to leave the kingdom, Jamyl replied. *He does plan to ride out with us in the morning; we're taking some of his Lendour men, after all. But I think Sir Llion will prevent him from following on.*

Well, do your own part to preserve Haldane honor, came the reply. *Meanwhile, I shall pass on this information to the Council.*

THE expedition departed early the next morning, as planned. Alaric rode with them as far as the river, along with Zoë, her father-in-law, and an escort of Lendour knights who would return with them. They watched at the ford as the queen's party headed northward toward Cardosa. Sé looked back and caught his eye as they turned, and nodded in unspoken agreement.

Riding back toward Cynfyn, Alaric had little doubt that Sé would succeed in his mission. He spent the return journey chatting with Zoë and Sir Pedur, who began acquainting him with developments since his last visit.

He passed the next week back at Cynfyn interacting with the men who held the castle for him, learning more of the responsibilities of each, sometimes sparring with some of them. Most days, he also spent time with his Chandos cousins, who adored him.

The firstborn, Kailan, was nearly nine, and Charlan a year younger, both of them active and inquisitive, very like their father Jovett and their mother Zoë. Their little sister, Alyce Maria, was only five, but did her best to keep up with the boys, and reminded Alaric of his own sister, Bronwyn. He hoped the two would meet, one day.

In the evenings, he presided over the high table with Sir Pedur and his wife, generally making himself available to the men and women who would be his future subjects.

But the waiting was tedious, with no real routine to occupy his time. He practiced with the squires and with some of the younger knights, and took his Chandos cousins out on rides about the countryside, also giving them pointers on riding and ring-tilting, but he had altogether too much time just to think, and to worry. He felt hopeful that with Sé along, the queen's request would prevail, but they were going into Torenth, where anything could happen. Not that Alaric was in any position to do anything about it. Pray, perhaps.

So with nothing to do regarding the queen's mission, he found his thoughts returning to the king. As the days passed, he imagined the king's festive ride downriver to Desse with his wedding party, the easy sail down the Eirian until they passed the southernmost point in Carthmoor, and then the cautious dash across open water to the Bremagne coast.

From there, they would have skirted the shore southward until they reached Rémigny, the Bremagni capital, where the royal bride awaited. He could not imagine that last part, because he had never been to Rémigny, but he had a vivid image in his mind of the king's beautiful and spirited bride.

Nor was he truly disappointed to be missing the royal wedding. As he had told the king, he had attended grand court occasions before. But this was the first time he could remember when the two of them had been so far apart, and for so long. It made him vaguely uneasy, though not for any specific reason he could articulate except that his father had made it clear that Alaric had an important destiny to fulfill with the king.

Nor was there anyone in Cynfyn with whom he could discuss such things, with Llion away. His Aunt Zoë might understand a little, and he knew he could trust her; but she was not Deryni, though she was married to one, and had been the closest of friends with Alaric's mother. He could only hope and pray that the king was safe and well, and that Llion and Sé and the others likewise were encountering no untoward difficulties.

So he counted off the days until Llion and Sé and the others were likely to return, and sometimes found himself fingering the medal Sé had left with him, rasping a thumbnail over the raised design and wondering where Sé had gotten it.

One side bore an equal-armed cross with smaller crosslets in the angles of the large cross; the other showed the haloed head of a saint. It could be just about any male saint—he had not thought to ask Sé at the time he was given charge of it—but he wondered whether it was meant to depict St. Camber, the patron of Deryni magic.

He supposed it was safe enough for a Deryni like Sé to wear it openly in the far eastern reaches of the Anvil of the Lord. Alaric had a St. Camber medal of his own back in Rhemuth, left to him by his mother, but he mostly refrained from wearing it because of the reactions it might provoke. Perhaps when he got back, if Sé's spell worked, Alaric could use his own medal in a similar fashion.

His waiting was rewarded a few nights later when, as he had for several nights before, Alaric lay down in his bed and settled into the receptive edges of trance the way Sé had instructed him, cupping the medal in his hand. He was on the verge of slipping into true sleep when he sensed Sé's touch in his mind.

Sé!

Nicely done, came Sé's response. *We have accomplished our mission, and all is well. We should be back to Cynfyn within the week.*

They gave up the bodies? Alaric asked.

They did. I shall tell you more when I see you.

This is excellent news. May I tell the others? He had an impression of amusement before the other responded.

Perhaps not the best of plans. While they do already know that you are Deryni, as am I, best not to flaunt your abilities. Some skills are best kept private.

Alaric immediately realized the wisdom of that advice, and sent his agreement.

I shall send a rider ahead when we are a day out from Cynfyn, Sé informed him. *Then you will have legitimate reason to know of our success, and to ride out to meet us. Until then, stand by each evening, as you have tonight, in case I have need to advise you further—though I do not anticipate such a need. We shall see you soon.*

With that, Sé ended the communication, with the wish that his student might sleep well. Alaric, for the first time since they had left, did sleep deeply and dreamlessly, and set about the next day's activities with renewed enthusiasm.

S EVERAL days passed without sign of the promised courier, but on the first day of June a lookout atop the castle wall announced the approach of a rider who, to Alaric's delight, proved to be Llion.

"They have the bodies," he called to Alaric and to Pedur Chandos and his wife as they met him at the gate, though Alaric already knew. "Everyone is well, and they'll be here in another day. I need a bed first, but we can ride out to meet them in the morning."

Llion declined to be drawn out by Sir Pedur and the other knights concerning exactly how the mission had been accomplished, pleading exhaustion; but when he had wolfed down a hasty meal and duly retired to the apartment that was his when in Cynfyn, Alaric went with him. There, Llion was more than willing to elaborate, at least to Alaric.

"I mayn't speak of this to anyone else," he said candidly. "In fact, I *cannot.* But as you might have supposed, Sé and Savion were largely responsible. Sigismund and even the duke seemed almost afraid of them. It makes me wonder what power the Anvilers have in the far east."

Alaric nodded thoughtfully. "I wish I knew more about them. But go on."

"There's little more I can say. The two stood flanking the queen while she made her request, saying not a word; the ducal court was silent. She appealed to the duke and his retainers as a grieving mother, and pointed out that, while she did not question Sigismund's grief, he had only known Xenia for a couple of years, while Richeldis had known her all her life."

Alaric shook his head in disbelieving admiration. "The queen is brave, I'll give her that. What did the Arkadians say, when she had made her case?"

Llion raised a droll eyebrow. "What do you think? When she had finished, Count Sigismund exchanged a glance with the duke, then nodded to the queen and said that he certainly would allow them to take the bodies back to Rhemuth.

"And that was it. With so many Deryni in the room, I suspect that there was a great deal more going on, but nothing that I could detect. And Sir Sé declined to comment, later on. That very afternoon, we were escorted to the cathedral and told to wait beside a new wagon that the duke provided. Sé and Savion accompanied Sigismund and a party of Arkadians inside, and they shortly emerged with a brightly painted coffin that was loaded onto the wagon. We left that very afternoon. It was as if they couldn't get us out of there fast enough."

"Or couldn't get Sé and Savion out of there fast enough," Alaric muttered. "I wonder what was threatened."

"I have no idea," Llion replied. "And I'm not certain I want to know."

"You said one coffin; I assume the baby was buried with Xenia?"

"So I assume. But I can't imagine that Sé didn't check to make sure."

"No, he would have checked," Alaric replied. "In any case, it will be good to meet up with them again tomorrow."

E and Llion departed just after dawn with an honor guard of fresh troops to escort the queen and her daughter, and met the royal party a few hours out from Cynfyn. That night, the coffin rested in the castle's chapel, where the queen summoned the household and asked Father Creoda to lead them in prayers for the deceased. Before Alaric could join the others, Sé quietly drew him apart. Savion was waiting in the yard with their horses, so Alaric knew the conversation would be brief.

"I imagine you'll want your medal back," he murmured, pulling its chain from beneath his tunic and taking it off.

"Thank you, I do." Sé closed the medal and chain in his hand and nodded to Alaric. "You did well—and you learn very quickly. You should find this skill useful in the future. And I am glad we were able to serve the queen in this way."

Alaric gave the Deryni knight a faint smile. "I don't suppose you're ever going to tell me how you managed to persuade the duke to let Xenia go."

"I don't suppose I am." Sé's answering smile confirmed that further questioning would be pointless. "But, time enough for such matters when you're grown," he went on, laying a hand on Alaric's shoulder in farewell. "For now, I am well pleased with your progress." His hand tightened momentarily on Alaric's shoulder, then released him. "God keep you, my young friend. Until next time."

With that, he was striding into the night and the torchlight near where Savion waited with the horses, to quickly disappear into the night.

T HE recovery party lingered at Cynfyn for two days more, to allow the queen and Alazais to rest, for they had learned on their return that there now was no reason to hasten back to the capital. In Alaric's absence, a messenger had arrived with word that the king was returned to Gwynedd with his new wife, who had entered Rhemuth at the center of a grand procession that wound its way up to the cathedral for a blessing of the couple and the crowning of Gwynedd's new queen, who had taken the Gwyneddan form of her name at her coronation: Jehana.

"Too late to worry about that now," the old queen said to Jamyl, on hearing the news. "Sadly, we have missed that celebration—and my return with the body of the king's sister will hardly be cause for the same kind of rejoicing. Meeting my new daughter-in-law can wait a few more days."

Alaric knelt with them for prayers that last evening, remembering the departed Xenia, only a few years older than himself, and mourning her sacrifice on the altar of political expediency. Alaric's grandfather Keryell and his Uncle Ahern lay beneath the floor here at Cynfyn: two Deryni earls to guard the dead princess. Alaric had never known either of them, but his mother had told him of the legacy they had left him. Before God, he vowed to be worthy of that legacy, and to serve the king to the best of his ability.

Chapter 40

"Ye have condemned and killed the just . . ."
—JAMES 5:6

T HEY departed for Rhemuth the next day, along with Sir Jovett and half a dozen of his knights who had assisted in the mission into Torenth. Thanks to the industry of Zoë and her mother-in-law during their absence, all in the party wore black mourning bands on their sword arms. Xenia's brightly painted coffin bore a black pall, now dusty from their journey. The horses pulling the funeral wagon sported black plumes in their headstalls.

The night before they were to reach Rhemuth, Jamyl sent a fast courier ahead to inform the king of their coming, and their success. The next day, just at noon, they approached the city walls and eastern gate to be met by an honor guard of Haldane lancers, with black crape banding their sword arms and more black fluttering from their lances.

The lancers formed up to either side of the gate, dipping their black-pennoned lances in salute as the wagon bearing their dead princess passed between their ranks. The king and his bride of only a few weeks awaited their arrival just before the gates, along with his remaining sister, his brother, and his uncle, all of them in blackest mourning. Both sovereigns wore their crowns, but no other adornment. As the cortege approached them, the dowager queen rode out from the rest and urged her mount toward her son, with Jamyl and Alaric closely following. She nodded to Brion and then to Jehana as she drew rein.

"We have returned with your sister and her child," she said to her son, head held high. "And dear Jehana, I am so sorry not to have been here to welcome you, but it did not seem fitting that a Haldane princess should lie in a foreign grave. When you are become a mother, you will understand."

"I do understand, madame," Jehana said softly, with a deep bow in the saddle. "The king was wise to send you on this mission. Who better than a mother, to appeal to those who kept her?"

"I did *choose* to go," Richeldis replied archly, with an inclination of her head. "My son did not *send* me. But you are right that he was wise not to try to stop me." Smiling, she leaned across to gently clasp Jehana's forearm. "You will learn these things in time, my dear. It is ill advised to stand between a queen and her children." She cast a weary smile at her other two children, at Nigel and Silke silently sitting their horses, then returned her attention to her eldest son.

"I hope our arrival will not dampen the joy of your wedding festivities. I ask only that your sister be accorded the honors due her royal status, so we may lay her to rest with her kin."

"Arrangements have already been made," Brion replied. "The archbishop will come to the palace tomorrow morning to consult with you regarding your wishes." He turned his attention to Jamyl, waiting attentively at the dowager queen's side. "And thank you for your services, Sir Jamyl. It cannot have been easy."

Jamyl only inclined his head in acknowledgment, as did Alaric, when the king nodded to him. His inclination was to say nothing of the assistance they had received from Sé and Savion, for he did not know how much Jamyl was prepared to tell. Jamyl seemed not to have any problem with Deryni, but would he protect Sé?

For now, though, that hardly mattered, because the king was kneeing his horse aside to allow the wagon catafalque to precede him.

Men with muffled drums fell in ahead of the wagon, beating out a slow march. Just inside the gates, a crucifer and thurifer and a score of green-robed monks from the cathedral chapter joined the procession, intoning prayers for the dead princess and her infant daughter.

The somber sounds accompanied them as the cortege made its slow way through the city and into the castle yard, where eight black-clad knights waited to carry the coffin into the chapel royal. There it would lie overnight to allow members of the royal household to pay their respects, before being transported back to the cathedral for a state funeral.

They buried Xenia and her daughter two days later, following a solemn Requiem Mass celebrated by the archbishop to commemorate her short life and that of her child. They laid her to rest in the cathedral crypt, beneath a ledger stone beside the sarcophagus that held the body of her father, King Donal, and near the bodies of brothers and sisters who had died before her. Alaric and Llion attended with the others involved in the recovery of the body, given an honored place near the family mourners.

Dinner that night was subdued, to no one's surprise. Alaric attended the old queen and Princess Silke, as he had for several years now, and the Redfearn twins continued their attendance on the king and his new queen.

Afterward, Prys and Airey followed Alaric to his quarters and there proceeded to tell him of their adventures of the past several months, and the latest gossip at court. The pair had become quite smitten with their new royal mistress during the wedding festivities in Bremagne and the journey home, as were the other squires and pages at court, and Alaric soon found himself quite prepared to let himself get caught up in their adulation for the new queen.

"She's beautiful and kind, and she likes to hunt . . . ," Airey said dreamily.

"Aye, and she loves to dance," Prys chimed in. "Her ladies are organizing dancing lessons for the squires and pages—and the knights, too, if they want to come. She brought about eight ladies, you know, and most of them are young and beautiful!"

Alaric, remembering what he had seen of the court at Millefleurs, could certainly believe that. He hoped the pretty Fallonese girl was not among them, though. She would be a complication he definitely did not need. For now, celibacy seemed by far the best choice.

"She's brought a couple of sisters, too," Airey added. "Religious ones, you know. You'll see them around, looking like crows in their black habits. I don't know what order, but they seem awfully somber, even though they're young. Well, one's young. The other is, well, older. Mathilde and Clemence, they're called."

"And there's a young priest, too," Prys chimed in. "His name is Father Aimone. I think he's sort of Llion's age, but he seems very strict. He says Mass for the new queen and her household every morning, first thing. I think he'd like all the squires and pages to attend, too, at least the ones who serve the queen, but Duke Richard says that isn't necessary for future knights. He says once a week is enough."

"I'd keep a low profile, if I were you," Airey said. "I don't think he much likes Deryni."

Alaric mostly listened to all of this information, and resolved to keep an open mind and decide for himself about the new queen's household.

Meanwhile, once Jovett and his knights set out for Cynfyn, the day after Xenia's funeral, Alaric tried to settle back into what had become the new normal. Llion escorted Alazais back to Morganhall to visit their daughter, but returned after only a few days, ready to resume his duties.

Training of the squires and pages continued, for Duke Richard still was in charge of that, but the king seemed sometimes preoccupied, seen often in the company of his new bride on long rides through the countryside, strolling in the gardens, sometimes simply disappearing for hours at a time in his apartments.

In the lengthening summer evenings, Alaric found himself continuing to serve the old queen, now partnered with a pair of younger pages whose diffidence told him that they were well aware of who and what he was. And while Airey and Prys continued to be friendly to him, some of the other squires had become more reserved.

"They're jealous because you got to go on the mission to Torenth," Airey told him.

"But I didn't go to Torenth; I only went to Lendour, my own county."

"You still were treated like a man," Prys replied. "They're still whacking at pells and sweating in the practice yard."

"But, so am I. So is Prince Nigel, so is the king."

"That's true," Airey admitted. "But you still got to go on a real mission, doing important work."

"That's because they needed my Lendour men," Alaric said. "Once we got to Cynfyn, they picked up a Lendouri escort and I got left behind with my cousins and my sister."

"But you did get to go to Cynfyn," Prys insisted.

Alaric could only sigh and shake his head, for the pair did not yet understand what Alaric himself was fast learning: that even nobles sometimes were called upon only to wait.

The king's attitude and behavior also were somewhat different, now that he was a married man. Alaric had expected some changes, but some of them still surprised him. The royal couple usually dined in the great hall with the court, presiding over divers entertainments and dancing into the darkness, but sometimes they took their meals in their apartments while Duke Richard presided with the dowager queen. Alaric was assured by Llion that this was normal behavior for newlyweds, but he missed some of the personal time he had spent with the king before.

Owing to the death of Princess Xenia, the king's birthday court was somewhat subdued that year, even with a new queen at his side, but the associated tournament was held as scheduled. Alaric duly attended, setting rings for the pages and squires and handling lances. And he squired for the king when he took to the field to demonstrate his prowess before his new wife. But he decided he would not ride against the other squires this time.

"You could best most of them, you know," Llion said, "even the ones nearly ready for knighthood."

"I probably could."

"Then, why not compete?"

"Well, let's just say that I prefer to lie low for a while."

"Because . . . ?"

"Because since we returned, I've sensed . . . some resentment, that I was allowed to help lead the recovery mission. Airey and Prys have noticed it."

"But you did *not* go with the king to his wedding," Llion pointed out.

"No, but I was sent on a very adult mission. It's true that they were my men being used, and that I was only providing the assistance appropriate from the Earl of Lendour, but there have been some remarks among a few of the older squires."

"From whom?"

"I'd rather not say."

Llion let out a heavy sigh. "I appreciate your discretion, but I think Duke Richard should be aware of such behavior."

"I can handle it, Llion."

"I'm sure you can. But I hope you aren't thinking to use your powers to do it."

"I won't do that."

"You're certain?"

Alaric shrugged and bit back a grudging grimace. "I won't do anything. At least nothing *overt*."

"See that you don't," came Llion's curt reply.

N O provisions were made that summer for Alaric to visit his lands of Corwyn or Lendour, for he had returned only recently from Lendour, and had spent time in Corwyn the previous year. Instead, late in July, he rode to Morganhall with Llion, for a brief outing that could incite no further resentment among his fellow squires, who likewise were allowed visits home during the summer months.

During their six weeks away from the capital, he and Llion also rode up to Culdi to visit Alaric's McLain cousins, taking Bronwyn with them. Kevin, now sixteen, had recently returned from more than a year at the court of the Duke of Claibourne, squiring for Duke Ewan and honing his fighting skills against Ewan's northern knights. Duncan was still at home, continuing his military training with his father's knights but also studying with his tutors and thinking increasingly about a priestly vocation.

"I'm only thinking about it," he told Alaric, during one of their private conversations up on the roof leads one night. "I'm only a second son, so I don't have to worry about one day inheriting a title and responsibilities. And there's this pull, this yearning toward . . . I'm not sure what. But I do know that when I'm at prayer, or even just sitting in the chapel by myself, I'm . . . more than content. Father Geordan and I talk."

"But he doesn't know what you are," Alaric said softly. "You know it's forbidden for our kind."

Duncan shrugged. "Those are the laws of men, not God's law. There used to be Deryni priests. Somehow, I don't think God cares about such restrictions. Do you really think that He would reject the service of a Deryni priest whom He has called to His service?"

"I would hope not," Alaric replied. "But be careful, Duncan."

Meanwhile, Alaric joined in the training regimen set for Kevin and Duncan, made that much more challenging by the addition of Tesselin as a weapons master and sparring partner. Alaric fought matches against all three during his stay in Culdi, and acquitted himself well.

"That was very well fought," Duke Jared told him, after watching a particularly intense exchange with Kevin, who was three years older, and nearly a head taller. "You're fighting well beyond your age. Who has been your sword-master of late?"

Alaric pulled off his helm and accepted the towel Jared handed him with a nod of thanks. "Well, Duke Richard, of course, and Llion. But I also spent time in Coroth and in Bremagne last summer, training with their squires and even with some of their knights. And remember that I was in Cynfyn for nearly a month, earlier this year. I've learned, by dint of many a bruise, that there are vast differences in fighting styles, when one goes outside Rhemuth."

"Well, all that exposure to different training serves you very well," Jared replied. "If I may, I should like to send Kevin to Coroth for a season. He's good, but one can always be better."

Alaric nodded. "He is certainly welcome at Coroth, for as long as he likes—or for as long as *you* like," he amended with a smile.

Jared also smiled, shaking his head. "You're sounding very grown-up," he mused. "Very like an earl, or even a duke. Travel becomes you. And the experience you had going to Cynfyn with the old queen certainly stood you in good stead."

Alaric had the grace to duck his head in appreciation. It was beginning to dawn on him that, at very nearly thirteen, perhaps he was nearly over the worst aspects of being treated like a child.

Certainly the news awaiting him and Llion when they returned to Morganhall was not for a child, and certainly not a Deryni child.

"*I require that both of you return to Rhemuth as soon as you receive this,*" the king's letter said, addressing Llion, "*and bring along an escort of knights from Morganhall to ensure your safety. There has been a disturbing development that may affect Alaric.*"

Nothing in the missive gave any clue as to what the threat might be, or why it was addressed to Llion rather than Alaric, but they left immediately for Rhemuth, taking along half a dozen of Alaric's household knights. When they arrived, the captain of the watch promptly escorted the pair to the king's withdrawing room, where pages brought a cold collation of bread and cheese and wine and then withdrew. Llion had begun pouring wine for both of them, and Alaric was carving himself a slab of cheese, but both of them came to their feet when Duke Richard came into the room, the king right at his heels. At their grim expressions, Alaric immediately lost all appetite.

"Sire?" Llion said carefully, looking to Richard as well.

"Sit," Richard said, himself taking a seat as Brion did the same. "And go ahead and eat, if you have the stomach for it, when you've heard the news. There has been . . . an incident up by Valoret."

"By Valoret?" Llion muttered. "Why do I have the suspicion that Archbishop de Nore is involved?"

"Because you're a very astute man," the king replied. "Tell them, Uncle."

Duke Richard allowed himself a heavy sigh. "Early in August, during an ordination ceremony at Arx Fidei Seminary, one of the new priests was discovered to be Deryni. Needless to say, he was immediately taken into custody by the ecclesiastical authorities."

"A Deryni priest!" Alaric breathed, stunned. "How, *discovered*?"

"No one knows," Richard replied. "The bishops would say that God revealed the man's true nature."

"What will happen to him?" Llion asked.

"Nothing good," Richard said. "Archbishop de Nore has convened a special ecclesiastical court in Valoret, where the man is being tried for heresy and defiance of the Laws of Ramos, which forbid Deryni to seek holy orders. If he is convicted, which seems certain, he will be executed."

Sickened to the point of nausea, Alaric could only stare sightlessly at his untouched food in shock, his mind churning with the implications. Only days ago, he and Duncan had been discussing this very subject, and Duncan had confided that he felt drawn increasingly to a priestly vocation of his own. But Alaric could never reveal that conversation to anyone in the room.

"They'll burn him won't they?" he whispered after a few seconds, trying to put from mind the stench of burnt flesh from all those years ago at Hallowdale.

"Aye, that does seem inevitable," Richard said. "Canon law is clear on the penalty, and the archbishop—well, I trust I needn't remind *you* why de Nore holds such an abiding hatred of Deryni. All apart from the Ramos laws."

"Because of my mother," Alaric managed to reply, looking up uneasily. "And that's why he hates me, in particular."

"Aye, but this is not about you," the king responded. "At least not directly. It's an ecclesiastical matter; and unfortunately, the archbishop is also Primate of All Gwynedd, and the last court of appeal in such cases. He will have seen this as a direct attack on the Church by Deryni, and will show no mercy."

"But—can nothing be done?" Llion asked.

The king shook his head. "Sadly, he *has* broken the law."

"Man's law, or God's?" Alaric said bitterly.

"Oh, man's law, to be sure," Richard replied. "But the Church is powerful, and the Laws of Ramos are still the laws of the land. It will take time and care to unravel them, especially so long as the people hate and revile Deryni."

"But that is for the future," the king said briskly. "I am also concerned that the public execution of a Deryni, condoned by the Church, may spark increased hostility to Deryni in general. That means that you will be even more under scrutiny than you have been. You have my protection, of course, but that is only effective if you stay close. And for God's sake, don't do anything that might draw attention to yourself."

"I understand, Sire," Alaric murmured with a nod.

THE next weeks were tense, as periodic reports trickled in regarding the trial proceeding in Valoret. Indeed, acts of reprisal against Deryni were already beginning to be reported, as news of the event spread outward from the cathedral city and outraged citizens went on the rampage, looking for Deryni to share the fate of the accused. Alaric learned that the young priest was called Jorian de Courcy, by all reports an able and pious student while in seminary, hailing from the mountain region bordering the Connait.

"De Courcy, de Courcy," Alaric heard Queen Richeldis murmur to the new queen over supper one night, while he was serving at the royal table. "I know that name. My late husband had a de Courcy on his great council for many years."

"Was he Deryni?" Queen Jehana asked, with an uneasy glance at Alaric.

"Oh, I don't think so," Richeldis replied. "But I believe there were de Courcys who served the Crown a century ago. I suppose there might have been Deryni blood there, though I've never heard about it. There was certainly never anything overt. And those de Courcys were always loyal to the Haldanes. Still, I doubt there is any connection with this unfortunate young man."

Alaric was called to help bring in the next course after that, and the discussion had turned to other topics by the time he returned.

But snippets of further information continued to surface at court, as the days passed. In early September, word arrived that, to no one's surprise, Jorian de Courcy had been condemned to death, though the bishops wished to continue his interrogation, in hopes that he might betray yet more Deryni of his acquaintance—for surely he must have had help, to infiltrate so close to the priesthood.

"Duke Richard said that they'll try to break his spirit next, even torture him," Llion reported to Alaric a few days later, after dining privately with the three Haldane princes. "They won't call it that, and they'll be careful to leave no marks on him, but since he has already been condemned, they can do to him whatever they like, in the name of preserving the purity of the faith. They'll want to learn more about how he got that close, to actually have hands laid upon him in ordination. And they'll want to know if there could be more Deryni in their ranks."

Alaric shook his head, sick at heart. Other than praying for the unfortunate Jorian, all he could do was keep up with his training, building his strength and skill against the day when the king's protection might not be enough. The other squires kept their distance, for the Deryni stigma

Alaric had always lived with was only reinforced by the ongoing rumors and speculation that were rife at court. He grieved for Jorian de Courcy, whom he had never met and now would never meet. But there was nothing he could do.

He turned thirteen at the end of September, though his natal feast was not the festive affair of previous years, spent in his own lands when possible. Alazais came down from Morganhall with Bronwyn and her own young daughter, to spend a few days with him and Llion, but Alaric knew he was poor company. Little was said publicly about a final disposition of Jorian de Courcy, but Alaric was aware that Jorian's eventual fate preyed on the mind of the king, who felt he dared not interfere with the rulings of the Church.

Word came at last that the execution would take place on the eleventh day of November, in the yard of the abbey school where he had been apprehended. The news made the coming event very real, far removed from the abstract notion of a judicial killing of a man who had done nothing except to obey the Word that called him to be a priest.

"They're really going to do it," the king said almost disbelievingly, when the messenger had delivered the official decree from Valoret.

"You knew they would," Duke Richard replied. "What made you think the outcome could be any different?"

Brion was shaking his head. "This shouldn't be. I've had inquiries made. From everything I've been able to learn, this Jorian de Courcy is a temperate, pious, and well-read young man who wanted only to serve God: precisely the kind of man we want in the priesthood.

"But they're going to kill him, in one of the most horrible ways yet devised. And do you remember what day that is, the eleventh of November? It's Martinmas, which is also the day that marks the beginning of slaughtering of animals for the winter." He snorted. "The slaughter of an innocent, more like."

But worse was to come, even before the execution day arrived. On the first day of November, the king and his uncle were signing and sealing correspondence in the withdrawing room, with the assistance of Prince Nigel and Alaric, when Jiri Redfearn intruded to report that a delegation from Archbishop de Nore was requesting audience with the king.

"How many?" the king demanded.

"Only two, Sire, but one is a bishop."

"Please tell me it isn't de Nore. . . ."

"No, Sire. He says his name is Seabert of Nyford," came the reply. "He mumbled the name of his companion, so I didn't catch it, but I wasn't about to give him the satisfaction of having me ask to repeat it. Appears to be another priest, though."

"Probably another of de Nore's staff, then." Brion sighed heavily. "Very well, I suppose I must see them, but I'll see them on my terms. Let them cool their heels for a little while. And meanwhile, here's what I want you to do."

Half an hour later, the king had changed his clothes for a stark black tunic, as had Duke Richard. He also had directed Jiri to summon Llion and Jamyl, whose younger brother had been a classmate of the doomed Jorian de Courcy and had witnessed his apprehension. All of them likewise had been instructed to put on black except for the two squires, Prince Nigel and Alaric, who stood uneasily to either side of the king in their crimson Haldane livery.

It was Sir Jiri who escorted the archbishop's envoys into the withdrawing room, where the king had seated himself on the only available chair, wearing the Eye of Rom in his right ear and a simple gold circlet set round about with cabochon rubies as big as a man's thumbnail, his sable hair scraped back severely in a warrior's knot.

"Sire, Bishop Seabert of Nyford and Father Gorony," Jiri announced.

Both men bowed, and the king inclined his head in perfunctory acknowledgment. Beneath their plain black working cassocks and traveling cloaks the newcomers were booted and spurred. The older of the pair clearly was the bishop, with an ornate pectoral cross gleaming on his breast. The younger man was slender and thirtyish looking, of middling height, altogether nondescript and benign in appearance. Brion thought he recognized him as one of de Nore's chaplains.

"Bishop. Father."

"Thank you for seeing us, Sire," the younger man said easily, with a slight inclination of his head. "I am Lawrence Gorony, chaplain to my lord Archbishop de Nore. He bids me confirm to Your Majesty that the

Deryni heretic Jorian de Courcy will undergo his purgation by fire on the eleventh day of this month." In the deadly silence, he paused to draw a leisurely breath.

"His Grace further wishes you to know that, while he does not oblige you to attend, this being a matter of Church discipline as well as civil law, he does order and require that the Deryni squire Alaric Morgan present himself on the eleventh day instant to witness the execution." His eyes flicked briefly to Alaric as he continued. "This is for the good of his immortal soul, and a demonstration of the fate awaiting any Deryni who attempts to defy Mother Church and the laws of this land."

As the king stiffened, and Alaric lifted his chin in defiance, Duke Richard broke in.

"The archbishop," he said icily, "does not 'order and require' *anything* of His Majesty or one of His Majesty's peers. You overstep yourself, priest, as does your master."

Gorony merely glanced aside at his companion and inclined his head slightly, stepping back half a pace, clearly deferring to the other's greater authority as the bishop closed a pale right hand over his pectoral cross, which also brought attention to his bishop's ring. Siebert was somewhat taller than Gorony, sturdily built but soft looking, with faded and thinning reddish hair, a long nose, and an abundance of freckles.

"Far be it from me to contradict a prince of the blood," Siebert said smoothly, "but Archbishop de Nore is Primate of All Gwynedd, and has the authority and duty to care for *all* the souls in his charge—even the tainted souls of the Deryni goats among his sheep." He briefly turned a disdainful eye on Alaric. "His Grace feels that witnessing the execution of a fellow Deryni with inappropriate aspirations will have a salutary effect on ensuring that said Alaric Morgan minds his own soul—such as Deryni may possibly *have* souls."

"Have a care, Bishop!" Llion warned, hand on the hilt of his sword.

"No, let be," Brion quickly said, lifting a restraining hand. "Since I have no intention of complying with the archbishop's *request*, we need not give it countenance."

"I would not presume to contradict my king," Siebert went on, "but this was not a mere *request* from His Grace; it was an episcopal directive, for the good of the Deryni boy's soul and yours, Sire. And if you accept it not, I am instructed to inform you that His Grace intends to exercise the full weight of his office to ensure that his directive is carried out."

"I trust that is not a threat, Bishop," Duke Richard said.

"Certainly not, Your Highness," Siebert replied. "Neither he nor I would presume to threaten our king. But he does wish me to tell you this." He returned his attention to the king. "If you refuse to order the boy to comply with his archbishop's directive, which is all for the regulation of his immortal soul, His Grace will be obliged to impose the penalty of excommunication, not only on him but on yourself, since Alaric Morgan serves you as squire, and you are responsible for all aspects of his conduct. And if it should come to pass that you remain still obdurate, interdict is not beyond—"

"I'll go!" Alaric blurted.

In the immediate silence produced by these two words, all eyes turned to Alaric Morgan.

"Forgive me, Sire, but I am well aware what happens when interdict is imposed. The people suffer greatly."

Siebert mostly controlled a prim and satisfied smile, sweeping his gaze disdainfully up and down Alaric's taut form, but the king lifted a restraining hand before the bishop could speak again.

"Uncle, please escort Bishop Siebert and Father Gorony to wait outside. The rest of you, please accompany them. I would have private converse with Lord Alaric."

Richard immediately moved to comply, followed by the others, but the king signed for Llion to remain. Not until the door had closed behind them did the king speak, beckoning Alaric closer.

"I cannot let you do this."

"Sire, I must."

"Alaric, it is a noble thing you are offering, to witness such an atrocity against one of your own people," the king said, "but I cannot ask you to do this."

"You are not asking me, Sire," Alaric said quietly. "I have decided that this is something I must do."

"Alaric—"

"No, Sire. Please do not try to dissuade me. Interdict is too big a price to pay, just to spare me witnessing something unpleasant."

" 'Unpleasant,' " Brion repeated. The king stared at him for a long moment, then inclined his head in acceptance, though the royal lips were pressed tightly together.

"Very well." He nodded to Llion. "Bring the others back in."

Bishop Siebert and Gorony duly filed back into the room, followed by the rest. Alaric remained standing beside the king, where Llion also took up his station.

"Tell your archbishop," the king said without further preamble, "that I will allow what he has requested. But it is only because *my* Duke of Corwyn has agreed to do it. And make no mistake: Alaric Morgan *is* the Duke of Corwyn, even though he has not yet attained his legal majority. Because of that, selected members of my court, suitable to his rank, will be allowed to accompany him. And if any harm comes to *any* of them, I shall regard it as an act of treason against my crown."

Siebert inclined his head slightly. "I remind Your Majesty that the Abbey of Arx Fidei is a place of religious sanctuary. Any who pass through its gates are guaranteed the protection of the Church."

"A singular reassurance to Jorian de Courcy, I am sure," the king muttered.

"Indeed." Siebert's expression was one of distaste. "But I am obliged to point out that de Courcy is a convicted heretic, a mocker of the law of God, as well as being Deryni." He glanced contemptuously at Alaric. "I trust that the Deryni Duke of Corwyn will comport himself appropriately, while under our protection."

"The Duke of Corwyn is a faithful son of the Church," Brion said. "I shall send one of my chaplains with him, to attest to that."

"Then, you need not fear for him, my lord," the bishop said, and inclined his head in leave-taking before turning to withdraw with his companion.

Chapter 41

"God hath delivered me to the ungodly, and turned
me over into the hands of the wicked."

—JOB 16:11

THE day appointed for the execution came far too soon. Two days before, Alaric made the journey to Valoret with Llion, Father Creoda, and Jamyl Arilan at the head of a small escort of Haldane cavalry. During the ride, a troubled Jamyl confided that his younger brother was a seminarian at Arx Fidei, and had been present when Jorian de Courcy was discovered.

"All the seminarians were shocked," Jamyl said. "Morale at the school is dismal; they still have not recovered. And all of them will be required to witness the execution. It makes one wonder how God could be present through all of this, and allow this to happen."

"Unfortunately," Father Creoda said, "God's laws and man's laws do not always coincide. But He is always present, even in the midst of adversity, and He will surely be with Father Jorian."

When Alaric said nothing, Creoda added, "He will be with you as well, young Morgan, and with all the young men at Arx Fidei."

"And what of the bishops?" Alaric muttered. "Does God condone what they are doing?"

Creoda shrugged. "We cannot know God's mind, my son. He gave us free will for a reason, even if we do not always understand it. But surely He will be with the bishops, in hopes that their hearts may soften, in the end."

"Enough to help Jorian?" Alaric retorted.

Creoda sighed and shook his head. "Probably not. But Jorian will not be alone when he leaves this life. This I know."

Alaric wished he could be as sure. But perhaps Creoda's prayers could ease Jorian's anguish. At least Jorian could have one priest praying for his soul.

They stayed the night before at a manor house belonging to one of the king's barons, not far from where the execution was to take place. Martinmas dawned clear and crisp, with hardly a hint of the chill of the coming winter. Alaric dressed all in black for the day, with a black cap covering most of his bright hair and a hooded black cloak further obscuring his identity. In a private act of defiance, he wore his mother's St. Camber medal under his tunic, along with his father's Lendour signet on its chain.

Llion and Jamyl likewise had donned stark black, unrelieved by even their knight's belts, though under their cloaks both men wore long dirks thrust through the backs of their belts, as did Alaric. Father Creoda looked surprised and faintly scandalized to learn that the three of them were armed, but he could not fault their caution.

"With luck, no one will realize we're anything other than a few outside clergy come to view the proceedings," Jamyl told him. "But I don't think the king would be pleased if we were to take Alaric in there without at least a chance of defense, if things should turn uglier than they already are."

Arrangements had been made for an escort of knights from the archbishop's household to conduct them from their lodgings to Arx Fidei. Alaric was less than pleased to discover that their commander was Sir Errol Seaton, the father of Cornelius: sent ostensibly because he was acquainted with all of them from his time at court. But at least Cornelius, now *Sir* Cornelius, was not among their number. Two of the Haldane cavalry trailed along behind, wearing black cloaks and plain harness without the badges of the king.

Several monks were waiting to accompany the four into the abbey precincts, though Sir Errol also remained with them, watchful and efficient, a hand resting on the hilt of his sword. As they made their way through the gates, Alaric fancied he could sense the man's hostility, and was glad that Llion and Jamyl flanked him. Even Father Creoda was a comfort, at his back.

Beyond the gates, their progress was slowed by a sea of dark-clad men, both young and old, ranged in ranks along the edges of the square and wearing the habits of several different religious orders. Most seemed to be seminarians. A smattering of lay folk had also been admitted to the abbey precincts, muttering and milling restlessly to either side of the gates. Mercifully, Sir Errol led them to a place against the north side of the square, where the four of them could stand with their backs against the wall.

But the center of the square provided the terrible focus for what was about to happen. There a stout stake protruded from a dense surround of kindling, extending outward twice the span of a man's arms. A clear path led through the kindling, between the stake and the broad steps leading into the abbey church. There, several men in the purple of bishops had already begun to congregate, some of them speaking quietly among themselves.

"Look at them, *lurking*," Llion muttered to Jamyl, surveying the gathering crowd. "And these others"—he jutted his chin at the other clerics lining the square. "Did they really bring in further witnesses from other seminaries?"

Jamyl nodded gravely. "That is my understanding."

"And all these 'men of God' have come to watch a Deryni *die*?" Alaric whispered, aghast.

"I fear they have," Jamyl said. "You heard what Bishop Siebert said, when he came to court. They intend to make an example of Jorian de Courcy, to remind other Deryni what will happen to those who defy the laws of the Church."

Alaric mostly suppressed a shudder, profoundly glad that he had no priestly vocation. He tried not to think about his cousin Duncan, who very likely did.

They watched with increasing apprehension as black-clad men and boys continued to take their places along the edges of the square, until finally a pair of liveried episcopal guards emerged from a door to the left of the church steps, followed by two black-clad and hooded executioners escorting a stumbling scarecrow of a man in chains. The prisoner was heavily bearded, in stark contrast to the clean-shaven clergy in the square, and wore only a scant and tattered loincloth. His hair had been hacked off close to his head so that no semblance of his former tonsure remained.

"Is that him?" Alaric whispered.

Jamyl nodded minutely. "I believe it is."

"Good God, what have they done to him?"

Jamyl only shook his head, unable to answer, and Llion folded his arms resignedly across his chest as Father Creoda crossed himself in shock.

"God help him," the priest whispered.

The prisoner staggered as the executioners led him out in front of the church steps to bow to the bishops before turning their prisoner to hustle him along the pathway left clear of kindling. At the same time, several more bishops emerged onto the steps through the great doors of the church, joining the others. One of them was accompanied by two men in the black attire of simple priests, and wore a stark black cope and a towering black mitre. The great crozier in his hand marked him as Archbishop de Nore.

"I think that's Gorony with de Nore," Jamyl whispered low as he half turned toward Creoda. "Father, do you know who the other man is?"

Creoda shook his head uncertainly. "Perhaps the abbot of this place. I do not know either of them."

Meanwhile, with nary a wasted motion, the two executioners had chained the condemned man to the stake with his back to the church, leaving only his arms free. Alaric could hardly believe what he was seeing, that they truly meant to do this terrible thing. Jorian, for his part, looked dazed, perhaps even drugged, hardly aware of what was going on around him.

"My brothers in faith," de Nore suddenly said, speaking from the front edge of the steps, "I have summoned you today to witness the purgation of a grave sinner, who has profaned the very sacraments we all hold sacred. The scourge of Deryni heresy is real, and it is a mortal danger. This heretic thought to bring it into the very bosom of the Church."

De Nore continued to drone on, sowing the familiar hatred, but Alaric had no stomach for it. Instead he returned his focus to the center of the square, where Jorian's executioners were backing off from the stake, using heavy rakes to close the path in the kindling.

Jorian himself, alone now in the center of the pyre, looked forlorn and pitiable, head bowed and arms hanging limply at his sides, like a man who had lost all hope. Did he pray for deliverance to the God Who had abandoned him to this fate? Alaric wondered.

But he knew there would be no mercy for Jorian in this life. He wondered whether there would ever be mercy for Deryni. He wished there were something he could do, that there were some way he could use his powers to free Jorian, but there was nothing—and he suspected that this was the reason de Nore had insisted he be here. He could feel the hatred beating all around him almost like a living and malevolent entity as the archbishop at last finished his rant and then strode purposefully down the stairs.

Utter silence settled over the square as de Nore halted at the edge of the kindling, briefly surveying the condemned man. The executioners had brought lighted torches to the edge of the pyre as the archbishop spoke, and handed one to the archbishop as he turned to one of them. Without further ceremony, de Nore thrust his torch into the kindling at his feet and stepped back, the two executioners moving in both directions to light the kindling in several other places.

A collective murmur whispered through the watching throng, punctuated by the crackle of dry wood catching fire and then the *whoosh* of flames quickly spreading all along the outer edges of the pyre and eating inward. Alaric flinched at the sound, anxiously scanning the assembled spectators: the grim-faced clergy, mostly impassive, some of them horrified, a few showing sanctimonious satisfaction. The seminarians from Arx Fidei almost universally looked sick at heart and aghast, for the doomed man was their classmate, whom they had thought they knew.

Less varied were the reactions of the lay folk present, almost all of whom seemed to display no indecision regarding what was being done. Catcalls and hoots of derision rippled among them as the flames intensified and as Jorian briefly lifted his hands in a futile warding-off gesture, though to no avail.

Alaric could hardly bear to look, but he knew that he owed it to Jorian, to be witness to this horror. Tears welled in his eyes as he prayed for Jorian's deliverance, vision wavering as the Deryni's bare arms fluttered in a final appeal to heaven, then sank to cross on the heaving chest, the head tipping back against the stake, though he uttered not a sound.

Just then, as Alaric yearned toward the doomed man, wishing he could do *something, anything,* to ease Jorian's suffering, he sensed the presence of another, also reaching out to Jorian—and reeled as power rebounded from the contact. In that same instant, Jorian briefly went rigid, then slowly slumped into the flames now surging all around him. And then, as death claimed its victim, from somewhere across the square a young voice cried out:

"Sacerdos in aeternam!"

Sacerdos in aeternam . . . a priest forever!

Already recoiling from the sudden perception of magical intervention, which most certainly had given Jorian merciful release in death, Alaric cast his startled gaze in the direction of the shouted phrase, wondering who could have dared to say it: *Sacerdos in aeternum.*

The three words embraced everything that Jorian de Courcy had lived and died for, that were proclaimed before God during every priest's ordination, from time immemorial. Though Jorian's persecutors had declared him heretic and excommunicate, and denied him the sacraments of his faith, and even stripped away his priestly faculties, won so dearly, they could not erase that indelible stamp set upon his soul at ordination, that this was God's priest forever. It might be small solace to Jorian, who now was past having to worry about sanctimonious men who felt compelled to kill what they did not understand, but God surely would receive the soul of this faithful priest.

And who had released Jorian? Alaric thought it must surely have been Sé, for he knew no other adult Deryni who might have gained access to the execution and been powerful enough to do what had been done. But was it? And could it have been Sé who had shouted from across the square, or had caused someone else to do so?

Whatever its source, the shout had silenced the hecklers, ignorant men who rejoiced in the death of a Deryni, but Alaric noticed that soldiers in the archbishop's livery were moving briskly among the men and boys gathered at that side of the square, obviously looking for the person who had cried out. Sir Errol was even eyeing Alaric suspiciously, though he seemed satisfied that Alaric knew nothing of what had happened.

Meanwhile, the fire had totally engulfed the stake in the center of the square, its roar punctuated by the snap and crackle of burning timber that underscored the horror of the deed. No other sound could be heard as the thick column of greasy black smoke rushed upward from the pyre, carrying with it the sweet stench of burning flesh.

Alaric managed not to disgrace himself by vomiting or fainting, but it took a great deal of effort, and he could see and hear others with less fortitude—which made his own struggle even harder. Even though he *knew* that Jorian's soul no longer inhabited the blackened husk writhing in the flames, that the movement came only of the physical reaction of mortal flesh with fire, his stomach told him otherwise. Even Father Creoda looked queasy, and mostly kept his eyes averted, fighting nausea.

The bishops retired momentarily, and the gathered seminarians were dismissed shortly after that. A few had fainted, and many of them were battling varying degrees of unwellness. As they shuffled from the square, to disappear inside the abbey precincts, the lay witnesses also began to leave. Cornelius Seaton approached briefly to speak with his father and then depart, though not before giving Alaric a sneering up-and-down glance that spoke volumes without him saying a word.

"You are free to go now," Sir Errol said to Father Creoda, with a curt nod to Llion and Jamyl. "Do you wish an escort back to your lodgings?"

"That will not be necessary," Jamyl said stonily. "Our men await us outside. Good day to you, sir."

With that, he pressed between Alaric and the priest and seized an arm of each, bearing them away from the horror of the square.

Alaric tried to watch for Sir Sé as they mounted up and rode out from Arx Fidei, but he saw no trace of him.

Chapter 42

"Kings' daughters were among thy honourable women . . ."
—PSALMS 45:9

LARIC knew he was but poor company on the ride back to Rhemuth, but what he had witnessed at Arx Fidei would not leave his thoughts. He took but meager comfort in his growing belief that someone, probably Sé, had given release to the dying Jorian, for a part of him remained convinced that, somehow, he should have been able to help. Though none of it was logical, his continued sense of helplessness made him even more determined to learn as much as he could, as quickly as he could, to change things for the future.

Of course, without another Deryni to teach him, that determination was more aspirational than practical, but it was all he had. Sadly, he sensed that such training was beyond the ability of his Aunt Vera.

If only he had some way to contact Sé, to ask about what he had done at the execution, how he had managed to give Jorian release—if, indeed, it had been Sé. But who else could it have been?

Unfortunately, Alaric had never figured out how to summon Sé. So far as he knew, Sé's periodic appearances came mostly in response to his own perceptions of Alaric's needs—though the Anviler knight did seem to have a knack for knowing when Alaric truly had need of him or his training. But even with the aid of Sé's medallion, Alaric's ability to interact with Sé had only ever been at Sé's instigation, passive on Alaric's part, never with Alaric initiating the contact.

But the medallion did raise a possibility. As they rode into Rhemuth at last, midway through November, Alaric found himself wondering whether he could reach out to Sé using the focus of his St. Camber medal, since he had used Sé's medal for that purpose. Of course, those had been very different circumstances, using Sé's medal while he made himself open to Sé's call. He resolved to do just that.

First, however, he knew he must report back to the king. His friend Ciarán MacRae was duty squire that day, and came to escort him to the king's withdrawing room before he could even dismount.

"He said to fetch you as soon as you returned," Ciarán told him, as they made their way through the great hall. "Duke Richard is with him."

"I'm not in trouble, am I?" Alaric said.

"Why would you be in trouble? You did a very brave thing, to go voluntarily to witness that execution." Ciarán paused a beat. "Was it as terrible as I imagine?"

Alaric could not look at Ciarán, almost stumbling as they went up the steps toward the withdrawing room.

"Far worse," he whispered. "Whatever you can imagine, it was worse. But thank you for asking."

He paused just outside the door, drawing a deep breath to brace himself, then rapped lightly on the door before entering. He found the king and his uncle bent over a sheaf of maps spread open on the worktable, but both of them straightened as Alaric hesitated just inside the door.

"Come in," the king said, gesturing him closer. "Welcome back."

Alaric automatically smoothed at his travel-stained riding leathers as he came into the room, suddenly aware that he was not yet in his livery.

"Please excuse my attire, Sire," he murmured. "I would have changed first, but Ciarán said you wished to see me."

"I do. Uncle, could you give us a moment?" he added, with a nod at Duke Richard. He then indicated that Alaric should take a seat with him before the fire, briefly warming his hands from its heat.

"I am very sorry that you felt obliged to go to Arx Fidei," he said at last. "It must have been—difficult. Do you wish to talk about it?"

Alaric sat, very deliberately intertwining his fingers and resting them on his knees, fixing his gaze on the crossed thumbs. "Not particularly." After a beat: "Have you ever seen a man burn, Sire? Or smelled it?"

He heard the king's quick intake of breath, and sensed him shifting in his chair. "No. No, I haven't."

"Nor had I, before Arx Fidei. Oh, I'd smelled it, as a child. There was Hallowdale, to somewhat prepare me." He blinked back angry tears. "On the way to recover Xenia and her baby, we bypassed that town, and again on the way back. Llion wouldn't let us stay there or even ride through it; he'd been with me, before. Both times, it seemed to me that I could still smell the reek of burnt flesh. For me, I doubt that will ever change." He shook his head, but did not look at the king as he continued.

"Did you know, there's a sound, too, when a person burns—beyond the screaming you might expect, though Jorian de Courcy didn't make a sound. You can hear the *whoosh* as the kindling flares up, the pop and crack of the wood igniting—and then, if you listen very closely, the sizzle . . . like meat searing on a spit. Except that it isn't meat on a spit; it's a human being." He briefly closed his eyes. "At least by then, Jorian was beyond pain, but I hope never again to witness such a sight."

"I should have been there," Brion whispered.

"And done what?" Alaric shook his head. "There was nothing you could have done, without defying the laws of the Church and the land, just as there was nothing *I* could do except be his witness. One day, perhaps it will be different." *But not yet,* he added to himself, *though someone did something, to give that poor man release.* But he could not say that to the king.

"I promise you that we shall work toward that day," Brion said quietly. "Meanwhile, I am more grateful than you will ever know. If you had not offered to comply with the archbishop's order, I might have—"

"No!" Alaric said hotly. "I would not have let you defy him! Sire," he added, less heatedly. "Not on my account. I told you, I know very well what happened when your father and my mother tried to defy the bishops. I was brought up on the tale. At least I could prevent *that,* even if Jorian couldn't be saved."

"And I thank you for that service, believe me." The king sighed heavily and got to his feet, resting the heels of both hands against the mantel to gaze into a fire that was far more benign than the one they had been discussing.

"I expect you'll want some time alone, after all of this," he said after a few seconds, not looking at Alaric. "Take as much time as you need. Take Llion and go home to Morganhall for a few weeks, if that will help. Stay until Twelfth Night, if you like."

"I won't run away," Alaric said flatly. "I wouldn't give de Nore that satisfaction."

The king turned to gaze at him silently, then gave a nod.

"Very well. I'll tell my uncle to expect you back to your regular duties in the morning."

ALARIC retired to his quarters to find that Ciarán had gone ahead of him to order up a hot bath. Once the servants had finished filling the tub, he stripped off his riding leathers and immersed himself in the hot water, trying to relax, but his thoughts kept returning to the horror at Arx Fidei. Vexed with himself, he sat upright and scrubbed himself with a vengeance, trying to scour away every last vestige of what he had witnessed. Then, after drying off and readying for bed, he retrieved his St. Camber medal and ensconced himself in his familiar bed, using the medal as a focus to try to contact Sé. He slid into sleep without any awareness of whether or not he had been successful.

SO," Llion said to him the following morning, as they broke their fast down in the great hall, "do you mean to take the king up on his offer?"

"What offer?" Alaric replied.

"To go away for a few weeks."

Alaric snorted. "What would it solve? I'd still be Deryni, and Jorian would still be dead, and the world would still be what it is."

"Then, you'll be returning to your duties as royal squire," Llion said. "Aye."

Llion nodded. "Probably the best decision. I'll plan to escort Alazais back to Morganhall on my own, then. I'll only be gone a few days. And I believe Jamyl is heading out to Tre-Arilan. There was a message waiting for him, from his wife. Apparently their young son is ill."

"Not seriously, I hope?"

"I don't know. In any case, the king has given both of us leave to return to our families for the nonce." He paused a beat. "You'll be all right on your own, will you?"

Alaric nodded. "Aye, it will be good to get back into training, though I haven't exactly been idle while I was away." He quirked an ironic smile. "Grown-up activities, one might say. But I suppose it might give me better credibility with the other squires."

"Yes, I suppose it might." Llion clapped Alaric on the shoulder. "Good luck to you, then. I'll see you in a few days."

LLION and Alazais duly left later that morning, as did Jamyl. Meanwhile, Alaric threw himself back into his training. His experiences of the past several months did, indeed, seem to change the way some of the other squires regarded him, though not necessarily for the better. After all, he was still Deryni, like the executed man.

He found his own attitude becoming more focused, intent, especially his martial training. If some of the youthful joy had gone out of his fighting, his more adult focus more than made up for it. Duke Richard himself sparred with him several times, and seemed pleased with his progress.

At least his domestic duties seemed little changed, as he resumed his place in the rota of squires who served the royal family at court. As before, he found himself often in attendance on the old queen—and sometimes on the new one, though Richeldis did make a point to draw him aside and warn him that her new daughter-in-law seemed very wary regarding the subject of Deryni.

"You know that that is not a problem for me," she said, "but Jehana . . . is very wary of you. And that chaplain she brought with her, and the two sisters . . ." She shook her head. "Just be careful."

DESPITE that warning, Alaric soon began to understand how the other squires and pages almost universally had fallen under the spell of the beautiful and accomplished Jehana, as the court now was styling her. With her youth and beauty, and her soft Bremagni accent, and her somewhat exotic Bremagni customs and attire, she had brought a breath of fresh air to the Gwynedd court. Princess Silke also seemed to have been doting on every word of the new young queen during his absence, and sparkled under her influence.

As for the king, Alaric had never seen him happier, or more content. Indeed, with a new wife to please, even the king's dress sense had changed. Where once Brion Haldane had favored mostly utilitarian attire unless a state occasion required otherwise, his sartorial choices now were beginning to reflect the more refined tastes of his stylish and vivacious wife. He seemed almost gregarious, and increasingly was often to be seen on the dance floor with the queen, when musicians played following supper.

Which, when Alaric thought about it, was hardly surprising, since he had observed that dancing was a popular pastime in the queen's native Bremagne. Indeed, the dancing classes hinted by Airey and Prys were a reality, he soon discovered, with even the knights being drawn into the festivities.

Before he knew it, he was attending lessons along with the others. Moreover, Duke Richard heartily approved of it, and had noted that dancing had the serendipitous side effect of improving the dexterity of a warrior's footwork during swordplay. The court's youngest squire proved a quick study, and enjoyed the dancing as well, which quickly put him in demand as a dancing partner.

By the time Twelfth Night approached, he had danced with most of the younger ladies of the court, some of them many times, and had become a favorite partner of Princess Silke.

The feast of Christmas came and went, along with Queen Jehana's first appearance at the St. Stephen's Day court, the day after. There, while the king proudly watched from one side, Jehana joined the old queen in distributing the traditional gifts of food and clothing to the city's poor. Princess Silke happily joined them, along with Alazais, who had returned to Rhemuth with Llion at the beginning of December with their young daughter.

Afterward, while the women sought warmth in the cathedral, Brion heard petitions on the cathedral steps, as was his usual wont. Alaric, for his part, attended on the king with Llion and Jamyl and mostly observed, beginning to be regarded as much a junior advisor as a squire now, after his initiative earlier in the year.

Twelfth Night court that year would prove more festive than most that Alaric could remember. Not only was Nigel to be knighted, but for the first time King Brion would have his own queen at his side.

Jehana had spent months planning the entertainments and the menu for the feast, and overseeing the preparation of new attire for the royal party. Her over-gown of pleated crimson velvet parted in the front to show exquisite embroidery of tiny golden lions all over the cream underskirt.

Richeldis, no longer Gwynedd's first lady, elected to adopt a more sober version of Jehana's ensemble, but done in dove-grey rather than Haldane crimson, with the lions done in red. Silke, speaking animatedly with a bevy of new maids of honor lined up along the wall right of the thrones, had acquired a new gown of crimson and gold. For the king, there was a new, long court robe with his rampant lion device couched in gold from neck to waist on the fine crimson wool, worn under his state mantle of fur-collared crimson wool.

Nor had Jehana stopped with garments. She had also delved into the royal treasury and ferreted out several little-used items of state regalia: a necklace of cabochon rubies set in ruddy gold, called the Haldana jewels; a pair of ornate, gem-encrusted diadems not worn in several generations, according to Queen Richeldis; and for the knighting of Prince Nigel, a pair of golden spurs once worn by Prince Malcolm Haldane.

"They're beautiful," Nigel murmured, running his fingers over the chasing carved into the gold. Alaric had looped their straps over the hilt of the new sword shortly to be presented to the king's brother. "Are you sure I should wear them? King Malcolm has awfully big boots to fill."

"Well, these are only his spurs, not his boots," Alaric replied with a droll grin. "But I'm sure you will rise to the challenge. God knows, I've fought you enough."

Nigel only chuckled, shaking his head slightly.

The two of them were standing at the back of the hall with the rest of the party that would escort Nigel to the throne, after Brion finished receiving the new squires. The king's younger brother looked quite solemn this morning, garbed for the ceremony in the traditional attire of all candidates for knighthood in Gwynedd: an unadorned black over-robe mostly covering a stark white under-tunic, with a scarlet mantle clasped around his shoulders.

Like many of the young men at court, he had adopted the longer hair favored at the Bremagni court, pulled back in the braided warrior's clout favored by men of fashion there; the new queen had brought a smart escort of bodyguards with her on her marriage, who had introduced the custom. The hairstyle suited Nigel, with his glossy sable hair and grey eyes, though it was more severe than his usual look.

Alaric glanced toward the head of the hall, where this year's crop of new pages were already garbed in their Haldane tabards and waiting to the left of the throne, looking both excited and nervous, though they had already endured the most frightening part, by speaking directly to the king. Brion, meanwhile, was receiving several new squires being promoted from the pages' ranks.

"Only three new pages this year," Nigel muttered, with a glance aside at Alaric. "And look at them. Were we ever that green?"

Alaric controlled a smile and shrugged. "I suspect we were, sir. *I* was. And you were a prince, so I just assumed that you knew what you were doing."

"Big assumption," Nigel replied with a wink, again peering up the hall, where his brother was receiving another squire, this one accompanied by a knight in a red court robe with heraldic adornments. "Hello, who's this? Can you make out the device?"

Alaric followed Prince Nigel's gaze and nodded. "Yes, sir, it's the Earl of Rhendall and his heir," he said confidently. "I met them briefly before court. Our new squire, the future earl, is called Saer de Traherne. He seems keen enough. Carries himself well. I understand that he'll be here for a few years. There's also a sister around here somewhere, but I don't see her just now. I believe she'll be joining the queen's household. The new queen."

"Saer de Traherne, eh? I wonder if he's any good with a sword."

"I expect you'll find out, soon enough," Alaric replied. "I assume you'll continue training with the squires?"

"Of course. One is always learning."

"Well, then."

As the king spoke with the Earl of Rhendall, and Queen Jehana helped young Saer don his Haldane livery, Duke Richard made his way back to where Nigel and Alaric were waiting, along with a senior squire carrying Nigel's furled personal banner.

"You're next," he said to his nephew. "Are you ready?"

Nigel straightened and tugged resolutely at the hem of his over-tunic. "Ready, sir."

At the head of the hall, the duty herald stepped to the front of the dais and rapped with his staff against the oak boards. The banner-bearer moved into position at Alaric's right and shook out the scarlet silk to reveal Nigel's crowned golden demi-lion. Richard and Nigel fell in behind them.

"Sire, His Royal Highness the Prince Richard Haldane Duke of Carthmoor begs leave to approach the throne with business to present before Your Majesties."

At the king's nod, the herald lifted his staff in summons. Taking his lead from the banner, Alaric lifted the sheathed sword with its spurs looped over the hilt and processed down the length of the hall, Richard and Nigel right behind him. The crowd parted before them as they came. Alaric moved slightly to the left and halted, the banner halting to the right, as Richard and Nigel came to the bottom step of the dais and stopped.

"Your Majesties," Richard proclaimed, "I have the honor to present my nephew, the squire Nigel Cluim Gwydion Rhys Haldane, as a candidate for knighthood."

Brion tried to maintain a serious expression, but he kept fighting an exuberant grin as he answered, "We are pleased to receive him. Let the candidate be invested with the spurs."

That was the signal for one of the new pages to bring a red velvet cushion to set before Nigel on the bottom step. As the prince knelt, the other two came to take the spurs from the sword Alaric held, kneeling then to affix them to Nigel's heels. The boys obviously had been well rehearsed, for they did so with little difficulty, even though the straps were new. They then drew back to stand with the other pages.

Brion rose at that, turning to draw the Haldane sword from the jeweled scabbard that Jiri Redfearn held. He cocked the blade over his right shoulder as he turned to his brother, glancing aside at the two queens, who had also come to their feet. Duke Richard had moved to Brion's other side, and stood proudly as the king lifted the sword in salute before bringing it down to touch Nigel's right shoulder.

"In the name of the Father, and of the Son"—the sword lifted to descend on Nigel's left shoulder—"and of the Holy Spirit"—the blade lifted to touch the crown of Nigel's head—"be thou a good and faithful knight. Amen."

Alaric, holding the sword with which Nigel would shortly be invested, clutched it to his breast as a shiver ran along his spine. He had witnessed many a knighting, but the words never failed to thrill him. His grin mirrored the king's as Brion kissed the holy relic in the sword's pommel, then passed it back to Jiri and offered his right hand to his brother to raise him up and embrace him.

"Arise, Sir Nigel, and be invested with the further symbols of your new rank."

He turned then to his new queen and his mother, who jointly girded Nigel with the white belt. When that was done, Alaric moved without prompting to present Nigel's sword to the king, who in turn presented it to his brother. Nigel kissed the hilt before slipping it into its hangers on his belt. He then dropped to his knees again and offered his joined hands to his brother and king, who took them between his own as Nigel recited the traditional words of fealty:

"I, Nigel Cluim Gwydion Rhys, knight and prince, do become your liege man of life and limb and earthly worship. Faith and truth will I bear unto you, to live and to die, against all manner of folk, so help me God."

"And I, for my part, will be a faithful liege unto you, Nigel Cluim Gwydion Rhys," Brion replied, "giving justice and protection for so long as you keep faith with me. So help me God."

With that he released Nigel's hands, then seized his shoulders and raised him up in an enthusiastic embrace, for the brothers were and always had been close. The cheers of the court resounded among the great hammer beams in affirmation as Brion drew his brother onto the dais with him, where he then proceeded to knight two more candidates. Alaric retreated to stand with the other squires.

A T the feast that followed, though Alaric dutifully did his shift of service as a junior squire, he was also free to indulge in the more pleasant aspects of a major feast day at court. Dancing followed the feasting, with the king and queen often leading the dances, and Alaric found himself often called onto the dance floor. Mostly, though, he was all but monopolized by Princess Silke.

He had seen but little of the princess since the previous spring, for she had taken up with her new sister-in-law on Jehana's arrival, and Alaric had been away for much of that time. Now fifteen, she seemed to be putting aside many of her childhood pastimes, though she still had time for Alaric, and drew him onto the floor yet again to partner her in one of the more raucous dances.

"I'm not entirely certain I like this business of acting like a lady," she confided after the dance, as she pulled him into a shadowed and less trafficked corner of the hall to cool down.

Alaric snorted. "Well, you certainly *look* like a lady, especially tonight. And you do seem to be enjoying your friendship with the new queen."

"Oh, it isn't Jehana who's the problem. It's dear Maman. Now that I'm a woman, she has started to talk about marrying me off to some horrible Llanneddi prince. She's terrified that I shall end up like poor Xenia."

"What, married to some Torenthi scoundrel?" Alaric said lightly. "I don't think they have many of those in Llannedd."

"No, silly. Dead in childbed—or worse, wed to some ancient prince who is only interested in my bloodline."

He took her hand in his and pressed it to his lips, smiling. "If I were a Llanneddi prince, I would be interested in more than your bloodline, fair princess."

"Well, you're a *Corwyn* prince," she said pertly. "Or a duke, which is almost the same thing. Come to think of it, wouldn't *that* set the cat among the pigeons, if I were to marry *you?*"

He shook his head, chuckling. "You know that could never be, princess, even if our hearts were so inclined."

"Why *not*? You're certainly noble enough. And my brother is very fond of you. *I* am fond of you."

He looked at her in astonishment, suddenly aware that she was half-serious.

"Silke, you know what I am," he whispered. "Even if the king approved, even if he *wanted* it, the people would never accept me as your husband. The *Church* would never accept it. You're the king's sister. Your life is not your own."

"Is it not?"

In emphatic reinforcement of her words, Silke seized his face between her hands and kissed him hard, pressing him farther into the shadows. As she opened her mouth to his, probing with her tongue, he found his arms embracing her, his taut body beginning to answer her urgency. But then, of a sudden, he remembered who and what he was, and who *she* was, and pulled away to lean against the wall, trembling.

"Silke, you mustn't do that," he breathed. "*We* mustn't."

"Would it be *that* terrible?" she returned.

"No, but we mustn't. We really mustn't."

She sighed and leaned against the wall beside him, face flushed. "I know that," she whispered. "Oh, Alaric, take me away from all this!"

"Silke, you know I can't. . . ."

Very soon after that, the newly knighted Sir Justis Berringer spotted them and approached to bow and extend his hand to her in shy invitation. "Princess, would you care to dance?"

She put on a proper smile and nodded her assent, also giving Alaric a cool nod of thanks as she returned to the floor on Sir Justis's arm. Alaric prayed that no one had seen Silke's momentary indiscretion, and determined not to let it happen again.

Nor was Sir Justis the only young knight with courting on his mind. A little later, now watching moodily from one of the window embrasures, Alaric spotted Prince Nigel partnering a vivacious, dark-eyed girl in a gown of burnished bronze, with a glossy mane of chestnut curls tumbling down her back. She was almost of a height with Nigel, who had

changed from his knighting attire to a short tunic of royal-blue velvet
worked around the hem with a border of running lions. As the pair
passed closer to him, twirling and springing in the pattern of the dance,
Alaric became aware of a familiar presence easing in to stand beside him.

"Pretty little thing, isn't she?" Llion murmured, close beside his left ear.

Alaric turned to see Llion and Alazais, who had not been at court
that morning but must have arrived only recently, for both were still in
travel cloaks.

"You're here."

"Only just," Llion replied, easing Alazais's cloak from her shoulders
and then removing his own, for the great hall, crowded with dancers, was
warm after the out-of-doors. "The road south from Morganhall was icy,
worse than we'd been led to expect. I had wanted to be here for Nigel's
knighting."

"Well, it was much like any other knighting," Alaric replied. "Except
that Nigel is a prince, of course. I think he'd be popular with the court
even if he weren't royal. We did seem a few short on pages and squires,
though."

Alazais leaned in to kiss her husband lightly on the cheek and took
her cloak from him. "If you two don't mind, I think I'll leave you to discussing male things while I pay my respects to Queen Richeldis."

Llion caught her hand and kissed it fondly, then turned back to Alaric
as she headed along the side of the hall toward the dais where the old
queen sat amidst the new maids of honor. Across the hall, the young
queen was still on the floor with her handsome husband.

"So, not many pages and squires, then?" Llion said, guiding Alaric
toward one of the bench seats.

"Only three new pages. And four squires, I think. I was at the back of
the hall while that was going on, waiting in Nigel's knighting party. But
one of the squires has come from the Earl of Rhendall's court: his son
and heir, as it happens."

"Ah, yes. Saer de Traherne. I knew he was coming; and his sister, too,
I think. Is she one of the young ladies attending the queens?"

Alaric shook his head. "I wouldn't know."

"Well, it's always good to have more ladies at court," Llion said. "And

Nigel seems to be enjoying himself. Or, *Sir* Nigel, as I suppose we should say now."

"He's danced with that one several times," Alaric said. "And many others."

"Yes, now that the king is married, I suspect his brother may have begun to think about a wife of his own," Llion said.

"Llion—" Alaric drew a deep breath to steel himself. "Llion, I have to tell you about something. I did a stupid thing. Well, maybe not stupid, because I don't think it was entirely my fault, but I let it happen."

Llion raised an eyebrow in surprise, then glanced out at the crowded hall.

"Do you want to go elsewhere, so we can have some privacy?"

At Alaric's nod, Llion rose and headed out of the hall, Alaric following at his heels. When they had gained the seclusion of a stairwell, Llion turned to face his charge. "Well?"

Sheepish, feeling like an errant child—though what had happened most certainly was adult—Alaric told him about the incident with Silke, leaving nothing out. "I didn't lead her on; I didn't. At least I don't think I did. But if anyone saw us . . ."

"If anyone saw you, I'm sure it will be all over court by morning," Llion said baldly. "With luck, no one noticed and this will come to nothing. You do realize that you put yourself in a situation that would have been easy to misconstrue?"

Alaric nodded miserably. "I didn't realize she felt that way. And I do feel sorry for her. In her own way, she's as constrained by her blood as I am."

"She is," Llion agreed. "She's a princess of the royal blood, sister of a king. That very much limits whom she can marry."

Alaric shrugged, waggling his head back and forth in a yes-and-no gesture. "I understand that. But I really didn't do anything *wrong* . . . did I?"

"If you're certain you didn't, why are you feeling so guilty?" Llion countered.

Sighing, Alaric ducked his head. "Are you going to tell the king?"

"Should I?"

"He should know, if we were seen and people begin talking."

"Let's wait and see if anything is said," Llion said after a beat.

Chapter 43

*"A violent man enticeth his neighbour, and leadeth
him into the way that is not good."*
—PROVERBS 16:29

T O Alaric's very great relief, his brief moment of indiscretion with the king's sister seemed not to have been noticed, and Silke did not mention it or even seek private conversation with him again. For his part, Alaric avoided situations that might place him in much scrutiny and threw himself back into his training. Fortunately, the weather made that easier.

Later in January, while the kingdom lay deep in the grip of a wet and miserable winter, the king betook himself on a private mission to Arx Fidei with Jamyl Arilan, to attend the Candlemas ordination of Jamyl's brother Denis. Rather than subject Alaric to a return to the site of Jorian's execution, he took his new squire, Saer de Traherne, for it seemed the better part of valor not to bring a known Deryni into the abbey's sacred precincts. Taking Saer also provided an opportunity for king and squire to get to know one another better, and for Brion to better assess Saer's strengths and weaknesses, set apart from his martial skills.

As for Alaric, the king gave him leave to travel to Culdi with Llion, for his cousin Duncan's thirteenth birthday. While they were there, Alaric told Duncan about Jorian's execution, begging him not to pursue his notion to seek ordination himself.

"But it isn't just a notion," Duncan said, during one of their several conversations late at night in Duncan's quarters. "I'm beginning to think

I'm called, don't you see? It isn't something that I deliberately set out to pursue."

"Then, don't pursue it."

"But I'm not sure I have any choice," Duncan countered. "I know I could have quite a satisfactory life as a duke's son and, eventually, as a duke's brother. But I don't think that's enough. There's something more that I'm meant to do. Don't you ever get that feeling about your future role as Duke of Corwyn?"

Alaric did, actually, though sometimes it was hard to reconcile his future rank with the very difficult task of growing into the job. He continued to press Duncan during his stay at Culdi, but when he and Llion left a week later, he suspected that his arguments had fallen on deaf ears.

They were back in Rhemuth by early in March, when the land had begun to green and spring was becoming more than just a hinted promise of better weather to come. To the relief of all concerned, no untoward incident had marred the ordination at Arx Fidei this time. Jamyl's brother was now Father Denis Arilan, gone into post-ordination retreat for a month, and both the king and his party had returned.

"I saw no sign of what had happened in November," Saer was telling the other squires that first night back, as Alaric allowed himself to drift closer to the conversation. "I'd heard about it, of course; Arx Fidei isn't that far from my father's lands. But it must have been a horrible way to die, even if the man *was*"—he glanced aside uneasily as Alaric quietly joined their number—"even if he was . . . what he was."

"Just say it, Saer," Fanton Murchison said coldly. "De Courcy was Deryni. He knew the penalty, if he got caught." His venomous glance at Alaric left no doubt about how he felt about the incident, or about any Deryni.

"Fanton, you are an ignorant *git*," Alaric muttered, with fury in his eyes. "And I hope you cannot *imagine* how horrible it was."

With that, he turned on his heel and stalked from the room, well aware that he probably would always have to contend with such sentiment. As for Arx Fidei, he suspected that his return probably was inevitable, if Duncan persisted in his apparent intention to seek holy orders.

But that was for the future, and perhaps Duncan would change his mind. He did not know why Jorian de Courcy had been discovered, but he could only hope that Duncan would be more fortunate, if he did decide to pursue the priesthood.

Meanwhile, his life as a Haldane squire continued, though his personal progress was such that several of the senior knights began giving him extra tuition incumbent on a future duke. Along with his daily weapons' drills and ride-outs, and practice at hand-to-hand combat, Alaric continued his immersion in ever more complex military strategy and tactics, and at Duke Richard's insistence now took on the seminal masterwork on tactics by Zimri Duke of Truvorsk, *A Betrayal at Killingford*. It was a difficult work, not usually even attempted for several more years—and most men never truly understood it—but Alaric seemed to have a natural insight into the material.

Soon he was being included in the impromptu scenarios Richard ran for his nephews and other promising young knights in the royal withdrawing room, analyzing classic battles and formulating new battle scenarios for their analysis. Alaric held back at first, being much junior to the others, but he soon began to make his own contributions to their discussions, much to the satisfaction of the three Haldane princes. (Some of the knights were less than enthusiastic about the arrangement, but none dared make any overt objection.) Very soon, Alaric also became the squire most often on duty when the king received petitioners regarding the security of the kingdom.

Thus it was that he was present when news arrived from Eastmarch that not only would change the king's summer plans, but would draw Alaric further into the adult responsibilities he so craved, though no one could have anticipated how the situation would escalate.

The very first hints of unrest in Eastmarch—occasional cattle raids into neighboring Marley and the odd border incursion—had reached Rhemuth the previous year, while the king was absent in Bremagne to take a bride. Duke Richard, as regent, had been vaguely aware of the reports coming out of the north, but his personal focus had been on the dowager queen's expedition into Arkadia to retrieve her elder daughter and grandchild. Accordingly, he had noted only in passing the sparse reports of a marriage between a minor northern baron and the daughter of one of Brion's earls. After all, the Lady Eulalia Howell had a brother who would become the next Earl of Eastmarch. Her bridegroom, Sir Rhydon Sasillion, was only the Baron of Coldoire, and not well-known at court.

Little had changed once the king and his mother returned from their respective missions. It was not until the following spring that more alarming news reached the capital: that Rorik Howell Earl of Eastmarch had defied royal writ and begun to invade neighboring Marley, aided by his new son-in-law. Perhaps it was the birth of an heir to his daughter and her new husband that had finally sparked the move.

"I knew Rorik was ambitious, but I wouldn't have taken him for a traitor," Duke Richard said to the king, when the news first arrived. He had been running a battle scenario for Brion and the newly knighted Nigel, with Alaric observing and manning the map table to move markers. "You'll have to go up there, you know."

Brion scanned down the letter again, shaking his head. Alaric stayed very quiet, lest the others remember his presence and send him from the room.

"It does seem inevitable," Brion said. "Rorik has just changed from a minor irritation to a serious problem. He's wanted Marley for years. What do you know about this baron who sent the letter, who says he's trying to protect my interests?"

"Arban Howell," Richard replied. "Baron of Iomaire, and a cousin of Rorik. I knew his father. A good man."

"The father, or the son?"

Richard shrugged. "Both, so far as I know. The father was definitely one of the good ones. I know the son less well."

"Well, he's throwing his levies against Rorik, so I suppose we'd better go rescue him—and the good folk of Marley." Brion gave an arch glance at his brother. "Fancy trying out that new white belt in the field?"

"I wouldn't miss it," Nigel said with a grin.

"Right, then. It's going to be a quick, hard dash to get there in time to make much difference, so we'll want cavalry." He cocked his head at Richard. "What do we have available on short notice?"

"Take the Haldane lancers," Richard said. "Sixty should give you enough clout, added to what Arban can field."

THE king's preferred captains for the northern expedition would have been Jamyl and Llion, but both men were away from the capital, and Brion dared not delay, because no one knew what allies Rorik of Eastmarch might muster. Accordingly, he chose Sir Jiri Redfearn and Lord Lester to accompany him and Nigel as military aides, Jiri for his political acumen and Lester for his tactical experience.

As squires for the expedition, he selected Alaric and Saer de Traherne. His wife of only a year was less than enthusiastic about his planned excursion, and decidedly unhappy that the Deryni Alaric Morgan was to accompany her husband, but her objections carried no weight with the determined king.

"I know you don't like him, Jehana—what he is," the king said. "Out of respect for your wishes, I have begun keeping him from personal service that might bring him into close proximity with you, but he is my Duke of Corwyn, and he deserves the best guidance and training that I can give him. He is coming with me."

The queen pouted and retired to her chambers with her chaplain and the sisters to pray for the king, but his plans did not change.

The king and his party left for the north the next morning, following Mass and a blessing of the troops before they rode out. Both Alaric and Saer were arrayed in proper battle harness like the adults, and exchanged delighted grins as they mounted up, thrilled to be going on their first real military expedition.

With hard riding and little sleep along the way, the royal party caught up with battle stragglers in Marley livery two weeks later, well into the southern borderlands of Eastmarch. They soon learned that, true to the intentions outlined in his call for help, Arban Howell had, indeed, gone to the aid of the hard-pressed Earl of Marley and also enlisted the assistance of border troops of Ewan Duke of Claibourne, Marley's neighbor to the north and west. Marley men handling the local mop-up operations directed them northward, where it was believed that their earl and his allies had finally run Rorik to ground.

A few hours later they encountered jubilant outriders who reported that, indeed, combined forces of Ryan Earl of Marley, Duke Ewan, and Arban Howell had finally entrapped Rorik at Elcho with a handful of his captains. Riding into the base camp where the loyalist leaders were quartered, they learned that Rorik and many of his officers were now in chains at Arban's camp. The enterprise looked to have cost Rorik not only his freedom but the life of his son Kennet, knighted only weeks before, who now lay dying in a surgeon's tent not far from the center of the base camp. Unfortunately, Earl Rorik's ambitious son-in-law, the brash Rhydon Sasillion, had managed to elude his would-be captors and had last been seen galloping hell-bent toward the Torenthi border.

When they at last reached the command tent, a duke, an earl, and a baron were waiting to greet them, all still in battle harness. They were, all of them, men in their prime. All of them looked extraordinarily pleased with themselves.

"My Liege, you arrive in good time!" Duke Ewan said to Brion, as he strode up to catch the king's reins and gentle the big grey so that Brion could dismount. "We have the Earl of Eastmarch in custody, and were considering whether to go ahead and try him. We do have the right of high justice, and there is no doubt of his treason. But having him executed by the king he betrayed tastes of far more appropriate justice!"

"Not a job I relish, but I suppose it must be done," the king murmured, as Nigel and the others swung down. "How were your own losses?"

"Not as bad as they could have been," the Earl of Marley chimed in, joining them. "And it is thanks to the Baron of Iomaire, who raised the alarm in time for help to be summoned." He gestured toward a dark-haired younger man, also striding toward them. "Look here, Arban, 'tis the king!"

Half an hour later, the king and the rest of his immediate entourage had walked the campsite with the baron, seen Earl Rorik and his captains in chains, and looked in on the dying Kennet Howell, whose passing was not coming easily. The battle-surgeon and his assistant were attending him, and had removed or cut away most of his armor, but a cloak was partially pulled over the heavy swathing of blood-soaked bandages around his middle. The surgeon's expression was grim as he glanced up at the king and shook his head.

"I'll go to him," Jiri murmured, and crouched to lay a hand on the fevered brow and bend close to Kennet's ear. Alone of those in the king's immediate party, Jiri had sons of an age with the wounded man.

"How bad is it?" the king asked the battle-surgeon, who had drawn back to give Jiri access. Alaric was standing close at Brion's elbow, tight-lipped as he gazed down at the young knight.

The surgeon shook his head. "He took a belly wound, Sire. Half his entrails were spilling out when we found him. Better if he had bled out on the field."

"Does he wish the coup?" Brion asked. "Senseless, for him to suffer this way."

"He hasn't asked yet, my lord."

But he was asking now, Alaric had no doubt. He watched as the young man fumbled his hand into Jiri's and pulled him close for a gasping, whispered exchange. He could see Jiri nodding and reaching with his free hand for the dagger in the small of his back, keeping it close against his leg as he and Kennet continued to converse.

"Take this and help his lordship," the surgeon murmured, pressing a basin into Alaric's hands. "This place is bloody enough already."

Alaric glanced at the king, question in his eyes, but Brion only nodded, "Do it," then turned to leave with his entourage.

Heart pounding, Alaric knelt beside Jiri and, at his gesture, pressed the basin in the angle of the dying man's shoulder. Young Kennet closed his eyes, lips moving in prayer, but Alaric still flinched at the gush of hot blood that sprang from beneath Jiri's blade and frothed into the bowl, instinctively cupping his one hand over the wound to keep most of the blood in the bowl as he bent closer. In that instant of hard contact against Kennet's neck, he could sense the dying man's surge of fear. Instinctively he found himself reaching out with his mind to ease him on his way.

"Courage," he whispered, bending closer. "It will soon be over. Let go and let it happen. Go with God. . . ."

After, as he and Jiri washed the blood from their hands in the new basin the surgeon's assistant brought, Jiri eyed him thoughtfully and nodded. "You did well, lad. Your first time?"

Alaric nodded.

"Even better, then. I'm afraid it doesn't get easier, but you do learn to endure it." Jiri glanced down at the motionless form now shrouded under a blanket. "It's harder when they're so young. But he's at peace now."

He wiped his hands dry on a rough piece of toweling, then handed it to Alaric. "We'd best go find the king. I think he means to deal with the rest of this today."

"You mean, the Earl of Eastmarch?" Alaric said.

"Aye."

THEY found Brion and his brother seated on camp stools in the main tent, conferring with the Duke of Claibourne and the Earl of Marley, along with Arban Howell and several of his captains. Saer, assigned as Nigel's squire, stood to his back. A sharp-faced young man in battle leathers stood behind Arban, a familial resemblance suggesting that he might be Arban's son.

"Ewan tells me that this is mostly your victory, Sir Arban," the king said, as Jiri and Alaric took up places behind him and Nigel. "Is it your opinion that we should execute the ringleaders?"

Arban Howell glanced briefly at his dusty boots, apparently somewhat surprised to have a duke defer to him, but his voice was resolute as he met the king's gaze again. "My cousin betrayed his fealty to you, my lord, and persuaded others to join him in treason. For that, he deserves to die. The penalty the law requires is that he be hanged, drawn, and quartered."

"I do not question the law," the king replied, and turned aside to Jiri. "Is the boy dead?"

Jiri inclined his head. "Aye, Sire. He asked for the coup, and I gave it."

"Then, the direct line ends with Rorik." Brion considered briefly, then rose, the others hastily following suit. "Very well, let's be done with it," he said. "Summon your officers and as many of the Eastmarch captains as may be assembled before this tent. Such trial as Rorik Howell may merit will be carried out before his men."

Half an hour later, in the long, late summer twilight, Brion emerged to a clear space before the command tent where camp stools had been set for himself and Nigel, Duke Ewan, Earl Ryan, and Arban Howell, whose squire now stood behind his seat. In the interval, Alaric had learned that he was, indeed, Arban's son and heir, called Ian. Jiri and a pair of lancers stood behind the king's chair with folded arms. Lord Lester had gone to see to the troops.

Alaric, for his part, was charged with holding the sheathed Haldane sword to the left of the king. Brion had thrown on a dusty crimson mantle over his battle harness, and Alaric had tidied the king's battle braid before setting in place a leather band studded with cabochon garnets: practical diadem for travel. At not quite four-and-twenty, Brion Haldane looked every inch the warrior-king.

As the king and his lords took their seats, about a dozen Eastmarch men were chivvied before them and made to kneel. At Brion's nod, the defeated Earl of Eastmarch also was brought before him, hands bound behind, and likewise made to kneel, to a murmur of consternation from among his men. Brion fixed all of them with his scrutiny, silence settling over the gathering as he surveyed them, then turned his gaze on Earl Rorik.

"Sir Jiri, please remind this assembly of the penalty for high treason against the Crown."

"My Liege," Jiri said slowly, the title underlining just what Rorik had transgressed, "the penalty for high treason is death: to be hanged, drawn, and quartered. More specifically, the condemned is to be hanged to the point of unconsciousness, then cut down and revived, his entrails drawn from his body while still living, the body then to be beheaded and hacked into four pieces, all of these to be displayed at the king's pleasure, in a place or places of his choosing."

A faint murmur of dismay had rippled through the assembled listeners during Jiri's recitation, and Rorik himself had gone a little pale, jaw hard clenched, though he lifted his head bravely.

"I have but one question, my lord," he said quietly. "What has happened to my son?"

"Your son has died," Brion said starkly. Although Alaric's hands tightened slightly on the scabbard of the Haldane sword, he decided that the king also had granted Rorik a small mercy, not to specify just how Kennet Howell had died.

Even so, Kennet's father briefly closed his eyes, ducking his head, then lifted his gaze to the king once more. "Then, I have no reason to continue living. I commend me to God's mercy, for I know that I can expect none from this court."

Brion let out a measuring breath, then rose and reached his right hand across toward Alaric, taking the hilt of the Haldane sword to draw it from its scabbard. As the blade emerged, the ruddy sky of a dying day glinted red fire along the blade, gleaming as he reversed the weapon to let its tip rest on the packed earth beneath his feet.

"Rorik Howell Earl of Eastmarch, for that you have forsworn your oaths of fealty to our person and our Crown, and have risen against us in treasonous rebellion, and have attempted to take by force the lands of another, and thereby caused the deaths of many innocents; so, therefore, do we, Brion Cinhil Rhys Anthony Haldane King of Gwynedd, sentence you to die for the crime of treason, the penalty for which is to be hanged, cut down while still alive, your entrails drawn from your body, and your body then to be quartered.

"This is the just sentence prescribed by law, witnessed by your peers and henchmen here present."

Rorik had blanched as the sentence was pronounced, despite his earlier defiance. Brion stared at him for a moment, then shifted his gaze back across the kneeling Eastmarch men.

"This is the just sentence, prescribed by the law," he said. "But I desire to be known as a merciful king as well as a just one. I therefore direct that the said Rorik Howell Earl of Eastmarch shall be hanged by the neck until dead. Only then will the remainder of the sentence be carried out." He cast a cool glance at the surprised Rorik. "Ordinarily, a silken rope is specified for the execution of an earl, but my urgency in coming here to relieve the good people of Marley did not permit me that luxury." He glanced back at one of his lancer guards. "Over there, I think," he said, with a jerk of his chin in the direction of a nearby grove of sturdy oaks. "Take him."

The stunned Rorik was immediately dragged to his feet and hustled back through the assembled men, his warders heading him toward the indicated trees, where other lancers were bringing up a horse and tossing a rope over a high tree limb. At the same time, Brion cocked the Haldane sword over his shoulder and began to head toward the execution site. Jiri and Alaric fell in behind him, his other noble companions accompanying them.

Meanwhile, some of Arban's men chivvied the kneeling Eastmarch men to their feet, to stand and watch as Rorik was briefly allowed to bow his head before a black-clad priest for blessing. The king and his party halted a dozen paces from the execution site. As the condemned man then was lifted onto the horse and the noose dropped around his neck and drawn tight, Alaric swallowed down a queasy churning in his stomach, for he had never witnessed an execution by hanging.

"Steady, lad," Jiri murmured from the side of his mouth, for Alaric's ears only. "It won't be as bad as a burning."

Alaric tried to keep reminding himself of that, as the rope was adjusted and tied off, and the lancer holding the horse's bridle glanced at the king. He had been told about the involuntary reflexes that took over with a man's sudden death, the voiding of bladder and bowels, but mere words were different from actually seeing it. He tried not to grimace as execution was carried out, and decided that Kennet Howell's death had been far easier than his sire's.

"You all right, son?" Jiri murmured close beside his ear.

Alaric dipped his head minutely in a nod. "Aye, sir."

"Good lad."

They returned then to the stools before the command tent, where the king handed his sword to Nigel and then drew Alaric with him inside as the others again assembled.

"I'm about to do something that I hope I won't regret," Brion said in a low voice. "I still haven't dealt with Rorik's captains, but I first want to make Arban Howell the new Earl of Eastmarch. That part will be fine. I am more concerned about the captains." He cast a wary glance back out the tent flap, then returned his attention to Alaric.

"This is asking a great deal of you, but I understand that, some years ago, your late uncle, Lord Ahern, performed a great service for my father, by standing at his side while formerly rebellious subjects in Meara re-swore their oaths of fealty. Ahern was Deryni, of course, and used his ability to Truth-Read, to ensure that those swearing intended to keep their oaths in the future. Can you do that for me, with the Eastmarch captains? I really don't want to execute them, if I can avoid it. There's been enough of death in this place."

Alaric's jaw had dropped as the king's intentions became clear, and he swallowed with difficulty against a suddenly dry throat.

"You want me to Read so many, all at once?"

Brion snorted. "No, just one at a time. But I think the mere threat of a Deryni standing at my elbow will probably be sufficient. And I do think you'd detect at least any overt bad intention. I know it's best if you can touch them, but they don't necessarily know that. And I have a little of the ability, so you won't be alone. Between us, we should be able to spot at least the worst of them."

Alaric slowly nodded. It was a gamble, but he knew that the king was, indeed, said to be able to Truth-Read, to some extent. And a convincing performance of his own should give him greatly enhanced credibility for the future.

"I'll do my best, Sire," he said with rather more confidence than he actually felt. "Do what you must do, and I shall follow your lead."

With a curt nod, Brion led the way through the tent flap and took back his sword from Nigel, cocking it over his shoulder. The others had risen at his return, and the Eastmarch captains again knelt before the tent.

"Lord Arban, please attend us," the king said, taking his place before his stool.

Arban glanced uncertainly at Duke Ewan, Earl Ryan, and even Prince Nigel in question, but they looked as mystified as he. Stepping before the king, Arban immediately sank to one knee, looking up a little nervously. His son stood uneasily behind his father's empty stool.

"Sire?"

"Arban Howell Baron of Iomaire. We find that we are in need of a new Earl of Eastmarch," Brion said formally. "Will you accept this office from our hand, and do us homage for the lands of Eastmarch?"

A pleased expression came over Arban's handsome face, and a murmur of approval whispered among the men behind him. "Sire, I do and I will!"

Smiling faintly, Brion lifted the Haldane sword to bring the flat of the blade down lightly on Arban's right shoulder. "Then we, Brion, King of Gwynedd and Lord of the Purple March, do create you Earl of Eastmarch, and lord of all its lands and folk, for yourself and your heirs." The sword lifted to arch to the left shoulder. "We confer on you all the rights, privileges, and responsibilities thereunto pertaining." He lifted the sword and handed it off to Alaric to be sheathed. "Will you now do homage for your lands, Arban Howell Earl of Eastmarch?"

At once Arban lifted his joined hands to set them between the king's, his voice steady as he swore the oath.

"I, Arban, do enter your homage and become your liege man for Eastmarch. Faith and truth will I bear unto you, to live and to die, against all manner of folk, so help me God."

"And I receive your homage, Arban Howell Earl of Eastmarch, and pledge you my loyalty and protection for so long as you keep faith with me."

So saying, the king released his hands and cast a speaking glance toward Ewan and Ryan. "Does one of you have the Eastmarch signet, I hope?"

Earl Ryan hastily rummaged in his belt pouch to produce the ring, taken from Rorik Howell at his capture. This Brion placed on Arban's left forefinger.

"Receive this ring as a seal of fidelity to the oaths you have sworn, and a symbol of your authority. And next, as I recall, I would invest you with the coronet, but you'll have to sort that out when you actually take possession of your lands." He smiled as he raised Arban up and embraced him briefly, then stepped back so that Ryan and then Ewan and Nigel could likewise congratulate the new earl, pounding him on the back in approval.

"One further matter, before we disperse," Brion said, as Arban returned to his stool to be embraced by his son. "I have not forgotten that there is the matter of the men who followed the former lord of Eastmarch into treachery." At his hard glance over the Eastmarch captains, all of them shrank back on their knees, looking very wary.

"There was another, of course, who encouraged them to rebel," Brion went on, hooking his thumbs in his white knight's belt, "and who was high enough in rank that his wishes could not lightly be disregarded. It is my understanding that Earl Rorik was aided and abetted in his treachery by his son-in-law, one Rhydon Sasillion, Baron Coldoire, who has fled."

"That is true, Sire!" one bold soul cried out from the ranks of the Eastmarch captains.

"Then, I name him traitor and attainted," Brion declared, "his lands confiscated, and I banish him for life, under pain of summary execution, should he ever set foot in my kingdom again.

"But, what to do about the rest of you?" he mused, as his gaze again roamed the cowering Eastmarch captains. "In strict justice, I could hang the lot of you, and no one would fault me." Alaric could feel the fear of the trembling men, and the mixed reaction of the other lords watching, no one daring to intervene.

"But I shall take the counsel of my new Lord of Eastmarch," Brion went on, turning to Arban. "How, if I were to agree to pardon any of these who will pledge you fealty, with their hand upon my Haldane sword?"

Arban rose, apparently both surprised and heartened, and nodded his acceptance. "These are my countrymen, Sire, and some of them my kin. They were ill led. I would spare them, on their oaths."

"Very well." The king gave a leisurely glance to the sheathed sword in Alaric's hands. "But be aware," he continued, "that if any man swears you falsely, my Duke of Corwyn will know it." He did not take his eyes from the men as he reached behind him so that Alaric could put the sword into his hands. "You know that he is Deryni. You know that he can tell when a man lies."

The king then handed the sheathed sword to Arban Howell, who came to stand between the two of them as witnesses, as the Eastmarch men came forward individually to lay their hands on the sword's pommel and swear fealty to their new earl. Alaric did not know for certain whether any of the men who knelt before Arban had serious misgivings; he could not detect any, though the setting was less than ideal.

Still, his very presence seemed to keep the men focused and earnest. And all of Brion's allies seemed reassured as the assembly began dispersing to their campsites for the night. Alaric, bone weary after the stress of their hard-scramble ride from Rhemuth and the emotions of the day, was glad to wolf down a share of the travel rations that Duke Ewan managed to produce for the king and his companions, and even more grateful for the pallet that was spread for him at the foot of the king's camp cot. If he dreamed that night, he did not remember in the morning.

Chapter 44

*"I have pursued mine enemies, and overtaken them: neither
did I turn again till they were consumed."*

—PSALMS 18:37

THUS the rebellion ended in Eastmarch. The next morning, Brion
dismissed the Claibourne levies with his thanks, wished his new
earl Godspeed, then turned over command of the royal lancers to
Lord Lester, Sir Jiri, and his brother Nigel, who would accompany the
men back to Rhemuth. Brion himself, impatient with the senselessness of
the past two weeks, and the blood and killing, decided to set out for
home along a different route, taking only his Deryni squire with him.

It was nearing dusk when the pair found a suitable campsite for the
night, in the curve of a small stream that ran along the road. They had
taken little opportunity to rest since their early departure, so riders and
horses alike were tired and travel worn. The horses smelled the water up
ahead and tugged at their bits as the riders drew rein.

"God's wounds, but I'm tired," the king said with a sigh, kicking
clear of his stirrups to stretch his legs for a moment, then sliding grate-
fully from the saddle. "I sometimes think the aftermath is almost worse
than the battle itself. I must be getting old."

Alaric only chuckled at that as he, too, dismounted and caught at the
royal reins to secure the horses, for at just short of twenty-four, the king's
lament concerning aging was hardly credible. Indeed, at that moment,
Brion Haldane seemed hardly older than his squire as he made his way to
the edge of the nearby stream and, pulling off helmet and coif, let himself
fall face-first to bury his head in the cooling water.

After a moment, he tugged loose the battle braid and shook out the sweat-soaked strands, letting the long black hair float in the current and then stream down his back just past his shoulders as he rolled over and sat up, obviously the better for wear. Alaric, having watered the horses and tethered them nearby, picked up his master's helm and coif and laid them by the chosen campsite, then returned to the king.

"Your mail will rust if you insist upon bathing in it, Sire," he said, kneeling beside the king and reaching to unbuckle the heavy sword belt.

Brion leaned back on both elbows to facilitate the disarming, shaking his head in bemused appreciation as Alaric began removing vambraces and gauntlets.

"I don't think I shall ever understand how I came to deserve you," he said. He shifted a leg so that the boy could unbuckle greaves and spurs and dusty boots. "You must think me benighted, to ride off alone like this, without even an armed escort other than yourself, just to be away from my men."

"My liege is a man of war and a leader of men," Alaric replied, smiling faintly, "but he is also a man unto himself, and must have time away from the pursuits of kings. The need for solitude is familiar to me."

"You do understand, don't you?"

Alaric shrugged. "Who better than a Deryni, Sire? Like Your Grace, we are also solitary men on most occasions—though our solitude is not always by choice."

"I suppose that's true," the king said thoughtfully. He fell silent as he allowed the boy to pull the lion surcoat off over his head, then got to his feet and let Alaric help him worm out of the leather hauberk with its lining of mail. Discarding padding and singlet as well, he made his way into the water and waded out to where he could submerge himself with a sigh. Alaric joined him after a while, gliding eel-like in the dappled shadows as the two of them swam.

When the light began to fail, the boy was on the bank without a reminder and pulling on clean clothes, packing away the king's armor, laying out fresh garb. Reluctantly Brion came to ground on the sandy river bottom and stood, slicking back the long black hair.

By the time he had dressed, there was a small wood fire crackling cheerily in the shelter of several rocks, and a rabbit spitted above the flames, and mulled wine in sturdy leather traveling cups. Wrapped in their cloaks against the growing night chill, king and squire feasted on rabbit and ripe cheese and biscuits only a little gone to mold after days in their packs.

"This is a welcome change from field rations," Brion said, lifting a rabbit haunch in salute.

Alaric smiled and returned the salute. "You're very welcome, Sire. You know, we could have stayed in camp another day. I wouldn't be surprised if Arban Howell's men managed to kill a cow or sheep or two."

"No, I think that Arban Howell probably was eager to take possession of his new lands. I don't envy him the task, but I think he will be an able caretaker in the north." He paused to swallow, then drank deeply from his cup. "I suspect you've learned a lot from this venture," he said then, with a sidelong glance at Alaric. "Had you ever seen a man hanged?"

Alaric shook his head. "No, Sire. Nor seen the coup given, up close. At least not to a man."

Brion nodded thoughtfully. "The first for both, then. Sadly, being who you are, I doubt that will be the last. You bore up well, though. Many squires of your experience, and even older ones, have done far worse."

Alaric tossed the gnawed bones from his rabbit into the fire. "I was forced to watch a man burn, Sire. After that, neither a hanging nor the coup could be much worse—at least watching it done to someone else." He quirked a sour grin at Brion. "Of course, if I were the object of either fate, I'm sure I should feel differently."

"True enough." Brion also tossed the last of his rabbit into the fire and sucked grease from his fingers. "But as a duke, it eventually will fall to you to condemn others to death, and sometimes to kill them. And with the best will in the world, as a warrior you will sometimes be called upon to give the coup." He picked up his cup and turned it thoughtfully in his hands. "Did you—use your powers to help that young man die?" he asked.

"If you mean, did I kill him?—no." Alaric shook his head, looking down into the flames. "But I felt his pain and fear, and I tried to ease *that*." He glanced away. "It didn't seem right, that I should use my powers to actually kill him. Besides, it was Sir Jiri he'd asked for the coup. It seems to me, that's a sacred trust."

"Yes, it is." Brion dashed the dregs of his wine into the fire and set the cup aside. "But we probably should try to get some sleep. We've another day of hard riding ahead of us tomorrow. We might even divert to Cynfyn for a day or two, if you fancy it."

"Would we dare to do that?" Alaric said, with a raised eyebrow. "They'd worry, back in Rhemuth, if you didn't return as expected. Duke Richard will already have some choice words for you, that you've taken off like this."

"I *am* the king," Brion replied with a droll sideways glance at him. "There have to be a few advantages to go along with all the responsibility."

"Right, then," Alaric said, grinning. "Cynfyn it is. Did you want any more of this cheese?"

"No, I've had enough," the king said. "I need sleep more than food, just now. Will you take the first watch, or shall I?"

"I'll take it," Alaric said, getting to his feet.

By the time he had tidied away their supper things and seen to the horses, also finishing off the last of the cheese, it was fully dark, though the glow of a rising moon behind the mountains to the east promised a well-lit night. Brion had fallen asleep almost immediately, head pillowed on his saddle, so Alaric took out his ward cubes, activated them, and set them around the perimeter of their immediate campsite, breathing an extra prayer to the great archangels of the quarters before he, too, settled down to sleep.

The moon was almost overhead when he was awakened by the tingle of the wards and the sound of hoofbeats approaching from the direction they had come. It was a lone horseman—that much Alaric could determine, even through the fog of sleep he was shaking off as he reached for his sword and scrambled to his feet. He had slept in his boots. A few feet away, he sensed Brion likewise stirring.

But it was not just any rider. As Alaric sought cover in the shadow of a nearby tree, sword sliding silently from its scabbard, he cast his senses beyond the wards, seeking out some clue as to who it might be, then straightened and let out a sigh as he resheathed his sword.

"It's Prince Nigel," he said, coming back to the king and, with a thought and a gesture, releasing the wards.

Brion, by now well used to relying on the boy's extraordinary powers, groped for his boots and then drew on his cloak, at the same time peering toward the moonlit trail.

"I wonder why he's followed us," he murmured. "It can't be for any happy reason."

"A Haldane!" a familiar voice called out.

"A Haldane, ho!" Brion shouted in response, stepping into the moonlight to show himself.

The newcomer reined back his lathered horse and half fell from the saddle, handing the reins to Alaric as the pair, squire and king, came to greet him.

"Brion! Thank God I've found you!" Nigel pulled off his helmet, then enfolded his brother in a quick embrace as Alaric secured the horse with the others. "I feared you might have taken another route."

The younger prince was in full battle harness, grimy and foam flecked from his breakneck ride, and his breath came in ragged gasps as he allowed Brion to lead him to a seat by the fire, which Alaric quickly coaxed back to life. Collapsing against Brion's saddle, he gulped the wine that his brother offered and, without attempting to speak, pulled off one gauntlet with his teeth before reaching deep into the breast of his surcoat. He drew a deep breath as he withdrew a much-creased piece of parchment and gave it over to his brother.

"This was delivered several hours after you and Alaric left us. It purports to be from Hogan Gwernach."

"Gwernach?" Brion's face went very still as he began unfolding the parchment. They certainly had not anticipated trouble this season from Hogan Gwernach, also called the Marluk, for one of his Tolan titles. The Festillic pretender had caused problems for Brion's father, and at Brion's own coronation, but little had been heard of him since losing his only trueborn son, two years before. As Brion flattened the missive, turning it first to the address penned on the outside, he tilted it toward the firelight, squinting to make it out.

"Alaric, can you give me some better light?" he murmured, hardly noticing as Alaric raised a clenched right fist to his lips, then opened the fingers to cup a softly glowing sphere of greenish handfire, brighter than the fire, which he brought closer to the king. Prince Nigel almost stifled his gasp, but said nothing as his brother peered at the crabbed script.

"Unto Brion Haldane Pretender of Gwynedd," the king read, making a moue. "Well, he doesn't mince words." He turned the parchment over and let his eyes scan quickly down the page, then nodded and began to read aloud.

"Unto Brion Haldane, Pretender of Gwynedd, from Hogan Gwernach Duke of Tolan, Festillic heir to the thrones and Crowns of the Eleven Kingdoms. Know that we, Hogan, have determined to exercise that prerogative of birth which is the right of our Festillic ancestors, to reclaim the thrones which are rightfully ours. We therefore give notice to you, Brion Haldane, that your stewardship and usurpation of Gwynedd is at an end, your lands and Crown forfeit to the House of Festil. We charge and require you to present yourself and all members of your Haldane line before our royal presence at Cardosa, no later than the Feast of Saint Asaph, there to surrender your person and the symbols of our sovereignty into our royal hands. *Sic dicto, Hoganus Rex Regnorum Undecim.*"

"*King of the Eleven Kingdoms?*" Alaric mostly contained a snort, then remembered who and where he was. "Pardon, Sire, but he must be joking."

Nigel shook his head. "I might agree with you, except that this was delivered by Rhydon Sasillion under a flag of truce."

"That treasonous dog!" Brion muttered.

"Aye, the very one." Nigel nodded. "He said to tell you that if you wished to contest this," he flicked a nail against the edge of the parchment in his brother's hand, "the Marluk would meet you in combat tomorrow near the Rustan Cliffs. If you do not appear, he says they will sack and burn the town of Rustan, putting every man, woman, and child to the sword. If we leave quickly, we can just make it."

"Our strength?" Brion asked.

"Just our sixty lancers, that we can be sure of. I sent fifty of them ahead to rendezvous with us at Rustan, and my own escort are probably an hour or so behind me; I did some hard riding. Earl Arban is also reassembling some of his troops, but I can't tell you how many. Most of his men had already headed for home. Duke Ewan had also already headed north, but I sent a rider anyway."

"Thank you. You've done well."

With a distracted nod, Brion laid a hand on his brother's shoulder and got slowly to his feet, gathering his cloak more closely around him against the chill. As he stood gazing sightlessly into the fire, head bowed in thought, the firelight gleamed on the great ruby in his right ear and on a wide bracelet of silver just visible on his right wrist. Alaric, with a glance at Prince Nigel, retrieved the king's lion brooch and rose to fasten it at Brion's throat as the king spoke.

"Nigel, you must understand that the Marluk does not mean to fight a physical battle with me," he said in a low voice. "Oh, there may be battle among our various troops in the beginning. But all of that is only prelude. Armed combat is not what Hogan Gwernach desires of me."

"Aye. He is Deryni," Nigel breathed. He watched Brion's slow nod in the firelight.

"But—it's been two generations since a Haldane king has had to stand against Deryni magic," Nigel went on, after a long pause. "Can you do it?"

"I—don't know." Brion, his cloak hugged close about him, sank down beside his brother once again, his manner grave and thoughtful. "I'm sorry if I seem preoccupied, but I keep having this vague recollection that there is something I'm supposed to do now. I seem to remember that Father made some provision, some preparation against this possibility, but—"

He ran a hand through tangled sable hair, the firelight winking again on the silver at his wrist, and Alaric froze, head cocked in a strained listening attitude, eyes slightly glazed. As Nigel noticed and nudged his brother lightly in the ribs, jutting his chin in Alaric's direction, the young squire sank slowly to his knees. Both pairs of royal eyes stared at him fixedly.

"Sire," Alaric finally whispered, "there is that which must be done, which was ordained many years ago, when I was but a babe and you were not yet king."

"By my father?"

"Aye. The key is—the bracelet you wear upon your arm." Brion's eyes darted instinctively to the silver. "May I see it, Sire?"

Without a word, Brion removed the bracelet and laid it in the boy's outstretched hand. The bracelet was of silver, once polished to a mirror sheen, but years of constant wear had given it a fine patina of tiny scratches and even a few gouges, slightly dulling its original luster. Even so, Alaric could sense the potency symbolized by the heraldic rose incised at the bracelet's center, and what lay *sub rosa*, under the rose. Steeling himself against the rush of memories he knew lay waiting to be unleashed, he laid his right hand over the rose and let himself remember.

He had been just four when he first saw the bracelet. Now, a decade later, he knew that what had happened that night had been precisely in aid of the moment now before him. Both his parents had been there, his mother heavily pregnant with his sister Bronwyn, but it was the king who directed what was to come.

His father had carried him from his bed and placed him on his feet before the old king, who sat before the fire in a heavy wooden chair. It was the king who had worn the bracelet that night, who had taken Alaric onto his royal lap and removed the bracelet, held it before him and turned it to the inside, where three runes shone in the firelight. As Alaric turned it now in different firelight, the runes took on a new meaning.

"This is a time which your royal father anticipated, Sire," he said softly, turning the bracelet in his hands so that it flashed firelight into the king's eyes. "There are things which I must do, and you, and somehow he knew that I would be at your side when this time arrived."

"Yes, I can see that now," Brion murmured, his eyes never leaving Alaric's. " 'There will be a half-Deryni child called Morgan, who will come to you in his youth,' my father said. 'Him you may trust with your life and with all. He is the key, who unlocks many doors.' He knew. Even then, your presence was by his design."

"And was the Marluk also his design?" Nigel whispered, his tone conveying resentment at the implied manipulation, though it hardly mattered now.

"*Ancient mine enemy,*" Brion murmured. "No, he did not cause the Marluk to be, Nigel. But he knew I might have to face him one day, and he planned for that. It is said that the sister of the last Festillic king was with child by her brother when she was forced to flee Gwynedd. The child's name was—I forget, not that it matters. Marek, I think. But his line grew strong in Tolan, and they were never forced to put aside their Deryni powers. The Marluk is said to be that child's descendant."

"And full Deryni, if what they say is true," Nigel replied, his face going sullen. "Brion, we aren't equipped to handle a confrontation with the Marluk. He's going to be waiting for us tomorrow with an army and his *full-Deryni powers.* And us? With luck, we'll have the sixty men of our lancer escort, *maybe* we'll have some of Arban Howell's men, *if* he can recall them in time, and you'll have—what?—to stand against a full-Deryni lord who has always wanted your throne!"

Brion wet his lips, avoiding his brother's eyes. "Alaric says that Father made provisions. We have no choice but to trust and see. Regardless of the outcome, we must try to save Rustan town tomorrow. Alaric, can you help us?"

"I shall try, my lord," Alaric said.

Disturbed by the near clash between the two brothers, and sobered by the responsibility Brion had laid upon him, Alaric upturned the runes on the underside of the bracelet and set his right forefinger beneath the first one, grubby fingernail underscoring the deeply carved sign. He could feel the Haldane eyes upon him as he whispered the word, "*One.*"

The word paralyzed him, striking him deaf and blind to all externals, oblivious to everything except the images flashing through his mind: the face of the old king seen through the eyes of a four-year-old boy—and the instructions, meaningless to the four-year-old, now engraving themselves in the consciousness of the young man he had become, as deeply as the runes inscribed on the silver in his hand.

A dozen heartbeats, a blink, and he was back in the firelight again, turning his grey gaze on the waiting king. The royal brothers stared at him with something approaching awe, their faces washed clean of whatever doubts had remained until that moment. The moonlight on Alaric's golden hair gave the illusion of a halo. Or was it an illusion?

"We must find a level area facing east," the boy said. His brow furrowed in concentration. "There must be a large stone in the center, living water at our backs, and—and we must arm ourselves, for there may be little time after we have finished."

Chapter 45

"For when men will not believe that thou art of a full power,
thou shewest thy strength . . ."
—WISDOM OF SOLOMON 12:17

I T was nearing first light before they were ready. A suitable location had been found in another bend of the stream not far above their camp, with water tumbling briskly along the northern as well as the western perimeter. To the east stretched an unobscured view of the mountains from behind which the sun would shortly rise. They had used the horses to drag a large, stream-smoothed chunk of granite into the center of the clearing, half the height of a man, and had set four flattened lesser stones a few paces out from it to mark the four cardinal compass points.

On these stones Alaric had set the bonded pairs of his ward cubes, previously serving as sentinels while they slept, now readied for a slightly different purpose. Neither prince had even seen ward cubes before, and certainly not the ritual by which Alaric prepared them; but they watched in awed silence, trusting that what he did was needful.

A final time Alaric walked the perimeter of their working area to make certain everything was correct. The brothers watched from close beside the center stone, seated on the ground, both of them now armed. Brion's sheathed sword lay close beside him. With Nigel's help, he had re-braided his hair and bound it in a warrior's knot, and again wore the garnet-studded leather circlet of a king.

In the scant shelter of the cloak clasped close around him, the king sat now with bowed head. A knot of blazing pine thrust into the ground at

his right provided additional illumination in the moonlight, but he saw
nothing, submerged in contemplation of what lay ahead. Alaric, with a
glance at the brightening sky, scooped fresh water into one of the leather
cups and set it close beside the center stone on the western side, then sank
to one knee beside the king.

"The dawn is nearly upon us, Sire," he said quietly. "I require the use
of your sword."

"Of course."

Picking up the sheathed weapon, Brion leaned on it to scramble to his
feet, aided by his brother. It had been their father's sword, and their
grandfather's. It was also the sword with which he had been consecrated
king nearly ten years before, and the sword with which he had been
knighted. Since that day, no man had drawn it save himself, or by his
command.

But without further hesitation, Brion unsheathed the blade, handing
off the scabbard to Nigel and formally extending the sword to Alaric
across his left forearm, hilt first. Alaric made a profound bow as he took
the weapon, appreciating the trust the act implied, then saluted both
royal brothers and moved to the other side of the center stone. Behind
him, the eastern sky was ablaze with pink and coral.

"When the rim of the sun appears above the horizon, I must ward us
with fire, my Liege," he said. "Please do not be surprised or alarmed at
anything you may see or feel."

"Very well."

As the two princes drew themselves to respectful attention, Alaric
turned on his heel and strode to the flat stone at the eastern limit of their
working place. Raising the sword before him with both hands, he held
the cross-hilt level with his eyes and gazed expectantly toward the eastern
horizon. Very shortly, as though the sun's movement had not been a
gradual and natural thing, dawn was spilling from behind the mountains.

The first gleam of sunlight on steel turned the sword to fire. Alaric let
his gaze travel slowly up the blade, to the flame now blazing at its tip and
shimmering down its length, then extended the weapon in salute and
brought it slowly to ground before him. Fire flared where blade touched

sun-parched turf—a fire that burned but did not consume. A ribbon of flame unfurled as he turned to the right and walked the boundaries defined by the wards, tracing the outline of a containing circle.

When he had finished, he was back where he began, with all three of them standing now within a faintly shimmering circle of golden light. With hands that shook only a little, Alaric saluted sunward once again, then jammed the sword into the turf at his feet, so that it stood sentinel to their work. Then he extended both arms and closed his eyes, visualizing the pairs of bonded ward cubes at the quarters of the circle, and calling out their names in completion of the warding spell.

"Primus, Secondus, Tertius, et Quartus, fiat lux!"

The words flared the cubes to life, igniting the containing circle so that, with a faint rushing sound, it extended upward in a golden dome as he opened his eyes to look around him. He contained a smile of satisfaction as he turned and made his way back to the center of the circle, where the two princes waited.

"I'll need that bracelet again," he said softly, holding out his hand to Brion.

Wordlessly the king handed it over, watching as Alaric laid his finger under the second rune.

"Two!"

In a moment of pregnant silence, no one moved or even breathed. Then Alaric blinked, back in normal consciousness, and handed the bracelet back to the king, who absently clasped it back to his arm.

"This next part is less familiar to me," Alaric admitted. He moved around to the west side of the center stone to hold his cupped hands above it, gazing fixedly at the space above them as he called up power.

Nothing immediately happened that could be seen, though he could feel energy building between his hands. King and prince and squire stared until their eyes watered, then blinked in astonishment as the space between Alaric's hands began to glow. Pulsating with the heartbeat of the one who called it, the glow coalesced in a sphere of cool, verdant light, very different from the handfire he had conjured earlier, swelling to head size even as they watched.

Slowly, almost reverently, Alaric lowered his hands toward the center stone and parted them to let the light flow onto the stone, watching as the light spread bright across the uneven surface. He hardly dared to breathe, so tenuous was the balance he maintained.

Carefully drawing back the sleeve of leather tunic and mail, he swept the edge of his right hand and forearm across the top of the stone like an adze, shearing away the granite as though it were softest sand. Another pass to level the surface even more, and then he was using both his hands to press out a gentle hollow in the center, the stone melting beneath his touch like morning frost before the sun.

Then the fire died away, and Alaric Morgan was no longer the master mage, tapping the energies of the earth's deepest forge, but only a boy of not-quite fourteen, staggering to his knees in exhaustion at the feet of his king and staring in wonder at his hands and what they had wrought. Already, he could not remember precisely how he had done it.

Silence, finally broken by Brion's cautious intake of breath as he tore his gaze from the sheared-off stone. Beside him a taut, frightened Nigel was staring at him and Alaric, white-knuckled hands gripping the royal sword's scabbard as though it were his last remaining hold on reality. With a nervous smile of reassurance, Brion laid a hand on his brother's, then returned his gaze to the young man still kneeling at his feet.

"Are you all right?"

The king's words jarred Alaric, but he managed a vague nod as he drew a deep breath in and out, briefly closing his eyes as he murmured a quick spell to banish fatigue. It still took a profound exertion of will to get shakily to his feet, aided by the king's hand under his elbow, but he definitely felt stronger as he lifted his gaze to the king's.

"I am well, my lord," he murmured, and held out his hand. "I'll have that bracelet again, if you please."

A little skittishly the king removed the bracelet once again and laid it in his hand. Focusing again, Alaric bent the bracelet open, as flat as he could, and laid it in the hollow he had made in the stone. The three runes, the last yet unrevealed, shone in the strengthening daylight as he stretched forth his right hand above the silver.

"*I form the light and create darkness*," the boy said steadily. "*I make peace and create evil: I the Lord do all these things.*"

He did not physically move his hand, though muscles and tendons tensed beneath the tanned skin as he flattened his palm and pressed downward. He did not touch the silver physically, but it nonetheless began to curve away, to conform to the hollow of the stone as though another, invisible hand were pressing down between his hand and the metal.

The bracelet collapsed on itself and grew molten then, though it gave off no heat. When Alaric pulled back his hand a few seconds later, the silver had bonded to the hollow like a shallow silver bowl, all marking obliterated save the third and final rune. After drawing a deep, steadying breath, he laid his forefinger under the sign and spoke its name.

"Three!"

This time, he gave but a fleeting outward hint of the reaction triggered by the rune: a blink, an interrupted breath immediately resumed. Then he took up the cup of water and turned toward Brion, gesturing with his eyes for Brion to extend his hands, which he did.

"Lavabo inter innocentes manus meas," he whispered, as he poured a little of the water over the king's hands, in a gesture familiar from the Mass. *I will wash my hands among the innocent.*

When the king had dried his hands on the edge of cloak Alaric offered, Alaric handed him the cup.

"Pour water in the silver to a finger's depth, Sire," he said softly.

Brion complied, then bent to set the cup on the ground. Nigel, without being told, moved to the opposite side of the stone and knelt, still clasping the scabbard to his breast.

"Now," Alaric prompted, "spread both hands flat above the water and repeat after me. Your hands are already holy, consecrated with chrism at your coronation just as a priest's hands are consecrated. I am instructed that this is appropriate."

With a swallow, Brion obeyed, his gaze locking with Alaric's, grey eyes to grey, as the boy began speaking.

"I, Brion, the Lord's Anointed . . ."

"I, Brion, the Lord's Anointed . . ."

". . . bless and consecrate thee, O creature of water . . ."

". . . bless and consecrate thee, O creature of water . . . by the living God,

by the true God, by the holy God . . . by that God Who, in the beginning, separated thee by His Word from the dry land . . . and Whose Spirit moved
upon thee."

"*Amen*," Alaric whispered.

"*Amen*," Brion echoed.

"Now, dip the fingers of your right hand in the water," Alaric began,
"and trace on the stone—"

"I know this part!" Brion broke in. His right hand was already parting the water in the sign of a cross as he, too, was caught up in that web
of recall established so many years before by his royal father. His every
gesture, every nuance of phrasing and pronunciation, was correct and
precise as he then moved to touch a moistened finger to the stone in front
of the silver.

"*Blessed be the Creator, yesterday and today, the Beginning and the
End, the Alpha and the Omega.*"

A cross glistened wetly on the stone, the Greek letters drawn confidently at the east and west aspects.

"*His are the seasons and the ages, to Him glory and dominion through
all the ages of eternity. Blessed be the Lord. Blessed be His Holy Name.*"

As he spoke, he had traced symbols of the elements in the four quad-
rants cut by the cross—Air, Fire, Water, Earth—and as he realized their
significance, the king drew back his hand as though stung and stared
aghast at Alaric.

"How—" He swallowed. "How did I know that?"

Alaric permitted himself a wan smile, by now all but resigned to acting upon memories and instructions he could not consciously remember.

"Just as I was, you have also been schooled for this day, Sire," he said.
"Now you have but to carry out the rest of your father's instructions, and
take up the power that is rightfully yours."

Brion bowed his head, the jewels on his leather circlet catching the
strengthening sunlight. "I—am not certain I know how. From what we
have seen and done so far, there must other triggers, other clues to aid
me, but—" He glanced up at the boy. "You must give me more guidance.
You are the master here, not I."

"No, Sire," the boy whispered, touching one forefinger to the water and bringing a shimmering droplet toward Brion's face. "*You* are the master."

The king's eyes tracked on the fingertip instinctively as it approached, closing as the droplet touched the center of his forehead. A shudder passed through the royal body, and Brion blinked. Then, in a daze, he reached to his throat and unfastened the great lion brooch that held his cloak in place, letting the red wool pool behind him, hefting the piece in his hand as the words came.

> Three drops of royal blood on water bright,
> to gather flame within a bowl of light.
> With consecrated hands, receive the Might
> of Haldane—'tis thy royal, sacred Right.

The king gazed unseeing at Alaric, at Nigel, at the red enameled brooch heavy in his hand. Then he turned the brooch over and freed the golden clasp pin from its catch, held out a left hand that did not waver.

"*Three drops of royal blood on water bright,*" he repeated. He brought the clasp against his thumb in a swift, sharp jab. As blood welled from the wound, he laid the brooch aside and squeezed the thumb, letting three dark drops fall upon the water—once, twice, thrice—to spread scarlet, concentric circles across the silver surface. A touch of tongue to wounded thumb, and then he was spreading his hands above the water, closing his eyes.

Stillness. A crystalline anticipation as Brion began to concentrate. And then, as Alaric extended his right hand above Brion's two and added his strength to the spell, a deep, musical reverberation, more felt than heard, throbbing through their minds. As the sunlight brightened, so also brightened the space beneath Brion's hands, until finally could be seen the ghostly beginnings of crimson fire flickering on the water. Brion's emotionless expression did not change as Alaric withdrew his hand and knelt.

"*Fear not, for I have redeemed thee,*" Alaric whispered, calling the words from memories not his own as the fire grew. "*I have called thee by*

*name, and thou art mine. When thou walkest through the fire, thou shalt
not be burned: neither shall the flame kindle upon thee. . . ."*

Brion did not open his eyes, but as Alaric's words faded into silence, the
king took a deep breath and slowly, deliberately, brought his hands to rest
flat on the silver of the bowl, heedless of the fire. Nigel gasped as his brother's hands entered the flames, but no word or sound escaped Brion's lips to
indicate the ordeal he was enduring. Head thrown back and eyes closed,
the king stood unflinching as the crimson fire climbed his arms and spread
over his entire body. But when the flames shortly died away, Brion opened
his eyes upon a world that would never appear precisely the same again,
and in which he could never again be merely mortal.

He leaned heavily on the altar-stone for just a moment, letting himself settle back into his body as he caught his breath. But when he lifted
his hands from the stone, his brother stifled an oath. Where the royal
hands had rested, the silver was black, burned away. Only the dark silhouettes remained, etched indelibly in the hollowed surface of the rock.

Brion went a little pale when he saw what he had done, and Nigel
crossed himself, but Alaric merely got to his feet and returned to the east,
throwing back his head and extending his arms before the Haldane sword
in a banishing spell, watching the canopy of golden light dissipate as he
turned his hands downward and lowered his arms.

But as he laid his hands on the hilt of the Haldane sword, he suddenly
realized that they were no longer alone. While they had worked their
magic, the men following Nigel had found the royal campsite: ten livery-
clad Haldane lancers with bows slung across their backs. They were gathered near the horses in as uneasy a band as Alaric had ever seen. Neither
Brion nor Nigel seemed to have noticed yet, apparently still caught up in
what had happened.

At once Alaric pulled the sword from the ground and hurried back to
the king to present it hilt first, hoping he would not get an arrow in the
back before he could surrender it, for the men would not take kindly to a
Deryni handling the precious Haldane sword. At the same time, Nigel
also noticed the men and touched Brion's elbow to warn him, jutting his
chin in their direction as his brother looked up. As Brion turned toward

them in surprise, hand now on the hilt of his sword, they went to their knees as one man, several crossing themselves furtively.

"Bloody hell," Brion murmured under his breath. "Did they see?"

Alaric gave a careful nod, keeping his hands in sight, away from his body. "So it would appear, Sire. I suggest that you go to them immediately and reassure them. Otherwise, the more timid among them are apt to bolt and run." He did not add that the men might well shoot *him*.

"They would run from *me*, their king?"

"You are more than a mere man to them just now, Sire," Alaric said uncomfortably. "They have seen that with their own eyes. Go to them, and quickly."

With a sigh, Brion took the scabbard from Nigel and sheathed the Haldane sword, giving it into his brother's keeping, then twitched at his battle harness and strode across the clearing toward the men, nervously wiping his hands against his thighs. The men watched his movements furtively as he came to a halt perhaps half a dozen steps from the nearest of them. Noting their scrutiny, especially of his hands, he lifted them to show the palms.

"You are entitled to an explanation," he said simply, as all eyes fastened on the hands, which bore no mark upon them. "As you can see, I am unharmed. I am very sorry if my actions caused you concern. Please rise."

The men got to their feet, only the chinking of their harness breaking the sudden stillness that had befallen the glade. Behind the king, Alaric quietly gathered up the king's cloak and the lion brooch and came after him, Nigel at his side with the royal sword. The men were silent, a few shifting uneasily, until one of the bolder ones cleared his throat and took a half step nearer.

"Sire."

"Lord Ralson?"

"Sire." The man shifted uneasily from one foot to the other and glanced at his comrades. "Sire, it appears to us that there was magic afoot," he said carefully. "We question the wisdom of allowing a Deryni to influence you so. When we saw—"

"What *did* you see, Gerald?" Brion asked softly.

Gerald Ralson cleared his throat again. "Well, I—we—that is, when we arrived, Sire, you were holding that brooch in your hand"—he gestured toward the lion brooch that Alaric held—"and then we saw you stab it into your thumb. You looked—not yourself, Sire. As if—as if something else was commanding you." He eyed Alaric meaningfully, and several of the other men moved closer behind him, hands creeping to rest on the hilts of their weapons.

"I see," Brion said. "And you think that it was Alaric who commanded me?"

"It appeared so to us, Majesty," another man rumbled, beard jutting defiantly.

Brion nodded. "And then you watched me hold my hands above the stone, and Alaric held his above my own. And then you saw me engulfed in flame—and that frightened you most of all."

The speaker nodded tentatively, and his movement was echoed by nearly every head there, along with low murmurs of frightened agreement. Brion sighed and glanced at the ground, looked up at them again.

"My lords, I will not lie to you. You were witness to very powerful magic. And I will not deny, nor will Alaric, that he lent me his assistance. And the Duke of Corwyn is, most definitely, Deryni."

The men said nothing, though a few exchanged glances.

"But there is more you cannot be aware of," Brion continued, keeping them snared in his grey Haldane gaze. "Each of you has heard the legends of my house—how, nearly two centuries ago, we returned to the throne of Gwynedd when the Deryni Imre was deposed. But do you really think that the Haldanes could have ousted a Deryni usurper without some power of their own?"

"Are you saying, then, that you are Deryni, Sire?" asked one bold soul from the rear ranks.

Brion smiled and shook his head. "No—or at least, I don't believe that I am. But the Haldanes do have very special gifts and abilities, handed down from father to son—or sometimes from brother to brother." His glance flicked briefly to Nigel, now standing at his right. "You know that we can sometimes tell when a man is lying, that we have great physical stamina.

"But we also have other powers when they are needed, which enable us to function *as if* we were, ourselves, Deryni. My father, King Cinhil, entrusted a few of these abilities to me before his death, but there were other abilities whose very existence he kept secret, for which he left certain instructions with Alaric Morgan, *unknown even to him*—and which were triggered by the threat of Hogan Gwernach's challenge which we received last night. Alaric was a child of four when he was instructed by my father, so that even *he* would not remember his instructions until it was necessary. And apparently I was also instructed.

"The result, in part, was what you saw. If there was a commanding force, another influence present within the fiery circle, it was my father's. The rite is now fulfilled, and I am my father's successor *in every way*, with all his powers and abilities."

"Your late father provided for all of this?" one of the men whispered.

Brion nodded. "There is no evil in it, Alwyne. You knew my father well. You know that he would never have drawn down evil."

"No, he would not," the man replied, glancing at Alaric almost involuntarily. "But, what of the Deryni lad?"

"Our fathers, mine and his, made a pact: that Alaric Morgan should come to court to serve me when he reached the proper age. That bargain has been kept. Alaric Morgan serves me and the realm of Gwynedd."

"But, he is Deryni, Sire! What if he is in league with—"

"He is in league with *me*!" Brion retorted, setting his left hand on Alaric's shoulder. "He is *my* liege man, just as all of you, sworn to my service since the age of nine. In that time, he has rarely left my side. Given the compulsions that my father placed upon him, do you really believe that he could betray me?"

Ralson cleared his throat, boldly moving a step forward and making a bow before the king could continue.

"Sire, it is best that we do not discuss the boy. None of us here, Your Majesty included, can truly know what is in his heart. You are the issue now. If you were to reassure us, in some way, that you harbor no ill intent, that you have not allied yourself with dark powers—"

"Do you require my oath to that effect?" the king said softly, letting his hand fall from Alaric's shoulder. The mildness of his response was, itself, suddenly threatening. "You would be that bold?"

Ralson nodded carefully, not daring to respond with words, and his movement was again echoed by most of the men standing at his back. After a frozen moment, Brion gave his brother a curt nod. At once Nigel unsheathed the Haldane sword and knelt to hold up the cross-hilt before the king. Brion laid his bare right hand upon it and faced his waiting men.

"Before all of you and before God, and upon this holy sword, I swear that I am innocent of your suspicions, that I have made no dark pact with any evil power, that the rite you have witnessed was benevolent and legitimate. I further swear that I have never been, nor am I now, commanded by Alaric Morgan or any other man, human or Deryni; that he is as innocent as I of any evil intent toward the people and crown of Gwynedd. This is the oath of Brion Donal Cinhil Urien Haldane, King of Gwynedd, Prince of Meara, and Lord of the Purple March. If I be forsworn, may this sword shatter in my hour of need, may all succor desert me, and may the name of Haldane vanish from the earth."

In silence he crossed himself slowly, deliberately: a gesture that was echoed by Alaric, Nigel, and then the rest of the men who had witnessed the oath. Then he set his hand on the hilt of the sword and took it from Nigel, raising it.

"Now: ride with me to Rustan!"

Chapter 46

"Thou wilt prolong the king's life . . ."
—PSALMS 61:6

THE rest of Nigel's lancers caught up with them while they were breaking camp, along with a score of Arban Howell's men led by Arban himself. All the day long, their expanded party clambered along the rugged Llegoddin Canyon Trace: a winding trail treacherous with stream-tumbled stones that sometimes shifted beneath the horses' hooves.

The stream responsible for their footing ran shallow along their right, sometimes spilling onto the trail and sometimes even crossing it. At least it was cool in the little canyon, the shade a refreshing respite from the glaring sun, but Alaric knew that the echo of steel-shod hooves would announce their approach long before they actually reached Rustan. Along the last few miles, the canyon walls closed in on them until the riders were obliged to go two abreast. Alaric thought it seemed a perfect place for an ambush, though his increasing knack for sensing danger gave them almost no warning.

Right after the track made a sharp turn through the stream again, it suddenly opened out to a wide, grassy meadow of several acres. Across the center waited a long and broad line of armored horsemen, nearly twice the number of Gwynedd's forces—and most of the king's men were still behind them.

The Tolan men were mailed and helmed with steel, their lances and war axes gleaming in the afternoon sun. Their white-clad leader sat a heavy sorrel destrier before them, lance in hand and banner bright at his back. The device on the banner gave little doubt regarding his pretension. Along with the ducal arms of Tolan—the ermine field with a red lion's *jambe* clutching a coronet—he had quartered royal Gwynedd.

An academic point, however. All around Alaric, Brion and Nigel and the others were drawing their swords, urging their horses forward so the men behind could crowd after them. Suddenly Alaric realized that this was real, no training exercise, that very soon the men ahead were going to try to kill him and those around him. Even as he drew his own sword, and as the men behind jostled to ride clear of the canyon's confines, the Festillic pretender lowered his lance and began the attack.

The thunder of their charge shook the ground, punctuated by the jingle of harness and mail, the creak of leather, the snorting and whinnies of the heavy Tolan warhorses and the lighter steeds of the lancers. As quickly as they could, the Gwynedd men fanned out to absorb the charge. Just before the two forces clashed, a man charging near the king shouted, "A Haldane!"—a cry that was picked up and echoed immediately by most of his comrades in arms.

Then all were swept into the melee, steel clashing, men and horses falling, horses screaming riderless and wounded as lances splintered on shield and mail and bone. As the fighting closed hand to hand, lances falling aside, cries of the wounded and dying punctuated the butcher sounds of sword and axe on flesh.

It was so very different from Duke Richard's drills: Alaric's first true battle. Somehow surviving the initial clash unscathed, he soon found himself locked shield to shield with a man twice his age and size, who pressed him relentlessly and tried to crush his helm with a mace.

Alaric countered by ducking under his shield and wheeling his horse to the right, hoping to come at his opponent from the other side, but the man was already anticipating his move and swinging in counterattack. At the last possible moment, Alaric deflected the blow with his shield, reeling as he tried to keep his seat and strike at the same time. But his focus had been distracted, and instead of coming in from behind, on the man's temporarily open right side, he only embedded his sword in the other's high cantle.

He recovered before the blade could be wrenched from his grasp—just—gripping hard with his knees as his horse lashed out with a steel-shod foreleg and caught the man in the knee. Then, desperately parrying a blow from a second attacker, he managed to cut the first man's girth and wound his mount, also kicking out at yet a third man who was approaching from his shield side. The first man hit the ground with a muffled clank of battle harness as his horse went down, and narrowly missed trampling as one of his own men thundered past in pursuit of one of Brion's wounded.

Another strike, low and deadly, and Alaric's would-be slayer was, himself, the slain. It was the first time Alaric had killed a man, but he dared not think about it just now. Breathing hard under his helmet, he wheeled to scan the battle for the king—and immediately had to defend himself from renewed attack by two men now afoot. He managed to finish them off, but less cleanly than he might have wished. He tried not to look at the ruins of the second man's face as he fell screaming. But on a battlefield, he realized there was little room for finesse; only survival.

The king himself was faring little better. Though still mounted and holding his own, Brion had been swept away from his mortal enemy in the initial clash, and had not yet been able to win free to press for single combat. Nigel was fighting at his brother's side, the royal banner in his shield hand and a sword in the other, but the banner mostly served to hamper Nigel and mark the location of Gwynedd's king. Just now, both royal brothers were under serious attack from half a dozen of the Tolan men.

As for the Marluk, Alaric finally spotted him on the far side of the fighting, sword now in hand, apparently content, for the moment, to concentrate his efforts on cutting down some of Brion's men and avoiding Brion's reputed superior skill. As the two Haldane brothers beat back their attackers, the king glanced across the battlefield and saw his enemy, unhorsed another of his opponents with a backhanded blow, raised his sword, and shouted the enemy's name:

"Gwernach!"

The pretender turned in his direction and jerked his horse to a rear, circling his sword above his head. His helmet was gone, either lost or discarded, and pale hair blew wild from beneath his mail coif.

"Leave him to me!" he shouted to his men, spurring toward Brion and cutting down another Haldane man in passing. "Stand and fight, usurper! Gwynedd is mine by right!"

The Marluk's men fell back from the Gwynedd line as their master pounded across the field. With a savage gesture, Brion waved off his own men and spurred his horse toward the enemy.

Now was the time both sides had been waiting for: the direct, personal combat of the two kings. Steel shivered against shields as the two men met and clashed in the center of the field, exchanging ferocious blows. Their men, suddenly aware of the shift in battle, gradually ceased their own fighting and drew back to watch, temporarily suspending hostilities. Alaric kneed his mount closer to Nigel, standing a little in his stirrups to see, praying that the king could survive.

For a time, the two seemed evenly matched, exchanging and parrying blows with ease, though both men clearly were tiring. The Marluk managed to take a chunk out of the top of Brion's shield, but Brion divested the Marluk of a stirrup, and nearly a foot.

Finally, Brion's sword found the throat of his opponent's mount. The wounded animal collapsed with a liquid scream, dumping its rider in a heap. Brion, discarding niceties in the interest of survival, tried to ride down his enemy then and there.

But the Marluk rolled beneath his shield on the first pass and nearly tripped up Brion's horse, scrambling to his feet and bracing, sword still in hand, as Brion wheeled to come at him again. The second pass cost Brion his mount as well, gutted by the Marluk's sword. As the horse went down screaming in a bloody tangle of entrails, Brion rolled clear and managed to end up on his feet, whirling to face his opponent.

Both men were breathing hard. Alaric could hear them panting inside their helmets. For several taut minutes the two circled one another and exchanged tentative blows as the rest of their forces eased cautiously closer to observe. Though the Marluk had the advantage of weight and height, Brion had youth and greater agility in his favor. The outcome, in terms of mere physical ability, was by no means certain.

Finally, after another inconclusive flurry of blows, the two again drew apart, visibly tiring, and the Marluk sketched an ironic salute in the direction of his opponent.

"You fight well, for a Haldane," he conceded, still breathless. He gestured with his sword toward the waiting men. "We are well matched, at least in steel. And even were we to cast our men into the fray again, it would still come down to the same, in the end: you against me."

"Or your power against mine," Brion amended softly, letting the tip of his sword sink to rest against the ground. "That *is* your eventual intention, is it not?"

The Marluk shrugged and started to speak, but Brion interrupted.

"No, you would have slain me by steel if you could," the king said. "To win by magic exacts a price, and might not give you the sort of victory you seek, if you would rule my human kingdom and not fear for your throne. The folk of Gwynedd would not take kindly to a Deryni king, after your bloody ancestors."

The Marluk smiled and shrugged again. "By force, physical or arcane—it matters little in the long reckoning. It is the victory itself which will command the people after today. But you, Haldane, your position is far more precarious than mine, dynastically speaking. Do you see yon riders, and the slight one dressed in blue?"

He gestured with his sword toward the far opening of the clearing, where a dozen watching riders surrounded a pale, blue-clad figure on a mouse-grey palfrey.

"Yonder is my daughter and heir, Haldane," he said smugly. "Regardless of the outcome here today, *she* rides free—you cannot stop her—to keep my name and blood and memory alive until another time. But you— your brother and heir stands near, his life a certain forfeit if I win." He gestured toward Nigel, then rested the tip of his sword before him once more. "And the next and final Haldane is your uncle, Duke Richard of Carthmoor: a childless bachelor of fifty. After him, there are no others."

Alaric cast a nervous glance at Nigel, watching with the Haldane banner beside him. What the Marluk had said was basically true. There were no other male Haldanes beyond Brion's brother and his uncle, at least for now; and the queen, thus far, had failed to quicken, though he knew it was not for want of trying. Brion seemed besotted with his new queen, and she with him.

Nor, indeed, was there any way to prevent the escape of the Marluk's heir, regardless of the outcome here. Even if Brion won today, the Marluk's daughter would remain a future threat. The centuries-long struggle for supremacy in Gwynedd would not end here—unless, of course, Brion lost.

He knew Brion was very much aware of that, too. They had known it before they worked the ritual that, God willing, had released the Haldane potential in Gwynedd's king and given him the knowledge and power to stand against the Festillic pretender. He found himself holding his breath as the king, in a gesture of disdain, cast aside his shield and then removed his helm, tossing it after the shield.

And then, displaying far more confidence than he probably felt, for he would never play for higher stakes than life and Crown, Brion Haldane slowly backed off a few paces and lowered the tip of his blade to the ground, carefully and decisively tracing a symbol in the dust.

"Hear me, Hogan Gwernach, for I, Brion Haldane, Anointed of the Lord, King of Gwynedd and Lord of the Purple March, do call thee forth to combat mortal, for that thou hast raised hostile hand against me and, through me, against my people of Gwynedd. This I will defend upon my body and my soul, to the death, so help me God."

The Marluk's face had not changed expression during Brion's challenge, but now he, too, cast aside his shield, pulled off his mail coif and arming cap, then strode out confidently, to set the tip of his sword to the symbol scratched in the dust and retrace its lines.

"And I, Hogan Gwernach, descendant of the lawful kings of Gwynedd in antiquity, do return thy challenge, Brion Haldane, and charge that thou art base pretender to the throne and the crown thou holdest. And this I will defend upon my body and my soul, to the death, so help me God."

With the last words, he began drawing another symbol over the first one. Alaric could not see what it was, but it caused Brion to start back and then dash the Marluk's sword aside with his own, using his boot to obliterate whatever his opponent had begun to draw. Alaric could not hear what Brion said then, as he restored the original lines, but he sensed the anger, and prayed that the king would not let that anger sway him to recklessness.

Fortunately, good sense prevailed. Whatever the king had said, it caused the Marluk to step back and salute sharply with his blade, a hard look on his face, then retreat perhaps a dozen feet as Brion did the same. As the king extended his arms from his sides, sword still in hand, Alaric saw his lips move: a warding spell, no doubt, for answering fire sprang up crimson at his back.

The Marluk answered with a similar defense, blue fire joining crimson to complete the protective circle. Nigel and the other men around Alaric gasped as it flared up in a containing dome of shimmering purple, and everyone moved back a few steps more.

With that preparation, both men raised their swords again, though the protecting dome partially obscured what went on within. Fire sizzled along both blades, vast bolts of energy beginning to arc from sword to sword between the men, ebbing and flowing as battle was joined. The dome brightened as they fought, containing energies so intense that all around it would have perished, had the wards not held it in. The air within grew hazy, so that those without could no longer see the principals who battled there.

So it continued for what seemed to Alaric like an eternity. The king's men and the Marluk's eyed one another with increasing nervousness. When, at last, the crackling haze in the dome began to flicker erratically and die down, naught could be seen within save for two ghostly, fire-edged figures in silhouette, one of them staggering drunkenly.

Even Alaric could not tell for certain which was which, though he thought he knew, and prayed he was correct. One of the men had fallen to his knees and remained there, sword lifted in a last, desperate warding-off gesture. The other stood poised to strike, though something seemed to hold him back.

For several heartbeats, the tableau remained frozen, the tension growing between the two. But then the kneeling man reeled sideward with a cry of anguish and let fall his sword, collapsing forward on his hands with head bowed in defeat.

The victor's sword seemed to descend in slow motion, severing head from body in one blow and showering dust and victor and vanquished with blood. The act quenched the fire almost to nonexistence, so that at last they could see that it was Brion who had survived.

At that, a cheer went up from the men of Gwynedd. At the mouth of the canyon beyond, a slender figure on a grey horse wheeled to ride away with her escort. Those of the Marluk's men who were still ahorse scrambled to follow after, some of them picking up men afoot as they fled. A few of the king's men briefly gave pursuit, but fell back as the rest of the Marluk's men began casting down their weapons and surrendering.

Brion could not have seen much through the haze that remained, for the dome seemed still intact, but he clearly was aware on some level that more was yet required of him. Staggering back to the center of the circle, he traced the dust-drawn symbol a final time and mouthed the syllables of a banishing spell.

Then, as the remnants of the dome collapsed inward and the fiery circle died away, he stabbed his sword into the cleansing earth and staggered to his knees, bracing both hands on the quillons to bow his head briefly before the cross-hilt. When he finally rose, at last becoming aware of the cheers of his men, he retrieved his sword and gazed briefly at the now-empty canyon mouth before turning to walk slowly toward the Haldane banner, leaving the headless body of his enemy behind him. The men fell silent and parted before him as he came, Gwynedd and Tolan men alike.

Most of Brion's men remained ahorse or on their feet, perhaps two score of them, and most of Earl Arban's men and Arban himself; far fewer of the Marluk's men, and nearly all of them were wounded. The silence was palpable as he passed among them, and many of them looked wary of him.

He stopped and turned to look around him—at the wounded of both sides struggling upright to stare at him, interspersed with more than a score who would never move again. Among those dead, the Marluk was but one more. Under the Haldane banner in Nigel's hand, Nigel and Alaric still sat their battle-weary steeds. He was relieved to note that Saer, Prince Nigel's squire, had survived the battle: afoot, but supporting himself on Nigel's stirrup.

In the silence after battle, Brion let his gaze fall on each man in turn, catching and holding each man's attention in rapt, unresisting thrall.

"We shall not speak of the details of this battle beyond this place," he said simply. The words crackled with authority, compulsion, and only Alaric Morgan, of all who heard, knew the force behind that simple statement. Though most of them would never realize it consciously, every man present had just been touched indelibly by Brion Haldane's special magic.

Chapter 47

*"For thou hast girded me with strength unto the battle: thou hast
subdued under me those that rose up against me."*
—PSALMS 18:39

I N what remained of the day, the king set his men to see to the
wounded, Gwynedd men and Tolaners alike. The Tolan prisoners
were detailed to bury the dead. Earl Arban's forces had lost three
men, but he elected to take them back to Eastmarch for burial; no pleasant task in the summer heat, but he wished not to leave behind any of
those whose welfare he so recently had sworn to protect.

"I understand," Brion told him, as Arban and his party prepared to
ride out. "Know that I appreciate that you came back to assist us, and I
value those men's lives. Did they have families?"

"I don't even know, Sire," Arban said with a shake of his head. "They
are so recently come to my service. . . . But I'll find out," he promised.

"Do," Brion said. "I shall have purses sent to their families, when you
send me word."

"Thank you, Sire."

When Arban and his men had gone, the Gwynedd men not tending
the wounded began to make camp, for it clearly was too late to even
think about heading out. At least there were three fewer graves to be dug,
and the Tolaners would be allowed to take away the body of their fallen
duke for burial with his own kin.

Once the others were buried, the Tolan men were sworn never to
raise arms against Gwynedd again, before being released to take their

wounded and depart. Lord Lester sent out pickets to guard the departure point toward Cardosa, to make certain they did not return.

Shortly before dusk, while the Gwynedd men were settling into camp for the night, cleaning weapons and supping on meager travel rations, Jamyl Arilan and Llion arrived in a cloud of dust with twenty more Haldane lancers, sent by Duke Richard to find the king and his brother.

"We thought you would be in Eastmarch," Jamyl said, throwing himself from his horse. "What happened here?"

Brion, who had been moving among the wounded with Alaric, came to join his friend as Llion dismounted with less alacrity, anxious eyes searching Alaric's form for any sign of injury.

"A few of our friends from Tolan decided to meet me here instead," the king said lightly. "Hogan Gwernach took particular pains to make me feel welcome." He paused a beat. "I'm afraid I wasn't feeling particularly hospitable."

Jamyl's eyes widened, and he came close to seize the king's arm. "Brion, what did you do?" he whispered.

"I'd prefer not to talk about it," Brion replied. "Suffice it to say that Hogan Gwernach is no longer a threat."

"What does that mean?" Jamyl insisted, searching the king's eyes. "Did you kill him?"

Brion pulled his arm away and glanced at the ground. "I did what I had to do," he whispered. "Now, leave it, Jamyl!"

"But—"

"Just leave it!" the king repeated, and turned away to hail one of the men who had just risen from helping tend the wounded. As he continued on to join the man, Jamyl resolved to find out precisely what the king had meant.

He soon deduced that the king had, indeed, killed Hogan Gwernach—*after* something else had happened. But finding someone who would talk about it proved more difficult than Jamyl had expected. Though he questioned several of Nigel's men who had joined him and the king at Rustan, none of them were inclined to provide details. It took more insistent persuasion later that evening, when he drew one of the knights well apart from the others and simply took control of his mind.

What he discovered was startling. Though the man's memories were, of necessity, focused on his own survival and defending the king, he had also been witness to something that clearly was magical in nature, once the king faced Hogan Gwernach in single combat. And it had not been the mere clash of conventional weapons that finally had won the day for Brion Haldane.

It has finally happened, he told Stefan Coram later that night, by means of a magical link to his Camberian Council colleague, with instructions to convey the information to the rest of the Council; he felt the news too important to wait for the chance to attend in person. *We have long suspected that Donal must have made some provision for his son to assume his powers, and that Alaric Morgan was probably involved. This seems to confirm that suspicion.*

But Brion will not discuss it? Stefan asked.

He will not. And he was savvy enough to set compulsions in the minds of the witnesses, so that they cannot *talk about it. I daren't press him, for fear that he now has the ability to discover what I am. And Alaric and Nigel are likewise off-limits—Alaric, because we know he's half-Deryni, and Nigel because we just don't know what abilities he might have, as a Haldane heir.*

Nor was Jamyl able to press the king by more conventional persuasion, because the next morning Brion announced his determination to continue on with only his squire, as had been his original intention.

"Nothing that happened here changes my travel plans," the king told Jamyl and his brother over a meager breakfast the next morning. "I still intend to make my way back to Rhemuth on my own. I need some time alone. I've told Alaric that we'll go by way of Lendour, and stop at Cynfyn before we head west toward home," he added, with a glance at Alaric, who was packing up their saddlebags in preparation for departure, listening but saying nothing. "It's been a while since I was there. I'd like to see how his regents are looking after things, and thank them for their assistance in bringing Xenia home."

Neither Jamyl nor Llion nor Nigel could dissuade him from his plan, or persuade him to take along additional guards.

"But I *will* take along Llion, if that will make you feel better," the king told them. "It's probably good to have another sword along. But we'll be safe enough in Lendour. And Alaric's Lendour folk need to see him in my company, and be aware what a fine young man he's becoming."

In the end, with further badgering from Jiri and Lord Lester as well, he did agree to take along a pair of lancers from Jamyl's contingent: fresh warriors, who also had not witnessed the battle at Rustan. It somewhat mollified both the older men, who had no choice but to take the rest of the men back to Rhemuth, along with Jamyl, Nigel, and Saer.

"But don't delay over-long," Jiri said. "You have a queen who requires your attention. And not to put too fine a point on it, but you need an heir of your body."

"Believe me, I am well aware of that," the king replied, smiling. "And I intend to continue working on that as soon as I return."

THEY rode away from the dismantling campsite in good spirits, Alaric and Llion to either side of the king and with the two lancers following behind. They traveled in silence at first, for the king had made it clear that he had much to think about following his defeat of the Marluk, but the five of them soon fell into an easy camaraderie, as they headed farther south. Alaric, too, welcomed the time to ponder what had happened, and the men he had killed.

For several days they traveled through the rolling plains of central Lendour, observing the crops nearing harvest, availing themselves of local hospitality, finally striking west toward the Lendouri capital. Half a day out, with the king's permission, Alaric sent one of the lancers ahead to advise of their approach.

Even with so scant a warning, a sizeable welcome escort turned out to greet them: most of his Lendour regents, led by Jovett Chandos and his father. Zoë was waiting with her three children and Jovett's mother when they entered the castle yard, all of them overjoyed to see him again, so soon. Zoë could hardly believe how much he had grown in a year.

"You are very nearly a man!" she exclaimed, as she drew him into a happy embrace. "But of course, you *are* nearly of age. Your mother would be so proud!"

"I hope so," he said, briefly allowing himself the luxury of her affection. He wondered, though, if his mother would have been proud to learn that her little boy had become a killer. It had been in defense of the king, but he still tried not to think too much about that; it was what knights did, though killing was not meant to be pleasant.

"I see that my cousins are following in my footsteps," he added, noting the new Lendour pages' livery on the two boys, Kailan and Charlan, who now were ten and nine. "When did this happen?"

"At Twelfth Night," Zoë replied. "Kailan could have started last year, but he wanted to wait so that he and his brother could begin their training together."

Alaric smiled. "They're fortunate to have one another. It's always good to have a partner to train with. When they're a bit older, perhaps we can arrange for them to spend some time at Rhemuth, or even at Coroth."

"I'm sure they would like that," Zoë replied, "though I should miss them terribly. What brings you here again so quickly? Are you here for long?"

"Only a day or two, I'm afraid," Alaric replied, glancing back to the king, who was busily greeting Alaric's regents. "We've just come from some—delicate military maneuvers up in Eastmarch. He'll tell you what he wants you to know, over dinner."

"That sounds ominous," Zoë said. She paused to stroke the hair of her youngest, the six-year-old Alyce Maria, who had come over to see her illustrious cousin. "Can you say hello to your cousin Alaric, love? He's grown so much, I wonder that you even know him."

At dinner that night, the king had little to say about their recent campaign other than to remark that a traitor had been executed and a would-be usurper defeated, but it soon became clear that the king had a purpose in coming to the Lendouri capital, besides just a social one. Sitting at the head of the table with Alaric at his right hand and Jovett at his left, he rose when supper had been mostly completed and called the room to order with a rap of his knuckles on the table, then came around to stand before the table, looking up the hall at the two long tables set along the walls, filled with Lendour retainers and their wives. Llion had risen at a nod from the king, and briefly disappeared from the room, to return with something wrapped in fine wool, several handspans across and a handspan thick.

"My lords and ladies," the king said, "if you would indulge a visitor to your hall, I should like to share an item of personal business with all of you tonight. Lord Alaric, would you please attend me?"

Puzzled, Alaric rose and moved to obey, also coming around in front of the table. When he exchanged a questioning glance with Llion, the young knight only smiled and shook his head slightly.

"As many of you will have gathered," the king continued, "I have been extremely well pleased with the progress of your young lord, as he grows toward manhood. I prefer not to dwell on details of our most recent campaign in the north, but I know you are well aware how he offered the services of many in this room to assist in the mission last summer, to bring home the remains of my sister and her child. Though he technically serves me as squire, his service has been far beyond what I normally would expect of one so young.

"Accordingly," he set one hand on Alaric's shoulder, "though he yet lacks a few months before he attains his legal majority, I have decided to confirm him as your earl tonight, before you all." Alaric's jaw dropped, and a ripple of pleased surprise murmured among those present. "He will still return with me to Rhemuth as my squire, for he yet has lessons to learn before he is ready for knighthood and the full exercise of his rank as earl, but I have no doubt that he will continue to impress us all. Here in Cynfyn, I feel confident that his regents will continue to see to the welfare of Lendour as they have hitherto."

As Alaric listened in astonishment, and the throng gathered in the hall broke out in cheers and whistles of approval, Llion folded back layers from the bundle of fabric in his arms to reveal the silver coronet that Kenneth Morgan had worn as earl.

"I believe it's appropriate to kneel now," the king said aside to Alaric, lifting the coronet to display it to the watching Lendour folk.

Speechless, Alaric sank to one knee and briefly bowed his head before the king, then looked up.

"Alaric Anthony Morgan," the king said, "I declare you of legal age in Lendour and confirm you in your rank as earl, by right of your father and of your mother." He set the coronet on Alaric's head, then rested both his hands on the boy's shoulders. "Frankly, I would also confirm you for Corwyn, if I dared, but I fear my great lords would have apoplexy if I gave them a fourteen-year-old duke. So that will have to wait until you reach the age of eighteen, and can be knighted. You already have your father's signet, I believe?"

Alaric nodded, pulling it from under his tunic. He wore it on the chain with his St. Camber medal, but he let the king remove it, then quietly tucked the chain and medal back inside his clothing.

After briefly displaying the gold signet to the watching crowd, the king slid the ring onto Alaric's left forefinger. "Wear this ring as a token of the fidelity you have pledged to me, and a symbol of your authority. Arise, Earl of Lendour."

After the excitement had abated a little, Alaric took his place at the head of the hall, his liege lord at his side, and formally received the fealty of his vassals in Lendour. He then confirmed his new councilors of state, formerly his regents. He knew little would change in the immediate future, as he prepared to return to Rhemuth with the king, but it was heartening to have received this recognition of his growing maturity.

THEY left two days later, and were back in Rhemuth by the end of July, having taken their time on the return journey. They sent no riders ahead on the day they approached Rhemuth's eastern gate, but entered unchallenged to wind their way past the cathedral square and up the processional road that led to the castle.

The guards at the gatehouse scrambled to attention as they realized it was the king, one of them sending a man running ahead to alert those at the hall. A hastily assembled guard of honor was waiting as they rode into the yard, and anxious squires came running to take their horses, Saer de Traherne among them. Duke Richard and Prince Nigel were waiting on the stairs, Richard with his hands on his hips.

"I hope," said the duke to his royal nephew, "that you are very satisfied with yourself. We expected you several weeks ago."

"As a matter of fact, I *am* satisfied," Brion retorted, as he swung down from his horse. "Come inside, Uncle, and I'll tell you all about it."

As Alaric, too, dismounted, he found himself wondering whether the king intended to tell his uncle *all* about what had happened during his absence from the capital. But as he and Llion followed the three Haldanes up the great hall steps and into the hall, and the royal pair headed on into the withdrawing room, it became clear that this was to be a private conversation.

But apparently not a bitter one, for the three men seemed amiable and content when they appeared at table that night in the great hall. Jehana, happily reunited with her handsome young husband, was glowing. Princess Silke, attended by a petite, dark-haired girl Alaric did not recognize, likewise looked contented enough, as did the queen dowager. Alaric, for his part, was not summoned to table service that evening, and was glad to be excused early to go to bed.

But the usual routine resumed the next morning, with weapons drill in the practice yard, and sparring with blunted steel, then a ride-out at midday. After the rigors of the field, and the miles they had covered in the preceding two months, Alaric easily performed as he was asked. Duke Richard observed him closely for several days, then drew him aside after himself putting Alaric through a live steel drill.

"You've changed," he said, removing his practice helm and accepting a towel from the page assigned to attend the squires and instructors. "Walk with me."

Alaric took a towel of his own and mopped at his sweaty face as he fell in beside the duke.

"I understand that you killed a man or two at Rustan," Richard said, glancing at him sidelong.

"I did, sir," Alaric said. "They were trying to kill me."

"As good a reason as I've ever heard," Richard replied. "No qualms, then?"

"No, sir."

"Good. And I must say that I was happy to hear that my nephew went ahead and declared you of age. Your performance of late entirely merits it. And it was the right thing to do it in front of your people. Though I must confess, I was somewhat concerned that he just went haring off without telling anyone where he was going."

"We did tell Sir Jiri and Sir Jamyl and Prince Nigel, sir. They knew we were returning by way of Lendour."

"But to go with just Llion and the two lancers," Richard replied. "Anything might have happened. It will be your job to help him keep out of trouble, lad."

Alaric managed to suppress most of a dubious snort. "Do you think I could stop him, sir, if he really wanted to do something?"

"Probably not," Richard conceded. "At least not yet. But you will have to try. And you *are* Deryni."

"I—don't think that either of us would be happy if I used my powers to do that, sir."

"No, probably not." He grimaced. "Well, just do your best."

CHAPTER 48

THE king's order not to speak of the events at Rustan was not universally obeyed. Jamyl continued to ferret out the truth, by questioning several eyewitnesses; and it can be assumed that at least a few others present had enough ability, from long-suppressed Deryni bloodlines, to resist the order and begin speculating.

The real trouble began when rumors regarding the magical nature of the king's confrontation with the Marluk began to reach the new queen. Queen Jehana's confrontation with the king, behind closed doors, would reverberate throughout the royal household and, indeed, the court.

"Stay in your quarters," Llion told Alaric, when the row first began.

"But—"

"The queen has learned of the magic the king used to defeat the Marluk," Llion said. "She knows that you were involved."

"But, no one was supposed to—"

"*Someone* has been talking," Llion said sharply. "Did he really think that no one would speak? There were scores of men who saw what went on."

Alaric swallowed hard and averted his gaze. "I had nothing to do with that part. I only helped the king awaken his power."

"That isn't the way the queen sees it."

"Is she—terribly angry with me?"

"*Livid* would be a better description. I heard things being thrown."

And matters got worse the next morning. Alaric slept but little that night, but was awakened early by the sound of horsemen assembling in the castle yard: most of Queen Jehana's Bremagni guards, mounted and armed, ready to ride.

And then, the spectacle of the queen herself, hurrying through the great hall in the midst of additional guards, dressed for travel all in black, with three of her ladies, her chaplain, her two religious sisters, and even Princess Silke among them. They halted for nothing as they made their way to the yard, even though the king and his uncle came hurrying after, much under-slept, to remonstrate with the still distraught Jehana.

"And where do you think you're going?" Brion demanded, though he did not try to lay hands on her. Her guards were well armed and armored, and looked to be in no mood to allow any interference with their royal mistress. "Jehana, you are a queen! You have duties and responsibilities. You cannot just go riding off into the countryside!"

"I need time to think!" she retorted. "I intend to seek sanctuary in a house of religion. Do not try to stop me! I will send word when I am ready to talk to you!"

"Let her go," Duke Richard said quietly, laying a staying hand on his nephew's shoulder. "She has ample men. She will be safe enough in a convent, and will come to her senses soon enough."

"Jehana!" the king cried after her. "Would you rather the Marluk had killed me? Try to understand!"

But the queen would not listen, and let herself be mounted on a swift palfrey and swept away in the midst of her men and household. Brion watched them go, then summoned Jamyl and Jiri with a stormy glance.

"Go after her. Take a squadron of lancers. Do not try to stop her, but report back to me as to where she has gone. My uncle is right. Perhaps she needs time to consider her anger."

THE king bided his time in the days and weeks that followed, moody and short-tempered. The old queen had taken to her chambers, emerging most nights to preside at table with the king, but disinclined to discuss the new queen's absence. From time to time, one of the lancers sent to follow Jehana returned to report her progress, heading east and then north, but thus far she had not taken refuge with any known religious house.

For his part, Alaric kept his head down and tried to avoid private converse with the king, for he felt responsible for the queen's absence. He kept to himself, save for required training, said little even to Llion, and took his frustrations out on his opponents at weapons practice. This behavior soon caught the notice of Prince Nigel.

"It isn't your fault, you know," the prince said after a particularly aggressive match in which Alaric had actually disarmed him.

"That I'm Deryni? No, it isn't. But I helped him to magic."

"And saved his life!" Nigel retorted. "I was there! Can you imagine what the Marluk would have done to him, if he'd had no magic?"

"So he saved his kingdom and lost his queen!" Alaric returned. "Do you think he's thanking me for that?"

"Well, let's see if he is," Nigel said, seizing his upper arm and marching him toward the withdrawing room. "Do *not* fight me on this, or you shall see what the wrath of an angry Haldane is all about. If *he* doesn't thrash you, I shall!"

The prince's outburst shocked Alaric to silence, and he meekly let himself be chivvied along, half stumbling as Nigel drew him up the steps behind the dais and right through the door to the withdrawing room. The king was within, conferring with Jiri Redfearn, who must have returned unbeknownst to Alaric. Sir Tiarnán and Llion were also present.

"Can't this wait?" the king snapped.

"No, I don't think it can," Nigel replied. "You have news?"

Brion shook his head. "Mostly more of the same." He glanced at the others. "Jiri and Tiarnán, out! Llion, you stay. And you"—he pointed to Alaric—"sit."

His gesture at a stool beside the map table left no doubt as to his wishes. As Alaric sat, the king hooked another stool closer with a booted foot and also sat, gesturing for Nigel to do the same. Llion came to stand near Alaric, looking very solemn, indeed.

"Now. What is the problem?" the king demanded.

"Alaric feels responsible for the queen's absence," Nigel said. "He believes that the magic he awakened in you has driven her off."

"Well, he isn't responsible. Magic *has* driven her off, but it was *my* magic." Brion paused to draw a deep breath and shifted his gaze to Alaric. "Do you really think I blame you?"

Alaric averted his gaze, nervously intertwining his fingers. "She's gone, isn't she? And it's because of my magic."

"No, it's because of *my* magic, and what I did with my magic." Brion shook his head. "I blame that blasted priest of hers, and those sisters. I should never have allowed them to come with her household."

"Sire, that is hardly realistic," Llion ventured. "The queen is a pious young woman. You cannot have forgotten the sisters who were present at your betrothal."

Brion snorted. "Busy old crows!"

"But you must have known she would bring some of them," Nigel said. "As I understand it, she was convent educated by those 'old crows.' I would have been surprised if she did *not* bring some of them along as part of her household. And a queen needs her own chaplain; it's logical that she should have brought her own."

"Well, the timing could hardly have been worse," Brion muttered. "First the de Courcy affair, then the expedition into Eastmarch. Perhaps it was all too much, coming from the background she did."

"Sire, may I ask what news Sir Jiri brought?" Llion asked.

Brion let out his breath in a huff. "She seems to have taken refuge in an abbey up by Shannis Meer, in the Rheljan Mountains. Saint Giles, it's called. Jamyl has set up a camp nearby, to wait her out."

"You won't go get her?" Nigel asked.

Brion shook his head. "No. Not yet, at any rate. She said that she needs time to think. I must allow her to do that. Within reason. But meanwhile, Alaric, it is nothing to do with you."

"Pardon, Sire, but it has *everything* to do with me."

"But nothing that you can do anything about," the king replied. "Just leave it for now, lad. I mean that."

• • •

THE king waited well into autumn, but received only monthly letters reiterating Jehana's revulsion at the magic given Brion by his Deryni squire. By October, following a cheerless celebration of Alaric's fourteenth birthday, it had become clear that serious changes would be required at court, if Brion's queen was to return.

"So far as I can tell, she wants Alaric out of my life, and certainly out of the capital," the king said, at a meeting that included his uncle, his brother, his mother, and also the bone of contention himself: the fourteen-year-old Alaric Morgan. Llion was also present, in the role of Alaric's personal knight.

"Will you allow her to hold you to ransom, then?" Nigel asked. "Brion, he is your Duke of Corwyn, your Earl of Lendour. Whether she likes it or not, he is a part of your life, part of the defense of your kingdom. It appears that, if she had her way, Alaric would simply cease to exist!"

"I've been thinking about that," the king replied. "And I've explored at least a temporary solution with Uncle Richard." He glanced at Richard, who inclined his head in encouragement. "How, if Alaric were to withdraw to Cynfyn for the next few years, to take up his full-time duties as Earl of Lendour? He could also travel to Coroth periodically, to interact with his regents there. Once he reaches the age of eighteen, I would come to Coroth and knight him, confirm him in the duchy. And by then, God willing, Jehana would have come to her senses."

Alaric had listened to the proposal in silence, and now looked to Llion for direction. The young knight sighed.

"I understand your reasoning, Sire," Llion said. "But, what of the rest of his training? He is still only fourteen."

"The bulk of his formal training is largely finished," Richard said. "From this point, he should be given practical experience to harden and temper him, as he continues to gain strength and ability. I'm told that riding border patrol provides excellent tempering—and I dare say, Corwyn has some of the more spectacular borders with our Torenthi neighbors. Both Cynfyn and Coroth have an abundance of highly competent knights, who could guide him from this point."

As Llion allowed that this might provide a reasonable solution in the short term, Brion pointed out another consideration.

"Your own position becomes somewhat more problematical," the king said, "for I know that you had agreed to take on the stewardship of Morganhall during Alaric's minority—and your wife and child are there. Perhaps you could move them to Cynfyn for the first year, until Alaric is settled there. And, it is entirely possible that, with time, the queen may soften her attitude, so that he could return to court, at least a few times a year. After all, the time will come eventually when he must take up the full-time governance of his own lands."

Alaric had listened in silence as his elders discussed his future, and allowed himself a long sigh, which drew all eyes to him.

"Your thoughts?" the king said quietly.

Alaric nodded. "I understand the delicate balances you are trying to maintain, sir, and I appreciate your efforts. While it would never be my wish to go into exile—and what you describe *is* exile, of a sort—this seems a reasonable solution for the moment." Llion started to speak, but Alaric held up a staying hand.

"No, let me speak. The king must have his wife back, and she has no use for me. This I understand. But it will not be forever, and I will not be a child forever. If I can serve the king in this way, at least for now, then I will."

WITHIN a week they were on their way: Alaric, Llion, and a troop of Haldane lancers as escort, traveling along that now-familiar route eastward along the River Molling. They arrived early in November, his Lendour men alerted by a courier who had gone before, and most welcome.

"We had not expected you again so soon," Zoë told him, as she led him and Llion into the hall at Cynfyn.

"Things have become more complicated," Alaric replied. "Could you please ask Jovett and Sir Pedur to join me in the council chamber? There is aught all of you should know."

Half an hour later, he had told them of the events at Rhemuth after his and the king's return, and of the queen's flight to Shannis Meer, and the king's difficult decision to send him from court.

"He still has no guarantee that the queen will return," he said in summary, "but he has hopes. He has hinted that he may move his Twelfth Night court here, as it puts him that much nearer the queen. If she declines to join him here—which is likely, since *I* am here—I suspect he will feel obliged to go to her in the spring and bring her out, by force, if necessary."

It was not a happy proposition, but one that must be considered.

URING the next several months, Alaric continued learning about the operation of his county council and working with the men who had been running his affairs. Sir Xander of Torrylin and Sir Yves de Tremelan, men knighted by his father, returned to Cynfyn from their family holdings to assist him, and to take on the task of ensuring that his military training continued. Shortly before Christmas, he received word that the king would, indeed, be joining him for Twelfth Night court.

The king duly arrived two days before Christmas, with Nigel and Jiri Redfearn in tow, along with half a dozen of his courtiers from Rhemuth. Jamyl briefly appeared two days after Christmas, but only to report that the queen had declined Brion's invitation to join him for Twelfth Night, and showed no signs of leaving St. Giles's Abbey before the spring. Furthermore, the weather was worsening.

Accordingly, Twelfth Night at Cynfyn was less attended than it might have been, even with the king present, but Zoë and her mother-in-law managed to put together a respectable feast to entertain Lendour's young earl and his royal guest.

After supper, with the king looking on, Earl Alaric witnessed the induction of two squires into service of his house. For the knighting that followed, of a sober young man called Ualtar Bryndisi, he directed that the candidate's spurs be buckled on by his Chandos cousins, Kailan and Charlan: excellent court service for the young pages.

Sir Jovett would have done the dubbing honors in the normal course of affairs, since Lendour's earl was not yet a knight—or the king, since he was present. But Brion deferred to his young host, and asked Alaric also to lay his hand upon the sword that created Ualtar a knight.

"Now swear your fealty to your earl, Sir Ualtar," the king told the newly dubbed knight. "It is his privilege and your honor."

Alaric's hands shook as he took Sir Ualtar's hands between his own and exchanged the traditional vows, but the experience was exhilarating, and only a foretaste, he knew, of what would gradually come to him as he took on increasing duties for the king.

But the king seemed not to take as much pleasure in the event, though he put on a brave face. After Twelfth Night, while the denizens of Cynfyn hunkered down in the face of a harsh winter storm, Brion Haldane brooded before the fire in Cynfyn's hall and made his plans.

The king and his party left Cynfyn late in January, as soon as weather permitted, to head north toward Shannis Meer and St. Giles's Abbey. Alaric did not go with him, much though he would have wished to spare the king the coming confrontation with Queen Jehana. Instead he traveled west with Llion, Xander of Torrylin, and Yves de Tremelan, for their presence had been requested in Culdi for the knighting of Duke Jared's eldest son, Kevin McLain.

It was an event well worthy of celebration, but more important to Alaric was Duncan's coming of age, when he also became a squire to his father, as Kevin had done. Alaric duly celebrated both events, but his late-night discussions up on the castle leads were with Duncan, regarding his strengthening call to priesthood, which only Alaric and Duncan's confessor yet knew about.

"You're still thinking to do it?" Alaric asked.

Duncan shrugged, a resigned look on his face. "Father Geordan has my studies tilted in that direction. Mother doesn't know. And Father . . ." He shuddered. "At least he doesn't know how much more dangerous it will be for me, being what I am." By tacit agreement, both of them tried to avoid using Deryni terminology whenever possible.

"Unfortunately, Mother *does* know that," Duncan went on, "though she's never said a word to him. But she also knows that many young men begin seminary and never finish, after discovering that they're actually called in other directions. I suspect she'll hope that's the case with me. What about you? What will happen to you, now that the queen has effectively banished you from Rhemuth?"

Alaric gave a heavy sigh. "The king came to me at Cynfyn for Twelfth Night, since it's closer to where the queen is holed up. When I left to come here, he was heading north to fetch her home." He shivered. "I don't envy him *that* trip."

"Nor I," Duncan whispered, then looked up at Alaric with more enthusiasm. "But, I have a bit of court gossip for you. Prince Nigel is to be married, in early June."

"Married? To whom?"

"A lady called Meraude de Traherne. She's sister to one of the king's squires, called Saer de Traherne. He's heir to the Earl of Rhendall. Apparently Duke Richard announced the betrothal at the Twelfth Night court he held in the king's absence. They say Nigel is quite smitten."

Alaric thought he knew who Duncan was talking about. "Well, I wish him all happiness." He quirked an ironic smile. "Now that the king is married, I suppose *everyone* will be getting married."

"Not you and me," Duncan replied, grinning. "Not me, anyway. Not if I'm going to be a priest."

"Not me, either, especially now that this has happened," Alaric said. "Do you know that Princess Silke actually suggested that she and I should marry?"

"No! Was she serious?"

Alaric shrugged. "Well, she doesn't want to be married off like her sister. Apparently the old queen has already picked out some Connaiti prince for her. But I did point out that no one would accept a marriage between the king's sister and a Deryni." He gazed off into the distance. "I understand that she went into retreat with the queen, in that convent up in the north."

"You don't think she'd take the veil, do you?"

Alaric shrugged again. "I don't know." He sighed. "I don't feel like I know much of anything, right now. Who would have thought I'd be effectively exiled from court?"

"So, you'll go back to Cynfyn?"

"What else can I do?"

He and his knights headed back to Cynfyn the following week, pass-
ing through Morganhall to check on affairs there and for Llion to pick up
Alazais and their daughter, since it appeared that he would be needed in
Cynfyn for the foreseeable future. They did not stop at Rhemuth, though
Alazais had heard that the queen was back in residence, and that domestic
matters were settling down.

A letter was waiting from the king at Cynfyn, delivered in his absence,
informing him that he and the queen were on their way back to Rhemuth.
Nothing was said of the queen's state of mind, or the king's heart. Alaric
was not invited to return to Rhemuth, and did not send an immediate
reply.

It was early summer before more joyous news at last arrived from
Rhemuth, that the queen finally was with child.

"He's obviously won her back," Alaric said to Llion, as the two of
them shared far too much ale later that night.

"So it appears," Llion agreed, topping up his cup. "I wonder what the
price will have been."

"You think she laid down conditions?"

"I should think that both of them will have done."

Alaric pondered that statement for a long moment, then drained his
cup and held it out for a refill.

"Let us hope that she carries a son."

"Indeed," Llion replied. "I should hate to think that we might have
to go through this for every child, until he gets it right." He lifted his
cup in salute. "To a prince!"

"To a prince!" Alaric replied.

THEY heard nothing directly from the king through the summer,
though occasional gossip did reach Cynfyn. Prince Nigel had, indeed, married the Lady Meraude de Traherne early in June, up in Rhendall, but though the king attended the marriage of this, his only surviving
brother, Jehana declined, lest the journey endanger her pregnancy. And
Princess Silke had not been seen at court since the queen's return, and

was believed to be considering a religious vocation at a convent of hospitallers.

Alaric snorted as he read the letter, originally sent to Llion and shared by him. "Silke, to enter religion! She told me she didn't want to marry where her mother chose, at that Twelfth Night I told you about. But I didn't think she'd do this."

"It doesn't appear that anything has been decided yet," Llion replied, "though it would serve them all right. Poor Silke never had a chance at marrying someone she actually fancied."

"Maybe she was serious, that *we* should marry," Alaric said. "Not that it could ever happen, even if we were both so inclined. I told her that— and that was before the queen ran away. Somehow, I think that a Deryni brother-in-law would be absolutely the last straw."

Llion allowed himself a tiny smile. "You're probably right." He lifted his cup again. "Here's to Princess Silke, God bless her. May she find refuge from her blood, and satisfaction in whatever life she chooses."

Alaric touched his cup to Llion's. "To Silke."

I T was not long after that when Alaric decided to move his growing household to Coroth for Twelfth Night court.

"I haven't been there in a while. And it's fairly obvious that the king will not call me back to Rhemuth for *this* year's Twelfth Night court. He has other things on his mind besides an exiled Deryni."

While they made arrangements for the move to Coroth, Llion sent ahead to Corwyn's regents, informing them of their duke's plans, and likewise sent a courier to Rhemuth.

"It's a courtesy, Alaric. You're one of his dukes. He needs to have at least a general idea where you are."

Alaric thought it unlikely that the king would be thinking about him at a time like this, when his heir was due to be born in only a matter of months, but he allowed the message to be sent. He had been in Coroth for several weeks when a breathless messenger came galloping up to the castle gates from the harbor below, where a fast galley flying the royal standard could be seen tying up to the quay.

"Your Grace, it's the king!" the messenger gasped, almost collapsing as he blurted out the news.

"You mean, a message from the king?"

"No, it's the king himself! He's here!"

It was, indeed, the king, who strode into the hall hardly an hour later looking inordinately pleased with himself as Alaric and his regents came to greet him.

"I had to get away, if only for a few days," Brion said, looking like an errant schoolboy. "The first few months were wonderful, when we first knew she was with child, but pregnancy has not been easy, for either of us."

"Well, you're here now," Alaric said happily. "What would you like to do?"

"Something I should have done months ago," the king replied.

What the king had in mind was audacious, but it was the main reason he had abandoned his pregnant wife and risked the quick journey to Coroth so close to her term. That evening, before sitting down to meat in the great hall, the king summoned Alaric's regents into his council chamber and announced that he had decided to go ahead and declare Alaric of age in Corwyn.

"The queen, quite frankly, abhors Deryni, and has made it clear that she will not tolerate your duke at court on any kind of long-term basis," he said. "But without his assistance last year, to release the magic set in place by my father, I probably would not be speaking to you this evening, because I most likely would be dead."

A whisper of reaction rippled among the assembled regents, subsiding as the king went on.

"I tell you this because you, in Corwyn, have long been accustomed to having a Deryni as your duke, and lesser Deryni among you." He nodded to the young Jernian Kushannan, whose paternal grandmother was said to have been Deryni. "You understand the benefits that can come of benevolent rule. You have watched Alaric grow from boy to young man, because his father and mine made certain that, periodically, he would live and train among you. I gather that you have been reassured by what you have seen." He glanced at Alaric. "Please stand."

Alaric slowly rose in his place at the king's right hand. At the king's behest, he had put aside his Haldane squire's livery and wore a faded black heraldic mantle with the green gryphon of Corwyn emblazoned on the left shoulder, which mostly covered a stark black court robe. The mantle, retrieved from storage and only a little moth worn, had once belonged to his great-great-grandfather, Stíofan Anthony de Corwyn, the sixth duke, along with the Corwyn dagger hanging at his hip. On his breast he wore his father's Lendour signet on its chain, though the St. Camber medal was inside his tunic.

"Alaric Anthony Morgan," the king said, "you are the son and heir of a loyal knight and a noble lady whose families have ever been unshakable in their defense of the Crown of Gwynedd." He held out his right hand to Alaric, who took it. "Now be my duke in Corwyn, following in their illustrious example of service and devotion, to rule and speak for me in Corwyn. I declare you of age in Corwyn."

A little overwhelmed, Alaric dropped to his knees and pressed his forehead to the king's hand, then lifted his gaze to the king's. As the men of the council pounded on the table in approval, to cries of "Hear, hear!" and "Huzzah!" the king raised him up to a hearty embrace.

"Do you think you need to swear me oaths again, after all that has passed?" he asked, grinning.

All but overwhelmed, Alaric glanced at his council in question. "I have sworn many oaths, but I should like to swear this one, if I may."

"Give the oath!" said Lord Hamilton, his seneschal, obviously pleased. "It is for us as well as you, lad."

Sobering, Alaric sank back to his knees and lifted his joined hands to the king, drawing breath as the royal hands enclosed his.

"I, Alaric Anthony Morgan, do enter your homage and become your man for Corwyn and for Lendour. Faith and truth will I bear unto you and your lawful successors in all things, so help me God."

"And I receive your homage most gladly, Alaric Anthony Morgan, recognizing you as Duke of Corwyn and Earl of Lendour, and I pledge you my loyalty and protection so long as you keep faith with me and my house."

Again, the pounding of hands flat on the table as Alaric's regents affirmed the oath, interspersed with several verbal murmurs of approval as the king then extended a hand toward Jamyl Arilan, who passed him a gold signet ring.

"This is a new seal I've had made especially," the king said, slipping it onto Alaric's left forefinger. "Since I wished to honor your father as well as you, I've had the double tressure from Kenneth's arms added to those of Corwyn, encircling the Corwyn gryphon." He smiled as Alaric glanced at the ring in pleased surprise. "Wear this as a seal of fidelity to the many oaths you have sworn in the past, and as a symbol of your authority."

He then took up a hammered gold circlet set around with emeralds, which Jamyl also offered, and set it on Alaric's brow. "And wear this princely coronet as a mark of my esteem and trust, and as a symbol of your rank. And stay down; there's one more thing," he added, and received from Llion a sheathed sword, which he laid across Alaric's hands.

"Finally, as a sign of my charge to defend the lands I have entrusted to you, I present you with this sword, which belonged to your Uncle Ahern. I wish I had known him better. May you wear it with honor and grow in honor. Arise, Alaric Morgan Duke of Corwyn."

Epilogue

". . . Unto us a son is given . . ."
—ISAIAH 9:6

HE following day, the king would ride out with Alaric Morgan to survey some of the lands just entrusted to him. And while inspecting ancient ruins long associated with Alaric's Deryni ancestors, Brion Haldane would receive news of the birth of a son, brought by courtiers traveling out from the king's capital by way of a second fast galley, sent out a day after him.

It was the powerful Ewan Duke of Claibourne who led the band, red hair flying wild and red beard a-glisten in the autumn sunlight, who seized the Haldane banner from its bearer as he saw the flash of the king's crimson riding leathers against the grey stone ruins and waved it joyfully as he approached at the gallop, shouting his paean to the heavens as the king and his Deryni duke stared in amazement and Duke Ewan's bellow finally reached them.

"Sire, you have a son! An heir for the throne of Gwynedd. The queen is safely delivered of a prince!"

And the king, his mouth agape in awe, seized Alaric's two hands and joyously danced him around in a half circle, shouting, "A son? My God, it was supposed to be another month! Alaric, do you hear him? I have a son. I have a son!"

OUT of deference to the queen, Alaric did not accompany the king back to Rhemuth that day, but he was present six weeks later, when the new prince was christened before all the court at Twelfth Night. He

did not dare to attend the christening itself, but the king brought the infant prince to him later that evening, in the withdrawing room, and
proudly laid the babe in his arms.

"Alaric Anthony Morgan Duke of Corwyn, I present my son and
heir: Prince Kelson Cinhil Rhys Anthony Haldane. Yes, the 'Anthony' is
from you. May you be to him as you have been to me: a protector and
mentor, and a staunch defender against those who would wish him ill."

"I swear it, my Liege," Alaric said softly, gazing down into the wide
grey eyes. "God willing, I shall keep him safe, and make of him a king
whose name will live in legend."

APPENDIX I

INDEX OF CHARACTERS

*Indicates a deceased character or one only mentioned indirectly

AEAN MORRISEY—a page promoted to squire.

*AHERN JERNIAN DE CORWYN, LORD—deceased Earl of Lendour and Heir of Corwyn, Deryni; brother of Alyce de Corwyn, uncle of Alaric, and briefly the husband of Zoë Morgan.

AIMONE, FATHER—chaplain brought to Rhemuth by Queen Jehana.

AIREY REDFEARN—twin to Prys, son of Sir Jiri Redfearn; page, then squire at the Haldane court.

AIRICH O'FLYNN, SIR—Earl of Derry, succeeded by Sir Seamus O'Flynn.

AIRLIE KUSHANNAN, LORD—Earl of Airnis, one of Corwyn's regents, father of Jernian.

ALARIC ANTHONY MORGAN—eight-year-old son of the late Alyce de Corwyn Morgan and Sir Kenneth Kai Morgan; half-Deryni.

ALAZAIS MORGAN—youngest daughter of Sir Kenneth Morgan by his first wife.

*ALICIA MCLAIN, LADY—stillborn daughter of Jared and Vera McLain.

ALIX HELENA, BARONNE DE HAUT-LEON—wife of Jamyl Arilan, Deryni.

ALPHONSE—a squire at Pwyllheli, then at Rhemuth; a keen archer.

ALUN MELANDRY, SIR—son of the murdered former royal governor of Ratharkin, and cousin of Sir Wilce Melandry.

ALWYNE—a Haldane lancer present at Brion's assumption of power.

*ALYCE JAVANA DE CORWYN MORGAN, LADY—deceased Heiress of Corwyn and Lendour, Deryni wife of Sir Kenneth Morgan and mother of Alaric and Bronwyn.

ALYCE MARIA CHANDOS—daughter of Zoë and Sir Jovett Chandos.

ALYS LITHGOW—daughter of Geill Morgan and Sir Walter Lithgow.

AMIELLE, LADY—Countess of Zaria, betrothed of Illann King of Howicce and Llannedd.

ANDREW TAIRCHELL MCLAIN, DUKE—Duke of Cassan, father of Jared.

ANSELM, FATHER—a chaplain at Rhemuth Castle.

ARBAN HOWELL, SIR—Baron of Iomaire, later Earl of Eastmarch; cousin of Rorik Howell Earl of Eastmarch.

ARRAN MACEWAN, SIR—a knight of Claibourne.

ARTHEN TALBOT, SIR—youngest son of Sir Lucien Talbot, royal governor of Ratharkin.

AUDE, PRINCESS—Dowager Princess of Meara, mother of Princess Caitrin.

AUDE, PRINCESS—second daughter of Meyric King of Bremagne, sister of Jehana.

AURELIA, MOTHER—Abbess of St. Brigid's.

BAIRBRE—maid to Vera Countess of Kierney, who also looks after Duncan and Kevin McLain.

BARRETT DE LANEY—blind member of the Camberian Council.

BAYARD—a brindle hound given to Alaric by the king for his fourth birthday.

BAYLOR DE PAOR, SIR—elder son of the Baron of Trurill.

*BEARAND HALDANE, KING SAINT—pre-Interregnum Haldane king who pushed back the Moorish sea lords and consolidated Gwynedd.

*BLAINE EMANUEL RICHARD CINHIL HALDANE, PRINCE—second son of Donal King of Gwynedd, 1083–1092.

BRICE DE PAOR, SIR—younger son of the Baron of Trurill, knighted by King Brion at Trurill.

BRION DONAL CINHIL URIEN HALDANE, KING—King of Gwynedd, eldest son of King Donal.

*BRIONA, PRINCESS—only child of the last Prince of Mooryn, wife of Prince Festil Augustus.

*BRONWYN MORGAN—a sister of Charlan Kai Morgan, who died in the service of King Javan Haldane.

BRONWYN RHETICE MORGAN, LADY—five-year-old daughter of Alyce and Kenneth Morgan, younger sister of Alaric.

BROTHEN DE PAOR, SIR—Baron of Trurill, father of Baylor and Brice.

CAERIESSE—one of King Brion's ships, named for the lost land that sank beneath the sea.

CALIX HOWARD, SIR—one of Kenneth Morgan's knights living at Morganhall, married to Alaric's former nurse, Melissa.

CAMILLE FURSTÁNA, PRINCESS—daughter of Prince Zimri Furstán and Chriselle, a Festillic heiress; aunt of Prince Hogan Furstán; also known as Mother Serafina, a nun at Saint-Sasile, an all Deryni monastic establishment.

*DUCHAD MOR—Torenthi Deryni general who unsuccessfully attempted to invade Gwynedd in 985 on behalf of the Festillic pretender of the day.

*DULCHESSE, QUEEN—childless first queen of Donal Haldane.

DUNCAN HOWARD MCLAIN, LORD—son of Jared Earl of Kierney and Vera Howard (secretly Alyce's twin sister), cousin of Alaric and Bronwyn, age eight.

EDGAR OF MATHELWAITE—a baron's son and heir, squire at Coroth.

EDMUND LORIS, BISHOP—newly elected Bishop of Stavenham.

ERMENGARD, SISTER—gatekeeper at the Abbey of St. Brigid.

ERROL SEATON, SIR—father of Cornelius, in service to his brother-in-law, Bishop Oliver de Nore.

ESMÉ HARRIS, BISHOP—Bishop of Coroth, and member of Corwyn's council of regents.

ESTÈPHE DE COURCY, SIR—a young cousin of Michon de Courcy.

EULALIA HOWELL, LADY—daughter of Rorik Earl of Eastmarch, married to Sir Rhydon Sasillion Baron of Coldoire.

EVAN SULLIVAN, SIR—father of Paget, a neighbor of Oisín Adair at Arkella, near Ratharkin and the Mearan border.

EWAN DE TRAHERNE, SIR—Earl of Rhendall, father of Meraude and Saer.

EWAN MACEWAN, DUKE—Duke of Claibourne.

FAAS OF GLYNDOUR—a local baron near Cloome and Castel Edain.

FANTON MURCHISON—a squire at Rhemuth.

FAXON HOWARD, BISHOP—an itinerant bishop, kin to Vera Howard McLain.

*FESTIL, KING—first of the Interregnum kings of Gwynedd, a younger son of the King of Torenth.

FISKEN CROMARTY, BISHOP—itinerant bishop elected Bishop of Marbury in 1096, in succession to Paul Tollendal.

FROILÁN LASCELLES, SIR—a young knight of Kierney in Jared's service.

GABRIEL, ARCHANGEL—guardian of the element of Water.

GARETH—a guard in the service of Bishop Oliver de Nore.

GEILL (MORGAN) LITHGOW—middle daughter of Sir Kenneth Morgan by his first wife, married to Sir Walter Lithgow, a knight of Kierney.

GERALD RALSON, LORD—a Haldane lancer present at Brion's assumption of power.

GEOFFREY DE MAIN, SIR—a young knight of Gwynedd, non-identical twin to Thomas.

GEORDAN, FATHER—Duchess Vera's chaplain at Culdi.

GEZELIN, COUNT—ruler of county of Fianna.

GILES—a groom at Coroth.

GILLES CHOPARD, SIR—son of Sir Miles Chopard, a Corwyn regent; knighted by Kenneth.

GODREDD COLBERTSON, CAPTAIN—an officer of the Marley heavy cavalry, father of Godwin.

GODWIN GODREDDSON—a senior squire at Rhemuth, budding tactician, knighted by King Brion at Rhemuth.

GRAHAM MACEWAN, LORD—eldest son and heir to Ewan Duke of Claibourne.

GRYPHON—a sleek Corwyn cargo cog.

HAKIM, PRINCE—heir to Qais Emir of Nur Hallaj.

HALLORAN DU JOUX, SIR—eldest son and heir of Morian, Deryni.

HAMILTON, LORD—seneschal of Coroth.

HARRY—a squire at Rhemuth.

HENRY, FATHER—a chaplain at Rhemuth.

HENRY KIRBY—first mate aboard the *Gryphon*, an avid cardounet player.

HIRAM—a page from Llannedd, a shirttail relative of King Ronan.

HOGAN GWERNACH, SOMETIMES HOGAN FURSTÁN, PRINCE—Festillic pretender to the throne of Gwynedd, posthumous son of Prince Marcus (nephew of Princess Camille/Sister Serafina) and Jonelle Heiress of Gwernach, by which right he was sometimes known in later life as Hogan Gwernach.

HORT OF ORSAL—Overlord of the Forcinn Buffer States. (See Létald.)

IAN HOWELL—son and heir of Arban Howell Baron of Iomaire (later Earl of Eastmarch), and squire to him.

ILLANN, KING—King of Howicce and Llannedd; brother of Queen Richeldis.

*IMRE FURSTÁN OF FESTIL—last Interregnum King of Gwynedd.

INNIS DE PIREK (PIREK-HALDANE), SIR—a senior squire at Rhemuth, knighted by King Brion.

*IOLO MELANDRY, SIR—murdered royal governor of Meara.

IRIS CERYS—a sister of Arc-en-Ciel.

IRIS JUDIANA, MOTHER—Superior at Arc-en-Ciel; daughter of a Bremagni duke, educated at Rhanamé.

IRIS ROSE—a sister of Arc-en-Ciel.

ISARN, PRINCE—Prince of Logreine.

JAMES OF TENDAL, SIR—hereditary Chancellor of Corwyn.

JAMYL ARILAN, SIR—nephew of the late Sir Seisyll Arilan, Deryni; a favored companion of King Brion.

JÁNOS SOKRAT, COUNT—a Torenthi courtier.

JARDINE HOWARD, SIR—a knight of Lendour, one of Duchess Vera's uncles.

JARED MCLAIN, EARL OF KIERNEY—only son and heir of Andrew Duke of Cassan; husband of Vera, father of Kevin and Duncan.

JASKA COLLINS, SIR—a young knight of Gwynedd, known for his horsemanship, in Kenneth's service.

*Jathan Joachim Richard Urien, Prince—youngest son of King Donal and Queen Richeldis.

Jehana Julienne Adélaïde de Besançon, Princess—eldest daughter of Ryol King of Bremagne.

*Jernian, Duke—fifth Duke of Corwyn, a comrade of Kings Nygel, Jasher, and Cluim.

Jernian Kushannan, Master—a page at Coroth, heir to Airlie Earl of Airnis, two years older than Alaric; an avid cardounet enthusiast, but with poor vision.

Jiri Redfearn, Sir—an aide to King Donal, father of twin pages Airey and Prys.

Jorian de Courcy, Father—Deryni priest discovered by the Church hierarchy and sentenced to be executed; from the mountain region bordering the Connait.

Joris Talbot, Sir—eldest son of Sir Lucien Talbot, royal governor of Meara at Ratharkin.

Joscerand, Prince—uncle to Crown Prince Ryol of Bremagne, half-brother to King Meyric.

Jovett Chandos, Sir—childhood friend of Alyce de Corwyn, secretly Deryni; close friend of Sir Sé Trelawney; husband of Lady Zoë Morgan.

Judiana, Mother—see Iris Judiana, Mother.

Julian Talbot, Sir—second son of Sir Lucien Talbot, royal governor of Meara at Ratharkin.

*Jurij Orkény—great Torenthi battle genius, author of *Failed Battle Tactics*.

Justis Berringer—page at Rhemuth, then squire, finally a knight.

Kailan Peter Chandos, Master—elder son of Zoë Morgan and Sir Jovett Chandos.

Károly Furstán, Prince—third son of King Nimur of Torenth; Crown Prince of Torenth.

Kennet Howell, Sir—son and heir of Rorik Howell Earl of Eastmarch.

Kenneth Kai Morgan, Sir—an aide to King Donal; widower of Lady Alyce de Corwyn, father of Alaric and Bronwyn, plus Zoë and two more daughters by a first marriage; Earl of Lendour for life, in right of his wife.

Kerensa Alathea, Princess—niece of Alberic King of Fallon.

*Keryell of Lendour, Earl—Deryni Earl of Lendour and husband of Stevana de Corwyn, Heiress of Corwyn; father of Alyce, Vera, and Ahern.

Kethevan von Soslán, Lady—morganatic wife of Hogan Gwernach, created Countess of Soslán.

Kevin Douglas McLain, Master—son of Jared Earl of Kierney by his first wife, Elaine MacInnis; Master of Kierney, later Earl of Kierney.

MICHAEL O'FLYNN, EARL OF DERRY—special counsel to the Duchy of Corwyn; father of Sir Seamus O'Flynn.

MICHAEL PIREK-HALDANE, SIR—elder son and heir of Quentin Pirek-Haldane Earl of Carthane, brother of Innis de Pirek.

*MICHON DE COURCY, LORD—deceased member of the Camberian Council.

MIKHAIL COUNT OF SANKT-IRAKLI—bookish younger son of Prince Hogan by Kethevan von Soslán, disallowed from the succession.

MIKHAIL VASTOUNI, PRINCE—sovereign Prince of Andelon, father of Sofiana, brother of Khoren; Deryni.

MILES CHOPARD, SIR—secretary to Corwyn's council of regents.

MORAG FURSTÁNA, PRINCESS—daughter of the King of Torenth, sister of Princes Károly, Wencit, Festil, and Torval.

MORIAN DU JOUX (AP LEWYS), SIR—Deryni in Meara, husband of Lady Cloris.

MURCHISON, BARON—holder of a manor house two days north of Rhemuth.

NESTA MCLAIN, LADY—sister to Kenneth Morgan's first wife, and aunt to his three daughters.

NEVAN D'ESTRELLDAS, FATHER—a chaplain serving as Duke Jared's battle-surgeon, from Bremagne.

NIGEL CLUIM GWYDION RHYS HALDANE, PRINCE—younger brother of Brion King of Gwynedd, and his heir presumptive.

NIMUR (NIMOUROS HO PHOURSTANOS PADISHAH)—King of Torenth.

*NIMUR FURSTÁN, CROWN PRINCE—late eldest son of Nimur King of Torenth.

NINIAN DE PIRAN, SIR—deputy to Duke Richard for training; heir to Earl of Jenas.

NIVELON, DUKE—Duke of Vezaire, a distant relative of the late Queen Dulchesse of Gwynedd.

NOLEN MACINNIS—a squire at Rhemuth, friend of Cornelius Seaton.

O'BEIRNE, BISHOP (NEIL)—Bishop of Dhassa.

OISÍN ADAIR—a horse breeder, member of the Camberian Council.

OLIVER DE NORE, BISHOP—elder brother of the late Father Septimus; Bishop of Nyford; uncle of Cornelius Seaton.

ORBAN HOWARD, SIR—"father" of Vera (de Corwyn) Howard.

PAGET SULLIVAN—son of Sir Evan Sullivan and page, then squire and knight, at Rhemuth; friend of Alaric.

PASCHAL DIDIER, FATHER—R'Kassan-trained former chaplain to Keryell Earl of Lendour and tutor to his children; Deryni.

PATRICK CORRIGAN, BISHOP—auxiliary bishop in Rhemuth.

PAUL TOLLENDAL, ARCHBISHOP—Archbishop of Valoret and Primate of All Gwynedd.

THOMAS, SIR—a senior Kierney knight.

THOMAS DE MAIN, SIR—a young knight of Gwynedd, non-identical twin to Geoffrey, noted for his swordsmanship.

*THOMAS RIORDAN, SIR—author of *Essential Cavalry Tactics*.

TIARNÁN MACRAE, SIR—a senior aide to King Donal.

TIVADAN, FATHER—Chancellor of the Exchequer of Corwyn.

TORVAL FURSTÁN, PRINCE—second son of the King of Torenth.

TRESHAM MACKENZIE—a Claibourne squire at Rhemuth, cousin to Ewan Duke of Claibourne.

TREVOR, PRINCE—second son of Meyric King of Bremagne, brother of Jehana.

TREVOR UDAUT, SIR—a young knight of Corwyn, son of Sir Laurenz Udaut; assigned to Kenneth Morgan's service.

UALTAR DE BRYNDISI, SIR—a young knight dubbed by King Brion at Cynfyn.

ULF CAREY, SIR—a young knight of Gwynedd, known for his keen horsemanship.

*ULGER DE BRINSI—a Thurian cardounet master, author of *Elements of Basic Strategy*.

URIEL, ARCHANGEL—guardian of the element of Earth.

URSULINE, PRINCESS—third daughter of Meyric King of Bremagne.

VARIAN LEMANDER, SIR—a newly made knight of Danoc.

VERA LAURELA (DE CORWYN) HOWARD MCLAIN, COUNTESS—younger twin sister of Alyce, but raised by and believed to be the daughter of Lord Orban Howard and Lady Laurela; wife of Jared Earl of Kierney and mother of Duncan.

VILIAM DE SOUZA—a squire at Coroth, heir of a baron; four years older than Alaric, a cardounet enthusiast.

VIVIENNE DE JORDANET, LADY—member of the Camberian Council.

WALTER LITHGOW, SIR—a knight of Kierney, husband of Geill Morgan.

WENCIT FURSTÁN, PRINCE—fourth son of King Nimur of Torenth.

WILCE MELANDRY, SIR—sheriff of Ratharkin.

WILLIAM MACCARTNEY, ARCHBISHOP—Archbishop of Rhemuth.

XANDER OF TORRYLIN, SIR—a young knight of Lendour.

XAVIER HOWARD—a new page at Coroth, a cousin of Duchess Vera.

XENIA NUALA JARONI SWYNBETH HALDANE, PRINCESS—first daughter and third child of Donal King of Gwynedd and Richeldis.

YSOMBARD, PRINCE—Prince of Thuria.

YVES DE TREMELAN, SIR—a young knight of Lendour.

ZAIZIE—family pet name of Alazais Morgan, Kenneth's youngest daughter by his first marriage.

*ZEFIRYN—an ancient Deryni sage of Caeriesse.

*ZIMAREK COUNT OF TARKHAN—elder son of Prince Hogan by his morganatic wife, a tournament champion.

*Zɪᴍʀɪ Dᴜᴋᴇ ᴏf Tʀᴜᴠᴏʀsᴋ—Torenthi author of a tactical work, *A Betrayal at Killingford*.

Zᴏë Bʀᴏɴwʏɴ (Mᴏʀɢᴀɴ) Cʜᴀɴᴅᴏs, Lᴀᴅʏ—eldest daughter of Sir Kenneth Morgan, a former student at Arc-en-Ciel; heart-sister (and stepdaughter!) to Alyce de Corwyn; widow of Ahern Heir of Corwyn, wife to Sir Jovett Chandos, mother of Kailan Peter, Charlan, and Alyce Maria Chandos.

APPENDIX II

Index of Places